CW01649810

'The nov [illegible] ulinary mingling, the mong [illegible] of peoples across old barri [illegible] pain and glory of an earlier era of globalization'—Shashi Tharoor, *The Washington Post*

'Ghosh is creating a Tolstoyan epic charting the fortunes of people tossed around oceans by the mighty currents of commerce and colonisation. Superbly placed, plotted and researched, *River of Smoke* is stunning'—*Times Crest*

'Ghosh's characters are minutely etched figures with varied personal histories, idiosyncrasies and sartorial choices. In their sheer wealth of detail, they are reminiscent of Madhubani's miniatures . . . A sensuous feast'—*Hindustan Times*

'Generous helpings of humour, adventure, history, romance, villainy and suspense are expertly blended into the narrative to make for a rich and entertaining read'—*Outlook*

'A sensory feast of tastes and flavours, colours and textures . . . Ghosh creates an unforgettable world novel'—*Mint*

'No writer in modern India has held a novelistic lamp to the subcontinent's densely thicketed past as vividly and acutely as Amitav Ghosh . . . *River of Smoke* is both a stirring portrayal of the past and, novelistically, a prescient beacon for the future'—*The New York Times Book Review*

'Ghosh's language flows with elegance through a wide variety of registers, from dialect to nautical vocabulary to the free indirect style . . . The inventive language lends the characters a life that surpasses mere information . . . Like a shrewd merchant, Ghosh understands that confluences of money and power bring people together in ways their masters could not have expected'—*Times Literary Supplement*

'The vast book has a Dickensian sweep . . . Mr Ghosh conjures up a thrilling sense of place . . . The lexicon of the novel—English, Hindi, Parsi, Malay, Chinese and pidgin—is a rich brew from cultures re-energised through imperialism and trade'—*The Economist*

'A richly detailed panorama of the Opium Wars . . . Through the depth of his research, lightly worn, Ghosh has captured the many cross-currents of a fascinating historical period'—*The Telegraph* (UK)

'A marvel . . . The novel's strength lies in how thoroughly Ghosh fills out his research with his novelistic fantasy . . . so that at their best the scenes read with a sensual freshness as if they were happening now'—*The Guardian*

'An enthralling yarn, swollen with minor stories but increasingly resonant in its moral clarity'—*The Independent*

'Ghosh revels in words like a child frolicking in the snow. He marvels at their shape, throws them in the air, tastes them on his tongue and sculpts them into different forms'—*Indian Express*

'His descriptions bring a lost world to life . . . Ghosh portrays his characters with integrity and dignity'—*Deccan Chronicle*

'A riveting read'—*People*

'Amitav Ghosh conjures plotlines out of trading routes, which, in his supple and compulsive imagination, come magically alive as the conduits for human history; they effect the exchange not just of silk and silver but of language and love and enmity'—*The Observer*

'The proliferating details, the incessant off-shooting of side stories, the swarm of Chinese, Indian, and Creole words that buzz among the text; these enrich and engorge, by turns, the theme of *River of Smoke*. Beneath the lavish ornamentation of Amitav Ghosh's massive new novel . . . is a panther-like tautness and thrill'—*The Boston Globe*

PENGUIN BOOKS

RIVER OF SMOKE

Amitav Ghosh was born in Calcutta and grew up in Bangladesh, Sri Lanka and India. He studied at the universities of Delhi and Oxford, and has taught at a number of institutions. *River of Smoke* is the second in the Ibis trilogy, which was shortlisted for the Man Asian Literary Prize and *The Hindu* Literary Prize in 2011. The first of the trilogy, the bestselling *Sea of Poppies*, was shortlisted for the Man Booker Prize in 2008. Ghosh's other works include *The Circle of Reason* (Prix Médicis Étranger Award), *The Shadow Lines* (Sahitya Akademi Award), *In an Antique Land*, *The Calcutta Chromosome* (Arthur C. Clarke Award), *Dancing in Cambodia and Other Essays*, *Countdown*, *The Glass Palace* (Grand Prize for Fiction at the Frankfurt International e-books Awards), *The Imam and the Indian* and *The Hungry Tide* (Best Work in English Fiction, Hutch Crossword Book Award). In 2007 he was awarded the Grinzane Cavour Prize and in 2010 the Dan David Prize.

Amitav Ghosh currently divides his time between Calcutta, Goa and Brooklyn.

BY THE SAME AUTHOR

The Circle of Reason

The Shadow Lines

In an Antique Land

The Calcutta Chromosome

Dancing in Cambodia and Other Essays

Countdown

The Glass Palace

The Imam and the Indian

The Hungry Tide

Sea of Poppies

RIVER OF SMOKE

AMITAV GHOSH

PENGUIN BOOKS

PENGUIN BOOKS
Published by the Penguin Group
Penguin Books India Pvt Ltd, 11 Community Centre, Panchsheel Park,
New Delhi 110 017, India
Penguin Group (USA) Inc., 375 Hudson Street, New York, New York 10014, USA
Penguin Group (Canada), 90 Eglinton Avenue East, Suite 700, Toronto,
Ontario, M4P 2Y3, Canada (a division of Pearson Penguin Canada Inc.)
Penguin Books Ltd, 80 Strand, London WC2R 0RL, England
Penguin Ireland, 25 St Stephen's Green, Dublin 2, Ireland
(a division of Penguin Books Ltd)
Penguin Group (Australia), 707 Collins Street, Melbourne, Victoria 3008, Australia
(a division of Pearson Australia Group Pty Ltd)
Penguin Group (NZ), 67 Apollo Drive, Rosedale, Auckland 0632,
New Zealand (a division of Pearson New Zealand Ltd)
Penguin Group (South Africa) (Pty) Ltd, 24 Sturdee Avenue, Rosebank,
Johannesburg 2196, South Africa

Penguin Books Ltd, Registered Offices: 80 Strand, London WC2R 0RL, England

First published in Hamish Hamilton by Penguin Books India 2011
Published in Penguin Books 2012

Copyright © Amitav Ghosh 2011

All rights reserved

10 9 8 7 6 5 4 3 2 1

This is a work of fiction. Names, characters, places and incidents are either the product of the author's imagination or are used fictitiously and any resemblance to any actual person, living or dead, events or locales is entirely coincidental.

ISBN 9780143419136

For sale in India, Nepal, Bangladesh and Bhutan only

Typeset in Sabon Roman by SÜRYA, New Delhi
Printed at Thomson Press India Ltd, New Delhi

This book is sold subject to the condition that it shall not, by way of trade or otherwise, be lent, resold, hired out, or otherwise circulated without the publisher's prior written consent in any form of binding or cover other than that in which it is published and without a similar condition including this condition being imposed on the subsequent purchaser and without limiting the rights under copyright reserved above, no part of this publication may be reproduced, stored in or introduced into a retrieval system, or transmitted in any form or by any means (electronic, mechanical, photocopying, recording or otherwise), without the prior written permission of both the copyright owner and the above-mentioned publisher of this book.

ALWAYS LEARNING

PEARSON

For my mother

on her eightieth

part one

~

Islands

one

~

Deeti's shrine was hidden in a cliff, in a far corner of Mauritius, where the island's western and southern shorelines collide to form the wind-whipped dome of the Morne Brabant. The site was a geological anomaly—a cave within a spur of limestone, hollowed out by wind and water—and there was nothing like it anywhere else on the mountain. Later Deeti would insist that it wasn't chance but destiny that led her to it—for the very existence of the place was unimaginable until you had actually stepped inside it.

The Colver farm was across the bay and towards the end of Deeti's life, when her knees were stiff with arthritis, the climb up to the shrine was too much for her to undertake on her own: she wasn't able to make the trip unless she was carried up in her special pus-pus—a contraption that was part palki and part sedan chair. This meant that visits to the shrine had to be full-scale expeditions, requiring the attendance of a good number of the Colver menfolk, especially the younger and sturdier ones.

To assemble the whole clan—La Fami Colver, as they said in Kreol—was never easy since its members were widely scattered, within the island and abroad. But the one time of year when everyone could be counted on to make a special effort was in midsummer, during the Gran Vakans that preceded the New Year. The Fami would begin mobilizing in mid-December, and by the start of the holidays the whole clan would be on the march; accompanied by paltans of bonoys, belsers, bowjis, salas, sakubays and other in-laws, the Colver phalanxes would converge on the farm in a giant pincer movement: some would come overland on ox-carts, from Curepipe and Quatre Borne, through the misted uplands; some would travel by boat, from Port Louis and Mahébourg, hugging the coast till they were in sight of the mist-veiled nipple of the Morne.

Much depended on the weather, for a trek up the windswept mountain could not be undertaken except on a fine day. When the conditions seemed propitious, the bandobast would start the night before. The feast that followed the puja was always the most eagerly awaited part of the pilgrimage and the preparations for it occasioned much excitement and anticipation: the tin-roofed bungalow would ring to the sound of choppers and chakkis, mortars and rolling-pins, as masalas were ground, chutneys tempered, and heaps of vegetables transformed into stuffings for parathas and daal-puris. After everything had been packed in tiffin-boxes and gardmanzés, everyone would be bundled off for an early night.

When daybreak came, Deeti would take it on herself to ensure that everyone was scrubbed and bathed, and that not a morsel of food passed anyone's lips—for as with all pilgrimages, this too had to be undertaken with a body that was undefiled, within and without. Always the first to rise, she would go tap-tapping around the wood-floored bungalow, cane in hand, trumpeting a reveille in the strange mixture of Bhojpuri and Kreol that had become her personal idiom of expression: Revey-té! É Banwari; é Mukhpyari! Revey-té na! Haglé ba?

By the time the whole tribe was up and on their feet, the sun would have set alight the clouds that veiled the peak of the Morne. Deeti would take her place in the lead, in a horse-drawn carriage, and the procession would go rumbling out of the farm, through the gates and down the hill, to the isthmus that connected the mountain to the rest of the island. This was as far as any vehicle could go, so here the party would descend. Deeti would take her seat in the pus-pus, and with the younger males taking turns at the poles, her chair would lead the way up, through the thick greenery that cloaked the mountain's lower slopes.

Just before the last and steepest stretch of the climb there was a convenient clearing where everyone would stop, not just to catch their breath, but also to exclaim over the manifik view of jungle and mountain, contained between two sand-fringed, scalloped lines of coast.

Deeti alone was less than enchanted by this spectacular vista. Within a few minutes she'd be snapping at everyone: Levé té! We're not here to goggle at the zoli-vi and spend the day doing patati-patata. Paditu! Chal!

To complain that your legs were fatigé or your head was gidigidi was no use; all you'd get in return was a ferocious: Bus to fana! Get on your feet!

It wouldn't take much to rouse the party; having come this far on empty stomachs, they would now be impatient for the post-puja meal, the children especially. Once again, Deeti's pus-pus, with the sturdiest of the menfolk holding the poles, would take the lead: with a rattling of pebbles they would go up a steep pathway and circle around a ridge. And then all of a sudden, the other face of the mountain would come into view, dropping precipitously into the sea. Abruptly, the sound of pounding surf would well up from the edge of the cliff, ringing in their ears, and their faces would be whipped by the wind. This was the most hazardous leg of the journey, where the winds and updraughts were fiercest. No lingering was permitted here, no pause to take in the spectacle of the encircling horizon, spinning between sea and sky like a twirling hoop. Procrastinators would feel the sting of Deeti's cane: Garatwa! Keep moving . . .

A few more steps and they'd reach the sheltered ledge of rock that formed the shrine's threshold. This curious natural formation was known to the family as the Chowkey, and it could not have been better designed had it been planned by an architect: its floor was broad and almost flat, and it was sheltered by a rocky overhang that served as a ceiling. It had something of the feel of a shaded veranda, and as if to complete the illusion, there was even a balustrade of sorts, formed by the gnarled greenery that clung to the edges of the ledge. But to look over the side, at the surf churning at the foot of the cliff, took a strong stomach and a steady head: the breakers below had travelled all the way up from Antarctica and even on a calm, clear day the water seemed to surge as though it were impatient to sweep away the insolent speck of land that had interrupted its northward flow.

Yet such was the miracle of the Chowkey's accidental design that visitors had only to sit down for the waves to disappear from view—for the same gnarled greenery that protected the shelf served also to hide the ocean from those who were seated on the floor. This rocky veranda was, in other words, the perfect place to foregather, and cousins visiting from abroad were often misled into thinking that it was this quality that had earned the Chowkey its name—for was it not a bit of a chowk, where people could assemble? And wasn't it something of a chokey too, with its enclosing sides? But only a Hindi-speaking etranzer would think in that vein: any islander would know that in Kreol the word 'chowkey' refers also to the flat disc on which rotis are rolled (the thing that is known Back There as a 'chakki'). And there it was, Deeti's Chowkey, right in the middle of the rock shelf, crafted not by human hands but by the wind and the earth: it was nothing but a huge boulder that had been worn and weathered into a flat-topped toadstool of stone. Within moments of the party's arrival, the women would be hard at work on it, rolling out tissue-thin daal-puris and parathas and stuffing them with the delectable fillings that had been prepared the night before: finely ground mixes of the island's most toothsome vegetables—purple arwi and green mouroungue, cambaré-beti and wilted songe.

Several photographs from this period of Deeti's life have survived, including a couple of beautiful silver-gelatin daguerrotypes. In one of them, taken in the Chowkey, Deeti is in the foreground, still seated in her pus-pus, the feet of which are resting on the floor. She is wearing a sari, but unlike the other women in the frame, she has allowed the ghungta to drop from her head, baring her hair, which is a startling shade of white. Her sari's anchal hangs over her shoulder, weighted with a massive bunch of keys, the symbol of her continuing mastery of the Fami's affairs. Her face is dark and round, lined with deep cracks: the daguerrotype is detailed enough to give the viewer the illusion of being able to feel the texture of her skin, which is that of crumpled, tough, weatherworn leather. Her hands are folded calmly in her lap, but there is nothing reposeful about the tilt of her body: her lips are pursed tightly together and she is squinting fiercely at the camera. One of her eyes, dimmed by cataracts, reflects the light blankly back to the lens, but the gaze of the other is sharp and piercing, the colour of the pupil a distinctive grey.

The entrance to the shrine's inner chambers can be seen over her shoulder: it is no more than a tilted fissure in the cliffside, so narrow that it seems impossible that a cavern could lie hidden behind it. In the background, a paunchy man in a dhoti can be seen, trying to chivvy a brood of children into forming a line so that they can follow Deeti inside.

This too was an inviolable part of the ritual: it always fell to Deeti to make sure that the youngest were the first to perform the puja, so they could eat before the rest. With a cane in one hand and a branch of candles in another, she would usher all the young Colvers—chutkas and chutkis, laikas and laikis—straight through the hall-like cavern that led to the inner sanctum. The famished youngsters would hurry after her, scarcely glancing at the painted walls of the cave's outer chamber, with its drawings and graffiti. They would run to the part of the shrine that Deeti called her 'puja-room': a small hollow in the rock, hidden away at the back. If the shrine had been an ordinary temple, this would have been its heart—a sanctum with an array of divinities that was centred upon one of the lesser-known deities of the Hindu pantheon: Marut, god of the wind and father of Hanuman. Here, by the light of a flickering lamp, they would perform a quick puja, mumbling their mantras and whispering their prayers. Then, after offering up handfuls of arati flowers and swallowing mouthfuls of tooth-tingling prasad, the children would scamper back to the

Chowkey, to be met with cries of: Átab! Átab!—even though there was never a table to eat off, but only banana leaves, no chairs to sit on, but only sheets and mats.

Those meals were always vegetarian and perforce very plain, for they had to be cooked on open fires, with the rudest of utensils: the staples were parathas and daal-puris, and they were eaten with bajis of pipengay and chou-chou, ourougails of tomato and peanut, chutneys of tamarind and combava fruit, and perhaps an achar or two of lime or bilimbi, and maybe even a hot mazavaroo of chilis and lime—and, of course, dahi and ghee, made from the milk of the Colvers' cows. They were the simplest of feasts, but afterwards when all the food was gone, everyone would lean helplessly against the stony walls and complain about how they'd banbosé too much and how their innards were growling and how bad it was to eat so much, manzé zisk'arazé . . .

Years later, when that escarpment crumbled under the onslaught of a cyclone, and the shrine was swept into the sea by an avalanche, this was the part that the children who had been on those pilgrimages would remember best: the parathas and daal-puris, the ourougails and mazavaroos, the dahi and ghee.

~

It was not till the feast had been digested and gas lamps lit that the children would begin to drift back to the shrine's outer chamber, to stare in wonder at the painted walls of the cavern that was known as Deetiji's 'Memory-Temple'—*Deetiji-ka-smriti-mandir*.

Every child in the Fami knew the story of how Deeti had learnt to paint: she had been taught by her grandmother when she was a chutki of a child, Back There, in Inndustan, in the gaon where she was born. The village was called Nayanpur and it was in northern Bihar, overlooking the confluence of two great rivers, the Ganga and the Karamnasa. The houses there were nothing like you'd find on the island—no tin roofs, and hardly any metal or wood anywhere to be seen. They lived in mud huts Back There, thatched with straw and plastered with cow-dung.

Most people in Nayanpur left their walls blank, but Deeti's family was different: as a young man her grandfather had worked as a silahdar in Darbhanga, some sixty miles to the east. While in service there he had married into a Rajput family from a nearby village, and his wife had come back with him when he returned to Nayanpur to settle.

Back There, even more than in Mauritius, each town and village had its points of pride: some were famous for their pottery, some for the flavour of their khoobi-ki-lai, some for the unusual idiocy of their inhabitants, and some for the exceptional qualities of their rice. Madhubani, Deeti's grandmother's village, was renowned for its gorgeously decorated houses and beautifully painted walls. When she moved to Nayanpur she brought the secrets and traditions of Madhubani with her: she taught her daughters and granddaughters how to whiten their walls with rice flour, and how to create vibrant colours from fruits, flowers and tinted soils.

Every girl in Deeti's family had a speciality and hers was that of depicting the ordinary mortals who frolicked around the feet of the devas, devis and demons. The little figures who sprang from her hand often had the features of the people around her: they were a private pantheon of those she most loved and feared. She liked to draw them in outline, usually in profile, supplying each with some distinctive mark of identity; thus, her oldest brother, Kesri Singh, who was a sepoy in the army of the East India Company, was always identified by a symbol of soldiering, usually a smoking bundook.

When she married and left her village, Deeti discovered that the art she had learnt from her grandmother was unwelcome in her husband's home, the walls of which had never been brightened by a stroke of paint or a lick of colour. But even her in-laws could not keep her from drawing on leaves and rags, nor could they deny her the right to adorn her puja-room as she chose: this small prayer-niche became the repository of her dreams and visions. During the nine long years of that marriage, drawing was not just a consolation, but also her principal means of remembrance: being unlettered, it was the only way she could keep track of her memories.

The practices of that time stayed with her when she escaped that other life with the help of the man who would become her second husband, Kalua. It was only after they had embarked on their journey to Mauritius that she discovered herself to be pregnant with Kalua's child—and the story went that it was this boy, her son Girin, who led her to the site of her shrine.

Back in those days, Deeti was a coolie, working on a newly cleared plantation on the other side of the Baie du Morne. Her master was a Frenchman, a former soldier who had been wounded in the Napoleonic Wars and was ill both in mind and body: it was he who had brought Deeti and eight of her shipmates from the *Ibis* to this far corner of the island to serve out their indenture.

This district was then the remotest and least populated part of Mauritius so land here was exceptionally cheap: since the region was almost inaccessible by road, supplies had to be brought in by boat and it sometimes happened that food ran so short that the coolies had to forage in the jungle in order to fill their bellies. Nowhere was the forest richer than on the Morne, but rarely, if ever, did anyone venture to climb those slopes—for the mountain was a place of sinister reputation, where hundreds, perhaps thousands of people were known to have died. Back in the days of slavery the Morne's inaccessibility had made it an attractive place of refuge for escaped slaves, who had settled there in considerable numbers. This community of fugitives—or marrons as they were known in Kreol—had lasted until shortly after 1834, when slavery was outlawed in Mauritius. Unaware of the change, the marrons had continued to live their accustomed lives on the Morne—until the day when a column of troops appeared on the horizon and was seen to be marching towards them. That the soldiers might be messengers of freedom was beyond imagining—mistaking them for a raiding party, the marrons had flung themselves off the cliffs, plunging to their deaths on the rocks below.

The tragedy had occurred only a few years before Deeti and her ship-siblings from the *Ibis* were brought to the plantation across the bay, and its memory still saturated the landscape. In the coolie lines, when the wind was heard to howl upon the mountain, the sound was said to be the keening of the dead, and such was the fear it evoked that no one would willingly set foot upon those slopes.

Deeti was no less fearful of the mountain than any of the others, but unlike them, she had a one-year-old to wean, and when rice was scarce, the only thing he would eat was mashed bananas. Since these grew in abundance in the forests of the Morne, Deeti would occasionally screw up her courage and venture across the isthmus, with her son tied to her back. This was how it happened one day, that a fast-rising storm trapped her on the mountain. By the time she became aware of the change in the weather, the tide had already surged, cutting off the isthmus; there was no other way to return to the plantation so Deeti decided to follow what seemed to be an old path, in the hope that it would lead her to shelter. It was this overgrown trail, carved out by the marrons, that had shown her the way up the slope and around the ridge, to the rock shelf that would later become the Fami's Chowkey.

To Deeti, at the moment when she stumbled upon it, the outer ledge had seemed as sheltered a spot as she was ever likely to find: this was where she would have waited out the storm, unaware that the shelf was merely the threshold of a refuge that was yet more secure. According to family legend, it was Girin who found the fissure that became the entrance to the shrine; Deeti had put him down, so she could look for a place to store the bananas she had collected earlier. She took her eyes off him for only a minute, but Girin was an energetic crawler and when she looked around he was gone.

She let out a shriek, thinking that he had tumbled over the ledge, on to the rocks below—but then she heard his gurgling voice, resonating out of the rocks. She looked around, and seeing no sign of him, went up to the fissure and ran her fingers along its edges before thrusting in her hand. It was cool inside, and there seemed to be space aplenty, so she stepped through the gap and almost immediately tripped over her child.

As soon as her eyes grew accustomed to the light she knew she had entered a space that had once been inhabited: there were piles of firewood stacked along the walls, and she could see flints scattered on the floor. The ground beneath was littered with husks and she almost cut her feet on the shards of a cracked calabash. In one corner there was even a scattering of ossified human dung, rendered odourless by age: it was strange that something that would have excited disgust elsewhere, was here a token of reassurance, proof that this cavern had once sheltered real human beings, not ghosts or pishaches or demons.

Later, when the storm broke and the winds began to shriek, she piled up some wood and lit a fire with the flints: that was when she discovered that some parts of the chalky walls had been drawn upon with bits of charcoal; some of the marks looked like stick figures, made by children. When the raging of the wind made Girin howl in fear, it was these older images that gave Deeti the idea of drawing upon the wall.

Look, she said to her son: dekh—he is here, with us, your father. There is nothing to fear; he is by our side . . .

That was how she began to draw the first of her pictures: it was a larger-than-life-size image of Kalua.

Later, in years to come, her children and grandchildren would often ask why there was so little of herself on the walls of the shrine. Why so few images of her own early experiences in the plantation? Why so many drawings of her husband and his fellow fugitives? Her answer was: Ekut: to me your grandfather's image was not like a figure of an Ero in a painting; it was real; it was the verité. When I managed to come up here, it was to be with him. My own life, I had to endure every sekonn of every day: when I was here, I was with him . . .

~

It was that first, larger-than-life image that was always the starting point for viewings of the shrine: here, as in life, Kalua, was taller and larger than anyone else, as black as Krishna himself. Rendered in profile, he bestrode the wall like some all-conquering Pharaoh, with a langot knotted around his waist. Under his feet, engraved by some other hand, was the name that had been thrust upon him in the migrants' camp in Calcutta—'Maddow Colver'—enclosed in an ornamental cartouche.

As with all pilgrimages, the Fami's visits to the shrine followed certain prescribed patterns: usage and custom dictated the direction of the circumambulation as well as the order in which the pictures had to be viewed and venerated. After the image of the founding father, the next stop was a panel that was known to the Fami as 'The Parting' (*Biraha*): there was no inscription or engraving below it, but every Colver spoke of it by this name, and even the youngest of the chutkas and chutkis knew that it depicted a critical juncture in the history of their family—the moment of Deeti's separation from her spouse.

It had happened, they all knew, when Deeti and Kalua were on the *Ibis*, making the Crossing, from India to Mauritius with scores of other indentured workers. Bedevilled from the start, the misfortunes of the voyage had culminated with Kalua being sentenced to death for a simple act of self-defence. But before the penalty could be administered a storm had arisen, engulfing the schooner and allowing Kalua to escape in a lifeboat, along with four other fugitives.

The saga of the patriarch's deliverance from the *Ibis* was often told amongst the Colvers: it was to them what the story of the watchful geese was to Ancient Rome—an instance when Fate had conspired with Nature to give them a sign that theirs was no ordinary destiny. In Deeti's depiction of it, the scene was framed as if to freeze forever the moments before the fugitives' boat was swept away from the mother-ship by the angry waves: the *Ibis* was portrayed in the fashion of a mythological bird, with a great beak of a bowsprit and two enormous, outspread canvas wings. The fugitives' longboat was to the right, only a foot or so away, and it was separated from the *Ibis* by two tall stylized waves. As a contrast to the schooner's bird-like form, the boat's shape was suggestive of a half-submerged fish; its size, on the other hand—perhaps to underscore the grandeur of its role, as the vehicle of the patriarch's deliverance—was greatly exaggerated, its dimensions being almost equal to those of the mother-ship. Each of the two vessels was shown to be bearing a small complement of people, four in the case of the schooner, and five for the boat.

Repetition is the method through which the miraculous becomes a part of everyday life: even though the outlines of the tale were well known to everyone, Deeti would always be confronted with the same questions when she led family expeditions to the shrine.

Kisa? the chutkas and chutkis would cry, pointing at this figure or that: Kisisa?

But in this too, Deeti had her own orderly ritual, and no matter how loudly the youngsters clamoured, she would always start in the same fashion, raising her cane to point to the smallest of the five figures on the lifeboat.

Vwala! that one there with the three eyebrows? That's Jodu, the lascar—he'd grown up with your Tantinn Paulette and was like a brother to her. And that over there, with the turban around his head, is Serang Ali—a master-mariner if ever there was one and as clever as a gran-koko. And those two there, they were convicts, on their way to serve time in Mauritius—the one on the left, his father was a big Seth from Bombay but his mother was Chinese, so we called him Cheeni, although his name was Ah Fatt. As for the other one, that's none other than your Neel-mawsa, the uncle who loves to tell stories.

It was only then that the tip of her cane would move on to the towering figure of Maddow Colver who was depicted standing upright, in the middle of the boat. Alone among the five fugitives he was depicted with his face turned backwards, as though he were looking towards the *Ibis* in order to bid farewell to his wife and his unborn child—Deeti herself, in other words, here depicted with a hugely swollen belly.

There, vwala! That's me on the deck of the *Ibis* with your Tantinn Paulette on one side and Baboo Nob Kissin on the other. And there at the back is Malum Zikri—Zachary Reid, the second mate.

The placement of Deeti's image was one of the most curious aspects of the composition: unlike the others, who all had their feet planted on their respective vessels, Deeti's body was drawn in such a way that she appeared to be suspended in the air, well above the deck. Her head was tilted backwards, so that her gaze appeared to be directed over Zachary's shoulder, towards the stormy heavens. As much as any other element of the panel, it was the odd tilt of Deeti's head that gave the composition a strangely static quality, an appearance that seemed to suggest that the scene had unfolded slowly and with great deliberation.

But any suggestion to this effect was sure to meet with an explosive rebuke from Deeti: Bon-dyé! she would cry; are you a fol dogla or what? Don't be ridikil: the whole thing, from start to fini took just a few minits, and all that time, it was nothing but jaldi-jaldi, a hopeless golmal, tus in dezord. It was a mirak, believe me, that the five managed to get away—and none of it would have been possible if not for that Serang Ali. It was he who set up the escape, that one; it was all his doing. The lascars were all in on it, of course, but it was so carefully planned that the Captain was never able to pin it on them. It was a marvel of a scheme, the kind of mulugande that only a burrburrya like the Serang could think up; they waited till the storm had driven the guards and maistries below deck and into their cumra. Then they sealed them inside by jamming their hatches. As for the officers, the Serang timed it so that they broke out during the change of watch, when both Malums were off deck. Ah Fatt the Cheeni, who was the quickest on his feet, was given the job of shutting the hatch of the officers' cuddy—what he did instead was to send the first mate to lanfer with a sandokann between his ribs—but that wasn't to be discovered until the boat was gone. Me, when Jodu let me out and I came on deck, I thought vreman I'd lost my sight. It was so dark nothing was vizib except when the lightning flashed—and tulétan the rain, coming down like hail, and the thunder, dhamak-dhamak-dhamkaoing as if to deafen you. My job was only to cut your granper down from the mast, where they had tied him, but what with the rain and wind, you can't imagine how difisil it was . . .

To hear this description was to assume that the scene had ended after no more than a few minutes of frantic activity—and yet, in almost the same breath that she gave this account of it, Deeti would claim also that the duration of the Parting had lasted for as much as an hour or two of ordinary time. Nor was this the only paradox of the experiences of that night. Later, Paulette would confirm that she had been beside Deeti from the moment when Kalua was lowered into the boat until the second when Zachary bundled them back below deck; in all that time, she swore, Deeti's feet had never left the *Ibis*, not for a single instant. But her insistence made no dent in Deeti's certainty about what had happened in those scant few minutes: she never varied in her avowal that the reason why she had portrayed herself as she had was because she had been picked up and whirled away into the sky, by a force that was none other than the storm itself.

No one who heard Deeti on this subject could doubt that in her own mind she was certain that the winds had lofted her to a height from which she could look down and observe all that was happening below—not in fear and panic, but in unruffled calm. It was as if the tufaan had chosen her to be its confidante, freezing the passage of time, and lending her the vision of its own eye; for the duration of that moment, she had been able to see everything that fell within that whirling circle of wind: she had seen the *Ibis*, directly below, and the four figures that were huddled under the shelter of the quarter-deck's companion-way, herself being one of them; some distance to the east, she had noticed a chain of islands, pierced by many deep channels; she had seen fishing boats, sheltering in the islands' bays and coves, and other strange unfamiliar craft, scudding through the channels. Then, in the same way that a parent leads a child's gaze towards something of interest, the storm had tipped back her chin to show her a craft that was trapped within its windy skirts—it was the *Ibis*'s fleeing longboat. She saw that the fugitives had made use of the stillness of the storm's eye to race across the water to the nearest of the islands; she saw them leaping from the boat, and then, to her astonishment, she saw them turning the boat over, and pushing it out where the current could seize it and carry it away . . .

All this—this succession of visions and images—had been granted to her, Deeti would insist later, in a matter of a few seconds. And it was plain enough that if her testimony were true, then the visions could not have lasted any longer than that—for the arrival of the storm's eye had provided a respite not only for the fleeing fugitives, but also for the guards and maistries. With the abating of the winds, they had begun to hammer at the jammed hatch of their cumra; it would take them only a minute or two to break through and then they would come pouring out . . .

It was Zikri-Malum who saved us, Deeti would add. If not for him, it would have been a gran kalamité—there was no telling what the silahdars and overseers might have done to the three of us if they had found us on deck. But the Malum, he got us on our feet and pushed us back into the dabusa, with the other migrants. Thanks to him we were out of sight when the guards and overseers burst out on deck . . .

As to what happened after that, they—Deeti, Paulette, and the others in the dabusa—could only guess: in the brief interval before the passing of the storm's eye and the return of the winds, it was as if another tempest had seized hold of the *Ibis*, with dozens of feet pounding across the deck, running agram-bagram, this way and that. Then, abruptly, the typhoon was upon them again, and nothing could be heard but the howling of the wind and the roar of the rain.

Not till much later did the migrants learn that Malum Zikri had been blamed for everything that had happened—the escape of the convicts, the desertions of the Serang and the lascar, the freeing of Kalua, even the murder of the first mate—the responsibility for all of this had been laid foursquare on his shoulders.

Down in the dabusa, the migrants knew nothing of what was happening overhead, and when at last they were allowed out again, it was only to be told that the five fugitives were dead. The longboat had been found, overturned and with a hole in its bottom, they were told by the maistries, so there could be no doubt that they'd met the fate they'd earned. And as for Malum Zikri, he was under lock and key, for the Captain had been forced to promise the enraged overseers that he would be handed over to the authorities when they arrived in Port Louis.

Dyé-koné, you can imazinn how this news affected us all and the gran kankann that was caused, with the lascars lamenting the death of Serang Ali, the girmitiyas mourning for Kalua, and Paulette weeping for Jodu, who was like a bhai to her, and for Zikri Malum too, because he was her hombo and she had set her heart on him. I was the only one there, let me tell you, whose eyes were dry, for I knew better. Listen, I whispered to your Tantinn Paulette, don't worry, they're safe, those five; it was they who pushed the boat back in the sea, so they'd be taken for dead and quickly forgotten. And as for Malum Zikri, don't worry about him either, tu-vwá, he'll have made some arrangements for you—just trust in him. And sure enough, a day or two later, one of the lascars, Mamdoo-tindal was his name, he gave your Tantinn Paulette a bundle of the Malum's clothes and whispered in her ear: 'When we get into port, put these on, and we'll find a way of getting you ashore.' I was the only one who wasn't surprised, for it was as if everything was coming to pass as I had seen, when the storm carried me abá-labá and showed me what was happening below . . .

There was never a lack of sceptics to question Deeti's account of that night. Most of her listeners had grown up on the island and could boast of a certain intimacy with cyclones:

not one of them had ever imagined, or could believe, that it might be possible to look at the world through the eye of a storm. Was it possible that she had imagined all of this in retrospect? Had she perhaps succumbed to a seizure or hallucination? That she could actually have seen what she claimed seemed doubtful even to the most filial among them.

But Deeti was adamant: didn't they believe in stars, planets and the lines on their palms? Did they not accept that any of these might reveal something of fate to people who knew how to unravel their mysteries? So then why not the wind? Stars and planets, after all, travelled on predictable orbits—but the wind, nobody knew where the wind would choose to go. The wind was the power of change, of transformation: this was what she had come to understand that day—she, Deeti, who had always believed that her destenn was ruled by the stars and planets; she had understood that it was the wind that had decided it was her karma to be carried to Mauritius, into another life; it was the wind that had sent down a storm to set her husband free . . .

And here she would turn to 'The Parting' and point to what was perhaps the most arresting aspect of its imagery: the storm itself. She had portrayed it so that it covered the upper part of the panel, stretching all the way across the frame: it was represented as a gigantic serpent, coiling inwards from the outside, going around and around in circles of diminishing size, and ending in a single enormous eye.

See for yourselves: she would say to the sceptics; isn't this proof? If I had not seen what I saw, how would I ever have imagined that a tufaan could have an eye?

two

~

As people go, the Colvers were not exceptionally credulous so if there had been no rational reason to suggest otherwise, most of them would have been content to regard 'The Parting' merely as an unusual family memento. It fell to Neel to show the Fami that there was at least one thing about Deeti's depiction of the Parting that was genuinely visionary: this was the fact that she had shown the storm to be wrapped around an eye. This bespoke an understanding of the nature of storms that was, for its time, not just unusual but revolutionary: because 1838, the year of that storm, was when a scientist first suggested that hurricanes might be composed of winds rotating around a still centre—an eye, in other words.

By the time Neel set foot on the Morne the notion that storms revolved around an eye was almost a commonplace—but the concept had made such an impression on Neel that he remembered very clearly his own first encounter with it, some ten years before. He had read about it in a journal and had been astonished and captivated by the image it conjured up—of a gigantic oculus, at the far end of a great, spinning telescope, examining everything it passed over, upending some things, and leaving others unscathed; looking for new possibilities, creating fresh beginnings, rewriting destinies and throwing together people who would never have met.

Retrospectively, the idea gave shape and meaning to his own experience of the storm—and yet, at the time, Neel had had no conception of its significance. How was it possible then that Deeti, an illiterate, frightened young woman, had been granted this insight? And that too at a time when only a handful of the world's most advanced scientists knew of it?

It was a mystery, there was no doubt of that in Neel's mind. This was why, in listening to Deeti's telling of the story, he began to feel that Deeti's voice was carrying him back into the eye.

. . . And now the Serang and the others are shouting in my ears: Alo-alo! Alé-alé! And your granper, heaven knows how big he is, how heavy and byin-bati. He goes to the side of the ship and I fall at his feet: Let me come with you, let me come, I beg him, but he pushes me away: No, no! You must think of the baby in your stomach; you cannot come! And then they all begin to climb into the boat—and all around us, the tufaan, raging, raging; a blink of an eye and the boat pulls away. Suddenly it is gone . . .

Neel could almost feel the planks of the boat shuddering under his feet, the rain driving against his face: it was so real that he was grateful when the children began to tug at his arm, bringing him back to the shrine: What happened next, Neel-mawsa? Were you afraid?

No, not then, he said. I am afraid now when I think of it—but when it was happening there was no time. The wind was blowing with such violence that it was all we could do to cling to the boat; it seemed as if at any minute the boat would be whirled away with all of us in it. But miraculously it didn't happen: when we were least expecting it, the storm's eye came upon us and the winds fell away. It was in that brief interval that we rowed the boat ashore. Once our feet were on the sand, our first thought was to pick up the boat and carry it to some safe place. But Serang Ali stopped us: No, he said, the best thing to do was to knock a couple of planks out of the bottom, overturn it, and push it back into the current! We couldn't believe it; it seemed like madness—how would we ever get off that island if we didn't have a boat? But the Serang brushed us off: there were boats aplenty on the island, he said, and to keep the longboat, with its tell-tale marking, would entail many risks. If it was found, people would know we were alive, and we'd be pursued till the end of our days—far better to let the world think we were dead; that way we would be written off and could start new lives. And he was right, of course—it was the best thing to do.

And then? What happened then?

The first night we spent under an overhang of rocks, sheltered from the full blast of the storm. We were, as you can imagine, in a strange state, battered in body, but alive, and better still, free. Yet, what were we to do with this freedom? Apart from Serang Ali none of us knew where we were. We thought we'd been washed up in some desolate place where we would surely starve. That was the most immediate of our fears, but it was not long before it was dispelled. By daybreak the storm was over. The sun rose upon a clear sky and on stepping out of our shelter we found ourselves in the midst of thousands of coconuts—they had been torn off by the wind and deposited on the ground, and in the water.

After we had eaten and drunk our fill Ah Fatt and I walked around to take stock of where we were: the island, or what we could see of it, was like a single enormous mountain; it rose sheer out of the sea, and where the land touched the water, the slopes were edged with dark rocks and golden sand. But everything else was forest—a dense jungle it should have been, but now, with the greenery having been stripped clear by the storm, it was just an endless succession of naked trunks and branches. It seemed to be exactly what we had feared: a completely desolate place!

Serang Ali, in the meanwhile, had not bestirred himself at all; he had curled up in the shade and was peacefully asleep. We knew better than to wake him, so we sat around and waited and worried. When at last he stirred you can imagine how eagerly we gathered around him: What do we do now, Serang Ali?

This was when the Serang revealed to us that the island was not new to him; in his youth, while working on a Hainanese junk, he had come here many times. It was called

Great Nicobar and it was by no means a deserted wilderness; on the far side of the mountain, down by the water, there were some surprisingly rich villages.

How so? we said.

He pointed at the sky, where flocks of swift-flying birds were wheeling and soaring. See those birds, he said, the islanders call them *hinlene*; they revere them because they are the source of their wealth. Those creatures look insignificant but they make something that is of immense value.

What?

Nests. People pay a lot of money for their nests.

You can imagine the effect this had on us three Hindusthanis! Your grandfather and Jodu and I all thought the Serang was making gadhas out of us.

Where in the world would people pay to buy birds' nests? we said.

China, he said. In China they boil and eat them.

Like daal?

Yes. Except that in China, it's the most expensive food of all.

This seemed incredible to us, so we turned to Ah Fatt: could this possibly be true?

Yes, he said, if these were the nests that were called 'yan wo' in Canton, then they were indeed of great value, as good a currency as any that existed in eastern waters—depending on their quality they were worth their weight in either silver or gold. A single chest of nests could fetch the equivalent of eight troy pounds of gold in Canton.

Our first thought was that we were rich, and that all we had to do was to find the nests and scoop them up. But Serang Ali quickly put us right. The birds nested in enormous caverns, he said, and each cave belonged to a village. If we walked in and helped ourselves we would never leave the island alive. Before doing anything we would have to seek out a village headman—*omjah karruh* they called them there—to ask permission, arrange a proper division of the proceeds and so on.

Fortunately the Serang was acquainted with such a headman, so we set off at once to look for his village. After a half-day's walk, we found the omjah karruh heading up the slopes of the mountain; although he had a large work party with him he was glad to see us for he urgently needed more hands.

It took an hour or so of strenuous climbing to reach the mouth of the cave, and there for a while we stood bedazzled, staring at an astonishing spectacle. The floor of the cavern was of a pale ivory colour, being thickly paved with droppings. The light of the sun, reflecting brightly off this surface, was shining upwards into a chamber that was vaster and higher than anything that any of us had ever seen. The walls, rising sheer for hundreds of feet, were lined with a numberless multitude of white nests; it was as if every exposed expanse of rock had been inlaid with shells of mother-of-pearl.

Although the great majority of the nests were high up, a few were not far off the ground. The first nest I looked at was at shoulder height and it had a bird sitting inside: the creature made no movement when I approached, nor even when I picked it up—it was smaller than my palm and I could feel its heart pounding against my fingers. It was but a modest little creature, black-brown in colour, with white underparts, and no more than eight inches in length, with a forked tail and sharply angled wings—I was to learn later that it was known as a 'swiftlet'. When I opened my hand it tried to flap its wings but was unable to launch itself: it was only when I threw it up that it streaked away.

The storm had wrought havoc upon this colony and a great number of nests were lying upon the floor. Once the feathers, twigs and dust were brushed off, the nests were seen to be of an almost iridescent whiteness; it was evident at a glance that they were made of a substance that was utterly different from the materials which other birds use in fabricating their dwellings—they had the look of works of exquisite craftsmanship, being constructed from fine filaments, laid in a circular pattern. They were so small and light that seventy together scarcely weighed as much as one Cantonese gan or a Chinese catty—about the equivalent of twenty-one English ounces.

We collected thousands of them and then helped to carry them down to the village. In return for our work, they allowed us to keep a certain quantity—not enough to make us rich, but certainly enough to afford us onward passages.

So there we were, with the wherewithal to travel onwards—and we discovered now that we had more choices than we had imagined. Northwards lay the coast of Tenasserim in Burma, and the busy port of Mergui; to the south lay the Sultanate of Aceh, one of the wealthiest realms in the region; and to the east, a few days' journey away, were Singapore and Malacca.

For all of us to travel together would have drawn unnecessary attention so we knew we would have to split up. Serang Ali wanted to go to Mergui and Jodu chose to go with him. Ah Fatt on the other hand, decided to head east, to Singapore, and then Malacca, where he had relatives—his sister and her husband had moved there some years before.

It was for your grandfather, Maddow Colver, and myself that the decision was hardest. His first thought was of working his way to Mauritius, in the hope of rejoining your grandmother. But he knew that it would not be easy, in a small place, to hide his identity, and in the event of his presence becoming known he was sure to be sent to jail, and perhaps even to the gallows. My situation was not dissimilar: my wife, Malati, and my son, Raj Rattan, were in Calcutta and I longed to go back there, mostly so I could take them away. But to return immediately might be dangerous since I would very probably be recognized.

We talked about it, thought about it, and in the end, because Mergui was closer, your grandfather decided to go with Jodu and Serang Ali. For myself the matter was decided by Ah Fatt: he and I had been through a great deal together and had become close friends. He urged me to travel with him, to Singapore and Malacca, so that was what I decided to do.

And that was how we parted: Serang Ali arranged for the three of them to travel to Mergui on a Malay proa that was heading in that direction. Ah Fatt and I waited till a Bugis trading schooner stopped by, on its way to Singapore.

And then? What next? What next?

Now, taking pity on Neel, Deeti came bustling along to scatter her brood: *Agobay!* Too many questions—do you want to make him fatigé, kwa? He's here for a konzé, na, not to do palab and panchay with you. Stop all this bak-bak and katakata—go and eat your parathas.

But once the children were gone, it became clear that Deeti's intervention had another purpose. Handing Neel a lump of charcoal, she said: It's your turn now.

To do what? said Neel.

To add to our walls. You are one of our original jahaz-bhais and this is our memory-temple. Everyone who has been here has added to it—Malum Zikri, Paulette, Jodu. It is your turn now.

Neel could think of no way to say no. All right, he said. I'll try.

He had never been much of a draughtsman, but he took the lump of charcoal from her and set hesitantly to work. One by one, the children returned, clustering around, shouting encouragement and asking each other questions.

. . . he's drawing a man, isn't he?

. . . yes, see, he has a beard; and a turban too . . .

. . . and isn't that a ship behind him? With three masts . . .

It was Deeti who gave voice to the mounting curiosity: Who is it?

Seth Bahramji.

Who's that?

Seth Bahramji Naurozji Modi—Ah Fatt's father.

And that, behind him? What is it?

His ship: it was called the *Anahita*.

~

Later there would be much discussion on whether the *Anahita* was struck by the same storm that had hit the *Ibis*. Such information as was available then made it impossible to come to any reliable determination on this: what was certain was that the *Anahita* was less than a hundred miles west of Great Nicobar Island, heading for the Nicobar Channel, when she too ran into bad weather. She had left Bombay sixteen days earlier and was on her way to Canton, by way of Singapore.

Until then the voyage had been uneventful and the *Anahita* had sailed through the few squalls that had crossed her path with a full suit of sails aloft. A sleek and elegant three-master, she was one of the few Bombay-built vessels that regularly outran the swiftest British- and American-made opium-carriers, even such legendary ships as *Red Rover* and *Seawitch*. On this voyage too she had posted very good times and seemed to be heading for another record run. But the weather in the Bay of Bengal was notoriously unpredictable in September, so when the skies began to darken, the Captain, a taciturn New Zealander, wasted no time in snugging the ship down. When the winds reached gale force he sent down a note to his employer, Seth Bahramji, recommending that he retire to the Owners' Suite and remain there for the duration.

Bahram was still there, hours later, when his purser, Vico, burst in to tell him that the cargo of opium in the ship's hold had broken loose.

Kya? How is that possible, Vico?

It's happened, patrão; we have to do something, jaldi.

Following at Vico's heels, Bahram went hurrying down, struggling to keep his footing on the slippery companion-ladders. The hatch that led to the hold was carefully secured against pilferage, and the rolling of the ship made the chains and padlocks difficult to undo. When at last Bahram was able to lower a lantern through the hatch, he found himself looking down upon a scene that defied comprehension.

The cargo in the after-hold consisted almost entirely of opium. Under the battering of the storm, hundreds of chests had broken loose and splintered, spilling their contents. Earthenware containers of opium were crashing into the bulkheads like cannonballs.

Opium, in this form, was of a mud-brown colour: although leathery to the touch, it dissolved when mixed and stirred with liquids. The *Anahita*'s builders had not been unmindful of this, and a great deal of ingenuity had been expended in trying to make the hold watertight. But the storm was shaking the vessel so hard that the joins between the planks had begun to 'bleed', letting in a slick of rain- and bilge-water. The wetness had weakened the hemp bindings that held the cargo in place and they had snapped; the chests had crashed into each other, spilling their contents into the sludge. Waves of this gummy, stinking liquid were now sweeping from side to side, breaking against the walls of the hold as the vessel rolled and lurched.

Nothing like this had ever happened to Bahram before: he had ridden out many a storm, without having a consignment of opium run amuck as it had now. He liked to think of himself as a careful man and in the course of thirty-odd years in the China trade, he had evolved his own procedures for stacking the chests in which the drug was packed. The opium in the hold was of two kinds: about two-thirds of it was 'Malwa', from western India—a product that was sold in the shape of small, round cakes, much like certain kinds of jaggery. These were shipped without any protective covering, other than a wrapping of leaves and a light dusting of poppy 'trash'. The rest of the shipment consisted of 'Bengal' opium, which had more durable packaging, with each cake of the drug being fitted inside a hard-shelled clay container, of about the shape and size of a cannonball. Every chest contained forty of these and each ball was nested inside a crib of poppy leaves, straw, and other remains from the harvest. The chests were made of mango-wood and were certainly sturdy enough to keep their contents secure during the three or four weeks it usually took to sail from Bombay to Canton: breakages were rare, and damage, when it occurred, was generally caused by seepage and damp. To prevent this, Bahram generally left some space between the rows so that air could circulate freely between the chests.

Over the years, Bahram's procedures had proved their worth: through decades of travelling between India and China he had never, in the course of a single voyage, had to write off more than a chest or two of his cargo. Experience had given him such confidence in his methods that he had not taken the trouble to check the hold when the *Anahita* was hit by the storm. It was the crashing of the runaway chests that had alerted the ship's crew, who had then brought the problem to Vico's attention.

Looking down now, Bahram could see crates crashing against the bulkheads like rafts against a reef; all around the hold, hard-shelled balls of opium were exploding upon the timbers, and gobs of the raw gum were hurtling about like shrapnel.

Vico! We have to do something; we have to go down there and secure the chests before they all break loose.

Vico was a large, round-bellied man, of darkly glossy complexion, with protuberant, watchful eyes. Born Victorino Martinho Soares, he was an 'East Indian' from the hamlet of Vasai, or Bassein, near Bombay; along with smatterings of many other languages, he also spoke some Portuguese and from the time he entered Bahram's service, some twenty years before, he had always addressed him as 'patrão'—'Boss'. Since then Vico had risen to the rank of purser, from which position he not only reigned over Bahram's personal staff but also functioned as an adviser, go-between and business associate. He had long made it his practice to invest a part of his earnings with his boss and as a result he had himself become a man of no inconsiderable means; he owned properties not just in Bombay, but also in several other places; a devout Catholic, he had even endowed a chapel in his mother's name.

It was not out of necessity therefore that Vico continued to travel with Bahram but for a number of other reasons, not the least of which was a desire to keep a close eye on his investments. He too had a substantial stake in the *Anahita*'s cargo and his concern for its safety was no less pressing than Bahram's.

You wait here, patrão, he said. I'll get some lascars to help. Don't go down there on your own.

Why not?

Vico was already on his feet but he turned back to add a warning: Because suppose something happens to the ship? Patrão will be trapped down there alone, no? Just wait for me—I'll be back in a minute.

This was good advice, Bahram knew, but not easy to heed under the circumstances. He was, at the best of times, a restless man: repose was a trial to him and at moments when he was neither speaking nor moving, the effort of self-containment would often result in a small storm of toe-tapping, tongue-clicking and knuckle-cracking. Now, leaning over the hatch, he was met by a cloud of up-welling fumes: the sickly-sweet smell of the raw opium had mingled with the bilge-water to produce a stifling, head-churning stench.

In his youth, when he had been slim, lithe and quick of foot, Bahram would not have thought twice about going down that ladder; now, in his late fifties, his joints had stiffened a little, and his waistline had thickened considerably—but his portliness, if it could be called that, was of the robust kind, his vigour and energy being evident in the golden glow of his complexion and the pink bloom of his cheeks. To wait for Fate to decide matters was not in his nature: throwing off his choga, he began to descend into the hold only to be shaken violently from side to side, as the ladder tilted and swayed.

Crooking his arm around the iron struts, he was careful to keep a tight grip on the handle of the lantern. But for all his caution he was not prepared for the gummy slime that lay underfoot. With the splintering of the crates, the stuffing of dry leaves and other poppy 'trash' had spilled out, melting into the sludge. As a result the deck planks had become as sodden and slippery as the floor of a cattle-midden, everything underfoot being coated in a vegetal mess, of the consistency of cow-dung.

When Bahram stepped off the ladder his feet shot out from under him, throwing him face-forward into a heap of dung-like sludge. He managed to turn over, pushing himself into a sitting position, with his back against a wooden beam. He could see nothing, for his lantern had gone out; in moments his clothes were drenched in the muddy sludge, from the tip of his turban to the hem of his ankle-length angarkha: inside his black leather shoes, opium was squelching between his toes.

There was something wet and cold plastered against his cheek. He raised a hand to wipe it off but just then the ship went into a steep roll and he ended up smearing the stuff on his lips and his mouth. Suddenly in the pitching darkness, with chests and containers sliding and crashing around him, his head was filled with the giddying smell of opium. He began to claw at his skin, in frantic disgust, trying to rid his face of the gum, but a wooden chest hit his elbow in such a way that yet more of the drug slipped through his lips.

Then a light appeared in the hatchway above and a voice called out worriedly: Patrão? Patrão?

Vico! Here! Bahram kept his eyes fixed on the lantern as it came slowly towards him, down the swaying ladder. Then the ship lurched again, and he was thrown sideways, under a wave of sludge. There was opium in his eyes, his ears, his nose, his windpipe—it was as if he were drowning, and in that instant many faces flashed past his eyes—that of his wife Shireenbai, in Bombay, and of their two daughters; of his mistress, Chi-mei who had died some years before, in Canton; and of the son he had had with her. It was Chi-mei's face that lingered; her eyes seemed to be gazing into his own as he sat up, coughing and spluttering; her presence seemed so real that he reached out towards her—only to find himself looking into Vico's lantern.

His hands went instinctively to his kasti—the seventy-two-thread girdle, sacred to his faith, that he always wore around his waist. Since his boyhood his kasti had been the talisman that protected him from the terrors of the unknown—but touching it now, he realized that it too was soaked in the sludge.

And then, above the roar of the storm, he heard a breaking, tearing, splintering sound, as if the ship were being torn apart. The ship rolled steeply to starboard, sending both Vico and Bahram sliding down the deck planks. As they lay sprawled in the angle between deck and bulwark, loose balls of opium came cannoning down to crash into the timbers. Each ball was worth a sizeable sum of silver—but neither Bahram nor Vico now had any regard for their value. The *Anahita* was listing at so steep an angle that it seemed all but certain that she would roll over on her beam.

But then, very slowly, the ship began to ease off, with the weight of her keel pulling her back from the brink of tipping over. In righting herself she rolled again, to the other side, and then again, before settling into a precarious balance.

Miraculously, Vico's lantern was still alight. When the vessel's pitching had slowed a little, Vico turned to Bahram: Patrão? What happened? Why did you look at me like that? What did you see?

Glancing at his purser, Bahram had a shock: Vico was covered in mud-brown sludge, from the crown of his jet-black hair to the toe of his boots. The sight was especially startling because Vico was usually extremely careful of appearances, dressing always in European clothes: now his shirt, waistcoat and breeches were so thickly encrusted with opium that they seemed to have faded into his skin. By contrast his large, prominent eyes seemed almost maniacally bright against the matt darkness of his dripping face.

What are you talking about, Vico?

When patrão reached out right now, he looked like he'd seen a ghost.

Bahram shook his head brusquely: *kai nai*—it was nothing.

But patrão—you were calling a name also.

Freddy's name?

Yes, but you were calling him by his other name—the Chinese one . . .

Ah Fatt?

This was a name that Bahram almost never used, as Vico well knew: Impossible—you must have heard wrong.

No, patrão, I'm telling you. I heard you.

There was a cloudiness in Bahram's head now and his tongue seemed to have grown heavier. He began to mumble: It must have been the fumes . . . the opium . . . I was seeing things.

Frowning worriedly, Vico took hold of Bahram's elbow and nudged him towards the ladder. Patrão must go to the Owners' Suite and take some rest. I'll look after everything here.

Bahram cast a glance around the hold: never before had his fortunes been so closely tied to a single consignment of cargo—and yet never had he felt so utterly indifferent to the fate of his merchandise.

All right then, Vico, he said. Bail out the hold and save everything you can; let me know what the damage is.

Yes, patrão; be careful now, go slowly.

The ladder seemed unaccountably long as Bahram made his way up. Whether this was because of the pitching of the ship or the giddiness in his head, he could not tell, but he made no attempt to hurry, climbing with great deliberation, pausing for breath between the rungs. He reached the top to find a half-dozen lascars waiting to go down, and they parted to make way for him, staring at him in wide-mouthed astonishment. Following their gaze, Bahram glanced down at himself and saw that he, like Vico, was so thickly caked with melted opium that his clothes had become a kind of second skin. His head was thumping and he stopped to steady himself before stepping over the coamings of the hatch. The taste of opium was not new to Bahram: during his stays in Canton he smoked a pipe every now and again—he was one of those fortunate people who was able to take it occasionally without suffering unconquerable cravings afterwards: he never missed it when he was away. But there was a great difference between inhaling the drug and ingesting it in this raw, gummy, semi-liquid state. He was completely unprepared for the sudden nausea and weakness; he had no thought now for the losses he had suffered in the hold; his eyes and his mind were focused instead, with an almost clairvoyant concentration of attention, on Chi-mei: everywhere he looked, his eyes conjured up her face. Like a Chinese lantern the image seemed to hang before him, lighting his path as he made his way aft through the cramped innards of the ship to the spacious, sumptuously appointed poop-deck where he and the ship's officers had their quarters.

The Owners' Suite lay at the end of a long gangway with many doors leading off it. A group of lascars was standing crowded around one of these doors, and on seeing Bahram approach, one of them, a tindal, said to him: Sethji—your munshi has been badly hurt.

What happened?

The rolling of the ship must have tipped him out of his bunk. Somehow his trunk got loose and crashed on him.

Will he live?

Can't say, Sethji.

The munshi was an elderly man, a fellow Parsi. He had dealt with Bahram's correspondence for many years. He could not think how he would manage without him; nor could he summon the energy to grieve.

Are there any other casualties? Bahram said to the tindal.

Yes, Sethji; we've lost two men overboard.

And what's the damage to the ship?

The whole head of the ship was ripped off, Sethji, all of it, including the jib.

The figurehead too?

Ji, Sethji.

The figurehead was a sculpture of *Anahita*, the angel who watched over the waters. It was a prized heirloom of his wife's family, the Mistries, who were the *Anahita*'s owners. He knew they would consider its loss a portent of bad luck—but he had portents of his own to deal with now, and all he could think of was getting into his cabin and taking off his clothes.

Make sure the munshiji is looked after; let the Captain know . . .

Ji, Sethji.

~

Neel did not need to have Paulette's contribution to the shrine pointed out to him: he spotted it himself—it was an outline of a man's head, drawn in profile, not unlike one of those cartoonish drawings in which human features are fitted into the inner curve of the crescent moon: the nose was a long, pendulous proboscis, the eyebrows jutted out like a ferret's whiskers, and the chin disappeared into a tapering, upcurved beard.

Do you know who that is? said Deeti.

Yes, of course I do, said Neel. It is Mr Penrose . . .

Mr Penrose's face was not easily forgotten: it was gaunt and craggy, with a jutting brow and a chin that curved upwards like the blade of a scythe. Tall and very lean, he walked with a bowed gait, his eyes fixed on the ground, as if he were cataloguing the greenery on which he was about to tread. Notoriously unmindful of his appearance, it was not unusual for him to be seen with straw in his beard and burrs in his stockings; and as for his clothes, he possessed scarcely a garment that was free of patches and stains. When deep in thought (which was often) his tapered beard and bristling eyebrows had a way of twitching and flickering, as if to announce the presence of a man who was not to be spoken to without good reason. This tic was by no means an accretion of age, for even as a child he had had a habit of 'starin and twitcherin', in a manner that was so like a polecat's that it had earned him the nickname 'Fitcher'.

Yet, despite all his tics and idiosyncrasies there was a gravity in his manner, a penetration in his gaze that precluded his being taken for a mere crank or eccentric. Frederick 'Fitcher' Penrose was in fact a man of unusual accomplishment and considerable wealth: a noted nurseryman and plant-hunter, he had made a great deal of money through the marketing of seeds, saplings, cuttings and horticultural implements—his patented moss-scrapers, bark-scalers and garden-scarifiers had a large and devoted following in England. His principal enterprise, a nursery called Penrose & Sons, was based in Falmouth, in Cornwall: it was reputed especially for its Chinese importations, some of which—like certain varieties of plumbago, flowering quince and wintersweet—had gained enormous popularity in the British Isles.

It was the plant-hunter's avocation that had brought Fitcher eastwards again, in his own vessel, the *Redruth*, a two-masted brig.

The *Redruth* sailed into Port Louis two days after the *Ibis*, after a voyage that had also been beset by misfortune and tragedy. No one on the brig had suffered more than Fitcher himself, and it was at the urging of his own crew that he decided to go ashore for a break; on the first clear day after the *Redruth*'s arrival two sailors rowed him ashore and hired him a horse so he could pay a visit to the Botanical Gardens at Pamplemousses.

It was largely because of the Botanical Gardens that Port Louis had been included in the *Redruth*'s itinerary. The Pamplemousses garden was among the earliest of its kind and counted among its founders and curators some of the most illustrious names in botany—the great Pierre Poivre, who had identified the true black pepper, had worked there, as also Philibert Commerson, the discoverer of bougainvillea. Had there existed such a thing as a route of pilgrimage for horticulturists the Pamplemousses garden would have been, without a doubt, one of its most hallowed stations.

Pamplemousses was not much more than an hour's ride from Port Louis. Fitcher had visited the garden once before, on the return leg of his first voyage to China: at that time the island was a French colony—now it was a British possession and much had changed in appearance. But, somewhat to his own surprise, Fitcher had no trouble in finding the road that led to the village. On the way, growing by the roadside, he noticed some fine specimens of a shrub known as 'Fire in the Bush', a handsome convolvulus that produced a great mass of flaming red flowers. At other times a find like this would have excited and exhilarated him; he would have dismounted to look more closely at the plants—but his state of mind now was not such as to allow this so he rode on without stopping.

Pamplemousses was upon him before he was aware of it.

The village was one of the prettiest on the island, with brightly painted bungalows, whitewashed churches, and cobbled lanes that tinkled musically under a horse's hooves. The houses and squares were much as Fitcher remembered, but when his eyes strayed in the direction of the Botanical Gardens, he received a shock that almost toppled him from his mount: where once there had been orderly, well-spaced trees and broad, picturesque vistas, there was now a wild and tangled muddle of greenery. He shook his head in disbelief and looked again, more closely: the gateposts were where he would have expected them to be, but there seemed to be nothing beyond but jungle.

Reining in his horse, Fitcher appealed to an elderly passer-by: 'Madam! The garden? D'ee know the way?'

The woman pursed her lips and shook her head: 'Ah, msieu . . . le garden is no more . . . depwi twenty years . . . abandonné by l'Anglais . . .'

She wandered off, shaking her head, leaving Fitcher to continue on his way.

Although Fitcher was saddened to learn that his own compatriots were responsible for the garden's decline, he was not entirely surprised. Since the death of Sir Joseph Banks, the last Curator of Kew Gardens, Britain's own botanical institutions had fallen into neglect, so it was scarcely a cause for wonder that a garden in a distant colony should be in a state of disrepair. Yet this did nothing to mitigate Fitcher's revulsion at the sight of the wilderness that loomed before him now: the untrimmed crowns of the garden's trees had grown into each other, forming a canopy so dense that the grounds beneath, with their flower-beds and flag-stoned pathways, were shrouded in darkness; along the peripheries of the compound, the greenery was as impenetrable as a wall, and the unclipped aerial roots of the banyans that flanked the main gateway had thickened into a forbidding barrier—a portcullis that seemed to be designed to keep intruders at bay. This was no primeval jungle, for no ordinary wilderness would contain such a proliferation of species from different continents. In Nature there existed no forest where African creepers were at war with Chinese trees, nor one where Indian shrubs and Brazilian vines were locked in a mortal embrace. This was a work of Man, a botanical Babel.

Yet, even as he was mourning the garden's demise, Fitcher was not unmindful of the fact that he had been presented with a rare opportunity. Abandoned or not, the grounds were sure to contain many rare plants, and since they no longer belonged to anyone, a collector like himself could scarcely be accused of robbery if he were to retrieve a few valuable specimens.

At the old gateway Fitcher tethered his horse to one of the rusted posts before stepping towards the thicket of banyan roots that barred the entrance. He had advanced only a few paces when he was brought up short—for he realized suddenly that the garden was not quite as abandoned as it looked: looking down at the ground, he discovered that the muddy soil had been trodden recently by a pair of shoes. Fitcher paused: he had heard that brigandage was still rife in some parts of the island so it was perfectly possible that the prints had been made by some dangerous cut-throat. But having been forewarned, Fitcher had taken the precaution of bringing a pistol and machete. After checking the pistol to make sure it was loaded he put it back in his pocket. Then, withdrawing his machete from the saddlebag, he advanced into the thicket with his eyes fixed on the trail.

The wet ground made it hard to be stealthy and Fitcher had to lift his knees and tread on his toes, like a tightrope walker, to keep his shoes from squelching in the mud. The trail of prints disappeared abruptly into a tangled thicket of undergrowth and greenery and Fitcher stopped to take stock: although no one was in sight, he could sense a presence, close at hand. More cautiously than ever he took a few more steps and, sure enough, a minute or two later he heard a sound that brought him to a standstill: it was the quiet but unmistakable scratching of a metal blade, digging into the earth.

The sound seemed to be coming from an opening between two rows of trees. Concealing himself behind a tall thicket of yellow bamboo, Fitcher started to work his way forwards. In a minute or two he found himself in a position where he could see the intruder's back: he was dressed in breeches and a loose shirt, crouching on his haunches, digging a hole in the ground—

possibly in preparation for burying some stolen loot, or perhaps even a corpse.

A few more sidewise steps gave Fitcher a better view, and he discovered now, to his puzzlement, that he'd made a mistake: what the fellow was digging was not a pit, but rather a shallow hole, like a gardener might make before planting a seedling. His implement, too, was not of a kind that would be of much help in hiding loot or digging a grave: it was a garden trowel—and from the depths of his long experience, Fitcher could tell that the man's hand was well-accustomed to this tool. Then the man shifted a little and Fitcher saw that he also had a receptacle with him—at first it looked like a small bucket, except that there was a little pin protruding from the top. On closer inspection, Fitcher realized, with something of a start, that this was a 'transplanter', the professional gardener's tool for moving tender plants from one location to another.

Now here was a brave lot of nothing. Was this a cut-throat affecting to be a gardener, or the other way around? Or could it be that the fellow was but another collector, helping himself to the garden's riches?

Fitcher was inclining towards the latter view when the gardener suddenly rocked back on his heels and half-turned his head: it was but a geek of his face that Fitcher caught, but it was enough to see that he was a young fellow, and no ruffian either but a kiddle-boy. He did not seem to be armed, and Fitcher could not imagine that any danger was to be anticipated from him.

Fitcher was trying to think of an unobtrusive way of revealing his presence when his foot landed on a length of bamboo, splitting it apart with a loud report. The youth spun around instantly and his eyes widened in alarm as they took in the sight of the ill-concealed naturalist and the glistening machete that was enfolded in his grip.

'Beg eer pardon, m'lad . . .'

Fitcher was embarrassed at being caught spying and he would not have thought it blameworthy in the gardener had he chosen to berate him—or even if he had hurled a projectile.

But instead of reaching for a stone, the youth's arms rose, as if of their own accord, and crossed themselves protectively over his coatless chest and unlaced shirt. This reaction confirmed the good opinion that Penrose had already conceived of the youth—for he too had been brought up to believe that it was indecent to appear in public without a jacket—and he began to advance with a quickened step, in order to make his excuses and introduce himself. But then, suddenly, the youthful gardener spun around and darted away, crashing through the undergrowth.

'Wait!' cried Fitcher. 'Listen, I mean'ee no harm . . .'—but the fellow was already lost in the greenery.

Glancing into the transplanter, Fitcher spotted the succulent stub of a bluish-grey plant—some kind of cactus, he took it to be—but there was no time for a closer look. Machete in hand, Fitcher went stroathing into the bushes in pursuit of the fleeing gardener.

Soon Fitcher was hacking through densely tangled greenery, with thorns and dashels clawing at his clothes. Although he had long since lost sight of the gardener, he went crashing ahead, until he broke free of the tangled undergrowth and found himself in a field of chest-high grass. On either side were towering talipots, arranged in straight lines, as if to flank an avenue. At the far end, rising out of the disordered foliage, were the remains of a small but well-proportioned cottage: tenacious saplings had taken root on its roof and its walls, tearing apart its tiles and timbers; a couple of shutters had been prised apart by creepers and were slapping against their frames with tired squeaks of their hinges.

Fitcher remembered the house, for it had been pointed out to him on his last visit: it was 'Mon Plaisir', built by the great Pierre Poivre himself. As he walked towards the cottage Fitcher's steps were slowed by a pilgrim's awe—here had lived the man who had lent his name to an entire genus, *Poivrea*. Fitcher could not help thinking that this was how an explorer might feel on beholding a ruined temple in the jungle—except that the irony, in this instance, was that the force that was devouring the temple was precisely the aspect of Nature that was enshrined within it.

Suddenly, just as Fitcher was about to step on the cracked flagstones of the threshold, a figure appeared in the main doorway. It was the young gardener: he was dressed all proper-fashion now, in a jacket and hat, but in his hands he was holding a stout stick.

Fitcher came to a halt. 'There's no need to be getting eerself in a spudder now.' Placing his machete on the ground, he stuck out his hand: 'I'm Frederick Penrose—they call me Fitcher. I mean'ee no harm.'

'That is for me to decide sir,' said the youth, briskly, ignoring his hand. 'And my jugement must wait until I know what has brought you here.'

His English, Fitcher noted, was perfectly fluent, yet there was something puzzling about it—not just the pallyvouzing idiom but also the intonation, which contained some notes that were strangely reminiscent of the speech of lascar crewmen.

'I await your answer, sir,' said the youth, with a hint of asperity.

Fitcher shifted his feet and scratched his beard. 'Well,' he said, 'maybe both of us have come for the same thing.'

The youth frowned, as though he were trying to make sense of this statement, and on looking at him closely, Fitcher realized that he was even younger than he had thought, so young that his cheeks still had their adolescent bloom: indeed he was of an age at which many another fellow would have betrayed some apprehension, if not fear—yet there was no tremor in his voice, nor any other sign of the midgetty-morrows.

'I do not understand, sir,' said the gardener, 'how you can speak of our purposes being the same when you do not know the raisons for my being here?'

'It's just that I see'd'ee back there,' said Fitcher, 'digging a hole to pitch that cactus.'

At this the gardener narrowed his eyes for a moment, and then a slight smile appeared on his face. 'I think you are misled, sir,' he said. 'It is a long while since I touched a cactus.'

It was Fitcher's turn to be puzzled now: he could not understand why the lad would go to the trouble of dissimulating over a matter like this. 'What're ee getting at, boy?' he said a little testily. 'Ee had a cactus in eer hands back there. I see'd'ee with m'own eyes—ee can scarcely disknowledge it.'

The youth shrugged in a matter-of-fact way. 'It is of no great consequence sir: just a simple méprise. Your error is so common that it may be easily forgiven.'

'What's that then?' Fitcher was not used to being patronized in matters botanical and he bridled. 'D'ee think I'm so green a gardener I wouldn't know a cactus?'

The youth's smile widened. 'Since you are so sure of yourself, Mr Penrose, perhaps you would care to lay with me a wager?'

'That's what ee're after, is it?'

Although not a betting man, Fitcher plunged a hand into his pocket and pulled out a silver dollar. 'Here I'll wager ee this—and I hope ee can match it too.'

'Come then,' said the lad cheerfully. 'I will show you the parent plant, and you will see for yourself.'

He gestured to Fitcher to follow as he plunged into a forest of chest-high grass. Fitcher tried to stay close, but the fellow was going like a mail coach and there was no keeping up with him. In the end he came to a stop and called out: 'Where've ee gone tozing off to now?'

'Here.'

Fitcher headed towards the sound, and found the young gardener kneeling beside a stone bench that was covered with moss. At the foot of the bench was a spiky plant that was being slowly strangled by a blanket of vines: one glance at the bulbous clumps and tiny thorns, and Fitcher knew that he had indeed made an embarrassingly amateurish error.

'You see, Mr Penrose,' said the boy, triumphantly, 'it is not a cactus but a spurge. The very one that prompted Linnaeus to give this race the name *Euphorbia*. It is King Juba's spurge—a fine specimen it must once have been, but I fear it has not much longer to live. That is why I am trying to propagate it elsewhere.'

Fitcher sank shamefacedly on to the bench. 'Ee've shown me up for a druler, I won't deny it.' He reached into his pocket and took out the coin. 'E've won eer wager fair and square.'

Without another word the youth stretched out his hand. When Fitcher dropped the dollar into it, he snatched it back and stood staring at the piece of eight as if he'd never seen one before.

'Where'd'ee live then?' said Fitcher.

'Why sir,' said the youth, 'I live right here—in that house.'

'In the cottage ee mean? But it's a ruin, innit?'

'By no means, sir,' said the gardener. 'Come, I will show you.'

Now, once again, Fitcher was in for a wild coursey through the chest-high grass, chasing after the gardener as he raced towards the ruins of 'Mon Plaisir'. He arrived grunting and cabaggled, to find him waiting by the door.

'One can see for oneself,' said the youth, gesturing at the interior with proprietary pride, 'this house is not quite as much the ruin as the outside suggests.'

Fitcher had only to look through the door to see that this was true—for despite the drifts of dust on the floor and the spangled nets of cobwebbing that stretched from wall to wall, it was clear that the cottage had not succumbed to the onslaught of the elements. But of furniture, as of any other accoutrements of habitation, Fitcher could see no sign.

'But where d'ee sleep?'

'There is no lack of space, sir. See.'

The youth pushed open a door and Fitcher found himself looking into a room that had been carefully dusted and rearranged: the floor was clean and the air was scented with the pleasing aroma of boy's-love—clumps of the shrub hung suspended from the mantel and the window frames. At the centre of the room lay a pile of sheets and curtains, heaped up like after-grass to form a pallet. A chair and a table stood in one corner, both wiped free of dust. On the tabletop lay a leather-bound sheaf of papers, parted at a page that immediately drew Fitcher's eye—prominently featured on it was a brightly coloured illustration of a plant.

Not to take a closer look would have been impossible for Fitcher: he stepped over and peered closely at the page—the illustration was hand-drawn and it featured a long-leafed plant that was unfamiliar to him. The text beneath was in French and Latin and he could make almost nothing of it.

'Is this eer doing then?'

'Oh no! I did only the drawings, sir—nothing else.'

'And the rest?'

'It is the work of my . . . my uncle. He was a botanist and he taught me everything I know. Alas he died before he could finish the manuscrit, so he left it to me.'

Fitcher's eyebrows began to quiver with curiosity now: the community of botanists was so small as to be almost a family; every member had some acquaintance with the others, either in person, or by name and reputation. 'Who was he then, this uncle of eers? What was his name?'

'Lambert, sir. Pierre Lambert.'

A half-throttled cry burst from Fitcher's throat and he sank into the chair. 'Well . . . I . . . Monzoo Lambert! . . . did'ee say he was eer uncle? What was your relation to him?'

Once again the gardener began to stammer and stutter. 'Why, sir . . . he was the brother of my father . . . so I . . . I am his nephew, Paul Lambert. His daughter, Paulette, is my cousin.'

'Is she now?'

Although Fitcher Penrose was, by his own account, something of a misanthrope, he was by no means unobservant: suddenly things began to fall into place—the guilty surprise with which the 'boy' had crossed his arms over his chest, the flower-strewn bedroom. He looked again at the illustration on the open page and made out a signature.

'Whose was the drawing, did ee say?'

'Why sir, it is mine.'

Fitcher bent low over the page. 'But the signature, if I'm not wrong, says not "Paul" but "Paulette".'

~

Apart from Bahram himself, Vico was the only other person who knew that the *Anahita* was carrying three thousand chests of opium in her after-hold. Bahram and Vico had gone to great lengths to keep this a secret, fudging the bills of lading, rotating the stowage crews, and disguising some of the crates. To let the facts be widely known would have been imprudent on many counts, making insurance more difficult to obtain and increasing the risks of piracy and pilferage—for this shipment was not merely the most expensive cargo that Bahram had ever shipped; it was possibly the single most valuable cargo that had ever been carried out of the Indian subcontinent.

Bahram was one of the very few merchants who had the connections and reputation to assemble such a shipment, being almost without peer in his experience of the China trade: rare was the Indian merchant who could boast of travelling to Canton more than three or four times—but Bahram had made the journey fifteen times in the course of his career. In the process he had built, almost single-handedly, one of the largest and most consistently profitable trading operations in Bombay: the export division of Mistrie Brothers.

Although this firm was one of Bombay's most prominent establishments, it had by tradition been quite narrowly specialized, with few interests outside shipbuilding and engineering. The export division was Bahram's personal creation and it was he who had built this small unit into a worthy rival of the famous shipyard. In doing so he had faced no little resistance from within the firm; if he had persevered, it was largely because of his deep and abiding loyalty to his father-in-law, Seth Rustamjee Pestonjee Mistrie—the patriarch who had accepted him into the family, and given him his start in the world.

As with many others whose fortunes are transformed by advantageous unions, no one set greater store by the reputation of the family he had married into than Bahram himself: in his case, his regard for the Mistries was tinged also with a great deal of gratitude, for it was they who had given him an opportunity to rise above the humble circumstances into which he had been born.

There had been a time once when Bahram's own family had also been prosperous and well-respected, occupying a place of distinction in their hometown of Navsari, in coastal Gujarat; his grandfather had been a well-known textile dealer, with important court connections in princely capitals like Baroda, Indore and Gwalior. But in his waning years, after a lifetime of prudence, he had made a slew of rash investments, incurring an enormous burden of debt. Being a man of steely integrity he had taken it upon himself to pay off every loan, down to the last tinny, coproon and half-anna; as a result, the family had been reduced to utter penury, with no more than a handful of cowries in their khazana—too few, as the saying went, to string together on an arm's-length of thread. Forced to sell off their beautiful old haveli, they had moved into a couple of rooms on the edge of town, and this had proved fatal for the old man as well as his son, Bahram's father, who was a consumptive and had suffered from lifelong ill health; he did not live to see Bahram's navjote—his ceremonial induction into the Zoroastrian faith.

Fortunately for the boy and his two sisters, their mother had learnt one lucrative skill in her girlhood: she was an exceptionally good needlewoman, and the shawls she embroidered were much prized and admired. When word of the family's plight spread through the community, orders came pouring in, and by dint of thrift and hard work, she was able not only to feed her children, but also to provide Bahram with the rudiments of an education. In time her renown spread as far as Bombay, fetching her an important commission: she was asked to supply embroidered wedding shawls for the daughter of one of the foremost Parsi businessmen of the city—none other than Seth Rustamjee Pestonjee Mistrie.

The two families were not unknown to each other, for the Mistrie business had also been founded in Navsari—its origins lay in a small furniture workshop which the Modis, in their heyday, had lavishly patronized and supported. Attached to the workshop was a shed for building boats: although small to begin with, this part of the business had quickly outstripped every other branch. After winning a major contract from the East India Company, the Mistries had moved to Bombay where they had opened a shipyard in the dockside district of Mazagon. On taking charge of the firm, Seth Rustamjee had built energetically upon his inheritance, and under his direction the Mistrie shipyard had become one of the most successful enterprises in the Indian subcontinent. Now, his daughter was to marry a scion of one of the richest merchant families in the land, the Dadiseths of Colaba, and the wedding was to be celebrated on a scale never seen before.

But a few days before the beginning of the festivities, with all the arrangements made and anticipation at its height, fate intervened: one of the Dadiseths' associates in Aden had presented the prospective bridegroom with a fine Arab stallion, and the boy, who was only fifteen, had insisted on taking it for a ride on the beach. Disoriented after the long journey across the sea, the horse was sorely out of temper: galloping headlong on the sand, the boy was thrown and killed.

For the Mistrie family the boy's death was a double disaster: not only did they lose the son-in-law of their dreams, they had also to reconcile themselves to the knowledge that the tragedy would make it difficult, if not impossible, for their daughter to make a good marriage: her prospects were sure to be contaminated by the stain of misfortune. When they began to send out feelers once again, their apprehensions were quickly confirmed: the girl's plight occasioned much sympathy without eliciting any acceptable offers of marriage. When it became clear that no proposals would be forthcoming from within their circle, the Mistries reluctantly took their search beyond the city, to their ancestral town, where they presently found their way to Bahram's mother's door.

Although they had fallen on hard times, this branch of the Modis was acknowledged to be of respectable pedigree, and Bahram himself was a sturdy, good-looking lad, more or less educated, and of an appropriate age, being almost sixteen years old. Hearing good reports of him, the Seth met with Bahram during a trip to Navsari and was favourably impressed by his eagerness and energy: it was he who decided that the boy would be an acceptable match for his daughter, despite the disadvantages of a rough-edged demeanour and a poverty-stricken upbringing. But the circumstances being what they were, the proposal that was sent to Bahram's mother was qualified by certain stipulations: since the boy had no money and no immediate prospects for advancement, the couple would have to live in Bombay, in the Mistrie mansion, and the groom would have to enter the family business.

Despite the undreamt-of advantages offered by this match, Bahram's mother did not press it on him; the hardships of her life had given her many insights into the world, and in discussing the conditions that accompanied the proposal, she said: For a man to live with his in-laws, as a 'house-husband'—a *gher-jamai*—is never an easy thing. You know what people say about sons-in-law: *kutra pos, bilarã pos per jemeinã jeniyãne varmã khos*—rear a dog, rear a cat, but shove the son-in-law and his offspring into the gutter . . .

Bahram laughed this off as a piece of rustic wisdom that had no application to people as wealthy and sophisticated as the Mistries. He himself was impatient to quit his rustic surroundings, and he knew that an opportunity like this one was unlikely ever to be presented to him again: his mind was made up almost from the first, but for form's sake, he let a week go by before asking his mother to accept the proposal on his behalf.

And so, with appropriately muted celebrations, the marriage came about, and Bahram and Shireenbai moved into an apartment in the Mistrie mansion on Bombay's Apollo Street.

Shireenbai was a shy, retiring girl whose spirits had been permanently dimmed by the tragedy that preceded her marriage; her demeanour was more of a widow than a bride, and she seemed always to be shrouded in melancholy, as though she were mourning the husband she should have had. Towards Bahram she was dutiful, if unenthusiastic, and since he had not expected much more, they dealt with each other well enough and had two daughters in quick succession.

If there was little passion in Bahram's relationship with Shireenbai, there was also little rancour—but such could not be said for his dealings with the rest of her family. The Mistries' sprawling compound housed a great many people, including Shireenbai's parents, her three brothers, their wives and their children—and with the notable exception of the patriarch, they seemed mostly to be united in their wariness of the penniless provincial who had come into their midst: it was as though a bumptious and somewhat uncouth poor relative had insinuated himself into their home with an eye to dispossessing them of it.

That Bahram was sometimes clumsy in his ways, he himself would not have gainsaid, any more than he would have denied that his rustic Gujarati and inadequate English were something of an embarrassment within the urbane confines of the Mistrie mansion. But these were no more than minor issues; the truth was that he would not have been quite so much of a misfit had he not been so utterly bereft of the aptitudes that the Mistries expected of their menfolk. They were a lineage of builders and master-craftsmen, who prided themselves on their technical skills. Shireenbai's father, Seth Rustamjee, had made it his mission to prove that Indian-made vessels—which Europeans commonly spoke of as 'country-boats' or 'black-ships'—could perform as well as, if not better than, any in the world. Not only had the Seth been personally responsible for several significant innovations in shipbuilding techniques, he had also trained his apprentices to stay abreast of technological advances in this rapidly changing field. Bombay was regularly visited by some of the sleekest and most sophisticated foreign-made vessels: by befriending the artisans and repairmen who serviced these ships, the Mistries kept themselves informed of all the latest technical improvements and nautical gadgetry, which they quickly adapted and refined for their own use. Indeed, their ships were so advanced in design, and built at such little cost, that many European fleets and shipowners—even Her Majesty's Navy—had begun to send commissions to Mistrie & Sons in preference to the shipyards of Southampton, Baltimore and Lübeck.

If the Mistries had succeeded in making their firm into a formidable force within a fiercely competitive industry, it was because they had kept their attention closely fixed upon their chosen fields of expertise. To fit into such a specialized organization required, of a newcomer, certain skills and abilities that Bahram did not possess: tools did not sit well in his fidgety hands, details bored him, and he was too individualistic to stay in step with a team of fellow workers. His tenure as an apprentice shipwright was a short one and he was quickly shunted off to a dingy daftar at the back, where the firm's accounts were tabulated. But this suited him no better for neither numbers nor the men who worked with them were of the least interest to him: shroffs and ledger-keepers seemed to him to be painfully constrained in their vision of the world, devoid of imagination and entrepreneurship. His own gifts, as he saw them, were of a completely different kind; he was good at dealing with people, staying abreast of the news, and was blessed moreover with a sharp eye for sizing up risks and opportunities: not for him the tedium of coin-sifting and column-filling—even while serving time in the daftar, he was careful to keep himself informed of other openings, never doubting that he would one day chance upon a field of enterprise that was better suited to his talents.

It wasn't long before Bahram knew exactly what he wanted to do: the export trade between western India and China was growing very fast, and offered all kinds of opportunities—not just of profit but also of travel, escape and excitement. But he knew that to persuade the Mistries to enter this arena would not be easy; in matters of business they were deeply conservative and disapproved of anything that smacked of speculation.

Sure enough when Bahram first brought up the matter of entering the export trade, his father-in-law had reacted with distaste: What? Selling opium overseas? That's just gambling—it isn't something that a firm like the Mistries' can get involved in.

But Bahram had come prepared. Listen sassraji, he had said. I know you and your family are committed to manufacturing and engineering. But look at the world around us; look at how it is changing. Today the biggest profits don't come from selling useful things: quite the opposite. The profits come from selling things that are not of any real use. Look at this new kind of white sugar that people are bringing from China—this thing they call 'cheeni'. Is it any sweeter than honey or palm-jaggery? No, but people pay twice as much for it or even more. Look at all the money that people are making from selling rum and gin. Are these any better than our own toddy and wine and sharaab? No, but people want them. Opium is just like that. It is completely useless unless you're sick, but still people want it. And it is such a thing that once people start using it they can't stop; the market just gets larger and larger. That is why the British are trying to take over the trade and keep it to themselves. Fortunately in the Bombay Presidency they have not succeeded in turning it into a monopoly, so what is the harm in making some money from it? Every other shipyard maintains a small fleet to engage in overseas trade; isn't it time for the Mistries to set up an export division of their own? Look at the returns that some other firms are getting of late, by exporting cotton and opium: they have been doubling and even tripling their investments with every consignment they send to China. If you give me permission I will be glad to make an exploratory voyage to Canton.

Seth Rustamjee was still unpersuaded. No, he said, this is too big a departure from the firm's practices. I can't allow it.

So Bahram went back to his old accounting job but his performance was so poor that Seth Rustamjee called him back into his daftar and told him, bluntly, that he was becoming a complete *nikammo*—a worthless man. In the shipyard he had proved worse than useless; at home he seemed unable to get along with most of the family—if he carried on like this he would soon become a burden on the family.

Bahram lowered his head and said: Sassraji, everyone makes mistakes. I am just twenty-one; give me a chance to go to China and I will prove myself. Believe me, I will always try to be worthy of you and your family.

Seth Rustamjee had looked at him long and hard and then given him an almost imperceptible nod: All right, go then, let's see what comes of it.

And so Mistrie & Sons had financed Bahram's first voyage to Canton—and the results had astonished everyone, not least Bahram himself. For him, of all the surprises of that journey, none was greater than that of the foreign enclave of Canton, where the traders resided. 'Fanqui-town', as old hands called it, was a place at once strangely straitened yet wildly luxurious; a place where you were always watched and yet were free from the frowning scrutiny of your family; a place where the female presence was strictly forbidden, but where women would enter your life in ways that were utterly unexpected: it was thus that Bahram, while still in his twenties, found himself gloriously and accidentally entangled with Chi-mei, a boat-woman who gave him a son—a child who was all the more dear to him because his existence could never be acknowledged in Bombay.

In Canton, stripped of the multiple wrappings of home, family, community, obligation and decorum, Bahram had experienced the emergence of a new persona, one that had been previously dormant within him: he had become Barry Moddie, a man who was confident, forceful, gregarious, hospitable, boisterous and enormously successful. But when he made the journey back to Bombay, this other self would go back into its wrappings; Barry would become Bahram again, a quietly devoted husband, living uncomplainingly within the constraints of a large joint family. Yet, it was not as if any one aspect of himself were more true or authentic than the other. Both these parts of his life were equally important and necessary to Bahram, and there was little about either that he would have wanted to change. Even Shireenbai's unemotional dutifulness, her scarcely hidden disappointments, seemed indispensable within the contours of his existence, posing as they did, a necessary corrective to his natural ebullience.

Such was Bahram's success that he could very well have hived off from the Mistrie firm and set up a trading firm of his own—but this he was never seriously tempted to do. His compensation, for one thing, was so generous as to leave no room for complaint. But even more than his earnings, Bahram enjoyed the perquisites that went with serving as a representative of one of Bombay's most highly regarded companies: the fact of being able to command some of the finest lodgings in Canton, for example, and of having a near-unlimited allowance for his personal expenses. And then there was the comfort and prestige of having at his disposal a ship like the *Anahita*, which his father-in-law had built with his own hands, specifically for his use, so that it served almost as his personal flagship: few traders, in Canton or elsewhere, could boast of travelling in such unmatched luxury.

Besides, breaking off from the Mistrie firm would inevitably have entailed a change of residence as well—and Bahram knew that Shireenbai would never agree to leave the family mansion. Every time he had ever suggested it, she had burst into tears. How can you speak of leaving? *Ay apru gher nathi?* Isn't this our house too? You know my mother wouldn't survive it if I left. And what would I do during those months and years when you're away in China—alone on my own, with no man by my side? It would be different of course if *gher ma deekra hote*—if there was a son in the house, but . . .

So Bahram had been content to remain within the Mistrie fold, quietly building up his part of the business, grooming it into a worthy sibling for the family's shipyard. But strangely, Bahram's success did nothing to soften Shireenbai's brothers' view of him: on the contrary, it added an element of fear to their long-held suspicions, for they now began to resent their father's growing reliance on him.

If the younger Mistries' attitude was puzzling to Bahram, it was not so to his mother, who accounted for it by reaching into her ditty bag of proverbs. Don't you understand why they're afraid? she said. What they're saying to each other is: *palelo kutro peg kedde*—it's the pet dog that bites you in the leg . . .

As so often before, Bahram had laughed at her homespun wisdom—but in the end it was she who was proved right.

Through all his years of working for Mistrie & Sons Bahram had assumed, with his father-in-law's encouragement, that he would one day be given full control of the division he had founded and nurtured. But then, unexpectedly, the Seth had a stroke that left him paralysed and unable to speak. For many months he hovered between life and death, throwing the family, and the firm, into turmoil. The will that he was rumoured to have made was never found, and after his death his sons and grandsons quickly came to be embroiled in a struggle over the future of the firm. Neither Bahram nor Shireenbai played any part in this tussle, for her inheritance was held in trusteeship by her brothers, and Bahram himself did not possess enough of an equity stake to be considered a principal.

Bahram's first inkling of what was afoot came when he was summoned to a meeting with his brothers-in-law. Sitting around him in a semicircle, they told him that they had come to a decision about the future of their company; the shipbuilding business had been in decline for a long time and they had now resolved to liquidate the whole firm in order to provide the brothers and their children with seed capital to start other businesses. Since the export division, and the fleet, were now the most valuable parts of the company, they would be the first to be sold. It was unfortunate of course that he, Bahram, would have to go into retirement; but in recognition of his contribution, the firm would certainly award him an extremely generous financial settlement—and it was true after all, that he was in his fifties now, with both his daughters married and well-provided-for. Had he not reached a point in his life when a luxurious retirement would seem like a fitting end to a brilliant career?

In other words, he, Bahram, who had contributed so much to the firm was to be shut out of the succession and pensioned off.

That the Mistries might be willing to sell off their hugely profitable export unit was a possibility that Bahram had never contemplated. Nor could he abide the thought of retirement;

never to go to sea again, never to return to Canton would be to diminish his life by half or more; it would be as good as a living death. Three years had already passed since his last visit to China, and in the meanwhile his son, who was now in his early twenties, had disappeared and Chi-mei had died. For that reason alone it was impossible for him to think of renouncing Canton forever; he would never be able to live with the torment of not knowing what had become of his boy.

But why now? said Bahram to his brothers-in-law. Why do you want to sell the export division at a time when it's poised to do better than ever before? Why not wait a few years?

The Mistrie brothers explained that they had of late heard many troubling rumours about the situation in China; there was even talk that the Emperor would soon impose a total ban on opium imports. A period of prolonged uncertainty seemed to be looming ahead, which was why many Bombay businessmen were washing their hands of the China trade. As for themselves, they had always felt that this enterprise was overly risky and speculative; they had now concluded that it would be best to get rid of the export division before it became a drag upon the rest of the firm.

Bahram's response was to stare at his brothers-in-law in frank astonishment: being much better informed about the situation than they, he had given the rumours and gossip much more attention than they had. The conclusion he had reached was exactly the opposite of theirs; it seemed to him that the present conditions offered an unmatched commercial opportunity, the like of which came only once or twice in a lifetime. Similar rumours had circulated in 1820 and Seth Rustamjee had tried to dissuade Bahram from shipping any opium that year. Not only had Bahram insisted on going, he had shipped his biggest consignment to date; things had turned out exactly as he had expected and he had made an immense profit. It was this coup that had pushed him into the select group of foreign merchants who were known in Canton as *daaih-baan*—or tai-pans, as they liked to style themselves.

Bahram had good reason to think that the same thing would happen again this year: he had recently learnt that a group of senior mandarins had submitted a memorial to the Emperor of China, recommending the legalization of the opium trade. It seemed likely that this would soon be acted upon: the state stood to earn huge revenues if it taxed the trade, and the mandarins too would make enormous profits. The demand for opium was sure to increase vastly afterwards.

Bahram could have told the Mistrie brothers about this if he had wished; he could also have told them that he had planned to ship an unusually large consignment of opium this year, in the expectation of making a great deal of money for the firm. But he did neither; instead he came to a decision that he should have made many years ago: for much too long had he used his wits, his nerves and his experience to make money for his brothers-in-law; it was time now to do it for himself. If he pooled all his resources, cashed in his savings, mortgaged his properties, sold Shireenbai's jewellery and borrowed from his friends, he would surely be able to double or treble his capital, allowing him to set up his own company. The risk had to be taken.

He gave his brothers-in-law a polite smile. No, he said. No you will not sell off the export division.

What do you mean?

You will not sell it off because I will buy it from you myself.

You? they cried out in unison. But think of the cost . . . there are the ships . . . the *Anahita* . . . the crews and their salaries. . . . the insurance . . . the daftars . . . the warehouses . . . the working capital . . . the fixed expenses.

They fell silent and goggled at him, until one of them found the breath to ask: And do you have the funds?

Bahram shook his head. No, he said. I don't have the funds right now. But once we settle on a price, I give you my word that you'll have the money within a year. Until that time, I ask that you leave the export division intact, and in my charge, to run as I see fit.

The brothers had glanced at each other uneasily, unsure of how to respond. To settle the matter, Bahram had pointed out, gently: You have no choice, you know. Everybody in Bombay knows that I have built this division from nothing. No one would buy it against my advice. You would not realize a fraction of its true price.

Right then there was a sound overhead. It was caused merely by the fall of some weighty object on the floor above—but Bahram was familiar with the superstitions of his audience and he seized his opportunity. Laying his hand on his heart, he said: *Hak naam te Saahebnu*, Truth is the name of the Almighty.

Just as he had expected, this ended the argument: the Mistries accepted his terms and Bahram went immediately to work.

Over the years he had nurtured and cultivated an extensive network of connections among the petty traders, caravan-masters and moneylenders who were responsible for transporting opium from the market towns of western and central India to Bombay. Now his couriers and emissaries fanned out to Gwalior, Indore, Bhopal, Dewas, Baroda, Jaipur, Jodhpur and Kota, spreading the word that there was only one Seth in Bombay who was offering a fair price for opium this year. In the meanwhile, in order to raise the money for these purchases, Bahram liquidated his savings and drew upon every source of credit that was available to him. When these measures proved inadequate, he mortgaged—in the teeth of his wife's opposition—their jointly owned lands and sold off their gold, silver and jewellery.

But even after all this, he would not have succeeded in putting together a shipment that was equal to his ambitions: that he was able to do so was the result of an unforeseen development. By the end of the monsoons, when the bulk of the trading fleet usually left for Canton, the rumours of impending trouble in China had grown so insistent as to send commodity prices spiralling downwards. When everyone stopped buying, Bahram stepped in.

That was how he succeeded in assembling the shipment that ran amuck in the storm of September 1838. Its total value, if the price was what Bahram expected it to be, would be well over a million Chinese taels of silver—equivalent to about forty English tons of the precious metal.

How much of this was lost in the storm? As he lay in his bed, in the Owners' Cabin, dazed by the after-effects of the opium, Bahram was tormented with anxiety. Every time Vico made an appearance he would ask: How much, Vico? *Kitna?* How much is gone?

Still counting, patrão; don't know yet.

When at last Vico was ready with his final count it proved to be both better and worse than expected: his estimate was that they had lost about three hundred chests—about ten per cent of their cargo.

To lose the equivalent of five tons of silver was a devastating blow, undoubtedly, but Bahram knew it could have been much worse. With the insurance factored in, he still had enough left to pay off his investors and earn a handsome profit.

It was only a question now of how he played his cards; they were in his hand and the table was ready.

~

To watch a girl cry was very difficult, almost unbearable for Fitcher. After tugging mightily at his beard, and clearing his throat many times, he said, suddenly: 'Ee may be surprised to hear this, Miss Paulette, but I was acquainted with eer father. Ee features him mightily, I might say.'

Paulette looked up and dried her eyes.

'But that is incroyable, sir: where could you have met my father?'

'Here. In Pimple-mouse. In this very garden . . .'

It had happened over thirty years ago, when Fitcher was on his way back to England after his first voyage to China. The journey had been a difficult one: his old-fashioned 'plant-cabin' had been damaged in a hailstorm; the plants had been spattered with seawater and battered by winds. Having already lost half his collection, he had made the journey to Pamplemousses in a state of despair. But there, in one of the storage sheds near the garden's entrance, he had made the acquaintance of Pierre Lambert: the botanist was young, freshly arrived from France, and on the way over he had begun to experiment with a new kind of carrying case for plants: he'd removed a few panels from the casing of an old wooden trunk and replaced them with panes of thick glass. He gave Fitcher two of these cases and would accept no payment.

'I always wanted to thank eer father, but I never saw him again. Right sorry I am to know that he's gone.'

At this Paulette's composure dissolved and her story came pouring out: she told Fitcher that her father's death, in Calcutta, had left her destitute; she had decided to travel to Mauritius, where her family had once had connections and had succeeded in smuggling herself on to a coolie ship, the *Ibis*; the journey had been calamitous in many ways but because of the kindness of a few crew-members she had been able to make her way safely ashore; the vessel's second mate, Zachary Reid, had lent her the clothes she was wearing, but he was now under arrest and soon to be shipped off to Calcutta to stand trial for mutiny; finding herself penniless, she had walked to the Botanical Gardens, where her father had once worked—but only to find it abandoned; having nowhere else to go she had taken shelter in the abandoned cottage and had spent the last few days there, foraging for food.

'So what will ee do now? D'ee know?'

'No. Not yet. But I have managed well enough so far, and I do not see why I should not get by for a while longer.'

Fitcher coughed, cleared his throat and turned around to face her. 'And what if—what if I were to offer ee something better, Miss Paulette? A job? Would ee think of it at all?'

'A job, sir?' she said warily. 'Of what kind, may I ask?'

'A gardening job—except that it'd be on a ship. Ee'd have eer own cabin, all fitted out for a young lady. Ee'd have a bosun's pay, and nothing charged for the victuals neither.' He paused. 'I owe it to eer father.'

Paulette smiled and shook her head. 'You are very kind, sir, but I am not a lost kitten. My father would not have wanted me to take advantage of your generosity. And for myself too, sir, I must confess that I have grown weary of living on charity.'

'Charity?'

Fitcher was suddenly aware of a strange bedoling in certain parts of his body: it was as though he were being assailed by an unfamiliar illness, with symptoms that he could not remember having experienced before—a strangled feeling in the gullet, a palsied shaking of the hands, a fierce itching of the eyes. Sinking into the chair he raised his fingers to his throat and was bewildered to find drops of moisture dripping off the end of his beard. He looked at the wet ends of his fingers as though they had metamorphosed into something inexplicable—like tendrils sprouting on the ends of thorns.

Fitcher was not the kind of man who wept easily: even as a boy he had been able to endure dry-eyed any number of blows, cuffs and kicks. But now it was as if a lifetime of anguish was pouring out of him, streaming down his face.

Paulette went to kneel beside him and looked worriedly into his face. 'But sir, what is it? If I gave offence, believe me it was not my intention.'

'Ee don't understand,' said Fitcher, through his sobs. 'It's not out of charity that I offered ee the job, Miss Paulette. Truth is, I had a daughter too. Her name was Ellen and she was travelling with me. Since she were little she always wanted to go to China, to collect, as I had done. Month ago, she took ill and there were nothing we could do. She's gone now, and without her I don't know if I have it in my heart to go on.'

He removed his hands from his face and looked up at her: 'Truth is, Miss Paulette, it's ee who'd be doing a kindness for an old man. For me.'

three

For many years Bahram had regarded the fledgling township of Singapore as a junglee joke.

In the old days, when sailing through the Straits, Bahram had made a point of stopping not at Singapore but at Malacca, which was one of his favourite cities: he liked the location, the severe Dutch buildings, the Chinese temples, the whitewashed Portuguese church, the Arab souq, and the galis where the long-settled Gujarati families lived—and food-lover that he was, he had also developed a great partiality for the banquets that were served in the houses of the city's Peranakan merchants.

In those days Singapore was just one of many forested islands, clogging the tip of the straits. On its southern side, at the mouth of the river, there was a small Malay kampung: ships would sometimes drop anchor nearby and send their longboats over for fresh water and provisions. But the island's jungles were notorious for their tigers, crocodiles, and venomous snakes; no one lingered any longer than was necessary.

When the British chose that unpromising location for a new township, Bahram, like many others, had assumed that the settlement would soon be reclaimed by the forest: why would anyone choose to stop here when Malacca was just a day's sail away? Yet, as the years went by, despite his personal preference for Malacca, Bahram had been forced to yield, with increasing frequency, to his ship's officers, who claimed that the port facilities were better in Singapore—Mr Tivendale's conveniently situated boatyard was especially to their liking: they frequently cited it as the best in the region.

It was to this boatyard that the *Anahita* made her way after the storm: although she had lost her jib-boom and her figurehead, her other masts were intact and she was able to cover the distance in less than a week. Because of the lingering effects of the raw opium he had ingested, Bahram was unable to stir from his bed through this part of the voyage. For several days afterwards he suffered from opium-induced nausea: the attacks were more intense than anything he had ever experienced before, worse than his worst bouts of sea-sickness. Once or twice every hour his stomach would be knotted by spasms that made him feel as if his body were trying to eject his guts by pushing them out through his mouth. These seizures were so enfeebling that at times he could not turn on his side without Vico's help.

When the *Anahita* reached Singapore Bahram was still too weak to leave his bedroom; he chose to remain on board while the ship was being repaired and refurbished. This was no great trial, for the comforts offered by Mr Dutronquoy's hotel, the only respectable hostelry in town, were far exceeded by those of his own surroundings. The Owners' Suite on the *Anahita* was perhaps the most luxurious to be found outside a royal yacht: apart from a bedroom it also included a saloon, a study, a bathroom and a water-closet. Here, as in many other parts of the *Anahita*, the bulkheads were decorated with motifs from ancient Persian and Assyrian art, carved in relief upon the wooden panels: there were grooved columns like those of Persepolis and Pasargadae; there were bearded spear-carriers, standing stiffly in profile; there were winged farohars and leaping horses. In one corner of the cabin there was a large mahogany desk, and in another, a small altar, with a gilt-framed picture of the Prophet Zarathustra.

The suite's bed was one of its most luxurious features: a canopied four-poster, it was so placed that Bahram could look out at the harbour through the cabin's windows. He was thus able to appreciate, as never before, how quickly Singapore was changing.

The Tivendale boatyard was situated at the mouth of the Singapore River, between the port's inner harbour, which was in the estuary, and the outer anchorage, which was in the bay beyond. Being anchored between the two, the *Anahita*'s stern tended to swing with the flow of the tides: when it faced outwards, hundreds of bumboats and tongkang lighters would come into view, swarming around the ships anchored in the bay. On their way back to shore the boats would sometimes pass so close to the *Anahita* that Bahram would hear the voices of the Chulia boatmen talking, shouting and singing in Tamil, Telegu and Oriya. When the *Anahita*'s stern came about, a panoramic view of newly built godowns and bankshalls would appear in front of him. Sometimes the *Anahita* would sweep so far around that he would even be able to look upriver towards Boat Quay, where the smaller 'country boats' discharged their goods and passengers.

The activity was unending, the boat traffic constant, and in watching it Bahram began to understand why several businessmen of his acquaintance had recently bought or rented godowns and daftars in Singapore: it seemed very likely that the new settlement would soon overtake Malacca in commercial importance. This evoked mixed emotions in Bahram: he had a suspicion that this British-built settlement would not be an easy-going place like the Malacca of old, where Malays, Chinese, Gujaratis and Arabs had lived elbow to elbow with the descendants of the old Portuguese and Dutch families. Singapore had been so designed as to set the 'white town' carefully apart from the rest of the settlement, with the Chinese, Malays and Indians each being assigned their own neighbourhoods—or 'ghettoes' as some people called them.

What would become of this odd new town? The one thing that was for sure was that it would be a good place for buying and selling: the reports Vico brought back from his forays ashore confirmed that bazars and markets were springing up all around the settlement—Vico's particular favourite was a weekly open-air mela where people came from near and afar to sell and exchange old clothes.

From Vico's accounts, as from his observations of the traffic on the river, it was clear to Bahram that Singapore was rapidly evolving into one of the principal waystations of the Indian Ocean: this was why he was not greatly surprised to learn that an old friend of his, Zadig Karabedian, was in the city—Vico had run into him as he was walking down Commercial Street.

Arré Vico! said Bahram. Why didn't you bring Zadig Bey back with you?

He was going somewhere, patrão. He said he would come as soon as possible.

What's he doing in Singapore?

He's on his way to Canton, patrão.

Oh? Bahram sat up eagerly. Has he booked a passage already?

Don't know, patrão.

Vico, you have to go and find him, said Bahram. Tell him he has to travel with us, on the *Anahita*. I won't take no for an answer. Tell him to come aboard as soon as possible. Go na, jaldi!

Zadig Karabedian was one of Bahram's few true intimates. They had met twenty-three years before, in Canton. Zadig was a watchmaker by trade and travelled often to various ports in the Indian Ocean and the South China Sea, to sell clocks, watches, music boxes and other mechanical devices—known collectively as 'sing-songs', these articles were in great demand in Canton.

Although Zadig was Armenian by origin, his family had been settled for centuries in Egypt, where they lived in the old Christian and Jewish quarter of Cairo. Legend had it that one of Zadig's ancestors had been sold to the Sultan of Egypt as a boy: after rising in the Mamelouk ranks he had arranged to bring some of his relatives to Cairo where they had prospered as craftsmen, tax collectors and businessmen. Since then they had developed close business connections with Aden, Basra, Colombo, Bombay and several ports in the Far East, including Canton.

Zadig, even more than other members of his clan, was an inveterate traveller, and was fluent in many languages, including

Hindusthani. He had a great talent also for something that Bahram liked to call *khabar-dari*—keeping up with the news—and it was partly because of this that their paths had crossed in Canton.

The year was 1815, and the first reports of the French defeat at Waterloo had reached southern China in late November. The news was received with great relief by most of the European community. Many merchants who had delayed their return to Europe because of the war, now changed their minds and decided to make their way back; this caused all kinds of disruption, not the least of which was a shortage in bills of exchange. Because of the greatly increased demand it became especially hard to obtain bills that were payable in India: all of a sudden Bahram found himself faced with the prospect of having to travel to England in order to realize his profits for the season.

To Bahram this was no great disappointment: he had never been to Europe before and the prospect of travelling there was exciting beyond measure—but on trying to obtain a berth, he discovered that westward passages were in critically short supply. It was then that a Parsi friend put him in touch with Zadig Karabedian.

Being an avid student of Continental politics, Zadig had foreseen the outcome of the Hundred-Days' War and had even found a way to profit from it. It so happened that he too was travelling to England, and having guessed that there would be a great demand for westbound passages that season, he had reserved the other bunk in his cabin, in the expectation of making it over to a travelling companion, someone who would be both congenial and willing to pay a substantial dastoori. After some hard but amicable bargaining, he and Bahram were able to settle on mutually satisfactory terms and they boarded the Hon'ble Company Ship *Cuffnells* at Macau on 7 December 1815.

Zadig was tall, with a long, thin neck, and a face that had the look of being permanently frostbitten because of the webbing of cracks that radiated outwards from the twin spots of colour on his bright, pink cheeks. Once under weigh, Bahram and Zadig found themselves spending most of their time in each other's company: their cabin was deep in the vessel's bowels, and to escape the stench of the bilges the two traders spent as much time as they could on deck, leaning over the rails and talking, with the wind in their faces. They were both in their mid-thirties and they discovered, to their great surprise, that they had more in common than would seem reasonable for two men who had grown up continents apart. Like Bahram, Zadig had risen in the world as a result of an unequal marriage—in his case he had been chosen to marry the widowed daughter of a wealthy family that was related to his own. He too knew what it was to be regarded as a poor relative by his in-laws.

One day as they were leaning over to watch the *Cuffnells*' frothing bow-wave, Zadig said: When you are away from home, living in China—how do you deal with . . . with your bodily necessities?

Bahram was never at ease discussing such things and he began to stutter: *Kya?* . . . what do you mean?

There is nothing shameful in this, you know, said Zadig; it is not just the jism that has its needs but also the rooh, the soul—and a man who feels himself to be alone in his own home, does he not have a right to seek companionship elsewhere?

Would you call it a right? said Bahram.

Right or not, I don't mind telling you that I—like many others who must travel constantly—have a second family, in Colombo. My 'wife' there is a Ceylonese burgher and although the family I have had with her is not mine by law, it is as dear to me as the one that bears my name.

Bahram looked at him quickly before dropping his eyes. It is very hard, isn't it?

There was something in his tone that made Zadig pause. So you have someone too?

With his head lowered, Bahram nodded.

Is she Chinese?

Yes.

Is she what they call a 'sing-song girl'—a professional?

No! said Bahram vehemently. No. When I met her she was a washerwoman, a widow. She was living on a boat, with her mother and daughter; they made their living by taking in laundry from the residents of the foreign enclave . . .

Bahram had never talked about this with anyone: to speak of it was such a release that having started he could not stop.

Her name was Chi-mei, he told Zadig, and he, Bahram, was a newcomer to Canton when he met her; as the youngest member of the Parsi contingent he was often asked to run errands for the big Sethjis; sometimes he would even be sent to the waterfront to inquire after their laundry. That was how he first came across Chi-mei; she was scrubbing clothes in the flat stern of her boat. A scarf was tightly tied over her hair, but a few ringlets had escaped their bindings and lay curled on her forehead. Her face was pert and lively, with glinting black eyes, and cheeks that glowed like polished apples. They locked eyes briefly and then she quickly turned her face away. But later, when he was about to head back to the factory he glanced at her over his shoulder and caught her looking in his direction again.

When he was back in his room, her face kept coming back to him. This was not the first time that Bahram had been plagued by fantasies about the girls who worked on the waterfront—but this time his longings had a keener edge than ever before. Something about the way she had looked at him had lodged in his mind and kept pulling him back towards her sampan. He began to visit the laundry-boats on invented errands and it happened a couple of times that he saw her blush and look away on catching sight of him: this was his only way of knowing that she had come to recognize him.

He noticed that her sampan seemed to have only two other occupants, an old woman and a little girl: there were never any men around. He was obscurely encouraged by this, and finding her alone one day he seized his chance: 'You name blongi what-thing?'

She blushed: 'Li Shiu-je. Mistoh name blongi what-thing ah?'

It wasn't till later that he understood that she'd told him to call her 'Miss Li': at that moment it was enough to know that she was fluent in Fanqui-town's idiom.

'Me Barry. Barry Moddie.'

She rolled this around her tongue. 'Mister Barry?'

'Yes.'

'Mister Barry blongi *Pak-taw-gwai*?'

Bahram knew this phrase: it meant 'White-Hat-Ghost' and was used to refer to Parsis because many of them wore white turbans. He smiled: 'Yes.'

She gave him a shy nod and slipped away into the sampan's cabin.

Already then, he knew that there was something special about her. The boat-women of Canton were utterly unlike their land-bound sisters: their feet were unbound and often bare, and there was nothing demure in their demeanour; they rowed boats, hawked goods, and went about their work with just as much gusto, if not more, than their menfolk. In monetary matters they were often unashamedly grasping, and newcomers like Bahram were always warned to be careful when dealing with them.

Unlike some of the other washerwomen Chi-mei never asked for cumshaws or bakshish. She bargained vigorously for her dues but was content to leave it at that. Bahram tried to overpay her once, pushing a few extra pieces of copper into her hands. She counted it carefully then came running after him. 'Mister Barry! Give too muchi cash. Here, this piece catchi.'

He tried to give it back but this only made her angry. She pointed to the gaudy flower-boats that were moored nearby. 'That piece boat sing-song girlie have got. Mister Barry can catchi.'

'Mister Barry no wanchi sing-song girlie.'

She shrugged, dropped the coins in his palm and walked away.

He was a little shamefaced when he saw her next and this seemed to amuse her. After the washing had been handed over, she whispered: 'Mister Barry? Catchi, no-catchi, sing-song girl?'

'No catchi,' he said. And then gathering his courage together, he said: 'Mister Barry no wanchi sing-song girl. Wanchi Li Shiu-je.'

'Wai-ah!' she laughed. 'Mister Barry talkee bad-thing la! Li Shiu-je no blongi sing-song girl ah.'

The strange diction of pidgin was still new to Bahram, and it added an inexplicable erotic charge to these exchanges: he would wake up and find himself talking to her, trying to explain his life: 'Mister Barry one-piece wife have got; two-piece girl-chilo also have got . . .'

When he next went to pick up some clothes he found a way of inquiring into her marital status. Pretending that the bundle was too heavy for him, he said: 'Li Shiu-je have husband-fellow? If have, he can carry maybe.'

Her face clouded over. 'No have got. Husband-fellow have makee die. In sea. One year pass.'

'Oh? Mister Barry too muchi sad inside.'

Soon after that Bahram also suffered a bereavement. He received a letter from his mother telling him that his youngest sister had died, in Gujarat. She had been ill for months but they had thought it best not to inform him since he was so far away and would worry to no good effect. But now that the unthinkable had happened there was no reason why he should not know.

Bahram had doted on this sister and he became so distraught that he could not bring himself to share the news with any of the other Parsis in Canton. He retreated into his cubicle and neglected the duties he was expected to perform for the senior members of the Bombay contingent. One day he was berated by a senior Seth for not having paid proper attention to the washing. At the end of the tirade the Seth handed him a torn turban-cloth.

Look—this is all your fault; see what has happened!

Bahram was in no state of mind to argue with the Seth: he walked out of the factory and headed for Chi-mei's sampan. It was after nightfall but he found his way to the sampan without difficulty. For some reason she was alone.

'Mister Barry, chin-chin. What thing wanchi?'

'Li Shiu-je have done too muchi bad thing.'

'Hai-ah! What thing have done ah?'

'Have cuttee cloth.'

'What-place cloth have cuttee ah? Mister Barry can show?'

'Can. Can.'

The only lamp in the sampan was inside the cabin: it was a cramped, low space, but there were so few possessions in it that it did not feel crowded. Sitting crouched under the hooped roof, Bahram unfolded the fabric, looking for the part that was torn. The turban-cloth was many yards long, and soon it was all over them, tangled around their arms.

Profanities began to pour from Bahram's mouth—*bahnchod! madarchod!*—and suddenly she caught hold of his arms.

'Stop, stop, Mister Barry. Stop.' Raising a fold of the fabric, she wiped something off his face.

'Mister Barry trouble have got? Blongi sad inside?'

His throat was dry but he managed to say: 'Yes. Too muchi sad. Sister have makee die.'

She was sitting close to him, with her shoulders half turned in his direction. He dropped his head on the curve of her neck and to his astonishment she did not push him away. Instead she began to stroke his back with one hand.

Never before had he taken so much comfort in being touched: desire and lovemaking were nowhere in his thoughts; what he felt above all was gratitude.

Soon it became clear that she had come to some kind of decision in regard to him. She whispered in his ear, telling him he could not stay now, because her mother and daughter would be back in a few minutes. But she would send him word soon, through a messenger: 'He boy-chilo—my relative. He name blongi Allow.'

Two days later Bahram felt a tug on the hem of his choga. He turned around to find a little boy standing behind him. A drop of mucus hung pearl-like beneath his nose, and he was wearing a dirty tunic and ragged pyjamas. He looked like any of the urchins who wandered around the foreign enclave, begging for coins and offering to run errands.

'Name blongi Allow?'

The boy nodded and began to walk towards the waterfront. He had a tripping gait and seemed often to be on the point of falling over on his face: his walk was so distinctive Bahram had no trouble keeping sight of him in the dark. They came to a sampan that had no lights burning inside. Allow gestured to Bahram to climb in and he clambered over the foredeck. Chi-mei was waiting in the darkened cabin. She motioned to him to be silent and they sat quietly next to each other while Allow undid the moorings and rowed the sampan upriver, towards White Swan Lake. Only then did she unroll a mat.

'Come, Mister Barry.'

He had never been with any woman other than his wife: to almost the same degree that he was assured and combative in his business dealings, he was shy and reticent in all matters intimate or personal. His previous undressings had been solemn and silent; here Chi-mei kept giggling as she helped him take off his turban, slip off his choga and untie his pyjamas. When she tried to pull off his sacred waist-strings he whispered: 'This piece thread blongi joss-pidgin thing. No can take off.'

She uttered a yelp of a laugh. 'Waa! Joss-pidgin thread also have got?'

'Have. Have.'

'White Hat Devil have too muchi big cloth.'

'White Hat Devil have nother-piece thingi too muchi big.'

The cramped space, the hard edges of the timbers, the rocking of the sampan and the smell of dried fish that percolated up from the bilges created an almost delirious urgency. Lovemaking with Shireenbai was a clinical affair and their bodies seemed hardly to touch except where necessity demanded. Bahram was utterly unprepared for the sweat, the stickiness, the slippages and mistaken gropings, the sudden fart that burst from her when he least expected it.

Afterwards, when they were lying in each other's arms, they heard the sound of fireworks and thrust their heads out of the covering. Something was being celebrated in a lakeside village and rockets were arcing through the sky. The blazes of colour above were so brilliantly mirrored upon the dark surface of the water that the sampan seemed to be suspended within a glowing sphere of light.

When the boat turned shorewards, Bahram was not in the least surprised to hear her say: 'Now Mister Barry give cumshaw. Lob-pidgin have makee do. Eat chicken must pay. Mister Barry must give daaih-big cumshaw.'

For half an hour they bickered over how much money he would part with—and the bargaining was sweeter than any love-talk could possibly have been. It was the language he knew best, the language he used all day, and he was able to say much more with it than he could have with endearments. In the end he gladly gave her everything he had.

When he was about to go ashore she said: 'Mister Barry must give Allow cumshaw also.'

Bahram's pockets were empty, and he laughed. 'No more cash have got. Later can give Allow cumshaw.'

The boy had followed him back to his lodgings, and Bahram, in a fit of generosity, had rewarded him with a gift that had brought a beaming smile to his face: he had given him half a cake of Malwa opium and told him to sell it immediately. 'Buy shoes, buy clothes, eat rice. *Dak mh dak aa?*'

Dak! Mh-goi-saai! The boy had run off with a delighted grin on his face.

After that Bahram and Chi-mei had begun to meet regularly, once or twice a week. These 'lob-pidgin' sessions were always arranged through the boy, Allow. Bahram would see him running around the enclave, with the other lads, and all it took was a raised eyebrow, a glance. He would go to the waterfront in the evening and there she would be, in the sampan.

From the first Bahram tried to be generous, even extravagant, with her. At the end of that season, before leaving for Bombay, he asked her what she wanted and when she said she needed a bigger boat he gladly agreed to pay for it. When he returned at the start of the next season he came laden with gifts. At the end of each sojourn he made sure that she had enough for herself and her family—her daughter and mother—to live on until his next visit. Not for a moment did it occur to him to wonder whether she took other lovers when he was away: his trust in her was absolute and she never gave him any cause to doubt her faithfulness.

In March 1815, a few days before Bahram's departure for Bombay, Chi-mei took his hand and put it on her stomach: 'Look-see here, Mister Barry.'

'Chilo?'

'Chilo.'

He felt just as joyful as he had when he learnt of Shireenbai's pregnancies: his only concern was that she might try to abort the baby. To make it easier, he paid for her to leave Canton and go downriver, so that it would be possible for her to tell people that the baby had been given to her to adopt.

Such was his excitement about the child that he only spent four months in Bombay that year, returning to China at the end of the monsoons. On reaching Macau, instead of waiting for a passage-boat to take him upriver he hired a 'fast-crab' to whisk him to Canton through the back-channels of the Pearl River delta.

And there was the baby, swaddled so as to leave the genitals proudly exposed: when she put the child in his arms he had hugged him so tight that a warm jet had shot out of the boy's tiny gu-gu, wetting his face and dripping off his beard.

He laughed. 'He name what-thing?'

'Leong Fatt.'

'No.' Bahram shook his head. 'He name blongi Framjee.' They had bickered amicably for a while without reaching an agreement.

This had happened only three months before Bahram met Zadig. The exchange was still fresh in his mind when he was telling his new-found friend the story. When he came to the end he began to laugh and Zadig chuckled too: So what is the boy's name?

She calls him Ah Fatt. I call him Freddy.

Is he your only son?

Yes.

Zadig gave him a congratulatory pat. Mabrook!

Thank you. And how many children have you had with your other wife?

Two. A boy and a girl: Aleena and Sargis.

Zadig became pensive as he said the names. Resting his elbow on the deck rail, he put his chin on his fist: Tell me, Bahram-bhai, do you ever think of leaving your family—your legal family—so that you can live with your other family: Chi-mei I mean, and the child she's given you?

The question shocked Bahram. No, he said. Never. I could never think of it. Why? Is it something you've considered?

Yes I have, said Zadig. I think of it often, to tell you the truth. They have no one but me—and my other family, in Cairo, they have everything. As the years go on, I find it harder and harder to be away from those who really need me. It wrings my heart to be away from them.

The gravity of his tone surprised Bahram; he could not imagine that a responsible man of business would seriously contemplate breaking his ties with his family and his community: in his own world such a step would, he knew, bring not only social disgrace but also financial ruin. It amazed him that an apparently sound man, a husband and a father, would even admit to entertaining such a schoolboyish notion.

You know what they say, Zadig Bey, he said in a teasing tone. No sensible man will let his lathi rule his head.

It isn't that, said Zadig.

So what is it then? Is it a matter of—what do they call it—*ishq*? 'Love'?

Call it *ishq*, call it *hubb*, call it *pyar*, call it what you will. It's in my heart. Isn't it the same for you?

Bahram thought about this for a bit and then shook his head. No, he said. For me and Chi-mei it's not love. We call it 'lob-pidgin' and I like it better that way. The other thing—I wouldn't know how to say it to her. Nor could she say it to me. When you don't have a word for it how can you know if you feel it?

Zadig gave him one of his long, appraising glances.

I feel sad for you, my friend, he said. In the end, you know, that is all there is.

All there is? Bahram burst out laughing. Why you're mad, Zadig Bey! You're making a joke, no?

No. I am not, Bahram-bhai.

Well then, Zadig Bey, said Bahram lightly. If that's what you think then you'll have to leave your first wife, won't you?

Zadig sighed. Yes, he said. Some day that is what I will have to do.

Neither then nor afterwards had Bahram believed that Zadig would actually do it—but so he had, a few years later. He had settled a large sum of money on his other family, in Cairo, and had bought a spacious house in the Fort area in Colombo. Bahram had visited him there soon after: his mistress was a matronly woman of Dutch descent and so far as he could tell, their children were happy, healthy and well brought up.

The following year Bahram had taken Zadig to meet Chi-mei and Freddy, in Canton. Chi-mei had served them a fine meal and Freddy, who was a toddler then, had charmed Zadig. After that Zadig had made it his practice to visit them every time he travelled to China. On his return to Colombo he would often send Bahram news about them.

It was through one of these letters that Bahram had learnt of Freddy's disappearance and Chi-mei's death.

~

In the end it was the *Redruth* that settled the matter for Paulette—the brig cast a spell that put an end to whatever doubts she may have had about Fitcher's offer.

If ships could be built in the image of their owners, then there would be no question about whom this one belonged to—she was like an extension of Fitcher's very being. Like Fitcher, the *Redruth* was lean and angular, with sharply upcurved lines—her bowsprit even had a way of 'twitchering and shaking' that was strangely reminiscent of her owner's brow. Even the sound of the wind, blowing through the *Redruth*'s rigging, seemed different from that of any other vessel: if ships could speak, then the *Redruth*, Paulette imagined, would express herself in a voice that recalled Fitcher's broad accent and whistling vowels.

But it wasn't any of this that set the *Redruth* apart from every other sailing vessel: it was the greenery on her decks. Plants were not of course an uncommon sight on sailships: most carried a few, either for nutrition, or decoration, or merely because a touch of green was always a welcome sight on the high seas. But the *Redruth*'s stock of flora extended far beyond the usual half-dozen pots: her decks were stacked also with a great number of 'Wardian cases'. These were a new invention: glass-fronted boxes with adjustable sides, they were, in effect, miniature greenhouses. They had revolutionized the business of transporting plants across the seas, making it much easier and safer; the *Redruth* had scores of them on board, securely tied down with cables and ropes.

The greenest part of the ship was the quarter-deck: here stacked along the deck rails, and around the base of the mizzen-mast, were rows of pots and cases. To provide additional protection for the plants, Fitcher had designed an ingenious arrangement of movable awnings; these could be adjusted, as desired, to provide shade, sunlight, and protection from rough weather. When there was rain, the awnings turned into water-traps: with so many plants on board, the *Redruth* needed more fresh water than other ships, and Fitcher was loath to let a single drop go waste.

The *Redruth* also had its own, unique procedures for dealing with waste: refuse from its galleys was not indiscriminately emptied overboard; everything that might serve as plant nutrition was carefully separated from the remains of the salted meats that were the mainstay of the crew's diet. Tea leaves, coffee grounds, rice, bits of old biscuit and hard tack—all this was dumped in an enormous barrel that was suspended over the stern. This container was covered with a tight-fitting, waterproof lid, but on hot, windless days the smell of decomposing matter was sometimes strong enough to elicit protests from nearby vessels.

Inevitably, what with the green of the plants and the glare of the glass-fronted cases, the *Redruth* presented an appearance that was much mocked by bystanders: it was not uncommon for harbour-fronters to ask whether she was one of those famous 'asylum ships' that were reputed to be carrying lunatics to faraway islands. But in fact the brig, like her owner, was eccentric only in appearance: it quickly became evident to Paulette that there was nothing at all fanciful about the *Redruth*; on the contrary, every element of her functioning was determined by the twin motives of thrift and profit. Her consignments of greenery, for instance, required no significant outlay of capital, no tying-up of finances, and yet the returns they offered were potentially astronomical. But at the same time her goods were such as to be proof against both pilferage and piracy, their true value being unknown to all but a few.

Nor was there anything at all haphazard about the *Redruth*'s cargo. All her plants had been hand-picked by Fitcher himself: most were from the Americas and had only recently been introduced to Europe and were thus unlikely yet to have reached China. Amongst this assemblage of flora were antirrhinums, lobelias and georginas, introduced from Mexico by Alexander von Humboldt; also from Mexico were the 'Mexican Orange' and a beautiful new fuchsia; from the American Northwest there was *Gaultheria shallon*, a plant both ornamental and medicinal, and a magnificent new conifer, both introduced by David Douglas—Fitcher was certain that the latter species would appeal especially to the pine-loving Chinese. Shrubs were not neglected either: the flowering currant, in particular, was a species for which Fitcher had very high hopes. This one plant, he told Paulette, had repaid all the costs of Mr Douglas's first American expedition—luckily, no one had yet thought of introducing it to China.

Fitcher's intention was to exchange these American plants for Chinese species that had not yet been introduced to the West. The idea seemed ingenious and original to Paulette, but

Fitcher adamantly denied its authorship. 'Have ee ever heard of Father d'Incarville?'

After a little thought, Paulette said: 'Is he perhaps the one after whom the Incarvillea are named? With the beautiful trumpet flowers?'

'That's the one,' said Fitcher.

D'Incarville was a Jesuit, said Fitcher, who spent several years at the court of the Emperor, in Peking. As with other foreigners his movements were severely restricted and he was not allowed to collect plants outside the city; nor was he allowed to visit the royal gardens. Seeking to change this, he conceived the idea of proposing a botanical exchange: he wrote home to France asking for European flowers, and his correspondents sent him tulips, cornflowers and columbines. But none of those caught the Emperor's fancy—he chose instead a humble touch-me-not.

'If that, then why not what we've got here on the *Redruth*?'

The *Redruth*'s functioning thus profoundly belied her appearance, for she was the creation neither of a crazed scientist nor a deluded dreamer. She was actually something much plainer: the handiwork of a diligent nurseryman—not a man who was a speculative thinker, but rather a practical solver of problems, someone who looked upon Nature as an assortment of puzzles, many of which, if properly resolved, could provide rich sources of profit.

This cast of mind was completely novel to Paulette. To her father, who had taught her what she knew of botany, the love of Nature had been a kind of religion, a form of spiritual striving: he had believed that in trying to comprehend the inner vitality of each species, human beings could transcend the mundane world and its artificial divisions. If botany was the Scripture of this religion, then horticulture was its form of worship: tending a garden was, for Pierre Lambert, no mere matter of planting seeds and pruning branches—it was a spiritual discipline, a means of communicating with forms of life that were necessarily mute and could be understood only through a careful study of their own modes of expression—the languages of efflorescence, growth and decay: only thus, he had taught Paulette, could human beings apprehend the vital energies that constitute the Spirit of the Earth.

Fitcher's way of looking at the world could not have been more different: yet, it seemed to Paulette that in some strange way, he was more a part of the natural order than her father had ever been. Like a gnarled old tree, growing upon a stony slope, Fitcher was unshakeable in his determination to extract a living from the world: this was how he had grown rich, and it was also why his riches meant very little to him; he had no use for luxuries, and his wealth was a source not of comfort, but of anxiety—it was a burden, like the sacks of cabbages that had to be hoarded in the cellar for seasons of scarcity.

When she came to know him better, Paulette understood that Fitcher's ideas and attitudes were outgrowths of his upbringing. The son of a Cornish greengrocer, he had been born into a wind-pierced cottage on the outskirts of Falmouth, within sight of the sea. His father was once a sailor on a 'fruit-schooner'—one of those swift, sleek vessels that linked the orchards of the Mediterranean to the markets of Britain—but an accident, and a crippled right arm, had forced him to alter his mode of livelihood: he had taken to hawking fruits and vegetables, some of which he obtained from his former shipmates. There were five Penrose children and the family's circumstances being what they were, they could only intermittently attend school: when the boys were not helping their father, they were expected to earn a few pennies by working in nearby farms and gardens. It was thus that young Fitcher came to the attention of the parish doctor, who happened to be, in his spare time, a keen amateur naturalist: noticing that the boy had a way with plants, he introduced him to botanizing and lent him books. Thus was inculcated an appetite for self-improvement that served the boy well when he, in turn, was hired as a crewman by the captain of a fruit-schooner. He quickly acquired a knack for tending to the schooner's delicate Mediterranean cargoes—oranges, plums, persimmons, apricots, lemons and figs. As with most other merchant ships, fruit-schooners permitted each seaman to carry a certain amount of cargo on his personal account, to trade for his own profit. When the weather was suitable, Fitcher would make use of his quota to ship saplings, fruit trees and garden plants, some of which fetched good prices when the schooner visited London.

The habits of that time had stayed with Fitcher and had been crucial to the building of his fortune. It had taken him many years of patient application to build the Penrose nurseries into a major force in the world of British horticulture and to remove himself from the helm, even if temporarily, had not been easy. But as a purveyor of exotic flora, Fitcher was all too well aware that the business of gardening, even more than most, demanded ceaseless innovation—partly because the time it took for a new flower to go from sublime rarity to vulgar weed was growing steadily shorter; and partly because the market was crowded with increasingly aggressive competitors. Among Penrose & Sons' many rivals, perhaps the most formidable was the Veitch nursery, in nearby Devon: tireless in seeking out new wares, the Veitches would often help to fund exploratory voyages and expeditions. Fitcher too had helped to finance the travels of several would-be collectors, but never with satisfactory results: some of these wanderers had vanished with his money; some had lost their minds or died frightful deaths; and of those who returned, few had brought back anything of value. One such, a promising young Cornishman, had kept his best finds for himself, but only to sell them to the Veitches later—a betrayal that was all the more painful to Fitcher because his Devonshire rivals were not even true West Country people but transplanted Scotsmen.

These experiences had convinced Fitcher that he would do a better job himself, and probably at a lesser cost: he had, after all, personally collected many of his nursery's most successful offerings, in southern China, and that too at a time when he was inexperienced and starved of resources. He knew he would be able to accomplish a great deal more if he returned to China in a vessel of his own—but such a journey would require at least two or three years, and could not be undertaken until his familial responsibilities had been properly discharged. He had married late, and his wife had died an untimely death, leaving him with three children—twin boys, and a girl who was much younger than her brothers. To fob his children off on relatives was inconceivable to Fitcher; and to contract a marriage of convenience, for the purpose of providing his offspring with a caregiver, was even more so. So he had accepted, reluctantly, that his plans would have to be put in abeyance until his sons were of an age to take over the running of the business. In the interim he had made careful preparations for the voyage, even designing and commissioning the *Redruth*, which was named after his wife's birthplace.

The Penrose boys were capable young men, with good heads for business, and plenty of common sense besides. In listening to Fitcher, Paulette came to understand that the only cause for disappointment the boys had ever given him was that neither of them had any interest in botany or natural history: to them plants were no different from doorknobs, or sausages, or any other object that could be sold for a price on the market.

Of the Penrose children Ellen was the only one to inherit Fitcher's interest in the natural world. This was just one of the reasons why she was particularly dear to her father (she was also, Fitcher confided, the very image of her mother, Catherine, of whom it had often been said that 'her face was her best limb'). Although not robust in constitution, Ellen had been insistent on claiming a place in the *Redruth*. When Fitcher tried to dissuade her, by listing the dangers of a long voyage, she had countered by citing the career of Maria Merian, the legendary botanical illustrator who had travelled from Holland to South America at the age of fifty-two—and there was little Fitcher could say in response, for it was he who had encouraged Ellen's botanical interests by gifting her reproductions of Merian's paintings of the flowers and insects of Surinam.

Ellen had showed herself to be, in her quiet way, just as tenacious and determined as Fitcher himself. In the end Fitcher had been forced to relent: one of the *Redruth*'s cabins had been refurbished for Ellen's use and the brig had set sail in the spring, with a crew of eighteen, and a weighty cargo of plants and equipment. With favouring winds, the *Redruth* had made good time to the Canary Islands, where the wild flowers on the slopes had delighted Ellen. She had insisted on going ashore to climb a hill—and it was there, probably, that she had contracted the fever that was to reveal itself several days later, when the brig was well out to sea. Nothing in Fitcher's pharmacopeia could mitigate this illness and Ellen had died when the *Redruth* was but a day from the island of St Helena. Fitcher had buried her in a hillside graveyard that was carpeted with bellflowers and lobelias.

When Fitcher led Paulette to the locked door of Ellen's cabin, she understood, without having to be told, that many weeks had passed since anyone had stepped into it.

'It's eers now Miss Paulette. In the trunks ee'll find some clothes of Ellen's too: eer welcome to them if they're of any use t'ee.'

With that Fitcher shut the door, leaving her to settle in.

The cabin was neither large nor lavish, but it had a snug little bunk and a desk. It was provided moreover with all the facilities that a lone young woman would need to be comfortable amidst a shipful of men: a water-closet and porcelain basin, for instance, as also a copper tub that was attached ingeniously to the ceiling, with rivets.

Beside the bunk was a bookcase, and its contents gave Paulette some idea of the kind of person that Ellen Penrose had been: there was a much-thumbed Bible, a life of John Wesley, a Methodist hymnal and several other books of a devotional nature. Apart from these there was also a small collection of botanical works, including a book of Maria Merian's illustrations. But of fiction and verse there was not a single volume: it was easy to see that Ellen Penrose had been no more inclined to romance and poesy than was her father.

This impression was reinforced by the clothes that Paulette found in the trunks: they were plain and sensible, with a minimum of frills, lace and other fripperies. The collars of the dresses were high, with not an inch of neck exposed, and the colours were severe, black being the predominant hue. When she tried one on, Paulette saw that it had been cut for someone who had a fuller figure than herself—but there was a sewing box in one of the trunks and she had no trouble in making the necessary adjustments.

Still, it was not without some hesitation that Paulette prepared to appear before Fitcher in his daughter's clothes. But Fitcher paid no attention to her changed appearance; he was tending to an ailing Douglas fir and all he said was: 'Get eerself a pair of shears.'

It wasn't till a few days later that he remarked off-handedly: 'Ellen would've been happy ee know, to see her clothes being put to good use.'

Paulette was caught off-guard. 'Well sir . . . I don't know how to thank you . . . for everything . . .'

A catch in her throat prevented her from saying any more and she was glad of it, for even these few words of gratitude were enough to cast Fitcher into spasms of embarrassment. His face turned bright red and he began to mutter under his breath: 'Can't be in the glumps now Miss Paulette; not when there's a job to be done.'

It took only a day or two for Paulette to feel completely at home on the *Redruth*: the crewmen were so glad to be relieved of their plant-tending duties that they accorded her an even warmer welcome than their employer. Having quickly found her place on the brig, Paulette's chief concern in the days before the *Redruth* left Port Louis, was for Zachary. But this too was allayed to some degree after a fortuitous encounter, on the harbour front, with Baboo Nob Kissin Pander; he told her that Zachary was still in custody, awaiting transhipment to Calcutta, where he was to be questioned in relation to the incidents on the *Ibis*:

'No need to worry, Miss Lambert—Mr Reid will be fine. Captain Chillingworth is having big soft-corners for him. He will provide supporting testimony and case will be collared out. I am also there. I will keep weather-eye.'

This greatly reassured Paulette. 'Please tell him, Baboo Nob Kissin, that I am well, and have been most fortunate. I have met a famous gardener, Mr Penrose. He is some kind of archimillionaire and is travelling to China to collect plants. He has asked me to be his assistant.'

'So you are going to China is it? I pray god you may have safe journey.'

'You too, Baboo Nob Kissin. And please tell Zachary that I hope to see him soon, wherever I am . . .'

~

For Neel and Ah Fatt, the journey to Singapore was exceptionally slow: the Bugis schooner they had boarded at Great Nicobar was on its way back from the Hajj, and was obliged to make many stops along the Sumatran coast, to drop off the pilgrims. As a result the trip was prolonged by several days. They reached Singapore at low tide, so the schooner had to drop anchor in the outer harbour. Instead of waiting for the tides to change, the passengers pooled their coins together to hire a Chulia lighter to take them upriver to Boat Quay.

The mouth of the river was clogged with vessels—proas, sampans, junks, lorchas and dhows. In this ragtag flotilla of sea- and river-craft one vessel stood out: a medium-sized three-master of superb craftsmanship. She was anchored off the river mouth and was so positioned that the lighter had to pass close by her starboard beam. The ship's chiselled lines and rakish profile seemed to call special attention to the damage she had suffered; through the bandaging of nets that swathed her prow the evidence of her injury was clearly visible: there was a huge cavity where her jib-boom and figurehead should have been.

Many heads turned to stare at the decapitated ship and Neel noticed that Ah Fatt, in particular, was mesmerized by the sight of the damaged vessel—he gazed at it so fixedly that his knuckles turned white on the gunwales.

By the time they reached Boat Quay it was dark. They crossed the river, intending to seek out one of the many doss-houses where lascars, coolies and other working men could rent some floor space for a couple of coppers. But then Ah Fatt changed his mind. Walking along the embankment, he said: 'Hungry! Come, we find kitchen-boat.'

Kitchen fires were burning on many of the small boats that lined the shore, and on several of them groups of people—mainly Chinese men—could be seen eating and drinking. Ah Fatt stopped to appraise each in turn but none seemed to satisfy him. After walking on for a bit he came suddenly to a halt and gestured to Neel to follow him across a gangplank: his decision was made without hesitation, although on what basis Neel could not tell, for this boat seemed, if anything, somewhat darker and less frequented than the others.

'Why this one? How is it any different?'

'Never mind. Come.'

The boat was manned by a round-faced younger woman and a couple who looked as though they might have been her grandparents; they seemed to have finished for the day, and the older man was reclining on a mat when Ah Fatt shouted a few words across the gangplank. Whether these were greetings or questions, Neel could not tell, but their effect, in any event, was magical, instantly transforming the somnolent boat: the older couple broke into welcoming smiles while the younger woman beckoned energetically as she answered Ah Fatt.

'What is she saying?'

'She say Uncle and Aunt go to sleep now, but she happy make food.'

The warmth of the welcome seemed all the more surpising to Neel because both he and Ah Fatt looked like penniless vagabonds, in their threadbare pyjamas and soiled tunics, with their bundles slung over their shoulders. 'What did you say to them?' he asked. 'Why do they seem so happy to see you?'

'Spoke in boat language,' said Ah Fatt, in his laconic way. 'They understood. Never mind. Time to eat rice. And drink. We drink Canton-grog.'

The kitchen-boat was of a curious shape: it looked as though its mid-section had been carved out, leaving it with a raised stem and stern. At the rear was a wooden 'house' with a heavy door, and at the other end, between the bows, there was a thatch-covered area with open sides: this was where customers ate, sitting around a couple of raised planks that served as tables. The carved-out midsection was where the cooking was done: the cook had only to rise to her feet to put the food upon the 'tables'.

After they had seated themselves, Ah Fatt leant into the well of the kitchen space and had a brief exchange with the young woman. The conversation ended with him pointing to the roof of the 'house', where clusters of live chickens dangled upside down, trussed by their feet. The woman reached up and picked a chicken off the roof, plucking it from its covey as though it were a fruit on a vine. There was a brief squawking and flapping and then the bird, now headless but still trussed, was dropped over the side of the boat, to flap its wings in the river. Slowly the sound died away and a minute later bits of offal went into a fish-basket that was suspended beside the boat, producing a boiling, thrashing noise. There followed the hissing of hot oil, and soon a dish of fried liver, gizzards and intestines appeared before them.

The tastes were so vivid that Neel dispensed with chopsticks and fell upon the food with his hands. Yet Ah Fatt, despite having declared himself to be hungry, seemed hardly to notice the dish—no sooner had he finished talking to the cook than his eyes and his attention returned to the jibless vessel across the river.

'Why do you keep staring at that ship, Ah Fatt?' Neel said at last. 'What's so special about it?'

Ah Fatt shook his head as though he had been woken from a trance. 'If I tell, you not believe me.'

'Tell me anyway.'

'That ship belong . . . my family. My father.' Ah Fatt gave a hoot of laughter.

'What do you mean?'

'Only that. It belong my father family.'

A fiery, sour-smelling liquor had appeared before them now, and Ah Fatt poured some into a small white cup. Then he took a sip and laughed, in the way he sometimes did when he was embarrassed or uneasy. Whether this was a sign of seriousness or frivolity, Neel could not tell, for with Ah Fatt the outward manifestations of inner states were not as they were with other people: in the few months that he had known him, Neel had discovered that where Ah Fatt was concerned, bouts of apparently childlike silliness could sometimes be symptoms of seething anger, while a spell of brooding silence could betoken nothing more portentous than a fit of drowsiness.

Now despite the laughter, Neel could sense that Ah Fatt was not joking, or at least, not entirely: between him and the ship across the river there was some powerful but conflicted connection, some link that he was trying to resist.

'What's the ship's name then?' he said, on a note of challenge, half-hoping that Ah Fatt would not know the answer.

The reply came back without a missed breath: 'Name: *Anahita*. In Father's religion, that the name of the goddess of water. Like our A-Ma. Before, had statue in front, of goddess. It was—what do you call it—?'

'. . . the figurehead?'

'Figurehead. Gone now. Family will be sad. Especially Grandfather, who built ship.'

'"Grandfather"?' said Neel. 'On your father's side, you mean?'

'No,' said Ah Fatt. 'On side of Father's Elder Wife. Seth Rustamjee Mistrie: famous shipbuilder of Bombay . . .'

He was interrupted by the cook, who stood up to hand over a dish of browned chicken feet. Ah Fatt picked out a piece and offered it to her with his chopsticks, and after a few moments of laughter and joking, she allowed him to slip it between her teeth. Then she slapped his hand away, with a giggle, and he turned back to Neel.

'Sorry,' he said, his eyes shining. 'Long time see no woman. No chance do jaahk.' He laughed and poured more liquor into their cups. 'Only see you. Two of us, feet tied like chickens.' He pointed at the trussed birds on the boat's roof and laughed again.

Neel nodded: 'It's true.'

Through their time at sea they had been so closely bound and confined that it was impossible to move or turn except in tandem. Neel had never spent so much time with another human being, in such close proximity, never before experienced such extended intimacy with another physical presence—and yet now, as often before, he had the feeling that he knew nothing at all about Ah Fatt.

'Do you mean to tell me,' said Neel, 'that you're related to Seth Rustamjee Mistrie?'

'Yes,' said Ah Fatt. 'Through Father. His Elder Wife is Seth's daughter. For a long time even I did not know . . .'

Ah Fatt was almost at the end of his boyhood when he found out that he had connections, relatives, in faraway Bombay. As a child he had been told that he was an orphan, that his mother and father had died when he was a newborn, and that he was being brought up by his widowed Eldest Aunt—his Yee Ma. This was the story that was told to everyone who knew them, on the Canton waterfront and in Fanqui-town. There was nothing about Ah Fatt's looks to betray his paternity, not even his complexion, a sun-weathered tint being not uncommon among boat-people. Growing up, he did not think of his family as being different from the others around him, except in one respect, which was that they had a rich benefactor, 'Uncle Barry', a 'White-Hat-Alien' from India, who happened to be his godfather, his 'kai-yeh'. Uncle Barry had been his father's employer, he was told; after his parents' death he had felt a great obligation to their orphaned child; this was why he gave Yee Ma money for his upkeep, and brought presents for him from India, and paid for his teachers and tutors.

Yee Ma did not encourage Uncle Barry's ambitions for the boy: nor did she approve of spending so much money on such things. To arrange schooling for a boat-child was no easy matter and Uncle Barry had to pay generously to organize it: he wanted the boy to be literate in Classical Chinese as well as schoolroom English; he wanted him to grow up 'respectable', to become a gentil-man, who would be able to move easily with the merchants of Fanqui-town, impressing them with his sporting talents as well as his knowledge. Yee Ma could not see the point of all this: she would have preferred that Uncle Barry give her the money and leave the boy alone. What use was calligraphy to him when boat-people were banned by law from sitting for the Civil Service examinations? What was he to do with boxing and riding lessons when boat-people were barred even from building houses ashore? She wanted him to grow up like any boat-child, learning to fish and sail and handle boats.

Yet, in her dreams, if not in her waking state, Yee Ma must have accepted that he was not really a boat-child for she often had nightmares in which the boy was attacked by a dragon-fish—a sturgeon. As a result she would not let him in the water.

Like other boat-children Ah Fatt grew up with a bell attached to his ankle, so his family could always keep track of him; like them he had to sit in a barrel when the boat was moving; like them, he had a wooden board tied to his back, so that he would float if he fell in. But the other children lost their boards and bells when they were two or three—Ah Fatt's stayed on till long afterwards, making him a target of mockery. On the Canton waterfront little boys would earn money by diving in the river to amuse the Aliens, fishing out the coins and trinkets they threw in the water. Ah Fatt too wanted to do these things, to swim with the boat-children, to dive and earn coins—but to him alone, these things were strictly forbidden because of the spectre of the lurking dragon-fish.

But Yee Ma must have known also that it would be impossible to keep a child of the *seui-seung-yan* from the water.

'From time they—we—are little, we float . . .'

Ah Fatt broke off as bowls appeared before them, with balls of minced chicken swimming in a clear broth: using his chopsticks, he pointed at one of the bobbing morsels. 'Like that we learn to swim. The *pun-tei*—the land-people—they mock us and say we have fins instead of feet. Me too, I learn to swim, when Yee Ma is not there; sometimes I also go to dive for coins with others. Then one day she find out, and she pull me from the water. Beat me, shaming in front of everyone. So much shame, I think I throw myself in the river, and if dragon-fish comes, that also good. I think: she doing this because I have no parents. I think: if I her child, she not beat like this. I think: better run away. I make plans, I speak with beggar-men, but Older Sister find out. Then she tell me everything: that Yee Ma not aunt, but Mother. That "Uncle Barry" not kai-yeh, but Father. I could not ask Mother because I know she beat Older Sister for telling me. I wait until Uncle Barry come next time, and when alone, I ask: Is true you are Father, and Yee Ma is Mother? At first he say, no, not true. But I ask again, and again, and then he begin to cry and admit everything. He say, yes, all true; he Father and he have other family in Bombay.'

Ah Fatt fell silent and gestured to Neel to pick up his cup. After they had drained their liquor Neel too was silent for a bit. It was only after Ah Fatt had filled the cups again that he said quietly: 'It must have been a shock? To find out about all this? In that way?'

'Shock? Yes. Maybe.' Ah Fatt's voice was flat and emotionless. 'At first I just want to know. Know about Bombay. About Elder Wife. About sisters. You can think how strange for me all this. When I small, we live in boat like this one; we also poor people, like these. Just poor boat-people, sometime no food, we eat wind. Then one day I hear my father *hou-gwai*, rich man, rich White-Hat Devil. Now I think I know why my mother beat me—I not real China-yan, I her secret shame, but still she need me, because of money Father give. But does not matter now. Have got another family. I want know all about it. I ask Father, but he say nothing. Does not like to speak of it. He tells about Malacca and Colombo and London, but not Bombay. I read in books that "Western Island"—India—have gold and magic and I want to go—I want fly there like Monkey King. But this in my head—my feet in kitchen-boat, where I live. So when I hear of Father's ship, *Anahita*, I am mad to see it.'

'Did it come to Canton?'

'No,' said Ah Fatt. 'Big ships can-na come to Canton—just like they can-na come up this river. Too shallow. They must anchor at Huang-pu—Whampoa in English. Many boats go up and down so I know about ship: I know has set record for season—seventeen days from Bombay to Canton. When Father come, I say: take me, take me to your ship, and he turn red, shake head. He afraid if he take me then ship will carry news back to Bombay. Elder Wife will find out about me and there will be trouble. Ship not his, he tell me; belong to father-in-law and brothers-in-law. He like paid servant and must be careful. But this mean nothing to me; I do not care. I tell him I want to go, or I will shame him. I will go Whampoa myself. So then he says, yes, he will take. But he sends me with Vico, his purser—does not go himself. Vico shows me ship, tell me stories. And it is like I saw in my head—a palace, better even than mandarin-boat. You cannot believe till you see . . .'

He broke off to point to the *Anahita*'s raised quarter-deck, which was lit by the glow of a binnacle lamp. 'Look, near stern—third mast, what do you call it?'

'The mizzen-mast?'

'Yes. That mast like tree. Around its roots, on quarter-deck, there is carved bench, where people can sit. Grandfather built like that, to be like banyan tree in village. Vico tell me that. Afterward, when I see *Anahita*, always I think that *my* bench . . .'

Again now the cook interrupted, placing bowls of steaming rice on the plank, along with the rest of the chicken, prepared in a half-dozen different ways. The smells were tantalizing, but Neel was so absorbed in Ah Fatt's recollections that he paid no mind to the food.

'Did you go back to the ship again?'

'No—did not go, but saw many times. At Lintin Island.'

'Did you go there to see your father?'

'No. Father never in Lintin.' Seeing the puzzlement in Neel's eyes, he said: 'Look-see here, I show you . . .'

Using his chopsticks, Ah Fatt expertly dismantled a piece of chicken and picked out the wishbone. Laying it on the plank, he pointed to the yawning jaws: 'This like mouth of Pearl River, which lead to Canton.' Then, picking some grains of rice from his bowl he scattered them across the gap with his chopsticks. 'These like islands—have many here, like teeth rising from sea. Teeth very useful to pirates. Also to foreign merchants, like Father. Because foreign ship cannot bring opium to Canton. Forbidden. So they pretend they do not bring to China. They go here'—his chopsticks moved to point to a grain of rice that lay halfway between the jaws of the wishbone—'to Lintin Island. There they sell opium. When price is settled, dealer send out boat, quick boat, with thirty oar—"fast-crab".' Ah Fatt laughed, and his chopsticks flashed as he flipped the wishbone into the water. 'That how I go to Lintin—in "fast-crab".'

'Why? What were you doing there?'

'What you think? Buying opium.'

'For whom?'

'My boss—he big opium-seller, have many fast-crab, many leng work for him, many hing-dai. We are one big gaa and he is our Daaih-go-daai, Big-Brother-Big, for our family. We call him Dai Lou. He Canton man, but he travel everywhere—even to London. He stay there long time and then he come back to start business, in Macau. He have many like me to work for him; he like to hire my kind.'

'What do you mean your kind?'

'*Jaahp-júng-jai*—"mixed-kind-boy".' Ah Fatt laughed. 'Many like that along Pearl River—in Macau, Whampoa, Guangzhou. In any port, any place where man can buy woman, there is many *yeh-jai* and "West-ocean-child". They too must eat and live. Dai Lou give us work, treat us well. For long time he like real Elder Brother to me. But then we have trouble. That why I have to leave Canton, run away. Can-na go back.'

'What happened?'

'Dai Lou, he have woman. Not wife but . . . how do you say?'

'Concubine?'

'Yes. Concubine. She very beautiful. Her name Adelina.'

'Was she European?'

'No. Adelie also "salt-prawn-food", like me: she also half Cheeni, half Achha.'

'Achha? What do you mean by that?'

'"Achha"—that what Canton-yan call you people. You Hindusthanis—there you all "Achha".'

'But "achha" just means "good". Or "all right".'

Ah Fatt laughed: 'Is opposite in Gwong-jou-talk. Ah-chaa mean "bad man". So you are Achha to me and Aa-chaa to them.'

Neel laughed too. 'So your Adelie was half Achha? Where was she from?'

'Her mother from Goa, but live in Macau. Her father Chinese, from Canton. Adelie very beautiful; she also like smoke opium. When Dai Lou travel, he tell me to look after. Sometime she ask me bite the cloud with her. We both half-Achha, but never seen India. We talk about India, about her mother, my father. And then . . .'

'You became lovers?'

'Yes. We both become *din-din-dak-dak*. Crazy.'

'And your boss found out?'

Ah Fatt nodded.

'What did he do?'

'What do you think?' Ah Fatt shrugged. 'Just like country have laws, gaa have rules. I know Dai Lou try to kill me so I hide with mother. Then I hear hing-dai come for me, so I run away. Go to Macau, and pretend to be Christian. Hide in seminary. Then they send me to Serampore, in Bengal.'

'And Adelie?'

Ah Fatt looked into his eyes and then pointed his chopsticks at the muddy waters of the river.

'She killed herself?'

He answered with a barely perceptible nod.

'But that's all in the past, Ah Fatt: don't you ever feel like going back to Canton now?'

'No. Can-na go back, even though Mother is there. Dai Lou have eyes everywhere. Can-na go back.'

'But what about your father then? Why don't you go to see him?'

'No!' Ah Fatt slammed his cup on the table. 'No. Don't want see Father.'

'Why?'

'Last time I see him, I ask him to take to India. I want go away. Away from Chin-gwok, away from Canton. I know if I stay, something happen with me and Adelie. And I know also, Dai Lou can find out and then he can do anything—to her and me. So I go to Father one day. I ask him to take to India, on *Anahita*. But he say: No, no, Freddy, cannot go. Impossible. After that I angry too. Very angry. I never see Father again.'

Despite the vehemence of Ah Fatt's tone, Neel could sense that the ship's influence on his friend was strengthening, its magnetic field growing steadily more powerful. 'Listen, Ah Fatt,' he said. 'Whatever may have happened between you and your father is in the past. Maybe he's changed: don't you think you should find out if he is on board the ship?'

'No need find out,' said Ah Fatt. 'I know. He is there. I know he is there.'

'How?'

'See flag? With columns? Is only up when Father there.'

'Then why don't you send him a message?'

'No.' The word came out of Ah Fatt's mouth like a small explosion. 'No. Don't want.'

Looking up, Neel saw that Ah Fatt's face, which had shown very little emotion so far, had suddenly crumpled into a stricken mask. But almost immediately Ah Fatt straightened his shoulders and shook his head, as if to clear it. Then, swilling back a shot of liquor, he said: 'Mister Neel, you make me talk too much. Now no more talk. We go sleep.'

'Where?'

'Here. In this boat. Lady say we can stay here.'

four

~

For the journey from Mauritius to southern China Fitcher chose to follow the shortest route, which was by way of Java Head, with a stop for re-provisioning at Anger, the port that faced the perpetually smoking cone of Krakatoa from across the Sunda Straits.

When the order to hoist sail was issued, the *Ibis* was still at anchor in Port Louis. On her way out of the harbour, the *Redruth* passed within a few hundred yards of the schooner. There was no one on deck, and the bare-masted *Ibis* looked tiny in comparison with the tall sailships that were anchored around it. It amazed Paulette to think that so small a vessel could play so large a part in so many lives; even when the *Redruth*'s sails filled with wind and sent the brig racing ahead Paulette could not tear her eyes away from the *Ibis*: it fell to Fitcher to remind her that she had a job to do.

'Look sharp Miss Paulette: no time to lowster at sea . . .'

This, Paulette soon discovered, was no exaggeration: the business of tending plants on a ship at sail was one that allowed for very little rest. Something always needed doing; it was like caring for a garden that was tethered to the back of a large and extremely energetic animal. Almost never was the *Redruth* on an even keel; the closest she came to it was when she was merely dipping and tilting; at other times her decks were rolling steeply from side to side and her nose was either plunging into the sea or shooting out of it. And each of these movements was a potential hazard for the plants: a slight change in the angle of light could expose some shade-loving shrub to the fierce heat of the tropical sun; a breaking swell could send up a jet of seawater that would come down on the pots as a drenching shower of salinity; and if the decks tipped beyond a certain angle, the Wardian cases could escape their cables and go caroming along the gangways.

For each of these contingencies, and many more, there were procedures and protocols, all devised by Fitcher himself: he was not a man to provide lengthy explanations of his methods and for the most part Paulette had to learn by watching and imitating. But sometimes, as he was working, he would begin to mumble to himself—and there was much to be learnt, Paulette discovered, from these near-inaudible disquisitions.

On the subject of soils for example: Fitcher would take a look at a plant that was wilting, even in the shade, and he would trace its ills back to the composition of the matter in which it was planted. Some soils were 'hot', he said, and some were 'cold', by which he meant that some types of earth heated up quicker than others and some tended to retain their heat over long periods. To redress the balance, as necessary, he kept several barrels of soil in reserve, some marked 'cool' and some 'hot': the former tended to be lighter in colour, being of a chalky composition, while the latter were generally darker, being peaty, with a greater amount of vegetal matter. When one or the other was needed he would send Paulette down to fetch him some, and then he would apply the remedy in carefully judged amounts.

Paulette was inclined at first to dismiss these notions of hot and cold soils as a far-fetched fancy—but there was certainly no denying that Fitcher's methods sometimes effected miraculous resuscitations.

Manure was another matter which Fitcher had studied in great depth. He was not by any means dismissive of some of the conventional materials that were used to enrich the soil—the *Redruth*'s holds contained many barrels of rape-cake, malt dust and ground linseed—but the fertilizers that interested him most were those that could be harvested or generated while under sail. Seaweed for instance: he believed that certain varieties of it could be turned, through a process of soaking, drying and pulverizing, into matter that was extremely beneficial for plants. Whenever the *Redruth* encountered a patch of seaweed, he would lower nets and buckets into the water to haul up some fronds: then, after picking out the undesirable varieties, he would soak the rest in fresh water and hang them up on the after-shrouds and the rigging. When dry, he would grind them in a mortar and apply the powder in pinches, as though it were a rare remedy.

The *Redruth*'s flock of chickens was another important source of plant food. One of Paulette's duties was to clear the droppings out of the coop every morning; this, said Fitcher, could be turned into a powerful fertilizer if mixed with water and fermented. The birds' carcasses were not neglected either: when a chicken was slaughtered for the table, every part of it was put to use, including the feathers and bones which were cut up into tiny bits before being added to the compost barrels that hung from the *Redruth*'s stern. Stray seabirds, Fitcher claimed, were even more useful in this regard since they could be chopped up whole. Whenever an exhausted auk or gull came down to the brig to rest there would be a furious scramble among the sailors—for Fitcher offered a small reward for captured birds.

Meat bones were another much prized composting ingredient: bones retrieved from the provisions' barrels were broken up with hammers and then added to the compost. Paulette had never imagined that animal bones could be used in this way, but Fitcher assured her that this was a common practice in London where butchers made good money by selling the by-products of their trade to farmers—not just bones, but also hair and horns. Even bone dust and bone shavings could be sold for a price; boiled down and powdered, they were turned into cakes that were rich in lime, phospates and magnesia.

Nor were fish and fish-bones exempted from these uses. Two or three fishing lines were always trailing behind the brig;

when a catch turned up and was large enough to be eaten Fitcher would part with it only on condition that it was carefully filleted so that the head, tail and bones could be composted; when the fish were too small to eat, he would slip them whole into the potting soil. In Cornwall, he said, refuse pilchards were considered excellent manure and were often ploughed whole into the earth.

One day a small plump porpoise was found entangled in the *Redruth*'s fishing lines. It was still breathing when it was hauled up and Paulette would have liked to set it free, but Fitcher wouldn't hear of it—he had read somewhere that Lord Somerville had used blubber to very good effect at his farm in Surrey. He was delighted to see the creature on the *Redruth*'s deck 'threshing about like a pilcher in a pan-crock'. To Paulette's dismay the porpoise was quickly slaughtered and stripped of its fat, which was put into a special barrel to decompose.

The only substances which Fitcher had voluntarily debarred from use were what he referred to—at least in Paulette's presence—as 'excrementations'. But this was merely a necessity, imposed upon him by the prejudices of the crew; he admitted unhesitatingly that for his own part he would gladly have made use of them. The value of liquid excrementations, he said, had been amply proven by chemists, who had demonstrated that all urine, human and animal, contained the essential elements of vegetables in a state of solution. As for the other kind, well, not for nothing was it said in Cornwall that old Fitcher Penrose 'was so near with his pennies that he'd skin a turd for its tallow'—he wasn't ashamed to admit that he himself had pioneered the use of night soil as manure in Britain. This was one of several Chinese horticultural methods that was new to him.

'Indeed, sir? Was there much else?'

'So there was,' said Fitcher. 'Dwarfing for example—they're right aptycocks at that. And greenhouses. Had them for centuries, and clever little vangs they are too, made of paper and wood. Then there's air-layering.'

Paulette had never heard of this. 'Pray sir, what is that?'

'It's when ee makes a graft directly on to a branch . . .'

This, said Fitcher, was a Chinese gardening method that he had popularized in Britain with great profit to himself: ducking into his cabin, he emerged with a piece of equipment that he had designed and marketed as the 'Penrose Propagation Pot'. It was about the size of a watering-can, except that it had a slit down the side to accommodate a tree-shoot. Facing the slit was a small hoop with which the pot could be affixed to a branch: it was the perfect implement for allowing a shoot to develop roots without planting it in the earth.

'Wouldn't never have thought of it if I hadn't of see'd it in China.'

These stories amazed Paulette. Fitcher was so unlike the plant collectors of her imagination, so peculiar in his appearance and mannerisms, that it was hard to imagine him as an intrepid traveller. But Paulette knew, from her father's accounts, that even Humboldt, the greatest collector of all, was utterly unlike his legend—stout, dapper, and so much the boulevardier that people who sought him out often thought they had encountered an impostor. Not that Fitcher was an explorer of the same ilk—but the *Redruth*'s assemblage of plants and equipment was ample proof of his seriousness, his competence, and indeed, his passion.

'Pray sir,' she said one day, 'may I ask what it was that first took you to China?'

'That ee may,' said Fitcher, with a twitch of his eyebrows. 'And I'll answer as best I can. It came about while I was sailing for a living, on a Cornish fruit-schooner . . .'

One summer, when the schooner was in London for a few days, it came to Fitcher's ears that a certain gent had made it known that he was looking for sailors who had some experience of dealing with plants. On making further inquiries, he was astonished to learn that the man in question was none other than Sir Joseph Banks, the Curator of the King's Garden at Kew.

'Sir Joseph Banks?' cried Paulette. 'Why sir, do you mean he who first described the flora of Australia?'

'Exactly.'

Fitcher had not neglected his scientific interests during his years at sea: the leisure hours that other sailors spent in smoking, gossiping and catchum-killala, he had devoted to reading and self-instruction. He did not need to be told that Sir Joseph had served as the naturalist for Captain Cook's first voyage, or that he was the President of the Royal Society, from which post he reigned unchallenged over a veritable empire of scientific institutions.

Such indeed was Fitcher's awe of the Curator that his first encounter with him got off to an unfortunate start. Sir Joseph was as grand a gent as ever he had set eyes on, dressed to death, from the powdered curls of his wig to the polished heel of his shoe. On being shown into his presence, Fitcher became acutely aware of the shortcomings of his own appearance: the patches on his jacket seemed suddenly to become more visible, as did the attack of acne that had caused his shipmates to compare his face to a pot of bubbling skillygale. He was at the best of times a shy man, and in moments of awkwardness his tongue grew so heavy that even his siblings had been known to joke that he could say neither bee nor baw without sounding awful broad.

But Fitcher need not have worried. Sir Joseph guessed immediately that he was from Cornwall and proceeded to ask a couple of questions about Cornish flora—the first was about the 'bladder-seed' plant, and the second about the flower called the 'coral necklace'—and Fitcher was able to describe and identify both of them correctly.

This was enough to satisfy the Curator, who rose from his seat and began to pace the floor. Then suddenly he came to a stop and said he was looking for someone to go to China—a sailor with some horticultural experience. 'Do you think you might be the man?'

Fitcher, ever stolid, scratched his head and mumbled: 'It hangs on the pay and the purpose, sir. Can't say nothing till I know a little more.'

'All right then: listen . . .'

It was well known, said Sir Joseph, that the gardens at Kew possessed sizeable collections of plants from some of the remotest corners of the earth. But there was one region which was but poorly represented there, and this was China—a country singularly blessed in its botanical riches, being endowed not only with some of the most beautiful and medicinally useful plants in existence, but also with many that were of immense commercial value. Just one such, *Camellia sinensis*—the species of camellia from which tea was plucked—accounted for an enormous proportion of the world's trade and one-tenth of England's revenues.

The value of China's plants had not been lost on Britain's rivals and enemies across the Channel: the major physick gardens and herbariums of both Holland and France had also been endeavouring to assemble collections of Chinese flora—and for considerably longer than Britain—but they too had not had much success. The reasons for the lack of progress were not hard to fathom and the most important of them, without a doubt, was the peculiar obduracy of the Chinese people. Unlike the inhabitants of other botanically blessed countries, the Celestials seemed to have a keen appreciation of the value of their natural endowments. Their gardeners and horticulturists were among the most knowledgeable and skilful in the world, and they guarded their treasures with extraordinary vigilance: the toys and trinkets that satisfied natives elsewhere had no effect on them; even lavish bribes could not persuade them to yield their riches. Europeans had been trying for years to obtain viable specimens of the tea plant, offering rewards that would have sufficed to buy all the camels in Araby—but the quest remained still unrewarded.

A further difficulty was the fact that Europeans were not permitted into the country's interior and were thus unable to wander about, helping themselves to whatever they chose, as they were accustomed to doing elsewhere: in China they were confined to two cities, Canton and Macau, where they were closely watched by the authorities.

Despite these obstacles, the major powers had not slackened in their efforts to obtain China's most valuable trees and plants. Britain was not without advantages in this race even though some of her rivals had the benefit of an earlier start: the Hon'ble East India Company's establishment in Canton was larger than any other, and in order to profit from the British presence, he, Joseph Banks, had persuaded some of the Company's more scientifically minded agents to assemble collections as best they could. This they had proceeded to do, and not without some modest success—but only to have their efforts confounded by yet another problem: it had proved damnably difficult to transport the plants from China to England. The vagaries of the weather, the seepage of salt water, and the many changes of climate were not the only dangers they had to contend with—a yet greater threat was the attitude of the seamen who looked after them—for as men go, mariners were probably the worst gardeners in existence. They seemed to regard the plants as threats to themselves, and would deny them water at the least sign of any scarcity; when their vessels were menaced by storms or shoals, the pots were treated no better than the most dispensable kinds of ballast.

All other expedients having proved unsatisfactory, Sir Joseph had decided, a couple of years ago, to send a properly trained gardener to Canton. The man chosen for the job was a foreman at Kew, a young Scotsman by the name of William Kerr. The fellow had done his job well enough for a while, but he seemed of late to have become somewhat restless: he had written to say that he was planning to go off to the Philippines next summer and he had requested Sir Joseph to send out a man who could be trusted to safely take home the collection that he had already put together, in Canton.

'So what do you say, my good fellow?' said Sir Joseph. 'Are you of a mind to travel on such a mission? If so I will undertake to secure a place for you on a Company ship that is to depart for Canton next week.'

Fitcher had accepted the assignment, and even though his departure and arrival in Canton were much delayed, the ultimate results of the voyage were good enough to earn him the patronage of the powerful Curator: a few years later he was sent out to China again, not just as a custodian this time, but as a replacement for William Kerr. It was this second voyage that was to establish Fitcher's reputation amongst botanists and horticulturists—for after spending two years in Macau and Canton, he had succeeded in bringing back many new plants. He had been careful to select varieties that were likely to prove hardy in Britain, and several of his introductions had quickly become established in English gardens: two varieties of wisteria, a seductive new lily, a fine azalea bush, an unusual primrose, a lustrous camellia and much else.

'Canton's placed many a foot on the ladder of fortune,' said Fitcher, 'and I was fortunate that mine was among them.'

'And what is Canton like, sir?' said Paulette. 'Are there gardens everywhere?'

Fitcher gave one of his rare laughs. 'Oh it's nothing like that—it's the busiest, most crowded city I ever saw. The biggest too, bigger even than London. It's a sea of houses and boats and the plants are in places ee'd never expect. On the roof of a sampan, pouring over the top of a kewny old wall, hanging down from some sheltered balcony. There are carts that roam the streets, loaded with flower pots; there are sampans plying the river, selling nothing but plants. On feast and festival days the whole city bursts into bloom and flower-sellers hawk their wares at prices fit to make an English nurseryman turn chibbol-coloured with envy. Why, I m'self once saw a boatload of orchids sell out in an hour and that too, with each blowth valued at a hundred silver dollars.'

'Oh how I long to see it, sir!'

Fitcher frowned. 'But that ee won't ee know.'

'Oh?' said Paulette. 'But why not?'

'Because European women aren't allowed to set foot in Canton. That's the law.'

'But sir,' cried Paulette in dismay, 'how can that be so? What of all the merchants who live there? Do they not have their wives with them? Their children?'

Fitcher shook his head. 'No. Foreign women can go no further than Macau—that is where they must remain.'

The discovery that she would not be able to travel to Canton came as a bitter disappointment to Paulette: it was as if a flaming sword had descended from heaven to shut her out of Eden, forever depriving her of the chance to inscribe her name in the annals of botanical exploration.

Paulette could feel tears starting into her eyes. 'But sir! Will I not be able to go with you to Canton then? Where shall I stay?'

'Many a respectable English family in Macau takes in lodgers. It'll just be for a week or two at a time.'

Paulette had imagined that she would be collecting plants in the wild. Now cheated of her opportunity she burst into tears. 'But sir, I will miss the best of it.'

'Come now, Miss Paulette,' said Fitcher. 'Ee needn't take it so hard. There's a passel of islands along the coast where ee'll be able to do some collecting. There's no cause to be upset. Look, I'll show ee . . .'

Fetching a chart of the south China coast, Fitcher pointed to the yawning mouth of the Pearl River and the hundreds of tiny islands that lay scattered across it. On the western hinge of the jaws lay the Portuguese settlement of Macau: this was where foreign ships had to go to obtain the 'chop' that would permit them to travel up the Pearl River to Canton. At the eastern end of the river mouth, lay a sizeable island called Hong Kong: it was a windswept, sparsely populated place and the people who lived there did not seem to mind if foreigners went ashore, men or women. Fitcher had been there once: it was the only time he had been able to collect in the field in China. He had found some fine orchids and had always wanted to go back, to give the island a thorough going-over.

'That's as good a place as ee could wish for Miss Paulette,' said Fitcher. 'Ee'll be able to botanize in the wild there, just as ee'd hoped.'

~

Zadig greeted Bahram, as always, with a wide-armed embrace and kisses on both cheeks. It was only when they stepped back to look at each other that Bahram realized that a great change—a transformation—had come over his old friend.

Arré Zadig Bey! he said. You've become a white man! A sahib!

Zadig was dressed in duck trousers, a high-collared shirt, and a jacket and cravat—he glanced at his clothes in some embarrassment and made a gesture of dismissal. Don't laugh too loud, my friend, he said. One day you may have to wear these things too. In a town like this it sometimes comes in useful.

They were in the saloon of the Owners' Suite, where two large Chinese armchairs had been arranged beside an open window. Ushering Zadig to one of the chairs, Bahram said: I hope you haven't become too European for some paan?

No, said Zadig smiling. Not yet.

Good! Bahram gestured to a khidmatgar, who went off to fetch his paan casket.

Zadig, in the meanwhile, had been looking around the saloon which he had visited many times before. I'm glad to see nothing's been damaged here, he said. It was terrible to see what happened to the front of the ship.

Yes, said Bahram. We were lucky it wasn't worse. I've never been in a storm like that one. Two of our lascars were swept away—and my old Parsi munshi was killed, just sitting in his cabin. Some of the holds got flooded too.

Was the cargo damaged?

Yes. We lost three hundred crates.

Of opium?

Yes.

Three hundred crates! Zadig raised his eyebrows. At last year's prices that would have fetched you enough to buy two more ships!

A khidmatgar appeared with a silver casket and set it on a teapoy. Opening the lid, Bahram took out a fresh green betel leaf and smeared it carefully with chalky lime.

It was the worst storm I've ever been through, said Bahram. When I heard about the flooding in the hold I went to see what could be done. There was so much water in there I got knocked over and a very strange thing happened.

Yes? Go on, Bahram-bhai, I am listening.

Bahram reached for an areca nut and sliced it with a silver cutter. For a moment, he said, I thought I was drowning. And you know na, what they say, about the things a drowning man sees?

Yes.

I thought I saw Chi-mei. That's one reason why I am so glad to see you, Zadig Bey. I want to know what you learnt about Chi-mei and Freddy when you were last in Canton.

Folding the betel leaf into a triangle, Bahram handed it to Zadig, who tucked it into his cheek.

I'm sad to say, Bahram-bhai, there's not much I can tell you. I went to the floating city to look for Chi-mei's kitchen-boat, but it wasn't there. So I sought out your old comprador, Chunqua, and he told me what happened.

Bahram picked up the nut-cutter again. Yes? Tell me.

Zadig hesitated. It's an ugly thing, Bahram-bhai, that's why I didn't want to write to you about it. I thought I should tell you in person.

Go on, said Bahram impatiently. What happened?

It seems there was a robbery. Some thieves boarded the kitchen-boat, and she tried to chase them away. That's how it happened.

Bahram's hand froze and the nut-cutter fell out of his fingers. Are you telling me she was murdered?

Yes, my friend, said Zadig. I am sad that it is I who have to tell you this.

And Freddy?

Chunqua could tell me nothing about him, said Zadig. He disappeared shortly before Chi-mei's death and has not been heard from again.

Do you think something may have happened to him too?

There's no knowing, said Zadig. But you should not jump to conclusions. He may just have left and gone off somewhere.

I heard that his half-sister had married and moved to Malacca—maybe he went to join her there.

Bahram thought back to his last meeting with Chi-mei, three years ago, on the last boat she had bought—a large and fanciful vessel with a stern that was shaped like an upraised fishtail. He had gone to say goodbye to her, before leaving for Bombay. Having long since fallen into a relationship of easy companionability with Chi-mei, he often went to her boat for his evening meal—they had become, in a way, something like a long-married couple. Chi-mei did not usually cook when Bahram went to visit: her specialities were restricted to the subtle fare of Canton and she knew that he liked spicier food. She would send someone off to other boats nearby, to fetch some Dan-dan noodles, and some 'Hotand-Numbing Chicken', and perhaps some fiery Sichuanese 'Married-Couple-Slices'. When the food came she would serve it to him herself, sitting opposite him and waving a fan to keep the flies away. Over the years she had grown a little portly, and her face had become plumper, but her clothes were still sack-like in cut and severe in colour. It annoyed him that she took so few pains over her appearance and he had asked why she never wore any of the jewellery he had given her. She had fetched a gold-and-jade brooch, pinned it to her tunic and given him a wide smile: 'Mister Barry too muchi happy now?'

Was it the jewellery they had come for, those thieves? He thought of her trying to fend off their knives, and an image appeared in front of his eyes, of a rent in the fabric of her tunic, where that brooch had been, and of blood welling up from her chest.

Bahram clasped his hands to his face: I can't believe it; I can't believe it.

Zadig came to stand beside him and put a hand on his shoulder. It is hard for you, isn't it?

I can't believe it, Zadig Bey.

Do you remember, my friend, said Zadig gently, all those years ago, when you and I talked of love? You said that what you and Chi-mei had was not love? That it was something else, something different?

Bahram brushed his hand across his eyes, and cleared his throat. Yes, Zadig Bey, I remember very well.

Zadig squeezed Bahram's shoulder: I think maybe you were wrong, no?

Bahram had to swallow several times before he could speak: Look, Zadig Bey, I'm not like you—I don't think about such things. Maybe it's true what you say—maybe what I felt for Chi-mei was the closest I'll ever come to these things you speak of: love, pyar, ishq. But what does it matter now? She's gone, isn't she? I have to carry on: I have a cargo to sell.

That's correct. You have to look ahead Bahram-bhai.

Exactly. So tell me, Zadig Bey, will you come to Canton with me? On the *Anahita*? I will give you a fine cabin.

Yes, of course, Bahram-bhai! It will be wonderful to travel again with you.

Good! So when will you come on board?

Give me a day or two and I will be back with my baggage.

After Zadig had left, Bahram could not bear to remain in his suite. For the first time since the storm, he decided to go up to the main deck.

He had been dreading the moment when he would see for himself the wound in the *Anahita*'s prow, and the sight proved even more shocking than he had expected. Although the jib had already been replaced, to Bahram's eyes the absence of the gilded figurehead was starkly evident.

I cannot stand it, Vico, he said. I must go down.

Bahram's horror was not so much for the loss itself, as for the effect it would have on the Mistries, most of all on Shireenbai, who was a keen votary of signs and portents. Bahram's refusal to heed omens and oracles had long been a source of contention between them: she had never made any secret of her belief that it was largely responsible for the greatest of the many disappointments of their marriage–her lack of a son.

Shireenbai had grown up in a family of powerful, self-willed men, and even though they both doted on their two daughters, she had long wanted a boy of her own. To this end she had visited many magical wells, touched a great number of miraculous rocks, tied uncountable threads and sought the blessings of a legion of pirs, fakirs, swamis, sants and saints. That none of these missions had resulted in success seemed only to strengthen her belief in the potency of these intermediaries. She would often plead with Bahram to participate in her efforts to find a cure: but why? *pante kain?* why won't you come with me?

Once, many years ago, she had overcome his objections and taken him to visit one of her gurus: she had somehow got it into her head that this man would be able to remedy her failure to bear a male child and she had insisted that Bahram go with her to see him. After resisting for months Bahram had finally relented when she pointed out that her child-bearing years were almost at an end; in the hope of buying some peace at home, he had agreed to visit the miracle-monger. This master of fecundity turned out to be a hirsute, ash-covered sadhu who lived in the jungles of Borivli, two hours from the city: he had asked Bahram many questions and had taken extensive readings of his pulse; then after much cogitation and coaxing he had announced that the cause of the problem had been revealed to him—it lay not with Shireenbai but with him, Bahram. The masculine energies of Bahram's bodily fluids had become depleted, he said, because of his domestic circumstances: it could scarcely be otherwise with a ghar-jamai—a man who lived under the roof of his wife's family was bound to be weakened by his dependency on his in-laws. To make him strong enough to sire a male child would be no easy task, but could be achieved if he, Bahram, were willing to dose himself with potions, apply certain ointments, and of course, contribute very large sums of money to the sadhu's ashram.

Bahram had been uncharacteristically patient in enduring this performance, but at the end of it he let his annoyance show by asking: Are you sure you know what you are talking about?

The old man, whose cataract-clouded eyes contained a surprising glint of shrewdness, had smiled at him sweetly and answered: Why? Do you have any reason to think that your seed is capable of begetting a male child?

Bahram had understood at once that the old man had sprung a carefully crafted trap. To denounce him as a fraud would surely have excited Shireenbai's suspicions, and expensive though the alternative might be, the cost was negligible in comparison with the price he would have to pay if it came to be known that he had already sired a son—a bastard. A short while ago, a similar revelation had caused an upheaval in the community: the man concerned, a trader of Bahram's acquaintance, had been expelled from the Parsi panchayat. Not only had he become a social outcast, a pariah to whom no Parsi would so much as rent a room, he had also been financially ruined because no one would do business with him any more; there was almost no price that Bahram would not have paid to prevent such an outcome.

Yet, when he tried to speak the words of denial he found himself gagging on them. It was one thing to skim over the subject in silence; but to actively deny his son's existence, to pretend that he had played no part in engendering the life of his own child—this was impossibly difficult. Fatherhood and family were a kind of religion to him, and it would be like denying his faith, erasing the sacred ties of blood that connected him, not only to his son but also to his daughters.

The sadhu, perhaps sensing his dilemma, said: You have not answered my question . . .

Bahram could feel his wife's eyes boring into him, and somehow, swallowing hard, he had managed to say: No. You're right; the fault must lie in my seed. I will take the treatment—all of it, whatever is necessary.

Over the next several months he had taken the sadhu's tonics, applied the ointments, paid whatever was asked for and lain with Shireenbai in the prescribed ways, at exactly the prescribed times. The effort was not entirely wasted, for Shireenbai had never again talked to him about her wish for a son—but on the other hand, the failure of the 'treatment' had seemed only to confirm her forebodings about the future. Her belief in signs and omens had grown even more fervent than before.

Never were Shireenbai's apprehensions more acute than when Bahram was about to set sail for southern China: in the weeks before she would make daily visits to the Fire Temple and spend long hours with the dasturs; the day and the hour of Bahram's departure would be dictated by her astrologers and since he refused to consult fortune-tellers himself, she would seek them out, commissioning all kinds of prophecies and divinations. The night before, if an owl were heard, she would insist upon a change of date; in the morning, she would rearrange the household to make sure that he passed through a carefully constructed labyrinth of auspiciousness—a maid would materialize in the stairwell, with a pot of water on her head; the malis would be dispersed across the garden, as if uninstructed, but with their arms filled with the right sorts of fruits and flowers; when Bahram was about to step into his carriage a fisherman would mysteriously appear, just in time to give him a glimpse of his catch. Shireenbai would even dictate the route to the docks, planning it so as to avoid the washermen at Dhobi-Talao—for a dhobi carrying unclean clothes was a sight to be avoided at all costs.

Yet, even at their worst, Shireenbai's superstitions and observances had never before amounted to much more than a source of distraction: they had certainly never posed a serious obstacle to Bahram's ventures—not until this year, when she had done everything in her power to prevent him from leaving. Don't go, she had beseeched him. *Tame na jao* . . . don't go, don't go this year. Everyone says there's going to be trouble.

What exactly do they say? Bahram responded.

There's been so much talk, she said. Especially about that British Admiral who was here with those warships.

Do you mean Admiral Maitland?

Yes, she said. That's the one. *Jhagro thase* . . . they say there may be fighting in China.

It so happened that Bahram was well aware of Admiral Maitland and his mission: he was one of the few Bombay merchants who had been invited to a reception on his flagship, the *Algerine*, and he knew very well that the fleet under

Maitland's command was being sent to China only as a show of force.

Listen, Shireenbai, he said. There is no need for you to worry about these things. It's my job to stay abreast of these developments.

But I'm only telling you what my brothers are saying, Shireenbai protested. They are saying China will stop imports of opium and that it may even lead to fighting. They are saying you should not go now: the risk is too great.

This had made Bahram bristle: Arré, Shireenbai, what do your brothers know about this? They should do their work and leave me to mine. If they had been doing business with China as long as I have they would know that there's been talk of war many times before and nothing has ever come of it—no more than it will now. If your father were alive today he would have supported me—but it's as they say, 'when the wise one goes, things fall apart . . .'

After her first line of argument proved ineffective, Shireenbai confessed to the other reasons for her concern: one of her astrologers had declared that the stars were aligned in such a way as to signal danger to all travellers; a diviner had seen portents of war and unrest; a trusted pir had warned of upheavals on the high seas. Persuaded of her husband's peril, Shireenbai enlisted their two daughters—both of whom were married by now, and blessed with several children—to add their entreaties to hers, begging him not to go. As a concession he twice agreed to postpone his departure in order that some propitious portents might be found. But after a fortnight of waiting none such were discovered, and at last, fearing that he would miss the start of the Canton trading season, he had set a date, declaring that he could wait no longer.

When the appointed morning arrived, everything had gone wrong: an owl was heard at daybreak, a dire augury; and then his turban was found on the floor, having fallen down at night. Worse still, while dressing to accompany Bahram to the docks, Shireenbai had broken her red marriage bangle. Bursting into tears, she had again implored him not to go: *Tame na jao*. You know what it means for a wife to break her bangle, don't you? Even if you care nothing for me: what about the family? Do you care nothing for your daughters and their children? *Jara bhi parvah nathi?* Do you care nothing at all . . . ?

There was something in her voice that made it impossible for Bahram to answer her in his usual indulgent way: in her pleas there was an urgency and despair which he had never heard before. It was as if she had at last accepted him as something more than a substitute for the husband she should have had; it was as if, after forty years of performing her marital duties with apathetic punctiliousness, her feelings for him had suddenly ripened into something else.

That it should happen now, that he should have to confront an emotion that was so raw, so naked, after a lifetime of coping with her disappointed, dutiful indifference, seemed profoundly unjust—had it happened even the day before, he might have told her about Chi-mei and Freddy, but with the ship waiting to weigh anchor it was impossible to speak of it now. Instead, he put his arm around Shireenbai as she sat doubled over on the edge of their bed, clutching her broken bangle. Her thin, angular form was draped from head to toe in pale, brocaded China silk; her sari was a relatively plain one, as it happened, yet the sheen of the fabric filled the room with a milky glow; she was wearing no jewellery other than her bangles and the only points of colour on her body came from the scarlet Jinliang slippers she wore on her feet—he had bought them for her in Canton, many years ago.

Slowly unfurling her fingers, Bahram removed the broken glass hoop from her hand. Listen Shireenbai, he said; let me go this one last time, and when I come back I will tell you everything. You will understand then why it was so necessary.

When you come back? But what if . . . ? She looked away, unable to finish the sentence.

Shireenbai, said Bahram, my mother used to say 'a wife's prayers will never be wasted'. You can be sure that yours will not.

~

Who were they to be?

The question weighed not just on Ah Fatt and Neel but on everyone who visited the weekly clothes market in the Chulia kampung, where many of Singapore's lightermen, coolies and petty tradespeople lived. This was one of the poorest quarters of the makeshift new frontier town, a mushrooming bustee of bamboo-walled shanties and pile-raised shacks, squeezed between dense jungle on one side and marshy swamplands on the other.

The market was held in an open field, adjoining one of the tributary creeks of the Singapore River. The road that led there was not much more than a muddy pathway, and most of the bazar's visitors came by boat. From the Malay and Chinese parts of town people came in perahus and hired twakow rivercraft, while sailors and lascars usually came directly from their ships, in brightly painted tongkang lighters, bearing the wares they hoped to sell or barter: sweaters knitted on 'make-and-mend' days; tunics of stitched selvagee and wadmarel; oilskins and pea-jackets recovered from the fernan bags of drowned shipmates.

Neel and Ah Fatt were among the few to come on foot and the bustle of the marketplace took them by surprise: after a long trudge along an unfrequented path, there it was, all of a sudden, a noisy melee of a mela, on the banks of a mangrove-edged creek. In appearance and atmosphere, the bazar was not unlike the weekly markets and fairs that gather around villages everywhere: it had its share of itinerant pedlars and hawkers, entertainers and snack-sellers, meat-hawkers and muff-mongers—but the clothes-stalls were the main attraction, and it was to those that most of the visitors went.

Amongst sailors and lascars the bazar was known as the 'Wordy-Market' which suggested that it had once been a market for *vardi*s, or soldiers' uniforms. Many garments of that description were still to be found there: certainly there were few other places in the world where a grenadier's mitre could be exchanged for a Mongol wind-bonnet, or an infantryman's shell-jacket for a pair of Zouave pyjamas. But these regimental items were not the market's only wares: over the two decades of its existence the Wordy-Market had gained an unusual kind of renown, not just within Singapore, but far beyond. In the surrounding peninsulas, islands and headlands it was spoken of simply as the 'Pakaian Pasar'—the 'Clothes-Market'—and was known to be a place where every kind of garment could be bought and sold—from Papuan penis sheaths to Sulu skirts, from Bengal saris to Bagobo trousers. Well-heeled visitors to the island might prefer to do their shopping in the European and Chinese stores around Commercial Square, but for those of slender means and pinched purses—or those with no coins at all, but only fish and fowl to barter—this market, listed on no map and unknown to any municipality, was the place to go: for where else could a woman exchange a Khmer sampot for a Bilaan jacket? Where else could a fisherman trade a sarong for a coattee, or a conical rain-hat for a Balinese cap? Where else could a man go, clothed in nothing but a loincloth, and walk away in a whalebone corset and silk slippers?

Some of these articles of clothing came from the impecunious pilgrims, missionaries, soldiers and travellers who passed through the port. But many arrived from much farther afield, having been robbed, purloined or pirated at distant corners of the Indian Ocean—for amongst those who regularly plied these waters, it was well known that there was no better place than the Wordy-Market in which to dispose of stolen garments. Here, even more than in other bazars, buyers were well-advised to examine their goods carefully because many were marked by bloodstains, bullet holes, dagger punctures and other unsightly disfigurements. Caution was especially necessary with the more sumptuous garments—panelled chaopao coats and embroidered chang-fu robes—for many of these were retrieved from tombs and graves, and would often, upon inspection, be found to have been gnawed by worms. But if there were risks in shopping here, they were amply offset by the rewards: in what other place could a deserter exchange his tricorn and gorget for a suit of English clothes? That such a place would not be allowed to continue for ever was clear enough, but while it lasted, the Wordy-Market was recognized to be a godsend by all.

It was Neel who heard of the clothes bazar, from a Kalinga boatman who lived in the Chulia kampung. It was welcome news, for he and Ah Fatt had arrived wearing whatever clothes they had been able to acquire in the outer islands—pyjamas, vests and some threadbare sarongs. These bedraggled garments clearly would not do if they were to avoid drawing attention to themselves but their purses had dwindled by this time and the clothes that were on offer in the town's shops were far beyond their means.

The Wordy-Market was the perfect solution to their plight; the first items they bought were cloth bags, and these they proceeded to fill, going from one stall to another, haggling in a mixture of tongues. Neel bought a European-style coat and some pyjamas, narrow and broad, a few sirbands and bandhnas to serve as turbans, and three or four light cotton angarkhas. Ah Fatt collected a similarly eclectic mix: a paletot, some shirts and breeches, several tunics, black and white, and a couple of Chinese gowns.

They were heading towards the shoe stalls when a voice came booming at them, loud enough to be heard over the din of the marketplace. 'Freddy! Bloody bugger . . .!'

Ah Fatt froze and the blood drained from his face. He kept on walking, without looking back, prodding Neel to keep pace. After a few steps, he said, in an undertone: 'Look-see who it is. What he look like?'

Glancing over his shoulder, Neel caught sight of a heavy-bellied man, impeccably dressed in European clothes: the face under the hat was very dark, the eyes white and protuberant, and he was hurrying after the two of them with an armload of newly purchased clothing.

'How he look?'

Before Neel could say anything, the voice boomed at them again: 'Freddy! Arré Freddy you bloody falto bugger! It's me, Vico!'

From the side of his mouth Ah Fatt hissed at Neel: 'You go on. Keep walking. We talk later.'

Neel gave him a nod and walked on at a steady pace, not stopping till he was a good distance away. Then, from the shelter of a stall, he turned to watch the two men.

Even from that distance it was clear that Vico was pleading with Ah Fatt, who seemed unconvinced and unresponsive. But in a while he unbent a little, and Vico, visibly relieved, gave him a hug before hurrying off towards the creek, where an elegant ship's cutter awaited him.

Neel waited a bit before intercepting Ah Fatt. 'Who was that?'

'Father's purser, Vico. I tell you about him, no?'

'What did he say?'

'He say, Father sick. He want me very much. I must go see him.'

'And you agreed?'

'Yes,' said Ah Fatt in his laconic way. 'I go to ship. Later today. They send boat for me.'

For reasons that he could not quite understand, Neel was deeply disquieted by Ah Fatt's plan. 'But we have to talk about this, Ah Fatt,' he said. 'What will you tell your father? When he asks where you've been these last few years what will you say?'

'Nothing,' said Ah Fatt. 'Will tell him nothing. Will tell him that I join ship and leave China three years before. At sea all this time.'

'But what if he finds out that you were in India? And about your jail sentence and all that?'

'Impossible,' said Ah Fatt. 'He can-na! After I leave Canton, all time I use different name. In jail they have only my body: no proper name, nothing. Nothing to connect me with all that.'

'And after that? What if he wants to keep you with him?'

Ah Fatt shook his head. 'No. He will not want me with him. He too much afraid Elder Wife will find out. About me.'

Then Ah Fatt had one of his odd moments of almost uncanny perceptiveness. Throwing his arm around Neel's shoulder he said: 'You afraid I am going to leave you alone, eh Neel? Do not worry. You my friend, no? I can-na leave you all lone in this place.'

That evening, after Ah Fatt had left to visit the *Anahita*, Neel went back to the kitchen-boat and sat waiting for a while. As the hours passed he began to doubt that Ah Fatt would return that night and he grew increasingly impatient with himself: what reason was there to feel that his own future hinged upon the outcome of Ah Fatt's meeting with his father? If it came to a parting of their ways, he would have to manage as best he could—that was all there was to it. He rose to his feet, and made his way aft, to the covered 'house' in the stern of the kitchen-boat. This was where he had spent the last couple of nights and he fell asleep almost as soon as he lay down.

Some hours later, he woke up, urgently needing to relieve himself. Opening the door, he found the moon shining brightly upon the river. Afterwards, as he was making his way back to the cabin, his eyes strayed to the prow of the boat—he saw now that two figures were seated there, reclining in the bows.

Instantly, Neel was fully awake. He made his way quietly forward, until the two figures were only a couple of yards away. They were reclining against the moonlit bulwark: one was Ah Fatt and the other was the girl who did the cooking.

'Ah Fatt?'

All he got in answer was a subdued grunt.

Stepping up to the bows, Neel saw that Ah Fatt was cradling a pipe in his hands.

'What's this you're doing, Ah Fatt?'

'Smoking.'

'Opium?'

Ah Fatt tilted his head back, very slowly; his face was pallid in the moonlight and there was a look in his eyes that Neel had not seen before, subdued and dreamy, yet not somnolent. 'Yes, opium,' he said softly. 'Vico give me some.'

'Have a care Ah Fatt—you know what opium does to you.'

Ah Fatt shrugged. 'Yen have catch me tonight: must bite bowl; must have tonight.'

'Why?'

'Father tell me something.'

'What?'

There was a pause and then Ah Fatt said: 'Mother dead.'

Neel gasped: he could see nothing of Ah Fatt's face, and nor was his voice expressive of any emotion. 'How did it happen?'

'Father say, thieves maybe.' He shrugged again, and said, on a note of finality, 'No use talk about such-thing.'

'Tell me more,' said Neel. 'You can't stop there. What else did your father say?'

Ah Fatt's voice seemed to fade, as though it were retreating down the shaft of a well. 'Father happy see me. He cry and cry. He say he worry about me too much.'

'And you? Were you happy to see him?'

Ah Fatt shrugged and said nothing.

'But what else? Did he tell you what you should do next?'

'He agree better I go to my sister in Malacca. He say after this season in Canton he give me money for start busy-ness. Just have to wait three-four month.'

Ah Fatt's attention was clearly drifting away now, and Neel realized that it would be hard to get much more out of him. 'All right,' he said. 'Maybe we should sleep now. Better to talk tomorrow.'

But as he was turning to leave Ah Fatt called out: 'Wait! Some news for you too.'

'What?'

'You want work for Father?'

Neel looked into his absent eyes and expressionless face, and decided that he was merely rambling. 'What are you talking about, Ah Fatt?'

'Father need munshi—to write letter and read paper. His old munshi dead. I tell him I know someone who can do this job. In jail I see you write letter, no? And you can write English, Hindusthani and all: true?'

'Yes, but . . .'

Neel clapped his hands to his head and sat down again, beside Ah Fatt. He knew nothing about Bahram Modi except what he had heard from Ah Fatt, and these accounts had given him plenty of cause for misgiving. At times he had been reminded of his own father, the old Zemindar of Raskhali: between the two of them also there had been little communication, for the Zemindar had spent much more time with his mistresses than at home. Their meetings, being infrequent, had involved much preparation and a great deal of anxiety: always, when the time came to enter his father's presence, Neel would find that his tongue was stilled by a peculiar combination of emotions—a mixture of fear, anger and a dull mulish resentment—all of which came flooding back now, at the thought of meeting Bahram.

And yet what a relief it would be to have a job, to stop living like a fugitive.

'Father want to see you tomorrow,' said Ah Fatt.

'Tomorrow!' said Neel. 'So soon?'

'Yes.'

'What did you tell him about me, Ah Fatt?'

'I tell him I meet you by chance here, in Singapore. All I know is you have done munshi-work before. He say he want see you tomorrow. Talk about job.'

'But Ah Fatt . . .'

Neel was for once at a loss for words, but Ah Fatt, in his strangely intuitive way, seemed to know what was going through his mind.

'You will like Father, Neel. All people love Father. Some say he great man. He see many thing, know many people, tell many story. He not like me you know. And I not like him.' He smiled. 'Only one time I am like Father.'

'When?'

Ah Fatt held up his pipe. 'You see this? When I have big-smoke, I become like Father. Great man who all people love.'

five

~

The coast of China was only a week away when Paulette learnt that apart from a trove of living plants the *Redruth* was also carrying a 'painted garden'—a collection of botanical paintings and illustrations.

The reason why this discovery came so late was because the pictures were not on display: they were neatly bundled in ribbon-tied folders and hidden away in the dingy little storeroom where Fitcher kept his plant presses, seed jars and other equipment. This was no accident: Fitcher was not artistically minded and the aesthetic merits of the pictures meant little to him. He regarded them primarily as tools, but of a special kind—for him they were clues to guide him in the search for new and unknown species of plants.

To use paintings to look for plants struck Paulette as a marvellously inventive yet curious procedure: what could be more unlikely than to search for new species not in Nature, but in the most rarefied realms of human artifice? But this was an old and proven method, Fitcher explained, and he was by no means its inventor: it dated back to the earliest European plant-hunters to work in China—among them a British botanist by the name of James Cuninghame, who had visited China twice in the eighteenth century.

In Cuninghame's time, travelling in China was a little easier for foreigners than it was later to become: on his first visit he had had the good fortune to spend several months in the port of Amoy. He had discovered there that Chinese painters were exceptionally skilled at the realistic depiction of plants, flowers and trees: this was fortunate for him because in those days no one could hope to bring live specimens from China to Europe by sea; the collector's aims were rather to amass stocks of seed and to assemble 'dried gardens'. To these Cuninghame had added another kind of collection, the 'painted garden': he had returned to England with over a thousand pictures. These illustrations had elicited much admiration while arousing also a great deal of scepticism—to eyes accustomed to European flora it had seemed unlikely, if not impossible, that flowers of such extravagant beauty could actually exist. There were some who said that these painted flowers were the botanical equivalent of phoenixes, unicorns and other mythical creatures. But of course they were wrong: in time the whole world would see that Cuninghame's collection had contained pictures of many of the most notable flowers the world would receive from China—hydrangeas, chrysanthemums, flowering plums, tree peonies, the first repeat-flowering roses, crested irises, innumerable new gardenias, primroses, lilies, hostas, wisterias, asters and azaleas.

'But it's for the camellia that Cuninghame most deserves to be known.'

Never had he understood, said Fitcher, why Linnaeus had chosen to name the camellia after Dr Kamel, an obscure and unimportant German physician. By rights the genus ought to have been called *Cuninghamia*, in honour of Cuninghame, for whom camellias had been a passion, a quest: it was he who sent back the first camellia leaf ever to be seen in Britain.

It was not merely because of their flowers that camellias were of special interest to Cuninghame: he believed that next to foodgrains this genus was possibly the most valuable botanical species known to man. This was not a far-fetched notion: the camellia family had, after all, given the world the tea bush, *Camellia sinensis*, which was already then the fount of an extensive and lucrative commerce. Cuninghame's interest in its sister plants was sparked by a Chinese legend, about a man who fell into a valley that had no exit: he was said to have lived there for a hundred years eating nothing but a single plant. This plant, Cuninghame was told, was of a rich golden colour and yielded an infusion that could turn white hairs into black, restore the suppleness of aged joints, and serve as a cure for ailments of the lungs. Cuninghame named it the 'Golden Camellia' and came to believe that it might surpass the tea bush in value if it could be found and propagated.

'And did he find it, sir?'

'It's possible, but no one knows . . .'

On his way back to England, after his second visit to China, Cuninghame had vanished without trace, off the coast of southern India. His collections had perished with him, and it came to be whispered later that he might have met an untimely end because of certain protected plants that were in his possession. Those rumours were further fuelled when a packet of his papers reached England intact: they had been mailed shortly before he embarked on his last voyage and they included a small picture of an unknown flower.

'The Golden Camellia?'

'Ee can see for eerself,' said Fitcher, in his laconic way. Reaching for a folder he extracted a card-like square of paper and handed it to Paulette.

The card was not large, and the picture inside was only about six inches square: it was painted with a fine brush, on paper that was covered with a faint yellow wash. In the background, lightly etched, was a landscape of mist-covered mountains; in the foreground was a twisted cypress tree, and under it, the seated figure of an old man with a bowl cupped in his hands. Next to him lay a branch with a few brilliantly coloured blossoms. The scale was too small for the precise shape of the petals to be outlined in any detail, but the blossom's colouring was strikingly vivid: a mauve that turned gradually into a sunburst of gold.

Facing the picture, on the opposite leaf of the card, were two columns of Chinese characters, running from top to bottom.

Paulette pointed to the writing: 'Is the meaning of these lines known, sir?'

Fitcher nodded and turned the card over. Written on the other side, in a faint but distinctive copperplate hand, was an English translation:

The petals on their green tinged stem shine like the purest gold.
A purple eye looks up from the centre, setting the bloom aglow,
It remedies the pain of ageing bones and quickens the memory and mind,
It puts to flight the death that festers in the lungs.

Inscribed under these lines were the words: Hsieh Ling-yun, Duke of Kang-lo.

The Duke of Kang-lo, said Fitcher, was apparently a real person, not some mythical hero. He had lived in the fifth century of the Christian era and was regarded as one of the greatest of Chinese naturalists; these lines of his were thought to mean that not only could this flower reverse the effects of ageing, it could also be used to battle one of humanity's most dreaded enemies: that scourge of the lungs—consumption.

Many years after Cuninghame's death his papers had come into Sir Joseph's hands. He too had come to be convinced that the Golden Camellia might be one of the greatest of all botanical discoveries: the plant-hunter's Grail. This, said Fitcher, was one of the reasons why he had decided to send a trained horticulturist to Canton, at public expense—William Kerr.

'But Mr Kerr did not find the camellia?'

'No—but he did find evidence of it.'

The last consignment of plants that Kerr had sent back to Kew was exceptionally large, and to make sure of its safe arrival he had hired a young Chinese gardener to escort it to London. This boy's name was Ah Fey, and although only in his teens he was exceptionally clever and remarkably skilled—he had succeeded in transporting the collection almost intact. On arriving at Kew he had also handed Sir Joseph a small 'painted garden'—a set of several dozen botanical illustrations made by Cantonese artists. Amongst them Sir Joseph had found a picture of an unknown flower, a camellia that was remarkably like the bloom depicted in Cuninghame's painting.

Now, pulling another folder off the shelf, Fitcher took out a picture and handed it to Paulette. 'Here—have a look.'

The picture was painted not on paper but on another material, something thicker, stiffer and of a pristine and polished smoothness: it was a substance made from the pith of a reed, Fitcher explained, and was much favoured by Cantonese painters. The sheet was about the size of a foolscap page and at its centre was a startlingly vivid burst of colour. The vibrancy of the image was enhanced also by the manner in which the painting had been crafted, with many layers of paint being applied upon the pith so that the subject seemed to stand out in relief against the smooth surface—it was a perfectly formed double blossom, with its petals arranged in several concentric circles. At the heart of the bloom lay a closely packed whorl of stamens that seemed to be lit from beneath by a glowing circle of mauve; this tint spilled over on to the base of the petals, with the colours changing gradually as they moved away from the centre. The outer part of the corolla was a brilliant sunburst of gold.

Paulette had never seen such extraordinary variations of colour in a single bloom. 'It is very beautiful, sir—so much that one must doubt that such a flower really exists.'

'Can't fault ee for that,' said Fitcher. 'But if ee look at the way the parts are drawn ee'll see that they seem to be sketched from a live specimen. Wouldn't ee say?'

Now, looking at the picture again, Paulette saw that the picture's composition was not unlike that of a European botanical illustration: it had been so configured as to include many telling details. She focused her gaze on the leaves, of which two were depicted in the painting: they were elliptical in shape with beautifully defined drip-tips; the petioles were carefully drawn and the mid-ribs and veins were clearly indicated under the shining, glossy epidermis. A bud was also featured, with its head emerging from a wrapping of sepals, packed tightly together like fish-scales.

'Was it Sir Joseph who showed this picture to you?'

'So it was.'

Shortly after Ah Fey's arrival at Kew, Fitcher had once again received a summons from Sir Joseph Banks. On presenting himself before the Curator he had learnt that apart from plants and pictures, William Kerr had also sent a letter with Ah Fey, asking to be relieved of his post in Canton. He had spent several years there already and was desperate to leave. Since he had collected more than two hundred new species, Sir Joseph had decided to reward him by granting his wish: a new post would be created for him in Ceylon.

'But much useful work remains to be done in Canton,' said Sir Joseph. 'Indeed I have received intelligence of a flower that may be a greater prize than any of Kerr's discoveries. For this reason, among others, I have decided that the next man I send to China will go not as a representative of Kew, but as the emissary of a group of private investors.'

With that Sir Joseph had handed Fitcher the recently received picture of the Golden Camellia.

'I need hardly tell you, Penrose, that all this is in the strictest confidence.'

'No, sir.'

'So what do you say, Penrose? You're a steady kind of fellow, aren't you? Are you of a mind to make a name for yourself? And some money too?'

Fitcher knew right then that one way or another the offer would upend his life: three years had passed since his first voyage to China. On his return, he had been given a job at Kew, and had risen to the rank of foreman. On the strength of that he had married the girl he had set his heart on years before, in Falmouth, and she was now pregnant. Fitcher was loath to leave his wife at such a time, but it was she who persuaded him to accept the Curator's offer: she could go back, she said, to her parents for the two or three years it would take for Fitcher to return. In Falmouth, where a great number of women were married to sailors, this was a predicament shared by many and she would manage well enough; an opportunity like this was not to be forgone.

So, it happened that Fitcher set off on his second voyage to Canton. After two years he returned with the trove of plants that was to make his reputation and lay the foundations of his fortune—but the Golden Camellia was not in that collection.

'So you never found any trace of it sir?'

'No,' said Fitcher.

Sir Joseph had not been willing to entrust either of the camellia paintings to Fitcher: he had travelled instead with copies of the originals. Neither was particularly well-executed, and both had deteriorated during the long trip to China.

'It's different now that I've got the pictures,' said Fitcher as he put the paintings back in their folders. 'I know where to start.'

~

Within a minute of stepping on board, Neel saw that it was no exaggeration to describe the *Anahita* as a 'palace-boat'. Not that she was exceptionally large or imposing in size: at a mere hundred and twenty feet, she was smaller than many of the long-keeled European and American ships that were anchored in Singapore's outer harbour. But these larger ships, well-trimmed and trusty though they might be, were all workaday trading vessels; the *Anahita* had more the appearance of a pleasure yacht, a rich man's folly. Her brass fittings gleamed in the sunlight and her holystoned decks glowed with polish. Except for the absence of a figurehead, no sign of the damage she had recently suffered was anywhere to be seen. Not a rope or hawser was out of place, and a newly fitted bowsprit jutted proudly from her prow.

As he looked around the main deck, Neel's eyes were drawn to the bulwarks: from the outside they had looked like solid lengths of timber, but now that he was on board, he saw that they were ornamented, on the inner side, with a series of panels that featured motifs from the art of ancient Persia and Mesopotamia: winged lions, fluted columns and striding spear-bearers. He would have liked to examine the designs more closely, but there was no time for Vico kept hurrying him towards the poop-deck. 'Come, munshiji. Patrão waiting.'

With its saloons, cabins and staterooms, the poop-deck was by far the most lavishly appointed part of the vessel. During the day, much of it was lit by a soft, natural light, filtering in from above through a series of ornamental skylights. As a result, the interior was free of the gloomy dankness that was so common inside wooden ships: instead it had a spacious, airy feel. The main corridor was panelled in mahogany and was hung with framed etchings of the ruins of Persepolis and Ecbatana. Here too Neel would have liked to linger, but Vico moved him briskly along until they came to the door that led to the Owners' Suite. Then he raised a hand to knock.

Patrão, the munshi's here—Freddy sent him.

Bring him in.

Bahram was at his desk, dressed in a light cotton angarkha and jootis of silver-threaded brocade; the beard that framed his jaw was neatly trimmed and he was wearing a simple, but impeccably tied turban.

In the Seth's face, with its fine, high-bridged nose and dark brow, Neel could see the provenance not only of Ah Fatt's good looks, but also of some of his other attributes—his sharp-eyed intelligence, for instance, as well as a certain element of will: a determination that bordered on ruthlessness. But there the resemblance ended, for in Bahram there was no trace of Ah Fatt's wounded vulnerability: his manner was voluble, good humoured and disarmingly effervescent. This, Neel could see, was no small part of his charm.

Arré, munshiji, he cried out, gesticulating with both his hands. Why are you standing there like a tree? Come closer, na?

The cadences of his voice instantly dispelled Neel's memories of his meetings with his father: he saw at once that Bahram bore no resemblance at all to the old Zemindar—or indeed to any of the wealthy and influential men he had known in his previous life. In Bahram there was none of the world-weary boredom and sensual exhaustion that marked so many of those men; on the contrary, his restless manner, like his rustic accent, spoke of an energetic and unaffected directness.

'What is your good-name?'

Neel had already decided to name himself after his new trade: Anil Kumar Munshi, Sethji.

Bahram nodded and pointed to a straight-backed chair. Achha, munshiji, he said. Why don't you sit on that kursi over there, so we can look each other in the eye?

As you wish, Sethji.

In stepping up to the chair, Neel had a vague intuition that this was a test of some kind—a gambit which Bahram used in interviewing certain kinds of employees. What exactly was being tested he could not think, so he did as he had been instructed and seated himself on the chair, without preamble.

This was evidently the right thing to do, for Bahram responded with an outburst of enthusiasm. Good! he cried, giving his desk a delighted slap. *Ekdum theek!* Very good!

What exactly he had done right, Neel did not know, and it was Bahram himself who enlightened him. 'Glad to see,' he said in English, 'that you can manage chair-sitting. Can't stand those floor-squatting munshis. In my position, how to put up with daftari-fellows who are always crawling on the ground? Foreigners will laugh, no?'

Ji, Sethji, said Neel. He bowed his head deferentially, mimicking the manner of the munshis he had himself once employed.

'So you have seen the world a little, eh munshiji?' said Bahram. 'Done a chukker or two? Tasted something other than daal-bhat and curry-rice? Munshis who can manage chair-sitting are not easy to find. Can you handle knife-fork also? Little-little at least?'

Ji, Sethji, said Neel.

Bahram nodded. 'So you met Freddy, my godson, here in Singapore, is it?'

Ji, Sethji.

'And what you were doing before that? How you arrived here?'

Neel sensed that this question was intended not only as an inquiry into his past, but also as a test of his English—so it was in his clearest accents that he recounted the story he had prepared: that he was a member of a family of scribes from the remote kingdom of Tripura, on the borders of Bengal; having fallen out of favour with the court, he had been forced to make a living in commerce, working for a succession of merchants as a munshi and dubash. He had travelled from Chittagong to Singapore with his last employer who had died unexpectedly: this was why his services were now available.

The story seemed to hold little interest for Bahram, but he was clearly impressed by Neel's fluency. Pushing back his chair he rose to his feet and began to pace the floor. 'Shahbash munshiji!' he said. 'Phataphat you are speaking English. You will put me to shame no?'

Neel understood that he had unwittingly put the Seth on his mettle. He decided that from then on he would use Hindusthani whenever possible, leaving it to Bahram to speak English.

'You can write nastaliq, also?'

Ji, Sethji.

'And Gujarati?'

No, Sethji.

Bahram seemed not at all displeased by this. 'That is all right. No need to know everything. Gujarati I can manage myself.'

Ji, Sethji.

'But reading-writing is not all it takes to make a good munshi. Something else also there is, no? You know about what I am talking?'

I'm not sure, Sethji.

Bahram came to a halt in front of Neel, clasped his hands behind his back, and leant down so that his eyes were boring into Neel's. 'What I am talking is trust—shroffery—or sharaafat as some would say. You know the words no, and meanings also? For me munshi is the same as shroff, except that he deal with words. Just as shroff must lock the safe, so must munshi lock the mouth. If you are working for me, then everything you read, everything you write, all must be locked inside your head. That is your treasury, your khazana.'

Then, Bahram walked around the chair, placed his hands on Neel's neck and turned his head from side to side.

'You understand no, munshiji? Even if some dacoit tries to twist your head off, safe must stay closed?'

The tone of Bahram's voice was playful rather than threatening, yet there was something in his manner that conveyed a faint sense of menace. Although discomfited, Neel managed to keep his composure. Ji, Sethji, he said. I understand.

Good! said Bahram cheerfully. But one more thing you should know: writing letters will not be the biggest part of your job. More important by far is what I call 'khabar-dari'—getting the news and keeping me informed. People think that only rulers and ministers need to know about wars, politics and all that. But that was only in the old days. Nowadays we are in a different time: today a man who does not know the khabar is a man who is headed for the kubber. This is what I always say: the news is what makes money. Do you understand me?

I'm not sure, Sethji, Neel mumbled. I don't understand how the news can be of help in making money.

All right, said Bahram, pacing the floor. I will tell you a story that may help you understand. I heard it when I visited London with my friend, Mr Zadig Karabedian. It was twenty-two years ago—in 1816. One day someone took us to the Stock Exchange and pointed out a famous banker, one Mr Rothschild. This man had understood the importance of khabar-dari long before anyone else, and he had set up his own system for sending news, with pigeons and couriers and all. Then came the Battle of Waterloo—you have heard of it, no?

Ji, Sethji.

The day the battle was fought everyone was nervous in the London Stock Exchange. If the English lost, the price of gold would fall. If they won it would rise. What to do? Buy or sell? They waited and waited, and of course this banker was the first to know what had happened at Waterloo. So what do you think he did?

He bought gold, Sethji?

Bahram gave a belly-laugh and clapped Neel on the back. See, that is why you are a munshi and not a Seth. Arré budhu—he began to *sell*! And when he started to sell everyone thought, wah bhai, the battle is lost, so we'd better sell too. So the price of gold went down, down, down. Only when the time was right did Mr Rothschild step in to buy—and then he bought and bought and bought. You see? It was just that he knew the news before anyone else. Later some people told me the story is not really true—but what does it matter? It is a story for the times we live in, na? I tell you, if I had had the courage, I would have gone up to that man and touched his feet. You are my Guruji! I would have said.

Bahram had been pacing all this while, but now he came to a stop in front of Neel: So do you see munshiji, why khabardari is important for a businessman like me? You know, no, that we are going to Canton? When we get there you will have to be my eyes and ears.

Neel took alarm at this: In Canton, Sethji? But how? I don't know anyone there.

Bahram shrugged this off. You don't need to know anyone. You can leave that part to me. What you have to do is to read two English journals that are published in Canton. One is called the *Canton Register* and another is the *Chinese Repository*. Sometimes other papers also come out but you don't have to bother with them—only these two are of interest to me. It will be your job to go through them and make reports to me. You must cut out all the phoos-phaas and just give me what is important.

Here Bahram reached over to his desk and picked up a journal. Here, munshiji, this is a copy of the *Repository*. My friend, Mr Zadig Karabedian, has lent it to me. He has underlined some bits—can you tell me what they say?

Ji, Sethji, said Neel. He ran his eye over the lines and said: It seems that these are excerpts from a memorial written by a high-ranking Chinese official and sent to the Emperor.

Yes, said Bahram. Go on. What does he say?

'"Opium is a poisonous drug, brought from foreign countries. To the question, what are its virtues, the answer is: It raises the animal spirits and prevents lassitude. Hence the

Chinese continually run into its toils. At first they merely strive to follow the fashion of the day; but in the sequel the poison takes effect, the habit becomes fixed, and the sleeping smokers are like corpses—lean and haggard as demons. Such are the injuries which it does to life. Moreover the drug maintains an exorbitant price and cannot be obtained except with the pure metal. Smoking opium, in its first stages, impedes business; and when the practice is continued for any considerable length of time, it throws whole families into ruin, dissipates every kind of property, and destroys man himself. There cannot be a greater evil than this. In comparison with arsenic I pronounce it tenfold the greater poison. A man swallows arsenic because he has lost his reputation and is so involved that he cannot extricate himself. Thus driven to desperation, he takes the dose and is destroyed at once. But those who smoke the drug are injured in many different ways.

'"When the smoker commences the practice, he seems to imagine that his spirits are thereby augmented; but he ought to know that this appearance is factitious. It may be compared to raising the wick of a lamp, which, while it increases the flame, hastens the exhaustion of the oil and the extinction of the light. Hence the youth who smoke will shorten their own days and cut off all hope of posterity, leaving their fathers and mothers and wives without anyone on whom to depend; and those in middle and advanced life, who smoke, will accelerate the termination of their years . . ."'

Stop! Bas! Enough.

Bahram snatched the journal out of Neel's hands and tossed it on a table.

All right, munshiji, it is clear that you can read English without difficulty. If you want the job it is yours.

~

If there was one thing Paulette had learnt about Fitcher it was that he was a methodical man. This was why she was not surprised to discover that he had prepared, long in advance, a plan to trace the provenance of the camellia paintings. His hopes were centred especially on the illustration acquired by William Kerr: the picture was no more than thirty-odd years old and had almost certainly been painted in Canton—it was perfectly possible in fact that the painter was still alive.

'But you will need an expert to identify the artist, sir, will you not?'

'So I will,' said Fitcher.

'And do you know of anyone?'

'No, but I know of someone who may be able to help.'

The man Fitcher had in mind was an English painter who had been living in southern China for many years: he was said to be well-connected and extremely knowledgeable. Fitcher intended to call on him in Macau, at the earliest possible opportunity.

'And what is his name, sir?'

'Chinnery. George Chinnery.'

'Oh?'

Paulette's attention was instantly riveted but she was careful to feign a tone of indifference as she asked: 'Indeed, sir? And how did you hear of him?'

'From a friend of his . . .'

The name had been suggested to him, said Fitcher, by a regular client of his Falmouth nursery—one Mr James Hobhouse, a portraitist who had known Chinnery in his youth. The artist had been living in southern China for over a decade, Mr Hobhouse had told him, and was reputed to be intimately acquainted with the painters of Macau and Canton.

Hobhouse had known Chinnery at the Royal Academy, where they had been contemporaries of J.M.W. Turner. Chinnery had himself once been regarded as a painter of the same calibre, but he was a man of changeable moods: wilful and witty, amorous and extravagant, he was this minute in a high good humour, and in a deep dudgeon the next. None of this was out of keeping for a member of that clan, Mr Hobhouse had added, for the Chinnerys were a family in which unusual talent seemed often to be combined with odd and excessive behaviour.

The artist had certainly inherited more than his measure of the family's traits. The promise of a brilliant career was not enough to keep him in London. He had taken himself off to Ireland, where, like many a feckless youth before him, he had ended up marrying his landlord's daughter. She had given him two children in quick succession which was perhaps too strong a dose of family life for his flighty stomach; he had taken off again, leaving his wife to cope with the infants as best she could. His destination now was Madras, where his brother was then living; after five years in that city, he had moved on to Bengal, settling eventually in Calcutta. There, in the capital of British India, he had met with tremendous success, being universally acclaimed as the greatest English painter in the East. When word of his triumph trickled back to England his family had decided to make their way to India to join him—first his daughter Matilda, whom he had last seen as a child, and who was now a young woman; then his luckless wife, Marianne; and finally his son John, who had hopes of embarking on a military career. But the move brought misfortune with it: within a year of his arrival, John was carried off by a tropical fever, and the loss had all but unhinged Chinnery, embittering him against his wife, the very sight of whom became unendurable to him. Once again he took to his heels, moving about as far as possible—to Macau, a place that had suggested itself, or so the wags said, because in the event of his wife's pursuing him any further he could always take refuge in Canton, where he would be safe from all foreign women.

In southern China, said Mr Hobhouse, his old friend appeared to have found a niche that was to his liking, for he had remained there for the last thirteen years, a length of time that was, for him, an eternity. Now, at the age of sixty-four, safe from marital pursuit, he seemed to be content in the company of sea-captains, travelling merchants, opium traders and other itinerants. They for their part, seemed to regard his work with the greatest approbation: so many, and so lucrative were his commissions that he was reported to have created an atelier in order to keep pace with the demand, training his house-boys and servants in his methods of painting.

Did it matter to Chinnery that he, who had once been thought of as the equal of Romney, Raeburn and Hoppner, should be languishing in a place that was so far from the salons of Europe, a distant backwater where he had to serve a clientele of the grossest philistines? That he affected to be indifferent to such considerations needed hardly to be said—yet it was rumoured that the cognoscenti's neglect of his work, in London, had filled him with so much bitterness that he had taken to the opium pipe in order to escape his distress. Whether or not this was the usual idle blather of the canting-crew Mr Hobhouse would not say: but even though he was unwilling to venture an opinion of his own on this subject, he did express the hope that Fitcher would look into the matter and throw some light on it when he returned to Britain.

Paulette listened to the tale in silence, and was careful to do nothing that might suggest that she knew anything at all about the artist or his career—but in point of fact, the Chinnery name was not unknown to her: far from it. Indeed, on at least one aspect of the painter's life she was far better informed than was Fitcher: this was the matter of his other family—the two sons he had begotten with his Bengali mistress, Sundaree, during his twelve-year sojourn in Calcutta.

Paulette's acquaintance with George Chinnery's 'natural' sons had arisen out of a fortuitous connection between Sundaree and her own beloved nurse, Tantima. Tantima was Jodu's mother and she had looked after Paulette since her infancy: it so happened that she hailed from the same village as Sundaree, on the banks of the Hooghly. The two women had renewed the bonds of their childhood in Calcutta, when they both found themselves presiding over the households of unconventional and somewhat addle-pated sahibs. But there the commonalities ended, for Paulette's father, Pierre Lambert, was always something of an outcast within white society, and his circumstances, as a mere Assistant Curator of the Botanical Gardens, were never anything other than extremely modest.

George Chinnery, on the other hand, had earned fabulous sums of money while in Calcutta and his household was as chuck-muck as any in the city, with paltans of nokar-logue doing chukkers in the hallways and syces swarming in the istabbuls; as for the bobachee-connah, why, it had been known to spend a hundred sicca rupees on sherbets and syllabubs, in *one week* . . .

An adoring lover, Chinnery had lavished luxuries upon his cherished Sundaree, giving her an outhouse on the grounds to share with the two sons she had borne him. She had also been given her own little retinue of retainers: a khaleefa, several ayahs and khidmatgars, and even a paan-maker, who did nothing but fold betel leaves to suit her tastes. This arrangement had suited them both—Sundaree, because it allowed her the freedom to eat and live according to her fashion; and Mr Chinnery because it meant that his precious little passion-pit was readily available when needed, yet safely out of sight when sahibs and ma'ams came to visit.

Sundaree was herself quite a colourful figure and had once enjoyed her own share of fame and glamour: the daughter of a village drum-beater, she had made a name for herself as a singer and dancer—this was how she came to Mr Chinnery's attention, for he had paid her to sit for him after attending one of her performances. On becoming pregnant with his child, Sundaree had stopped performing and taken with gusto to a life of indulgence, bedecking herself with expensive textiles and unusual kinds of jewellery. In her prime, she had had no compunctions about ma'aming it over Tantima, pitying her for her cramped quarters and cluck-clucking over the straitened circumstances of the Lambert household.

But all this had changed dramatically when it came to be known that the artist's other family was soon to descend on Calcutta. As with many another bohemian, Chinnery was in some ways, extremely conventional—the possibility that his legal wife and children might learn about his Bengali ewe-mutton and her two kids, threw him into a panic. The delectable little butter-bun of the day before suddenly metamorphosed into a gravy-making gobble-prick: she and her two boys were summarily evicted from their quarters and packed off to a tenement in Kidderpore, where a khidmatgar would visit them occasionally to hand over a monthly tuncaw.

The arrangement deceived no one, of course, for amongst the sahibs of the city Mr Chinnery's private life was a matter of almost as much interest as the fluctuation of prices at the Opium Exchange. Marianne Chinnery had found out about her husband's other family soon enough, and to her great credit she had tried to ensure that they were provided for and that her husband did his duty by them. She had even arranged a church christening for the two little boys: known to their friends as Khoka and Robin, they were christened 'Henry Collins Chinnery' and 'Edward Charles Chinnery' respectively—which became a source of great hilarity to their playmates, who continued, of course, to use their Bengali nicknames.

More usefully perhaps, Marianne Chinnery had also prevailed upon her husband to take the boys into his studio, so that they might learn his trade, and both of them had spent a few years working under their father's tutelage. Unfortunately for them, this interlude in their lives was not to last long: they had not yet reached their teens when their father fled the city, abandoning both his families.

This was a double blow, for by that time Marianne Chinnery too had lost interest in Khoka and Robin: perhaps the death of her own son had made it more difficult for her to deal with them; perhaps her daughter, having married an English District Magistrate, had pressed her to sever a connection that might be an embarrassment to her husband; or perhaps it was merely that greater exposure to colonial society had coarsened her own sensibilities. In any event, after George Chinnery's departure, Sundaree and the two boys were more or less abandoned to their fate: the little money the painter sent was not enough to live on, and Sundaree had had to supplement her income by cooking and cleaning for a succession of British families. But Sundaree was a formidable woman in her own right: despite all her difficulties, she had done what she could to ensure the continuation of her sons' training in the arts—other than the paintbrush, she liked to say, there was nothing to keep them from sharing the lot of every other street-chokra in Kidderpore.

Of the two Chinnery boys, Khoka, the older, was a strapping, swarthily handsome lad, with light brown hair and a personable manner. He was an easy-going sort of chuckeroo who had a certain facility with the brush even though he had no great interest in art—had he not happened to have a painter for a father, no lick of paint would ever have stained his fingers. His brother Robin could not have been more different, either in appearance or in disposition: with his rounded cheeks, prominent eyes, and coppery hair, Robin was said to closely resemble his father; like him, he was plump, and short in stature. Unlike his brother, Robin was endowed with a genuine passion for the arts—a love so fervent that it all but overwhelmed his own very considerable gifts as a draughtsman and painter. Feeling himself to be incapable of creating anything that would meet his own high standards, he directed most of his energies towards the study of the works of other artists, past and present, and was always looking around for prints, reproductions and etchings that he could examine and copy. Curios and unusual objects were his other passions, and at one time he was a frequent visitor to the Lambert bungalow, where he had spent hours rummaging around in Pierre Lambert's collection of botanical specimens and illustrations. Although he was several years older than Paulette, there was a childlike aspect to him that made the difference in age and sex seem immaterial: he kept her informed about the latest fashions, bringing her little odds and ends from his mother's dwindling collection of clothes and trinkets—perhaps a payal to tie around her ankles, or bangles for her wrist. Paulette's lack of interest in ornaments always amazed him, for his own pleasure in them was such that he would often string them around his own ankles and wrists and twirl around, admiring himself in the mirror. Sometimes they had both dressed up in his mother's clothes and danced around the house.

Robin had also taken it on himself to further Paulette's artistic education. He would often bring over books with detailed reproductions of European paintings—his father had left many of these behind and they were among his most treasured possessions. He never tired of poring over them, and being gifted with unusually strong powers of visual recollection, he was able to reproduce many of them from memory. On learning that Paulette was making illustrations for her father's book, he had gone to some lengths to tutor her, showing her the tricks of mixing colours and drawing a clean line.

Paulette's relationship with Robin was not an easy one: as a tutor he was often insufferably overbearing and the ferocity of his disapproval, when she erred with pencil or brush, was such that it led to many quarrels. But at the same time she was also hugely entertained by his gaudy clothes, his unpredictable shrieks of laughter and his love of scandal—and she was sometimes strangely touched by his attempts to wean her from her hoydenish ways and turn her into a lady.

For all these reasons, Robin Chinnery had, for a time, been a large presence in her life—but that had come to an abrupt end when she was about fifteen. Around that time he had developed a strange fixation on Jodu and had decided to launch upon a project—a painting—in which Jodu and Paulette were to feature as the principal figures. The composition was inspired, he said, by one of the great themes of European art, but when Paulette asked what this was he would not tell her. She didn't need to know, he said, and it didn't matter anyway because he was re-interpreting it, and giving it a new spirit.

Paulette and Jodu were not at all enthusiastic about the project and their reluctance to participate grew stronger still when they discovered that they would have to spend hours standing still. But Robin's pleas were too heartfelt to be brushed aside—this, he declared, was his opportunity of creating a masterwork, of forging his own identity as an artist—so they had taken pity on him and relented. For a fortnight or so, they had obeyed his instructions, standing side by side while he laboured at his easel. Through this time he never once allowed them to look at what he was doing: if they asked he would say, wait, wait, it's not time yet; you'll see it when it's ready to be seen. In these sessions both Jodu and Paulette had worn their usual clothes, a gamcha or langot in his case, and a calf-length sari in hers, and although, at his pleading, they had sometimes wrapped these coverings a little tighter than they might otherwise have done, they had never once gone without them—neither of them could have imagined such a thing.

This was why, when at last they managed to sneak a look at the unfinished picture, they were doubly outraged to discover that they had been painted stark naked, with not a thread of clothing on their bodies. Not only that, they had been made to look utterly ridiculous in other ways as well, and shameless too, for they were shown to be standing under an enormous banyan tree, staring directly at the viewer as if to flaunt their nakedness—as though they were Naga sadhus or something. What was more, Paulette's skin was painted an ashy-white colour and she was shown to be holding a mango (under a banyan tree!), while Jodu was an inky shade of black and had a cobra rearing up above his head. Fortunately Paulette's mango was so positioned as to conceal that part of her which she would least have wanted the world to see—but Jodu was not so lucky with his cobra: even though the snake had its tail wound around his waist it did not cover what it could so easily have done; that part of his body could not only be clearly seen, it was painted in such vivid detail that it gave the clear impression of being uncircumcised, which added in no little measure to Jodu's sense of injury.

The whole thing was so shocking and outrageous that Jodu, who was always quick to anger, flew into a rage and snatched the canvas off the easel. Robin was not his match in strength and could do nothing except plead with Paulette to intervene. Stop him, I beg you, he had said; I've painted you as Adam and Eve, in all the beauty of your innocence and simplicity; no one will ever know that it is you—please, I beg you, stop him!

But Paulette was almost as incensed as Jodu was, and far from heeding Robin she had boxed his ears and then helped Jodu rip the canvas to shreds. Robin had watched silently, with tears running down his face, and at the end of it, he had said: You wait and see; you'll pay for this, some day . . .

After this the visits had ceased and from then on, Paulette had not followed the Chinnery boys' doings closely. The little she knew of their subsequent careers came from Tantima's occasional asides: she remembered hearing, a couple of years later, that Sundaree had fallen ill and that Khoka, the older boy, had been sent off to England as the personal emissary of the Nawab of Murshidabad.

Left to fend for himself in Calcutta, Robin had succeeded in using his talents in such a way as to enmesh himself in a scandal: he had started producing 'Chinnery' paintings. He was so familiar with his father's style and methods that it was no great challenge for him to turn out canvases in the same manner and he succeeded in selling several of these, at great profit, claiming that they were works his father had left behind. But eventually the fraud was discovered, and rather than face a jail sentence in India, Robin had followed the example of his uncle William—he had fled the country. Rumour had it that he had run off to join his father, but where exactly he had gone, Paulette did not know. It was not till she learnt from Mr Penrose that George Chinnery had taken up residence in Macau that it occurred to her that this was presumably where Robin had gone—which meant that she might well run into him if she were to accompany Mr Penrose to the painter's house. Given the circumstances of their last meeting she could not rule out the possibility that he might indeed find an opportunity to exact his revenge.

Although she remembered Robin with great warmth, and had often regretted the loss of his friendship, she knew also that he had a waspish, gossipy side and was perfectly capable of inventing stories that might cause a rift between herself and Fitcher. In considering all this, she let slip the moment when it would have been easiest to speak frankly to Fitcher about her connection with Robin. Something else came up and the opportunity was lost.

~

At Bahram's insistence, both Neel and Ah Fatt stayed with him while the *Anahita*'s repairs and refurbishments were being completed: each had a cabin to himself—an almost unimaginable luxury after the privations of the last many months. Day and night they were plied with food: every morning at breakfast, Bahram would summon his personal khansamah, Mesto—a dark giant of a man with a shining bald head and well-muscled arms—and confer with him on what was to be served to his godson for lunch and dinner. Each meal was a feast of a different kind, sometimes Parsi, with mutton dhansak and brown rice; okra cooked with fish roe and *patra-ni-machhi*, fillets of fish steamed in banana leaves; sometimes Goan, with shrimp rissoles and chicken xacuti and fiery prawn xeque-xeques; sometimes East Indian, with a mutton-and-pumpkin curry and sarpatel.

But the situation was not without its discomforts: Neel had to be careful at all times to maintain the pretence that he and Ah Fatt were casual acquaintances who had met by chance in Singapore; and he also had to be vigilant about concealing his awareness of Ah Fatt's real relationship with Bahram. This was not always easy for there were times when Bahram was himself unable to keep a firm hold on his god-parental mask: being spontaneous and affectionate by nature he would suddenly fold Ah Fatt into his arms and give him a huge hug; or else he would call him 'beta' or 'deekro' and pile food on his plate.

The fact that Ah Fatt was often unresponsive, and sometimes even resentful, of these displays of affection seemed to have little effect on Bahram. It was as though he were living, for the first time, the life he aspired to—in which he was a patriarch in his own right, passing on his wisdom and experience to his son.

To Neel there was something touching about the very clumsiness and excess of Bahram's expressions of affection. He understood why they irritated Ah Fatt, and he understood too why he might regard them as scant compensation for the long years of neglect during which he had felt himself to be disowned and unacknowledged by his father.

But to Neel what was most striking about Bahram's relationship with Ah Fatt was not its faults but rather the fact that it existed at all. In his previous life, in Calcutta, Neel had known many men who had fathered illegitimate children: not one of them, so far as he knew, had shown any trace of kindness in their treatment of their mistresses and their progeny; he even knew of some who, fearing blackmail, had had their babies strangled. His own father, the old Zemindar, was said to have begotten a dozen bastards, with a succession of different women: his method of dealing with the situation was to pay the women a hundred rupees and pack them off to their villages. Amongst men of his class this was considered normal and even generous; Neel himself had taken it so much for granted that he had never given it any thought—it had certainly never occurred to him to think of his father's bastards as his own half-siblings. On succeeding to the Zemindari he could easily have inquired into the fate of his illegitimate half-brothers and sisters—yet the notion had never so much as crossed his mind. Looking back, Neel could not avoid acknowledging his own failings in regard to this aspect of his past, and this in turn led him to recognize that Bahram's conduct in relation to Ah Fatt and his mother was not just unusual but quite exceptional for a man of his circumstances.

None of this was easy to explain to Ah Fatt.

'For Father "Freddy" like pet dog. That why he pat and hug and squeeze. Father care only for himself; no one else.'

'Listen, Ah Fatt, I know why you might think that. But believe me, most men in his situation would just have abandoned you and your mother. That would have been the easy thing to do; it is what ninety-nine men in a hundred would have done. It says something for him that he didn't do it. Don't you see that?'

Ah Fatt would dismiss these arguments with a shrug—or at least he would pretend to—but it was clear to Neel that despite all his grievances his friend was exhilarated to find himself where he had never been before: at the centre of his father's attention.

As the days passed, Ah Fatt seemed to grow quieter and more despondent, and Neel knew that it was not just the prospect of being parted from his father that was gnawing at him but also the knowledge that he would not be accompanying Neel to Canton. One day, while they were pacing the quarter-deck, Ah Fatt said, with more than a trace of envy in his voice: 'You lucky man. You go to Canton—number-one city in whole world.'

'In the world?' said Neel in surprise. 'Why do you say that?'

'No place like it, anywhere. You look-see for yourself.'

'You miss it, don't you?'

Ah Fatt allowed his chin to sink slowly into his chest. 'Too much. Miss too much, Canton. But can-na go.'

'Is there anyone you would like to send a message to? Anyone I should meet?'

'No!' Ah Fatt spun around on his heels. 'No! In Canton you can-na talk about me. Must take care, too much care, all times. No lo-lo-so-so. Can-na talk of Ah Fatt.'

'You can trust me Ah Fatt. But I wish you were coming too.'

'Believe me, Neel. I also wish.' Ah Fatt put a hand on Neel's shoulder. 'But be careful there, my friend.'

'Why?'

'In China people say "everything new comes from Canton". Better for young men not to go there—too many ways for them to be spoiled.'

SIX

For the last stretch of the journey to China, Fitcher set a circuitous course, keeping the *Redruth* clear of notorious pirate haunts like the Ladrone Islands. This stretch of water was unlike any that Paulette had ever beheld, dotted with thousands of craggy, apparently deserted islands. The islets were wild and windblown, with clumps of greenery clinging to their steep, rocky slopes; some were as picturesque as the names by which they were identified on the charts: 'Mandarin's Cap', 'the Quoin', 'Tortoise Head' and 'the Needle Rocks'.

As the coastline approached, many vessels of unfamiliar shape and rigging hove into view: lorchas, junks, batelos and stately Spanish Manilamen. Occasionally English and American vessels would also appear, and one morning Fitcher recognized a passing brigantine. The vessel's skipper was an acquaintance of his, so he decided to go over to have a word with him. He was rowed across in a gig and returned an hour later, looking unusually perturbed, his brow fretfully a-twitch.

'Bad news, sir?' said Paulette.

Fitcher nodded: the brigantine's skipper had told him that it had become very hard to procure the chops that permitted foreign vessels to enter the Pearl River. Even to enter the harbour at Macau had become a tricky affair and most foreign ships were choosing instead to take shelter at the opposite end of the river mouth, in the strait that separated the island of Hong Kong from the promontory of Kowloon.

After some thought, Fitcher decided to follow the course that had been recommended to him by the skipper: instead of making for Macau, as originally planned, the *Redruth* tacked about and headed in another direction.

Soon a ridge of jagged mountains came into view, rising sheer out of the sea. This, said Fitcher, was Hong Kong: few houses were visible on the shore and even fewer trees; it was a wild, gale-swept place, not unlike the other islands nearby, only bigger, steeper and taller. The name Hong Kong, Fitcher said, meant 'fragrant harbour': this struck Paulette as a strangely whimsical description for such a desolate and forbidding place.

The *Redruth* dropped anchor in a bay that was overlooked by the tallest peak in the island. There were several other foreign ships there; a small flotilla of bumboats and pilot-boats was swarming around them, ferrying provisions and passengers between the ships and the mainland.

Early the next morning Fitcher took a pilot-boat to Macau, leaving Paulette in charge of the *Redruth*'s floating garden. He returned a day later, looking thoroughly despondent.

Captain Charles Elliott, the British Representative in Macau, had treated him to a gloomy summation of the present situation. It appeared that the Emperor had sent down a series of edicts, commanding the provincial government to act forcefully against the opium trade. In response they had seized and burned the 'fast-crab' boats that had once roamed the Pearl River, transporting opium directly from ship to shore. Many English traders had assumed that the situation would soon go back to normal again—in the past too there had been brief periods of increased vigilance, but they had never lasted for more than a few months. But it was different this time: a few dealers had tried to rebuild their boats and the mandarins had burned them again. That was just the beginning. Next the mandarins had begun to arrest local opium-dealers; some were thrown in prison, some were executed. Their shops and dens were seized and the opium was burned. Then the regulations for travel on the Pearl River were tightened and as a result chops had become very difficult to obtain. Only those foreigners who were vouched for by the merchants' guild, in Canton, could hope to get chops at this time: since Fitcher had no such connections he was unlikely to be granted one in the immediate future. Such being the circumstances, Captain Elliott had recommended that Fitcher keep the *Redruth* at anchor near Hong Kong for the time being, to await a more favourable turn of events.

All through Fitcher's recital, Paulette had been listening for the name 'Chinnery'. Not having heard it, she said: 'And did you meet anyone else, sir?'

Fitcher glanced at her, and after a moment's silence, muttered: 'So I did. I also went to see Mr Chinnery.'

'Oh? And it was a useful visit, sir?'

'Yes. But not in the way I had expected.'

Mr Chinnery had received Fitcher in his studio, which was on the uppermost floor of his residence, at number 8, Rua Ignacio Baptista: a large, sunlit room, it was hung with several excellent portraits and landscapes, including one that was in the process of being finished by a pair of Chinese apprentices.

Within a few minutes Fitcher understood that Mr Chinnery had invited him into his studio in the expectation of receiving a commission for a portrait. When Fitcher explained that he had come in regard to an entirely different matter—a mission that concerned a pair of plant-pictures from Canton—the artist's expression had grown a little peevish. He favoured the camellia paintings with no more than a cursory glance before declaring them to be inconsequential little gew-gaws: the daubings of Canton's painters were not worthy of the attention of a serious man, he had declared; indeed, the scribblers who produced botanical illustrations and the like could scarcely be called artists at all—they were but counterfeiters and copyists who produced cheap souvenirs for travellers and seamen.

'Art is a dead letter in China, sir, a dead letter . . . !'

Fitcher had understood that he had found the artist in one of his dark moods: he had decided to excuse himself, perhaps to return another day. But when he stood up to leave, the artist, perhaps repenting of his ill-humour, had asked if Fitcher knew the way to the jetty, where he was to catch his boat. When Fitcher said no, he did not, Mr Chinnery offered to send someone with him, to show him the way: it so happened, he said, that he had a nephew staying with him, his brother's son; he had arrived from India some time ago and had quickly learnt his way around the city.

Fitcher had gratefully accepted this offer, whereupon Mr Chinnery had summoned his nephew, who proved to be a young man in his mid-twenties. He bore a close family resemblance to the artist: their faces, with their prominent eyes and knob-like noses, were so similar that they could have been avatars of each other, separated only by age, and also, perhaps, by a slight tint of complexion, which in the case of the younger man, was a little swarthier. So alike, in fact, were the two Chinnerys that if Fitcher had not known better he would have taken them to be father and son rather than uncle and nephew: nor was the likeness merely a matter of appearance—on the way to the jetty Fitcher learnt that the young man was also an artist, much in the mould of the senior Mr Chinnery. Indeed Mr Chinnery had been his first teacher, said the youth: now following in his footsteps, he was planning to go to Canton in search of commissions; through his uncle's influence he had already secured a chop and intended to leave in a few days.

On hearing this, Fitcher had been struck by an idea: he had shown young Chinnery the two camellia paintings and had asked him if he might be interested in making inquiries about them while he was in Canton. Young Chinnery had responded enthusiastically and in the course of the short walk to the jetty they had reached an agreement: Fitcher would pay him a retainer in exchange for regular reports on his progress; in the event of success there would be a substantial reward.

The one thing about the arrangement that had worried Fitcher was the prospect of being parted from his paintings. But this concern too had been quickly addressed: it turned out that the younger Mr Chinnery prided himself on his skills as a copyist. He had asked to keep the pictures only for a couple of days: it would take him no longer than that to make copies of them, he had said, and as soon as he was done he would deliver the originals to the *Redruth* in person.

'And may I ask sir,' said Paulette hesitantly, 'what was the name of this nephew of Mr Chinnery?'

'Edward—Edward Chinnery.' Here Fitcher paused to tug awkwardly at his beard. 'But he said ee'd know him as Robin.'

Paulette caught her breath: 'Oh did he?'

'Young Chinnery was very pleased, I might say, to hear that ee were here; said ee'd been like a sister to him once but there'd been a falling-out over some trivial thing. Said he'd sorely missed eer company—but he called ee by some other name—what was it? Pug-something?'

'Puggly?' Paulette had clasped her hands to her cheeks in mortification, but she dropped them now. 'Yes—he has many nicknames for me. Robin was . . . is . . . indeed a close friend. Please forgive me sir. I should have told you—but there was a most unfortunate incident. Shall I tell you of it?'

'Ee needn't trouble eerself with that Miss Paulette,' said Fitcher with one of his rare smiles. 'Mr Chinnery has told me already.'

~

The cry caught everyone unawares: *Kinara!* Land ho! China ahead! *Maha-Chin agey hai!*

Bahram and Zadig were up on the *Anahita*'s quarter-deck when the lascar on lookout duty began to wave and shout. They went to the dawa bulwark and shaded their eyes and soon enough the straight line of the horizon began to crack and splinter, giving way to the silhouette of a jagged landscape. Ahead lay the tip of Hainan, China's southernmost extremity, and for a while the *Anahita* sailed close enough to the island that Bahram was able to study it through a spyglass: it was not much different, in appearance, from Singapore and some of the other islands they had passed on the way, with steep hills, dense forests and fringes of golden sand along the shores.

Shortly after the sighting the officers called all hands on deck and put them on high alert: the waters around Hainan were notorious for pirates, and every vessel that came into view had to be treated as suspect. Lookouts were posted agil and peechil and the topmen were sent scrambling aloft.

Tabar lagao! Gabar uthao!

With stunsails on the yardarms and sky-sails atop every mast, the *Anahita* leapt before the wind, her cutwater plunging between swell and trough, her beams banking steeply as she tacked. The island vanished as the ship swung out to sea, but only to reappear towards sunset, when a cloud-wreathed mountain was spotted again.

The sight exhilarated Bahram, reminding him of another journey and another island he had visited, on the far side of the globe, some twenty-two years before.

Tell me, he said to Zadig. Do you remember that time? When we met the General?

Zadig laughed: Of course, Bahram-bhai. Who could forget it?

It happened in February 1816, when Bahram and Zadig were on their way to England on the HCS *Cuffnells*. Two months after leaving Canton they reached Cape Town where they were met by a startling piece of news: Napoleon Bonaparte had been exiled to a tiny island in the Atlantic. This came as a surprise, since the rumour, at the time of their departure from Macau, was that the Duke of Wellington had hanged the Emperor from a tree, at Waterloo. They were now astonished to learn that Bonaparte was being held captive on St Helena. This was their next port of call and the possibility of catching a glimpse of the erstwhile dictator caused a ferment of excitement among some of the ship's passengers.

Bahram's knowledge of European politics was quite limited at the time, and he was not among those who were greatly affected by the news. But for Zadig it was as if a bolt of lightning had struck the timbers beneath his feet: at the time of Bonaparte's invasion of Egypt, Zadig was a boy of fifteen, living in his family-house, which was in Masr al-Qadima, or Old Cairo. He remembered vividly the panic that had gripped this suburb when it came to be known that a French army had seized Alexandria and was marching on the capital. When the dust of battle rose above the pyramids, he was among the many who scaled the Church of the Mu'allaqa to listen to the sound of cannonfire, booming across the river.

Bonaparte's victory had affected Zadig in many ways, large and small: he had started taking French lessons, for instance, and he and his cousins had begun to ride horses, which was something that they, as Christians, could not have done before: he was never to forget his first trot around Cairo's Ezbekiya Gardens. It was then also that he acquired the skills that would launch him in his trade, being taken on as an apprentice by a French watchmaker.

Among Zadig's relatives there were many others whose lives were altered by the invasion: a couple of his cousins happened to have a smattering of French and they became interpreters for the invading army; others had found jobs in the newly established printing press. One perennially impoverished uncle, Orhan Karabedian, an artist, experienced a particularly dramatic change of fortune. As a painter of icons he had always found it hard to make ends meet, subsisting mainly on church commissions; now he was besieged by French officers who wanted souvenirs of Coptic Egypt—it made no difference to anyone that he was an Armenian and not a Copt.

The French invasion also led, indirectly, to Zadig's marriage: one branch of his mother's family became particularly prosperous by securing an enormously lucrative contract for the supply of wine and pork products to the French army. When Napoleon decided to march northwards, into Palestine and Syria, they deputed their youngest son-in-law, who had only recently joined their business, to accompany the invading army's baggage train. The young man was to die at Jaffa, a year later, of the plague. After the period of mourning was over, the family decided that their young daughter could not spend the rest of her life as a widow—and it was thus that Zadig's marriage came about.

While Napoleon was in Egypt, Zadig saw him only once, but at quite close quarters. It was when the Consul was on his way to visit the Nilometer, to preside over the ceremony that marked the start of the annual floods. Joining the crowd of spectators, Zadig had been astonished to discover that Napoleon was a full head shorter than himself.

Now, as the *Cuffnells* approached the venue of the former Emperor's exile, many long-forgotten memories stirred in Zadig's head. His feelings might have been even stronger if he had believed that he might actually meet the man in the flesh—but this he dismissed as an impossibility. Bonaparte was sure to be the most closely guarded prisoner in the world, he told Bahram; to think of seeing or meeting him was mere foolishness—yet, it was not long before they discovered that some of their fellow passengers harboured that very hope.

The *Cuffnells* was mainly a cargo ship and the only other passengers on board were four English couples. The geography of the ship, as much as anything else, ensured that Zadig and Bahram had little to do with the British passengers: their cabin was deep in the vessel's belly, close to the bilges; they ate their meals with the serangs, tindals, silmagoors and other petty officers, and when they needed to stretch their legs they did so within the confines of the main deck. The English couples, on the other hand, were travelling in the poop-deck and roundhouse, where the ship's officers also had their quarters. They dined at the Captain's table and spent their leisure hours on the quarter-deck, which could only be stepped upon by order or invitation.

Despite these barriers, the passengers were not unacquainted with each other for the main deck was the crossroads of the ship and it sometimes happened that they would find themselves face-to-face there. Then they would exchange bows and curtseys, salaams and greetings—although perfectly cordial, these ceremonies were a little stiff, the awkwardness of the respective parties being emphasized by the contrast in their costumes, the one being dressed in trousers, pelisses and surtouts, and the other in robes and ample headgear.

Although their interactions were few, Bahram and Zadig were not wholly unaware of the doings of their fellow passengers: often, while passing below the quarter-deck, they would hear snatches of the conversations that were being conducted over their heads. Beneath the companion-ladder there was a small alcove, under a ventilator: when the discussions above concerned some matter of unusual interest, this was a convenient place from which to listen.

After the *Cuffnells*' departure from Cape Town they overheard many conversations about the former dictator.

'Never could I have imagined that I would so desire to gaze upon this man, this creature, who was once a veritable bugbear . . .'

'Indeed it is astonishing that one should wish to look upon such a fiend—but I confess that I too am sorely tempted.'

'And how could you not be, my dear? To observe a monster in his lair is not an opportunity afforded to many.'

After a week or so at sea, the conversations on the quarter-deck took a new turn: instead of merely speculating about the possibility of catching an accidental glimpse of Napoleon, the English passengers began to discuss the various expedients by which a visit to his house might be arranged.

All foolishness, said Zadig dismissively. Unless they grow wings and fly like birds, they will see nothing of Napoleon.

Some three weeks after the *Cuffnells*' departure from Cape Town, a mountainous eyrie of an island appeared on the horizon: this was St Helena. Even from a distance it was clear that the British navy had mounted extraordinary precautions: there were so many vessels patrolling the island that it looked as if some great naval battle were shortly to be fought off its shores.

The sight of the island, and the warships around it, provoked a fresh outburst of excitement on the quarter-deck: 'To think that there lurks the Creature who agitated the world . . .'

'. . . grasped the sceptres of the finest Kingdoms . . .'

'. . . annihilated entire armies, at Jena and Austerlitz . . .'

Bahram and Zadig were down in their listening-post, and they understood that the notion of visiting the ex-Emperor had now blossomed into a fully fledged plan: evidently one of the

Englishmen had connections in the Admiralty and had drafted a letter to the authorities asking for permission to call on the former Consul; what was more, the Captain of the *Cuffnells* had been enlisted to deliver this letter with his own hands, thereby adding the weight of his authority to their cause.

The approach to shore took inordinately long because of the security precautions, and the *Cuffnells* was still miles from the island when she was stopped by a sloop o'war. Through a battery of speaking-trumpets, the officers of the *Cuffnells* were subjected to a prolonged interrogation before being allowed to proceed to the harbour. This incident gave the Captain pause, and he was heard to remonstrate with his compatriots, warning them that even if Napoleon himself were to entertain their request, it was most unlikely that the authorities would allow them to call upon the prisoner. But the ladies were not easily discouraged, and the *Cuffnells* had no sooner dropped anchor than they set up a great clamour for the Captain to fulfil his promise. Accordingly the Captain's ketch was lowered and he was rowed off to Jamestown with a letter of request in hand.

On the Captain's return it was evident from his deportment that he did not have anything encouraging to impart: Bahram and Zadig managed to reach their listening-post in time to hear him say that Napoleon was so strictly guarded that it was harder to gain access to him than to breach a fort.

'When the Bonaparte first arrived he observed to the Admiral that since it was impossible to escape from this island, his sentries and pickets might as well be removed. "No, no, General," said the Admiral to this: "You are a cleverer fellow than I, so here they must be, and an Officer must see you every twelve hours." And such has been the rule ever since.'

Living under these tight precautions, said the Captain, the Bonaparte was rarely disposed to entertain guests. He had previously refused all such requests, repeatedly expressing his reluctance to meet even with senior officers of the Admiralty. The chances of his being open to a social visit from a group of passing passengers was next to nil—but nonetheless the Captain had done his duty and handed over their letter.

The next day the Captain's gloomy prediction was confirmed; two uniformed visitors came aboard to announce to the hopeful passengers that their request had been summarily refused: the General had declared himself to be indisposed and incapable of receiving visitors.

This met with an outcry, not merely of disappointment but also of indignation and disbelief.

'Oh the Beast! After all he has done, does he not owe the world a debt?'

'But surely, sir, he must lack for company in this lonely place . . . he who has been used to the most glittering society, the most sparkling conversation . . . ?'

'He has been heard to say, madam, that he wishes he had perished in the snows of Russia. Or of a bullet, at Leipzig.'

'Oh, a fitting death it would have been too . . .'

So it went on, for quite a while, with opprobrium and entreaty being uttered in equal measure until at last the visitors tired of their hosts' importunities and rose to leave. Their descent was so precipitate that Bahram and Zadig had very little time to distance themselves from their alcove. Zadig managed to whisk himself off, but Bahram found himself face-to-face with the visitors, at the foot of the companion-ladder. Although startled, he managed to respond with some aplomb, performing a stately bow and assuming an air of nonchalance. This retrieved the situation, and he was answered in kind by the visitors. As he was completing his dignified retreat, Bahram had the satisfaction of knowing that he had made a considerable impression, for the visitors could be heard exchanging whispers with their hosts:

'The one with the turban—is he what they call a Raja?'

'Better still—he is a prince of ancient Persia . . .'

'A pure-blooded Parsee—directly descended from Xerxes and Darius . . .'

Bahram smiled to himself, thinking of how his mother would have laughed.

The next day it came to be known that the *Cuffnells* would have to remain in St Helena somewhat longer than expected because of a minor problem with equipment. For Bahram and Zadig, who were tired of their shipboard quarters and eager to get to their destination, the news caused only annoyance. But the British contingent, on the other hand, responded with a renewed surge of optimism: having learnt that Napoleon liked to go for long walks in the vicinity of his lodge, they arranged to hire horses to take them up to the hills. Zadig predicted that this expedition would prove as futile as all their other efforts—but he was wrong, for the members of the riding party returned with their hopes refreshed. Although they had not seen Bonaparte himself, they had encountered someone who had said that he might well be able to make the necessary arrangements. This gentleman happened to be one of the Quartermasters charged with the provisioning of the General's household; what was more, he was an acquaintance of one of the passengers and had quickly revealed himself to be the most civil, the most obliging of men: he said that the General had recently evinced some interest in the *Cuffnells* and he offered to convey their request directly to the Grand Marshal Bertrand, who was the General's companion in exile. He assured them that they would have their answer the following day.

Sure enough the next day brought the Quartermaster to the *Cuffnells* at noon. Not long afterwards a lascar came down to tell Bahram that his presence was required above, on the quarter-deck.

No such invitation had ever been extended to Bahram before and he was taken aback. Are you sure? he said to the lascar. Who sent you?

The sahibs and ma'ams, came the reply.

Achha? Chalo. Tell them I'm coming.

Donning a fresh angarkha, Bahram climbed the ladder to the quarter-deck and was greeted with an unprecedented display of warmth.

'Oh Mr Moddie, please do take a seat.'

'And you are well today? Not peaked by the weather I trust?'

'No, no,' Bahram hastened to reassure them. 'My health is pink. Please tell, how to be of service.'

'Well Mr Moddie . . .'

After some initial awkwardness, and several roundabout remarks, the Quartermaster came at last to the point. 'I am sure you are aware, Mr Moddie, that Napoleon Bonaparte is a prisoner on this island. Some of your shipmates are most desirous of meeting with him and he has agreed to receive them. But upon one condition.'

'Yes?'

'Bonaparte has stipulated that he will see the others only if he can meet with you first, Mr Moddie.'

'Me? But why?' Bahram cried in astonishment.

'Well, Mr Moddie, it has come to the Bonaparte's ears that there is a Zoroastrian prince on the *Cuffnells*.'

'Prince?' Bahram's eyes widened. 'What Prince? Why he wants? What he will do with Prince?'

The Quartermaster cleared his throat before launching on an explanation: 'It appears, Mr Moddie, that the Bonaparte had once fancied himself as the Alexander of our age. It was his intention to proceed eastwards from Egypt to Persia and India, in the footsteps of the great Macedonian. He had even dreamt, it seems, of encountering Darius at the gates of Persepolis, as had Alexander . . .'

To Bahram, as to many of his kin, there was no name more hateful than that of the two-horned Greek. The blood rushed to his head and he cried out: 'Chha! What you are talking Alexander-shalexander? You know what that dirty fellow did? Looting palaces, burning temples, haraaming wives—what he did not do? Even boys he was budmashing. Now this new one has come, you think I will go meekly to visit? You think I am mad or what?'

The flustered Quartermaster hastened to reassure him. 'You have no cause for concern, none at all: the Bonaparte intends you no harm. He is, after all, a Frenchman, not a Greek. And he is interested not only in your sect, but also in learning about the conduct of your business in China. He has been known to remark you know, that it is better that China remains asleep, for the world is sure to tremble when she awakes.'

This mystified Bahram who said: 'What you are saying? This fellow thinks Chinese are sleeping too much, is it?'

'Oh no,' said the Quartermaster. 'I am sure he was speaking only metaphorically. I meant only to suggest that he is keen to inform himself about that country. That is one of the reasons why he wishes to meet with you.'

Bahram was in quite a belligerent mood now and was not disposed to do anyone's bidding. 'Arré! One minute I am Darius, next minute I am Kublai Khan? What does he think? Let him catch some Chinaman. Why I should go?'

'Oh please, Mr Moddie,' pleaded one of the English ladies. 'Will you not reconsider?'

Somewhat mollified, Bahram drummed his fingertips together as he thought about his next step: to be summoned by a man who had only recently been an Emperor was undeniably flattering—but it occurred to him also that it might not be wise to single-handedly confront a General who had routed vast armies. He could almost hear his mother whispering in his ear in Gujarati: If you put your head on a grindstone, then you must expect the pestle.

Bahram scratched his beard and said: 'I also have one condition. If I go, my good friend, Mr Karabedian, must accompany me.'

His interlocutors exchanged doubtful glances. 'But why is that necessary?'

'Because,' said Bahram, 'he is talking French, no? He will be my translator.'

'I'm afraid it may not be possible,' said the Quartermaster, with a show of firmness. 'The Bonaparte did not, I might point out, include your friend in his invitation.'

'All right then! Bas! Why to waste time?' Gathering his robe together, Bahram made as if to rise. 'I will take leave now.'

'Oh but wait! Mr Moddie, please!'

The intervention of the ladies settled the matter, and it was agreed that the party would set off at ten the next morning.

Zadig had, of course, followed the entire exchange from the listening-post and he was deeply grateful to be included in the expedition—so much so that Bahram was even able to negotiate a small reduction in the remaining dues for his berth.

But it was as much for his own sake as Zadig's that Bahram had been so firm in demanding his friend's inclusion: Bahram's instincts told him that certain protocols would have to be followed in waiting upon an Emperor, even a deposed one, and he was at a loss to imagine what the appropriate etiquette might be. He had visited several Rajas and Maharajas and even a titular Badshah—Shah Alam II, who was then the occupant of the tottering Mughal throne in Delhi. These experiences had taught him that kings and emperors were fiercely jealous of their dignity, no matter how diminished their circumstances.

Zadig was, of course, more widely travelled than Bahram and was better informed about courtly procedures—but even for him, this was an unprecedented situation, and on some aspects of protocol he was almost as uncertain as Bahram. What were they to wear, for instance? Both men had a complement of European-style coats and trousers in their trunks but neither of them was at all eager to exchange his accustomed clothing for those tight-fitting, tailored garments. Besides, reasoned Zadig, Napoleon was sure to be disappointed, was he not, if his Persian prince turned up attired like a colonial clerk? Better, then, to dress in familiar attire—and fortunately they were both in possession of a few garments that would not have looked out of place at any court. In Zadig's case, these consisted of a sumptuous burumcuk caftan and a gold-embroidered Yerevan waistcoat; for Bahram they were a silver-grey 'Mughalai' pyjama with an ornamental *izarband* drawstring; it was worn with a knee-length jama of cream-coloured silk, embroidered with gold badla. This ensemble was completed by a resplendent outer garment, worn in the fashion of a coat—a choga of blue silk, with a raised collar made of strips of golden kimkhab ribbon. As for headgear, for Zadig the question was easily resolved, by the choice of a tall, sable calpac—but for Bahram, this issue threatened to be the trickiest part of the preparations. His ceremonial turban was over ten feet long and he knew it would be no easy feat to deal with so much cloth in a cabin that was barely large enough for two men to turn around in.

But their costuming proved less onerous than they had feared: by serving as each other's valets they were able to squirm and wriggle into their clothes well before the Captain's ketch was declared to be ready to ferry their party ashore, to Jamestown.

This was the island's principal settlement and it presented an appearance that was at once pictureseque and strikingly unusual: the town consisted of a double row of prettily coloured houses that ran along the floor of a steep, V-shaped valley. As it receded into the interior of the island, the valley led the eye directly to a hill that was topped by a modest lodge: here lay the site of Napoleon's imprisonment.

Transportation, in the form of a train of horses, had already been arranged, and the party set off at a brisk trot, winding their way upwards through the town's narrow, cobblestoned streets. The house that had been allotted to the former Emperor was called Longwood and it was located on one of the island's highest elevations, about five miles from the capital. The path was narrow but scenic, and every turn brought into view alternating vistas of a glittering blue sea and wooded hillsides, covered with fern-draped trees. Climbing steeply, the visitors passed through orchards and massed clumps of wild flowers before reaching a point where the way was blocked by a picket of British soldiers. A tumbledown cottage stood nearby: they were informed that this was the residence of the Count Henri Gratien Bertrand, Grand Marshal of the Palace and former commander of the Irish corps of the French army.

Here they dismounted, and their arrival being announced, the Marshal came out to meet them—and he proved to be not at all the ogre that some had feared but a distinguished-looking man with extremely winning manners. After greetings had been exchanged, the Marshal led the visitors towards the cottage, promising to introduce them to someone they would find very interesting. The women interpreted this to mean that they were soon to be in the presence of the Fiend himself and were reduced to fluttering agitation—needlessly it turned out, for the Marshal had merely been teasing them: it was his wife who was waiting inside the shack, and they were all charmed by her engaging manners and fluent English. She seemed particularly pleased to meet Zadig, and brought out a camel-hair shawl: it had been given to her, she said, by the Empress Maria Louisa who had bought it from an Armenian trader for three hundred guineas. This led to a lively discussion and the English passengers were soon on the best of terms with the Countess, who was half-Irish and half-Creole. So charmed, indeed, were they, that they expressed no disappointment when Marshal Bertrand informed them, somewhat apologetically, that it was his duty to now take the two Asiatic visitors to the General, for a private conversation: if the others had no objection to remaining awhile in the Countess's company, he would briefly take their leave. The English visitors readily gave their assent, so Bahram and Zadig rose to their feet and followed the Marshal out of the cottage.

Longwood stood on the summit of the hill, and the path that led up to it was steep and winding. When the house came into view, the two visitors were taken aback: it was just a bungalow, impressive neither in size nor appearance. Its one distinguishing feature was a steeply gabled portico; if not for the soldiers who were posted around the grounds, it could have been mistaken for the home of a family of modest circumstances.

At the bottom of the garden, there was a tent manned by a platoon of soldiers. Several other visitors were waiting there, but on the Marshal's word, Bahram and Zadig were waved through before the rest. After a few more steps, the Marshal came to a halt and pointed them in the direction of what seemed to be a flower garden: he now needed to retrace his steps to his own dwelling, he said, but they would have no difficulty in finding the General—at this time of day he liked to stroll in the gardens and they were sure to see him on their way up.

The last part of the climb had been quite strenuous, and both Zadig and Bahram were now breathing heavily and perspiring under their robes.

'What kind of Emperor he is?' Bahram muttered, under his breath. 'No chobdar even to receive his guests.'

Despite the Marshal's reassurances they saw no sign of the General, and the flowers, when they reached them, proved to be a mere sprinkling of daisies and asters.

'At least he could put some roses, no?' said Bahram in disgust. 'Emperor-shemperor and all?'

They hurried on and were making their way through a vegetable patch when they caught sight of someone approaching. Not only was this man a personage of commanding aspect, he also had a star pinned to his breast. They both assumed that he was Bonaparte himself.

To encounter an Emperor in a manure-strewn cabbage patch was a contingency for which Bahram was wholly unprepared; deciding that he would copy everything that Zadig did, he drew back a little, and kept his eyes fixed upon his friend. Had he proceeded to kneel in the mud, Bahram would certainly have followed suit, no matter what the damage to his clothing; but the gesture that Zadig performed was somewhat more difficult to emulate: reaching for his hat, he bared his head. Only for an instant did Bahram toy with the idea of removing his own headgear; just in time he realized that it would be no easy matter to unravel ten feet of cloth: Emperor or not, he decided he was not going to pull off his turban. Instead he merely bowed deeply from the waist.

Much to their chagrin, their efforts were wasted: the gentleman in question was not Napoleon at all, but an officer-in-waiting—and what was more, he seemed to take no small pleasure in their discomfiture. 'The General is ready to receive you,' he instructed them, smiling slyly. 'So please compose yourselves.'

~

The weather being exceptionally fine, chairs were laid out amongst the pots and plants on the *Redruth*'s quarter-deck, in preparation for Robin Chinnery's visit: it was from the shade of the deck's protective awning that Paulette observed the visitor as he came up the side-ladder to be welcomed on board by his host.

From the moment she set eyes on Robin it was evident to Paulette that he had changed a great deal since she had seen him last—almost as much perhaps as she had herself, except that in his case the alteration was principally a matter of attire and bearing. He was still a small, portly fellow with a knob of a nose, protuberant eyes and pouting, hibiscus-hued lips—but the flamboyantly colourful clothes, the diaphanous scarves and glittering trinkets, were all gone: they had been replaced by a dark, sober suit, of the kind that he himself had once been accustomed to mock as the 'livery of the English shipping-clerk'. His jacket and trowsers were dull to a fault, the collar of his shirt was neither high nor low, and on his head, he, who had liked to wear sparkling bandhnas and multicoloured pugrees, was now wearing a plain black hat.

The bag that hung from his shoulders was also a far cry from the embroidered satchels and jewelled reticules that he had carried in the past: it was a leather case with a brass clasp. Seeing him reach into it, Paulette listened from afar as he took out a slim portfolio.

'Your pictures, Mr Penrose: I did not trouble to copy the older one as it is lacking in detail. But here is my copy of the other—I wager you'll not be able to tell it apart from the original.'

'Ee're right there, but I'm not a betting man.'

From the evidence of Robin's voice it seemed to Paulette that his accent had changed just as much, if not more than his appearance: he had lost all trace of a Bengali intonation. When he cried out 'And Paulette? Where is she?' it was in the rounded tones of the English pucka sahib.

'Waiting for ee up there,' said Fitcher, pointing to the quarter-deck. 'Go on up. I know the two of ee have a lot to talk about so I'll give ee a few minutes on eer own.'

Now, Robin uttered a little shriek—'Why there she is, my darling Puggly!'—giving Paulette a glimpse of her friend's earlier more familiar self. And then, as he came racing up the companion-ladder he was almost the Robin of old, chattering away in Bengali: *Arré Pagli, toké kotodin dekhini!*—haven't seen you in so long! Come here, you . . .

Paulette threw her arms around him and the feel of his soft and bosomy embrace was like a remembered taste, dissolving upon the tongue; she recalled the savour of the times they had spent together, bantering, teasing, arguing and gossiping and she understood, all of a sudden, that Robin was perhaps the closest friend she had ever had—for Jodu was more a sibling than a friend.

Oh Robin, I'm so happy to see you—it's been so long.

Too long; far too long! cried Robin. 'I've missed you so much my sweet, dear Puggly.'

Have you forgiven us, Robin? Jodu and me?

'Oh yes,' said Robin, releasing her from his embrace. 'It is all in the past now. You were just children, and not, if I may say so, my dear Miss Pugglesford, particularly *distinguished* in your tastes, so how could you be expected to understand Art? The fault was mine really, I blame myself . . . although I cannot deny that your vandalism was indeed something of a *blow* at the time. I had invested a great deal in that painting and the loss of it sent me into something of a decline—and that, I am sorry to say, led to a *most* unfortunate outcome. My poor, sweet mother, who was, as you know, too good and trusting a soul for this world, became so alarmed at my state that she arranged—would you believe it, Puggly dear?—for me to be *married*!'

Really? And what came of it?

'I'm afraid it didn't *take*, Puggly dear, for I'm not a *marrying* kind of man, besides which she—my bride—was a perfect *fright* and inspired utter *terror* in all who crossed her path.'

Eki? So what did you do?

'I did what any Chinnery would have done, Puggly dear: I took to my heels. And of course the first thought in my mind was to escape to Canton, just as Mr Chinnery had done, for it is the one place where a sahib may count on being safe from mems. To get away was no easy feat though, I can tell you that, for a passage to China is not *cheap*, by any means . . . but fortunately I had a couple of paintings at hand, done in the Chinnery manner and lacking only a signature. Once that was rectified I had no trouble selling them and I was sure Mr Chinnery would forgive me this desperate measure. But alas, nothing has turned out quite as I had expected: Mr Chinnery positively *berated* me for forging his signature—and worse still, it turned out that he was not living in Canton after all, but in Macau, which is nothing but a dull, mofussil town. It is the kind of place where everyone pretends to be exceedingly genteel and this fever seems to have seized Mr Chinnery as well: my arrival put his nose severely out of joint—would you credit it, Puggly dear, he insists that I pretend to be his *nephew*, and has absolutely *forbidden* me to appear in public in any but the dullest kinds of costume. I try to be obedient but he still keeps *haranguing* me to go back to Calcutta—to be reconciled with my wife he says, although he knows perfectly well that she has run off to Barrackpore with a bandmaster. Of course I am no fool, and I know full well that he only wants to be rid of me—but I was *determined* not to leave without spending a season in Canton, and he could not shake me from my resolve.'

But why, Robin? Why is it so important to you to go to Canton?

Robin let out a long sigh. 'I shrink from telling you, Puggly dear. I fear you will laugh at me.'

Certainly not. *Bol!* Tell me.

'Well Puggly dear, mine has not been, as you know, a life that could properly be described as *happy*—and to no one is this state more attractive than to those whom it is consistently denied: suffice it to say that I have become quite convinced that Canton is the place where I am most likely to find some small measure of contentment.'

In Canton? cried Paulette. But why there, of all places?

'Well Puggly dear, I am old enough now to know that I am not destined to enjoy any of the usual forms of domestic felicity. In all likelihood I will live out my days as a bachelor, and I fear that mine may be a lonely lot unless I succeed in finding a Friend—someone to whom I may be a true and devoted Companion. All the artists I most admire had Friends to sustain them in their endeavours—Botticelli, Michelangelo, Raphael, Caravaggio. In reading about them it has become apparent to me that the lack of a Friend has been a tragic want in my life: without one, I shall never achieve anything of significance. But as you know, Puggly dear, it has never been easy for me to make friends—I am not like other men and people do sometimes tend to think me a little *odd*. Even when I was a little chokra no one would play with me, not even my brother—oh if only I had a penny for all the times I was beaten by the other boys! I'd be a rich man, I promise you.'

But Robin, is it not a strange thing to go to Canton in search of friendship?

'Oh by no means, my dear Puggly! I have it on excellent authority that there is no better place on earth for Friendships than Canton's foreign enclave: nowhere else is there such a number of incorrigible bachelors. It is no hardship for them, you know, to live in an enclave that is forbidden to women; since there is also a great deal of money to be made in Canton, it is, I believe, a most *amenable* place for confirmed solitaries like myself. I am told that at certain times of year bachelors flock there like birds to a wintering hole: indeed some of Mr Chinnery's own friends have told me so. I have often quoted them to him but this only seems to infuriate him—he says that I am exactly the kind of man who is likely to succumb to the temptations of Canton and he can never countenance such a fate for his own flesh and blood. He was so adamant that I *despaired* of going. Indeed he would never have agreed, I suspect, if I had not threatened to use the only weapon in my quiver: I told him that if he did not use his influence to obtain a chop for me, I would *expose* him to his genteel friends and reveal *everything* about his treatment of my mother, my brother and myself. At that he relented and so, Puggly dear, it has all been arranged: I am to spend the season at Markwick's Hotel in Canton!'

Oh how I envy you, Robin! said Paulette. I wish I could be there with you.

Putting an arm around her, Robin gave her a hug. 'And so you *shall* be, my sweet, sweet Pugglagolla. I shall write to you as often as I can—boats go back and forth between Canton and the Outer Islands all the time so I will have no difficulty in sending letters. I will make sure that you see Canton through my eyes!'

Will you really, Robin? Can I hold you to it?

'Of course you can—you must not doubt it for a moment.' As if to seal the pledge, Robin gave her hand a squeeze. 'And now Puggly dear, I want to hear all about *you* . . . You and that budmash brother of yours. Tell me all—I must know *everything*!'

~

Bahram and Zadig had their first glimpse of the General as they came around a corner: Bonaparte was standing amidst a copse of trees, surveying the valley below. He was a thickset man, a little shorter than Bahram, and he was leaning forward a little, with his hands clasped behind his back. He was much stouter than Bahram had been led to expect: his belly was a sizeable protuberance and seemed scarcely to belong on someone whose life had been so extraordinarily active. He was dressed in a plain green coat with a velvet collar and silver buttons, each imprinted with a different device; his breeches were of nankeen, but his stockings were of silk, and there were large gold buckles on his shoes. On the left side of his coat was a large star, emblazoned with the Imperial Eagle, and on his head he was wearing a cocked, black hat.

At the approach of his visitors, Bonaparte removed his hat and bowed briskly, in a manner that might have seemed perfunctory in another man, but which in his case seemed merely to indicate that time was short, and there was nothing to be gained by wasting it on superfluous niceties. It was his gaze, most of all, that Bahram was to remember, for it was as penetrating as a surgeon's knife, and it cut into him as if to lay bare the flimsy nakedness of his bones.

Once he began to speak it was evident that the General, military man that he was, had been at some pains to inform himself about his two visitors: he clearly knew that Zadig was to be the interpreter for it was to him that he turned after the introductions had been completed.

You are named 'Zadig' *hein*? he said, with a smile. Is it taken from Monsieur Voltaire's book of the same name? Are you too a Babylonian philosopher?

No, Majesty; I am Armenian by origin, and the name is an ancient one among my people.

While the two men were conversing with each other, Bahram took the opportunity to observe the General closely. His build reminded him of one of his mother's Gujarati sayings: *tukki gerden valo haramjada ni nisani*—'a short neck is a sure sign of a haramzada'. But he noted also his piercing gaze, his incisive manner of speaking, his sparing but emphatic use of his hands, and the half-smile that played on his lips. Zadig had told him that Napoleon was capable of exerting, when he chose, an extraordinary charm, almost a kind of magic: even the barriers of language, Bahram saw now, could not diminish the power of his hypnotic appeal.

Soon it became apparent that Bahram himself was now the subject of the conversation, and he knew, from the General's darting glances, that he was going to be in for a lengthy interrogation. It was odd to be spoken of without knowing what was being said and Bahram was glad when Zadig turned to him at last and began to translate the General's words into Hindusthani.

It was in the same language that Bahram answered—but Zadig was by no means a passive interpreter and since he was more knowledgeable than Bahram about many of the subjects that were of interest to Napoleon, the conversation was quickly triangulated. For much of the time Bahram was merely an uncomprehending spectator. It wasn't until much later that he was to understand everything that was said—yet in retrospect he remembered it all, with perfect clarity, as though he and Zadig had been listening and speaking with the same ears and the same tongue.

Napoleon's first set of questions, Bahram recalled, were of a personal nature and embarrassed Zadig a little: the scourge of Prussia had declared that he was forcibly impressed by Bahram's appearance and could see in his face and beard, a resemblance to the Persians of antiquity. In his costume, however, he saw no such similarity, for it seemed to be of the Indian type. He was therefore curious to know what aspects of the civilization of ancient Persia had been preserved by the Parsis of the present day.

Bahram was well prepared for this question, having often had to deal with similar queries from his English friends. The General was right, he answered; his clothing was indeed mostly that of Hindusthan, except for two essential articles: his religion required every adherent, male and female, to wear, next to their skin, a girdle of seventy-two threads called a kasti, and a vestment known as a sadra—and Bahram was wearing both of these, under his outer garments, which were, as the General had rightly surmised, no different from those which any other man of his country and station would have worn upon such an occasion. This adaptation in outward appearance, accompanied by the preservation of an inner distinctiveness, could also be said to extend to other aspects of the life of his small community. Where it concerned matters of belief Parsis had clung faithfully to the old ways, making every effort to adhere to the teachings of the prophet Zarathustra; but in other respects they had borrowed freely from the customs and usages of their neighbours.

And what are the principal doctrines of the Prophet Zarathustra?

The religion is among the earliest of monotheistic creeds, Your Majesty. The God of its holy book, the Zend-Avesta, is

Ahura Mazda, who is omniscient, omnipresent and omnipotent. At the time of Creation Ahura Mazda is said to have unleashed a great avalanche of light. One part of this aura submitted to the Creator and was merged into him; the other part turned away from the light and was banished by Ahura Mazda: this dark force came to be known as 'angre-minyo' or Ahriman—the devil, or Satan. Since then the forces of goodness and light have always worked for Ahura Mazda while the forces of darkness have worked against Him. The aim of every Zoroastrian is to embrace the good and to banish evil.

Napoleon turned to look at Bahram: Does he speak the language of Zarathustra?

No, Your Majesty. Like most of his community, he grew up speaking nothing but Gujarati and Hindusthani—he did not even learn English until much later. As for the ancient language of the Zend-Avesta, it is now the exclusive preserve of priests and others versed in Scripture.

And what of the Chinese language? the General asked. Living in that country, have the two of you made any attempt to familiarize yourselves with that tongue?

They answered in one voice: No, they said, they spoke no Chinese, because the common language of trade in southern China was a kind of patois—or, as some called it, 'pidgin', which meant merely 'business' and was thus well suited to describe a tongue which was used mainly to address matters of trade. Even though many Chinese spoke English with ease and fluency, they would not negotiate in it, believing that it put them at a disadvantage in relation to Europeans. In pidgin they reposed far greater trust, for the grammar was the same as that of Cantonese, while the words were mainly English, Portuguese and Hindusthani—and such being the case, everyone who spoke the jargon was at an equal disadvantage, which was considered a great benefit to all. It was, moreover, a simple tongue, not hard to master, and for those who did not know it, there existed a whole class of interpreters, known as linkisters, who could translate into it from both English and Chinese.

And when you are in Canton, said the General, are you allowed to mix freely with the Chinese?

Yes, Your Majesty: there are no restrictions on that. Our most important dealings are with a special guild of Chinese merchants: it is called the Co-Hong, and its members bear the sole responsibility for conducting business with foreigners. In the event of any wrong-doing it is they who have to answer for the behaviour of their foreign counterparts, so the relationship between the Chinese merchants and the others is, in a way, very close, like a partnership almost. But there exists also another class of intermediaries: they are known as 'compradors' and they are responsible for supplying foreign merchants with provisions and servants. They are also charged with the upkeep of the buildings in which we live, the Thirteen Factories.

Zadig had said the last three words in English, and one of them caught the General's attention: Ah! 'Factory'. Is the word the same as our *factorerie*?

This was a subject that Zadig had inquired into and he was not at a loss for an answer: No, Your Majesty. 'Factory' comes from a word that was first used by the Venetians and then by the Portuguese, in Goa. The word is *feitoria* and it refers merely to a place where agents and factors reside and do business. In Canton, the factories are also spoken of as 'hongs'.

They have nothing to do with manufacturing then?

No, Your Majesty: nothing. The factories belong, properly speaking, to the Co-Hong guild, although you would not imagine this to look at them, for many of them have come to be identified with particular nations and kingdoms. Several even hoist their own flags—the French Factory being one such.

Striding briskly on, the General gave Zadig a sidewise glance: Are the factories like embassies then?

The foreigners often treat them as such, although they are not recognized to be so by the Chinese. From time to time Britain does indeed appoint representatives in Canton, but the Chinese do not countenance them and they are allowed to communicate only with the provincial authorities: this too is no easy thing, for the mandarins will not receive any letters that are not written in the style of a petition or supplication, with the appropriate Chinese characters—since the British are reluctant to do this, their communications are often not accepted.

Napoleon laughed briefly and the sunlight flashed on his teeth: So their relations founder on the barriers of protocol?

Exactly, Your Majesty. Neither side will yield in this matter. If there is any nation that can match the English in their arrogance and obstinacy, it is surely the Chinese.

But since it is the English who send embassies there, it must mean that they need the Chinese more than they are themselves needed?

That is correct, Your Majesty. Since the middle years of the last century, the demand for Chinese tea has grown at such a pace in Britain and America that it is now the principal source of profit for the East India Company. The taxes on it account for fully one-tenth of Britain's revenues. If one adds to this such goods as silk, porcelain and lacquerware it becomes clear that the European demand for Chinese products is insatiable. In China, on the other hand, there is little interest in European exports—the Chinese are a people who believe that their own products, like their food and their own customs, are superior to all others. In years past this presented a great problem for the British, for the flow of trade was so unequal that there was an immense outpouring of silver from Britain. This indeed was why they started to export Indian opium to China.

Glancing over his shoulder, the General raised an eyebrow: Started? *Commencé?* You mean this trade has not always existed?

No, Majesty—the trade was a mere trickle until about sixty years ago, when the East India Company adopted it as a means of rectifying the outflow of bullion. They succeeded so well that now the supply can barely keep pace with the demand. The flow of silver is now completely reversed, and it pours away from China to Britain, America and Europe.

Now the General came to a halt under a tree with strange hairy leaves: plucking two of them he handed one each to Bahram and Zadig. You will no doubt be interested, he said, to learn that this tree is called the 'She-Cabbage Tree' and exists nowhere else on earth. You may keep these leaves as souvenirs of this island.

Zadig bowed and Bahram followed: We thank you, Majesty.

They had come quite a distance from the house by this time, and the General now decided to turn back. For a moment it seemed—somewhat to Bahram's relief—that his attention had wandered from the matters they had been discussing before. But once they began to walk again it became clear that he was not a man to be easily distracted.

So tell me, messieurs, do the Chinese perceive no harm in opium?

Oh they certainly do, Your Majesty: its importation was banned in the last century and the prohibition has been reiterated several times. It is in principle a clandestine trade—but it is difficult to put an end to it for many officials, petty and grand, benefit from it. As for dealers and traders, when there are great profits to be made, they are not slow to find ways around the laws.

Napoleon lowered his gaze to the dusty pathway. Yes, he said softly, as though he were speaking to himself; this was a problem we too faced, in Europe, with our Continental System. Merchants and smugglers are ingenious in evading laws.

Exactly so, Your Majesty.

Now, a twinkle appeared in the General's eye: But how long do you think the Chinese will suffer this trade to continue?

It remains to be seen, Your Majesty. Things have come to a pass where a cessation in the trade would be a disaster for the East India Company. Indeed it is no exaggeration to say that without it the British would not be able to hold on to their Eastern colonies; they cannot afford to forgo those profits.

Quelle ironie! said Napoleon suddenly, flashing his visitors his arresting smile. What an irony it would be if it were opium that stirred China from her sleep. And if it did, would you consider it a good thing?

Why no, Your Majesty, responded Zadig immediately. I have always been taught that nothing good can be born of evil.

Napoleon laughed. But then the whole world would be nothing but evil. Why else *par example* do you trade in opium?

Not I, Your Majesty, said Zadig quickly. I am a clockmaker and I play no part in the opium trade.

But what of your friend? He trades in opium, does he not? Does he believe it to be evil?

This question caught Bahram unawares and he was temporarily at a loss for words. Then, gathering his wits, he said: Opium is like the wind or the tides: it is outside my power to affect its course. A man is neither good nor evil because he sails his ship upon the wind. It is his conduct towards those around him—his friends, his family, his servants—by which he must be judged. This is the creed I live by.

Napoleon directed his piercing gaze at Bahram: But a man may die, may he not, because he sails upon the wind?

The thought withered on his lips for Longwood had come into view, and an aide was seen to be hurrying down the path in search of the General.

Bonaparte turned to Zadig and Bahram and swept his hat off his head: *Au revoir messieurs, bonne chance!*

part two

Canton

seven

Nov 7, 1838
Markwick's Hotel, Canton

Dearest Puggly, I am *transported*! Canton, at last—and what an age it took! I came in a passage-boat—a *most* curious vessel, shaped like a caterpillar and just as slow. How I envied the rich fanqui shipowners who went breezing past us in their fine sloops and sleek yawls! I am told the fastest of them can make the journey from Macau to Canton in a day and a half. Needless to say, it took our caterpillar more than twice that length of time, and at the end of it we found ourselves in Whampoa which is yet some twelve miles from Canton.

Whampoa is an island in the Pearl River, and the waters around it serve as the last anchorage for foreign ships. These vessels are not permitted to approach any closer to Canton so here they must stay while their holds are filled and emptied. This is a sore trial for their poor crewmen because there is little of interest in Whampoa other than a fine pagoda: I have the impression that the village is to the Pearl River what Budge Budge is to the Hooghly—a ramshackle cobbily-mash of godowns, bankshalls and customs-khanas. Bored sailors and lascars, marooned for weeks on their stationary ships, occupy themselves by counting the days till their next shore leave in Canton.

Fortunately one need not tarry long in Whampoa, for there are ferries to Canton at all times of night and day. The river is crowded here with vessels of curious shapes and fantastical designs yet you do not immediately have the impression of approaching a great city. To your left lies an island called Honam: being laid out with gardens, estates and orchards it is exceedingly pastoral in appearence—this too is reminiscent of the approaches to Calcutta where the fields and forests of Chitpur lie across the river from the city. But the number of sampans, lanteas and salt-junks have been increasing all this while and soon there are so many of them lying at anchor on both sides of the river that they are like a continuous barricade, blocking the shore from view. Then, above the masts and sails, appear the city's ramparts—immense walls of grey stone, capped, at intervals, with watch-towers and many-roofed gateways. Calcutta's Fort William seems *tiny* in comparison with this vast citadel: its walls run for miles and miles; you can see them rising up a hill and coming together to meet at a majestic five-storeyed tower. It is called the Sea-Calming Tower (is that not the most *poetic* name?) and I am told that the soldiers who guard it will allow visitors to enter if offered a satisfactory cumshaw: the view is said to be extraordinarily fine, with the whole city lying spread out beneath your feet, like an immense map. It takes only an hour or two to walk to the tower, skirting around the city walls, and I am determined to go—otherwise I will see nothing at all of the citadel. It is utterly *forbidden* for a foreigner to step through any of the city gates—which does *so* make one long to go in! Oh well . . . there is more than enough to see and paint anyway, for all around the city walls there are suburbs—the citadel is but the flagship of the city of Canton and it has a flotilla of lesser vessels anchored around it.

You may not credit it, Puggly dear, but the greatest of Canton's suburbs is the river itself! There are more people living in the city's floating bustees than in *all* of Calcutta:

fully *one million* some say! Their boats are moored along the water's edge, on either side, and they are so numerous you cannot see the water beneath. At first this floating city looks like a vast shanty town made of driftwood, bamboo and thatch; the boats are so tightly packed that if not for the rolls and tremors that shake them from time to time you would take them for oddly shaped huts. Closest to the shore are rows of sampans, most of them some four or five yards in length. Their roofs are made of bamboo, and their design is at once very simple and *marvellously* ingenious, for they can be moved to suit the weather. When it rains the coverings are rearranged to protect the whole boat, and on fine days they are rolled back to expose the living quarters to the sun—and it is *astonishing* to observe all that goes on within them. The occupants are all so *busy* that you would imagine the floating city to be a waterborne hive: here in this boat someone is making bean-curd; in another, joss-sticks; in that one noodles, and over there something else—and all to the accompaniment of a great cacophony of clucking, grunting and barking, for every floating manufactory is also a farmyard! And between them there are little watery lanes and galis, just wide enough to allow a shop-boat to pass; and of these there are more than you would think could possibly exist, for they are manned by hawkers and cheap-jacks of every sort—tanners, tinkers, tailors, coopers, cobblers, barbers, bone-setters and many others, all barricking their wares with bells, gongs and shouts.

Fanquis say the floating city is a rookery for bandits, bonegrabbers, sotweeds, bangtails and scumsuckers of every sort—but I confess that this makes me all the more eager to explore it. It is so very *eye-catching* that I long to try my hand at a few nautical paintings, in the manner of Van Ruysdael perhaps, or even Mr Turner (but that would never do, alas, for Mr Chinnery turns positively *green* at the very mention of that name).

And so at last to the foreign enclave—or 'Fanqui-town' as I have already learnt to call it! It is the farthest extremity of the city, just beyond the citadel's south-western gate. In appearance Fanqui-town is not at all as you might expect: indeed it is so different from what I had envisioned that it fair took my breath away! I had imagined the factories would be prettily primped with a few Celestial touches—perhaps a few curling eaves or pagoda-like spires like those that so beguile the eye in Chinese paintings. But if you could see the factories for yourself, Puggly dear, I warrant they would remind you rather of pictures of places that are very far away—Vermeer's Amsterdam or even . . . Chinnery's Calcutta. You would see a row of buildings with columns, capitals, pilasters, tall windows and tiled roofs. Some have colonnaded verandas, with the same khus-khus screens you see in India: if you half close your eyes you could think yourself to be on the Strand, in Calcutta, looking at the bankshalls and daftars of the big English trading houses. The colours are quite different though, brighter and more varied: from a distance the factories look like stripes of paint against the grey walls of the citadel.

The British Factory is the largest of the thirteen; it has a chapel with a clock-tower and its bell keeps time for all of Fanqui-town. It also has a garden in front and an enormous flagpole. Some of the other factories have flags flying before them too—the Dutch, the Danish, the French and the American. These flags are larger than any I have ever seen and the poles are immensely tall. They look like gigantic lances, plunged into the soil of China, and they rise high above the factory roofs, as if to make sure that they are visible to the mandarins within the city walls.

As you may imagine, already on the ferry I was thinking of how to paint this scene. I have not started yet, of course, but I know it will be a stern challenge, especially where it concerns the matter of depth. The factories are so narrow-fronted that to look at them you would think they could scarcely accommodate a dozen people. But behind each façade lies a warren of houses, courtyards, godowns, and khazanas; a long, arched corridor runs the length of each compound, linking the houses and courtyards—at night these passageways are lit with lamps, which gives them the appearance of city streets.

Some say the factories have been constructed in accordance with a typically Chinese pattern of building, where any number of pavilions and courtyards may sit within the walls of a single compound; but I've also heard it said that the factories are a bit like the colleges of Oxford and Leiden, with halls and houses grouped around many linked quadrangles. Were I a painter of Persian miniatures, I would paint the façades head-on, and then I would create an angle behind them such that the pattern of the compound's interior would be made visible to the eye. But it is not to be thought of, for it would be a great *scandal*: Mr Chinnery would be horrified and I would have to spend *years* doing exercises in perspective.

I am getting ahead of myself: I have yet to bring you to Fanqui-town's landing ghat, which is called—and this is true I swear—'Jackass Point' (the fabled Man-Town must, in other words, be entered through the Point of Jack's Unspeakable). Yet this suppository is no different from our Calcutta landing ghats: there is no jetty—instead there are steps, sticky with mud from the last high tide (yes, my darling Puggleshwaree, the Pearl, like our beloved Hooghly, rises and falls twice a day!). But even in Calcutta I have never witnessed such a goll-maul as there is at Jackass Point: so many people, so much bobbery, so much hulla-gulla, so many coolies, making such a tamasha of fighting over your bags and bowlas! I counted myself fortunate in being able to steer mine towards a lad with a winning smile, one Ah Lei (why so many Ahs, you might ask, and never any Oohs? On the streets of Macau too you will come across innumerable young men who will pass themselves off as 'Ah Man', 'Ah Gan' and the like, and if ever you should ask what the 'Ah!' signifies you will learn that in Cantonese, as in English, this vocable serves no function other than that of clearing the throat. But just because the bearers of the 'Ah' are usually young, or poor, you must not imagine that they possess no other name. In their other incarnations they may well be known as 'Fire Breathing Dragon' or 'Tireless Steed'—whether accurately or not only their Wives and Friends will know).

Ah Lei was neither dragon nor steed; he was less than half my size. I thought he would be crushed by my luggage but he hoisted it all on his back with a couple of flicks of his wrist. 'What-place wanchi?' says he to me, and I tell him: 'Markwick's Hotel.' And so, following my young Atlas, I stepped upon the stretch of shore that forms the heart and hearth of Fanqui-town. This is an open space between the factories and the river-bank: the English speak of it as 'The Square', but Hindusthanis have a better name for it. They call it the 'Maidan' which is exactly what it is, a crossroads, a meeting-place, a piazza, a promenade, a stage for a tamasha that never ends: it is a scene of such activity, such *animation*, that I despair of being able to capture it on canvas. Everywhere you look there is something utterly strange and ever so *singular*: a storm of chirruping approaches you, and at its centre is a man with thousands of walnut-shells hanging from shoulder-poles; on closer inspection you discover that each walnut has been carved into an exquisite cage—for a cricket! The man is carrying thousands of these insects and they are all in full song. You have not taken more than a step or two before another tempest of noise approaches you, at a trot; at the centre of it is a grand personage, perhaps a Mandarin or a merchant of the Co-Hong guild; he is seated in a kind of palki, except that it is actually a curtained sedan chair, suspended from shoulder-poles; the men who carry the chair are called 'horses without tails' and they have attendants running alongside, beating drums and clappers to clear the way. It is all so new that you stare too long and are almost trampled underfoot by the tail-less stallions . . .

And yet it is a *tiny* place! All of Fanqui-town—the Maidan, the streets and all thirteen factories—would fit into a small corner of the Maidan in Calcutta. From end to end the enclave is only about a thousand feet in length, less than a quarter of a mile, and in width it is about half that. In a way Fanqui-town is like a ship at sea, with hundreds—no, thousands—of men living crammed together in a little sliver of a space. I do believe there is no place like it on earth, so small and yet so varied, where people from the far corners of the earth must live, elbow to elbow, for six months of the year. I tell you, Pugglissima mia, were you to stand in the Maidan and look at the flags of the factories, fluttering against the grey walls of Canton's citadel, I am certain you too would be *overcome*: it is as if you had arrived at the threshold of the last and greatest of all the world's caravanserais.

And yet, in a way, it is also so familiar: Everywhere you look there are khidmatgars, daftardars, khansamas, chuprassies, peons, durwans, khazanadars, khalasis and lascars. And this, my dear Puggly, is one of the greatest of the many surprises of Fanqui-town—a *great number* of its denizens are from India! They come from Sindh and Goa, Bombay and Malabar, Madras and the Coringa hills, Calcutta and Sylhet—but these differences mean nothing to the gamins who swarm around the Maidan. They have their own names for every variety of foreign devil: the British are 'I-says' and the French are 'Merdes'. The Hindusthanis are, by the same token, 'Achhas': no matter whether a man is from Karachi or Chittagong, the lads will swarm after him, with their hands outstretched, shouting: 'Achha! Achha! Gimme cumshaw!'

They seem to be persuaded that the Achhas are all from one country—is it not the most diverting notion? There is even a factory that is spoken of as the 'Achha Hong'—of course it has no flag of its own.

~

Neel's days began early in the Achha Hong. Bahram was a man of settled habits, and his retainers and employees had to arrange their time to suit his will and convenience. For Neel this meant that he had to rise while it was still dark, for it was he who bore the responsibility of making sure that Bahram's daftar was cleaned and made ready in exact accordance with his wishes. The Seth would not tolerate any imprecision in this matter: the room had to be swept at least half an hour before he made his entry, so as to give the dust time to settle; Neel's desk and chair had to be placed exactly so, pushed against that corner of the far wall and nowhere else. Making sure of all this was no mean feat, for it involved waking and chivvying many others, some of whom were not at all inclined to take orders from a munshi as young and inexperienced as Neel.

The daftar was as strange a room as any Neel had ever seen: it looked as though it had been transported to China from some chilly part of northern Europe—its ceiling was high and raftered, like that of a chapel, and it even had a fireplace and mantel.

It was Vico who told Neel how the Seth had come into the occupancy of his daftar. In his early days in Canton, Bahram, like most other Parsi merchants, had resided in the Dutch Factory: the story went that in the distant past in Gujarat, the Parsis had been of great help to merchants from the Netherlands—later they, in turn, had offered the Parsis shelter when they began to trade with China. Back in Surat, Bahram's grandfather too had once had a trading partner from Amsterdam, and it was this connection that had first brought Bahram to the Dutch Factory. But Bahram had never much cared for that hong; it was a dull, solemn kind of place where a loud laugh or raised voice could fetch disapproving glares and even dumbcowings. Besides, as one of the youngest members of the Bombay contingent, Bahram had almost always been assigned the dampest and darkest rooms in the complex. Nor did it add to his comfort that so many other Parsis were living in that hong—including many elders who believed it to be their duty to keep an eye on him—so when he learnt that a fine apartment had become available in another building, he had wasted no time in going to take a look.

It turned out that the establishment in question was the Fungtai Hong, which was a 'chow-chow' or miscellaneous factory. The Fungtai's frontage was modest by comparison with some of its neighbours. Like all the factories it was not really a single edifice, but rather a row of houses, connected by arched gateways and covered corridors, each building being separated from the others by a courtyard. The houses were not all of the same size: some were small, while others were large enough to be divided into several apartments, each with its own kitchen, godown, daftar, khazana and living quarters. The houses at the rear were generally the least desirable: being separated from the Maidan by numerous corridors and courtyards they were darker and dingier than those in front; some were like tenements and their cell-like rooms were occupied by the poorest of Fanqui-town's foreign sojourners—small-time traders and money-jobbers, servants and minor daftardars.

The most desirable lodgings in Fanqui-town were those that looked out on the Maidan, but these were few in number since the buildings were so narrow-fronted. They were considered a great luxury and were priced accordingly but even then it was very rare for an apartment with a view to become available. So when Bahram saw that he was being offered a suite that looked out on the Maidan he was quick to put down an advance. Since then, he had rented the same suite on every subsequent visit, adding a few more rooms each time, to accommodate his growing entourage of shroffs, khidmatgars, daftardars and kitchen staff.

Later, following Bahram's example, many other Bombay merchants had started to gravitate towards the Fungtai, which was how the factory came to be known as the 'Achha Hong'. But the distinction of being the first Parsi to move there belonged to Bahram, and now, having sojourned there for more than two decades, he occupied the best rooms in the building as if by right: his establishment included a godown, a kitchen, a khazana, and several small cubicles and dormitories to accommodate his entourage of fifteen employees. His own apartment was on the top floor, and it consisted of a spacious but gloomy bedroom, a frigid bathroom and a dining room that was only used on special occasions. And then, of course, there was the daftar, with its fine view of the Maidan and the river—over the years, its mullioned window had become one of the minor landmarks of the foreign enclave and many an old resident had been known to point it out to newcomers: 'Take a dekko up there; that's where Barry Moddie has his daftar.'

But Bahram was not, of course, the only merchant ever to use that room: in years when he chose to remain in Bombay over the trading season, it was rented out to others. Several of the apartment's former occupants had left behind traces of their tenancy, for it often happened, at the end of a season, that a merchant would find himself burdened with more possessions than he could conveniently carry home: in those circumstances, the easiest thing to do was to leave them behind. In this fashion a large collection of miscellaneous objects had accumulated in the daftar: waist-high figurines with nodding heads, pagodas carved out of wood, lacquered mirrors, a silver urn that was actually a nutmeg grater, and a glass bowl with a perpetually circling, goggle-eyed goldfish. Many of these things belonged to Bahram, including an enigmatic boulder that sat in one of the room's darker corners, blanketed in dust: it was large, grey and so pock-marked with holes that it looked as if it had been eaten from within by maggots.

'You know who gave that thing?' said Bahram to Neel one morning, pointing to the boulder. 'It was Chunqua, my old comprador. One fine day he comes here and says he has brought a present to do chin-chin. So I said, all right, why not? So then six fellows come up carrying this rock. Must be some joke, I thought: the fellow has hidden some jewel or something inside—now suddenly he will pull it out and make a big surprise. But no! He tells me his great-great-grandfather has brought it from Lake Tai, which is famous for stones—(just imagine, hah? for rocks also these Chinese fellows have "famous places": like laddoos and mithais for us). But after the rock was brought back to his house, his forefather decided the damn thing wasn't ready yet. See, no, how these fellows think? God had made this rock long ago, but that is not enough. So what they did, you know? They placed it under their house roof, so water could fall on it and make patterns. So much time these fellows have, hah? Not like you and me: no one is doing jaldi-jaldi and chull-chull. Ninety years the bloody rock sits under the roof, and then Chunqua decides it is ready at last and he brings to me as a chin-chin gift. Arré-baba, I thought to myself, what I will do with this damn-big rock? But can't refuse also or his feelings may be hurt. And can't take home either, or Beebeejee will dumbcow. "What?" she will say; "nothing else you can find in China, you are bringing me sticks and stones? What sort of budmashee you are learning there?" So what to do? I had to leave here.'

The rock was not the only object in the room to be imbued with a private significance for the Seth: his desk was another. This was, without a doubt, a beautifully made piece of furniture, a polished assemblage of red-tinted padauk wood and gleaming Paktong hardware. The front opened out to reveal a double row of arched pigeonholes, separated by columns that were carved to look like gilded book-spines. Below the writing surface lay nine solid drawers, each fitted with a brass handle and keyhole.

The desk's keys were all in Bahram's safekeeping, except for the largest which opened the front—Neel too was entrusted with a copy of this one, for it was his job to unlock the desk in the morning and to make sure that it was stocked with Bahram's chosen writing materials. The goose quills that the Seth professed to like were not hard to supply—but ink was a different matter, for Bahram would not put up with anything ordinary. While in Canton, he insisted on having at his disposal a finely carved inkstone, a couple of high-quality inksticks, and a little pot of special 'spring' water—all this so that he might, if the need arose, grind his own ink, in the patient, meditative fashion of a Chinese scholar. Given the fidgetiness of Bahram's disposition, this was the unlikeliest of conceits, but no matter—the ink-making materials, like the quills, had to be placed in exactly the same spot every day, near the top, left-hand corner of the desk. The irony was that neither the desk nor the ink-making materials ever saw much use since Bahram rarely sat down while he was in the daftar; his time there was spent mainly in pacing the floor, with his hands clasped behind his back; even when he had to sign a document, he usually did it standing by the window, with one of Neel's well-worn quills.

Only when he was eating his breakfast did Bahram make extended use of a chair. This meal was an elaborate affair, a ceremony that had evolved over many years: it was presided over by Mesto the cook, and it was served not in Bahram's private dining room, but on a marble-topped table in a corner of the daftar. Shortly before the Seth entered the daftar, Mesto would cover the table with a silk cloth; then, once Bahram was seated, he would lay before him an array of little plates and bowls, containing perhaps some *akoori*—eggs, scrambled with coriander leaves, green chillies and spring onions; some shu-mai dumplings, stuffed with minced chicken and mushrooms; maybe a couple of slices of toast and some skewers of satay as well; possibly a small helping of Madras-style congee, flavoured with ghee; and a small dish of *kheemo kaleji*—mutton minced with liver. And so on.

Bahram's breakfast always ended with a beverage that Mesto claimed to have invented himself: the drink was made with tea leaves but it bore no resemblance to the *chàh* that was commonly served in Canton—indeed it was considered so revolting by the Achha Hong's Chinese visitors that the very smell of it had made a couple of them vomit ('Just look,' said Vico, disparagingly, 'these fellows are happy to eat snakes and scorpions but milk they cannot take!').

Although it was Mesto who prepared the beverage, the responsibility for procuring the ingredients fell to Vico—and this was no small matter, since one of the drink's most important requirements was milk, a commodity that was harder to obtain, in Canton, than myrrh or myrobalans. The foreign enclave's main source consisted of a few cows that belonged to the Danish Hong; since many of the European merchants could not do without cream, butter and cheese, the Danes' entire supply was spoken for as soon as it had squirted into the pail. But the tireless Vico had discovered another provider: directly across the river from the foreign enclave, on Honam Island, lay an immense Buddhist monastery which housed a sizeable contingent of Tibetan monks. Being accustomed to buttered tea and other comestibles that required milk, the Tibetans kept, as a substitute for yaks, a small herd of buffaloes: these were the animals that provided the milk for Mesto's beverage. He boiled it with a measure of dark Bohea leaves and a sprinkling of cloves, cinnamon and star anise—all this was rounded off with a few handfuls of cheeni, the refined Chinese sugar that had recently become popular in Bombay. The resulting confection was called 'chai' or 'chai-garam' (the latter being a reference to the garam masala that went into it): Bahram could not do without it, and tumblers were brought to him at regular intervals, providing the punctuation for the passage of his day.

Chai was the beverage of choice not just for Bahram but for the whole of the Achha Hong, and everyone in Bahram's entourage listened keenly for the voices of the peons who came through periodically, chanting: Chai-garam, chai-garam! Particularly eagerly awaited was the mid-morning tumbler of chai, which was usually served with a snack. Of these the one that was most commonly provided was a Uighur speciality called a *samsa*—these were small triangles of pastry, stuffed usually with minced meat; baked in portable tandoors they were sold hot in the Maidan and were easy to procure. Being the ancestor of a popular Indian snack, they were consumed with much relish in the Achha Hong and were spoken of familiarly by their Hindusthani name—*samosa*.

Like everyone else in the Achha Hong, Neel too was soon looking forward eagerly to his mid-morning samosa and chai-garam. But to him the sound of these unfamiliar words was just as savoury as the items that bore their names. He found that he was constantly learning new words from the others in Bahram's entourage: some, like 'chai', came from Cantonese, while others were brought in from the Portuguese by Vico—like 'falto' for example, meaning fraudulent or false, which became *phaltu* on Achha tongues.

Even as he was settling in, it became clear to Neel that No. 1 Fungtai Hong was a world in itself, with its own foods and words, rituals and routines: it was as if the inmates were the first inhabitants of a new country, a yet unmade Achha-sthan. What was more, all its residents, from the lowliest of broom-wielding kussabs to the most fastidious of coin-sifting shroffs, took a certain pride in their house, not unlike that of a family. This surprised Neel at first, for on the face of it, the idea that the Achhas might form a family of some kind was not just improbable but absurd: they were a motley gathering of men from distant parts of the Indian subcontinent and they spoke between them more than a dozen different languages; some were from areas under British or Portuguese rule, and others hailed from states governed by Nawabs or Nizams, Rajas or Rawals; amongst them there were Muslims, Christians, Hindus, Parsis and also a few who, back at home, would have been excluded by all. Had they not left the subcontinent their paths would never have crossed and few of them would ever have met or spoken with each other—far less thought of eating a meal together. At home, it would not have occurred to them to imagine that they might have much in common—but here, whether they liked it or not, there was no escaping those commonalities; they were thrust upon them every time they stepped out of doors, by the cries that greeted them in the Maidan: 'Achha! Aa-chaa?'

To protest the affront of this indiscriminate lumping-together served no purpose: the urchins cared nothing for whether you were a Kachhi Muslim or a Brahmin Catholic or a Parsi from Bombay. Was it possibly a matter of appearance? Or was it your clothes? Or the sound of your languages (but how, when they were all so different)? Or was it perhaps just a smell of spices that clung indifferently to all of you? Whatever it was, after a point you came to accept that there was something that tied you to the other Achhas: it was just a fact, inescapable, and you could not leave it behind any more than you could slough off your own skin and put on another. And strangely, once you had accepted this, it became real, this mysterious commonality that existed only in the eyes of the jinns and jai-boys of the Maidan, and you came to recognize that all of you had a stake in how the others were perceived and treated. And the longer you stayed under that roof, with the Maidan at your door, the stronger the bonds became—because the paradox was that these ties were knotted not by an excess of self-regard, but rather by a sense of shared shame. It was because you knew that almost all the 'black mud' that came to Canton was shipped from your own shores; and you knew also that even though your share of the riches that grew upon that mud was minuscule, that did not prevent the stench of it from clinging more closely to you than to any other kind of Alien.

~

The familiar sound of the chapel clock was as reassuring to Bahram as the view from his daftar's window: when he looked outside, at the Maidan, the scene was much as it had ever been—teams of touts swarming about, trying to find customers for the shamshoo-dens of Hog Lane; sailors and lascars pouring in through the landing ghat at Jackass Point, determined to make the most of their shore leave; bands of beggars standing under the trees and at the entrances to the lanes, clattering their clappers; porters scuttling between godowns and chop-boats; barbers plying their trade at their accustomed places, shaving foreheads and braiding queues under portable sunshades of bamboo matting.

Yet, despite the appearance of normality, it had been clear to Bahram from the moment he entered the Pearl River that things had indeed changed in China. In the past he would have left the *Anahita* at Lintin Island, at the mouth of the river: this was where cargo ships always went, on making the voyage over from India. But this time there was not a single ship to be seen at the island, only two old receiving hulks, one American and the other British. In years past it was from the decks of these mastless vessels that opium had been spirited away by fast-crabs. To watch those slim, powerful boats shooting through the water, sixty oars rising and falling in unison, had once been one of the most thrilling sights of the Pearl River. Now there was not a single fast-crab anywhere to be seen on the estuary. The hulks, whose decks had been hives of activity in the past, were abandoned and seemed almost to be keeling over.

Having been forewarned, Bahram had left the *Anahita* at Hong Kong, anchored in the narrow strait that separated the island from the headland of Kowloon. This too would have been inconceivable in the past, for ships had usually avoided that channel for fear of piracy. This year the whole opium fleet was anchored there, so there was at least the comfort of knowing that they would be able to provide some security for each other.

The conditions at the river's mouth had led Bahram to expect that Canton too would be drastically changed: he had been heartened to find Fanqui-town carrying on more or less as usual. It was only when his eyes strayed towards the floating townships of the Pearl River, as they did now, that he was reminded of one important respect in which the city was irrevocably changed, at least in relation to himself. By force of habit his eye went straight to the place where Chi-mei's boat had always been stationed: it was off to the right, where the Pearl met the North River to form a wide expanse of water known as White Swan Lake—over the last couple of decades Chi-mei had somehow succeeded in holding on to that mooring-place, even though she had changed vessels several times. In the early years, when her kitchen-boats were nondescript and modest in size, Bahram had been hard put to pick them out from the hundreds of vessels that were moored along the riverbank. But with the passage of time her boats had become bigger and more distinctive, and the last had been so eye-catching that he had been able to spot it without difficulty from the window of his daftar: it was a brightly painted vessel, with two decks and a stern shaped like an upcurved fishtail. His eyes had become habituated to seeking it out when he went to the window: when there was smoke spiralling up from the cooking fires, he knew that Chi-mei had lit her stoves and the day's work had begun—it was as if the rhythms of that boat were a mysterious but necessary counterpoint to those of his own daftar.

On arriving in Canton Bahram had half-hoped and half-expected to find Chi-mei's boat still in its accustomed place; it was, in a sense, his own property too, since he had contributed liberally to its purchase: he would have liked to be able to dispose of it himself.

The matter had been much on his mind during the last leg of the journey, from Whampoa to Canton, and he had intended to take it up with his comprador, Chunqua, at the earliest opportunity. But when he arrived at Jackass Point, Chunqua's familiar face was nowhere to be seen: Bahram and his entourage were received instead by one of Chunqua's sons, who went by the name of Tinqua. It was from him that Bahram learnt that his old comprador had died some months before, after a long illness—and as was the custom his sons had inherited their father's clients.

Bahram was shaken by the news: Chunqua had been his comprador for a long time; they had started working together when they were both in their twenties, and they had accompanied each other into prosperity and middle-age. The bonds of trust and affection between them had been very deep: they had known each other's families and when Bahram was away it was Chunqua who had looked after Chi-mei and Freddy; he had kept an avuncular eye on the boy's upbringing and it was through him that Bahram had sent them money and gifts.

The loss of Chunqua meant the severing of yet another of Bahram's ties to Canton: he had known his comprador's sons since their childhood but he could not imagine any of them taking their father's place—least of all Tinqua, who was a flighty young man, with little interest in his work. When Bahram asked him about Chi-mei's boat he replied off-handedly that it had been sold—to whom he did not know.

Every time Bahram stepped up to the window now his eyes would stray automatically to the place where the boat had been moored in the past—and when they didn't find what they were looking for, a twinge would shoot through him, making him flinch.

It was strange that the absence of a single vessel could create a gap in such a densely crowded landscape.

The other pole of Bahram's life in Fanqui-town was not visible from his window: it was the Canton Chamber of Commerce, which had its premises inside the compound of the Danish Factory.

The Chamber was a more significant body than was suggested by its name: not only did it regulate and speak for the merchants of the foreign enclave, it also controlled the heartbeat of Fanqui-town's busy social life. Many of the foreign merchants in Canton had spent time in India and were accustomed to the amenities offered by the Byculla Club, the Bengal Club and the like. There being no similar establishment in Canton, the Chamber of Commerce had become willy-nilly the nearest equivalent. It occupied one of the largest buildings in Fanqui-town: House No. 2 in the Danish Factory. On the ground floor were the Chamber's offices and the Great Hall, which was large enough to accommodate meetings of the entire General Body. The social facilities were on the floor above: this part of the building was known as 'the Club' and those members who were willing to pay the extra dues could avail themselves of a smoking room, a taproom, a library, a reception room, a veranda, where tiffin was served when the weather permitted, and a dining room with windows that looked out on a tidal sandbank called Shamian.

The building had yet another floor, above, where lay several sumptuous suites and boardrooms. These were closed to all but a few—the President and the members of the powerful Committee that ran the Chamber. Officially this body was known as the 'Committee of the Chamber'—but in Fanqui-town everyone spoke of it simply as 'The Committee'.

There was one respect however in which the Chamber differed quite markedly from the Bengal and Byculla clubs: the exclusion of Asiatics was here a matter of discretion rather than procedure. This policy was necessitated by the peculiar circumstances of the Canton trade, in which a very large proportion of the incoming goods were shipped from Bombay and Calcutta. Since many of the supply chains, especially of Malwa opium, were controlled by Indian businessmen it was acknowledged to be impolitic to enforce too rigidly the racial norms that were followed by the clubs of the Indian subcontinent. Instead, the Chamber's dues were fixed at very elevated levels, ostensibly to discourage undesirables of all sorts. It was the custom moreover for the Committee to include at least one Parsi—usually the most senior member of the community then in residence in Canton. Among the Bombay merchants this was a hugely coveted appointment, a coronation of sorts, because the Committee was in effect the foreign enclave's unofficial Cabinet.

Bahram had been in Canton only a week when Vico came up to the daftar with a letter that was stamped with the seal of Mr Hugh Hamilton Lindsay, the current President of the Chamber of Commerce and thus also the head of the Committee. Being well-versed in the conventions and usages of Fanqui-town Vico had a fair idea of what the letter was about. He grinned broadly as he held it up: Look, patrão, see what has come!

The letter was not unexpected, of course, but Bahram was still conscious of an almost childlike thrill when he cracked the seal. This was what he had dreamt of when he first came to Canton, decades ago: to be recognized as the leader of Canton's Achhas.

He smiled: Yes, Vico—I've been invited to join the Committee.

Accompanying the letter was a handwritten note inviting Bahram to a dinner where several other members of the Committee would be present.

Bahram looked up to find Vico grinning as though the triumph were his own. Arré patrão! See what you have become now? You are a Seth of Seths—a Nagar-seth, a Jagat-seth! The whole world is at your feet.

Bahram tried to shrug off the tribute but when he glanced at the letter again his chest swelled with pride: he folded it carefully and slipped it into the chest-pouch of his angarkha, where it lay close to his heart; it was proof that he had now joined the ranks of such great merchants as Seth Jamsetjee Readymoney and Seth Jamsetjee Jeejeebhoy; it was confirmation that he, Bahramji Naurozji Modi, whose mother had made ends meet by embroidering shawls, had become a leader amongst a group that included some of the world's richest men.

The next morning, Zadig walked into the daftar, with his arms wide open: Arré, Bahram-bhai! Is it true that you've been invited to join the Committee?

It did not surprise Bahram that Zadig was abreast of the news. Yes, Zadig Bey, it's true.

Mabrook Bahram-bhai! I'm really glad.

Oh it's no great thing, said Bahram modestly. The Committee is just a place for people to talk. Behind the scenes it'll be the same people making all the decisions.

Zadig answered with an emphatic shake of his head. Oh no Bahram-bhai. That may have been true in the past, but it's going to change very soon.

What do you mean? said Bahram.

Haven't you heard? said Zadig with a smile. William Jardine has decided to leave Canton. He is going back to England!

This took Bahram completely by surprise: William Jardine had been for at least a decade the most influential man in Fanqui-town. His firm, Jardine, Matheson & Company, was one of the largest players in the Canton trade and he had for years been pushing aggressively to expand the Chinese opium market. In India, too, Jardine had an extensive network of friends and was idolized by many; within Bombay's business circles Bahram was one of the few to be less than smitten with him. This was because Jardine had close ties with a rival Parsi firm and this alliance had caused Bahram many headaches in the past. For Bahram, Jardine's departure was a thing so fervently to be wished for that he could not believe that it might actually happen.

Are you sure, Zadig Bey? Why would Jardine leave for England? He hasn't been home in years.

The choice isn't his any more, said Zadig. The Chinese authorities have come to know that his company has been sending ships to the northern ports of China, looking for new outlets for opium. The rumour is that they're planning to throw Jardine out of the country. Rather than face extradition he will leave on his own.

With Jardine gone, said Bahram, everything will change in the Chamber.

Yes, said Zadig with a smile. I think you'll find yourself making many new friends. In fact I wouldn't be surprised if you received some overtures even from Mr Dent.

Dent? Lancelot Dent?

Who else?

Lancelot Dent was the younger brother of Thomas Dent, who had founded one of Canton's most important business houses: Dent & Company. Bahram had known Tom Dent for a long time: a Scotsman of the old school, he was thrifty, modest and unpretentious; he and Bahram had always got on well with each other and for some years they had worked as partners, competing successfully with the formidable Jardine, Matheson combine. But some nine or ten years ago, Tom Dent's health had begun to fail and he had returned to Britain, leaving the company in the hands of his younger brother—and Lancelot Dent was an entirely different kind of man, glib of tongue, nakedly ambitious, resentful of his competitors and dismissive of those he considered less gifted than himself. His friends were few and his enemies legion, but even the worst of them could not deny that Lancelot Dent was a brilliant and far-sighted businessman: it was public knowledge that under his leadership the profits of Dent & Company had overtaken those of Jardine, Matheson. Yet, despite his commercial successes, Lancelot Dent had never commanded much influence in Fanqui-town; unlike Jardine, who was charming as well as ambitious, he was an awkward, abrasive man, with little talent for endearing himself to others. He had certainly never gone out of his way to befriend Bahram—and for his part, Bahram too had kept his distance, for he had had the impression that the younger man regarded him as a quaint old character with superannuated notions.

I've hardly exchanged a word with Lancelot Dent since Tom left for England.

Zadig laughed. Yes, but you weren't on the Committee then, Bahram-bhai, hai-na? You wait and see. He'll be chatting you up very soon. And nor will he be the only one.

Why do you say that?

The Angrezes—and I mean by that the Americans as well as the British—are not all of one mind right now. There's a lot of confusion about what has been happening here these last few months. Jardine and his party have been pushing for a show of force from the British government. But there are other views too: there are some who think this is just a passing phase and the opium trade will soon be back to what it was.

But that is possible, isn't it? said Bahram. After all, the Chinese have made noises about putting a stop to the trade before. For a few months there's a big tamasha about it and then it all goes back to normal.

Zadig shook his head: Not this time, Bahram-bhai. It's different now; I think the Chinese are serious this time.

Why do you say that, Zadig Bey?

Just look around you, Bahram-bhai. Did you see a single fast-crab on your way down to Canton? When they were first seized and burned some people said it was only a gesture, and new boats would be back on the river in a couple of months. But no. Some of the retailers did try to rebuild their crabs, and the mandarins burned them again. In the last few weeks they have arrested hundreds of opium-dealers; some have been thrown in prison, some have been executed. It's become almost impossible to bring opium ashore. It's reached a point where the fanquis have started doing something they had never done before: they have begun transporting the drug themselves. They hide it in their cutters and pinnaces and send it upriver with their lascars. That way, if the boats are caught, they'll pass it off on the lascars.

But the risk is slight, no? said Bahram. After all, the Chinese don't usually interfere too much with boats that belong to foreign ships.

But that too is changing, Bahram-bhai, said Zadig. It's true that the Chinese have always been very careful in dealing with us foreigners: they've avoided confrontation and violence to a degree that is hard to imagine in any other country. But in January this year they stopped an Englishman's boat and when they found opium inside it, they confiscated the goods and expelled him from China. And you know of course what happened when Admiral Maitland came here with his fleet? The Chinese would meet neither the Admiral nor Captain Elliott, the British Representative. It was the usual business about protocol and kowtowing and all the rest. The fleet left having achieved no purpose other than to provoke and anger the Chinese. Now on both sides there is confusion and anger. The Chinese are determined to stop the opium trade but they are divided on how to do it. And the British too are not sure of how to respond.

Zadig gave Bahram a smile. That is why I am glad I'm not in your place, Bahram-bhai.

Why, exactly?

Because the Committee is where these battles will be fought. And you will be in the middle of it. You may even be the one who sways the balance. After all, the opium that is traded here comes almost entirely from Hindusthan. Your voice will carry great weight.

Bahram shook his head. You are putting too much on my shoulders, Zadig Bey. I can only speak for myself—not for anyone else. Certainly not for all of Hindusthan.

But you will have to do it Bahram-bhai, said Zadig. And not just for Hindusthan—you will have to speak for all of us who are neither British nor American nor Chinese. You will have to ask yourself: what of the future? How do we safeguard our interests in the event of war? Who will win, the Europeans or the Chinese? The power of the Europeans we have seen at work, in Egypt and in India, where it could not be withstood. But we know also, you and I, that China is not Egypt or India: if you compare Chinese methods of ruling with those of our Sultans, Shahs and Maharajas, it is clear that the Chinese ways are incomparably better—government is indeed their religion. And if the Chinese manage to hold off the Europeans, what will become of us, and our relations with them? We too will become suspect in their eyes. We who have traded here for generations, will find ourselves banned from coming again.

Bahram laughed. Zadig-bhai you've always been too much of a philosopher; I think it's because you spend so much time staring at those clocks of yours—you look too far ahead. You can't expect me to make decisions based on what might happen in the future.

Zadig looked Bahram straight in the eye. But there is another question too, isn't there, Bahram-bhai? The question of whether it is right to carry on trading in opium? In the past it was not clear whether the Chinese were really against it. But now there can be no doubt.

There was something in Zadig's voice—a note of disapproval or accusation—that made Bahram smart. He could feel himself growing heated now, and having no wish to provoke a quarrel with his old friend, he forced himself to lower his voice.

How can you say that, Zadig-bhai? Just because an order has come from Beijing does not mean that all of China is for it. If the people were against it, then the opium trade wouldn't exist.

There are many things in the world, Bahram-bhai, that do exist, despite the wishes of the people. Thieves, dacoits, famines, fires—isn't it the task of rulers to protect their people from these things?

Zadig Bey, said Bahram, you know as well as I do that the rulers of this country have all grown rich from opium. The mandarins could stop the trade tomorrow if they wanted to: the reason they have allowed it to go on is because they make money from it too. It's not in anyone's power to force opium on China. After all, this is not some helpless little kingdom to be kicked around by others: it is one of the biggest, most powerful countries on earth. Look at how they constantly bully and harass their neighbours, calling them 'barbarians' and all that.

Yes, Bahram-bhai, said Zadig quietly. What you say is not untrue. But in life it is not only the weak and helpless who are always treated unjustly. Just because a country is strong and obdurate and has its own ways of thinking—that does not mean it cannot be wronged.

Bahram sighed: he realized now that one of the ways in which Canton had changed for him was that he would not be able to speak freely to Zadig any more.

Let's talk about other things, Zadig-bhai, he said wearily. Tell me, how is business?

~

From the deck of the *Redruth* the island looked like a gigantic lizard, with its immense, rearing head thrust into the sea and its mountainous spine curving into a curling tail.

The brooding peaks and cloud-wreathed crags were like a magnet to Paulette from the start. The attraction was difficult to explain for there was little of interest to be seen on those desolate scrub-covered slopes. The vegetation was sparse and lacking in interest: such trees as there may once have been had been hacked down by the people who lived in the impoverished little villages that were scattered around the island's rim. They had done a thorough job of it too, for almost nothing remained now but a few stunted trunks and wind-twisted branches. Apart from that, the slopes seemed to offer nothing but scree and scrub—and the two were sometimes almost indistinguishable in colour, now that the greenery had turned a dull autumnal brown.

To the north of the bay where the *Redruth* was anchored lay several villages, on the shores of the promontory of Kowloon. A couple of times a day bumboats would paddle across the channel to offer provisions: chickens, pigs, eggs, quinces, oranges, and many different kinds of vegetables. The boats were mostly rowed by women and children, and except when it came to the matter of bargaining, the villagers were usually quite friendly. But when on land their attitude changed; they had had bad experiences with drunken foreign sailors and as a result they were apt to treat landing parties with suspicion and even outright hostility. The few foreigners who had rowed over to Kowloon had had an uncomfortable time of it, being followed everywhere with chants of *gwai-lou, faan—gwai* and *sei-gwai-lou!*

On Hong Kong, by contrast, visitors could be sure of being left alone since it was so sparsely inhabited. The stretch of land that lay closest to the *Redruth* for instance was empty of habitation. The nearest hamlet was a good distance away: it was not much more than a clump of dilapidated little hutments, surrounded by rice fields. Although there was little there to attract mainlanders, the island offered something of inestimable value to the foreign ships: good clean drinking water, which was to be had in abundance from the many clear streams that came tumbling down from the island's peaks and crags.

Once every day, and sometimes more, a gig, loaded with empty barrels, would make the journey over from the *Redruth* to the narrow strip of pebbled beach that ran along the bay. Paulette would often accompany the sailors and while they were filling their barrels and washing their clothes she would wander along the beach or climb the slopes.

One day she followed a stream for a good half-mile, clambering up the steep, boulder-strewn nullah that guided it down from the peak. It was hard going, with little reward, and she was about to turn back when she looked ahead and spotted a hollow in the hillside, some hundred yards further up. There were white smudges on its sides, and on looking more closely she saw that a cluster of flowering plants was growing inside. She took off her shoes and pressed on, climbing over an escarpment of jagged rock and tearing her skirt in the process. But it was well worth it for she soon found herself looking at a bunch of exquisite white blooms: she had seen their like before, in Calcutta's Botanical Gardens: they were 'Lady's Slipper' orchids—*Cypripedium purpuratum*.

She went bounding down in delight and the next day she brought Fitcher with her. This time they went higher still and were rewarded with another find, hidden between two boulders: a pale red orchid. It was new to Paulette but Fitcher identified it at a glance: *Sarcanthus teretifolius*.

They had climbed a fair distance now and when they sat down to catch their breath Paulette was startled by the splendour of the vista below: the tall-masted ships looked tiny against the blue band of the channel; beyond lay the crags of the Chinese mainland, stretching into the hazy distance.

'You are so fortunate, sir,' said Paulette, 'to have wandered in the forests and mountains of China. How thrilling it must be to botanize in these vast and beautiful wilds.'

Fitcher turned to her with a startled expression. 'Wander? What can ee be thinking of? Ee don't imagine, d'ee, that I was collecting in the wild in Canton?'

'Were you not, sir?' said Paulette in surprise. 'But then how did you find all those new plants? All your introductions?'

Fitcher gave a bark of a laugh. 'In nurseries—just as I would have at home.'

'Really, sir?'

Fitcher nodded: traipsing through forests was out of the question in China since foreigners were not allowed to venture beyond Canton and Macau. The only Europeans who had seen anything of the flora of the interior were a few Jesuits, and a couple of naturalists who had had the good fortune to accompany diplomatic missions to Peking. Every other would-be plant-hunter was confined to those two southern cities, both of them populous, bustling, noisy places, in which nothing 'wild' had existed for centuries.

'But what about Mr William Kerr?' said Paulette. 'Did he not introduce the "heavenly bamboo" and *Begonia grandis* and the "Lady Banks Rose"? Surely they did not come from nurseries?'

'Oh yes,' said Fitcher. 'They did.'

Everything that Billy Kerr had collected, said Fitcher, indeed most anything that any plant collector had obtained in China—all the begonias, azaleas, moutans, lilies, chrysanthemums and roses that had already transformed the world's gardens—all these floral riches had come from just one place: not a jungle, nor a mountain, nor a swamp, but a set of nurseries, run by professional gardeners.

Paulette, who had been listening in rapt attention, let out a gasp. 'Is it true, sir? And where are they, these nurseries?'

'On the island of Honam, opposite Canton.'

At the western end of the island there was a stretch of well-watered ground, said Fitcher. That was where the nurseries were: foreigners called them the 'Fa-Tee Gardens'. It cost eight Spanish dollars to get a chop to go there—and they were only open a few days in the week.

'And what are they like, sir, these nurseries?'

Fitcher opened and closed his mouth several times as he pondered this. 'They're a maze,' he said at last, 'like the mizzy-maze at Hampton Court. Every time ee think ee've seen everything, ee'll find that ee've scarcely begun. Ee're just wandering around, gaking at what ee're allowed to see, mazed, like a sheep in a storm.'

Paulette clutched her knees and sighed. 'Oh I wish I could see them for myself, sir.'

'But that ee won't,' said Fitcher. 'So ee may as well put it out of eer mind.'

eight

~

Nov 14, Markwick's Hotel

Dearest Puggly, don't you hate it when people write letters from faraway places without telling you about their lodgings? My brother, when he went to London, wrote not a word about his quarters which drove me quite to distraction—for silly painterly fellow that I am, I can see nothing until I see *that*. And it strikes me now that I am guilty of the same thing—I have told you nothing at all about my room.

Well, my dear Lady Puggleminster, you shall know all about Mr Markwick's hotel: it is right in the heart of Fanqui-town, halfway between our two principal thoroughfares, which are known, conveniently, as Old China Street and New China Street. Although they are called streets you must not imagine them to be wide or extensive roadways, like Chowringhee or the Esplanade. Fanqui-town's streets go no further than the width of the enclave, which measures only a few hundred feet. I am not sure our streets should even be known by that name, for they are like a set of parallel mews, running between the factories: they lead from the Maidan to the outer boundary of the enclave, which is marked by a busy roadway called Thirteen Hong Street.

Within the enclave there are only three streets and one of them is actually a tiny gali, like you might see in Kidderpore. It is called Hog Lane and it is so narrow that two men can scarcely pass abreast without rubbing up against each other—and I must say Puggly dear that one is sometimes witness there to the most *unseemly* sights. The passageway is lined with ill-lit dens and foul-smelling shacks: they serve brews that go by such names as 'hocksaw' and 'shamshoo' (the latter, I am told, is doctored with opium and flavoured with the tails of certain lizards). These dens are very popular among the sailors and lascars who come up to Fanqui-town on their shore-leave days. Having spent weeks at anchor in Whampoa the poor fellows are half crazed with boredom and so eager to spend their drink-penny that they do not even take the trouble to sit down while they imbibe. Indeed no chairs or benches are provided for them, but only ropes, strung up at the height of a man's chest. The function of these peculiar articles of furniture (for such indeed they are) was revealed to me when I saw a half-dozen seafarers hanging from them, with their arms flung over, dribbling vomit from their mouths. The ropes serve to keep them upright after they have cast up their accounts—should they fall on the floor they would probably drown in their own regurgitated swill. Some of these liberty-men spend the whole of their shore leave in this fashion, swaying on their feet, their bodies slumped over the ropes and unconscious to the world.

I need scarcely add that drink is not all that is offered in these dens. One has only to step into the Lane to be besieged by ponce-shicers. 'Wanchi gai? Wanchi jai? What kind chicken wanchi? You talkee my. My savvy allo thing; allo thing have got.'

You must not imagine, my dear Miss Pugglemore, that your poor Robin would ever dream of availing of these offerings. Yet it would be idle to deny that there is something strangely thrilling about a place where every desire can be provided for and every want met (though not perhaps always to complete satisfaction: just yesterday, as I was walking by, a sailor disappeared into the shadows of Hog Lane with a creature that looked like a painted hag. A moment later the nautical knight let out a dreadful yell: 'God help me shippies! A travesty has me in hand, and it'll be down the chute with my fore-tackle if I'm not cut loose!').

New China Street is positively genteel in comparison to Hog Lane, although it is only a clamorous, crowded gali, like those around Calcutta's Bow Bazaar: here too shops are stacked upon shops; here too touts will tug at your clothes until you begin to wonder what their intentions are. The older fanquis are not daunted by this and will clear a path by laying about with their whangees—but since I cannot conceive of carrying one I generally try to stay clear of this street.

By comparison with our other roadways Old China Street is a haven of cleanliness and quiet: it is in fact more an arcade than a roadway, being lined with shophouses. Some of the shophouses are quite tall but they are dwarfed by the walls of the factories that flank the street. The gap overhead is covered with a kind of matting, which is laid down so artfully that below, at the level of the street, it is always cool and shady, like a pathway in a forest. As for the shops, they are utterly beguiling and their wares are laid out in the most charming fashion, on shelves and in glass-topped cases. There are shops for lacquerware, pewterware, silk and souvenirs of all kinds (the most ingenious of these are some amazing multi-layered balls, carved out of whole blocks of ivory, with the outer shell enclosing others of diminishing size). The name of every merchant is written above the door, in English and Chinese, and there is always a sign to mark his calling: 'Lacquer Merchant', 'Pewter Seller', 'Ivory Carver' and the like. Many other banners, pennants and painted signs are strung above the shops and when there is a breeze the whole street shimmers and flutters with colour. It is quite *wonderfully* picturesque.

The shopkeepers are, to my mind, even more diverting than their shops. One of my favourites is Mr Wong, the tailor; he is so friendly, and so eager to show off his wares that it seems cruel to go by without stopping for a cup of tea. He is a most *antic* creature: this morning, while I was sitting there he rushed out to wave to a group of sailors. 'Hi! You there Jack!' he shouted. 'You there Tar! Damn my eyes! What thing wanchi buy?'

The sailors were several sheets to the wind and one of them shouted back: 'What do I want to buy? Why you mallet-headed porpoise, I want to buy a Welsh wig with sleeves on it.'

Mr Wong never doubts that he has every article of clothing a fanqui could possibly want, so he pointed at once to a green gown. 'Can do, can do! Look-see here,' he cried. 'Have got what-thing Mister Tar wanchi.'

At this the sailors went into convulsions of laughter and one of them cried out: 'Damn my eyes! That thing is no more a Welsh wig than you are the Queen of England!'

Mr Wong, I need hardly say, was quite *crushed*.

At the far end of Old China Street, on the other side of Thirteen Hong Street, is the Consoo—or 'Council House'. It is built in the style of a mandarin's 'yamen' which is an elaborate kind of daftar. It is surrounded by a high wall, beyond which rise the upswept roofs of many halls and pavilions. The buildings are graceful in appearance, yet most fanquis regard the Consoo House with an apprehension that borders on dread—for that is where they are summoned when the mandarins wish to call them to account!

But why, in heaven's name, am I rattling on about the streets and the Consoo House when I meant to tell you about Markwick's Hotel? Well, it is not too late! Without another word I shall seize you by the hand—there!—and lead you towards my room.

Mr Markwick's Hotel is in the Imperial Factory which is one of the most interesting of the Thirteen Hongs. It is so called because it was once linked to the Austro-Hungarian Empire, and even though there are few Austrians to be seen in it now, the double-headed eagle of the Hapsburgs is still affixed to the gateway (for which reason the factory is known to locals as the 'Twin-Eagle Hong').

Mr Markwick runs his hotel in partnership with his Friend, Mr Lane. They both came out to China as boys, to work for the East India Company (Mr Markwick was a steward and Mr Lane a butler), and they have been Friends *forever*. They are a curious couple and look as though they belong in some childish ditty, for Mr Lane is short and fat and rather jolly, while Mr Markwick is tall and lugubrious and seems always to be sniffing, even when he is not. On the ground floor of their premises they run a shop where they sell all kinds of European goods and products: Hodgson's ale, Johannisberger wines, Rhenish clarets, umbrellas, watches, sextants and suchlike. They also run a coffee room, which is considered a great curiosity by the enclave's Chinese visitors; and of course there is a dining room too, and the fare it provides is most interesting, for Mr Markwick is a dab hand at adapting Chinese dishes for European tastes. One of his offerings is called 'chop-shui' and it is so popular amongst the seafaring tribe that he has been offered *vast* sums of money for the recipe, but he will not, on any account, part with it. He also sells a delicious sauce of his own invention, flavoured with Chinese condiments: it is known as Markwick's ketjup and old China hands cannot live without it.

The 'hotel' occupies the floors above and is spread over several houses. The buildings must have been quite grand once, but they have long since run to seed and are woefully in need of care. It is a warren of a place, with many dim hallways and cobwebbed vestibules (this suits me very well, I must admit, for it is easy to conceal oneself when some cranky-looking foreign-ghost goes lumbering by). The rooms are damp and sparsely furnished but by no means inexpensive for they cost a dollar a night! I would certainly not have been able to afford to stay at the hotel had I been required to pay the normal rate, but I have been most *singularly* fortunate Puggly dear: Mr Markwick was not, I think, very eager to have me mingling with his other guests (a man who sniffs the wind as diligently as he does cannot,

I imagine, have failed to pick up some of the tittle-tattle about me and my uncle) so he offered me a kind of attic, which is tucked away on the roof and costs less than half the price of the other rooms! But oh! I wish you could see it Puggly dear, for I think you would love it as much (or almost) as I do. Although small and draughty (I think it was once a chicken-coop), it is filled with light because it has a large window and a small terrace. The window is, to my mind, the room's best feature: I tell you, my sweet Puggly, I could spend the *whole day* sitting beside it, for it looks out on the Maidan, and it is like watching a mela that never ends, a tamasha to outdo all others in chuckmuckery.

The other great boon of this room is that it has given me a *most* extraordinary neighbour: he is an Armenian and lives on the floor below. He has been everywhere and speaks more languages than the best of dubashes. A man more imposing in presence and more pleasing in address I do not think I have ever met (. . . and no, my dear Marquise de Puggladour, just in case you are tempted to speculate, he is not the One—he is old enough to be my father and seems to be possessed of paltans of children). He reminds me a little of our Calcutta Armenians: he grew up in Cairo and learnt watchmaking from a Frenchman who went to Egypt with Napoleon (you may not credit it but Mr Karabedian has actually *met* the Bonaparte!). He describes himself as a 'Sing-song Man'—because he trades in watches, clocks and music-boxes which are all spoken of as 'sing-songs' in the Canton jargon. Such is the demand for them that Mr Karabedian is able to sell his best musical clocks for thousands of dollars (one has even been sent to the Emperor, in Peking!). After he has sold all his foreign sing-songs Mr Karabedian buys a great quantity of locally made clocks and watches—they are perfectly serviceable and produced at such little cost that he is able to sell them for a handsome profit in India and Egypt.

Mr Karabedian has been coming to Canton for a very long time and knows all the gup-shup—which tai-pans are at odds with each other, who is befriending whom, and which sets of people you cannot invite to dinner together (and yes, my dear Puggly, even in this tiny place there are many Sets and Cliques and Factions). There are even Royals of a sort, or at least there is an uncrowned King: he is Mr William Jardine, a great Nabob of Scottish origin. He is a personable man, tall, and, considering that he is in his mid-fifties, surprisingly youthful in appearance. Mr Chinnery has painted a portrait of him which is much celebrated: I confess I admired it too, at least until I saw Mr Jardine in the flesh. Now it seems to me that Mr Chinnery flattered him more than a little. If I were to paint Mr Jardine I would do it in the manner of the Velázquez portraits of Phillip the Fourth of Spain. Mr Jardine has an equally smooth and glowing face, and there is in his gaze the same certainty of power, the same self-satisfaction.

Mr Karabedian says he came to Canton as a doctor but grew tired of medicine and went into the Trade instead. He has made *millions* through it, mainly by selling opium—he is so industrious he keeps no chair in his office for fear of encouraging idle prattle and slothfulness. His company is called Jardine & Matheson, but his partner is an unremarkable man and Mr Jardine is rarely seen with him: when he walks abroad it is almost always in the company of his Friend—one Mr Wetmore who is Fanqui-town's great dandy, always exquisitely dressed. You should see how people scatter before them when they take their turns around the Maidan: there is so much salaaming and hat-raising that you would think Mr Jardine was the Grand Turk, out for a stroll with his most beloved BeeBee. Mr Jardine and Mr Wetmore are ever so solicitous with each other and Mr Karabedian says that at Balls (and yes, there are many of those in Fanqui-town) they always reserve the waltzes and polkas for each other, even though everyone *clamours* for their hands. But this touching attachment may alas be nearing its end. Mr Karabedian says that Mr Jardine is soon to make the 'ultimate sacrifice', by which is meant, leaving Canton and moving to England to get married. Mr Jardine is most reluctant to do this, not only because of his Friend but also because he has spent much of his life in the East and is deeply attached to it.

As you know, Puggly dear, nothing is of interest to me if I cannot see and paint it. I had never imagined that politics would ever fall into that class of things—but in listening to Mr Karabedian I have begun to conceive of an epic painting: it is a *delicious* thought for I could include in it many details from the gallery of pictures I carry around in my head. Just think of it! In Mr Jardine I have already found a window through which I can smuggle in a small touch of Velázquez; Mr Wetmore, on the other hand, would be perfect for an essay in the manner of Van Dyck. And there will be room for a Brueghel too, right beside Mr Jardine—for Fanqui-town has a Pretender as well as an uncrowned King! He is Mr Lancelot Dent—and despite his absurd name he is indeed a great magnate.

You may remember, Puggly dear—I once showed you an engraving of a wonderful painting by Pieter Brueghel the Younger? It was a picture of a couple of village lawyers: I recall in perfect detail the face of the younger man, puffed up with conceit and brimming with intrigue. This indeed is Mr Dent: Mr Karabedian says he is just as rich as Mr Jardine and controls even more of the flow of opium; he has apparently been content for many years to hover in the background because he has been preoccupied with building up his fortune. But having done so, he has now set his sights on Mr Jardine's crown. Mr Karabedian says that as a student at Edinburgh Mr Dent came under the influence of some obscure doctrine concerning the wealth of nations; he is now both a disciple and apostle of it and seeks to impose it on everything and everyone he encounters. Repellent though he is, I confess I feel a twinge of pity for him sometimes: can you imagine a more horrible fate than to be enslaved to a doctrine of *trade* and *economy*? It is as if a tailor had come to be convinced that nothing exists that does not fit the measure of his tape.

The more I think of my painting, the larger it becomes: there are so many people here who simply *cannot* be left out. The mandarins for example: there is one who is known to fanquis as 'the Hoppo'—and from the name you would imagine him to be some kind of kangaroo. But no, he is merely the Chief Customs Inspector of Canton—but his gowns and necklaces are so magnificent that you would think him to be Kublai Khan himself. And then there are the merchants of the Co-Hong—they are the only Chinese who are allowed to conduct business with foreigners. They are immensely rich and they wear the most *breathtaking* clothes: silken gowns with magnificent embroidered panels, and caps with glass beads that denote their rank.

And do you remember, Puggly dear, how in Calcutta I would spend long hours copying Mughal miniatures? Well, it has proved to be a most *fortunate* thing—for there is in Canton someone who would need to be painted in just such a fashion. He is a fabulously rich Parsi merchant from Bombay, Seth Bahramji Naurozji Modi. He is one of the great personages of Fanqui-town and a splendid figure he is too: he puts me in mind of Manohar's famous painting of the Emperor Akbar—with a turban, a flaring angarkha, a stoutish belly, and a fine muslin cummerbund.
Mr Karabedian is a great friend of his and says that all the factions are now desperately eager to win over the Seth.

You see, Puggly, what a great challenge my epic tableau has already become? And I have shown you only a small part of it. There are so many others: the editor of the *Canton Register*, for instance—Mr John Slade. He is *hugely* fat and has the look of a gargantuan salad, composed of diverse elements of the vegetable and animal kingdoms: what a *treat* it would be to paint him in the fashion of Archimboldo—his face as florid as a pomegranate; his whiskers glistening like the tail feathers of a dead pheasant; a belly with the contours of an ox's haunch and a neck like that of a bull. Mr Slade's voice is so loud that it has earned him the nickname of 'Thunderer'—and I can attest that it is well-deserved: I can hear him in my room when he is at the other end of the Maidan!

Then there is Dr Parker, who flaps about like a raven but is a most amiable man and runs a hospital where many Chinese patients are treated. And there is a Mr Innes who is some kind of Highland Chieftain and strides about the Maidan like a Crusader, picking fights with all who have the temerity to cross his path. Mr Karabedian says that he is persuaded that all his endeavours are willed by a Higher Power, even the selling of opium!

But in Fanqui-town this conviction is not unusual, even with the missionaries. There are several of them here—a horrid Herr Gut-something who is always hectoring everyone; and a Reverend Bridgman, who is insufferably priggish. I confess I detest these Missionaries, and it is not, I promise you, because they treat me with the pitying solicitousness that is the due of a Child of Sin. Mr Karabedian says they are utter *hypocrites* and he has seen them, with his own eyes, distributing Bibles from one side of a ship while selling opium from the other. But there is this at least to be said for them that they present a marvellous opportunity for an exercise in the Gothic style—what *fun* it would be to show them up for the ghouls and charlatans that they really are!

And that is still not the end of it, for I certainly could not leave out Mr Charles King. He does not, properly speaking, constitute a faction, being but a party of one—yet by virtue of the example he sets, he is counted a considerable force in Fanqui-town. He is the representative of Olyphant & Co., which is, according to Mr Karabedian, the only firm in Canton that has *never* traded in opium! Of course he gets no credit for this from the other fanquis—on the contrary he is *reviled* for his rectitude, and is forever being accused of toadying up to the mandarins. But neither threats nor mockery can sway Mr King: even though he is a mere *stripling* compared to the venerable grey beards who rule over Fanqui-town he has held stubbornly to his course—which takes, as you may imagine, no little courage in a pasturage where every other creature meekly follows the bellowing bulls who lead the herd.

Mr King is not quite thirty but he is already the Senior Partner in his firm (the founder, Mr Olyphant has long been gone from Canton). But to look at Mr King you would never think him to be a businessman—silly creature that I am, I cannot deny, Puggly dear, that one of the reasons why I am drawn to Mr King is that he bears a striking resemblance to the painter who stands higher in my esteem than any other modern Artist: the magnificent and tragic Théodore Géricault.

I have only ever seen one likeness of Géricault, a pen-and-ink drawing by a Frenchman whose name I cannot remember—it shows him in his youth, with dark curls tumbling over his brow, an *exquisitely* dimpled chin, and a gaze that is marvellously dreamy and yet a-glow with passion. Anyone who has ever studied that portrait will surely gasp (as I did) if they happen to set eyes on Mr King—for the likeness is quite *startling*!

You will remember, dear, that I once showed you a copy of Géricault's masterpiece 'The Raft of the *Medusa*'? You may recall also that we were so affected by his depiction of the plight of the doomed castaways on the raft that the print became quite *damp* with our tears? Only a man who had himself experienced great tragedy could create such a moving portrait of suffering and loss, we agreed: well, this is yet another aspect of Mr King's resemblance to the Artist of my imagination—for there attaches to him an air of the most *plangent* melancholy. So striking is this element of his appearance that it does not come as a surprise to learn (as I did from Mr Karabedian) that he has indeed suffered an almost unendurable loss.

It appears that Mr King's family circumstances were such that he had to leave his home, in America, when he was very young. He was sent to Canton when he was but seventeen years old—he was then even paler and more delicate in appearance than he is now, and was thus subjected to all manner of bullying and ballyragging by the rowdier fanquis. The tenor of their taunts will be apparent to you from the nickname he was given then—'Miss King' (and you may not credit it, Puggly dear, but this appellation is still in use, being frequently whispered behind his back. This is not the least of the reasons why I am so much in sympathy with Mr King for I am myself no stranger to such names ('Lady Chin'ry'! 'Hijra'!)). I too know very well what it is to be tormented by packs of loutish budmashes (oh, if you only knew, Puggly dear, of all my encounters with langooty-ripping thugs; of the many times I have had to fight bare-chuted with badzats . . .).

But Mr King was luckier than I—Providence took pity on him and granted him a Friend. A year or two after he came to Canton, it happened that another American lad travelled to China to join the same firm. His name was James Perit and he was by all accounts a Golden Youth, brilliant in intellect, of charming address, and blessed with uncommon good looks (I have seen a picture of him—and had I not known that it was painted in Canton I would have thought the sitter was none other than Mr Gainsborough's 'Blue Boy'!).

I do not know if this is all in my own head, Puggly dear (and I think it may well be so, because I am, as you know, an unregenerate dreamer)—but I am persuaded that my Géricault and the Blue Boy enjoyed the most perfect Friendship in the short time that was to be granted to them. But it would not last—for barely had James Perit reached the age of twenty-one when he contracted a virulent intermittent fever . . .

Well I will not draw it out, my darling Pugglee-ranee (the blots on this page will show you how much this tragedy *affects* me). Suffice it to say the Golden Youth was struck down—he now lies buried in the foreign cemetery on French Island, not far from Whampoa.

Poor Mr King—to be given a taste of a kind of happiness that is rarely granted to mortals, only to have it snatched away! He was utterly stricken with grief and has since dedicated himself to religion and good works (Mr Karabedian says that in a town that *teems* with hypocrites, Mr King is one of the few true Christians).

I will not conceal from you, Puggly dear, that before I knew of all the circumstances, it did occur to me to wonder, for a few precious moments, whether Mr King might not be the Friend I have dreamed of. But of course this is the most absurd of idle fancies: Mr King is impossibly high-minded and must regard me as a flighty, frivolous creature and a pagan as well (for none of which could I, in all conscience, blame him). Yet, I am not without consolation, for Mr King is nothing if not kind and treats me always with the greatest courtesy and consideration—he has even assured me that he will soon commission a portrait! He does not strike me as at all the kind of man who likes to hang his own likeness upon his walls so I suspect that his intention is to make a good Christian out of me—but I do not care: I cannot tell you how eagerly I await this commission!

As for the others I think they must gossip a great deal about me (Mr Karabedian says he has never known a place where there's more buck-buck than Fanqui-town). It is not uncommon for eyes to be sharply averted and voices to suddenly drop when I pass by. As to what is being said I need scarcely conjecture for many people here, especially the grandees, are well acquainted with Mr Chinnery for he has painted most of them: suffice it to say that I have so come to dread their sneers that I keep away from all who are within my Uncle's circle of acquaintance.

Well it is my lot and I must bear it. I console myself with the thought that I shall have some small measure of revenge when my painting is done.

But do not imagine for a moment, Pugglecita mi amor, that I have forgotten about the task that you and your benefactor enjoined upon me. I daily nurture the hope that I will meet someone who may be able to cast some light upon Mr Penrose's camellias.

And it would be remiss of me to conclude this without acknowledging receipt of your letter and thanking you for keeping me abreast of the happenings on the HMS *Redruth*. I was *delighted* to read about all the lovely plants you have found on this island of yours! Who would have thought that a place of such barren aspect would be so rich in greenery? And who, for that matter, would have imagined that my own sweet Puggly would one day take on the guise of an intrepid explorer?

As for the query with which you ended: why, of course, you can certainly depend on me to do whatever I can to help you with your spoken English! But in the meanwhile, I do strongly urge you to exercise some care in your choice of words. There is nothing wrong of course in speaking words of encouragement to the crew of the *Redruth*, especially when they do their job well, but you must be prudent in how you phrase what you say. Knowing you as I do, I understand very well that your motives were wholly innocent when you congratulated the bosun for his fine work on the ship's prow. But you should know Puggly dear, that it is not wholly a matter for surprise that he was taken aback by your well-meant sally: I confess that I too would be quite *astonished* if a young lady of tender years were to felicitate me on my dexterity in 'polishing the foc-stick'. Far be it from me to reproach you for your spontaneity, Puggly dear, but you must not always assume that it is *safe* to transpose French expressions directly into English. The English equivalent of *bâton-à-foc*, for instance, is definitely not 'foc-stick'—it is 'jib-boom'.

And no, dear, nor were you well-advised to tell the baffled bosun that your intention was only to compliment him on his skill with 'the mighty mast that protrudes from the front'. You should know, my dear Princesse de Puggleville, that sometimes it is not *wise* to persist in explaining oneself.

~

Bahram's methods of work were not easy for Neel to deal with. Back in the past, when he had himself employed a host of scribes and secretaries, in his own daftar, he had seldom needed to communicate at any length with his crannies, munshis and gomustas, since they were far better schooled than he in the time-hallowed canons that dictated the form and content of a zemindar's letters. Later, after his conviction for forgery, when he was awaiting transportation in Calcutta's Alipore Jail, he had earned himself many favours by composing missives for other inmates—but these too had required little effort, for his fellow convicts were mainly unlettered men, and no matter whether they were writing to a relative at home, or to a chokra in the next ward, they had deferred to Neel's literacy and left it to him to invent their words and shape their thoughts.

Such being his experience of letter-writing, Neel was caught unawares by the demands of Bahram's correspondence: the Seth's letters rarely followed any set forms and usages, being mostly intended to keep his associates informed of the situation in southern China. And nor could Neel expect any deference from the Seth, who seemed to think that a munshi was a minor flunkey—one who belonged, in the order of importance, somewhere between a valet and a shroff, his principal duties being those of tidying up his employer's verbal attire, and of picking through the coinage of his vocabulary to separate what was of value from what was not.

Neel's job was further complicated by the Seth's habits of dictation: he always composed on his feet and his restless pacing seemed to add to the turbulence of his words, which often came pouring out in braided torrents of speech, each rushing stream being silted with the sediment of many tongues—Gujarati, Hindusthani, English, pidgin, Cantonese. To stop the Seth when he was in full flow was inconceivable, and to pose a question about this phrase or that, or to ask the meaning of one word or another, was to risk an explosion of irritability—queries had to be deferred till later or, better still, referred to Vico. In the interim all Neel could do, to make sense of this gurgling snowmelt of sound, was to pay close attention, not just to what Bahram said, but also to the gestures, signs and facial expressions with which he amplified, enlarged upon, and even negated the burden of his words. This unspoken idiom could not be lightly ignored: once when Neel rendered a sentence as 'Mr Moddie affirms that he would be glad to comply', Bahram took him to task for his negligence—'Whatré? You didn't see, how I was doing with my hand, like-this, like-this. How you take that to mean "yes"? You cannot see it is "no"? Just dreaming or what?'

And then there was the window, which was a perennial source of disruption in the daftar: even though Neel's desk was in the far corner of the room, there was always a rich medley of sound to cope with, wafting in from below: the barriking of barrowmen and the drunken bellowing of sailors on the dicky-run; the keening of moochers and the clattering of clapperdudgeons; the whistling of tame songbirds, being promenaded in their cages and outbursts of gong-banging to mark the passage of consequential personages—and so on. The cacophony that welled out of the Maidan changed from minute to minute.

If the window was a source of disruption for Neel, it was far more so for his employer, who would often break off in mid-sentence and stand there as if hypnotized. Outlined against the frame, in his dome-like turban and wide-skirted angarkha, the Seth's form was so regal that Neel was sometimes led to wonder whether he was deliberately striking a pose for the benefit of the strollers on the Maidan. But Bahram was not a man who could stand still for long: after staring moodily into the distance, he would again begin to pace the floor, furiously, as though he were trying to outrun some hotly pursuing thought or memory. But then, glancing outside once more, he would spot some friend or acquaintance and his mood would change: leaping to the window he would thrust his head out and begin to shout greetings, sometimes in Gujarati (*Sahib kem chho?*); sometimes in Cantonese (*Neih hou ma Ng sin-saang? Hou-noih-mouh-gin!*); sometimes in pidgin ('Chin-chin, Attock; long-tim-no see!'); and sometimes in English ('Good morning, Charles! Are you well?').

When his attention returned to his letter, he would frequently find that he had forgotten what he had intended to say. His face would cloud over and his tone would grow sharp as if to imply that the interruption was somehow Neel's fault: 'Achha, so then read the whole thing to me—from the beginning.'

The arrival of the mid-morning samosa and chai was the signal for Neel to leave the daftar. From then on the Seth's attention would be claimed by a procession of other employees—shroffs, khazanadars, accountants, and the like. Neel, in the meanwhile, would repair to his tiny, smoky cubicle, beside the kitchen, to make a start on the job of turning the Seth's thoughts and reflections into coherent prose—in Hindusthani or English as the case demanded. Although frequently difficult and always time-consuming, the process was rarely tedious: often, while copying out the finished compositions in his best nastaliq or Roman hand, Neel would be struck by how strangely challenging Bahram's correspondence was. In the Seth's letters, there were none of the flourishes, formulae and routine expressions that had played so large a part in his own correspondence, back when he was himself the master of a daftar; Bahram's concerns were all about the here and now; whether prices would rise or fall, and what it would mean for his business.

And yet, what exactly was this business? The strange thing was that despite all the time he spent with Bahram and all the letters he wrote for him, Neel had only a hazy idea of how his enterprise functioned. That most of his profits came from opium was clear enough, but exactly how much of it he traded, who he sold it to and where it went—all this was a mystery to Neel, for Bahram's letters rarely made any reference to such matters. Could it be that unbeknownst to Neel, there were certain code words in the letters? Or could it be that he filled in some details in his own hand, in Gujarati, on the margins of the sheets that Neel handed to him? Or was it that certain letters were written for him by his other daftardars, men who were better acquainted with the functioning of the business? The last seemed the likeliest possibility, but somehow Neel was not persuaded of it: it seemed to him, rather, that all of Bahram's employees—with the possible exception of Vico—knew only as much as they needed to and no more. Bahram's daftardars were like the parts of a watch, each doing what was required of him but unaware of the functioning of the whole: only the Seth himself knew how the ensemble was put together, and for what purpose. And nor was this an accident: it was rather a function of some inborn skill that enabled him to manage his subordinates in such a way that they each worked efficiently within their own spheres while he alone was responsible for the whole.

This too made Neel think back on his own experience of presiding over a daftar, and it was only now that he understood exactly how bad he had been at the job: most of his employees had known more about his affairs than he had himself, and all his attempts to curry favour with them had had exactly the opposite effect. This realization, in turn, engendered an appreciation of Bahram's talents that soon developed into a kind of exasperated admiration: there was no denying that the Seth was often maddening to work for, with all his little peccadilloes and eccentricities; yet there could be no doubt that he was a businessman of exeptional ability and vision: indeed it seemed quite likely to Neel that Bahram was, in his own sphere, a kind of genius.

It was evident too that Ah Fatt had been right to describe Bahram as a man who was widely liked, even loved. From his employees he commanded an almost fanatical loyalty, not only because he was a generous paymaster and fair in his dealings, but also because there was something in his manner that conveyed to them that he did not consider himself to be above, or better, than anyone on his staff. It was as if they knew that despite his wealth and his love of luxury, the Seth remained at heart a village boy, reared in poverty: his irritability was regarded as more endearing than offensive, and his occasional outbursts and dumbcowings were treated like vagaries of the weather and were never taken personally.

Nor was Bahram's popularity restricted to the Achha Hong: writing notes of acceptance was another of Neel's duties so he knew very well how much the Seth was in demand at the enclave's gatherings.

The intensity of Fanqui-town's social whirl was a source of constant amazement to Neel: that a place so small, and inhabited by such a peculiar assortment of sojourners, should have a social life at all seemed incredible to him, let alone one of such intensity. Astonishing, too, that all this activity was generated by such a paltry number of participants—for the foreign traders and their Chinese counterparts, counted together, added up to no more than a few hundred men (but then, as Vico once pointed out to Neel, these buggers were, after all, some of the world's richest men; 'and over here, they are all squeezed together, with hardly room to turn around. No families, nothing to do—they have to make their own fun, no? When no wife there is at home, who thinks of sitting down at his own table? And what kind of falto will go to bed early when there is no one who will scold?').

Nor was it only the Seths and tai-pans and big merchants who knew how to enjoy themselves: while the heads of houses were at their banquets, their employees too, would throw parties of their own, in which food and drink flowed just as freely as at the tables of their bosses (and were indeed often obtained from the same kitchens and parlours). Afterwards, they would stroll around the waterfront, comparing the merits of the entertainments that were on offer in the various hongs—and it was not unusual for them to conclude that they had contrived to entertain themselves with far greater success than their supposed superiors.

Vico's connections in Fanqui-town were no less impressive than Bahram's: he knew people in every factory and was often out till the small hours of the morning. His love of food and liquor were legendary in the Achha Hong and no one liked to boast about it more than he himself: he was one of those men whose pretensions consist only of exaggerating the grossness of their own instincts and appetites; to listen to him was to imagine that he liked nothing better than to spend his days in bed, eating, drinking, farting and fornicating.

So consistent was his description of this fictional self that it took Neel a while to understand that Vico was, in some ways, the opposite of what he pretended to be: industrious, energetic, a faithful husband and a devout Catholic. That he was also a man of many resources, endowed with all kinds of unexpected affiliations, was made apparent only through throwaway remarks and references—for example, to his connection with Father Gonsalo Garcia, the East Indian missionary who had been crucified near Nagasaki, in Japan, along with a number of other Catholics, including five other members of the Franciscan order. The martyr had been beatified by Pope Urban VIII and in his birthplace he was already venerated as a soon-to-be saint: as it happened, this was none other than Vico's own village—Bassein, near Bombay—and his was one of several local families who were reputed to be distantly related to the family of the venerable friar.

Because of their network of co-religionists, in rural China, members of the Catholic missionary orders were often extremely well informed about what was happening in the country: some of them occasionally visited Canton, to tend to the needs of the Catholics of the foreign enclave, and despite their reputation for secrecy, they were not impervious to the magic of Vico's charmed connections.

Vico's connections were often useful to Neel too, for apart from note- and letter-writing, the most important part of his job was khabar-dari—news-gathering. Through his first few weeks in Canton, Neel despaired of being able to cater to the Seth's insatiable appetite for news. Knowing no one in the city, and possessing no sources of news other than the *Canton Register* and the *Chinese Repository* he was reduced to scouring old issues in the hope of finding something of interest to report. Of the two publications, the *Repository* was the more scholarly, the bulk of it being dedicated to long articles on subjects like the habits of scaly anteaters and witchcraft among the Malays. Such matters were of no interest to Bahram: he had as much scorn for abstractions as for useless facts.

'Don't want any bloody professory, understood, munshiji? News, news, news, that's all. No bloody "hereuntos" and "thereunders": just the khabar. Samjoed?'

The *Canton Register* was both newsy and polemical, and was therefore of more interest to Bahram, especially because the editor, John Slade, was also a regular at the Chamber of Commerce. But this meant that he was often aware of the *Register*'s contents even before they saw print.

'Munshiji,' the Seth would snap irritatedly, 'why you are telling me all this stale news? If I ask for milk will you give me curds?'

Sometimes, taking pity on Neel, Vico would hand over things that he knew would be of interest to the Seth. It was thus that Neel was able to announce one morning: Sethji, I have something you will want to hear.

What is it?

Sethji, it is a memorial submitted to the Son of Heaven. The *Register* has published a translation. I thought you would want to know about it, because it is a discussion of how to put a stop to the opium trade.

Oh? said Bahram. All right. Start then.

'"From the moment of opium first gaining an influx into China, your majesty's benevolent grandfather, known as the Wise, foresaw the injury that it would produce; and therefore he earnestly warned and cautioned men against it, and passed a law interdicting it. But at that time his ministers did not imagine that its poisonous effects would pervade China to the present extent. In earlier times, the use of opium was confined to the pampered sons of fortune, with whom it became an idle luxury. But since then its use has extended upwards to the officers and the belted gentry, and downwards to the labourer and the tradesman, and even to women, monks, nuns and priests. In every place its inhalers are to be found and the implements required for smoking it are sold publicly in the face of day. Its importation from abroad is constantly on the increase. Anchored off Lintin and other islands, are special vessels for the storage of opium. They never pass the Bocca

Tigris or enter the river, but depraved merchants of Kwangtung, in collusion with the militia, send boats called 'scrambling dragons' and 'fast-crabs' to carry silver out to sea and smuggle the opium into the realm. In this way the country is drained to the annual amount of thirty million taels of silver and upwards. The value of the legitimate trade, in the import of woollens, clocks and watches, and the export of tea, rhubarb and silk, is less than ten million taels annually and the profit from it does not exceed a few millions. The total value of the legitimate trade is therefore not a tenth or twentieth part of the gains derived from the opium traffic. It is evident from this that the chief interest of the foreign merchants is not in the legal trade, but in the trafficking of opium. This outpouring of wealth from China has become a dangerous sickness and your ministers cannot see where it will end . . ."'

Suddenly, pushing his food away, Bahram rose to his feet. Who has written this?

A senior wazir of the court, Sethji.

Bahram began to pace the room: All right; go on. What else does he say?

Sethji, he is discussing the different proposals for stopping the flow of opium to China.

What are they?

One suggestion is to blockade all Chinese ports, to prevent foreign ships from entering or doing business.

What does he say about that?

Sethji, he says this method would not work.

Why not?

Because China's coast is too long, Sethji, and it is impossible to close it off completely. The foreigners have established close connections with Chinese traders and officials, he says, and because there is so much money to be made, there is sure to be a lot of corruption. The officials will collaborate with the merchants in finding ways of bringing opium into China.

Hah! Bahram began to stroke his beard as he paced. Go on. What else does he say?

Another proposal is to stop all trade and all interactions with foreign merchants. But this too, he says, will not work.

And why is that?

Because the foreign ships will merely gather offshore, and their Chinese associates will send out fast-boats to smuggle in the opium. This method has no chance of success, he says.

Bahram came to a stop beside the bowl in which the daftar's goggle-eyed goldfish circled endlessly in pursuit, of the streaming ribbons of its tail.

So what is his own suggestion? What does he want the Court to do?

It seems, Sethji, that the Chinese officials have been making a study of how the Europeans deal with opium. They have found that in their own countries, the Europeans are very strict about limiting its circulation. They sell the drug freely only when they travel east, and to those people whose lands and wealth they covet. He cites, as an example, the island of Java; he says that the Europeans gave opium to the Javanese and seduced them into the use of it, so that they could be easily overpowered, and that is exactly what happened. It is because they know of its potency that the Europeans are very careful to keep opium under control in their own countries, not flinching from the sternest measures and harshest punishments. This, he says, is what China must do too. He proposes that all opium smokers be given one year to reform. And if after that they are found still to be using, or dealing, in the drug, then it should be treated as a capital crime.

What does he mean by that?

The death penalty, Sethji: *mawt ki saza*; everyone who uses the drug or deals in it, he says, should be sentenced to death.

The Seth gave a snort of disbelief: 'What kind of bakwaas you are talking? Must be some mistake.' He came stalking over to Neel and looked over his shoulder. Where is all this? Show me.

Here, Sethji. Holding the journal open, Neel rose to his feet, to show Bahram some passages that he had marked.

See, Sethji? It says: 'a transgressor should be punished by the exclusion of his children and grandchildren from the public examinations, in addition to the penalty of death . . .'

'Bas! You think I can't read Angrezi or what?'

Bahram's frown deepened as he scanned the passage, but then suddenly his face cleared and his eyes lit up. 'But it is just a memorial, no? Written by some bloody bandar of a baboo. Hundreds of these they must be writing. Emperor will throw and forget. What he cares? He is Emperor, no, busy with his wives and all? Mandarins will not tolerate any change—or else where they will get cumshaw? How they will fill their pipes? Those bahn-chahts are the biggest smokers of all.'

~

Bahram had known Hugh Hamilton Lindsay, the current President of Canton's General Chamber of Commerce for many years. A rubicund man with a silken blandness of manner, he was connected to the Earls of Balcarra, a prominent Scottish dynasty. He had been in China some sixteen years and was widely liked, being universally regarded as a good fellow who never gave himself any airs. Bahram had dined with him many times and knew him to be an excellent host: what was more, he knew him also to be a discerning judge of food.

It was thus with a pleasurable sense of anticipation that Bahram picked out his clothes for Mr Hamilton's dinner. In place of an angarkha he chose a knee-length white jama of Dacca cotton: it was discreetly ornamented with jamdani brocade, and the neck and cuffs were lined with bands of green silk. Instead of pairing this with the usual salwar or pyjamas, Bahram settled on a pair of black Acehnese leggings, shot through with silver thread. The weather being still quite warm he picked, as an outer garment, a cream-coloured cotton choga embroidered with silver-gilt *karchobi* work. The ensemble was completed by a turban of pure malmal muslin. Then, as Bahram picked up a slim cane with an ivory knob, the valet-duty khidmatgar misted the air with a puff of his favourite *raat-ki-rani* attar; after lingering in the fragrant cloud for a moment, Bahram made his way to the door.

The dinner was to be held in the Chamber's dining room, which was only a five-minute walk from the Achha Hong. But it was the custom, in Canton, for people to hire lantern-bearers to light their way when they were invited out to dine, even if they were going only a short distance. Bahram had employed the same bearer for decades: known to foreigners as Apu, this man had an uncanny ability to divine when he was needed. He also seemed to possess some occult faculty of persuasion that enabled him to keep at bay the cadgers and chawbacons of the Maidan. This evening, as on so many before, Apu arrived punctually, just before sundown, and Bahram set off shortly afterwards: with his embroidered choga flapping in the breeze, and a paper lantern glowing above his white turban, he was about as striking a figure as any—but such were his lantern-bearer's powers that he was the only passer-by not to be besieged with importuning cries of 'Cumshaw, gimme cumshaw!'

The bustle and noise of the Maidan transported Bahram's spirits, taking him back to his earliest days in Canton: he paused to look around him—at the looming bulk of the Sea-Calming Tower, in the far distance; at the grey walls of the citadel, running like a curtain, behind the enclave; and at the narrow-fronted factories, glowing in the last light of day: the hongs' arched windows seemed to be winking at him, their colonnaded porticoes smiling as if to greet an old friend. The sight made Bahram's chest swell in proprietorial pride: after all these years it still thrilled him to think that he was as much a part of this scene as any foreigner could ever hope to be.

At the gates of the Danish Hong, two turbaned chowkidars were standing guard. They were from Tranquebar, near Madras, and they bowed when they saw Bahram: as the doyen of the Achha community of Canton, he was well known to them. Murmuring salaams they ushered him through the gates and into the factory.

Crossing the courtyard that led to the Chamber's premises, Bahram could see that many of Mr Lindsay's guests had already gathered in the Club: the reception room and the dining room were both brightly lit and he could hear voices and the clinking of glasses. At the entrance to the reception room Bahram paused to peek in: few colours other than black and white could be seen on the men inside and he knew that with the candlelight sparkling on the silver and gold threads that were woven through his garments, his entrance would make a considerable impression; he ran a hand over the skirt of his choga, fanning it out so as to show it off to best advantage.

On stepping in, Bahram met with a warm reception. He knew almost everybody present and greeted many of them with hugs and even kisses. He knew there was no danger of being rebuffed: such exuberance might be looked upon askance in a European but in an Oriental of sufficient rank it was likely to be seen rather as a sign of self-assurance. As a young Achha in Canton Bahram had noticed that such effusions were almost a prerogative of seniority amongst the Seths; he had noticed also that his elders often imposed their physical presence on others as an expression of their power. It was oddly satisfying to know that he too had arrived at a point in his life when his hugs and thumps and kisses were universally welcomed, even by the starchiest Europeans.

Now the host, Mr Lindsay, appeared at Bahram's side, murmuring his congratulations and welcoming him into the Committee. Soon Bahram was led off to admire the full-length portrait of Mr Lindsay that was now hanging amongst the pictures of the Chamber's past presidents.

'You will recognize, of course,' said Mr Lindsay proudly, 'the hand of Mr Chinnery.'

'Arré, shahbash!' said Bahram, dutifully admiring the painting. 'So nicely he has done, no? Put sword in your hand and all. Like a hero you are looking!'

A glow of pleasure suffused Mr Lindsay's rosy face. 'Yes, it is rather fine is it not?'

'But why so soon, Hugh? Your time as President is not over, no?'

'Actually,' said Mr Lindsay, 'I have just a few months left.' Now, leaning closer, he whispered: 'Between the two of us, Barry, that is the occasion for this dinner—I intend to announce the name of my successor.'

'The next President?'

'Yes exactly . . .'

Mr Lindsay was about to say more but he happened to look over Bahram's shoulder and immediately cut himself short. With a quick 'Excuse me' he took himself off and Bahram turned around to find himself facing Lancelot Dent.

Dent's appearance had changed considerably since Bahram had seen him last; a slight man, with a narrow face and receding jawline, he had grown a sandy goatee, probably to extend the length of his chin. He was now brimming with an affability that Bahram had never seen in him before.

'Ah Mr Moddie! Congratulations on your appointment—we are delighted to have you amongst us. My brother Tom sends you his very best wishes.'

'Thank you,' said Bahram politely. 'I am extremely glad to have your blessings and good wishes. And of course you must call me Barry.'

'And you must call me Lancelot.'

'Yes. Certainly, Lance . . .' The name was not easy to say but Bahram managed to get through it in a rush: 'Of course, Lancelot.'

The gong rang, to summon the guests to the dining room, and Dent immediately slipped his arm through Bahram's. There were no place cards on the table, and Bahram had no option but to take the chair next to Dent's. Seated to his left was John Slade of the *Canton Register*.

Slade had long been a fixture on the Committee so his presence at the dinner came as no surprise. Apart from editing the paper, he also dabbled in trade—although without much success. He was reputed to have run up significant debts, but such was the fear inspired by his acid tongue and scathing pen that rare indeed was the creditor who attempted to reclaim a loan from the Thunderer.

But there was no thunder in Mr Slade's mien now as he greeted Bahram: his large, flushed face creased into a smile and he muttered: 'Excellent . . . excellent . . . very pleased indeed to have you on the Committee, Mr Moddie.'

Then his eyes wandered across the room and his face hardened. 'Which is more than I can say of the Bulgarian.'

This completely baffled Bahram. Following Slade's gaze he saw that the Thunderer was looking at Charles King, of Olyphant & Co.: this was an American firm, and Bahram knew for sure that Mr King was an American himself.

'Did you say "vulgarian", Mr Slade?'

'No. I said Bulgarian.'

'But I thought Mr King was from America. You are sure he's Bulgarian?'

'It is not impossible, you know,' said Slade darkly, 'to be both.'

'Baap-re-baap! American and Bulgarian also? That is too much, no?'

Here Dent came to the rescue and whispered in Bahram's ear: 'You must make some allowances for our good Mr Slade: he is a stickler for proper usage and has a great detestation of corrupted words. He particularly dislikes the word "bugger", which is so much in use among the vulgar masses. He believes it to be a corruption of the word "Bulgar" or "Bulgarian" and insists on using those instead.'

This further deepened Bahram's puzzlement for he had always assumed that 'bugger' was the *anglice* of the Hindusthani word *bukra*, or 'goat'.

'So Mr King is having goats, is he?' he said to Mr Slade.

'It would not surprise me at all,' said Mr Slade mournfully. 'It is common knowledge that a congenital Bulgar will Bulgarize anything that takes his fancy. *Amantes sunt amentes*.'

Bahram had never heard of anyone keeping goats in Fanqui-town, but it stood to reason that if someone did it would be a representative of Olyphant & Co.—for that firm had always been the odd one out in Fanqui-town, choosing to do business in eccentric, money-losing ways. What was more, the firm's managers had even had the effrontery to criticize others for refusing to follow their lead: not surprisingly, this did little to endear them to their peers.

Bahram was one of the few tai-pans who was actually on good terms with Charles King—but this was because he usually discussed things other than business. He knew very well that the Olyphant agent inspired deep hostility within the upper echelons of Fanqui-town, and was astonished to see him amongst the members of the Committee.

Bahram turned to Dent with a puzzled frown: 'Is Charles King also on the Committee?'

'Yes, indeed he is,' said Dent. 'He was invited to join because he is a great favourite of the mandarins. It was felt that he would be able to represent our views to them. But it must be admitted that it has not turned out well: instead of advocating our issues to them, he unfailingly does exactly the opposite. He is forever trying to bully and hector us into obeying his Celestial patrons.'

At this point the Club's stewards entered with the first course. The stewards were all local men, with braided queues, round caps and sandalled feet. Their tunics were in the Club's colour, blue, and were worn over grey, ankle-length pyjamas.

Unlike the stewards, many of the Chamber's cooks were from Macau: when freed from the obligation of producing the kind of fare that was most in demand in the Club's dining room—roast beef, Yorkshire pudding, haggis, steak-and-kidney pies and the like—they were capable of serving superb Macahnese food. Now, looking at the plate that had been set before him, Bahram was delighted to see that it contained one of his favourite dishes: a bright green watercress soup called Caldo de Agrião. With it was served a variety of condiments and sauces, as well as a fine Alvarinho wine from Monçao.

Bahram was absorbed in savouring the wine and the soup when Mr Slade's voice boomed across the table. 'Well Mr Jardine, since no one else will dare ask, it falls to me to bell the cat. Is it true, sir, that you intend soon to return to England?'

The soup was suddenly forgotten and every head turned to look towards Mr Jardine who was sitting at the other end of the table, between the host and Mr Wetmore. A quizzical smile appeared on his unlined face and he said quietly: 'Well Mr Slade, I was planning to make my intentions public at the end of the evening, but since you have presented me with this opportunity, I will seize it. The answer is, in short: Yes, I am indeed planning to return to England. The date has not yet been decided but it will probably be in a month or two.'

A silence fell, leaving many spoons suspended in the air. Before anything else could be said Mr Lindsay broke in, speaking in his usual rounded, measured tones: 'The urge to seek the joys of marriage and fatherhood is powerful in all men. We cannot expect Mr Jardine to forever defer his happiness in order to provide us with his unrivalled leadership. We are fortunate in having had him with us for as long as we have. It behoves us now to wish him luck in finding the bride he deserves.'

This was met with nods and a quiet chorus of Amens and Hear-hears, which Mr Jardine acknowledged with a smile: 'Thank you, gentlemen, thank you: I will certainly need your good wishes. I have so little experience of the petticoat company that I should consider myself fortunate if I succeed in finding a lady who is fat, fair and forty. It is as much as a man of my age has a right to expect.'

Amidst the roar of laughter that followed, the soup plates were whisked away and a number of dishes were laid upon the table. Inspecting them closely, Bahram recognized many of his favourite Macahnese specialities: croquettes of bacalhao, boulettes of pork, a spiced salad of avocado and prawns, stuffed crabs and a fish tart.

The food did not long distract Mr Slade: having made quick work of a couple of glasses of wine and several platefuls of crab, codfish and pork balls, he again addressed Mr Jardine: 'Well sir, since so many of us at this table are old bachelors and perfectly content with our lot—as indeed you too seemed to be until quite recently—you will perhaps forgive us for wondering whether the attractions of the marital bed are the sole cause of your departure from our midst.'

Mr Jardine raised an eyebrow. 'Pray Mr Slade, I am not sure I understand you.'

'Well sir,' said Mr Slade in his booming voice, 'let me put the matter plainly then: it is widely rumoured that you have drawn up a detailed war plan and are hoping to persuade Lord

Palmerston, the Foreign Secretary, to make use of it. Is there any truth to this?'

Jardine's smile did not waver in the slightest: 'I fear you overestimate both my foresight and my influence, Mr Slade. Lord Palmerston has not called on me for advice or assistance—although you may be sure that if he did I would not hesitate to offer it.'

'I am glad to hear it, sir.' Mr Slade's voice grew louder. 'And if you should happen to meet Lord Palmerston I beg you to speak your mind to him, on behalf of all of us.'

'What exactly would you have me say, Mr Slade?'

'Why sir,' said Slade, 'my views are no secret: I have stated them repeatedly in the *Register*. I would have you tell His Lordship that he has disappointed us, at every turn. He is no doubt a man of exceptional ability so we had hoped he would understand the importance of trade and commerce to the future of the Empire. Yet every measure he has taken so far for the protection and promotion of the British trade to China has failed utterly and disgracefully. I would urge him to recognize that it was a mistake to appoint a man like Captain Elliott to be the Representative of Her Majesty's government in China. Captain Elliott has attained his position solely because of his connections in Society and Government—he understands nothing of financial matters and as a military man he can never adequately appreciate the principles of Free Trade. It follows therefore that he cannot honestly represent the interests of men such as ourselves. Yet it is we who, through our taxes, pay the salaries of men like him—a class of official parasites that seems to be forever increasing in number. This is unconscionable, sir, and it must be made plain to His Lordship. I would urge him to change his policy; to stop reposing his trust in soldiers and diplomats and other representatives of the government. This is a new age, and it will be forged and shaped by trade and commerce. His Lordship would do better to make common cause with men like us, who are here and who are acquainted with the conditions of this country; he should trust our leading merchants to represent our own best interests. His Lordship should be cautioned that if he intends to proceed as he began, then the future for British subjects in this country is gloomy and dark indeed: if not for his inaction, the situation here would never have come to the present pass. He should be warned also that if he continues along his present path he himself will not escape opprobrium. He will find that he has paid too dear for his ministerial whistle if its price is the sacrifice of the honour and interests of his own country.'

There was a dazed silence, which helped the stewards to serve another course: even though Bahram's attention had been distracted by Mr Slade's thunderous peroration, he did not fail to recognize that the dish that had now appeared on the table was the great glory of Macahnese cuisine—*Galinha Africana*—grilled chicken, napped with a coconut sauce that was redolent of the spices of Mozambique.

No one else paid any attention to the chicken. From the other end of the table, Mr Lindsay directed a frown at Mr Slade. 'You must consider yourself lucky, John, that you were born in England. In some countries a man might well lose his head for taking such a tone with his leaders.'

'Believe me, sir,' said the Thunderer, 'I know very well the value of my freedoms. Nothing would give me greater pleasure than to see them conferred upon the uncountable millions who groan under the yoke of tyranny—most notably the wretches who suffer the rule of the Manchu despot.'

'But Mr Slade!' It was the voice of Charles King. 'If freedom is merely a stick for you to beat others with, then surely the word has lost all meaning? You have blamed Lord Palmerston, you have blamed Captain Elliott, you have blamed the Emperor of China—yet you have not once taken the name of the commodity that has brought us to the present impasse: opium.'

Slade's heavy jowls quivered thunderously as he turned to face his interlocutor. 'No, Mr King,' he said. 'I have not mentioned opium, nor indeed have I spoken of any of your other hobby horses. And nor will I until your Celestial friends candidly admit that it is they who are the prime movers in this trade. In supplying them with such goods as they demand we are merely obeying the laws of Free Trade . . .'

'And the laws of conscience, Mr Slade?' said Charles King. 'What of them?'

'Do you imagine, Mr King, that freedom of conscience could exist in the absence of the freedom of trade?'

Before Charles King could respond Jardine broke in: 'But all the same, Slade, you're coming it a bit strong, aren't you? I cannot see that it will serve any purpose to address the Foreign Secretary so harshly. And as for Captain Elliott he is merely a functionary—we should not ascribe to him greater consequence than is his due.'

Slade opened his mouth to respond, but was distracted by the entry of the dessert, which was a rich and creamy 'sawdust pudding'—*serradura*, topped with a crisp layer of toasted crumbs.

Mr Lindsay was quick to seize this opportunity and struck his knife upon his glass.

'Gentlemen, in a minute we will drink to the Queen. But before that I have some good news to share with you. As you know, my term as President of the Chamber runs out in a few months. It is of course the custom for the outgoing President to name a successor. I am happy to announce that our next incumbent will be someone who will ensure that Mr Jardine will remain with us in spirit even after his departure. For he is none other than Mr Jardine's dearest friend: Mr Wetmore.'

Many hands began to clap and Mr Wetmore rose to his feet in acknowledgement.

'I am moved, deeply moved, to be trusted with the responsibilities of leadership at a time like this.' There was a catch in his voice and he paused to clear it. 'It is some consolation, if I may say so, for the loss of Mr Jardine.'

This too was answered with a burst of clapping. Even as he was joining in the applause, Bahram noticed that his two neighbours were exchanging smiles and glances that seemed to say: 'Did I not tell you so?'

Under cover of the noise Dent leant close to Bahram's ear: 'You see, Barry, how things are disposed of amongst us?'

Bahram decided to answer cautiously. 'Pray, Lancelot, what is your meaning?'

Dent's voice, although low, became very intense: 'We are at a critical juncture, Barry, and I do not think we have the leadership we need.'

He cut himself short as Mr Lindsay rose to his feet, glass in hand. 'Gentlemen, the Queen . . .'

After the toasts had been drunk Mr Lindsay declared that the evening was not over yet, far from it. At a signal from him the sliding doors that connected the dining room to the reception room were thrown open: inside were three fiddlers, setting up their music stands. They struck up a waltz and Mr Lindsay gestured to his guests to rise. 'Come, gentlemen, this would scarcely be a Canton evening if it did not end with some dancing. I am sure Mr Jardine and Mr Wetmore will lead the way, as they have so often in the past.'

Now, as the guests began to pair off around the table, Bahram realized that he would have to choose between Mr Slade and Mr Dent. He turned hurriedly to his right: 'Shall we dance, Lancelot?'

'Why certainly, Barry,' said Dent. 'But can I have a minute of your time before that?'

'Of course.'

Linking his arm with Bahram's, Dent led him out to the wide balcony that adjoined the dining room. 'You must know, Barry,' he said in a low voice, 'that we are facing a crisis of unprecedented magnitude. It should come as no surprise that the Grand Manchu has decided to demonstrate his omnipotence by prohibiting the entry of opium into this country. It is in the nature of tyranny for tyrants to be seized by fancies, and it is clear that this one will stop at nothing to enforce his whim: arrests, raids, executions—the monster is willing to use every instrument of oppression that is available to him. None of this is perhaps surprising in a heathen despot—but I am sorry to say that there are some in our community here who would gladly march to the tyrant's tune.'

'Are you referring to Charles King?' said Bahram.

'Yes,' said Dent. 'My fear is that in Mr Jardine's absence he will attempt to seize control of the Committee. Fortunately he has little support and Mr Jardine's adherents will not allow them to prevail. Yet, the means by which Mr Jardine and his people propose to solve our problems are not much different: they speak of Free Trade and yet their intention is to invite the armed intervention of none other than Her Majesty's government. To me this is not merely a contradiction of the principles of Free Trade, but a mockery of them: it is my belief that whenever governments attempt to sway the Invisible Hand, whenever they attempt to bend the flow of trade to their will, then must free men fear for their liberties—for that is when we know that we are in the presence of a power that seeks to make children of us, a force that seeks to usurp the sovereign will that God has bestowed equally on all of us. A pox on both their houses I say.'

Bahram's instinctive suspicion of abstractions was now aroused. 'But Lancelot, what would *you* do about the present situation? Are you having any definite plan?'

'My plan,' said Dent, 'is to trust in the Almighty and leave the rest to the laws of Nature. It will not be long before mankind's natural cupidity reasserts itself. I hold this to be Man's most powerful and most noble instinct: nothing can withstand it. It is only a matter of time before it overwhelms the proud ambitions of those who seek to govern from on high.'

Bahram began to fidget with the hem of his angarkha. 'But Lancelot . . . see, I am an ordinary man of business; can you please explain what you are trying to say in a simple way?'

'All right,' said Dent. 'Let me put it like this. Do you think the demand for opium in China has abated merely because of an edict from Peking?'

'No,' said Bahram. 'That I doubt.'

'And you are right to doubt it, for I assure you it has not. The absence of food does not make a man forsake hunger—it only makes him hungrier. The same is true of opium. I am told that the price being offered for a chest of opium in the city is now in the region of three thousand dollars—five times what it was a year ago.'

'Is it really?'

'Yes. Can you imagine what that means, Barry? The cumshaws that every mandarin, guard and bannerman received a year ago are now also potentially many times higher.'

'That is true,' said Bahram. 'You have a point.'

'How long before the mandarins see reason? If the Emperor's edicts and prohibitions are not rescinded, what is to hold them back from fomenting rebellion? If he does not disavow his whim, what is to prevent lesser men from rising up against the power-maddened Manchu, who is not even of their own race? How long can it be before they see where their own interests lie?'

'But that is the problem, Lancelot,' said Bahram. 'Time. Let me be frank with you. I have a shipful of opium anchored off Hong Kong and I need to dispose of it quickly. I do not have much time.'

'Oh I understand very well,' said Dent with a smile. 'Believe me I am in exactly the same position—even more so because I have more than one shipload to dispose of. But ask yourself this: what is the alternative? If the Olyphants have their way then we will lose our cargoes in their entirety; if Jardine and his people win out what will it profit us, you and me? It will be a year, or perhaps two, before an expeditionary force arrives. Do you think the investors who have entrusted us with their capital will wait quietly while an English fleet sails halfway around the world?'

'No, it is true; they would not wait that long,' said Bahram. 'But tell me, Lancelot, what is *your* solution? What would *you* do about this problem?'

'It's quite simple,' said Dent. 'You and I need to be able to dispose of our opium at our convenience and it is essential that the Chamber does nothing to stand in our way. It is vital that we do not allow it to become a shadow government seeking to usurp our individual freedoms. But to make sure of this I will need your help. In the months to come we will face tremendous pressure. Governments on both sides of the world will attempt to bend us to their will. At this time, above all, it is essential that we prepare to resist—and unless we stay together we will all be swept aside.' He placed his hand on Bahram's arm. 'Tell me, Barry—can I count on your support?'

Bahram dropped his eyes: he could not see himself aligning either with Jardine or with the representatives of Olyphant & Co.—yet there was something about Dent that led him to doubt that he would be able to carry the majority of his peers with him.

'Tell me, Lancelot: do you think you are having as much support as will be required?'

Dent was silent for a moment. 'I own I would be more confident if Benjamin Burnham were here already. I could certainly count on him and I do believe that with his help and yours I would be able to sway the Committee.'

'Mr Burnham of Calcutta?' said Bahram. 'Is he also on the Committee?'

'Yes,' said Dent. 'As you know, it is the custom to include one representative from the Calcutta agency houses. I was able to ensure that the seat was kept for Benjamin: he and I understand each other very well. He is on his way to Canton now and once he is here, I will feel far more confident.' He paused to clear his throat. 'But of course we will still need you, Barry—and you are, after all, an old ally of Dent and Company.'

Bahram decided it was far too early to show his hand. 'I certainly hold your company in the highest esteem,' he said in a non-committal way. 'But as for these other matters I will have to do some thinking.'

There was a break in the music now, which provided Bahram with an opportunity to end the conversation. Cocking his head towards the reception room he said: 'Ah, waltz is over! Now polka is starting. Shall we go in?'

If Dent was put out by the abrupt change of subject he did not show it. 'Certainly,' he said. 'Come. Let us go in.'

As they stepped inside, Bahram spotted a large, hulking figure leaning negligently against the sliding doors of the reception room with a tankard of beer clutched in one hand.

'Why, it is Mr Innes,' said Dent.

'Was he invited? I did not see him earlier.'

'I doubt that Mr Innes would be stopped by the lack of an invitation,' said Dent with a laugh. 'He will brook no hindrance from anyone but the Almighty Himself.'

Bahram had only a nodding acquaintance with Innes but he knew him well by repute: although well-born he was a wild, wilful character, who did exactly as he pleased. He was a brawler, forever getting into fights, and in Bombay no respectable merchant would deal with him for he was regarded as an inveterate troublemaker. As a result he was forced to obtain his consignments of opium from petty dalals—and thieves and dacoits too, for all that anyone knew.

He was surprised now, to hear Dent speaking of Innes with approbation.

'It is men like Innes who will resolve our present difficulties,' Dent said. 'These are the free spirits who will thwart the designs of tyrants. If there is anyone who can be considered a crusader in the cause of Free Trade it is he.'

'What do you mean, Lancelot?'

Dent's eyebrows rose in surprise. 'Are you perhaps unaware, Barry, that Innes is the only man who is still transporting cargoes of opium into Canton? He believes it to be God's will, so he continues to bring the chests upriver in his own cutters, defying the Emperor's ban. It wouldn't be possible of course if he did not have local allies—everyone is paid off on the way, the customs men, the mandarins, everyone. He has had no trouble so far—it is proof that the natural cupidity which is the foundation of human freedom will always prevail against the whims of tyrants.'

Dent leant closer to Bahram's ear. 'I will tell you this in confidence Barry: Innes has disposed of several dozen cases for me in the last few weeks. I would be glad to speak to him on your behalf.'

'Oh no,' said Bahram quickly. It made him cringe to think of what would be said of him in Bombay if it ever came to be known that he was dealing with a man like Innes. 'Please do not trouble yourself, Lancelot. That will not be necessary.'

To Bahram's alarm, Innes seemed to have guessed that he was being talked about for he turned around suddenly, with a scowl on his face. All of a sudden Bahram was seized by the notion that Innes would ask him to dance. This so panicked him that he grabbed Dent's hand: 'Come, Lancelot,' he said. 'It is time to dance.'

nine

~

Markwick's Hotel, November 21

My dear, dear Begum of Pugglabad, Good news! At last I am able to report some *progress* in the matter of your camellia. It is not a great step, but it is a step nonetheless—and I am *hopeful*, not just in regard to your painting but to that other quest, even closer to my heart . . . !

But I will come to that later: suffice it to say that none of this would have come about if I had not done something I should have done *ages* ago: I have finally summoned the courage to visit the most celebrated artist in Canton: Mr Guan Ch'iao-chang.

And now that I have done it, I positively *berate* myself for not having gone earlier: how could I have been such a *gudda*? But I must not be too hard on myself for the fault is not mine alone: the blame goes, in large part, to my Uncle.

You will have heard from Mr Penrose that Mr Chinnery holds the painters of Canton in utter scorn and positively *bridles* if they are spoken of as Artists. He regards them as the merest craftsmen, no better than the potters and tinkers who set up shop by the roadside. And in this he is not alone: this is the opinion also of Chinese connoisseurs; they too are dismissive of the Canton style of painting which is indeed *utterly* different from the manner that commands admiration in China. Nor are the painters of Canton of the same ilk as the great Chinese artists of old: they are not from famously cultivated families and they are neither great scholars nor high-ranking officials nor illuminati. They are the kind of people whose forebears were malis and peasants and khidmatgars and labourers in workshops—humble, strong and *virile*. Mr Karabedian has made a study of the subject, for some of the craftsmen he buys watches from are of the same stock. He says that the Canton studios grew out of—would you believe it?—*porcelain kilns*, the very ones that made China-ware famous around the world! It was the practice for fanquis to send patterns and pictures to Chinese porcelain-makers; these were then used to decorate the pottery that was made here for European markets (is it not the most *delightful* absurdity to think of all those hausfraus rushing out to buy 'China' thinking it to be marvellously foreign when all the while the designs were provided by their own countrymen?).

These workmen became expert at creating images that appealed to Occidentals and in time they turned their hands to other things: they made paintings on snuff-boxes and trays and tiles and sheets of glass; they copied portraits from lockets and amulets and made little miniatures—and these trifles so delighted the sailors and sea-captains who visited Canton that they brought them their favourite pictures to copy: miniatures of their wives and children, as well as landscapes and portraits—some brought etchings of famous Euopean paintings and these too were reproduced with extraordinary skill. Mr Karabedian says that some Canton painters have gained so intimate a familiarity with the Masters of Europe that it is no great matter for them to invent Tiepolos and Tintorettos that have never before seen the light of day—and in so perfect a manner that if the artists themselves were to behold these paintings they would think them to be their own! Many such paintings have already been taken to Europe and sold says Mr Karabedian; he is even willing to wager that a day will come when many a canvas thought to have been painted in Venice or Rome will be found to have been made in China! Yet

Canton painters are without honour in their own country for their work does not accord at all with Chinese High Taste.

You can imagine, dear Puggly, the effect these revelations had on me! I understood at once why Mr Chinnery held these artists in such low regard: it is because Canton's studios produce a *bastard* art—a thing no more likely to be loved by its sire than is its human avatar (and who could know this better than I?).

You will understand why a sense of kinship with these artists began to germinate within me: I felt myself to be utterly in sympathy with them—and this bond was greatly strengthened by the knowledge that some of them had even learnt from the same teacher as I: none other than Mr Chinnery himself! Yes, my dear Puggly, in light of what I have said about my Uncle's opinion of these painters it may amaze you to learn that a good number of them have served as apprentices in the Chinnery atelier. But in Mr Chinnery's eyes this earns them no more merit than is gained by the paintbrushes that pass through his hands—for these apprentices serve merely as instruments (just as I and my brother once did) filling in here a patch of paint and there a lick of colour: not for a moment could he imagine them to be partaking of that feast to which he gives the name 'Art'.

You will see why the discovery that these apprentices are perfectly capable of creating canvases of their own would be discomfiting for him; you will understand why his distrust and dislike would be directed most particularly at the one who enjoys the greatest renown: Mr Guan—who is known to fanquis as Lamqua. (Why always the 'qua' you might ask? Some say the syllable originated in the surname Guan and some claim that it is a version of some title—it is impossible to make any sense of it so I have ceased to try. But this I can tell you—that no place has such an abundance of quas and quacks and quiddities as Canton—Howqua, Mowqua, Lamqua, why there may well be a Jenesequa for all I know!)

But to return to Lamqua: he too spent time at the atelier on the Rua Ignacio Baptista, and Mr Chinnery claims the credit for having taught him *everything*. But this cannot be accurate for Lamqua is himself from a family of painters: his grandfather was one of the most famous of Canton's artists—Guan Zuolin, who is known to fanquis by the most absurd name you could ever conceive: Spoilum (Mr Karabedian has shown me a few of his works, which are scattered around Fanqui-town, and I can attest that they are indeed quite extraordinary, particularly some portraits painted on glass). But Mr Chinnery will not allow that Lamqua may have learnt anything from his forebears; he insists that he came to him in the guise of a house-boy with the explicit intention of stealing his secrets. Whether there is any truth to this I cannot say, but this I can tell you—that when I was preparing to leave for Canton Mr Chinnery gave me to understand that there now exists between the two of them a great bitterness: he warned me not to enter Lamqua's studio on any account for I would most assuredly be rudely evicted and might even be set upon with cudgels. And nor was this the whole of it: most of Canton's painters are related to each other, he said, so I would do best to stay away from all of them.

So there you have it, my darling Pugglee-beebee: you will understand now why I was careful to avoid the very people whom I should have sought out immediately upon arrival—and if it were not for Mr Karabedian I might still be slinking past their studios with my face half-hidden. But good, kind man that he is, Zadig Bey (as I have learnt to call him) took it on himself to persuade me that I have nothing to fear: Lamqua is a most *amiable* man, he said, and harbours no resentment against his old teacher—the grudge is held entirely by Mr Chinnery who is furious because Lamqua has made enough of a name for himself that some clients who might otherwise have made their way to the Rua Ignacio Baptista now seek him out instead (that Lamqua charges less than half the price Mr Chinnery demands probably plays some part in this).

You can imagine then with what an eagerly beating heart I followed Zadig Bey to Lamqua's studio. This establishment was not of course unknown to me: it is only a short distance from my hotel, and as a matter of fact it is quite impossible to walk through Old China Street without noticing it. For right above the door there hangs the most *intriguing* sign: it says—'Lamqua: Handsome Face-Painter'.

The studio is a three-tiered shop-house like many others on the street: the front is made of wood, and the upper floors have sliding windows of finely carved fretwork. During the day, the windows are often pulled back and you can see the bowed heads of the apprentices inside, bending over their tables with their brushes and pencils—and I swear to you, dear Puggly, that it is apparent at a glance that they are exactly what is promised by the sign below: handsome face-painters.

Can you think, my darling Pugglepuss, how thrilled I was to walk through that door? Aladdin at the entrance of his cave could not have been more excited than was I! And nor was I disappointed—for everywhere I looked there was something either curious or interesting or utterly *novel*. In glass-fronted cases lay dozens of paintings, all made in the studio: pictures of everything that might interest visitors, both Chinese and foreign—for just as foreigners want pictures of Fanqui-town because it looks to them so indescribably Celestial, so too do the Chinese covet them because the same sight is in their eyes utterly Alien. Between the two of them they have created an enormous market for views of Canton—and apart from these there are innumerable pictures of animals, rural scenes, pagodas, plants, catgut-scrapers, monks and fanquis. Some of these pictures are painted on little cards, not much larger than your palm, and are sold for a few cash; they have become such a craze they are being copied everywhere—Zadig Bey says in Europe they are all the rage and are spoken of as 'postal cards'.

Also offered for sale are laquered paint-boxes and bundles of paper: I had always thought this was rice-paper, but Zadig Bey revealed to me that rice has nothing to do with it—the pith of a certain reed is taken out and beaten flat; it is then treated with alum, which preserves the colours and keeps them marvellously vivid over many years. Then there are brushes: some have no more than a single hair and some are as thick as my wrist; and they are made from the hairs of a fantastic bestiary of animals, some of them completely *unknown* to the world.

From the shop you ascend to the next floor by means of a narrow staircase—a ladder really, with banisters running along one side. You step off it to find yourself in the very heart of the workshop. There are several long tables, like those used by carpenters and tailors. The apprentices are seated on benches and each has his own work-space on which all his materials are neatly arranged; nowhere do you see a careless splash of colour or an unmindful smudge of ink. They sit with their heads bent over, their queues coiled around their caps, and they do not in the least mind being observed—for they are so intent upon their work that they are totally unaware of your presence.

And now was revealed one of the most important secrets of their picture-making: stencils! There is a stencil for everything—for the outlines of ships, trees, clouds, scenery, clothing. Zadig Bey says these stencils are sold by the dozen and can be bought in the market: every studio keeps hundreds of them at hand. By varying their placement and position, the painter can achieve all manner of interesting effects.

To watch the progress of a single painting is an astonishing thing: it starts its journey at one end of the table, as a blank sheet of paper, and is quickly prepared with a wash of alum. As it passes down the bench, going from hand to hand, it acquires outlines, colours and more washes of alum and yet more colours, until it arrives at the other end as a complete painting! And all this in a matter of minutes. It is *breathtaking*—a veritable manufactory of image-making!

Zadig Bey says the methods of these studios hark back to the porcelain kiln, where a single cup or saucer may pass through as many as seventy hands, one tracing outlines, one painting the rim, one applying the blues and another the reds—and so on. He insists that the world owes these studios a great debt because they have made possible what people of modest means could only ever dream of: to possess likenesses of themselves and their dear ones, and to have real paintings on their walls. (I cannot understand why we have no such studios in Bengal: indeed, Puggly dear, I think it quite possible that my fortune may lie in creating something similar there . . .)

All this and you have yet to meet Lamqua himself: you climb another ladder, not unlike the one before, and suddenly you are in the sanctum sanctorum of this temple of Art, right inside the Master's studio. He has a sitter present—a ruddy-faced Swedish sea-captain, in this instance—so you have a few minutes' leisure in which to observe him at his work. The artist has a look of prosperity, with a full face, a comfortable stoutness in the waist, and a high-domed head. He is wearing a plain, workmanlike gown, and he has tied his queue into a glistening black bun. But his way of working is not much different from that of a European painter: he has a palette and brush in his hands and stands in front of a canvas that is placed upon an easel. The studio is small, but there is a skylight overhead that fills it with brightness: everything is neat and in its place—there is no disorder, no impatient brush-smudges nor any unruly splashes of colour. On the walls hang dozens of portraits, some recently finished and others that have, for one reason or another, never been collected (among these is a *most* melancholy portrait of a midshipman—it is unfinished and destined to be forever so because the boy died of the typhus while it was being painted).

Yet the one thing Lamqua will not do—and a very strange thing it is too, considering the sign that hangs above his door—is to make a man handsomer than he is. On no account will he leave out blemishes, warts, birthmarks, yellowed teeth, rheumy eyes, cauliflower ears, noses a-bloom with grog-blossom and so on—indeed some of the men on his wall are perfect *frights*.

And as I was looking around who should I see? Myself! Or rather Mr Chinnery, painted in a most engaging way: one has only to look at the picture to know that the painter harbours no grudge against the sitter.

Lamqua must have seen me looking at the likeness, for he pointed to the picture and said to me: 'Same-same.' Then, even without my being introduced he proceeded to chin-chin me, folding his hands together and addressing me as 'Mr Chinnery': he said that he had heard that I had come to Canton and would have invited me to visit his studio but had refrained from doing so for fear of further annoying my Uncle. He then proceeded to inquire after Mr Chinnery's health and asked about his work, saying that it was a matter of great regret to him that he was no longer able to visit his studio, especially because he had heard that Mr Chinnery had recently completed a most unusual landscape, which he would dearly have loved to see.

I confess I found this most *affecting* for I do consider it utterly *unjust* that Mr Chinnery should treat Lamqua in such a fashion: so strong was this feeling that I felt I had to do *something* about it, so I asked for a piece of paper and a pencil.

As you know, my dear Pugglovna, I have been blessed with an excellent memory for pictures, so I was able, in a short while, to conjure up a perfectly passable impression of the painting in question (a view of Macau). Zadig Bey said afterwards that it was indiscreet of me to do this as one of Mr Chinnery's chief complaints against Lamqua is that he copies the style of his paintings. But I own that I do not give a fig for this argument: it seems to me that a man who is *shamefully* neglectful of the Lives that issue from his loins has no right to be protective of the Works he creates with his hands.

And this brings me, my dear Puggly, to the matter which is of greatest interest to you: your camellias. For Lamqua was so delighted with my little offering that he asked at once if there was anything he could do for me. This emboldened me to hand him Mr Penrose's picture: I told him that it belonged to a friend who was keen to know about the subject and provenance of this painting.

It took Lamqua but a moment to declare that he had never seen this particular flower—but that did not prevent him from minutely examining the picture. He turned it over, again and again, feeling the paper and even moistening the edges. He said he was almost certain, from the style, that the picture had been painted in Canton; and the condition of the paper suggested to him that it was about thirty years old. Yet he was hesitant to hazard a guess as to who the painter might be: he gave me to understand that the illustrators who make a speciality of botanical and zoological paintings have always been a little removed from the general run of Canton's artists; they do not as a rule serve apprenticeships in studios as do most others; instead they are employed by visiting European botanists and collectors, who train them in the methods that are particular to their work. For this reason too their work is rarely seen in China—their pictures are usually shipped off to Europe along with the accompanying botanical collections.

Here Lamqua paused to reflect for a while. Then he said that although he could assist me no further himself, he knew of someone who might be able to do so: he was a collector of plants and pictures and an authority on both subjects. He, if anyone, would be able to point me in the right direction.

And who, pray, was this collector? Zadig Bey knew his name although I did not: he is one of the great magnates of the Co-Hong guild, a *fabulously* wealthy merchant who goes by the name of Punhyqua. Lamqua knows him well and said one of his apprentices would make arrangements to take me to him.

This apprentice was then sent for—and that, Puggly dear, was when it happened! When he stepped in I knew, within minutes, that this was no ordinary meeting: a Palpitation went through me, and my hands flew to my chest, as if to quell the pounding of a drum.

His name is Jacqua and you must not think that I am speaking of an Adonis, or of a golden, peach-plucking Botticelli youth: no, not at all. Jacqua is not tall and nor is he athletic in build, but there is in his face a luminous quality, in his eyes a glitter of calm and directed intelligence that no paintbrush could ever capture. Indeed I confess there is no image in my memory, no picture nor portrait, to which Jacqua conforms! It is not often that I meet such a person (no one knows better than you, Puggly dear, how many pictures are stored in my head), but when I do it is always strangely thrilling, for I know that I am in the presence of the New, standing upon the precipice of a discovery, a fall, an adventure . . .

Oh my sweet Princess of Pugglovia, if I thought you knew how, I would ask you to *pray* for me . . . for I do think it possible that I may at last have encountered the One—the True Friend I have always sought.

And I should add that this was not the only heaven-sent encounter of the week: I have also found the most *astonishing* courier—you will see for yourself when you meet him.

~

One morning, when the air was brisk but not yet cold, Bahram looked out of the daftar's window and saw that most of the locals had exchanged their summer wardrobes for heavier clothing: gone were the cotton tunics and pyjamas, the light slippers and silk caps—they had been replaced by quilted robes and embroidered leggings, thick-soled shoes and fur hats.

Bahram knew exactly what had happened: the Governor of the province must have been seen in his winter clothes the day before: this was always the signal for everyone else to follow suit and unpack their winter clothes. It was just like the British in India—except that here the Governor had to await a signal from faraway Peking. The strange thing was that considering how far the capital was and how different the climate, the change of wardrobe in Canton was never out of kilter with the north by more than a few days.

Sure enough, a couple of days later a chilly wind began to blow from the north and the temperature suddenly plummeted: in the daftar it was so cold that charcoal-burning braziers had to be brought in.

The change in weather brought in its train rumours of changes of another kind. In the afternoon Zadig dropped in to say that he had picked up some interesting gossip: the present Governor of the province, who had been so zealous about seizing opium, burning crab-boats and prosecuting dealers, was being recalled to the capital: apparently a new official was to be appointed in his place.

Fanqui-town had been so beset by rumours, of late, that Bahram was careful not to invest too much hope in this report. For a few days he asked around discreetly and although he was unable to find any direct confirmation, he did learn that many others had heard the same reports—indeed there was so much speculation on this subject that the rumour seemed to have crossed the boundary that separates conjecture from news. And the consensus, at least among the Committee, was that the change was a hopeful sign.

This was hugely encouraging to Bahram. Over the last couple of weeks he had received several anxious inquiries from the Bombay businessmen who had invested in the *Anahita*'s cargo: they had heard reports of the damage the vessel had suffered and had written to ask when they might expect to recoup their funds. Bahram's answers had been apologetic but reassuring, informing them that the Canton market had been unusually dull of late but was expected to improve soon. He had not had the heart to tell them that the *Anahita* was still anchored near Hong Kong, with her holds almost full; nor had he let them know that he had yet to receive a single feeler from an interested buyer. Now, emboldened by the rumours of changes in the provincial administration, he decided that the time had come to inform his investors that some positive portents had at last been glimpsed on the Chinese firmament.

Take a new letter, he said to Neel. Start with the usual opening and then continue with this: As you know, the Canton markets have been very dull of late because of certain policies pursued by the present Governor. But your humble servant wishes to inform you that a change of direction has been signalled by the highest authorities in China. It is widely believed that the present Governor is soon to be recalled to the capital. The name of his replacement is not yet known, but I need hardly explain that this is a most welcome sign. It is possible that conditions here may soon return to normal, in which case it is not unreasonable to expect that we may also be able to dispose of our cargoes at a time when there is a great deal of pent-up demand . . .

At this point there was a loud knocking on the daftar's door.

Patrão! Patrão!

Vico? What is it?

The door opened just wide enough to admit Vico's head: Patrão, there's someone to see you.

Now?

Bahram was both surprised and annoyed by the interruption: it had long been his practice to reserve the first hours of his workday for his correspondence, and his standing instructions to his staff were that no visitors were to be admitted to his daftar until after his mid-morning chai break.

What is this nonsense, Vico? A visitor at this time? I've just started a letter.

Patrão, it is one Ho Sin-saang. His full name is Ho Lao-kin.

This did nothing to mollify Bahram: Ho Sin-saang? Who's that? Never heard of him.

Advancing a little further into the room Vico made a barely discernible gesture, with his forefinger, to indicate that he could say no more while the new munshi was in the room.

Bahram turned reluctantly to Neel: That's all for now, munshiji—you can go to your cumra. I will send for you when I am ready.

Ji, Sethji.

Bahram waited till the door had closed again: So what is this about, Vico? Who is this 'Ho Sin-saang'?

Patrão, he says you used to know him many years ago.

Arré, Vico, there are thousands of Ho Sin-saangs in Canton. How can I remember every one I've met? Especially if it was long ago?

Vico shifted his feet uncomfortably: Patrão, he says he was related to Madame . . .

To Chi-mei? Bahram's eyes widened in surprise. But I don't remember that she had any relatives with the surname Ho.

Maybe you knew him by a different name, patrão. These Chinese fellows are always changing their names—one minute it's Ah-something and next minute it's Sin-saang this and Sin-saang that.

Did he mention any other name?

Yes, patrão. He said you might remember him as Ah-Lau or Allow or something like that.

Allow? The name stirred a ripple of recollection in Bahram's memory. Turning his back on Vico he went to the window to look down on the Maidan. As usual, swarms of snot-nosed mosquito-boys were roaming about, in their grey mud-spattered clothes and conical hats, besieging strolling foreigners with cries of: 'I-say! I-say! Achha! Mo-ro-chaa! Gimme cumshaw lan-tau!'

Suddenly he remembered the face of one such urchin, a waist-high jai with a tripping walk—the fellow who had acted as a messenger for Chi-mei.

Bahram turned back to Vico: I think I remember this fellow Allow. But it must be over twenty years since I last saw him. Where did you come across him?

In the Maidan, patrão. He came up to me and asked if I worked for you. I said yes, so then he said he needed to see you on an urgent matter.

What kind of matter?

Business, patrão.

What kind of business? What does he do?

He does *maal-ka-dhanda*, patrão—deals in the kind of cargo we need to sell. Middle-level I think; not a wholesaler. Has a couple of dens of his own, and also owns a pleasure-boat.

Bahram had been pacing furiously for the last few minutes but now he came to a sudden stop. A dealer, Vico? he said, his voice rising in anger. You let a dealer into my house?

Between the two of them it had always been understood that no one associated with the lower end of the trade would be allowed to enter their own premises. Business of that kind was taken care of outside the hong, by Vico—and in years past even Vico had rarely had to deal with small-time vendors, den-keepers and the like, since the cargo was usually disposed of offshore, either at Lintin Island or even further out to sea.

Bahram had never once had any dealings with the legions of unsavoury people who were involved in the inner workings of the trade. That someone from that world should seek an interview with him, in his own daftar, was as astonishing to him as the fact that Vico had actually allowed him in.

Vico, have you gone mad? Since when have people like that been permitted to enter this hong?

Vico patiently stood his ground. Listen, patrão, he said. You know as well as I do that we haven't been able to move any maal these last few weeks: it's not like it used to be before. I've spoken to this man and he has an interesting proposal. I think you should listen to it.

But here? In my daftar?

Where else, patrão? It's better here, no, than outside, where you might be seen by anyone?

And what if someone had seen him coming here?

No one saw, patrão: I brought him the back way. He's waiting downstairs. Now tell me: what do you want me to do? If you're scared to take the risk I will tell him to go.

Bahram went to the window again and looked down at the hurrying porters and eager food-vendors; the bustling beadles and quick-fingered jugglers. The Maidan's brashness and energy were a reproach to his own caution: he could not abide the thought that he had lost his venturesomeness—wasn't it his appetite for risk that had brought him to where he was? He took a deep breath and turned around. All right, he said to Vico: show him in. But make sure the munshi and the others don't see him.

Yes, patrão.

On one side of the daftar there was an arrangement of straight-backed Chinese armchairs. This was where Bahram liked to receive visitors, and he had just seated himself when the door opened to admit Vico and the visitor: a small man, he was dressed unostentatiously, but not inexpensively, in a quilted jacket and a gown of plain, dove-coloured silk. His waist-length hair was dressed with a red ribbon and his head was crowned with a round black hat.

'Chin-chin, Mister Barry,' he said, stepping jauntily across the room. 'Fa-tsai! Fa-tsai!'

It was his stride rather than his face that Bahram recognized, suddenly recalling a stocky little fellow, walking on the balls of his feet and looking as though he might, at any minute, fall face-forward on his nose. The snub-nosed face had grown plump and middle-aged but the walk had somehow retained its sprightly spring. The wheedling cadences of his voice had not changed either: hearing him speak, Bahram was reminded of the days when he would materialize suddenly from within the crowds of the Maidan and whisper: 'Chin-chin, Mister Barry, Number-One Sister tolo come tonight ah . . .'

These memories, so unexpected in this context, provided a kind of jolt that made it impossible for Bahram to be quite as stiffly formal as he would have liked. 'Chin-chin Allow! Chin-chin. Fa-tsai!'

This seemed to delight the visitor, who cried: 'Waa! Mister Barry remember, ah?' He smiled, showing several gold teeth and made a rowing motion with both hands. 'Allow take

Mister Barry and Number-One Sister to White Swan Lake. Remember?'

'Yes.' Bahram recollected now, with painful clarity, that it was this fellow who had rowed Chi-mei and him to the lake when they went there for the first time: he had sat in the stern, patiently working the yuloh, while he and Chi-mei lay together in the cabin below, awkwardly tugging at each other's clothes.

'Remember, later I come to Mister Barry house and he give me cumshaw? Big cumshaw?'

'Yes. Remember.'

In the meanwhile Allow's face had turned grave, as if to reflect Bahram's expression. 'Allow too muchi sad inside, Mister Barry. Too muchi sad Number-One Sister makee die.'

Bahram narrowed his eyes. 'What happen to Number-One Sister? Allow savvy, no-savvy?'

Allow answered with a vehement shake of his head. 'No-savvy. Allow that-time go Macau. Too muchi sorry, Mister Barry.'

'So talkee me,' said Bahram. 'Sittee, sittee here. Allow what thing wanchi? Tell maski, chop-chop. No time have got.'

Hai-le! came the answer, accompanied by a vigorous affirmative nod. 'Allow have ear-hear Mister Barry have come China-side with plenty, plenty big cargo. Is, is-not true? Mister Barry have, no-have plenty cargo ah?'

'Is true. Cargo have got. Plenty big cargo-la.'

'Galaw, Mister Barry talkee allo is inside his heart: what-thing he thinki do with cargo? This-time cannot do-pidgin in Canton. Cannot sell. Mister Barry savvy, no-savvy ah?'

'Savvy. Savvy.' Bahram gave him a nod.

'One piece mandarin have got in Canton, makee too muchi bobbery-la? Floggee, nik-ki, cuttee head. He too muchi damn sassy, galaw. This time cargo no can sell-la.'

Bahram looked at Allow carefully, sizing him up: it was clear that he was referring to the present Governor and his attempts to enforce the embargo—but he was also probably probing to see how much Bahram knew about the situation.

Bahram shrugged in a casual way, to indicate that he was not particularly worried. 'Allow have no ear-hear? This piece mandarin go back soon-soon. Mister Barry can waitee. Maybe new mandarin blongi better. No makee bobbery.'

'Haih me?' Allow made a face of almost comical alarm. 'Mister Barry no-savvy ah? After this piece mandarin go, next one may be muchi more bad galaw. My friend come Beijing. He say people there talkee that Pili-pili—that mean Empe-ro—have chosen already one-piece mandarin. He come soon-soon. He blongi next . . .'

Here, unable to retrieve the word he needed, Allow broke off to take a small pamphlet out of the sleeve of his gown. This was not the first time that Bahram had seen someone consulting this booklet, so he knew what it was—a glossary called 'Foreign Devil-Talk'.

Bahram waited patiently until his visitor had leafed through hundreds of Chinese characters to arrive at the one that he needed.

'Governor. Pili-pili have find new Governor for Canton. He this-time Governor Hukwang. In that-place he stoppee allo opium-pidgin. Pili-pili wanchi do same-same Guangdong. So new Governor come. His name Lin Zexu.'

The mention of a name aroused Bahram's suspicions: the likelihood that a man like Allow would be in possession of such detailed information seemed very small: it was probably just another bargaining tactic. He decided to call his visitor's bluff and smiled broadly: 'Allow savvy name also?'

To Bahram's surprise Allow nodded vigorously. 'Savvy, savvy.'

'Can write name?'

'Can. Can.'

At a gesture from Bahram, Vico fetched a piece of paper and a pencil and Allow laboriously drew a couple of characters on it. Handing the sheet to Bahram, he said: 'This-piece mandarin, Lin Zexu, he too muchi iron-face—teet-meen man. After he come Mister Barry will be in tiger-mouth la. Allow also. Cargo no can get. Allo pidgin finish—*leih an*—no makee joke, Allow. More better, Mister Barry sell this-time, fitee-fitee. Before Lin Zexu come.'

Allow's knowingness and insistence had begun to irk Bahram. His tone sharpened. 'What-for Allow talkee so fashion? He wanchi makee pidgin? Wanchi buy cargo?'

Allow answered with a gesture of self-deprecation. 'No can buy allo cargo. Allow small man—no can catchi so muchi cash. Allow wanchi hundred-piece case la. No can take more. What you wah ah? Do, no-do pidgin?'

The number gave Bahram pause: one hundred cases was less than a twentieth of his cargo, but at this point it would represent a substantial sale. Yet the most important problem remained unchanged: how was the shipment to be brought to Canton?

'How Allow can bring hundred-piece case from ship to Canton ah? Mandarin can catchi no? Then too muchi bobbery for Mister Barry.'

Here Allow glanced at Vico who leant forward to intervene.

Listen, patrão, he said to Bahram in an urgent undertone: I have already discussed all this with our friend here. There's only one man who is bringing cargoes down at this time—Mr James Innes. His lascars have been transporting it to Whampoa, in his own cutters, hidden under other goods—cotton, furs, coins and so on. He has an understanding with one of the big dealers. They've paid off all the officials along the route. He has had no trouble so far and now he is planning to bring a shipment directly to Canton—we can arrange for him to bring ours too. If you give permission, I will go to the *Anahita* and oversee the whole thing. You won't have to get involved too much. All you have to do is to go to Mr Innes's apartment for a few minutes, at the end, to confirm delivery. Mr Innes will let you know when the time comes. That's all—I've worked it out.

Bahram paused to consider this: he had done business with distasteful people before, and he would certainly be able to deal with Innes, if it came to that. But it would only be worth the risk if the price was right. Without looking in Allow's direction, he said to Vico: How much is our friend offering?

Vico smiled and pushed himself up from his chair. He'll tell you himself, he said. It's best you settle it with him; I'll wait outside.

As Vico stepped away, Bahram turned to Allow. 'For one-piece chest how muchi dollar?'

Allow smiled and held up a hand with the thumb turned down and four fingers extended.

'Four?' said Bahram in a carefully neutral voice. 'Four thousand dollars? *Sei-chin maan?*'

Allow's smile grew wider as he nodded in affirmation.

Bahram rose to his feet, crossed the room, and pushed the window open, allowing the crisp air to cool his face.

The sum was even higher than Dent had suggested, more than six times the usual price. The proceeds would go a long way to paying off his creditors; he could almost see himself dictating the letters he would send them: Your faithful servant is pleased to report that despite a very dull market he is able to honour some of his obligations . . .

'Mister Barry . . .'

He spun around to find Allow standing right behind him, smiling thinly. 'Mister Barry,' he said, in a quietly suggestive voice, 'Mister Barry savvy no-savvy Allow have buy boat blongi Number-One Sister ah?'

'You? You have buy boat blongi Chi-mei?'

Allow bowed and grinned. 'Yes, Allow have buy. After Number-One Sister makee die. Why Mister Barry no come on boat one day ah? Go White Swan Lake, like olo time? Catch one-two piece pipe la? Have got number-one-chop gai-girlie. Mister Barry can do all waan. Man must do laap-pidgin sometime or catchi sick, get too muchi olo. Allow give Mister Barry top-chop sing-song girlie, just like Number-One Sister . . .'

To hear Chi-mei spoken of in this way was more than Bahram could tolerate. He spun around to face Allow, his eyes blazing: 'Wailo Allow!' he shouted. 'What-thing you talkee? Number-One Sister no blongi sing-song girl. She blongi good woman—work hard; care for boy-chilo. She no blongi sing-song girlie. Allow savvy no-savvy ah?'

Allow backed away, his eyes widening. 'Sorry! Very sorry, Mister Barry. Me too muchi sad inside, say bad thing.'

The door flew open and Vico burst in. *Kya hua?* he said. What's happened, patrão?

Bahram was shaking now, and he leant towards the window again, turning his back on his visitor.

Take him away, Vico, he said, with a brusque gesture of dismissal. Tell him I can't do it. I don't want to get mixed up with people like Innes and this fellow here. There are just too many risks.

As you say, patrão.

At the door Allow stopped to look back. 'Mister Barry,' he said, 'you thinkee what I say. You wanchee, still can do-pidgin. Any time, Allow ready. Better do-pidgin before new Governor come.'

Bahram was so angry now that a slew of half-remembered Cantonese obscenities spewed from his lips: *Gaht hoi! Puk chaht hoi . . .*

A few minutes later Vico came back, accompanied by the new munshi, and Bahram exploded: What sort of staff have I got? Why do I never get any proper news from either of you? Why do I have to find out everything from others?

What do you mean, patrão? What news?

The news about the new Governor; this Lin Jiju or Zexu or whatever. Why didn't I hear about this from one of you?

~

It was Vico who showed Neel a way to stay ahead of the news: See, munshiji, the *Register* comes out every Tuesday, but the printing and preparation are done on Sunday and Monday. Sometimes even earlier.

But what good is that to me? said Neel.

Obvious no? said Vico. You have to go where it is printed.

There were only two English printing presses in Canton, Vico explained. One was in the American Hong and belonged to Protestant missionaries; the other was on Thirteen Hong

Street and was owned and run by a Chinese man who had for many years worked as an apprentice to a well-known Macau printer, Mr De Souza, Goan by origin. Vico knew him well, and through him had also come to be acquainted with his assistant, Liang Kuei-ch'uan, who went by the fanqui-name of Compton. Vico knew for a fact that Compton was always looking for proofreaders.

Can you read proofs in English munshiji?

Neel had, for a while, co-edited a literary magazine; he was able to answer, with some confidence: Yes, I can.

Then I'll take you to meet Compton, said Vico. His shop is like a bazar for the news.

Compton's shop was on Thirteen Hong Street, the road that separated Fanqui-town from the city's southern suburbs. One side of the street was lined by the rear walls of the foreign factories, some of which were fitted with small doorways to connect them with the busy thoroughfare. On the other side stood innumerable shops and shop-houses, large and small, each of them bedecked with banners and pennants that advertised the goods within: silk, lacquerware, ivory carvings, false teeth and the like.

Compton's print-shop differed from its neighbours in that it had no counters and no goods on offer. Visitors stepped into a room that smelled of ink and incense, and was crammed with reams of paper. The press was nowhere in sight; the printing was done somewhere deep inside the building.

Neel and Vico entered to find a boy dozing upon a pile of old *Register*s. A glance at the visitors was enough to send the fellow scampering through a door; when next seen he was hiding behind the legs of the portly, harried-looking man who presently emerged from within.

'Mr Vico! *Nei hou ma?*'

'*Hou leng*, Mr Compton. And you?'

Compton had a round full face, the shape of which was perfectly echoed by the lenses of the spectacles that sat precariously upon the end of his nose. He was dressed in a grey gown that was partly covered by an ink-smeared apron, and his queue was coiled into a tight and workmanlike bun.

'And is this your pang-yauh, Mr Vico?' Compton squinted at Neel with the worried frown of the chronically short-sighted. 'Who is he, eh?'

'Mr Anil Munshi. He is Seth Bahramji's letter-writer. You are looking for a proofreader, no?'

Compton's eyes grew unnaturally large behind his thick glasses. 'Gam aa? Proofreader! Is true?'

'True.'

Within minutes Neel was sitting on a bale of paper, scrutinizing the proofs of the next issue of the *Register*. By the end of the day, he and the printer were on first-name terms: Compton had asked him to drop the 'Mr' and he had become Ah-Neel. He left the shop with a string of cash wrapped around his wrist and was back again the next day.

Compton had another set of proofs ready, and while looking through them Neel asked: 'Have you heard anything about a new Governor? One Lin Tse-hsü?'

Compton glanced at him in surprise: 'Haih-a! Gam you have heard the talk also?'

'Yes. Do you know about him?'

Compton smiled. 'Maih-haih! Lin Zexu is great man—one of best poet and scholar in China. He is man with big mind, open mind—always want to learn new things. My teacher his friend. Speak of him a lot.'

'What does he say?'

Compton lowered his voice: 'Lin Zexu not like other mandarin. He is a good man, honest man—best officer in country. Wherever there is trouble, there he is sent. He never take cumshaw, nothing—jan-haih! He become Governor of Kiangsi while he is still very young. In two years he stop all opium trade in that province. People there call him *Lin Ch'ing-t'ien*—that means "Lin the Clear Sky".'

Compton paused and put a finger on his lips. 'Better not tell this to your master bo. He will get too much worried. Dak?'

Neel nodded: Dak! Dak!

Soon Neel took to dropping by the print-shop when he had time to spare, and sometimes Compton would lead him down the passageway that separated his shop from his living quarters. This part of the building was two storeys high, with the rooms arranged around a courtyard. Although the courtyard was paved with stone tiles, a profusion of potted plants, trees and vines gave it the feel of a garden. The washing that fluttered overhead, strung between the rails of the upstairs balconies, provided a canopy of shade; on one side was a cherry tree, with leaves that were beginning to turn colour.

When Neel entered this part of the house the womenfolk would disappear, but the children, of whom there were many, would remain. Often Neel would see faces he had not seen before, and this gave him the impression of an extended family, frequently augmented by visitors: he was not surprised when Compton told him that his ancestral village lay at the mouth of the Pearl River, at Chuenpi, which was why he often had to play host to visiting relatives.

Compton himself was not Canton-born and nor had he grown up in the city. As a boy he had spent much of his time on the water: his father had made his living as a ship's comprador, and the family had usually spent the trading season travelling between the Bogue and Whampoa, in the wake of foreign vessels.

The job of a ship's comprador was different from that of a factory comprador; the latter, like the dubashes of India, were responsible for providing supplies to foreign traders after they had taken up residence in Canton. Ships' compradors were more like ship chandlers, procuring provisions and equipment for the vessels that engaged their services. Unlike factory compradors, who had close links with the merchants of the Co-Hong, ships' compradors worked on their own and had no powerful patrons to rely on. Theirs was a fiercely competitive business: as a boy, at the start of each season, Compton and his father would take it in turns to keep a lookout for the opium fleet, from a hill near their house. When the first vessel was spotted, they would go running down to the harbour to unmoor the family sampan. Then would begin a wild race against the rest of the bumboat fleet. The first boat to reach the incoming vessels stood the best chance of being taken on as the comprador, especially if the captain happened to be known to the family; if they were quick and lucky, they would secure a contract that would keep them busy for the next several weeks.

Compton's family had been in the business long enough to be known to the skippers and crews of many foreign ships and some would hire them every time they returned to southern China. Among their oldest and most loyal customers were the vessels of a Boston-based firm, Russell & Co. Through them their family had acquired a large American clientele, many of whom gave them letters of recommendation to show to other American ships; some of their customers stayed in touch with them long after they had stopped sailing, and some even sent them little gifts and tokens with younger seafaring relatives. In this way the family had acquired letters from a Mr Coolidge, a Mr Astor and a Mr Delano, all of whom, they had later discovered, were from families that were of the first importance in America. A Canton trader called William Irving had even given them a book, *Tales of the Alhambra* written by his uncle, Washington Irving: unfortunately Compton had no memory of this man; to him he was just one amongst hundreds of friendly travellers who had given him lessons in English.

From the time he could walk, Compton had accompanied his father on his visits to foreign vessels. He was a winning child and was always made much of by the seamen and ship's officers. At Whampoa, where inbound ships had to spend several weeks at anchor, time always hung heavy on the hands of the crewmen and they would amuse themselves by speaking English with the boy. A quick learner, Compton became an invaluable asset to his family, winning them many clients with his fluency. In time this talent also earned him a job at the De Souza print-shop, in Macau. But printing was not all he did there: during his apprenticeship, he had also conceived the idea of combining his knowledge of English and Chinese to produce a glossary of the Canton jargon, for the use of his own countrymen.

The title of this short booklet was translated for Neel as 'The Red-Haired-People's-Buying-and-Selling-Common-Ghost-Language'. It was more commonly known however as 'Ghost-People-Talk'—*Gwai-lou-waah*—and it sold very well, far better than its author could ever have imagined, and the proceeds had allowed Compton to set up his own print-shop in Canton.

Several years after its publication the popularity of 'Ghost People-Talk' was still undiminished: many vendors and shopkeepers kept a copy at hand, for reference, so its cover was a familiar sight in Fanqui-town. It featured a drawing of a European in eighteenth-century costume, with knee-breeches, stockings, a three-cornered hat and a buckled coat. The figure held a thin cane in one hand, and in the other something that might have been a handkerchief—this at least was the surmise of Compton himself. Handkerchiefs had once been an object of fascination for people in China, he explained to Neel; many had believed that Europeans used them to store and transport their snot—in much the same way that thrifty Chinese farmers carried their excrement to the fields.

The cover of 'Ghost-People-Talk' had caught Neel's eye long before he met Compton and he had sometimes wondered about the booklet's contents. He was astonished to learn that it was a glossary—and was delighted also to discover that the author was none other than his part-time employer.

Of the book itself, Neel understood very little since it was written entirely in Chinese. But being besotted with words of all kinds, Neel had fallen headlong in love with Chinese writing: for him Canton offered no greater pleasure than the ubiquitous presence of the ideograms, on shop-signs, doorways, umbrellas, carts and boats. He had already learnt to recognize a few of them: the 人 character for example, which was easy to remember because its two legs represented its meaning—'man'. Similarly 'big', which was, in its mysteriously evocative way, merely a man with arms extended; and 'dollar', the sign for which was omnipresent in Fanqui-town, being featured on innumerable shop-signs. Having once come to know the characters, he saw them everywhere: they would leap out at him from the most unexpected places, waving their limbs as if to catch his attention.

In leafing through 'Ghost-People-Talk' Neel was surprised to find that the first entry featured two ideograms he had learnt to recognize: one was the character for 'man' and the other the sign for 'dollar'. The pairing of 'man' and 'dollar' puzzled him. Was it perhaps a subtle philosophical statement?

Compton laughed at this. 'Mat-yeh?' he said. 'What, don't you see? "Dollar" is *maan* in Cantonese.'

Neel was greatly taken by the ingenuity of this: instead of using phonetic symbols, Compton had suggested the pronunciation of the English word by using a character that sounded similar when pronounced in the Cantonese dialect. For longer and more complicated words, he had joined together two or more one-syllable Cantonese words: thus 'today' became 'to-teay' and so on.

'And all this you did yourself?'

Compton nodded proudly and added that it was his practice to revise and enlarge the booklet every year, thus ensuring its continuing sale.

Thinking about this later, in the privacy of his cubicle, Neel realized that there was something providential about his meeting with Compton: it was as if Fate had conspired to bring him into the orbit of a kindred spirit, a man who valued words just as much as he did himself. Looking through Ghost-People-Talk it occurred to him to wonder why no glossary of pidgin existed for the benefit of people who spoke English. Or for that matter Hindusthani? Surely the foreigners who sojourned in Fanqui-town needed to understand the enclave's lingua franca just as much as their hosts did? And if an English version of Ghost-People-Talk could be produced, surely it would also command a substantial market?

In the middle of the night, he sat up in his bed. Of course such a book had to be written—and who better to do it than he himself, in collaboration with Compton?

The next day, as soon as his duties in the daftar were done, he went hurrying over to Thirteen Hong Street. On reaching Compton's shop he announced: 'I have a proposal.'

'Ngo? What is it then?'

'Listen, Compton . . .'

It turned out that the idea of producing an English version of 'Devil-Talk' had already occurred to Compton. Looking for a collaborator, he had approached several Englishmen and Americans. They had all laughed at him, contemptuously dismissing the idea.

'They think-la, pidgin is just broken English, like words of a baby. They do not understand. Is not so simple bo.'

'So will you let me do it?'

Yat-dihng! Yat dihng!

'What does that mean?' Neel inquired a little nervously.

'Yes. Certainly.'

Do-jeh Compton.

M'ouh hak hei.

Neel could already see the cover: it would feature a richly caparisoned mandarin. As for the title, that too had already come to him. He would call it: *The Celestial Chrestomathy, Comprising A Complete Guide To And Glossary Of The Language Of Commerce In Southern China.*

~

Collecting plants on Hong Kong proved to be more of a challenge than either Fitcher or Paulette had expected. The island's slopes were precipitous on every side and the ridge that ran along most of its eight-mile length was nowhere less than five hundred feet in height: it was topped with several peaks that rose to over a thousand feet, and the tallest of them, in Fitcher's estimation, was perhaps only a little under two thousand feet. The soil was granitic and glinted underfoot with quartz, mica and felspar; on steep slopes it had a way of slipping and sliding so that a slightly misplaced shoe could send an avalanche roaring down a treeless gully. In some stretches the decomposed granite was covered with mould and ferns, which gave it a deceptive look of solidity; a moment's carelessness could lead to a nasty slip or a fall.

The steep gradients and rocky slopes were hard on Fitcher's ageing joints and at the end of a day's collecting he was often in pain. By refusing to acknowledge the physical toll of his advancing years he frequently made matters worse for himself: he would plan miles-long expeditions, insisting that he was accustomed to walking such distances on the Cornish moors and making no allowances for the difference in terrain. Having once set off he would soldier on to the very end, despite Paulette's remonstrances, earning himself hours of agony afterwards.

As the weather turned colder, Fitcher's hips and knees grew still stiffer and his pains worsened to the point where even he had to accept that if he was going to continue collecting on the island, it would not be on foot. But there were no vehicles on Hong Kong and no roads either; even paths were few, for the island's villages and hamlets were dotted along the shoreline and their inhabitants travelled between them mainly by boat.

Horses would have provided an easy solution to their predicament, but there were none on the island—at least not to their knowledge: the only draught animals on the fields were bullocks and buffaloes. A sedan chair might also have provided a solution, but Fitcher would not hear of it: 'Botanizing in a carry-cart? I hope eer funning, Miss Paulette . . .'

The answer arrived with Robin's next letter: the courier was a *louh-daaih*, or 'laodah'—the master of a junk, and not much different in appearance from the other leathery Cantonese seamen who skippered the vessels of those waters. Sturdy of build, he had the bow-legged gait and weather-sharpened gaze of an experienced sailor. He was dressed in the usual boatman's pyjamas and quilted tunic. His queue was short and flecked with grey, and his head was topped with a conical sun hat of the kind that was to be seen on every boatman's head.

But when he began to speak Paulette was struck dumb. *Nomoshkar*, he said in Bengali, joining his hands together. Are you Miss Paulette? Your friend, Mr Chinnery, has sent you a letter, from Canton.

It took Paulette a few seconds to recover from her surprise. Then, after thanking him profusely, she said: *Apni ke?* Who are you? Where did you learn to speak Bangla?

I lived in Calcutta for a long time, he said with a smile. I went there as a sailor and jumped ship, to get married. Over there people called me Baburao.

And now you live in Canton, do you, Baburao-da?

Yes; when I'm not out on my boat, that is.

He turned to point to his vessel, which was anchored nearby, and explained that he travelled regularly between Canton and Macau and frequently acted as a courier, dropping off letters and packages at various points along the way.

If you need anything let me know; I may be able to help.

Paulette could tell, from his demeanour, that this was not an idle boast: he looked like the kind of man who was spoken of, in Bengali, as *jogaré*—a resourceful improviser, with his ears close to the ground.

Tell me, Baburao-da, she said, do you think it might be possible to find a couple of horses here, on the island?

Baburao scratched his head and thought a little. Then his face brightened: Why yes! he said. I know a man who lives on the island. He has some horses. Would you like to meet him?

So it was arranged: the next day Baburao came by in a sampan and rowed Paulette and Fitcher to a picturesque little village on the shores of an inlet. The horse-owner was duly found, the horses were examined and a reasonable price was quickly arrived at. But when everything was almost settled an unforeseen problem arose: the owner possessed only two saddles and both were of the Chinese type, with a high pommel and cantle.

Fitcher took one glance and shook his head: 'Ee'll never be able to manage that in eer skirts, Miss Paulette.'

Paulette had already thought of a solution but she knew she had to be careful about how she put it across.

'Well sir,' she said, 'skirts are not the only clothes in my possession.'

'Eh?' Fitcher frowned.

'You will remember, sir, that when we met at Pamplemousses, I was wearing a shirt and a pantalon. Mr Reid had lent them to me and I still have them.'

'What?' barked Fitcher. 'Dress up as a man? Is that what ee've got in mind?'

'Please sir, it is the only sensible thing. Is it not?'

Fitcher's face went into a deep scowl, tying itself into so tight a knot that the tip of his beard came within a few inches of touching the twitching tips of his eyebrows. But then, having thought the matter through, he unclenched his jaws.

'Since ee've set eer mind on it—we'll try it tomorrow.'

So they returned the next day, with Paulette dressed, once again, in Zachary's clothes, and even Fitcher had to concede that it was a happy solution. The horses carried them to a height of over a thousand feet, where they came upon more orchids: pale rose 'bamboo orchids', *Arundina chinensis*, and a small primrose-yellow epiphyte, growing in a nullah—the first was already familiar to Fitcher, but not the second.

'Why Miss Paulette, I think ee may have found something new there. What'd ee like to call it?'

'If it were up to me, sir,' she said, 'I would call it *Diploprora penrosii*.'

ten

~

Markwick's Hotel, Nov 26

Dearest Puggly, so much *news*! So many *developments*—and not least in regard to your camellias . . . but I will not speak of that immediately for fear that the rest of this letter would be wasted on you. And I do want you to know, dear Puggly, that I have never been so *happy* as in these last few days . . .

Lamqua has given me the run of his studio and I have spent many joyful hours there. I sit beside Jacqua, on the apprentices' bench, and have become an *expert* in the art of using stencils. He has taught me some of his little tricks, like that of painting flesh tones on the *reverse* side of the paper—you would not believe what a marvellously lifelike translucence this lends to the skin! But some of the things he can do I do not think I could even *attempt*. His pictures are not large, yet when he paints clothing you sometimes have the impression of being able to see the very *threads* of the garments. If you could see how it is done I warrant you would declare it an *astounding* sight: he holds not one but two brushes in his hand, the first being just thick enough to hold a droplet of colour. The second is so fine that it has no more than a single hair and by flicking this against the other brush he transfers the paint to the paper—in such a manner as to create filaments of paint that are scarcely visible to the eye!

Sometimes Jacqua and I go for walks, in Fanqui-town and the suburbs beyond, and he tells me a little about his Family. He has such an elfin look that I had taken him to be younger than I—can you imagine my surprise when I learnt that he is actually a little *older*, in his mid-twenties, and is not only *married*, but also the father of two children—a boy of seven and a girl of five (he has shown me their portraits, which he has painted himself: they are perfect angels and would not be in the least out of place on the ceiling of a Mantegna chapel). His wife has bound feet and I should *so* love to see a picture of her but he pretends that he does not have one (or if he does he will not show it to me) because of course she is in purdah (which seems to be almost as strict here as it is at home amongst certain classes). Their house is, I think, not unlike the rambling family compounds of Calcutta, with many courtyards, and more uncles and aunts and cousins than you can count—but with this difference: that many of Jacqua's brothers and cousins are also painters—for they too are a Studio family.

But I must not go on . . . I know you are impatient to learn about your camellias and I have kept you waiting long enough.

Unfortunately, my dear Puggly, it took *inordinately* long to hear back from Punhyqua, the Hongist, because he has removed to his country estate, for a change of air! But yesterday Jacqua told me that Punhyqua had at last sent a letter, asking that we visit him at his country retreat, which is on Honam Island. And so we went this morning . . . and that is why I have set myself down to write to you this very day, because I knew that if I did not get to it at once, I would be *overwhelmed*, and might never summon the energy to do it—for it was all *exceedingly* strange and wonderful and new! Even the boat we went in was of a kind I would never have imagined that I would ever step on of my own accord—for it was a *coracle*! These are round shells, made of plaited reeds and straw: they are often to be seen on the Pearl River, spinning giddily across the water with children clinging on inside, looking as if they were being swept away in a giant basket. In ours there were no children but instead two young women, each armed with an oar. This too is a common sight in Canton, for many of the boats on the river are handled by girls and women—and you must not imagine these females to be delicate, foot-bound creatures, too timid to look a man in the eye. They are absolute *harpies* and will say things that bring a blush to the cheeks of the most hardened Tars. The tenor of their raillery will be clear to you when you learn what they said to me as I came aboard. Needless to say, coracles are *extremely* unsteady and when you step in they lurch violently under your weight. To save myself from falling in the water I had to fling an arm around one of the girls. Far from being outraged she gave a great shriek of laughter and said: 'Na! Na! Morning-time no makee like so. Mandarin see, he squeegee me. Wait litto bit. Nightee time come, no man can see!' Then there followed gales of laughter and they kept on teasing me in the most shameless way—yet, all this while, our little craft was spinning through the floating city, and all around us were tea-boats and rice-boats and sampans, moored so as to form streets and lanes.

Winding through these waterways, we emerged into the channel that is kept open in mid-stream to permit the flow of traffic: suddenly we were darting past ponderous barges and enormous pole-junks, stacked high with bamboo. It seemed impossible that we should evade a collision and I clung so tightly to the sides of the coracle that my knuckles turned a *deathly* white—but our two oarswomen were so utterly insensible to the perils around us that from time to time, even as they were rowing and steering, they would cool their faces with their fans.

Honam is on the other bank of the river. I think I have mentioned this island to you before; it lies opposite the city of Canton and is of considerable size, extending sixteen miles from end to end. Jacqua told me that there are some who believe the island should be called not Honam but

Honan—which is the name of another province in China. As with everything here, there is a complicated story behind it, something about a mandarin who caused snow to fall on the island by planting pine trees from Honan. It sounds *most* unlikely—but I think perhaps the story is meant to point to the contrast between the two banks of the river, which is indeed so marked that they might well belong to different provinces. The north bank, where Canton lies, is as crowded a stretch of land as you will ever see, with houses, walls, bustees and galis extending for miles into the distance; Honam, by contrast, is like a vast park, green and wooded: several small creeks and streams cut through it and their shores are dotted with monasteries, nurseries, orchards, pagodas and picturesque little villages.

Our destination lay deep in the interior of the island and to get there we had to turn into a winding creek. Presently, while passing through a stretch of jungle, we came to a jetty, projecting out of a muddy bank. The place is desolate, with no habitation anywhere in sight, but here you must leave your boat and follow a winding path that leads into the forested interior of the island. Then you come to a long wall, shaped like a wave and extending into the far distance. There is only a single gateway in sight, circular in shape, like a full moon. Placed in front of it is an arrangement of feathery pine trees and utterly *fantastical* boulders: to look at them you would think they were anthills, they are pierced with so many holes and hollows and fissures—but they are grey in colour and their appearance is created not by insects but by the action of water.

The gate was locked and while we were standing outside, waiting to be let in, I learnt from Jacqua that Punhyqua's estate is regarded as a fine example of the southern style of garden-making. You can imagine, Puggly dear, the eager expectation with which I slipped through that circular portal—and indeed it was as if I had arrived in some other kingdom, a place of the most *extravagant* fantasy: there were winding streams, spanned by hump-backed bridges; lakes with islands on which dainty little follies sat precariously perched; there were halls and pavilions of many sizes, some large enough to accommodate a hundred people and some in which no more than one person could sit. The trees too were fantastically varied, some tall and sturdy, soaring proud and erect; some tiny and stunted with their branches trained as if to illustrate the flow of the wind. At every turn there was a new perspective to baffle and delight the eye: it was as if the very ground had been shaped and contorted to create illusory vistas.

Suddenly I understood why Chinese artists paint landscapes on scrolls: you would see nothing of a garden like this if you painted it in perspective. On a scroll it would unfold in front of you, from top to bottom, like a story—you would see it like it *happened*; it would unroll before your gaze as if you were walking through it.

And then, Puggly dear, I had an idea, a Notion, that froze me in my steps. Should my epic painting be a scroll instead? (Of course I would have to find a fitting name for it, since an 'epic scroll' does not sound quite right, does it?) But is it not a stroke of Genius? Events, people, faces, scenes would unroll as they happened: it will be something New and Revolutionary—it could make my reputation and establish me for ever in the Pantheon of Artists . . .

You will understand, my dear Puggly-wallah, why my mind was in such a *tumult* that I was aware of nothing else until I entered the presence of our host, Punhyqua.

You must not think I was completely unprepared for the meeting: in the days preceding I had been to some trouble to inform myself about this magnate. His family, Zadig Bey had told me, has been conducting business in Canton for *hundreds* of years and one of his ancestors was among the founders of the Co-Hong guild, in the middle years of the last century. Yet they are not from the province of Canton—they hail from another maritime province, Fujian, where lies the port of Amoy—and despite their long residence in the city they are careful to maintain many of the ways and customs of their ancestors. They are now among the wealthiest of the Co-Hong families, and Punhyqua himself has a mandarin's rank and is entitled to wear certain buttons in his cap: he is said to be a great sensualist, with a vast harem of wives and concubines, and an epicure too, famous for his banquets.

These accounts had led me to wonder whether Punhyqua might not be a little like our Calcutta Nabobs—insufferably conceited and consequential. But I need have had no fear on this score: he is a grandfatherly man with a kindly twinkle in his eyes. There is not a chittack of conceit about him. When we came upon him he was taking his ease in an airy pavilion, with windows of blue and white glass. He was dressed in the simplest way, in a quilted jacket and a robe of plain cotton, and he was lying on a kind of divan, with a little teapoy at his side. He greeted us in the most hospitable way and inquired at some length after Lamqua, and after Jacqua's family. Then he asked about Mr Chinnery, whom he knows well, having had his portrait painted by him. I happened to express some curiosity about this work, which, like many of Mr Chinnery's Chinese paintings, was unknown to me, so he had it fetched from his house—and it proved to be one of my Uncle's finest, executed in his Grand Manner, with many dabs and flourishes.

Only after these preliminaries had been completed did I show him the camellia paintings—and you would have been thrilled, dear Puggly, to observe his response, for his face lit up in such away that you could not doubt that he had recognized something. At once he summoned a retainer and sent him racing off along the winding pathways. I thought for sure the man would return with a potted camellia and thereby put an end to our search. But no! He came back with a roll of silk, from the inside of which there emerged a picture that was very similar to the one I had brought with me—the flowers were arranged at different angles, which changed the composition slightly, but even to my unpractised eye it was evident that the blooms were of the same variety. As for the colours, the brushwork and the paper, they were like enough to suggest that the two pictures had been painted by the same hand and at about the same time.

I can see you now, my dear Puggly-mem, sitting with your brow furrowed and holding your breath as you ask: whose *was* this hand?

I regret to say you are shortly to be disappointed . . .

. . . for Punhyqua did not *know* who the illustrator was: the only thing he could remember was that he was a young Canton painter but employed by an Englishman—a botanist or gardener who had come to Canton some thirty or thirty-five years before. And strange to say, it was this man—the fanqui—who had given Punhyqua the picture and for the same reason that Mr Penrose has entrusted me with his: that is to say, in the hope that it might help in tracing the flower. But the variety was unknown to Punhyqua, and despite making extensive inquiries he has been able to learn nothing about it. So far as he knows the Englishman was never able to find any trace of it either.

Now once again, I can see you asking yourself: so who was this fanqui, this Englishman in whose footsteps you follow?

And you may be sure that I did not neglect to put this question to my host—but to no avail alas, for he could not remember the man's name (which is not surprising, I suppose, after a gap of thirty years!).

This is all that I would have to tell you today, if not for a most *fortunate* circumstance. As we were preparing to take our leave of Punhyqua, another magnate of the Co-Hong was shown in. I recognized him at once, because Mr Chinnery has painted him too, and I happen to have chanced upon one of the preparatory sketches: he is Mr Wu Ping-ch'ien who is the very greatest of the Co-Hong merchants, known to fanquis as Howqua.

Howqua is the oldest of the Hongists and also the richest by far. Zadig Bey says that his fortune amounts to thirty million Spanish dollars—can you imagine, Puggly dear, if you were to melt that amount of silver, you would have a lump that would outweigh twelve thousand people! Yet to look at Howqua you would never imagine that he was one of the world's richest men: Zadig Bey says that he is famed both for his generosity and his asceticism (he is known to have once torn up a promissory note in the sum of seventy-five thousand dollars, out of pity for an American who was unable to pay it back and was desperate to go back home!). And as for his habits, Zadig Bey says that he will sit through a hundred-course banquet without touching more than a morsel or two. He certainly has the look of an ascetic, very thin, almost skeletal, with sunken cheeks and deep-set eyes.

So there they sat, these great magnates of finance, who between them would be able to buy half of the city of London if not more—joining their heads together to pore over your camellias! They remembered that the Englishman was an odd, strange fellow, very fond of the opium pipe; they recalled that he had been none too popular among his countrymen and had gone off to live on Honam Island, in a small hut. In the end it was Howqua who remembered his name (although I cannot believe he said it right): for it sounded, Puggly dear, like C-u-r—and it is hard to imagine that he could have been called that. But perhaps Mr Penrose will know if ever there was a botanist in Canton who had a name like that?

And oh, my dear Baroness von Pugglenhaven, I cannot end this without thanking you for the letter you sent with Baburao: it was perfectly *enchanting*! I was entranced by the vision it conjured up—of you galloping across Hong Kong dressed in your beau's clothes! I should tell you that you made a great impression also on Baburao: he swears that you make an even better sahib than a ma'am!

~

The invitation to the banquet could not have come at a better time: with fresh rumours swirling through Fanqui-town every day, it had become a matter of mounting frustration for Bahram that he had not been able to have a quiet talk with any of the leading Co-Hong merchants. To obtain an appointment with one of them would not have been difficult, but Bahram knew that they would not speak candidly in their places of business: an encounter at some well-attended event, out of the earshot of spies and informers, was far more likely to lead to a useful conversation.

In times past, such meetings would have come about with dependable regularity, for the Co-Hong merchants were second to none in their conviviality, and were often among the most enthusiastic participants in Fanqui-town's gatherings. But this year, they had become much more reticent: when attending events in the foreign enclave, they were stiff in demeanour and were usually accompanied by large entourages. In the past they had themselves regularly hosted large and elaborate banquets, but now these much-awaited fixtures had also become rare events: this was why Bahram was glad to receive one of the red, beautifully ornamented envelopes that were always used for such invitations. He was even more pleased when he opened the envelope and saw that the invitation was from Punhyqua, for a banquet to be held at his estate on Honam Island: Bahram could remember a time when Honam Island, on the far side of the Pearl River, had been the site of some of Canton's most memorable feasts—and none more so than those hosted by Punhyqua, who was a renowned gourmet.

On the morning of the banquet, as was the custom, yet another red card was received, as a reminder, and a few hours later, Bahram set off across the Maidan, in the direction of Jackass Point, with Apu, his lantern-bearer, in train. As always there were dozens of boats lined up along the landing ghat, disgorging passengers and cargo, and it was something of a challenge to negotiate the muddy steps.

The one good thing about Jackass Point was that the crowds that poured through it were always in a hurry: of the usual loiterers and bonegrabbers there were very few here, so a man who was not particularly pressed for time could usually find some spot where he could stand and look around, without being noticed or accosted; it was in one such corner that Bahram positioned himself while Apu went off to arrange for a boat and boatman.

Watching the crowds surge past, Bahram remembered his first visit to Honam Island, decades ago, when he was all of twenty-two: he recalled how he had stared, open-mouthed and unashamed, at the exquisite pavilions, the carved griffins, the terraced gardens and landscaped lakes—he had seen things whose very existence he could not have imagined. He remembered how eagerly he had attacked the food, delighting in the unknown aromas and unfamiliar tastes; he remembered the heady taste of the rice wine, and how it had seemed to him that he had stepped into some kind of waking dream: how was it possible that he, a penniless chokra from Navsari, had wandered into a place that seemed to belong in some legendary firdaus? It seemed to him now that he would gladly trade all his years of experience, all his knowledge of the world, to be granted once again an instant of such incandescent wonder—a moment in which, even in the midst of so many new and amazing things, nothing would seem more extraordinary than that he, a poor boy from a Gujarat village had found his way into a Chinese garden.

He was woken from this daydream by a disturbingly familiar voice: 'Mister Barry! Chin-chin!'

'Allow?'

'Chin-chin Mister Barry! What-side you go now ah? Honam?'

Bahram was annoyed and unsettled to find Allow at his elbow. It seemed hardly possible that such an encounter could happen by accident in the midst of this surging crowd; it occurred to Bahram to wonder whether Allow might have been forewarned that he, Bahram, was planning to cross the river today. But of course there was no way of knowing.

'Yes,' he said, curtly. 'Go Honam.'

Allow treated him to a broad, insinuating smile. 'What for Mister Barry no talkee Allow eh? Can takee Honam. Mister

Barry savvy Allow have one-piece nice boat, no?' He raised a hand to point to the waterside. 'There—look-see.'

Turning to look where Allow was pointing, Bahram met with a shock. He recognized the boat at a glance, even though it was much changed: it was the last 'kitchen-boat' that Chi-mei had bought—the very one on which she had been killed. It had since been re-fitted and repainted, in the gaudy colours of a pleasure-boat—red and gold—but it was still recognizable because of its distinctive stern, shaped like an upraised fishtail. The main deck, which had once housed Chi-mei's eatery, was now tricked out with brightly decorated windows; the upper deck, which had served as her living quarters, had been turned into a richly ornamented pavilion. At its fore was a balcony-like gallery: Bahram and Chi-mei had often sat there in the past, on a pair of old chairs. These had been replaced by a divan with a canopy of billowing silk.

'Mister Barry likee?'

Bahram answered with a brusque nod: 'Yes. Likee.' It irked him to think that Allow had probably bought the boat cheap; he had clearly done well with it.

Allow bowed and smiled and nodded energetically. 'Can take Mister Barry Honam chop-chop. Boat can go fitee-fitee.'

Only now did Bahram notice that the boat was rigged out with sails as well as a complement of six oars: while in Chi-mei's possession it had always stayed at its moorings—never once had he seen it move.

'Why Mister Barry no go Honam with Allow?'

Bahram was momentarily tempted to accept Allow's offer. But his instincts told him that this was merely a ploy to wheedle him into a deal—and besides he wasn't in the right state of mind to deal with the memories and associations the boat was sure to evoke.

'No, Allow,' said Bahram. 'No can go. Have got boat already; lantern-boy have gone get.'

And here, providentially, Apu returned, having secured a boat, so Bahram was able to make his escape without another word.

~

The banquet of that night was to be held in a pavilion with tall windows and a roof that had the profile of a bird in flight. It overlooked a lotus pond that was illuminated by paper lanterns that glowed like dozens of little moons.

At one end of the pavilion there was a stage where seated musicians were playing on stringed instruments; occupying the centre were several tables, each surrounded by chairs. The furniture was all covered with scarlet tapestries, and an array of tiny dishes and bowls had been laid out on each table: they contained almond milk, roasted nuts, dried and candied fruit, watermelon seeds and oranges, cut into sections. Each place was set with a battery of dishes and implements—porcelain saucers, spoons, and drinking cups; toothpicks, wrapped in red-and-white paper; and of course ivory chopsticks, resting upon ebony stands.

Punhyqua belonged to a family that had old and deep connections with the merchants of Bombay: once, when the firm was being subjected to a severe 'squeeze' by a mandarin, a group of Parsis had advanced him a loan on generous terms: without this assistance the house might not have survived. Punhyqua had never forgotten this and Parsis were always treated with special respect at his table: tonight, as on other occasions in the past, Bahram was placed in the seat of honour, to the left of the host.

The meal began with a round of toasting during which the drinking-cups were filled and refilled several times with warm rice wine. Then the first set of plates was set upon the table and Punhyqua began to describe each of the dishes in turn: here were some 'ears of stone', much loved by monks; they were made from a kind of fish, and were cooked with black vinegar and mushrooms; that tangled heap over there was a mound of crisp-fried shellfish; this quivering lump was a flavoured jelly made from the hooves of deer; those tidbits there were called 'Japanese leather' and had to be macerated for days before they could be eaten; here was a bowl of succulent roasted caterpillars, of a kind to be found only in sugar cane fields.

'Barry you like-no-like ah?'

'Too muchi like! *Hou-sihk! Hou-sihk!*'

Unlike some of the other foreigners at the table, Bahram did not hesitate to taste any of these dishes: he liked to say of himself that he had no prejudices in regard to ingredients and cared only about flavours and tastes. He was glad to pronounce that to an unbiased palate such as his, there could be no doubt of which was the best of these dishes—the plump, cane-sweetened caterpillars.

Then came the fashionable new pottage known as 'Buddha Jumps over the Wall': it was a Fujianese delicacy and had been prepared by a chef who had been specially brought in for that purpose. It had taken two days to prepare and included some thirty condiments—crisp shoots of bamboo and slippery sea-cucumbers; chewy tendons of pork and juicy sea scallops; taro root and abalone; fish-lips and mushrooms—a symphony of carefully harmonized contrasts of texture and taste, it was reputed to have lured many a monk into breaking his vows.

After this there was a brief lull, during which several toasts were drunk. By now the atmosphere of camaraderie had grown warm enough that Bahram felt free at last to lean over to Punhyqua. 'Is tooroo that new mandarin come to Canton soon-soon? One Lin . . . Lin . . .'

He could not remember the name but it didn't matter: it was clear from Punhyqua's reaction that he knew exactly who he was talking about. The tycoon's eyes widened and he lowered his voice to a whisper: 'Who tolo? That-piece news what-place you hear?'

Bahram made a vague gesture. 'Some fellow tolo. Is tooroo maski?'

Punhyqua's eyes wandered around the table, taking in the other guests. Then he shook his head ever so slightly. 'Not now. Later we talkee. In quiet place.'

Bahram nodded and returned his attention to the food. Another set of dishes had appeared now, containing rolls of sharks' fin and squares of steamed fish; candied birds' nests and chopped goose livers; fried sparrow heads and crisp frogs' legs; morsels of porcupine, served with green turtle fat, and parcels of fish gizzards wrapped in seaweed—and each preparation, miraculously, was more delicious than the last. Savouring the sublime tastes, Bahram fell into a kind of reverie, from which he stirred only to nod every time a server came to ask: 'Wanchi grubbee?'

After two hours of continuous banqueting the diners were given a brief respite in which to prepare themselves for the delicacies that were yet to come. While the other guests went off to recover from the last thirty courses Bahram stayed in his seat, having been detained by a discreet tap from one of Punhyqua's inch-long fingernails.

Presently, when it became possible to leave the table unobserved, Punhyqua pushed his chair back and led Bahram out of the hall and over a bridge to a little island that was topped by an octagonal pavilion. Stepping inside, he motioned to Bahram to seat himself on a stone bench, while he crossed over to a similar one on the other side of the pavilion. Then, holding up his hands he clapped them lightly and almost instantly a linkister appeared: stepping discreetly to Punhyqua's side he stood in the shadows, effacing himself so completely that nothing remained of him but his voice.

Wah keuih ji . . . said Punhyqua, and the linkister began to translate: 'My master ask: from who you hear new mandarin come to Canton?'

'Doesn't matter.' Bahram shrugged. 'But it is true?'

'He say: surprise you hear so soon. No one know for sure anything, except that Emperor has called Governor of Hukwang province to Beijing: his name Lin Zexu . . .'

Although he was not personally acquainted with Lin Zexu, said Punhyqua, he knew a good deal about him for he too was from Fujian province. He came from a family that was poor but highly respected, having produced many reputed officials and statesmen. Lin was himself a brilliant scholar, and had passed his Civil Service examinations with distinction at an unusually early age. Rising quickly through the ranks of officialdom, he had earned a reputation for exceptional ability and integrity: not only was he known to be incorruptible, he was one of the few men in the realm who was unafraid of expressing opinions that ran contrary to the views of the Court. Whenever there was a serious problem—a flood, an uprising of disaffected peasants, a breach in some essential dike—it was to Lin that the government turned. Thus it happened that while still in his forties Lin Zexu had been appointed to one of the most coveted posts in the country: the governorship of Kiangsi province. It was there, apparently, that he had had his first encounter with British opium smugglers.

'Mr Moddie remember a ship call *Lord Amherst*?'

'Yes,' Bahram nodded. 'I remember.'

Bahram recalled the affair of the *Lord Amherst* with exceptional clarity because he had himself been involved in it, in a small way. It had happened six years ago: the *Lord Amherst* was one of many British ships to be sent to forage along the northern coast of China, in the hope of finding new ports through which to funnel opium and other foreign goods into the country. The British had long chafed against the constraints that were imposed upon them by the Chinese authorities, and of these none was felt to be more restrictive than the rule that compelled foreign traders to limit their activities to Canton: the thinking was that if only some means could be found of circumventing this regulation then the volume of trade could be vastly expanded.

The *Lord Amherst*'s mission was thus to try to establish links with people who might be inclined to subvert Chinese laws and regulations. It was a risky task, but the potential for profit was very great; the merchants who succeeded in entering these new, virgin markets were sure to earn enormous rewards. By virtue of his standing in the community, Bahram was one of the few non-British merchants to be invited to invest in the venture, and since such an opportunity could not be allowed to go begging he had added fifty crates to the *Lord Amherst*'s cargo.

But the mission had not gone well. Hit by bad weather, the *Lord Amherst* had been forced to take shelter in a Chinese port. When asked by the local authorities what their ship was doing so far north, the officers had said that they had been blown off course while sailing from Calcutta to Japan; a perfectly reasonable answer, except that they happened to be carrying pamphlets, printed in Chinese, that left little doubt of their actual intention. The officers had also taken the prudent precaution of lying about the ship's name, so that in the event of a protest from the government the East India Company would be able to deny ownership—but this too had not turned out too well, for somehow the Chinese officials, in their usual bothersome way, had succeeded in ascertaining the facts.

Here Punhyqua broke in and addressed Bahram directly. 'That-time Lin Zexu, he Governor Kiangsi. He savvy allo this-thing. Maybe he thinkee, English-fellow speakee too muchi lie, allo time.'

Bahram laughed. 'Is tooroo,' he said. 'England-fellow speakee plenty lie. But he just like us: he likee cash.'

In any event, the matter of the *Lord Amherst* had evidently made a deep impression on Lin Zexu. On taking up his next post, in Hukwang, he had launched a massive campaign to eradicate opium—and being the man he was, his efforts had met with far greater success than any before. Indeed he had become such an expert on opium-trafficking that he was one of the select few to be asked to submit reports on opium to the Son of Heaven—and his memorial on the subject had proved to be the most comprehensive ever written.

Now, once again, Punhyqua leant forward. 'Mr Moddie, Lin Zexu, he savvy allo,' he said. 'Allo, allo. He have got too muchi spy. He sabbi how cargo come, who bringee, where it go. Allo he savvy. If he come Governor Canton too muchi bad day for trade.'

'But nothing has been decided yet, no?'

'No. Not yet,' said the linkister. 'But Emperor meet Governor Lin many time already. He give him permission ride horse in Beijing. Is big sign. People say, Emperor has told that he cannot face shadow of ancestor until opium business is rooted from China.'

'But others have tried before, no?' said Bahram. 'Even the present Governor is trying: raids, executions, searches—all the time we hear. But still it goes on.'

Punhyqua leant forward again and tapped Bahram's knee with a fingernail. 'Governor Lin not like other mandarin,' he said. 'If he come to Canton, too muchi trouble Mr Moddie. If cargo have got, better sell now, jaldi chop-chop.'

~

'Why,' said Fitcher, scratching his chin, 'it must be Billy Kerr they were speaking of.'

Paulette looked up from Robin's letter. 'But sir, surely the man who introduced the world to the Tiger Lily and the Chinese Juniper and Christmas Camellia was not a smoker of opium?'

'Oh he had his share of troubles, did poor Billy Kerr . . .'

Kerr had been in China a couple of years already when Fitcher met him for the first time, in Canton, in the winter of 1806. He was in his mid-twenties then, a little younger than Fitcher: a tall, strapping Scotsman, he had more energy and ambition than he could put to good use. He had arrived in Canton bearing the gaudy title of 'Royal Gardener' but only to find that it carried no weight in the British Factory, which was as starchy in its own way as a manor house. A gardener was, after all, just a servant and was expected to comport himself as such, remaining below stairs and refraining from intruding upon his superiors.

It was true certainly that Billy had been born with dirt beneath his fingernails—his father had been a gardener before him, and probably his grandfather too. But Billy was a sharp, hard-working fellow who had applied himself to his books and his botany with a mind to bettering himself. His position in the British Factory didn't jibe with his idea of his own consequence and he was a little bit forward at times: as a result, instead of finding a place at the high table, he was fed a steady diet of snubs and slights. Nor did it help that his salary, which, at a hundred English pounds a year, would have been perfectly adequate elsewhere, was a trifling sum in Canton: Billy could not even afford to pay for his own washing.

'Billy was a forthy fellow, prickly as a hedgy-boar.'

One summer he had run off to the Philippines, in defiance of Sir Joseph's instructions. Unfortunately for him the voyage had turned into a disaster: the collection he had put together in Manila was destroyed by a typhoon, on the way back to China.

Billy took it hard: the journey was but a few months behind him when Fitcher arrived in Canton. Fitcher could see that he had been greatly affected: one sign of it was that he had moved out of the British Factory, cutting himself off from his compatriots. A Chinese merchant had granted him the use of a plot of land, near Fa-Tee, and he had built himself a little shack there. Fitcher had visited him once and so far as he could tell, Kerr's existence was one of hermit-like solitude. His 'house' consisted of a single room, surrounded by clusters of saplings and rows of experimental plant-beds. His only companion was the boy he had hired to help with his garden, Ah Fey: he was some thirteen or fourteen years old at that time, and by dint of his service with Kerr, he already spoke fluent English.

'Is that the same Ah Fey who brought the camellia picture to England?'

'Yes. The very one.'

Although Ah Fey had successfully discharged his mission, his departure from Canton was not without a price for Kerr: deprived of his only companion he had become more isolated than ever. When Fitcher saw him next he was in a poor state: his skeletally thin frame and haunted eyes were clear signs that he was in an advanced stage of addiction. Desperately eager to be on his way, he had left Canton within a couple of days of Fitcher's arrival. Fitcher was never to see him again: he died of a fever shortly after his arrival in Colombo.

'And what of Ah Fey?'

'Ah, that's a strange story now . . .'

On returning to England, three years later, Fitcher had learnt that Ah Fey's time at Kew had not been a happy one: he had quarrelled with the foremen and fought with the family he was living with. A local clergyman had taken the little savage into his house, in the hope of saving his soul by awakening him to the Lord. In return, Ah Fey had burgled his house and disappeared.

For many years after that, reports were heard that Ah Fey had changed his name and was living in the slums of East London, pushing a costermonger's barrow.

'Did you ever see him yourself?'

'No,' said Fitcher. 'Last I heard of him, he was working his way back to China, on a ship. But that was a long time ago now—over twenty years if memory serves me right.'

~

By the time all eighty-eight courses of the banquet had been served and the last toasts drunk, the diners' wine-cups had been filled and refilled so many times that there was scarcely a guest present who was entirely steady on his feet. It remained only to thank the host and say the final chin-chins: then Bahram headed back towards the estate's landing jetty with some of his English and American friends. They strolled down to the water arm-in-arm, with dozens of lantern-bearers lighting their way, and it was agreed by all that the warmth and conviviality of the night had been such as to place it among the finest banquets of all.

On reaching the jetty there was one last burst of leave-taking and then they parted. As the others headed off in their skiffs and wherries, Bahram looked around for his own boat and found, to his annoyance, that it was nowhere to be seen. The surrounding shores were thickly wooded and with nightfall, a fog had begun to rise off the creek. Not much was visible from the jetty and after waiting a few minutes, Bahram went back to the shore and walked a little way along the banks to see if his boatman had perhaps fallen asleep in some quiet mooring spot. His investigations took him first in one direction and then another, but to no avail, and on returning to the jetty, he found it still deserted and wreathed in wisps of fog: the other guests were all gone and the lantern-bearers were on their way back to the estate—their lights could be seen, bobbing up and down on their poles, a long way off.

What was he to do now? This was a place where there were no boats for hire, and no passers-by to ask for help. He was about to turn around, to follow the lantern-bearers back to Punhyqua's estate, when he heard, to his great relief, a distant tinkling, like the sound of a boat's bell. It seemed to be coming up the creek, making its way slowly through the fog: the boatman must have wandered off and got lost somewhere; what he needed was a proper dumbcowing, something that would make him forget his mother's name for a while. As he stood waiting, Bahram began to dredge from his memory every Cantonese obscenity he had ever heard, stringing them together for the tirade that he would unleash when the fellow arrived.

But the boat which presently appeared was not the one that had brought him there: it was brightly illuminated, by a constellation of paper lanterns, and its outlines could be seen, through the fog, as it approached the jetty: its stern was carved to look like a gigantic fishtail, rising out of the water in an elegant curve.

Astounded, Bahram stared at the apparition, wondering whether it might not be part of some sort of wine-induced hallucination. Then he heard a voice calling across the water: 'Mister Barry! Mister Barry!'

It was Allow again: the bahenchod must have paid off the boatman and sent him away, so that he might have another opportunity to obtain a deal. That was clear enough—what was less plain was how he had known that he, Bahram, would be here, on this out-of-the-way jetty? Why had the lantern-bearers, usually so solicitous, slipped away so quickly? Could it be that Allow had some informer amongst Punhyqua's people?

Or was it just the wine that was inspiring these visions of plots and conspiracies?

No matter, he was where he was—standing on a jetty in some jungly place—so it was no use getting too prickly. And the truth was that whether out of sheer relief, or because of the warming effects of the wine, he was very glad to see the boat, and Allow too. But of course, it wouldn't do to betray this, so he cleared his throat and let loose in Cantonese: *Diu neih Allow! Diu neih louh mou! Diu neih louh mou laahn faa hai!*

'Sorry, Mister Barry. Very sorry.'

'Allow, you bloody bahnchoding bahn-chaht, where my boat? You talkee man and send away?'

'Allow too muchi sorry, Mister Barry. Allow wanchi makee nice surprise—give ride in Allow boat. Just I get little-bit late.'

'You makee too muchi bobbery for Mister Barry. Look-see here: Mister Barry alone in jungle. What if snake did catchi?'

The boat had pulled up to the jetty in the meanwhile, so Allow stepped out and gave Bahram a deep bow. 'Sorry, Mister Barry, very sorry ah. Come now, Allow takee Mister Barry to Achha Hong.'

There was no option now but to accept this invitation, but Bahram had no intention of pretending to be grateful. Ignoring Allow, he stalked brusquely up the gangplank to the stern of the vessel.

Ahead lay the large, hall-like room that had once housed Chi-mei's eatery. The entrance had been transformed into an opulent gateway, with dragons and phoenixes writhing upon the door jambs. One of the doors was half-open and Bahram could see the figure of a woman inside, silhouetted against a red lamp. The sight startled him, reminding him suddenly of Chi-mei. He had a vision of her, hurrying through that hallway to greet him, calling out, in her high, tinkling voice: 'Mister Barry! Mister Barry! Chin-chin.'

He came to a stop but Allow was close behind him and he made as if to usher Bahram towards the entrance. 'Mister Barry no wanchi come in?'

Bahram turned his eyes away from the shadowed woman: he was not a sentimental man and it did not come naturally to him to dwell on the past; he had tried hard not to waste time in grieving uselessly for Chi-mei and he did not want to be haunted by his memories.

'No, Allow,' he said. 'No wanchi go in there. Wanchi go upstairs. Over there.'

Pointing to the deck above, Bahram started down the gangway that led to the staircase. Only when his hands were on the rails did it occur to him that this too might not be a good idea: the upper deck was the part of the boat he knew best—that was where Chi-mei had had her living quarters and it was there they had been accustomed to sit, of an evening, when he came to visit.

The thought came to him that she had possibly died up there: could it be that her killers too had mounted these stairs? He considered asking Allow if he knew exactly where she had been struck down, in which part of the boat. But as the query took shape in his mind he knew he would not be able to say: 'What-place Number-One Sister makee die?' The words seemed to belittle her death.

And besides, what good would it do to know?

Halfway up the stairs, Bahram faltered again: it might be better, he knew, to turn around, to find some other place to sit. But a morbid curiosity had taken hold of him now and he could not go back: he mounted the steps quickly and when his head emerged at the top he was hugely relieved to see that Chi-mei's room was completely transformed, almost unrecognizable: its walls were painted red and gold and it was lit by an array of tasselled lamps. Her bed, chairs, closets and altar were all gone and their place had been taken by the usual flower-boat furniture—elaborately lacquered couches, stools, teapoys and the like.

Bahram walked straight through the room to the canopied divan on the foredeck. He was tired now and the prospect of sitting down was most welcome. Removing his shoes he sank back against a bolster.

Although the river was cloaked in fog the sky was clear. Looking up at the stars Bahram thought what a pity it was that he and Chi-mei had never taken this boat out on the river together. Then Allow came padding up to the divan and bent down to whisper in Bahram's ear: 'Mister Barry wanchi gai-girlie? Number One "silver chicken" have got. She *sei-méi* girlie—first chop in all four flavour, foot-lick also. Anything wanchi, can do.'

Bahram was infuriated by the crudeness of the proposition. 'No, Allow,' he snapped. 'No wanchi sing-song girlie. *Mh man fa! Heui sei laa!*'

'Sorry, Mister Barry. Very sorry.' He withdrew quickly, leaving Bahram alone.

The boat had begun to move now and as its prow parted the fog the ripples of the bow wave went lapping through the water like misty shadows. Many of the boat's lanterns had been extinguished and the few that were still lit had been dimmed by the mist, their glow reduced to faint pinpricks of light. The fog was so dense that everything was blurred in outline, and muted too, in colour and sound: the splash of the oars was barely audible.

Now Allow appeared again, bearing a tray that was covered by an embroidered cloth.

'What-thing have brought?'

Seating himself on the divan, Allow plucked the cloth cover off the tray to reveal a finely carved ivory pipe, a long needle, and a carved opium box.

'What-for all this thingi?' said Bahram. 'I no wanchi eat smoke.'

'No problem, Mister Barry. Allow sittee here, catch litto-piece cloud. If Mister Barry wanchi, can talkee Allow.'

Bahram tried to keep his eyes fixed on the fog-cloaked water, but his gaze kept returning to Allow as he dipped the point of the needle into the gum and then held it over the wick of a lamp. The opium sputtered and caught fire and then Allow began to draw on the pipe, pulling the smoke into his lungs with a thirsty, whistling sound. A whiff of it blew towards Bahram and the sweetness of the smell astonished him—he had forgotten how different it was from the odour of raw chandu, how fragrant and heady.

'Mister Barry wanchi litto-bit? Too muchi good inside.'

Bahram said nothing, but nor did he object when Allow handed him the pipe and lit the flame again. He put the mouthpiece between his lips and Allow placed a tiny, sizzling droplet of opium in the bowl. Bahram drew the smoke in once, twice, and almost at once he could feel his body growing lighter. The cares and anxieties that had been rattling around in his head these last many days slowly ceased their remorseless clattering—it was as if he were a ship that was steadying itself after being battered by a furious gale.

Allow removed the pipe from Bahram's hands and picked up the tray. 'Mister Barry rest now. Allow come back soon-soon.' He took himself off, with the implements, and Bahram lay back, revelling in the supreme contentment that only opium could confer: that marvellous god-like lightness in which the body and the spirit were freed from gravity, of all kinds.

The fog was all around him now, and his weightless body seemed to be floating upon a cloud. He closed his eyes and let himself drift away.

How long he lay like that he did not know but there came a moment when he understood that he was no longer alone on the divan: someone was sitting by his feet—a woman. He knew she had been sent up from the deck below, and at first Bahram felt distinctly annoyed with Allow for disobeying his instructions. Had the woman been the usual type of sing-song girl, perfumed and painted and decked out with cheap jewellery, he would have sent her packing at once; he might even have shouted and lost his temper. But that was not the kind of woman she was: her clothing was as plain as could be—grey trousers and a tunic—and far from being coquettish or flirtatious she had draped a shawl over her head, as if to protect herself against the thick, smoky mist that was rising off the river. Nor did she make any move towards Bahram; she sat motionless at the bottom of the divan, with her feet drawn up and her arms clasped around her knees. There was something oddly comforting about her presence and Bahram's initial annoyance with Allow turned slowly to gratitude; he was a budmash, of course, but a good fellow really, very considerate in his own way.

The woman seemed perfectly content to stay where she was and in the end it was Bahram who beckoned to her to approach him. When she made no response he sat up against the bolster and reached for her hand. He was pleased to find that it was not the hand of a sing-song girl—it was accustomed to hard work, with rough calluses on the palm. Her sleeve was wet so he pushed it back and lifted the inside of her wrist to his nose; there was not the faintest whiff of perfume about her; she smelled like the river, of woodsmoke and silted water. Something stirred in Bahram, some deep need, some yearning that had gone so long unacknowledged that he had forgotten its very existence. He tugged at her arm and when she seemed to resist, he turned his body around and laid his head against her: it was almost as if he were back with Chi-mei now, in that bubble of impossible absurdity they had once inhabited together, floating side by side in that coracle which had no proper name, which wasn't love but wasn't quite 'lob-pidgin' either.

'Come,' he said. 'Come; I give cumshaw. Plenty big cumshaw.'

When she made no move he was seized with the fear that she would refuse him. To test her, he brushed her cotton-clad nipple with his lips; there was a wetness in the cloth that surprised him, but he was so glad she hadn't pushed him away that he thought nothing of it. He undid the buttons and laid his face between her small, firm breasts and breathed deeply, sucking in the smell of smoke and water.

Her hands were on him too now, roaming through the folds of his clothing with the ease of familiarity, parting his choga, undoing the ties of his angarkha, gently lifting the sadra from under the strings of the kasti, loosening the top of his leggings and slipping down, to touch him in his secret places. Almost without effort, she drew him into her, pivoting her body so that her covered face was turned away from him, and his cheek was pressed against the back of her wet, moist neck.

In all his life he had never experienced a lovemaking that was so protracted, so complete and yet so frictionless; it was so pure a union that it was as if neither of them was burdened with bodies; skin, flesh, muscles, sweat—none of this seemed to divide them and when it ended it was as if he had tumbled over a waterfall and was being carried down, very slowly, by a misty cloud.

To let her go now was impossible: he held her tightly, still resting his cheek against the back of her neck. He could feel the boat turning, and he raised his head just long enough to see that they had come to the end of the creek. The Pearl River lay ahead, and the fumes from the cooking fires, on the thousands of vessels that lined the shores, had melted into the fog that was rising off the surface of the water. The mist was thick but fast-flowing, with so many visible eddies and currents that it was as if the river itself had turned into a surging torrent of smoke.

Bahram closed his eyes and laid his cheek against her neck; once again he was weightless, afloat in the mist. He allowed himself to drift along, on the river of smoke, and when his sleep broke he was amazed to find that his arms were empty and she was gone.

'Mister Barry! Mister Barry! We come Jackass Point.' Allow was standing over him, with a lantern. He grinned playfully as Bahram stirred on the divan. 'Mister Barry likee?'

Bahram nodded. 'Yes,' he said gruffly. 'Likee.' He sat up, fumbling with his choga. The dew seemed to have settled heavily on his clothes; everything was damp and smelled faintly of the river. Cloaking himself in his choga, Bahram retied the drawstrings of his clammy pyjamas. He was reaching for the fastenings of his angarkha when his hand brushed against the inner pocket where he carried his money; it was damp, but he could tell from its heft that it was still filled with coins—he had half-expected that it would be empty, and it surprised him to find it untouched. He would not have minded if she had helped herself to the silver—he had promised her a cumshaw after all, and would have gladly given her all his money.

Bahram looked up at Allow: 'Where girlie have gone? Allow can call?'

'Call who, Mister Barry?'

'That-piece girlie. Allow have sent, no?'

A mystified look came into Allow's eyes.

'Allow no have sent sing-song girlie. Mister Barry say no wanchi girlie. He angry me, no?'

'Yes, but Allow have sent anyway, no?'

Allow doggedly shook his head. 'No. Allow no have sent.'

Bahram put his hands on Allow's shoulders and shook him gently. 'Listen: Mister Barry no angry Allow. Mister Barry too muchi happy Allow have sent this-piece sing-song girlie. Mister Barry only wanchi know: she blongi who? Name blongi what? Mister Barry wanchi give cumshaw.'

Allow's snub-nosed face broke into a broad smile.

'Mister Barry have see smoke-dream,' he said, with a knowing grin. 'Opium pipe have bring Mister Barry sing-song girlie.'

Releasing Allow, Bahram fell back against the cushions: his head was still fogged with smoke and he could not think properly. Perhaps Allow was right; perhaps that was all it was—an opium-fuelled dream, conjured up by the pipe. That would explain why he hadn't seen her face, and also why it had seemed so perfect—like the imaginary night-time couplings of adolescence.

'Allow talkee tooroo? No have sent girlie?'

'Tooroo, tooroo,' said Allow, nodding vigorously. 'No have sent girlie. Mister Barry have look-see dream. Mister Barry sleepee allo time, after pipe to Jackass Point.' He pointed at the jetty, which was just visible through the roiling currents of smoke.

Bahram shrugged. 'All right, Allow,' he said. 'Mister Barry go Achha Hong now.'

Allow nodded and bowed. 'Allow walkee Mister Barry.'

Slipping on his shoes Bahram stood up to go. But with his first step he trod upon a puddle of water and his feet slipped out from under him. He would have fallen if Allow hadn't caught hold of him.

'How water have come here? No rain have got.'

Looking down, Bahram saw that there was not just one little puddle on the deck but several: they formed a wet trail, leading from the side of the deck that overlooked the river right up to the corner of the divan.

Allow too had seen the puddles, each separated from the other by the space of a footstep. For an instant his face stiffened into a frightened scowl. But then, recovering quickly, he said: 'That blongi nothing, Mister Barry. Come from fog. Happen allo time.'

'But fog no can makee puddle.'

'Can. Can. Come, we go now. Too muchi late.'

Bahram followed Allow down, to the gangplank and over the jetty. The Maidan was empty of people and wreathed in fog. In the distance, amongst the row of factories, the Achha Hong was the only one that still had many lights burning. Bahram knew that Vico and the others had probably begun to worry about his whereabouts.

They were halfway across the Maidan when Allow broached the subject of opium again: 'Mister Barry wanchi do cargo-pidgin with Allow? Like we talkee that time? Still can do if Mister Barry wanchi.'

Bahram had been expecting something like this all the while, and had the deal been proposed a few hours ago he would have refused it without hesitation. But somehow it was no longer possible to say no. 'All right, Allow,' he said. 'We do cargo-pidgin. Tomorrow Vico come talkee Allow. Then Vico takee boat to go *Anahita*, makee bandobast. We do cargo-pidgin.'

eleven

~

Markwick's Hotel, December 2

Dearest Puggly, I was utterly *absorbed*—and astonished as well—by your letter and your account of the career of poor Mr William Kerr. But I promise you, what I have to tell will surprise you even more—as for Mr Penrose he will be *astounded*, for I have made the most *startling* discovery. But I will save that for later; first I must tell you how it came about.

You will remember how the Hongists, Punhyqua and Howqua, had promised to give me an introduction to Lynchong, the nurseryman in Fa-Tee? Well, several days went by with no word from anyone and I was beginning to think I would have to set off for Fa-Tee on my own. But this morning Mr Markwick knocked on my door to announce a Visitor. He was positively *glowering*: for he has no love of Visitors, you know, especially local people—he thinks many of the townsmen who frequent the Maidan are la-lee-loons (which is 'dacoit' in pidgin). As a consequence anyone he considers Undesirable is made to wait at the top of the stairs below. Mr Markwick is often uncharitable in his assessments, but this was one instance in which he could not be accused of being too harsh a judge. The Visitor was a shifty-looking man with a large mole and a long queue: he bowed and smiled in a manner at once obsequious and insistent, as men do when they have something disreputable to offer, and I feared at first that he might be some kind of tout. But it turned out that he had been sent to accompany me to Fa-Tee, by Mr Lynchong, who was, he said, his Dai Lou or 'Boss-man'.

He introduced himself as Ah-med, but I think his name might be plain old 'Ahmed' for he did confide in me that his father was a Black-Hat-Devil, which means that he was probably an Arab or Persian (I certainly would not have suspected it if he had not said so, for I could see nothing in his appearance to suggest that he was anything other than Cantonese).

Half-Arab or not, Ah-med had a sampan waiting on the river, and wanted to leave at once.

I would have liked Jacqua to come too for I could not conceive how I would speak with Mr Lynchong, and nor did I much fancy the prospect of a long boat-ride with Ah-med. But Ah-med brushed this off and said we should leave right now, chop-chop, and no linkister would be needed because 'Boss-man speakee first-chop English—too muchi good'. Not for a moment did I believe this and nor did I like to be rushed, but there was nothing to be done: I went to my room to fetch the camellia painting and then followed him to his sampan.

Fa-Tee is not far from Fanqui-town, being situated at the tip of Honam Island, where the Pearl River debouches into White Swan Lake. But to get there one must traverse the width of the floating city. Right next to Fanqui-town lies a sandbank called Shamian: moored around it are a number of 'flower-boats'—these are vessels where men go to be entertained by women. I know you are no melting Miss, my dear Madame de Puggligny, so I will not mince words with you (although I do not recommend that you read this to Mr Penrose)—these boats are, in point of fact, nothing other than floating bordellos! The sight of them made Ah-med wax lyrical in a way that led me to wonder whether he did not have some connection with them—for the descriptions he gave me and the offers he made were such, Puggly dear, that the thought of repeating them to you brings the blush even to a cheek like *mine*: suffice it to say that it was revealed to me that I had, for the asking, a choice of ladies from Hubei and Honan and Macau; of wide-bosomed grandmothers and slender maidens; of songstresses whose voices would caress my ears and seamstresses whose nimble fingers would sew me into stitches.

But no, said I, to Ah-med's evident disappointment. As if in revenge, he pointed to a spot in the distance. 'Lookee that side,' he cried; 'that place cuttee head! Cuttee head!'

Whatever could he be talking about? It took me a minute or two to understand that he was pointing to the public execution grounds, which are also situated on the river.

I confess I was transfixed. Zadig Bey has told me about the grounds: on execution days many people, including fanquis, go there to watch—some factories have even been known to organize boat parties! It seems *utterly* revolting, does it not? But of course hundreds of people go to watch the hangings in Calcutta, and I know the same is true also of London and many other cities—so one cannot pretend to be shocked that it happens here too. But since I, for one, have no taste for such things, I had promised myself I would stay away—yet now that it was in sight I must admit I *gaped* in fascination.

It is a narrow stretch of open ground, right by the river, so you can see it all quite clearly from a boat. Instead of a gallows there are other devices and contraptions—for example a kind of chair, to which men are tied before their heads are lopped off. There is even an apparatus that looks like a cross, but it is actually used for *strangling* people: the condemned man is tied, with his arms outspread, and then a cord is pulled tight around his neck.

Although it was a good distance away, I thought I discerned a corpse hanging upon one of those crosses. It made me feel quite *faint*—but now that I have seen it I do not regret it at all: I knew at once that this too must figure somewhere on my scroll and for a long while afterwards I could think of nothing but how to paint it.

Thus was I preoccupied when Ah-med announced that we had come to Fa-Tee. I had expected this to be an area of open gardens extending down to the waterside but it was nothing of the kind; the shore was pierced by a multitude of muddy creeks and channels, not unlike those we see around Calcutta, and on the banks were many trees that we see also in Bengal: banyans, bodhis and silk-cottons. We turned into a creek and from time to time we passed large, fortress-like compounds, where nothing was visible beyond the walls except, on occasion, a few tiled roofs. Then we came to a jetty around which were moored many boats of different kinds—sampans, scows, lanteas and even a large, brightly painted pleasure-boat.

Beyond lay a compound not unlike those we had passed on the way. The wall that ran around it was tall, grey, and so forbidding in appearance that you would think you had come to a prison or an arsenal. So little did this place accord with my conception of a nursery that I thought at first there had been some mistake. But when Ah-med led me to the entrance it became clear that I had indeed arrived at the right destination—for hanging beside the gate was a sign with a few English words inscribed above the Chinese lettering: 'Pearl River Nursery'.

Ah-med took me inside and showed me to a bench; then after taking my card, he vanished through a small doorway at the back. There were many gardeners and nurserymen around me but they were busy with their work and paid me no attention. I found myself at liberty to look around at leisure.

The nursery is contained within a large, rectangular courtyard and is enclosed on all sides by a wall. Although blank and featureless on the outside, the inner surfaces of the walls are elaborately ornamented with tiles and geometrical designs. The floor too is covered with tiles, from end to end: not a single patch of unpaved soil is anywhere to be seen. Every plant in the place—and there must be *thousands*—grows in a pot: never will you see so many pots of so many different designs, gathered in one place—shallow saucers, rounded bowls with fluted lips, enormous vat-like urns planted with plum trees; porcelain tubs as brilliantly coloured as the flowers that bloom within them.

Pots, pots, pots—that is all you see at the outset. But then, as your eye grows more accustomed to the surroundings, you notice that the containers have been skilfully grouped to create an impression of a landscape, complete with winding paths, grassy meadows, wooded hills and dense forests. You see also that these natural features are endlessly mutable: you notice here a freshly made grove; you see over there a grassland that was perhaps an orchard until recently. It becomes clear then that the courtyard can be reconfigured with the passing of the seasons, or perhaps even to suit the daily moods of its custodians.

It is indeed a marvellously ingenious way of organizing a nursery!

As I was wandering around, taking all this in, I came to the door through which Ah-med had exited a short while before. I discovered now that this door had a tiny peephole, cunningly hidden behind a small shutter. Putting my eye to the shutter I saw a rush-covered marshland and a path winding through it. At the other end of the path lies another walled compound, far larger than the nursery—it has the look of a citadel.

While I was standing there, with my eye to the hole, the gates of this fortress suddenly swung open. They stayed open long enough for some ten or eleven men to step out, and during this time I was afforded a glimpse of the interior: I could not see much but I had the impression of a luxuriant garden, with pavilions and waterways. Then the gate swung shut again and the group of men began to walk towards the nursery. One man was walking slightly ahead of the others, with his hands clasped behind his back: from the deferential way in which the others were hanging back, it was clear that this was the 'Boss-man', Lynchong.

He has, it must be said, an arresting face, and having been afforded the opportunity I did not neglect to make a close study of it.

You may think it odd Puggly dear, that I should say this of a China-man, but I swear to you, Puggly dear, it is true: Lynchong looks like one of those Renaissance cardinals whose portraits the Italian Masters were so often made to paint! The similarities in clothing are obvious enough—the cap, the gown, the jewellery—but the resemblance extends also to the beak-like nose; the fleshy jowls; the piercingly sharp eyes, hidden behind heavy lids—here, in other words, is a face filled with cleverness and corruption, cruelty and concupiscence.

I stepped away from the door just soon enough to avoid being detected. By the time it opened I had moved to a distance that allowed me to pretend that I had been browsing amongst the pots all the while.

Lynchong was alone, except for Ah-med: the others—khidmatgars, peons, lathiyals or whatever they were—had been left to cool their heels outside. He stood observing me for a minute or two, with a look of keen appraisal, and I was just about to chin-chin him, in pidgin, when he spoke his first words to me—and I promise you, Puggly dear, if the ground beneath my feet had turned to water I could not have been more surprised. For what he said was: 'How're you going on there, Mr Chinnery?'—and the pronunciation was as you would expect of someone who had spent *years* wandering the streets of London!

I managed to summon the presence of mind to say: 'Very well, sir. And you?'

'Oh you know how it is,' he said, 'up and down, like the weather yardarm.'

Ah-med, in the meanwhile, had produced two chairs: Lynchong took one of them and assigned me to the other. Hardly had I absorbed my surprise at his earlier sallies than he began to speak again.

He was glad to meet me, he said; his name was Chan Liang, but I could call him Lynchong, or Mr Chan or whatever I wished: he was not partikler about this matter. And then, like a busy man of affairs, he turned with no further ado to the matter at hand: 'I'm told you have something to show me.'

'So I do,' I said and proceeded to hand him the picture of the camellias.

The heavy-lidded eyes flickered as he looked at it, and an odd expression passed over his face. He tapped the picture with a fingernail that was at least two inches long.

'Where'd you get this?' he demanded to know and I told him it belonged to a friend who had asked me to make inquiries on his behalf. 'Why?' said he, in the same brusque way. I did not particularly care to be spoken to in that tone, so I told him it was because my friends wished to acquire a specimen for a botanical collection.

What would they pay? he asked me now, and I told him their intention was to propose an exchange, for they had with them an extensive collection of botanical novelties from the Americas.

Now a glitter came into his eyes, and his long fingernails began to scratch his palm as if to soothe the itch of acquisition. 'What plants do they have? Have you brought any with you?'

No, said I. The plants were on board a ship that was anchored offshore, near Hong Kong.

'That's not much good to me, is it now? How'm I to know if they're worth an exchange? These camellias, they're monstrous rare they are—only to be found in the endermost places. I'm not one to trust to the figaries of chance, Mr Chinnery: I need to see the wares on offer.'

What was to be done now? I was at a loss for a moment and then an idea came into my head. I said: 'Why sir, my friends could send me pictures to show you; one of them is a talented illustrator.'

He thought about this for a moment and then said yes, this would be all right, as long as I could show him the pictures soon—for it would take a while to have the golden camellias transported to Canton from the mountains where they grew.

'I will write immediately, sir,' I promised. 'I do not doubt that I will have some pictures to show within the week.'

He had begun to fidget busily now, so I thought the interview was at an end and made as if to rise. But he stopped me by extending one of his long fingernails. 'Let me ask you something, Mr Chinnery,' he said. 'This friend of yours—the one who owns that picture—is it possible that his name is Penrose? I forget his Christian name but I think they called him "Fitcher".'

Can you imagine my surprise, Puggly dear? I promise you, through the duration of our conversation I had not *once* uttered Mr Penrose's name: how was it possible then that this man should know about the ownership of a picture that had travelled halfway around the world?

But he undeniably did.

'Yes, sir,' I said. 'The owner is indeed Mr Penrose.'

'I remember him well—has a face like a pox-doctor, don't he, old Fitcher Penrose?'

'So you know him, sir?'

'That I do,' came the answer. 'And he knows me too. When you write to him please tell him Ah Fey sends his most respectful salaams. He'll know how the beer got in the bottle.'

So there you have it, Puggly dear: this was not the first time that Lynchong, or Mr Chan, or whatever you wish to call him was seeing Mr Penrose's camellia picture: for he is none other than Ah Fey, the gardener who accompanied William Kerr's collection to London!

Perhaps, my dear Lady Pugglesbridge, you will understand now why I am *consumed* with curiosity about this man. So take pity on me and send me pictures of your best plants as soon as you possibly can: I cannot wait to renew my acquaintance with Mr Chan.

~

As with a strictly run joint family, the rhythms of Bahram's establishment were unvarying and unnegotiable. This was why Neel was knocked momentarily off-tempo when Vico, who was the orchestrator of this intricate symphony, announced that he was going to be away for a few days.

'You will have to manage Patrão while I'm gone,' said the Purser, with a big grin. 'Don't be gubbrowed; you can do it.'

'Where are you going?'

'To *Anahita*, just for some work only.'

'But isn't she anchored off the outer islands?'

'Yes,' said Vico, picking up his bag. 'I will have to hire bunder-boat from Amunghoy or Chuen-pee.'

Only in Vico's absence did Neel begin to appreciate the importance of the purser's role in the running of Bahram's affairs. As the head of the firm the Seth was more an admiral than a captain, with his eyes turned to the far horizon and his attention focused upon long-term strategies. It was Vico who skippered the flagship and no sooner was his steadying hand lifted from the helm than the vessel began to lose its trim: the 'mess'—a smoky but well-heated part of the kitchen, where the two dozen members of the staff took their meals—was no longer properly cleaned, and food stopped appearing at the accustomed times; the lamps in the corridors became sooty and the kussabs neglected to light them at the usual hours; the khidmatgars and peons took to mudlarking in the grog-kennels of Hog Lane, often returning so late that they could not get up in time to prepare the daftar, in the prescribed fashion. This was a matter in which Bahram had been very strict in the past, but now he seemed neither to notice nor care that his instructions were being disregarded. It was as if a giant pair of dice had been cast up in the air—everyone, from the Seth to the lowliest topas, seemed to be holding their breath as they waited for the spinning cubes of ivory to come back to earth.

Yet, not a word was said, in Neel's hearing at least, about the precise nature of the task that had taken Vico to the *Anahita*. The rest of the staff were a close-knit team and although of disparate communities and backgrounds, they all hailed from the hinterlands of Bombay; as an outsider from the east—and one who had jumped rank to boot—Neel knew that he was the subject of some suspicion and had to be careful about how he comported himself. He asked no untoward questions and when matters of business were being discussed in languages unknown to him—Gujarati, Marathi, Kachhi and Konkani—he did his best not to appear unduly curious. But he did not neglect to listen attentively, and he soon came to the conclusion that his colleagues knew no more about Vico's mission than he did; if they were on edge it was not because they were aware of the purser's assignment: rather, it was because they had learnt, through long habit, to attune themselves to their employer's moods—and there wasn't a soul in No. 1 Fungtai Hong who did not know that the Seth's state of mind had been, of late, strangely precarious.

One sign of this was that he had stopped going out in the evening: every day, as the sun dipped towards White Swan Lake, Bahram would ask Neel what invitations he had accepted and after the list had been read out—and lists indeed they were, for it was not unusual for a reception to be followed by a rout and then a late whist-supper—he would ponder the matter for a minute or two before brusquely dismissing it.

Send out chits with the lantern-wallah, tell them I'm . . .

'Indisposed?'

Anything you like.

As the days dragged on, with no news being received from Vico, it became clear to everyone that the Seth's nerves were fraying ever thinner under the strain. His fidgeting became increasingly agitated and he took to venting his impatience indiscriminately, on whoever happened to be at hand—which was, more often than not, his unfortunate munshi.

News of these eruptions would spread quickly through the Achha Hong, and for a while afterwards everyone would act as though they were performing a collective penance, walking on tiptoe and speaking in English.

The two shroffs were always the first to offer their condolences:

'. . . what to do? Sethji is like that only . . .'

'. . . in life agonies and sufferings are always there . . .'

'. . . pray God and bear up the burden . . .'

One morning, while Bahram was toying with his breakfast, Neel began to read out an excerpt of an Imperial edict, issued in Beijing: '"The Controller of the Board has reported that the habit of smoking is on the increase even though the Viceroys and Governors of every Province have been authorized to conduct raids and make seizures of Opium. Alas the mandarins are careless and manage matters unskilfully. If they have seized any Opium it is only a miserably small quantity and I fear they are not all upright . . ."'

What is this? snapped Bahram.

Sethji, it is a hookum-nama issued by the Son of Heaven, in the capital: a translation has been published in the last issue of the *Register*.

Pushing aside his unemptied plate, Bahram rose from the table: Go on, munshiji. Let me hear the rest.

'"After this the Viceroys and Governors of every province must sternly and distinctly demand that their people obey the commands; and they must also order their civilian and military officers to vigorously search all traitorous merchants who are engaged in the traffic of Opium. And all people who keep Opium shops in the Cities must be apprehended and brought before the Tribunals."'

Glancing up from his notes, Neel saw that on rising from the breakfast table Bahram had done something that was very rare for him—he had seated himself at his desk.

'Why you have stopped?' said Bahram. 'Carry on: what else does Emperor say?'

'"The Viceroys and Governors of every Province must exert themselves to eradicate the evil by the very roots; a single person must not be allowed to slip through the net of the law; if they dare to wink at, or conceal, or lose opportunities of apprehending, or other evils of that sort, then they will be punished by a new law, and further their sons and grandsons will not be allowed to appear at the examinations. If, on the other hand, the district Mandarins show intelligence and ability in conducting this business they will be promoted according to the new law. Let this be promulgated through every Province for the information of all people. *Respect this!*"'

Here Neel was interrupted by a curious grinding noise, like the gnashing of teeth. Looking up in surprise, he saw that the sound was emanating not from Bahram's mouth, but rather from his hands—he had positioned his carved inkstone in front of him and was furiously kneading his long-neglected inkstick. Whether this was to give release to his agitation or to calm himself, Neel could not decide, and a moment later the inkstone, unsteadied by the increasing violence of the Seth's motions, went hurtling off the desk. A jet of black ink flew up, drenching the Seth's immaculate choga and splashing all over his papers.

Bahram jumped to his feet, looking down at himself in horror. 'What bloody nonsense! Who has told these Chinese fellows to make ink like it is masala? Crazy buggers!' Turning a pair of angry, disordered eyes at Neel, he pointed to the inkstone: 'Take it away! I never want to see it again.'

Ji, Sethji.

Neel was moving towards the door when it flew open of itself: a peon was outside, a sealed note in hand.

An urgent chit had just been delivered, the man said. The bearer was downstairs, waiting for a reply.

From Bahram's response it was clear that he had long been awaiting this note. All thought of the inky mishap was instantly erased from his mind, and his voice turned brisk and businesslike: Munshiji, I need you to go down to the khazana. Kindly ask the shroffs to prepare a purse of ninety taels: tell them to pick out 'number-one first-chop coins'. And tell them also: none of the coins must carry my mark.

Ji, Sethji. Bowing out of the daftar, Neel headed quickly down the stairs.

Like every other counting-room in Fanqui-town, the Seth's khazana was on the ground floor. A small airless room with a massive door, it had only one heavily shuttered window, with thick steel bars. This was the exclusive domain of the firm's two shroffs and no one else was allowed inside: here they would sit shroffing for hours, creating an unceasing metallic melody, with streams of coins tinkling through their hands.

Fanqui-town's most commonly used coin was the one that had the widest currency in the world: it was the Spanish silver dollar, also called the 'piece of eight' because it was valued at eight reals. The dollar contained a little less than an ounce of fine silver and was embossed with the heads and arms of recent Spanish sovereigns. But among the pieces of eight that circulated in Canton, very few retained the designs that had been stamped on them at the time of their minting. In China, while passing from hand to hand, every coin was marked with the seals of its successive owners. This practice was considered a surety for buyers as well as sellers, for anyone who complained of a bad coin could be sure of having it replaced so long as it could be shown to be marked with the seal of its last owner.

When space ran short, more was created by flattening the coin with a hammer. In due time, the cracked and battered coins would be broken into bits, to be kept in bags and placed upon the scales when a transaction required silver of a certain weight. As coins aged, they became more and more difficult to pass off, even when their content of silver remained unchanged; new coins, on the other hand, were called 'first-chop dollars' and were so prized they were valued above their weight.

Although ubiquitous, the Spanish dollar was used principally for small everyday exchanges; commercially important transactions were usually conducted in Chinese coinage, of which the smallest was the 'cash' (or *chen*). Made of zinc and copper these coins had a square hole in the middle, and could be strung together in large numbers: a string of a hundred cash was known, in English, as a 'mace' and when people went shopping they usually carried one or two of these, wearing them like bangles on their wrists and arms.

The cash was a beautiful coin, to Neel's eyes, but it was too heavy to be carried in bulk and counted for little, being worth even less than an Indian paisa. The tael was the Chinese coin that was of real value: it contained about a third more silver than the Spanish dollar and was the unit most often used for the purposes of large-scale commerce.

The fact that Bahram had asked for a purse containing taels rather than dollars was significant in some way, Neel knew, but he could not quite surmise what: the sum was not large enough to pay for a significant quantity of goods but was yet much too big for an everyday purchase.

To discuss the matter with others in the hong was unthinkable, of course, so Neel assumed that the answers to these questions would remain forever obscure to him. But a little while later, after he had delivered the ninety taels to the Seth's bedroom, encased in a leather purse, he went to the daftar to fetch his papers and found an oddly encrypted message on his desk. A scribble had appeared on the sheet of paper that he used as an ink-blotter: a closer glance showed it to be in the Seth's sloping hand.

Evidently, his own desk being splattered with ink, Bahram had decided to make use of Neel's. After penning a reply to the note he had received, he had dried the ink on the blotting sheet. Now, peering at the sheet, Neel was able to decipher a few words:

. . . Innes . . .

. . . to confirm . . . will bring purse . . . Eho Hong at eleven . . .

Yrs Bahr . . .

~

Bahram knew exactly what he had to do that morning; Vico had coached him carefully on the details. He was to go over to James Innes's apartment, which was in the Creek Factory. The money was to be handed over only after the delivery of the first set of crates: it wasn't intended to be Innes's fee—that would be paid later—it was meant for cumshaws, to be distributed to the local officials who had made the shipment possible. The first delivery was to be a trial run and Vico would not be accompanying it; he planned to stay back, in Whampoa, to make sure that the next set of crates was properly transferred, from the yawl that had brought them down from Hong Kong, to a pair of cutters.

Vico had planned everything so that Bahram's presence in the Creek Factory would only be required for an hour or so—not a great length of time, certainly, but Bahram had never much cared for the Creek Factory and he would have been glad if his vigil were shorter still. Although he had never lived in that hong himself he had a more-than-passing familiarity with it for it adjoined his first place of residence in Canton, the Dutch Factory. The two buildings were separated only by a wall but they could not have been more different. While the Dutch Factory was sombre to a fault, the Creek Factory was a boisterous, freewheeling place inhabited by determined and headstrong Free-Traders—men like Jardine and Innes.

The Creek Factory was spoken of as such because it was flanked by a narrow waterway: it was the last building on that side of Fanqui-town—on the other side of the creek lay the godowns of the Co-Hong merchants. The creek gave the hong a distinctive character because many of its lodgings had little quays of their own, providing direct access to the river.

The Creek Factory's residents often said they liked it because of its proximity to the water, but this had never made any sense to Bahram. The so-called creek from which the factory took its name, was really just a nullah—a combination of open sewer and tidal stream. The nullah was one of the principal conduits for the city's refuse, and at low tide, when it shrank to a trickle and its banks were exposed to plain view, a more noxious sight was hard to imagine. The tides would often deposit the carcasses of dogs and piglets in the refuse-clogged mud and there they would lie, buzzing with flies and creating a vomit-inducing stench until they swelled up and exploded.

This 'view' had never held any appeal for Bahram and he could not imagine that it did for many of the factory's other residents either: it was perfectly clear that for men like James

Innes the Creek Factory's attraction lay rather in the fact that the nullah gave them direct access to the river; they all lived in apartments that were furnished with docks as well as godowns, so that shipments could be delivered to their doors without having to be carried across the Maidan. The fact that the offices of the chief Canton customs inspector was situated close to the entrance of the Creek Factory, at the very mouth of the nullah, made no difference: the customs men—or 'tidewaiters' as they were called—would all have been taken care of well before the arrival of the shipment.

Bahram knew that such shipments were delivered regularly to the Creek Hong so the chances of anything going wrong were very small—but he still could not stop fretting, about things large and small. He pulled out an almanac that Shireenbai had given him and looked to see if the day and the hour were auspicious—it disquieted him further when he saw that they were not. Then he looked at the fine clothes that had been laid out for him, on his bed, and decided that they were too elaborate for the task at hand. With his turban and choga he would be conspicuous anyway, and the last thing he wanted was to draw attention to himself with unnecessary finery.

After some thought he settled on a nondescript old caftan that he hadn't worn in years. Then, while his turban was being tied, it occurred to him that it might be a good idea to loosen the tail-end, so that it could be pulled across his face, if needed—an absurd little precaution perhaps, but at that moment he was not in a mood to dismiss any measure that might provide a little peace of mind. But nor could he bring himself to ask the khidmatgar to do it—everybody on his staff knew that he always wore his turban tightly tucked; if word got out, the whole hong would be talking about it—so he decided to do it for himself and asked the fellow to step out.

And of course the dolt took it as a reprimand and began to wring his hands and moan—*Kya kiya huzoor?* What did I do wrong?

At this, Bahram's temper snapped and he shouted: *Gadhera!* You think I can't do anything for myself? Just go, *chali ja*!

The man backed away, whimpering, and Bahram felt the sting of a painful twinge of regret: the fellow had been with him a long time, maybe twenty years; he'd come as a boy, he remembered, and now already there were wisps of grey in his moustache. On an impulse, he reached into the chest pocket of his angarkha and took out the first coin that brushed against his fingers: it was a whole dollar, but no matter—he held it out to the man.

Here, he said. It's all right; take this. You can go now. I'll do the rest myself.

The man's eyes widened and then filled with tears. Bowing low, he took hold of Bahram's hand and kissed it. Huzoor, he said, you are our *maai-baap*, our parent and sustainer. Without you, Sethji . . .

Bas! said Bahram. That's enough; you can go now. Chal!

Once the door was shut, Bahram turned to the looking glass and loosened a fold of his tightly wound turban. He was about to tuck it back in, lightly, when he saw that his hand was shaking. He stopped and took a deep breath; it was alarming to see how frayed his nerves were, how brittle his temper—but then, who would have thought that a day would come when he, Seth Bahramji Naurozji Modi, would be reduced to fashioning a veil out of the tail-end of his turban?

Before leaving his bedroom Bahram decided to wrap the leather purse inside the folds of his cummerbund: it weighed heavily on his waist but was safely hidden, under his woollen choga. As he was about to open the door, it occurred to him that it might be a good idea also to carry a cane: he armed himself with a stout Malacca, topped with a porcelain knob. His eyes fell on his watch and he saw that it was almost eleven. He stepped quickly out of the room and found the munshi waiting at the top of the stairs.

Sethji, is there anything you want me to do this morning?

No, munshiji. Bahram came to a stop and gave him a smile. You've been working hard of late. Why don't you take the morning off?

Ji, Sethji.

On reaching the bottom of the staircase, Bahram found several members of his staff milling about and whispering in the hallway.

. . . huzoor shall we come with you?

. . . do you need any help, Sethji?

Bahram knew that if he was not firm with them, they would follow anyway, so he held up a finger and wagged it sternly: No. No one is to come with me—and I don't want anyone trailing after me either.

At this, they dropped their eyes and slunk off and Bahram made his way to the door. Once he was outside, in the fresh air, he took some comfort from the everyday bustle of the square: the barbers were hard at work, shaving foreheads and braiding queues under their portable sunshades; clouds of fragrant smoke were rising from the barrows of chestnut-sellers and a troupe of travelling acrobats was performing for an audience of wide-eyed jais. Looking towards Jackass Point Bahram was relieved to see that it was less crowded than usual. This sometimes happened when there was a long interval between dockings, so he thought no more of it and set off at a brisk pace, swinging his cane.

Between the Maidan and the creek lay the British and Dutch Hongs. These two factories had gobbled up the patches of land in front of them and turned them into private gardens. As a result, all foot traffic between the Maidan and the creek was funnelled through a narrow lane—this crowded walkway was known to Achhas as Chor Gali, 'Thieves' Alley'.

Bahram had personal experience of the 'claw-hands' of Chor Gali: once, many years ago, while making his way through the lane, he had been robbed of fifty dollars; the purse had been cut out of the lining of his choga while he was battling the crowds, the job being done so neatly that he hadn't even noticed until he was at the customs office. Passing through the alley today he was careful to keep a hand on his purse, as a surety against the sharping-tribe.

On reaching the end of the lane, Bahram glanced quickly towards the customs office—it was a modest brick building, right at the mouth of the nullah. Adjacent to it was a yard of beaten earth. The yard was quiet today, with only a few coolies and vendors loitering about: from where Bahram stood, nothing could be seen of the river, which was screened off by the office. He toyed momentarily with the idea of walking up to the bund to make sure that nothing untoward was under way on the river. But on thinking the matter over, he decided it would be better not to draw attention to himself. Swinging his cane, he headed straight for the Creek Factory's entrance, a few feet to his left.

Several years had passed since Bahram had last stepped into the Creek Factory but nothing seemed to have changed: a long dark corridor lay in front of him, smelling of mildew and urine. Innes had taken an apartment in House No. 2 and the entrance to it lay on the right. Striding up to it, Bahram rapped on the door with the knob of his cane. There was no answer so he knocked again. Shortly afterwards the door swung open and he was ushered into Innes's apartment by a manservant.

Ahead lay a long, narrow room, of the sort that served as living quarters for many a small-time trader in Fanqui-town—except that this one was in a state of wild disorder: dishes encrusted with stale food lay piled on a small dining table and the chairs and settees were heaped with soiled bedclothes. Grimacing in distaste, Bahram turned his eyes to the far end of the room.

As with many apartments in the Creek Factory, this one had a small balcony that overlooked the nullah: so strong was the smell of stale food and unwashed clothing that Bahram decided that this was one instance in which the smell of the creek might actually be preferable to the stench of the room. He was about to step outside, on to the veranda, when Innes came running up the steep staircase that connected his living quarters with his godown, on the floor below: his face was unshaven and he was wearing a jacket and a pair of breeches that looked as though they had not been changed in several days. Glowering at Bahram he said, without preamble: 'I hope you've brought the brass, Mr Moddie.'

'Why, of course, Mr Innes,' said Bahram. 'You will have it after the shipment is safely delivered.'

'Oh, it's a-coming all right,' said Innes.

'You are sure? Everything is all right?

'Yes, of course. It has been ordained and will surely come to pass.' Innes stuck a Sumatra buncus in his mouth and raised a match to the tip. 'The tide is coming in so they should be here any minute.'

Bahram found himself warming to Innes: there was something heartening about his brutish self-confidence. 'Your spirits are high, Mr Innes. I'm glad to see it.'

'I am but an instrument of a higher will, Mr Moddie.'

There was a sudden shout from below stairs: it was Innes's manservant. 'Boat! Boat ahoy!'

'That'll be them,' said Innes. 'I'd better go down to see to the unloading. You can wait on the balcony, Mr Moddie—if you don't mind a bit of a stinkomalee that is. You'll get a good dekko of everything from up there.'

'As you wish, Mr Innes.' Bahram opened the door to the balcony and stepped outside.

With the tide in flood, the nullah had filled with water and was now at a level where a boat could easily be docked beside Innes's godown. Glancing downwards, Bahram saw that Innes and his servant had stepped outside, and were standing on the quay, craning their necks to look up the creek. Turning his gaze in that direction, Bahram saw that a boat had slipped in from the river and was moving slowly down the narrow waterway, past the Hoppo's office: it was a ship's cutter, rowed by a lascar crew, and guided by two local men.

Even with the tide running high, the creek was so narrow that the cutter's progress was painfully slow—or so at least it seemed to Bahram, whose forehead had begun to drip with sweat. When at last the boat pulled up at the quay, he breathed a deep sigh and wiped his face with the tail-end of his turban.

'You see, Mr Moddie?'

It was Innes, standing astride the dock, triumphantly puffing on his buncus: 'What did I tell you? All delivered, safe and sound. Is this not proof that it was predestined?'

Bahram smiled. The gambit had paid off after all; all things considered, it was remarkable how easy it had been to arrange the whole thing—and with so little risk too, without the opium ever even entering his own hong or passing through his godown. His one regret now was that he had not contracted to send more cases.

Bahram raised a hand, in congratulation. 'Shahbash, Mr Innes! Well done!'

~

It wasn't often that Neel had the morning to himself, and he knew exactly what he was going to do with it: it had been a while since he had last paid a visit to Asha-didi's kitchen-boat, and his mouth began to water at the very thought of it.

This eatery was an institution among the Achhas of Canton: visiting it was almost a duty for the innumerable sepoys, serangs, lascars, shroffs, mootsuddies, gomustas, munshis and dubashes who passed through the city. This was because Asha-didi's kitchen-boat was the one establishment, along the entire length of the Pearl River, that provided fare that an Achha could enjoy with untroubled relish, knowing that it would contain neither beef nor pork, nor any odds and ends of creatures that barked, or mewed, or slithered, or chattered in the treetops: mutton and chicken, duck and fish were the only dead animals she offered. What was more, everything was cooked in reassuringly familiar ways, with real masalas and recognizable oils, and the rice was never outlandishly soft and sticky: there was usually a biryani or a fish pulao, some daals, some green bhaajis, and a chicken curry and tawa-fried fish. Occasionally—and these were considered blessed days—there would be pakoras and puris; even vegetarian fare could be cheaply obtained at Asha-didi's if suitable notice were provided—and hers was not the bland stuff of Canton's monasteries, but as chatpata as anyone might wish.

Some Achha visitors to south China subsisted for weeks on boiled greens and rice for fear of inadvertently ingesting some forbidden meat—or worse still, some unknown substance that might interrupt the orderly working of the bowels—and for them Asha-didi was a figure who inspired not just gratitude but the deepest devotion. But Neel had another reason to frequent her eatery: for him the foods of her kitchen were spiced by an additional reward: the pleasure of speaking Bengali.

Asha-didi's fluency in Hindusthani and Bengali often came as a surprise to Achhas for there was nothing about her to suggest a connection with their homeland. Slim and straight-backed, she dressed in the simple work-clothes that were commonly worn by Cantonese boat-women—a blue tunic, calf-length pyjamas, a conical sun hat and perhaps a quilted vest, to ward off the winter cold. When seated on her stool, with her fingers flicking through an abacus, and a time-stick burning at her elbow, she fitted so neatly into the setting of Canton's waterfront that Achhas were often taken aback when she greeted them in a familiar tongue—Hindusthani, perhaps, or Bengali, both of which she spoke with perfect ease. Often, their mouths would fall open and they would ask how she did it, as though her fluency were a trick, performed by a conjuror. She would answer with a laugh: You know there's no jadoo in it; I was born in Calcutta and grew up there; my family is still settled there . . .

Asha-didi's father had moved to Bengal soon after she was born: he was one of the first Chinese immigrants to settle in Calcutta—a rare Cantonese amongst a largely Hakka group. He had originally gone there to work as a stevedore, in the Kidderpore docks, but after his family came out to join him, he had entered the victualling business, setting up a small enterprise that catered to the Chinese crewmen of the ships that passed through the port, supplying noodles, sauces, pickled vegetables, sausages and other provisions that were necessary to their well-being.

The making of the victuals was done at home, with the help of every member of the family, including the children, of whom Asha-didi was the eldest. One day, when she was not quite a girl but not yet a woman, Asha-didi happened to open the door for a young sailor called Ah Bao, who had been sent there to top up his ship's provisions, in preparation for making sail the next day. It was a busy morning, and she was powdered with flour and garlanded with wet noodles; Ah Bao's mouth had fallen open when he set eyes on her. He had mumbled something in Cantonese and she had responded in kind, telling him to say what he wanted and make it quick—*faai di la!* Her response, if not her appearance, should have caused him to disappear forever—but the next day he was back again: he had jumped ship, he explained, because he wanted to offer his services to the family.

Of course Asha-didi's parents knew exactly what he was up to, and they were none too pleased—partly because they guessed from the boy's speech that he was a boat-fellow by origin; and partly because they had long had another, more suitable, groom in mind for their eldest daughter. But despite all that, Asha-didi's father had decided to take him in anyway, and not out of charity either, but only because he was a shrewd merchandiser who prided himself on his business acumen. He reckoned that the young sailor might have something valuable to offer, something that was vital to any ship chandler's business: the ability to take a boat out on the river, to vie for the custom of newly arrived ships. Until then, he had handled this job himself, but he was no boatman, and had always had to hire Hooghly River khalasis to operate his sampan, being regularly cheated in the process. Could it be that this young fellow would know how to manage the boat, on the crowded river? The answer was by no means self-evident, for the sampans of the Hooghly were quite different from the craft from which they took their name: the 'three-board' *saam-pan* of the Pearl River. Being upcurved both in stem and stern, the Hooghly version of the vessel was more like a canoe in shape and handled quite differently.

But Ah Bao was born to the water, and rare indeed was the boat that could defeat him: the sampan posed no challenge to him and he conquered it easily. Nor was oarsmanship the only useful skill that he had learnt on the Pearl River: the ghat-serangs and riverfront thugs who tried to put the squeeze on him found that he had dealt with their like all his life; and those who yelled jeers and taunts at him—*Chin-chin-cheenee!*—discovered that he was no stranger to budmashing, barnshooting and galee-gooler. He quickly gained the respect of the other boatmen, and became a familiar figure on the waterfront: people called him Baburao.

Soon Baburao was so indispensable to the family business that no one could remember why he had been considered an unsuitable groom for Eldest Daughter: objections evaporated, messages went back and forth between the families and matters were arranged to everyone's satisfaction. After the banquet, which was held on a budgerow, the couple settled into a room in the family compound and that was where Asha-didi gave birth to five of their nine children.

Although Baburao settled into his new life with gusto, Calcutta was not to him what it was to his wife. He had grown up on the vessel from which his family made their living; a junk that plied the coastal trade routes around Canton, with his father as its laodah. Theirs was a small craft, and even though it was neither speedy nor especially comfortable, to Baburao it was home. When it came to his ears that his father was thinking of selling the junk he did not hesitate for a moment: letters and gifts travelled regularly between Calcutta and Canton by way of the sea traffic between the cities; Baburao went from ship to ship until he found an acquaintance who could be trusted to persuade his father to hold off for just a little while longer. The money for passages was raised with the help of the community and a few months later the couple set sail for China with their children.

After the move, it was Asha-didi who found herself in the position of having to communicate with her family through nautical go-betweens, and when a serang or a seacunny showed up, bearing gifts and messages, it seemed only natural to offer him something that she herself was often homesick for—an Achha meal, of the kind she had grown accustomed to eating in Calcutta. As word of her cooking spread, more and more

Achhas began to seek her out, not just lascars, but also sepoys, sentries and daftardars. As the number of visitors grew, so did the costs of feeding them and a day came when Baburao said, in exasperation, that if they were going to be feeding so many people they might as well make some money from it. The more they thought about it, the more sense it made: after all, Baburao's junk could be used to procure supplies from Macau, where masalas, daals, achars and other Achha comestibles were easy to find, because of the sizeable Goan population. And did they not have before them the example of Asha-didi's parents, who had done well by filling a similar need, providing foods that were hard to procure in a foreign place?

The success of the eatery had allowed Asha-didi and her family to set up other business ventures, but for herself the kitchen-boat remained her principal passion; she was never more content than when seated at her accustomed place—between the cash-box and the cooking-fires.

Having always seen Asha-didi in that seat, that was where Neel's eyes went when he stepped on to the prow of the boat and passed through the pavilion that formed the eatery's entrance: for him, one of the pleasures of seeing her was that each meeting was an occasion for a fleeting renewal of the jolt of surprise he had experienced the first time she greeted him in Bengali, with some perfectly casual phrase, something like *nomoshkar*, *kemon achhen?*—words that would have seemed banal in a Calcutta alleyway, but had the sound of a magical mantra when pronounced on a Canton kitchen-boat.

But today, within moments of stepping on the boat, it became clear to Neel that the surprises that awaited him were of a different order: not only was Asha-didi not in her usual place, a couple of her daughters-in-law were bustling about, pulling the windows shut: it appeared that the eatery was being closed down—even though it was only mid-morning and the day had just begun.

Low-slung and rectangular, the kitchen-boat was a barge-like vessel with raised pavilions at both ends; in the middle was a long shed, with benches running along the sides and a single, common table in between—this was where meals were served. Looking through the doorway, Neel saw that Asha-didi was at the back of the boat, helping to put out the cooking-fires. She happened to look up and was evidently startled to see Neel, for she came hurrying down the length of the boat. Her first words, when she reached him, were not those of her usual greetings: instead, with an abruptness that was almost rude, she said: *Ekhaney ki korchhen?* What are you doing here?

Neel was so startled he could only stammer: I just came to eat . . .

Na! She cut him short. You shouldn't be here now.

Why not?

The authorities have just sent word, telling us to shut down.

Oh? said Neel. But why?

She shrugged: They just want to make sure there's no trouble around here.

This puzzled Neel. What kind of trouble? he said. I just came through the Maidan and I didn't see anything amiss on the way.

Really? She pressed her painted lips together and raised an eyebrow: And did you look towards the river?

No.

Look then.

She put a hand on his elbow and turned him around, so that he was facing the river: he saw now that the open channel in mid-stream, usually so busy at this time of day, had emptied of traffic. All the tubs, coracles and sampans had scattered to either side to make way for two war-junks that were converging on Fanqui-town from different directions.

War-junks were rarely seen in this stretch of water and they made an arresting sight: they had castellations at either end and were strung with a great number of flags and pennants. One of them was quite close, and as it approached Neel saw that it was bearing a sizeable contingent of troops—not the usual soldiery to be seen around the city, but tall Manchu guardsmen.

What is happening? said Neel. Do you know?

Asha-didi looked over her shoulder and then gestured to him to bend lower.

I don't know for sure, she whispered, but I think there's going to be some sort of raid. On one of the factories.

Suddenly alarmed, Neel said: Which one, do you know?

She smiled and gave his arm a reassuring pat: Not yours, don't worry. It's the farthest one: do you know it?

Do you mean the Creek Factory?

She gave him a nod and then added: Yes. The Eho Hong.

It took a moment before the words registered. What was that? he said. Is that what you call the Creek Factory? Are they the same?

She nodded again. Yes. That is the Eho Hong; they are the same.

~

Standing on the balcony Bahram kept careful watch as the lascars unloaded the crates from the cutter. Those that belonged to him were only a small part of the consignment, but he was able to recognize them from afar because they still bore the stains of the storm. He began to count them, and had just reached six, when a sudden banging of gongs drew his attention away from the dock and back to the river. Spinning on his heels, he found that he could not see past the creek's mouth any more; the opening to the river had been blocked by a huge vessel—some kind of junk—which had silently positioned itself at the entrance to the nullah.

Then he saw why the gongs had suddenly started to beat: they were the accompaniment for the debarkation of a platoon of Manchu troops; the soldiers were filing off the junk and forming a column in the yard of the Hoppo's office; the ranks in the lead had already begun to run in the direction of the Creek Factory.

Could it be a raid? For a moment Bahram stared in stunned immobility. Then he managed to say: 'Innes! Innes! Look . . .'

The sweat began to pour from Bahram's brow, soaking his turban. His breath was coming in gasps, and he could no longer think; all he knew was that he had to get away. He brushed his hand against his cummerbund, to make sure that his leather purse was still in its place. Then, pulling the end of his turban across his face, he stepped away from the balcony and hurried through the apartment. As he passed the staircase, he heard Innes's voice, downstairs, railing at someone—the lascars or his servant—he couldn't tell who.

How would Innes cope with the soldiers? Bahram couldn't think, and it didn't matter anyway; Innes had no family and no reputation to lose; he was a hardened budmash; he'd manage perfectly well—and even if he didn't, he could count on being backed up by British gunboats. He, Bahram, had no such surety, and could not afford to linger another moment.

Stepping into the courtyard Bahram hurried over to the arched gateway that led to the inner recesses of the factory's compound. As he was passing through it, he glanced over his shoulder, in the direction of the factory's entrance. Through the gateway he caught sight of a troop of guardsmen, trotting across the customs yard, advancing upon the Creek Factory at a run.

Turning away, Bahram began to walk quickly in the other direction. Along with the Fungtai and a few other hongs, the Creek Factory had a rear entrance that opened out on Thirteen Hong Street. Bahram knew that if he could cross the next couple of courtyards without being seen by the soldiers he'd be able to make his escape from the hong.

The soldiers' boots could be heard now, coming through the factory's entrance. As he was stepping into the next courtyard Bahram stole a backward glance and caught sight of half a dozen soldiers, silhouetted against the light: with their pointed plumes they looked unnaturally tall, like giants.

No time, no time . . . as he walked along the corridor, Bahram could hear the soldiers hammering on Innes's door with their weapons. Now other doors were opening and people were pouring out to see what the commotion was about. Bahram checked his pace, measuring his stride with his cane, keeping his head low, as people ran past him in both directions: some were hurrying away from the noise, and others rushing towards it. He kept his eyes down and watched the paving stones, with the end of his turban between his teeth, paying no heed to those who jostled his shoulders and elbows. So careful was he to avert his gaze that it was only when his shadow appeared under his feet that he realized that he was out of the compound.

He was standing on Thirteen Hong Street, which was lined with shops, many of them familiar to him from past visits; he knew that if he went into one of those establishments he would be able to sit down and steady himself. But even as he was thinking of which way to go, he saw that the shops were emptying and people were rushing out to see what was happening in the Creek Factory.

Nearby lay a stone bridge that crossed the nullah at a right angle, overlooking the Creek Factory. This was where most people seemed to be heading, and Bahram allowed himself to be carried along by the flow. On reaching the bridge, he braced himself against the parapet and found that he was looking in the direction of the little balcony that he had been standing on, just a few minutes before. The balcony was empty now, but the dock below was swarming with people, most of them soldiers: Innes was at the centre of the throng, his face red, the buncus still glowing in the corner of his mouth, shouting, waving his arms, trying to bluster his way out of the situation. You had to give it to him—he didn't lack for gall or guts, that fellow—but he was having a hard time of it; that was clear enough. Beside him a soldier was prising the top off a crate—one of his own, Bahram realized. When the planks came off, the soldier plunged his hands in and triumphantly lifted up a spherical black object, about the size of a cannonball—a container of the British Empire's best Ghazipur opium.

Bahram could feel himself choking. He raised a hand to his throat and tugged at the neck-cord of his choga as though he were struggling against a noose. As the choga loosened, so did his cummerbund; he could feel his purse beginning to slip and he let go of his cane so that he could fasten his hands upon his waist. People were surging all around him and he was being pushed towards the parapet. The purse was about to drop from his fingers when he felt a steadying hand upon his elbow.

Sethji! Sethji!

It was the new munshi, what was his name? Bahram could not remember, but rarely had he been so glad to see a member of his staff. He pulled the munshi close, and slipped the purse into his hands: Here hold this; be careful, don't let anyone see.

Ji, Sethji.

Bracing his shoulders, Bahram pushed against the crowd.

Come on, munshiji; come on.

Ji, Sethji.

Breaking free of the throng, Bahram began to walk towards the Fungtai Hong. Wrung out as he was, Bahram could only be grateful that his munshi had not troubled him with any questions—but he knew also that word of his presence at the melee was sure to get back to his staff. Better to think of some explanation right now, something that would scotch rumours and speculation before they got out of hand.

Bahram cleared his throat and slowed his pace. When Neel caught up with him, he put his hand on his elbow.

I was on my way to Punhyqua's hong, he said. To make a payment, you understand . . . for some silk. Then this commotion broke out, and I got swept along. That's what it was. That's all.

Ji, Sethji.

Fortunately, the lane that led to Punhyqua's town house was close by, which lent some credence to the story. But now, as Bahram turned to look in that direction, he encountered a spectacle that all but knocked the breath out of him: it was Punhyqua himself, marching down the lane, flanked by columns of soldiers. He was dressed in a fine *long pao* robe of maroon silk, with brocaded clouds above the fringed hems, and an intricately embroidered panel on the chest—but yoked to his neck was a heavy wooden board. The plank was large enough to make his head look like an apple, sitting upon a table.

Punhyqua's gaze caught his, for a brief instant, and then they both dropped their eyes.

The cangue! Bahram whispered in shock. They've put a cangue on Punhyqua! Like a common thief . . .

Behind the soldiers, further down the lane, Bahram could see members of Punhyqua's family—his sons, his wives, his daughters-in-law—standing in clusters, weeping, covering their faces. He had a vision of himself, in Punhyqua's place, being led out of the Mistrie compound on Apollo Street in the same way, under the eyes of his daughters and sons-in-law, his servants and brothers-in-law—with Shireenbai looking on—and his heart almost seized up. He could not imagine that he would be able to survive so public a humiliation: and yet, he knew also that if it came to such a pass, he, like Punhyqua, would have no choice in the matter; mere shame could not, after all, be counted on to provide the escape of death.

In a daze Bahram began to walk towards the Achha Hong, with Neel at his heels.

A cangue on Punhyqua! Bahram shook his head in disbelief. A man worth at least ten million silver dollars? The world has gone mad. Mad.

twelve

December 9, Markwick's Hotel

Oh my dearest Puggly, there has been the *most* frightful to-do here and it has led to such *extraordinary* happenings that I am all at sixes and sevens. So much has transpired that it seems impossible that it should have started only the day before yesterday—but so it did, and I can hardly credit it because the day had begun in such a *promising* way.

I had succeeded at last, you see, in persuading Jacqua to sit for me! And it took no little contrivance, you may be sure, for not only did I have to persuade *him*, but I had also to prevail on Lamqua to give him leave from his duties at the workshop. This he was most reluctant to do, for fear of exciting the resentment of the other apprentices, and it was not until I had offered a copy of another recent Chinnery canvas that the issue was settled in my favour. I brought Jacqua back to Markwick's Hotel like a trophy won in battle—and so flushed was I with triumph that I positively *slammed* the door on Mr Markwick (who had of course, followed at our heels, mumbling and muttering in the most *odious* way).

It was the very first time that Jacqua—or anyone for that matter—had been in my room and I confess I was a little worried that he might be upset by the disorder (for he is so very *neat* in everything). But on the contrary he was quite *entertained*—or so at least I like to think for he laughed out loud when a shoe was discovered on my only chair (but whether I am right to read this as a sign of amusement I do not know, for I have noticed that Chinese people do sometimes laugh when they are *shocked*). Fortunately the mishap did not prevent him from sitting on the chair or else I would have had a problem on my hands—for I had already resolved, you see, to depict him in a seated position, after the manner of Andrea del Sarto's 'St John the Baptist' (I'm sure I've shown you an engraving: it is truly the most *prodigious* picture—of a youth whose robe has been pushed down to his waist, baring a splendidly muscular and *utterly* unsaintly chest). Of course I was not so brazen as to suggest that Jacqua disrobe himself in like manner (I am not, as you well know, my darling Puggle-bunny, one of those feeble painters who needs to *see* a body in order to create its likeness)—and besides one does not wish to seem *forward* . . . apart from which it is also quite cold in my room, and it is not right, I think, to *incommode* one's Friends (but perhaps when it is a little warmer . . .).

I did however take the liberty of arranging Jacqua's limbs to my satisfaction and he bore this imposition with such good humour that I may have lingered on this task a little longer than I should have done. For scarcely had I repaired to my easel than we were interrupted by a great *uproar* in the Maidan. We both ran out to the terrace and were confronted with a *most* disquieting sight. A crowd had gathered in the Maidan and people were rushing about in disarray. At the centre of the tamasha was a paltan of Manchu sepoys with flags, pennants and plumes protruding from their helmets and uniforms. The paltan was marching through the Maidan in a square formation; in the midst of it some dozen or so prisoners could be seen, bound together by chains. Such was the press of people around the captives that not much was visible of them apart from their heads—and of these only a couple were tonsured and pigtailed in the Chinese manner: the rest were turbaned or bandannaed in an unmistakably Hindusthani fashion!

Achhas in chains? The local constabulary so rarely imposes itself upon foreigners that Jacqua was as amazed as I: he too had never seen anything like it before. Who could these unfortunate Achhas be? What was their crime?

Seized by curiosity, Jacqua and I ran down to the Maidan and thrust ourselves into the crowd.

It took Jacqua only a few minutes to learn what was afoot: the troops had raided Mr Innes's house, in the Creek Factory, and had caught him *in flagrante*, unloading opium from a ship's cutter. They had then arrested the men in the boat, amongst whom were two locals, who had served as guides. The rest of the crew were lascars and they too were now to be incarcerated in a chowki inside the walled city!

The two guides were bruised in body and their clothes were torn to bits. The lascars were unmolested but they too made a pitiable sight, in their bare feet and their thin cotton pyjamas and kurtis, with nothing to protect them from the cold but the bandhnas around their heads and the cumblies over their shoulders. They must have been gubbrowed out of their wits but they did not show it: they seemed stoic and resigned, in the usual Achha way. Even though I knew them to be smugglers and richly deserving of their fate I confess I could not help feeling some pity as I watched them shuffling along, with their eyes lowered: what would I have done, I wondered, were I in their place, surrounded by an angry crowd, in a strange city, being led off to a Celestial prison?

With Jacqua's help I pushed my way to the front of the crowd, which had in the meanwhile been pressing closer and closer to the guardsmen and their captives. The paltan was now entering Old China Street and in passing through this defile I was pushed abreast of one of the lascars. He was lean of build, but sturdy-looking and although he was hanging his head like the others, I had the impression he was quite young. I was close enough to see that the grimy bandhna around his head was a worn and faded gamchha, and this led me to wonder whether he might not be from Bengal, as lascars often are.

The clamour of the crowd seemed to grow louder as we passed through the shaded confines of the street. This distracted the guards and I was able to push still closer to the young lascar: I could see only the side of his face, but something about the cut of his jaw led me to think I had seen him somewhere before. The crowd was so thick I could not get a good look at him—but I swear to you, from where I stood he looked very much like that 'brother' of yours: your beloved Jodu.

But you must not worry, Puggly dear. In the first place I cannot be sure of who the boy was; and Jacqua assures me anyway that 'cuttee head' is not to be the fate of those lascars (I confess I had begged him to inquire, for this thought had not eluded me . . .)—but no, you may be assured it will not come to that; they have merely been incarcerated in the citadel.

Since that day, a semblance of normality has returned to Fanqui-town yet nothing has been quite the same. The Creek Factory, where Mr Innes lives, is under siege, with soldiers and guards posted all around it. You might ask why do they not enter the factory and seize Mr Innes? According to Zadig Bey, they will not do this because it has always been the custom here for the Co-Hong merchants to stand surety for the foreign counterparts. The authorities insist that it is the Hongists' duty to drive Innes out of Canton: if he chooses not to leave it is they who will be made to suffer—and the penalties that have been inflicted on them are indeed *frightful*.

I was to see proof of this with my own eyes when I made my next attempt to visit the Pearl River Nursery.

But I mustn't get ahead of myself: the antecedents of this little trip will be of interest to you as they pertain directly to your paintings.

The packet you dispatched last week was delivered to me four days ago—how lucky we are that a full set of illustrations had been readied by Miss Ellen Penrose (and I must say the illustrations are, if I may so, quite surprisingly *competent*). The packet could not have arrived at a better time—or so I thought—for it had been arranged, as you will remember, that Ah-med would fetch me from the hotel the very next day, exactly one week having passed since my last visit to the Pearl River Nursery. My desire to see Mr Chan being still undiminished it was with the greatest eagerness that I prepared myself for Ah-med's arrival. Having packed your pictures in a bag, I told Mr Markwick that I was expecting a visitor and was to be informed as soon as he appeared. Then I ensconced myself in my room and remained there for the next several hours.

The time was not spent unprofitably for I was able to make a start on Jacqua's torso—and yet you cannot imagine how *disappointed* I was, Puggly dear, when Ah-med failed to appear! I was quite *stricken*—but annoyed as well, and when the chapel clock struck six I decided I would wait no longer. I sought out Jacqua and told him I was *determined* to go to Fa-Tee on my own, the very next morning, in a hired boat. To my great delight he offered (as I had rather hoped he might) to accompany me and even said he would arrange for a boat.

So the next morning we set off, and you cannot conceive, my dear Puggly, how *expectant* I was. All the circumstances seemed exceedingly propitious: it was a fine day and the boat was not a horrid little coracle, managed by harpies, but a sampan rowed by a kindly old boatman. I own it was a little narrow, which meant that Jacqua and I had to sit side by side, and were often compelled to hold on to each other because of the lurchings of the vessel. But this only added to the interest of the journey so we decided to prolong it a bit by going a little way downriver. It was not till we were well past the usual landmarks—the Shamian sandbank, the Dutch Fort, the execution grounds—that it came to our attention that a huge crowd had gathered along the shore, in order to goggle at some kind of tamasha that was being staged upon a barge.

On approaching a little closer it became evident that the spectacle consisted of a man who had been put on public display, with a huge wooden pillory around his neck. Jacqua spoke to some passing boatmen and learnt that this man stood accused of being a confederate of the wretched Mr Innes: this was his punishment for conniving to smuggle opium into the city. The boatman said he might even be *beheaded* if Mr Innes did not leave the city!

We assumed of course that the man was a Thug or a Dacoit, much like Innes himself—so you will understand, Puggly dear, the extent of my *horror* when we came close enough to get a good look at the accused man. For the man was none other than Punhyqua, the eminent Hongist and connoisseur of flowers and gardens!

It was so distressing to see him thus, with a huge board around his neck and thousands of people leering at him that I *yearned* to be whisked away to Fa-Tee—but this too proved impossible. Scarcely had we turned around, to head towards Fa-Tee, when we came to a barrier where we were told that new rules had been put in effect and we could proceed no further without a special chop. So we turned back, and on returning to Markwick's I discovered that the journey would have been wasted anyway—for in the meanwhile Ah-med had come to the hotel to inform me that Mr Chan had left town on urgent business!

Since that time I have seen no further trace of Ah-med and nor have I received any word from Mr Chan—but this is not surprising perhaps for the atmosphere in Fanqui-town has become quite *alarmingly* charged. Mr Innes still refuses to leave and every day there are rumours of new sanctions and threats against him. One afternoon, placards were posted all around the Creek Factory, in Chinese and in English. I brought one away, as a keepsake, and I cannot resist the temptation to copy the words, for I know they will interest you:

'On the third of this month the foreign merchant Innes, with a daring disregard of the laws, clandestinely brought opium up to Canton in a boat which was seized by the government. He openly defies the Imperial mandates and displays the most supreme contempt for his own reputation. His conduct merits universal outrage. We decline therefore to do any more business with him and shall not suffer him to dwell in our buildings: we accordingly placard our resolve in the most explicit manner, that every reasonable man may be informed of it and take timely warning.'

Is it not quite the most *ominous* pronouncement? But such a man is Mr Innes that even this has made no impression on him.

The strangest part of the whole affair, says Zadig Bey, is that Mr Innes cannot have been acting alone—he must have had accomplices and it is quite possible that he would be able to lighten his burden of guilt if he were to spread the blame. But this he has resolutely refused to do, choosing instead to profess complete innocence of all the charges levelled against him (even though he was caught in the very act of unloading the opium on his own doorstep!). But Mr Innes claims the drug was put on his boat by the Chinese customs people (which is of course perfectly *preposterous*) and he will not accept the slightest measure of blame. This has put the Hongists in a terrible quandary. They have held many meetings and issued innumerable notices but to no avail, and they are now at their wits' end.

But a resolution may yet be reached. Zadig Bey has heard from his friend, Mr Moddie, that the Hongists have now requested a secret meeting with the Committee: they want Mr Innes to be present so they can confront him directly with their charges. They are hoping perhaps to shame the Chamber of Commerce into acting against Mr Innes—and it is most *earnestly* to be desired that something comes of it, my dear Puggle-minx, for in the interim the traffic on the river has dwindled to nothing and I do not know how or when I will find a boat to carry this letter.

~

Bahram had thought that the Committee's special session would be held in the Great Hall, on the ground floor of the Chamber's premises. But on presenting himself there he learnt that the venue had been changed, at the express request of the Co-Hong merchants: in view of the confidential nature of the proceedings they had asked that it be moved to more sequestered surroundings. Mr Lindsay had then decided to hold it in the President's personal saloon, on the third storey—this floor contained several private offices and meeting rooms and was closed to all but the President, the Committee and a few members of the Chamber's staff.

As he was approaching the saloon, Bahram heard a raised voice, echoing out of the saloon: 'No sir, I will not leave Canton and you cannot make me do it! Let me remind you that I am not a member of this Chamber. I am a free man, sir, and I obey no mortal voice. You would do well to bear that in mind.'

It was Innes, and the sound of his voice made Bahram check his stride.

Bahram had for days been dreading the thought of coming face-to-face with either of the two men who had it in their power to implicate him in the Creek Factory affair: Allow and Innes. But Allow had providentially disappeared—Vico had heard a rumour that he had fled the country—and as for Innes, this was the first time, after that day, that he and Bahram would be in the same room. Before stepping inside Bahram took a deep breath.

Charles King was speaking now: 'Mr Innes, if you value the freedom you boast of, then you must accept the consequences of your own actions. Do you not see what your exploits have led to? Do you not understand that you have brought disaster upon Punhyqua—and indeed on all of us?'

The President's saloon was a large, well-appointed room, with windows that commanded fine views of White Swan Lake and the North River. On the marble mantelpiece stood two magnificent Ming vases, and between them, facing each other, a pair of lacquered snuff-boxes. The members of the Committee had gathered at the far end of the room, around the mantelpiece: they were all seated, except for William Jardine, who was standing with his back to the mantel. Although Mr Lindsay held the title of President, it was clear from Jardine's attitude of command that it was he who would be presiding over the proceedings. A hint of a smile appeared on his smooth face now as he listened to the exchange between Innes and King.

'Punhyqua's plight cannot be pinned on me,' cried Innes. 'It is the mandarins who are to blame. You cannot hold me responsible for their idiocy.'

Everybody was so absorbed in the argument that only Dent seemed to notice Bahram's entry. He greeted him with a brisk nod and gestured to him to take the empty chair between himself and Mr Slade.

As he was sitting down Bahram heard Jardine intervene, in his usual placid, equable tones: 'Well Charles, you must admit that Innes has the right of it there. The Celestials have made a great muddle of it all, as always.'

'But sir,' responded King, 'the present situation has arisen solely because of Mr Innes's actions. It is in his power to resolve it—all he has to do is to leave. Considering the suffering and inconvenience his presence is causing surely it is only reasonable that he should depart immediately?'

This drew a forceful response from Mr Slade who had been stirring restlessly in his seat. 'No! Mr Innes's fate is not the only thing that is at stake here. There is a more important principle at issue and it has to do with the powers of this Chamber. Under no circumstances can this Chamber be allowed to dictate to any free merchant—that would be an intolerable encroachment upon our liberties.'

Dent had been nodding vigorously as Slade was speaking and now he spoke up too: 'Let me be perfectly clear: if the Chamber attempts to set itself up as a shadow government then I shall be the first to resign from it. This body was established to facilitate trade and commerce. It has no jurisdiction over us and it is of the utmost importance that this principle be preserved. Or else the Celestials will attempt at every turn to use the Chamber to bend us to their will. This is clearly why they have asked to meet us today—and in my opinion that gives us a very good reason to stand together in support of Mr Innes.'

'Support Innes?' A note of disbelief had entered Charles King's voice now. 'A crime has been committed and we are to support the perpetrator? In the name of freedom?'

'But nonetheless, Charles,' said Jardine calmly, 'Dent is right. The Chamber does not have jurisdiction over any of us.'

Charles King raised his hands to his temples. 'Let me remind you, gentlemen,' he said, 'of what is at stake here: it is Punhyqua's head. He has been a good friend to all of us and his colleagues of the Co-Hong are coming here to plead for his life. Are we going to turn them away on the grounds of a legalism?'

'Oh please!' retorted Slade. 'Have the goodness to spare us these Bulgarian melodramas! If you were not so wet behind the ears it would be evident to you that there are more . . .'

'Gentlemen, gentlemen!' Jardine broke in before Slade could finish. 'I must appeal to you to restrain yourselves. We may have our differences on this matter but this is surely not the time or place to air them.'

As he was speaking a steward had come in to whisper in his ear. Jardine gave him a nod before turning back to the others. 'I have just been informed that the Hongists have arrived. Before they are shown in I would like to remind you that no matter what our personal opinions, it is Mr Lindsay who must speak on our behalf—he and no one else. I take it this is clearly understood?'

Jardine's gaze swept around the room and came finally to rest on Charles King.

'Oh, is that how it is to be then?' said King, with an angry glint in his eye. 'You have already settled the matter between you?'

'And what if we have?' said Jardine calmly. 'Mr Lindsay is the President. It is his prerogative to speak on behalf of the Chamber.'

Mr King made a gesture of disgust. 'Very well then. Let us be done with this charade. Let Mr Lindsay say what he will.'

A steward entered now to announce the arrival of the Co-Hong merchants and everyone present rose to their feet. The delegation consisted of four merchants, led by the seniormost member of the guild, Howqua. All of them were wearing their customary formal regalia, with buttons, panels and tassels of rank displayed prominently on their robes and hats.

At any other time there would have been a great deal of chin-chinning between the Hongists and the fanquis but today, as if in deference to the gravity of the situation, the members of the delegation stood at the door, wearing severe, unwavering expressions, while their servants rearranged the seating in the saloon, placing four chairs side by side, in a row, facing the rest. Then the magnates marched straight in and seated themselves in stiffly formal attitudes, with their hands lying invisible on their laps. Their agitation was apparent only in the occasional fluttering of their sleeves.

Now, without any of the usual preambles and speech-making, a linkister stepped up to Mr Lindsay and handed him a roll of paper. When the seal was broken, the writing inside was discovered to be in Chinese—but Mr Fearon, the Chamber's translator, was at hand and he took the scroll off to an anteroom to make of it what he could.

In his absence, which lasted a good half-hour, very little was said: the elaborate refreshments that had been prepared for the visitors—syllabubs, cakes, pies and sherbets—were waved away by the Co-Hong merchants who sat immobile all the while, looking directly ahead. Only Charles King attempted to make conversation but such was the severity of the Hongists' expressions that he too was quickly quelled.

Every man in the room could remember exchanging toasts and gossip with the magnates of the Co-Hong, at innumerable banquets, garden parties and boat-trips. Everyone in that room was fluent in pidgin and they had all, on occasion, used that tongue to discuss things they would not have talked about with their own wives—their lovers, their horoscopes, their digestions and their finances. But now no one said a word.

Sitting on the left was the thin, ascetic Howqua: it was he who had presented Bahram with his beloved desk. On the extreme right was Mowqua, who had once entrusted Bahram with the job of purchasing pearls for his daughter's wedding; in the centre, was Moheiqua, a man so trustworthy that he had been known to refund the cost of an entire shipment of tea because a single chest had been found to be substandard.

The ties of trust and goodwill that bound the Hongists to the fanquis were all the stronger for having been forged across apparently unbridgeable gaps of language, loyalty and belonging: but now, even though the memory of those bonds was vitally alive in everyone present, no trace of it was visible in the faces that confronted each other across the room.

When Mr Fearon returned, the air seemed to crackle in anticipation of his report. Addressing himself to Mr Lindsay, the translator began by saying: 'I fear I have not been able to translate the communication in its entirety, sir, but I will endeavour to provide the gist. Fortunately it repeats some parts of the Co-Hong's earlier communications with us.'

'Please proceed, Mr Fearon. You have our full attention.'

Mr Fearon began to read from his notes: '"We, the merchants of the Co-Hong, have again and again sent to you gentlemen copies of the laws and edicts that regulate our trade in Canton. But you, gentlemen, thinking them of no importance, have cast them aside without giving them the least attention. A seizure has recently been made by the government of some opium which Mr Innes was endeavouring to smuggle into the city. In consequence of this one of our colleagues has been sentenced to the punishment of publicly wearing the cangue. You, gentlemen, have all seen or heard of this."'

The words sent a shiver through Bahram: the sight of Punhyqua, labouring under the weight of the cangue, still festered in his eyes. How many palms had Punhyqua greased over the years? How many beaks had he wetted? Over his lifetime he had probably distributed millions of taels amongst the province's officials; even the men who had come to arrest him had probably profited from his largesse at some time or another. And yet, it had not served to prevent his arrest.

Across the room Mr Fearon was still reading: '"We have established hongs for trading with you, gentlemen, in the hope of making a little money, and to ensure that all things go on peacefully and to our mutual advantage. But foreigners, by smuggling opium, have constantly involved us in trouble. Ask yourselves, gentlemen, whether in our places you would be at ease? There are surely some reasonable men among you. Trade has been suspended and now we are forced to demand some new conditions before reopening it, being determined no longer to suffer for the misdeeds of others. Hereafter, if any foreigner should attempt to smuggle opium, or any other contraband article into the factories, we shall immediately petition the government that such may be dealt with according to law, and that the offenders may be turned out of their lodgings. Furthermore, the foreign merchant, Mr Innes, being a man who clandestinely smuggles opium into Canton, His Excellency the Governor has directed, by edict, that he be driven out of this city."'

Inadvertently Bahram's eyes strayed towards Innes, who was looking out of the window with an oddly stricken expression on his face. The sight inspired a rush of sympathy in Bahram: if not for this man's silence he knew that he too might now be facing the prospect of a permanent exile from Canton.

What would it mean, never to see the Maidan again? To be forever banned from setting foot in China? He realized now, as never before, that this place had been an essential part of his life, and not just for reasons of business: it was here, in Canton, that he had always felt most alive—it was here that he had learnt to live. Without the escape and refuge of Fanquitown he would have been forever a prisoner in the Mistrie mansion; he would have been a man of no account, a failure, despised as a poor relative. It was China that had spared him that fate; it was Canton that had given him wealth, friends, social standing, a son; it was this city that had given him such knowledge as he would ever have of love and carnal pleasure. If not for Canton he would have lived his life like a man without a shadow.

He understood now why Innes was so insistent in professing his innocence: in this lay his only hope of being able to return to China, to Canton—to implicate others, as he could so easily have done, would have required an acknowledgement of guilt and thus an acceptance of permanent exile.

Across the room, Mr Fearon's voice rose: '"In case Innes perversely refuses to leave, we must pull down the building in which he lives, so that he may have no roof above his head. No foreigner must give him shelter, lest he himself become involved in trouble. We have to request that you circulate this amongst you and send it to your newspapers for publication. Know that all this is in consequence of an edict we have received from the Governor, in which he has threatened that all of us, merchants of the Co-Hong, shall wear the cangue unless Innes leaves Canton immediately. Time is short. If you do not act to expel Innes from the city the Governor is certain to carry out his threat."'

Here Mr Fearon stopped, and an uncomfortable silence descended upon the room.

It was Innes who broke it. 'Let me say once again, I am not guilty—or perhaps I should say rather that I am no more guilty than anyone else in this room, including these fine gentlemen of the Co-Hong. I see no reason why I alone should bear the blame for a situation and circumstance that has come about through the mutual consent and connivance of all of us. I will not be made a scapegoat and I will not leave to suit anyone's convenience. And nor is there anything the Chamber can do about it. You had better explain that, Mr Lindsay.'

Many pairs of eyes turned towards the President of the Chamber who now rose to address the Hongists.

'I would be grateful, Mr Fearon, if you would inform our esteemed friends and colleagues of the Co-Hong that the Chamber is powerless in this matter. As it happens Mr Innes is not even a member of this body: he is here today at my express invitation, but it must be noted that the Chamber has no jurisdiction over him. Mr Innes protests his innocence of the charges levelled against him. As a British subject he enjoys certain freedoms and we cannot make him leave the city against his will.'

Bahram smiled to himself as he listened: the arguments were marvellously simple yet irrefutable. Really, there was no language like English for turning lies into legalisms.

Scanning the room, Bahram saw that he was not the only one to be favourably impressed: Mr Lindsay's rejoinder had met with widespread approval among the fanquis. But on the other side of the room, as the import of Lindsay's words sank in, expressions of appalled disbelief began to appear on the faces of the Co-Hong merchants. They held a hurried consultation among themselves and then whispered again to the linkisters, who, in turn, had a brief palaver with Mr Fearon.

'Yes, Mr Fearon?'

'Sir, this is what I have been instructed to convey: "By the obstinate defiance of this one man, Innes, the whole foreign trade is involved in difficulties, the consequences of which may be truly great. We earnestly beg of you gentlemen to endeavour, by reasonable arguments, to make Innes leave Canton today. We have known each other for many years; you have done business not only with us, but also with our fathers and grandfathers. Should we be obliged to wear the cangue our reputations will be indelibly seared. With tainted characters, how shall we ever again be able to carry on the trade, either with natives or with foreign merchants? Ask yourselves, in the name of our long friendship . . ."'

Here the translator's rendition was cut short by Innes who jumped noisily to his feet. 'I have had enough of this!' he cried. 'I will not be defamed by a caffle of yellow-bellied heathens. They point their fingers at me, and yet heaven knows that they themselves have no equals in sinfulness and venery. They've slummed the gorger out of us at every turn; if they could put the squeeze on us this minute they'd do it in the twinkling of a bedpost. Why, I would not cross the room to spare them the cangue! It will only be a foretaste of the fate that awaits them in the afterworld.'

Innes's tone was so expressive that his words needed no translation; nor did the Co-Hong's delegation ask for any—Innes's defiance was self-evident.

One by one the Hongists rose to their feet, bringing the meeting to an abrupt end. The one exception was Howqua: at his advanced age he was too infirm to rise quickly from his chair. As his retainers were helping him up, he glanced at some of his fanqui friends, Bahram among them. On his face was an expression of mingled bewilderment and disbelief: his eyes seemed to ask how this situation could possibly have arisen.

There was something about the old man's uncomprehending regard that quieted even Innes. The foreign merchants stood in silence as the delegation withdrew.

They were not long gone when Innes turned upon the others: 'Oh look at all of you, sitting there with long faces while the stench of your hypocrisy fills this room! You who preside over the Sodom of our age dare to look at me as though I were the sinner! Between the lot of you there is no sin left uncommitted, no commandment unbroken—your every act is shameful in the eyes of the Lord. Gluttony, adultery, sodomy, thievery—what is exempt? I have only to look at your faces to know why the Lord willed me to bring those boats into this city—it was to hasten the destruction of this city of sin. If that purpose has been advanced then I can only be glad of it. And if my continuing presence brings the hour of retribution any closer, why then, I would consider it my duty to remain.'

He paused to look around the room and then spat on the floor. 'There's not one amongst you doesn't know that in comparison to all of you fine fucking gentlemen, I am an innocent—an honest man. And that, let me tell you, gentlemen, is the only reason why I might choose to leave Canton: it's because there's not one amongst you who deserves to keep company with James Innes.'

~

December 12

I cannot believe, dearest Puggly, that this letter has been sitting helplessly on my desk for so many days. But so indeed it has, because I have not been able to find a boat to take it to Hong Kong. Thanks to Mr Innes, who has still to leave Canton, the Trade is at a *complete* standstill.

But the strange thing, Pugglie-chérie, is that this has been a marvellously happy time for me—so much so that I would not be in the least sorry if the Trade were to remain frozen *for ever*! For I have never found so much joy in painting as I have had in these last few days. Jacqua comes to sit for me whenever he can, and I confess that I do not always work as speedily as I might—not only because his company is pleasing but also because it is exceedingly *instructive*. You may be surprised to learn that he was not in the least offended to see himself being depicted with an unclothed torso. Indeed he was kind enough to rectify and even *embellish* my efforts—which is how I discovered that he, and many other young apprentices at the studio, have made a deep study of anatomical painting. This is at the insistence of Lamqua, who goes frequently to Dr Parker's hospital, to paint patients who have undergone operations there. These paintings of Lamqua's are quite *extraordinary*—I have never in my life seen anything like them. They are of people with amputated arms and legs, and also of some who are suffering from dreadful diseases—and the miracle of it is that they are not in the least ghoulish or prurient, even though they are painstakingly detailed and unrelentingly accurate. I am sure I myself would swoon dead away if I had to gaze upon such injuries and lesions for any length of time (but I am, as you know, just a little bit *squeamish*). Yet Lamqua's pictures are so wonderfully sympathetic that I am inclined to think that to be painted by him is perhaps even a part of the patients' cure. He paints the human body as if mutilation and imperfection were not the exception but the *rule*, proof of life itself. It is a way of looking at anatomy that could never be learnt in a morgue or through the dissection of corpses—for the flesh is never without life nor the other way around.

Jacqua too has imbibed something of this unflinching yet tender regard for the body, and when he corrects me I sometimes feel that he is *reproving* me—for he laughs and says that I paint human flesh as a tiger might, as though it were *food*. This has made me think anew about the del Sarto torso on my canvas: I see that its flaws lie exactly in the perfection of the flesh, which renders nothing of the spirit of the subject and seems indeed to be utterly at odds with it.

But it is all to the good, for I do not in the least mind being criticized by Jacqua: it gives me a reason to start all over again and sometimes Jacqua will even allow me to sketch from *life*—which is, I find, a great deal more rewarding than trying to remember a painting which I have never even seen, except in reproduction.

But that is not all, mia cara Pugglazón. I have also received my first *commission*! And from whom, you might ask? Well, it is none other than Mr King, my young Géricault! He came up to me in the Maidan some days ago and said that he is often unoccupied nowadays because of the stoppage in Trade, so would I like to do his portrait while he has the time to sit for it? Of course I said yes, and I have spent several afternoons in the American Factory, where he has his lodgings.

Although he has been kind to me, Mr King is, I think, a reserved, even reticent man. We did not speak much at first, but then a very curious thing happened. One day I came across Mr Slade in the Maidan and he asked me if it was true that I was painting a portrait of Mr King. I said it was indeed true, so then he proceeded to *harangue* me, demanding to know whether I was not ashamed to associate with such a man—a creature of perverse and unnatural inclinations, who consorted with China-men and took their side against his own kind. I said I knew nothing about all that but Mr King had always treated me kindly, and I liked him very much. Mr Slade went away, harrumphing loudly, but I was greatly shaken and I could not refrain from mentioning this peculiar encounter to Mr King. To my surprise he laughed, a little scornfully, and owned that he was not entirely surprised. Mr Slade is exceedingly peculiar, he says: although his behaviour towards Mr King is often insulting in public, in private he often *besieges* him with protestations of Friendship—he has even been known to ask the barber for a lock of his hair! Mr Slade sees depravity and desire everywhere he looks, says Mr King, except within himself, which is where they principally have their seat. That a man of this sort, filled with rage and shallow invective, should command a following in Fanqui-town is a cause for *despair*, says Mr King.

Detestable as he is, I feel I should thank Mr Slade for breaking the ice between Mr King and myself. For Mr King speaks to me now with such a frankness that I feel I am well on the way to becoming his confidant (indeed he has asked me to call him Charlie!). And I am persuaded, Puggly dear, that he is *tormented* by all that is happening here! He thinks the foreign merchants are entirely to blame for the present Situation: opium has made them so rich they cannot conceive of managing without it; they do not understand that it has become impossible for the Chinese to continue to import it because thousands, maybe millions of people here have become *slaves* to it—monks, generals, housewives, soldiers, mandarins, students. Even more dangerous than the drug, says Charlie, is the Corruption that comes with it, for hundreds of officials are paid bribes in order to ensure the continuance of the trade. It has become a matter of life and death, Charlie says, because over the last thirty years the export of opium to China has increased *tenfold*. If the Chinese do not stop the inflow of opium their country will be eaten away from within—and in his darkest moments he thinks that this is exactly what the foreigners want, even though they speak endlessly of bringing Freedom and Religion to China. When confronted with evidence of their smuggling, they resort to the most absurd subterfuges, thinking the Chinese will be deceived and they never are. He fears that this latest affair, concerning Mr Innes, has brought things to such a pass that an Insurrection or an Uprising may well break out (and this is not excessive, Puggly dear, for I have asked Jacqua about it and he says it is perfectly true. He has friends who are positively *chafing* to set fire to the house Mr Innes lives in—they refrain from doing so only out of fear of the local constabulary).

. . . and oh dear Puggly, perhaps I should not have written those last lines, for even as I am sitting here, writing, I can see from my desk that another great Commotion is getting under way in the Maidan. I see bannermen trooping in, accompanied by gongs and pennants and fireworks. They have stationed themselves around the American flag, which is at the very centre of the Maidan, and they are driving people back with the butts of their spears, creating a kind of clearing. A crowd has begun to gather around them, and now more soldiers have appeared, a whole troop of them, and some mandarins too, in sedan chairs. I can scarcely believe it, but they have brought an apparatus with them! It looks exactly like the one I saw at the execution grounds—a sort of wooden cross.

My heart has risen to my throat, dear Puggly . . . I can write no more . . .

~

Neel was walking out of the Danish Hong, where he had gone to deliver a letter, when he was halted by an unexpected sound: a synchronized thudding of feet, accompanied by drums, gongs and exploding firecrackers.

Drawing abreast of the Danish Factory's cattle pen, Neel waited to see what would happen. A minute later a column of troops burst out of the mouth of Old China Street. Their rhythmically stamping feet sent a cloud of dust spiralling into the air as they trotted towards the tall pole that bore the American flag.

As it happened the flag was hoisted not in front of the American but the Swedish Factory for it was in that compound that the residence of the American Consul was located. Between the Danish Hong, which was at the far end of the enclave, and the Swedish, which was in the middle, lay six other factories: the Spanish, the French, the Mingqua, the American, the Paoushun and the Imperial Hong. It took only a few minutes for the sound of drums, gongs and firecrackers to penetrate to the interior of those factories. Then all at once, traders, agents, shroffs and merchants came pouring out.

It was ten in the morning, the busiest time of day in Fanqui-town. The early ferry-boats from Whampoa had arrived a couple of hours before, bringing in the usual contingent of sailors on shore leave. On reaching the enclave the lascars and lime-juicers had gone, as was their custom, straight to the shamshoo-shacks of Hog Lane, so as to get scammered as quickly as possible. Now, as word of the troop's arrival spread, they came running out to see what was under way. Neel could tell that many of them had taken on full loads of the stagger-juice; some were reeling and some were leaning heavily on the shoulders of their shipmates.

With the crowd swelling fast it took Neel a good few minutes to push his way through to the American flagpole, where a space had been cleared and a tent erected: a mandarin, ceremonially robed, was seated inside, with assistants hovering at his elbow. A few yards away, right under the flag, a squad of soldiers was nailing together a strange wooden apparatus.

Now again there was an outburst of gongs and conches and the crowd parted to admit another column of troops. They were carrying a chair that was attached to two long shoulder-poles. Tethered to this device was a man in an open tunic, bareheaded, with his hands tied behind his back. He was thrashing about, flinging his head from one side to another.

As the crowd churned around him, Neel picked up snatches of an exchange in an eastern dialect of Bengali.

Haramzadatake gola-tipa mairra dibo naki? . . . Are they going to throttle the bastard?

Ta noyto ki? Dekchis ni, bokachodata kemni kaippa uthtase . . . What else? Look how the fucker's shivering . . .

It turned out that Neel was standing shoulder to shoulder with two lascars from Khulna, a tindal and a classy. The tindal had a bottle in his hand: delighted to have come across a fellow Bengali, he put his arm around Neel's neck and held the bottle to his lips. Here, have a little sip, won't do you any harm . . .

Neel tried to push the bottle away but this only made the two lascars more insistent. The spirit trickled past his lips and left a burning trail behind it as it percolated through his body: he knew from the taste that the liquor had been especially doctored to produce a quick and powerful effect. Opening his mouth, he stuck out his seared tongue, fanning it with his hand. This hugely amused the two lascars, who put the bottle to his lips again. This time Neel's resistance was much more feeble: the heat of the shamshoo had risen from his stomach to his head now, and he too was suffused with a comradely warmth. They were good fellows these two, with their cheerful rustic accents; it was wonderfully comforting to speak Bengali with these friendly strangers. He flung his arms around their shoulders, and they stood three abreast, swaying slightly on their feet as they watched the preparations for the execution.

The shamshoo had made the lascars garrulous and Neel soon learnt that they were both employed on the *Orwell*, an East India Company ship that was presently lying at anchor in Whampoa. Their last voyage had been bedevilled by bad weather and they had escaped to Canton at the earliest opportunity, hoping to put it out of their minds.

The slurred voices of the lascars' limey shipmates could be heard over the hum of the crowd.

'. . . look at old Creepin Jesus over there . . .'

'. . . they's never going to nail him to no cross!'

'. . . bleedin blasphemy is what I call it . . .'

The movements of the condemned man, in the meanwhile, had grown even more frenzied than before. His head was the only part of his body that was not lashed to the chair and his unbraided pigtail was whipping from side to side; thick strands of hair were stuck to his face, glued fast by the drool that was dribbling from his mouth. Now, at a word from the presiding official, an attendant opened a box and took out a pipe.

'Fuckinell! An artichoke ripe?'

'. . . and I'll be blowed if it in't yong that's going into it . . .'

'Opium? But in'that why he's gettin the horse's nightcap though?'

The prisoner had caught sight of the pipe too now, and his whole body was straining towards it, the muscles of his face corkscrewing around his open, drooling mouth. As the pipe was put to his lips a silence descended on the crowd; the sound of his thirsty sucking was clearly audible. He closed his eyes, holding the smoke in his lungs, and then, breathing it out, he fastened his lips on the pipe again.

The eerie quiet was dispelled by an indignant cry: 'Sir, on behalf of my fellow Americans, I must protest . . .'

Turning his head, Neel saw that three gentlemen, attired in jackets and hats, were approaching the mandarin in the tent. Their words were lost in the ensuing hubbub, but it was clear that the exchange between the mandarins and the Americans was a heated one and it was lustily cheered by the sailors.

'. . . that's the ticket, mate! Donchyoo stand for it . . .'

'. . . you tell'im—put the squeak in his nibs . . .'

'. . . in't he ever so pleased with his little self?'

The dispute ended with the three Americans marching over to the flagpole and hauling down the flag. Then one of them turned to the crowd and began to shout.

'Do you see what is happening here, men? It is an outrage the like of which has never been seen in the history of this enclave! They are planning to stage an execution right under our flags! The intent is perfectly clear—they are pinning the blame for this man's death upon us. They are accusing us of being his accomplices! Nor is that all. By doing this here, in the Square, they are linking our flags with smuggling and drug running. These long-tailed savages are accusing us—the United States! England!—of villainy and crime! What do you say to that, men? Are you going to stand for it? Are you going to allow them to desecrate our flags?'

'. . . not on yer life . . .'

'. . . if it's a bull-and-cow they want, they can'ave it . . .'

'. . . got a porridge-popper waitin for whoever wants it . . .'

While the voices in the crowd were getting louder, the condemned man had fallen so quiet that he appeared to have become oblivious to his fate: his head had slumped on to his shoulders and he seemed to have lost himself in a dream. When two soldiers untied his bindings and pulled him to his feet, he rose without protest and went stumbling towards the apparatus that had been erected for his execution. He was almost there when he tipped his head back to look at it, as if for the first time. A choked cry bubbled up in his throat and his knees buckled.

'. . . don't he look like a dog's dinner . . . ?'

'. . . like a birchbroom in a fit . . .'

The voices were right behind Neel. Turning to look, he saw a burly seaman with an empty bottle in one hand. Slowly the man drew his arm back and then the bottle went curling over the crowd. It exploded near the soldiers, who spun around to face the crowd, arms at the ready. Their raised weapons elicited a howl from the sailors. 'Fucking peelers!'

The shouts of the two lascars were loud in Neel's ears: *banchod-gulake maar, maar* . . . !

Neel too was shouting obscenities now. His voice was no longer just his own; it was the instrument of a multitude, of all these men around him, these strangers who had become brothers—there was no difference between his voice and theirs, they had joined together and the chorus was speaking to him, telling him to pick up the stone that was lying at his feet, urging him to throw it, as the others were doing—and there it was, one amongst a hailstorm of stones and bottles, flying across the Maidan, hitting the soldiers on their helmeted heads, raining down on the mandarin in his tent. They were running now, taking the prisoner with them; the mandarin was fleeing too, sheltering behind the soldiers' upraised weapons.

Elated by their victory the sailors began to laugh. 'I say, Bill, we don't get such a lark as this every day!'

Having driven the execution party away, the mob now fell upon the things the soldiers had left behind—the wooden cross, the tent, the table and the chairs—and smashed them all to bits. Then they piled the remnants together, poured shamshoo on them and set the heap alight. As the flames went up, a sailor ripped off his banyan and threw it upon the bonfire. Another, egged on by his shipmates, tore off his trowsers and added it to the flames. A rhythmic clapping began, urging the half-naked sailors to dance.

The triumph of foiling the execution was no less intoxicating than the liquor, the flames, and the howling voices. Neel was so absorbed in the celebration that he could not understand why his new-found lascar friends had suddenly fallen silent. Even less was he prepared for it when one of them tugged at his elbow and whispered: *palao bhai, jaldi* . . . Run! Get away!

Why?

Look over there: it's a mob . . . of Chinese . . . coming this way . . .

A moment later a shower of stones came pelting down. One of them struck Neel on his shoulder, knocking him to the ground. Raising his head from the dust he saw that dozens, maybe hundreds, of townsmen had come pouring into the Maidan: they were tearing up the fences that surrounded the enclave's gardens, arming themselves with uprooted posts and palisades. Then he caught a glimpse of some half-dozen men running in his direction with upraised staves. Scrambling to his feet he raced towards the Fungtai Hong; he could hear footsteps pounding behind him and was grateful, for once, that the enclave was so small—the entrance was only a few paces from where he had fallen.

He could see the doors being pulled shut as he ran towards them. He did not have the breath to call out but someone recognized him, and held a door open, beckoning, gesturing, shouting: *Bhago munshiji bhago!* Run! Run!

Just as he was about to go through something struck him hard on the temple. He staggered in and collapsed on the floor.

He came to consciousness in his cubicle, on his bed. His head was throbbing, from the shamshoo as well as the blow. He opened his eyes to find Vico peering at him, with a candle.

Munshiji? How are you feeling?

Terrible.

His head began to pound when he tried to sit up. He fell back against his pillow.

What time is it?

Past seven at night. You were out for all of it, munshiji.

All of what?

The riot. They almost broke in, you know. They attacked the factories with battering rams.

Was anyone killed?

No. I don't think so. But it could have happened. Some of the sahibs had even brought out their guns. Can you imagine what would have happened if they'd shot at the crowd? Fortunately the police arrived before they could open fire. They put a quick end to it—cleared everyone out of the Maidan in a matter of minutes. And then, just as it was all settling down who should arrive?

Who?

Captain Elliott, the British Representative. He got word of the trouble somehow and came hurrying down from Macau with a team of sepoys and lascars. If the mob had still been in the Maidan his men would probably have opened fire. Who knows what would have happened then? Luckily it was all over by that time.

So what did he do, Captain Elliott?

He called a meeting and gave a speech, what else? He said the situation was getting out of control and that he was going to see to it personally that British boats were no longer used to bring opium into Canton.

Oh?

Sitting up slowly, Neel put a hand to his head and found that a bandage had been wrapped around it.

And Sethji? Is he all right?

Yes. He's fine. He's gone to the Club to have dinner with Mr Dent and Mr Slade. Everything's quiet now, the trouble's over. Except for the uprooted fences and broken glass in the Maidan, you wouldn't know it had happened.

~

'It is going exactly as I had predicted,' said Dent gloomily, looking at his plate. 'Instead of protecting our liberties Captain Elliott intends to join hands with the mandarins to deprive us of them. After his speech of today there can be no doubt of it; none at all.'

A steward had appeared at Dent's elbow as he was speaking, bearing a tray of Yorkshire pudding: Bahram was no lover of this concoction but it did not escape his notice that the version being offered today was quite different from the dining room's usual soggy staple—it was steaming hot and freshly risen.

Bahram had never known the Club's staff to be as solicitous as they had been that evening: it was as if they were trying to make amends for the chaos of the day. Earlier, one of the stewards had come up to him and whispered in his ear: knowing of his fondness for Macahnese food he had offered him items that were not usually served in the Club—crisp fritters of bacalhau, char-grilled octopus and roast-duck rice. Bahram had accepted gladly but now that the rice was in front of him, topped with succulent slices of mahogany-coloured duck, he found he had lost interest in it.

Slade's appetite, on the other hand, seemed only to have been whetted by the riot: having already wolfed down an enormous helping of roast beef, he now helped himself to some more.

'It is unconscionable, I tell you! Completely and utterly unconscionable that Captain Elliott should take it upon himself to issue these fiats. Why, it seems to be his intention to offer himself to the Celestials as the chief officer of their police and customs!'

'Shocking, is it not,' said Dent, 'that he should direct his strictures specifically at British traders?'

'It is but proof of his ignorance of the situation in China,' said Slade. 'He seems to be unaware that this so-called system of "smuggling" was pioneered by the Americans. Was it not a Boston schooner, the *Coral*, that first sent her boats upriver with opium?'

'So indeed it was!'

'And in any case Captain Elliott has no legal authority to issue extravagant pronouncements on our behalf. There has never been any express diplomatic convention between England and China. *Ergo* he is not invested with any consular powers. He is assuming powers he does not possess.'

Dent nodded vigorously. 'It is appalling that a man whose salary we pay should take it upon himself to impose Celestial misrule upon free men.'

Bahram happened to be facing a window and he noticed now that several brightly illuminated flower-boats had appeared on the misted waters of White Swan Lake; one passed close enough that he could see men lounging on pillows and girls plucking at stringed instruments. It was as if the turmoil of the day had never happened; as though it were all a dream.

Even at the time, as the events were unfolding under his own window, Bahram had found it hard to believe that these things were really happening: that a gibbet was being erected in the Maidan; that some poor wretch was to be executed within sight of his daftar. The semblance of unreality had grown even more acute when the condemned man was carried in. At one point, while twisting and writhing in his chair, the man had turned his head in the direction of the Fungtai Hong. Very little was visible of his face because of the hair that was matted on it, but Bahram had noticed that his eyes were wide open and seemed almost to be staring at him. The sight had shaken him and he had stepped away from the window. When he returned, the melee was already under way and the execution party had disappeared.

'What happened to that fellow?' Bahram said suddenly, interrupting Slade. 'The one they were going to strangle? Was he let off?'

'Oh no,' said Slade. 'I believe his reprieve lasted only an hour or two. He was taken to the execution grounds and quickly dispatched.'

'Sorry little wretch,' said Dent, 'he was nothing but a minion; a tu'penny ha'penny scoundrel like hundreds of others.'

Bahram glanced out of the window again: somewhere on the other side of White Swan Lake a village was celebrating a wedding with a display of fireworks; rockets were arcing upwards, each seeming to travel on two planes simultaneously, through the sky, and over the misted mirror of the lake's surface. Gazing at the spectacle, he was reminded of that night, many years ago, when he and Chi-mei had lain beside each other in a sampan that seemed to be suspended within a sphere of light; he remembered how he had reached for the silver in his pocket and poured it into her hands and how she had laughed and said: 'And Allow? Why no cumshaw for Allow?'

Bahram could not bear to look at the lake again. He glanced down at his plate and saw that the fat had begun to congeal on his untouched slices of duck. He pushed his chair back. 'Gentlemen,' he said. 'Please forgive me. I am not feeling quite pucka tonight. I think I should retire.'

'What?' said Slade. 'No custard? No port?'

Bahram smiled and shook his head: 'No, not tonight, if you please.'

'Of course. A good night's sleep will give you back your appetite.'

'Yes. Good night, Lancelot. John.'

'Good night.'

Bahram went quickly down the stairs, pulling his choga tight around his shoulders. On stepping outside the Chamber's premises he paused, of long habit, to look around for Apu his lantern-bearer. Ordinarily Vico, or someone else, would have made sure that Apu had been sent to fetch him—but today was no ordinary day, so he was not surprised to find the courtyard empty of lantern-bearers.

Setting off at a brisk pace, Bahram emerged from the Danish Hong to find himself alone on the Maidan, with a thick fog rolling in from the river. The waterfront was already obscured as was much of the Maidan, but pinpricks of light could be seen in the windows of all the factories.

In the distance, on the far side of White Swan Lake, fireworks were still shooting into the sky. On exploding the rockets created a peculiar effect in the fog, sparking a diffuse glow that seemed to linger in the tendrils of mist. During one of these bursts of illumination Bahram caught sight of a gowned man, some ten paces ahead. He could only see his back but there was no mistaking his walk.

'Allow?!'

There was no answer and the fog had gone dark in the meanwhile. But then another rocket exploded overhead and Bahram caught sight of him again. He raised his voice: 'Allow! Chin-chin! What-for Allow no speakee Mister Barry?'

Again there was no answer.

Bahram was quickening his pace when he heard Vico's voice, echoing out of the fog: Patrão! Patrão! Where are you?

He turned to see a lamp bobbing in the gloom.

Here, Vico!

Stay there, patrão. Wait.

Bahram came to a stop and a couple of minutes later Vico's lamplit face loomed out of the fog.

I was coming to fetch you, patrão, said Vico. The lantern-walas weren't around today and what with the fog and all I thought you might need a light. I was on my way to the Club when I heard your voice. Who was that you were speaking to?

Allow, said Bahram.

Who? Vico's eyes suddenly grew very large: Who did you say?

Allow. He was right in front of me. Didn't you see him?

No, patrão.

Vico put a hand on Bahram's arm and turned him in the direction of the Achha Hong.

It couldn't have been Allow, patrão. You must have seen someone else.

What do you mean, Vico? said Bahram in surprise. I'm almost sure it was Allow. He was just ahead of me.

Vico shook his head. No, patrão. It must have been someone else.

Why do you keep saying that, Vico? I'm telling you. I saw Allow.

No, patrão, you could not have seen him, said Vico gently. See, patrão, Allow had not run away as we had thought. It turns out that he had been arrested.

Oh? Bahram ran a finger over his beard. Have they let him off then? How is it that he was out on the Maidan?

Vico came to a stop and put his hand on Bahram's arm.

That was not Allow, patrão. Allow is dead. It was he who was to be executed in the Maidan this morning. The authorities have just announced the name: it was Ho Lao-kin—that was what Allow was called, remember? After the riot he was taken to the execution grounds. He was strangled this afternoon.

part three

Commissioner Lin

thirteen

~

January 4
1839!!

Never before has it happened to me, Puggly dear, that I have started a letter in one year and ended it in the next! It could not be helped, however, for the traffic on the river has been frozen all this while. But only this morning there was word that the ban may soon be lifted—and being thus reminded of this unfinished letter, I have retrieved these pages from the drawer in which they have languished since December 12th.

Having now re-read the last entry I have decided to leave intact the interrupted sentence with which it ended: for just as the half-eaten meals on the tables of Pompeii are proof of the unforeseen nature of Vesuvius's eruption, this little fragment too bears witness to the suddenness with which the riots of December 12th burst upon us in Canton.

Since news needs no boats to travel in, word of those events will, I warrant, have reached you before this letter. Instead of burdening you with my own account of the riots I am enclosing a copy of Mr Slade's report in the *Canton Register*. Suffice it to say that the events unfolded in front of my very eyes and in looking back it strikes me that it was a most *fortunate* turn of kismet that led to my being seated at my desk at the time of their commencement. I was thus preserved from Bodily Injury (which was not the case with some who were wandering abroad in the Maidan); and being granted a privileged point of vantage, I was spared the temptation also of venturing closer to the Scene.

It is surely no secret to you, my dear Puggla'zelle, that your poor Robin does not aspire to be a Hero, so you will not be surprised to learn that I did not *stir* from my room until order had been restored. In the late afternoon I was informed by Zadig Bey that Captain Elliott, the British Superintendent, had arrived in Fanqui-town and was shortly to address all the foreign residents. Being assured that there was no risk to my Person, I decided to accompany Zadig Bey to the meeting, which was to be held in the British Hong, across the Maidan from Markwick's Hotel.

The enclave was, by this time, perfectly tranquil, with guards posted everywhere and no sign of the usual vendors and loiterers. Yet, evidence of the recent Upheaval was littered around us; shards of glass glistened in the dust; fence posts lay scattered about, like twigs after a storm, having been uprooted and hurled against the factory walls; and the gates of some of the factories were so badly battered it seemed a miracle their hinges had not given way.

The American Hong in particular had suffered a great deal of damage: this is where Charlie resides and I was shocked to see that the windows of his daftar—the very room where he had been sitting for me—were shattered! I am of course something of a Worrier, Puggly dear, so you will understand how *relieved* I was when we came upon Charlie shortly afterwards and found him unharmed. He was however in a state of great agitation, having witnessed the riots with a sense of dire foreboding. The disturbances were proof, he said, that the foreign merchants are utterly mistaken in their belief that the populace is not in accord with their rulers on the matter of opium. They are, on the contrary, wholly supportive of the official measures against the drug; indeed there is immense public indignation at the impunity of the foreigner—else the people would not have turned upon us all at once, and we would not have needed police protection against them.

'The smuggling of opium has lost us the affections of the good, has made us panders to the appetites of the bad, and we may well fear lest we one day suffer by the outbreakings of passions to whose excitement we ourselves have ministered.'

Among the educated classes, many have come to be convinced, said Charlie, that the foreign traders are like children, and are unacquainted with reason (which they call *Taou-le*). That the mandarins had resorted to the extreme and unprecedented step of ordering an execution in the Maidan was a sure sign, he said, that they had abandoned all hope of being able to communicate with the foreign community through other, more reasonable, means.

We were all agreed, of course, that the method employed was a deplorable one—yet none of us doubted that it was indeed the mandarins' intention to awaken the fanquis to a reckoning of the consequences of their own actions. This was why, on entering 'Company Hall', where the meeting was to be held, we were all stricken with dismay: for no sign of remorse—or indeed even the faintest acceptance of culpability—was visible in the mien of the foreign merchants who had gathered within. Their attitude was expressive rather of an increased belligerence; their regrets seemed to be centred solely on their failure to mount a more aggressive defence of the enclave.

Such was the mood that we began to ask ourselves whether Captain Elliott had any chance of succeeding where the mandarins had failed. Would he even recognize the delicts of the fanquis? I was inclined to be hopeful: not being a trader himself it seemed likely to me that the Captain would see the Situation from a different point of view.

Zadig Bey was not sanguine. The most important thing to know about Captain Elliott, he said, is that he is a Pucka Sahib: the colonies are to him what water is to a fish—his element, his breath, his being. He is the son of a former Governor of Madras, the nephew of a Governor

General of India and has spent many years serving in the British Navy. Neither his birth nor his training are of such a kind as to dispose him to act against the interests of his peers.

And what manner of man is he? I asked, to which Zadig Bey replied: 'Everything you need to know about him you will see when he steps in front of you and begins to speak.'

Zadig Bey was not wrong.

When at last Captain Elliott appeared, he was in full uniform, with a sword strapped to his waist. This was well-judged, I think, for his appearance was certainly impressive enough to quiet the commotion and restore order to the hall. But that was more the doing of the Accoutrements than of the man himself—for even I, who have a talent for such things, am at a loss to conjure up the image of the Captain's face (although I can recall, with perfect clarity, the colours and cut of his clothing).

Captain Elliott is so Pucka, so much the soldierly Sahib, that his visage has become a part of his uniform—it seems to belong not to one man alone but to an entire platoon of men, all clad in blue, with close-cropped hair and trimmed moustaches. When he spoke, his voice too seemed to issue from the weather end of a naval quarter-deck: it was unemphatic and authoritative, the kind of voice that might be expected to exhort reason on everyone. And so it did: the mandarins must be reasonable, he said, and desist from strangling people in the Maidan; but the British Traders had to be reasonable too; they must desist from openly smuggling opium into Canton, in their own boats. The British government had strongly reprobated this practice, which brought disrepute on the Empire; he was determined to put a stop to it and would even offer his co-operation to the Chinese authorities in this regard &c. &c.

In other words, the Captain's objections were directed against the business of sending contraband up the Pearl River in British boats. Of the larger matters—the many opium ships that are anchored off the Outer Islands, and indeed, the whole question of sending the drug from India to China—he made no mention. And how indeed could he, considering that the making and selling of opium is sponsored and supported by the very Empire that he represents?

I confess I left Company Hall with a feeling of intense trepidation in my heart. Zadig Bey too was not reassured by what he had heard. He is convinced that the Situation has passed beyond the control of both Captain Elliott and the mandarins. The foreign merchants will brook no interference, he said, either from the Chinese or from the British Representative: they are convinced that the doctrine of Free Trade has given them licence to do exactly as they please. And amongst the people of Canton there is mounting anger at the impunity with which the foreigners defy the law: if not for the police, says Zadig Bey, the townsfolk would surely have torched the factories and driven the fanquis out of the city.

I thought then that Zadig Bey had overstated the matter a little. But it was not long before I discovered that he had not erred one whit in his estimation of the temper of the townspeople—and when you hear of how I made this discovery you will understand full well, Puggly dear, why I was, for many days afterwards, too downcast to leave my bed.

For this is how it happened:

It had been arranged between Jacqua and myself that he would come to sit for me on the afternoon of the 13th (the day after the Disturbances). I stayed in and waited, almost until sunset; when he failed to appear I went to Lamqua's studio to inquire after him. The moment I stepped in I knew something *frightful* had occurred, for instead of the usual smiling chin-chins I was greeted with sullen stares and peevish frowns.

Of Jacqua there was no sign and none of the apprentices would tell me what had become of him:

to learn what had come to pass I had to apply to Lamqua himself.

This is what I heard: on the morning of the riot Jacqua and his fellow apprentices were at their benches, in the studio, when the troops went marching past the studio. Their curiosity being aroused, they downed their brushes and ran out to the Maidan, disregarding Lamqua's pleas. So it happened that they were in the way when the foreigners went on the rampage: Jacqua had the misfortune to be set upon by a group of drunken sailors and lascars and sustained a blow that broke his arm.

You may imagine, Puggly dear, the *grievous* effect this had on me! I will not conceal from you that I *wept*! I would have gone at once to see my wounded Friend, but of course his home is within the forbidden city—and even if that were not so, I could not have gone. Lamqua told me that it would not be wise for a fanqui to venture abroad at that time, for fear of attracting the ire of the townsfolk.

And as if all this were not *crushing* enough already, I was waylaid, on my way out of the studio, by some of the apprentices. These boys, who had been so friendly before, now proceeded to *bombard* me with galees and Contumely. What exactly they said I cannot remember but the burden of it was that we fanquis were little better than dacoits and murderers; that we did not understand the restraints of civilization and did not deserve to live in Canton—&c. &c.

Knowing me as you do, Puggly dear, you will perhaps understand why I was quite *overwhelmed* and could not for many days bring myself to step out of my room. Christmas came and then the New Year and although I had received a few invitations, I remained inside. The thought of plunging into fanqui-dom again, and of perhaps encountering the men who had set upon Jacqua, made me feel, I confess, quite *desolate*.

Often enough in the past have I wished that I had never been born, but never has that sentiment resonated as strongly within my bosom as it did then. I told myself I should leave Canton, that it was Wrong and Unconscionable to remain in a place where one was unwelcome—but nor could I rid my mind of the thought that nowhere else would I find the Happiness I had enjoyed here. How could I abandon the one place that had offered me the treasure I had always sought and never found—Friendship?

If not for Zadig Bey I do not know what would have become of me—it was only because of him that I did not starve. Charlie too came to see me a couple of times, but he has had very little time to spare nowadays, being much preoccupied with the Situation: he has decided to take out a petition urging all foreigners to renounce the opium trade and surrender their stocks. Predictably, this effort has met only with anger and derision: as a result, poor Charlie is himself now mired in despond and in no position to bring cheer to his friends.

How long I would have remained in that state of despair I do not know, but I am certain that my time of affliction would have been greatly extended if not for Zadig Bey: on New Year's Day, he dangled before me the prospect of fulfilling a long-yearned-for desire—of seeing Canton from the heights of the Sea-Calming Tower. He had for some time been telling me that I should leave my room and that the Situation had greatly improved since the departure of the horrible Mr Innes (and yes, he has indeed left the city). I discovered now that he had even arranged a litter for me, anticipating perhaps that I might claim to be too enfeebled for a long walk. Being robbed of this pretext I could not refuse to go with him—and I am *inordinately* glad that I did not: for it is indeed a most *marvellous* experience to see the entire city spread out before your eyes!

You may remember, Puggly dear, that I once showed you a copy of El Greco's 'View of Toledo'? Try to imagine those grey walls greatly extended and so shaped as to form the outline of a gigantic bell: that will give you an idea of the contours of Canton's walled city. Inside, it is cross-hatched with innumerable streets and avenues: some of the roadways are like narrow galis while others are broad boulevards, spanned by triumphal arches: but no matter whether wide or narrow, the thoroughfares are all perfectly straight and intersect at right angles. The quarters and districts are easy to tell apart: the areas where the Manchu officials have their yamens are as evident to the eye as the neighbourhoods that contain the huddled hutments of the poor. The public places and monuments stand out like the tallest pieces on a chessboard, their positions being marked with cascading roofs and soaring spires.

Only now did I discover how fortunate I was in having an Amanuensis like Zadig Bey: he has studied the city closely and is familiar with all its landmarks. He had brought a spyglass with him and he pointed the sights out to me, one by one. The first, as I remember, was the mandir that marks the founding of the city—which happened, he said, at about the same time as Rome! And as with Rome, it is said that the gods had a hand in Canton's birth: five Devas are said to have descended from the heavens to mark a spot on the bank of the river: the immortals were mounted on rams, each with a stalk of grain in its mouth; these they gave to the people on the shore with the blessing: 'May Hunger Never Visit Your Markets'.

I must admit that the strange tale, and the sight of the forbidden city, lying outspread at my feet, had a powerful effect upon me. More than ever it made me conscious of my Alien-ness, of the distance between myself and this city. I remembered the galees those apprentices had hurled at me and it struck me that perhaps they had only been telling the truth: perhaps it was indeed an unforgivable intrusion for one such as myself to seek to impose his presence upon a place that is so singular, so ancient, so completely an outgrowth of its own soil.

But Zadig Bey would have none of it: the true surprise of Canton, he said, is that its streets and lanes are strewn with reminders of the presence of Aliens. 'Why,' he said, 'even the city's guardian deity is a foreigner—an Achha in fact!'

'Impossible!' I cried, but he insisted that it was so and to back it up he pointed his spyglass in the direction of a mandir nearby: it was the temple of the goddess Kuan-yin, who is said to have been a bhikkuni from Hindusthan, a Buddhist nun who chose not to become a Bodhisattva, as she might have done, so she could tend to the common people.

Is it not *stupefying*, Puggly dear, to think that Canton's tutelary spirit may have been a woman who had once worn a sari?

Scarcely had I recovered from the surprise of this when Zadig Bey pointed his spyglass in the direction of another temple, far away: Buddhists from Hindusthan had lived there for centuries, he said, the most famous of them being a Kashmiri monk called Dharamyasa.

Nor is this all! Down by the river stands a temple that was founded by the most famous of Buddhist missionaries—the Bodhidharma, who had come to Canton from southern India and was perhaps a native of Madras!

And that too was not the end of it: Zadig Bey's finger rose again to point to another roof, which belonged, he said, to a mosque—one of the oldest in the whole world, having been built in the lifetime of the Prophet Mohammad himself! It is a most remarkable structure, no different, in outward appearance, from a Chinese temple—all except for the minaret, which is like that of any dargah in Bengal!

But how is it possible, I said, that people from Hindusthan and Arabia and Persia were able to build monasteries and mosques in a city that is forbidden to foreigners?

It was then that I learnt it has not always been thus: there was a time, said Zadig Bey, when hundreds of thousands of Achhas, Arabs, Persians and Africans had lived in Canton. Back in the time of the Tang dynasty (they of the marvellous horses and paintings!) the emperors had *invited* foreigners to settle in Canton, along with their wives and children and servants. They were allowed their own courts and places of worship and were permitted to come and go as they pleased. Amongst the Arabs the city was so famous, said Zadig Bey, that it was known by a word that meant 'Olive'—*Zaitoon*. Even Marco Polo had visited it, he said; in fact he had probably stood where I was standing at that very moment!

Not content with these revelations Zadig Bey produced another, still more surprising.

Why, he asked me, do you know how the Pearl River got its name?

No, I said, so then he pointed his spyglass at an island in the river, not far from the foreign enclave: it is but a small outcrop of rock, with some crumbling ruins on it. Fanquis speak of it as 'the Dutch Folly'.

'But the Chinese have another name for it,' said Zadig Bey. 'They call it Pearl Island. It's said that there was nothing there until a jewel merchant from across the sea (whether he was an Arab or an Armenian or a Hindusthani, no one knows); but wherever he was from he was clumsier than a jewel merchant ought to be—he dropped the best of his pearls in the river. Now you've seen how muddy that water is? How quickly things disappear? Most things maybe, but not that pearl. It lay at the bottom, glowing like a lantern and slowly growing larger until it grew into an island. And from then on that waterway, which is properly spoken of as the "West River", became famous as the Choo Kiang or "Pearl River".'

You will understand how *dumbfounded* I was.

'I cannot credit it, Zadig Bey,' I cried. 'Surely you do not expect me to believe that the Pearl River may owe its name to an Achha?'

He answered with a nod. 'Yes,' he said. 'It is quite likely.'

'So what happened then?' I asked. 'Why did they go away? The Arabs, the Persians and the Achhas?'

'It is a familiar story,' said Zadig Bey. 'The Tang went into decline and people became discontented. There was hunger and unrest, and as is common at such times, the troublemakers looked to place the blame on the foreigners. One day a rebel army stormed into the city and killed them all—men, women and children, over a hundred thousand of them were slaughtered, in a great river of blood. The memory of it was so bitter and lingered so long, that for centuries afterwards no visitors would venture here from overseas.' Here he paused, with a proud smile. 'But when the foreigners did return it was my own people who were in the lead.'

'Armenians?' said I, and he nodded: 'Yes. Some came overland from Lhasa, where a large Armenian community has existed since late Roman times. Some came by sea, through Persia and Hindusthan. By the fourteenth century there were hundreds of them living here in Canton. One of them, a woman, even built an Armenian church.'

'Inside the walled city?'

'Possibly. But this was almost five hundred years ago, you understand. The walls were not where they are now.'

'But it was still possible, was it, for foreigners to venture inside the city?'

'Oh yes,' said Zadig Bey, 'it was only about a hundred years ago that foreigners were banned from entering the city.'

Now once again he pointed his spyglass at the Dutch Folly. 'When the Netherlanders first came to Canton,' he said, 'they needed a place to set up warehouses, just as the Portuguese had done in Macau. They were given that little island, so then they asked if they could build a hospital there, to treat their sick sailors. This was impossible to object to, so the Chinese said go ahead, and the Dutchmen began to bring ashore a great number of tubs and barrels—filled, they said, with provisions and building materials. But the tubs were strangely heavy and one of them got loose; it broke into splinters and out rolled a cannon! "How can sickman eat gun?" they were asked and of course they had no answer. Evidently, under the guise of setting up a hospital, the Dutchmen were busy building a fort! And even after the deception was discovered the Chinese did not attack or molest them. Instead they used the tactic that has since become their favourite weapon against the Europeans: a boycott. They stopped people from sending supplies, so the Dutch ran out of provisions and had to abandon the island. From then on the Chinese knew the Europeans would stop at nothing to seize their land—and one thing you have to say about the Chinese is that unlike others in the East they are a practical people. When faced with a problem they try to find a solution. And that over there was their answer: Fanqui-town. It was built not because the Chinese wished to keep all aliens at bay, but because the Europeans gave them every reason for suspicion.'

You cannot imagine, Puggly dear, what a *tonic* effect these discoveries had on me.

Canton appeared to me in an entirely new light: if only I could see Jacqua, I thought, surely I would be able to explain that I was not one of those fanquis who come with cannon, but rather one of those who have been drawn here by Art—by paintings and porcelain, as in the times of the Tang?

Happily these explanations proved unnecessary. For who should knock on my door the next day but Jacqua himself? He had bandages on his arm, tied by the bone-setter, but that did not prevent him from greeting me with a fond Embrace!

You can imagine, I am sure, how glad I was when I discovered that Jacqua had not for a moment thought to link me with the vile men who had set upon him in the Maidan: indeed, when he heard of the recriminations that had been heaped upon me by his colleagues, he was shocked. He reproached them so forcibly that they had made me a painting by way of apology—a view of the Maidan with Jacqua and I, strolling arm-in-arm! It is not perhaps a masterpiece, yet nothing I have ever owned has been so precious to me!

And so, my sweet rose of Pugglesbury, everything is well again: my Friend has been restored to me, my blue-devils have been banished, and I am so Happy I do not know how I shall ever bring myself to leave this place . . .

And do not imagine for a moment, my dear Puggly, that I have forgotten about your camellias—I have *not*! The moment the river is opened again I shall make another foray in the direction of Fa-Tee.

Oh, and I cannot send this off without mention of the incident you described in your last letter (your little squabble with the *Redruth*'s cook). You must not take it too much to heart, dear: it was not at all wrong of you to tell him that the galley smelled like a crêperie! The fault was entirely his for taking offence. I suspect the fellow has no French and did not understand that you were merely complimenting him on his pancakes. If he was upset it was probably because he thought (quite wrongly, of course) that you were comparing his kitchen to a tottee-connah (sometimes vulgarly spoken of in English as a 'crappery').

Really, dear, I would have loved to see the cook's face when you told him that you liked nothing better than the smell of fresh crêpes, warming in the pan. I am sure the *Redruth* has never seen its like!

~

Although Bahram was deeply attached to his faith, he was not fervently religious; nor did the practical considerations of his busy life allow him to be as meticulous in his observances as he would have liked. He was always careful, however, to keep a copy of the Khordeh Avesta beside his bed and he was never without a sadra and a kasti. When in Bombay he often accompanied Shireenbai on her daily visits to the Fire Temple and when Mullah Feroze delivered his homilies he made every effort to be in attendance. While in Canton, he tended personally to the altar in his bedroom, daily lighting incense under the portrait of the Prophet, regularly changing the flowers and fruit that lay under it and making sure that the wick of the *divo* was always lit. But most of all he tried, in his own acknowledgedly fallible way, to keep in mind the guiding principles that had been instilled in him in childhood—*Humata, Hukhta, Hvarshta*—'good thoughts, good words and good deeds'.

In his easy-going, yet respectful, approach to religion Bahram was not unusual amongst his peers; where he did differ from them was in a certain lack of credulity—in his circle of merchants he was one of the few who never sought the guidance of augurers, astrologers, fortune-tellers and the like. If he was an exception in this, it was mostly because he had always placed more trust in his own intelligence and foresight than in the divinations of kismet-doctors.

But now, as the chill of December turned into the numbing cold of January, he began to doubt, as never before, his ability to look ahead. Everywhere he turned there was confusion; every day there was a new pronouncement or edict to add to the uncertainty.

Sometimes, at night, when the fog came swirling in from the river, he would look out of his bedroom window and imagine that he was seeing Allow, down in the Maidan: the figure would appear to wave in the direction of his window, beckoning with his finger, signalling to Bahram to follow him to the water. In some part of his mind, Bahram knew his eyes were playing tricks on him—and yet, in that other part of him that had now become prey to all kinds of fears and fancies, Allow seemed always to be waiting in the shadows. Even in his head he could not bear to pronounce his names: Ho Lao-kin, Allow—the syllables, in their various iterations, had taken on the character of mantras that could summon the dead.

But no matter how hard he tried to expel them from his head, the echoes of those names kept making themselves heard.

One morning, at breakfast, the munshi said: Sethji, Mr Slade has written a long piece; he has strongly criticized Captain Elliott.

What for?

He is incensed that Captain Elliott openly spoke against the smuggling of opium on the river.

Read it out munshiji.

'"The clear inference of Captain Elliott's words is that he, and the English government, while they *reprobate the smuggling of opium on the river*, approve and encourage smuggling *outside* the river and on the coasts of China. To smuggle a hundred chests *outside* the Bogue is neither an offence nor a degradation; but to smuggle one chest or a few balls inside is both! Admirable consistency in the principles of government and public men! Admirable consistency in political and commercial morality! And how will Captain Elliott explain these orders of the English to the local government without implicating the *whole of the opium trade in the question*?"'

Here the munshi stopped to glance at Bahram. Shall I go on, Sethji?

Yes. Go on.

'"We have just heard that Captain Elliott has dispatched a petition to the Governor of Canton *through the Hong merchants*. He has thus betrayed the property and disgraced the character of British subjects to this lying, corrupt and unjust government. It is reported indeed that he has petitioned the Governor to place him in command of a Chinese cruiser in order that he may, in person, expel the British-owned boats from the river. This proceeding appears to us very likely a felony injurious to the Queen's prerogative, being the offence of serving a foreign prince without permission.

'"By custom, as is well known, *virtually all the Chinese laws were suspended in the case of foreigners, except in capital offences*. Let then the Chinese enjoy their opium pipes and the Emperor and his magnates proceed in their cruel and indefensible policy of sacrificing human life for the mere indulgence of a luxurious and debilitating habit until 'the spears and lances arise to avenge the misrule' of the dynasty."'

Now the munshi looked up again.

Sethji, he has mentioned you too.

Me? Bahram pushed his plate aside and rose quickly from the table. What does he say?

'"We never expected to see a superintendent of British trade lackeying the heels of the Governor of Canton, proffering his services against those whom by his office he is bound at least to endeavour to protect. When Captain Elliott has distinguished himself in the service of the mandarins, the next duty His Excellency will impose on him will probably be to deport Messrs Dent, Jardine and Moddie."'

What was that? said Bahram. Did Mr Slade say 'deport'?

Ji, Sethji. That is what Mr Slade has written. He implies that the execution of Ho Lao-kin was a signal . . .

Stop! Bahram clapped his hands to his ears. Munshiji—bas!

Yes, Sethji, of course.

Bahram glanced at his hands and saw that they were trembling slightly. To give himself time to recover, he dismissed the munshi.

You may go to your room, munshiji, he said. I will call you when I need you.

Ji, Sethji.

When the door had closed, Bahram walked over to the window and looked down at the Maidan. Of late it was less crowded than it had been and some of the men who came there did not seem to belong: they were not like the loiterers of old; they seemed alert and vigilant, as though they were keeping watch on the residents.

Now, as he stood by the window, Bahram had the impression that several pairs of eyes had turned to look in his direction. Had they been posted there to watch him? Or was it all in his head?

The worst of it was that it was impossible to know.

His gaze strayed towards the pole where the American flag had once hung. It had not been hoisted again since the day of the riots; nor had any of the other flags. Their absence had changed the appearance of the enclave, denuding it of some essential element of colour. The bare flagpoles were like reminders of that day—that morning when the gibbet was set up and the chair was carried in with . . .

The fellow's name was almost on his tongue when he bit it back: it was as if his mouth had been soiled by something unclean and alien: feeling the need to wash it out he crossed the corridor and opened the door of his bedroom. In keeping with Parsi custom, the doorway was garlanded with a *toran*—a beaded drapery that had been given to him by his mother at the time of his marriage. The toran had travelled with him on all his trips to China and over the years it had become a link with his past, a personal good-luck charm.

Bahram was about to step inside when he saw that the toran had slipped from its place, above the lintel, and had somehow become entangled in the door jamb. As he was trying to pull it free, the frail old threads broke and a shower of beads rained down on him. Bahram recoiled, in shock, mumbling under his breath: *Dadar thamari madad* . . . Help me, Almighty God.

Falling on his knees he began to pick up the tiny pieces of glass, digging them out of the cracks in the wooden floor and slipping them into the chest pocket of his choga.

One of the peons came to help. Sethji, let me do it . . .

No! cried Bahram, without so much as looking up. Get back! Stay away!

The thought of anyone else touching his mother's beads was intolerable to him; he stayed on his knees until the last of them was off the floor. Then he rose to his feet and saw that several khidmatgars had gathered in the corridor; they were standing in a knot, watching him silently.

He shouted: Chull! Don't you have any work? Get away from here. Go!

Slamming his bedroom door, he lay down. He could feel tears prickling behind his eyelids, so he turned and buried his face in his pillow.

The next day Vico reported that the city officials had sent around a notice asking all the foreign factories to seal up their rear entrances. It was a minor matter, yet it was deeply disturbing to Bahram; he could not help wondering whether it was directed specifically at himself. Could it be that he had been seen leaving the Creek Factory by the rear entrance? Or was it maybe that Vico had been spotted that day when . . . ?

Do you think they saw you, Vico? said Bahram. They have spies everywhere, you know. Maybe they were watching when you used the back entrance to bring that fellow here.

Do you mean Allow?

Bas! You know who I mean, Vico! There's no need to say the name.

Vico looked at him oddly before dropping his gaze: Sorry, patrão, sorry; I won't say it again.

But Vico too was powerless to silence the echoes of the name.

A few days later he came hurrying up to say: Patrão, Mr King is downstairs. He wants to see you.

Why?

I don't know, patrão. He didn't say.

The call was not unprecedented: Charles King had come by several times in the past, soliciting funds for the various charities that he was involved with. On a couple of occasions his conversations with Bahram had strayed in other directions too. Once, noticing the Farohar picture in the daftar, Mr King had asked Bahram about it: this had led to a long conversation about the nature of Good and Evil, and the eternal struggle between Ahura Mazda and Ahriman.

That discussion seemed very distant to Bahram in his present state of mind—yet he could not turn Charles King summarily away from his door: he was known to have good relations with the mandarins and it would not do to antagonize him.

Send him up, Vico.

Bahram spent the next few minutes composing himself, and when the visitor was shown in he was able to greet him with some semblance of his usual heartiness. 'Ah Charles! A pleasure indeed! Come in, come in!'

'A very good day to you, Barry.'

Bahram bowed and pointed to an armchair. 'Please be seated, Charles. Tell me, what can I do for you?'

'Barry, I've come to see you because I am troubled by the present situation in Canton. It seems to me that if things carry on like this then it is not improbable that Great Britain will interfere in China ere long. But for what? For the preservation of the revenue on opium in Bengal; for the protection of an article which it is a shame even to the Chinese pagan to consume.'

'But the trade has gone on like this for a long time, Charles,' said Bahram. 'Surely you do not expect an overnight change?'

'No, but change it must, Barry, and we must change too. You will remember that I proposed that we sign a pledge some time ago. I feel that it is more than ever necessary now and I intend to place it before the Committee again. Your support would mean a great deal.'

'A pledge? Regarding what?'

The visitor withdrew a sheet of paper from his pocket and began to read: '"We, the undersigned, believing that the opium trade with China is fraught with evils, commercial, political, social and moral; that it gives just offence to the Government of this country; arrays the authorities and the people against the extension of our commerce and the liberty of our residence; and defers the hope of true Christian amelioration; do hereby declare that we will not take part in the purchase, transportation, or sale of the drug, either as principals or agents."'

Mr King looked up and smiled: 'I had hoped to discuss this at a public meeting but unfortunately nobody came; nor did the pledge garner a single signature other than mine. But I think in light of recent events, many will be willing to reconsider the matter.'

Bahram had been shifting uncomfortably in his seat, and now he said: 'But the matter is not in our hands, Charles. Surely you do not think the traffic in opium would stop if we signed a pledge? Others will step in—because it is not we but the Chinese who are responsible for the trade. It is they who love opium after all.'

'I cannot agree with you, Barry,' said Mr King. 'It is the ready availability of opium that makes it attractive; it is the inflow of the drug that creates the addict.'

'But what do you propose we do Charles? There are thousands of crates of opium lying in ships offshore. What is to become of all this merchandise?'

'Well not to mince words, Barry, I feel that all existing stocks must be surrendered.'

'Really, Charles?'

Only for a moment did Bahram entertain the thought that the young man was joking—the glow of sincerity in his dark-browed face was enough to instantly dispel that notion.

Bahram cleared his throat cautiously and put his fingertips together. 'But Charles! What you are recommending is a very extreme step, no? You are aware I am sure, that many merchants have stocked opium only because there were indications that the Chinese government might legalize the trade. Some mandarins had circulated memorials recommending this, as you must know.'

'You are right, Barry,' said King. 'When the proposition to legalize the opium trade was first brought before the Chinese government we at Olyphant & Co. also thought that matters were fast tending to that result. But such has not proved to be the case. The memorials have been rejected and the Imperial opposition to the use of the "vile dirt" continues unabated. Whatever doubt there was on that score was settled, surely, on the morning of 12th December?'

'What do you mean?' said Bahram.

'You must be aware, Barry, that the Governor had a very specific intent in mounting the execution of Ho Lao-kin in the heart of our enclave.'

Bahram dropped his eyes and withdrew his hands into his choga: 'What was that intent, Charles?'

'You will surely have seen the Governor's letter on this subject? It was written in answer to the Chamber's accusation that he had disrespected the foreign flags. He said: The penalty of death to which Ho Lao-kin had subjected himself was the result of the pernicious introduction of opium into Canton by depraved foreigners; his execution, in front of the foreign factories was designed to arouse reflection amongst the foreigners—for foreigners, although born and brought up beyond the pale of civilization, *have yet human hearts*.'

Suddenly Bahram remembered how he—the condemned man—had turned to look in the direction of his window. He shuddered and his hand instinctively sought the reassurance of his kasti.

'Did you know, Barry, that the authorities are rumoured to have extracted an extensive confession from Ho Lao-kin? He is said to have told them that he had been inducted into the opium trade at a very young age, by a merchant who gifted him a ball of the drug. I have heard that when Ho Lao-kin learnt of his sentence he himself begged to be executed in the square.'

Bahram could not bear to listen any more. With a great effort he brought a smile to his face. 'Well Charles, this is all very interesting,' he murmured. 'I will certainly give your suggestions due consideration. But regretfully this is a rather busy time . . . I am sure you will understand.'

'Of course. I understand.'

Charles King left, looking rather puzzled, and Bahram went to his bedroom and lay down, with his hand resting on his kasti.

The next morning, there was an ominous piece of news: on stepping into his daftar Bahram discovered that Lin Tse-hsü was on his way to Canton.

Sethji, it has been confirmed, said the munshi. Lin Tse-hsü was given his appointment on the night of December the 31st, by the Son of Heaven himself.

So he is to be the next Governor, is he?

No, Sethji. He will be much more powerful than the present Governor. His position is that of 'Imperial High Commissioner'—'Yum-chae' in Cantonese. He will be more like a Viceroy than a Governor—he will be above the admirals, the generals and all other officials.

What is the reason for that?

Sethji, it is because the Emperor has specifically entrusted him with the job of ending the opium trade. Apparently when the Emperor gave Lin Tse-hsü the appointment he told him, with tears in his eyes, that after his death he would not be able to face his father and grandfather if opium-smoking had not been eradicated from the land.

Bahram came to a halt by the window: Are you sure this is not just gossip, munshiji?

Ji, Sethji. The outgoing Governor and Lieutenant-Governor have issued a joint notice. A very stern proclamation, addressed to foreign merchants. I've picked out some bits.

Go on.

'"In times past edict after edict has been directed against opium, and we, the Governor and Lieutenant-Governor, have often reiterated our commands and admonitions. But even to the last, gain alone has been your aim, and our words have filled your ears as the empty wind. At this time, the great Emperor, in his bitter detestation of the evil habit, has his thoughts hourly bent on washing it clean away. In the capital he has commanded the ministers of his court to deliberate and to draw up plans. Besides all this the Emperor has just now appointed a high officer as his special Commissioner, to repair to Canton in order to examine and adopt measures in reference to the affairs of the sea-port. The Commissioner is now not far off; his arrival is expected shortly. His purpose is to cut off utterly the source of this noxious abuse, to strip bare and root up this enormous evil; and though the axe should break in his grip or the boat should sink from beneath him, he will not stay his hand till the work is accomplished."'

'Does he say anything about what measures the Commissioner has in mind?'

Ji, Sethji.

'"We have already received, with the deepest respect, an edict commanding the admirals of every station, along with the commanders of the different garrisons and military stations, to dispatch squadrons of warships to seize the native smuggling boats and drive out the loitering foreign ships. It appears that several hundred seizures have already been made. As for those villains who have grown grey in this nefarious traffic, to them shall be awarded the most awful penalty of the law, as was the case with the criminal Ho Lao . . .'"

This time the munshi interrupted himself, without Bahram's having to say a word.

Maaf karna, Sethji; please excuse me.

Perversely, the apology only deepened Bahram's disquiet: what did the munshi know? Had the staff been discussing these matters below stairs?

His head began to throb and he decided to lie down for a bit.

That's enough for now, munshiji. I'll call you when I'm ready.

Ji, Sethji.

Not long after this there was a rare piece of good news: foreign-owned boats were once again being issued permits to leave and enter Canton. But when the traffic resumed it was learnt that the opium fleet, still at anchor off the outer islands, had been joined by several more vessels, recently arrived from Bombay and Calcutta.

Soon there was a slew of letters; among them were some that commented on the state of the markets in India. Bahram discovered to his shock that the poppy harvest of the last year had turned out to be the most bountiful ever; the markets of Calcutta and Bombay were awash with opium and the price of the drug had crashed. A great number of would-be merchants were now leaping into the trade.

For Bahram, the news was disastrous on many counts: it was galling enough to know that he could have purchased his cargo at half the price if only he had waited a few months; it was worse still that he no longer had the option of taking his consignment back to Bombay, in the event of its remaining unsold—the Indian prices were now so low that he would not recoup even a fraction of his costs.

A few days later a large new contingent of Bombay merchants poured into Canton. They were mostly Parsis with a sprinkling of Muslim and Hindu traders: the majority were young men, small-time businessmen who had no prior experience of Fanqui-town. Among them was a relative of Shireenbai's, Dinyar Ferdoonjee, a boy Bahram had not met in many years: he was taken by surprise when a tall, athletic young man, square-jawed and strikingly good-looking, walked into his daftar.

Dinyar?

'Yes, Fuaji.' Holding out his hand he gave Bahram an energetic handshake. 'How are you, Fuaji?'

Bahram saw now that he was wearing a pair of well-cut trowsers and a coat made of the finest Nainsook; his cravat was perfectly tied and on his head, instead of a turban, there was a glossy black hat.

Dinyar had brought presents from Shireenbai and his daughters, mostly new clothes for Navroze, the Persian New Year, which was coming up in March. After handing them over, he wandered around the daftar, examining its contents with a slightly amused smile. All the while he kept up a flow of chatter, in English, passing on greetings and messages from various people in Bombay.

Amazed by his fluency, Bahram said, in Gujarati: *Atlu sojhu English bolwanu kahen thi seikhiyu deekra*—Where did you learn to speak English so well, son?

'Oh Puppa kept a tutor for me—Mr Worcester. Do you know him?'

No.

Dinyar in the meanwhile had made his way over to the window and was looking down at the Maidan. 'Grand view, Fuaji! I'd love to rent this room some day.'

Bahram smiled: You'll have to get your business going first, deekra—a room like this is expensive.

'It's worth it, Fuaji. From here you can keep an eye on everything that's going on.'

That's true.

'That affair in December: you must have seen it all from up here, no?'

What affair?

'When they tried to execute someone down there? What was his name—Ho-something, wasn't it?'

Kai nai—Never mind.

Bahram sank back into his armchair and wiped his forehead. 'Sorry, beta—I have some work to finish . . .'

'Yes of course, Fuaji. I'll come by again later.'

For the rest of the day Bahram averted his eyes from the Maidan and stayed away from the windows. But just as he was about to go to bed, he heard an unfamiliar noise outside, a kind of chanting, accompanied by the tinkling of cymbals.

It was impossible not to look out now. Parting the curtains he saw that some dozen people had gathered at the centre of the Maidan. A clump of flickering candles was planted in front of them and the flames threw a dim light on their faces: they were all Chinese but not the kind of men who usually came to the Maidan—a couple of them were dressed in the robes of Taoist priests, including the man who was leading the chanting.

Suddenly Bahram remembered witnessing something similar on one of Chi-Mei's boats: she had always had a great dread of unquiet spirits and hungry ghosts and some trivial incident had led her to summon a priest. Looking out of the window now, Bahram began to wonder whether the men in the Maidan were performing an exorcism. But for whom? And why there—at the very spot where the gibbet had been erected that day?

He reached for the bell cord and tugged it hard, setting off an insistent clanging in the kitchen downstairs.

A few minutes later Vico came running up, wearing a look of concern. Patrão? What's the matter?

Bahram beckoned to him to come to the window.

Look at those people down there, Vico. See how they're chanting? And look there—isn't that some kind of priest, waving his hands and lighting incense?

Maybe, patrão. Who knows?

Isn't that exactly the place where they had brought that fellow that day?

Vico shrugged and said nothing.

What are they doing down there, Vico? Is it an exorcism?

Vico shrugged again and would not look into his eyes.

What does it mean, Vico? said Bahram insistently. I want to know. Have other people seen what I saw that night, in the fog? Have you heard of anything like that?

Vico sighed and pulled the curtain shut. Listen, patrão, he said, in the kind of tone that men use to soothe children. What is the point of thinking about all this? What good will it do, ha?

You don't understand, Vico, said Bahram. It would make me feel better if I knew I wasn't the only one who had seen it—whatever it was that I saw.

Oh patrão, leave it na?

Vico went to Bahram's bedside table and poured out a stiff measure of laudanum.

Here, patrão; take this, it will make you feel better.

Bahram took the glass from him and drained it at a gulp. All right, Vico, he said, climbing into his bed. You can go now.

With his hand on the doorknob, Vico came to a stop.

Patrão, you can't let your mind run away with you like this. There are so many who are depending on you, here and in Hindusthan. You must be strong, patrão, for our sake. You can't let us down; you can't lose your nerve.

Bahram smiled: a gentle warmth had begun to spread through his body as the laudanum took effect. His fears dissolved and a sense of well-being took hold of him. He could scarcely remember why he had felt so oppressed and frightened just moments before.

Don't worry, Vico, he said. I am fine. Everything will be all right.

~

The gold in Asha-didi's teeth glinted as she rose to welcome Neel into her floating eatery.

Nomoshkar Anil-babu! she said, ushering him past the painted portal. You've come at a good time. There's someone here you should meet; someone from Calcutta.

At the far end of the kitchen-boat sat a statuesque form, draped in a shapeless gown: the matronly figure, the bulbous head and the long, flowing locks were so distinctive that there could be no doubt of who it was. Neel came instantly to a halt, but it was too late to attempt an escape. Asha-didi was already performing the introductions: Baboo Nob Kissin, here is the gentleman I was telling you about; the other Bengali Baboo in Canton—Anil Kumar Munshi.

A frown appeared on Baboo Nob Kissin's bulging forehead as he looked up from his plateful of daal and puris. His eyes widened as they lingered on Neel and then narrowed; Neel could sense his bafflement as his gaze tried and failed to strip the beard and moustache from his face. He forced himself to stay calm and pasted a bland smile on his face. *Nomoshkar*, he said, joining his hands together.

Ignoring his greeting, Baboo Nob Kissin gestured to him to sit down. 'What is your good-name, please?' he said, switching to English. 'I did not catch. Clarifications are required.'

'Anil Kumar Munshi.'

'And what-type employments you are engaging in?'

'I am Seth Bahram Modi's munshi.'

The Baboo's eyebrows rose. 'By Jove! Then we are like colleagues only.'

'Why is that?'

'Because I am Burnham-sahib's gomusta. He is also tai-pan.'

It took all of Neel's self-control to conceal the shock that went through him at this. 'Is Mr Burnham here now?' he said, in a carefully expressionless voice.

'Yes. He has come in his new ship.'

'What ship?'

Once again, Baboo Nob Kissin's eyes narrowed shrewdly as his gaze raked over Neel's face. 'Ship is called *Ibis*. Might be you have heard of it?'

Now, fortunately, a plate of biryani was laid before Neel. He lowered his eyes and shook his head. '*Ibis*? No, I have not heard of it.'

Baboo Nob Kissin let out a sigh and when he spoke again it was in Bengali.

Baboo Anil Kumar, I will tell you about the *Ibis* while you eat. It was only last year that Burnham-sahib acquired this ship and the moment I set eyes on her I knew she would bring about a great change in my life. You may ask how I, an English-educated Baboo, could know such a thing at one glance. Let me tell you: this person you see in front of you is not who you think. Inside the visible body there is someone else—someone hidden, someone who in another birth was a gopi, a girl who played with cows and made butter for the butter-thieving Lord. I have long known this, just as I know also that some day, the visible body will drop off and the inner form will step out, like a dreamer emerging from a mosquito-net after a good night's sleep. But when? And how? These questions were much on my mind when I first saw the *Ibis* and I knew at once this ship would be the instrument of my transformation. On board there was a man by the name of Zachary Reid, a plain sailor you would think to look at him, but I knew at once that he too was not what he seemed. Even before I beheld him, I heard him playing the flute—the flute!—instrument of the divine musician of Vrindavan. I knew beyond a doubt his arrival was a sign, I knew I had to be on that ship—and by good fortune I was able to arrange for myself to be appointed the vessel's supercargo.

The ship was carrying over a hundred coolies and two qaidis. One of the two convicts was a Bengali—about your age I would say, Anil-babu. He had been a Raja earlier, but had lost all his money and committed forgery. He was taken away from his wife and son, his palace and his servants; he was packed off to jail, there was a trial and he was sentenced to transportation—seven years of hard labour in a prison camp in Mauritius. I had seen this man, this Raja, on the streets of Calcutta before his fall from fortune: he was like other zemindars, arrogant and lazy, corrupt and debauched. But ships and the sea have a way of changing people, would you not say so, Anil-babu?

Neel looked up from his biryani. Yes, maybe . . .

I don't know whether it was he or I who was most changed by the *Ibis*, but when I saw this one-time Raja in chains, on the ship, I felt a strange connection with him. My inner voice whispered in my ear: this is your son; this is the child you have never had. I tried to help him; I would go to see him and his fellow prisoner in their chokey and I would take them food and other things. As the supercargo, I had my own keys to the chokey; one night the qaidis asked me to leave the door open. This too I did, and that night, in the midst of a storm, this young man and some others tried to escape. Next day evidence was found that their boat had capsized and they had all perished. The blame for this incident fell, unfortunately, on the shoulders of the blameless Zachary Reid, who is still in Calcutta trying to clear his name. But for myself, I had to suffer another kind of punishment: I thought I had lost my new-found child—and I felt the pain of it so bitterly that when I returned to Calcutta I went to see his wife and son . . .

It was all Neel could do, now, to keep his eyes fixed on his biryani. Somehow he managed to keep his head lowered and his jaw working.

. . . the news of his death had already reached them, but you will be amazed to hear, Anil-babu, that the Rani, a woman deeply observant of Hindu custom, was not wearing widow's whites. Nor had she broken her bangles or removed the vermilion from the parting of her hair. I discovered then that even though her husband has been declared dead she was certain, in her heart, that he was alive. And I confess to you that she was persuasive enough to convince me too. She asked me to keep my eyes open for him on my travels. I told her that even if he was alive it was unlikely that I would recognize him. He was sure to have changed his name and his appearance; what was more, he would be extremely wary of revealing himself to me, knowing that I work for Mr Burnham, who is the cause of his dispossession and banishment. But she would not listen. She said: if ever, by some miracle, it should happen that your paths do cross, then you must tell him that you would never betray him, for he is still like a son to you, just as he is still my husband . . .

Stop! Neel looked around to make sure there was no one nearby. Then leaning forward, he said in a whisper: Is it true

Baboo Nob Kissin? Did you really see them? Malati, my wife, and my son Raj Rattan? Don't lie to me.

Yes. I saw them.

How is she, my wife?

She has managed better than you would think. She teaches your boy his letters and some of the local children too. Neither your wife nor your son doubt for a moment that you will return.

Tears came into Neel's eyes now, and he lowered his head to blink them away unseen. He remembered Malati's face as he had seen it the first time, on the night of their wedding, when he was fourteen and she a year younger. He remembered how she had hidden behind her veils, even when they were in bed; he remembered how she had turned her face away from him when he tugged at the coverings. He remembered also the day she came to see him in jail, in Calcutta: her ever-present veils were gone and it was as if he were seeing her for the first time. Not till then did he realize that the girl he had married had grown into a woman of uncommon beauty.

That Malati had managed to make the best of her circumstances did not surprise him; what amazed him was her refusal to accept the news of his death. How could she have known? Her certainty suggested a depth of feeling that left him beggared for words.

And my son, Raj Rattan?

He has grown, his mother says, even though it is less than a year since you left. He is a bold, sturdy fellow—she says he often threatens to run away to sea, in search of you.

Neel remembered the day when the police came to arrest him, at the Raskhali Palace in Calcutta. He had been flying kites with Raj Rattan, on the roof, and when he was called away, he had said to the boy: I'll be back in ten minutes . . .

I must take him some kites from China, he mumbled. They have beautiful kites here.

His mother says he makes his own now, from odd scraps of paper. She says he remembers you when he flies them.

For a while Neel could not trust himself to speak: the constriction in his throat was caused not merely by the reminders of his wife and son, but also by his remorse for his initial response to Baboo Nob Kissin. But for this strange man, so shrewd in some ways, and yet possessed of such inexplicable conceptions and attachments, he would not be here now, he would not have escaped from the *Ibis*. The Baboo was, in fact, almost a protective deity, a guardian spirit, and his presence in Canton was nothing to be feared: it was a gift.

I am happy to see you, Baboo Nob Kissin, said Neel, and you must excuse me for not revealing myself to you immediately. If I sought to deceive you, it was only because of Mr Burnham. If he finds out I am here, it will be all over for me.

There is no reason why he should find out, said Baboo Nob Kissin. I am the only one who knows and you can be sure I will not tell him.

But what if he recognizes me?

Oh you should have no fear of that, said Baboo Nob Kissin with a laugh. Your appearance is so much changed even I did not recognize you in the beginning. As for Mr Burnham, he cannot tell one native from another—unless you give yourself away he will not recognize you.

You are sure?

Yes, quite sure.

Neel breathed a sigh of relief: *Achha to aro bolun*—tell me more, Baboo Nob Kissin, tell me about my wife, my son . . .

~

In the latter part of January, as the date of William Jardine's embarkation for England approached, a consensus emerged amongst Jardine's friends and followers that his departure could not be allowed to look like a defeat, or worse still, an admission of guilt (for it was no secret that the 'Iron-Headed Rat' was regarded as an arch-criminal by the Chinese authorities). As a result, the preparations for his farewell dinner took on a defiant exuberance: long before the date arrived it was evident to all that it would be the most magnificent event ever seen in Fanqui-town.

The dinner was to be held in Company Hall, the largest and grandest venue in the foreign enclave. The hall was in the 'Consulate' which was the name by which House No. 1, in the British Factory, was known to foreigners.

The Achha Hong was separated from the British Factory only by the width of Hog Lane, and the approaches to the Consulate were clearly visible from Bahram's daftar. Although Bahram was not an intimate of Jardine's, he was by no means immune to the excitement caused by the upcoming dinner: so noisy and visible were the preparations that they even helped him overcome his growing aversion to the view from his window. Looking out again now he spotted, on several occasions, long lines of coolies, winding their way through the Maidan with buckets of vegetables and sacks of grain. One afternoon, hearing a sudden outburst of grunting and squealing, he rushed to the window and saw a herd of pigs racing through: the animals disappeared into the British Hong and were never seen again. The next day he was privy to an even more extraordinary sight: a long line of ducks was waddling through the Maidan, bringing all foot traffic to a halt; before the last bird had stepped off the duck-boat, at Jackass Point, the first had already reached the Consulate.

The very appearance of the British Hong began to change. Attached to Company Hall was an enormous, colonnaded veranda that extended over the entrance, overlooking 'Respondentia Walk'—the fenced-in garden in front of the factory. For the purposes of the dinner the veranda was to be turned into a temporary 'withdrawing-room': a team of decorators went to work, covering its sides with huge sheets of white canvas. After nightfall, with dozens of lamps glowing inside, the veranda became a gigantic lantern, glowing in the dark.

The spectacle was striking enough to draw sightseers from all over the city: Chinese New Year was not far away now and the illuminated Consulate became one more attraction for the growing number of pleasure-boats on the Pearl River.

In the meanwhile Bahram too had begun to make his own preparations for Jardine's farewell. As the doyen of Canton's

Achhas he deemed it his duty to ensure that the community did not go unnoticed at the event—if for no other reason than merely to remind the world that the commodity that had made Jardine rich, opium, came from India and was supplied to him by his Bombay partners. He came up with the idea of buying a farewell present for Jardine, by common subscription of the whole Parsi community. In a few days he succeeded in raising the equivalent of a thousand guineas: it was agreed that the money would be remitted directly to a famous silversmith, in England, with orders to prepare a dinner service, complete with Jardine's monogrammed initials. The gift would be publicly announced at the dinner, and the accompanying speech, Bahram decided, would be given by the most fluent English-speaker in the Bombay contingent—Dinyar Ferdoonjee.

By the evening of the dinner, expectations had been roused to such a pitch that it seemed impossible for the event to live up to its promise. But on entering the Consulate Bahram could find no cause for disappointment: the grand stairway was decorated with silk hangings and soaring floral arrangements; upstairs, in the improvised 'withdrawing-room', Jardine's initials glowed brightly upon the canvas hangings; in the hall, the Doric columns were garlanded with colourful blooms; the chandeliers overhead were ablaze with clusters of the finest spermaceti candles and the gilded mirrors on the walls made the room look twice as large. There was even a band: the *Inglis*, a merchant vessel anchored at Whampoa, had contributed a troupe of musicians: in celebration of Jardine's Scottish origins, the diners were regaled with a succession of Highland airs as they filed in to take their places.

Bahram had, from the first, taken charge of the Parsi contingent and he was gratified by the impression made by their white turbans, gold-embossed jootis and brocaded chogas. But so far as seating was concerned, he had decided that it would not be appropriate for a tai-pan like himself to be at an ordinary table, with the rest of the Bombay group. He had arranged to be seated with the Committee, at the head of the room.

On arriving at his table he found he had been placed between Lancelot Dent and a newcomer, a tall, stately looking man with a glossy beard that covered half his chest. He looked familiar but Bahram could not immediately remember his name.

Dent came to his rescue: 'May I introduce Benjamin Burnham, of Calcutta? Perhaps you've met before?'

Bahram had only a nodding acquaintance with Mr Burnham, but knowing him to be an ally of Dent's he shook his hand with cordial enthusiasm. 'You have come to Canton recently, Mr Burnham?'

'A few days ago,' said Mr Burnham. 'Had no end of trouble getting chops. Had to wait a while in Macau.'

Mr Slade was seated to Burnham's right, and he broke in now with a satirical smile. 'But your time in Macau was not ill-spent, was it, Burnham? After all, you did make the acquaintance of the exalted Captain Elliott.'

On hearing the British Representative's name, Bahram threw a quick glance around the room. 'Is Captain Elliott here with us tonight?'

'Certainly not,' said Slade. 'He has not been invited. And even if he had been, I doubt very much that he would have deigned to break bread with us. It seems that he regards us as little better than outlaws—why, he has actually had the temerity to write to Lord Palmerston describing us as such.'

'Really? But how did that come to your ears John?'

'Through Mr Burnham,' said Slade with a wink. 'By a stroke of singular genius, he has secured copies of some of Captain Elliott's recent dispatches to London!'

Mr Burnham promptly disclaimed the credit for this coup. 'It was my gomusta's doing. He's a pucka rascal but not without his uses. He is a Bengali, as is one of the copyists in Elliott's daftar—I need say no more.'

'And what does Captain Elliott say in his letter?'

'Hah!' Slade pulled a piece of paper out of his pocket. 'Where should I begin? Well, here's a fine little sample. "It is clear to me, my Lord, that the opium traffic will grow to be more and more mischievous to every branch of the trade. As the danger and shame of its pursuit increases, it will fall by rapid degrees into the hands of more and more desperate men and will stain the foreign character with constantly aggravating disgrace. Till the other day, my Lord, I believe there was no part of the world where the foreigner felt his life and property more secure than in Canton; but the grave events of 12th December have left behind a different impression. For a space of near two hours the foreign factories were within the power of an immense and excited mob, the gate of one of them was absolutely battered in and a pistol was fired, probably over the heads of the people for it is certain that nobody fell. If the case had been otherwise, Her Majesty's government and the British public would have had to learn that the trade with this empire was indefinitely interrupted by a terrible scene of bloodshed and ruin. And all these desperate hazards have been incurred, my Lord, for the gains of a few reckless individuals, unquestionably founding their conduct upon the belief that they are exempt from the operation of all law, British and Chinese."'

Slade's face had turned red as he was reading and an exclamation of disgust now burst from his lips. 'Pah! This from a man who is supposed to be our own Representative! A man whose salary we pay! Why, he is nothing but a Judas—he will bring ruin upon us.'

'John, you are too ready to take alarm,' said Dent calmly. 'Elliott is nothing but a functionary, a catspaw. The question is only whose purpose he will serve, ours or the mandarins'.'

A roll of drums now announced the arrival of the first course, a rich turtle soup. As it was being served the band struck up a lively tune, and under cover of the music Bahram turned to his neighbour: 'I believe, Mr Burnham, the market has fallen very low in Calcutta. Were you able to make any significant purchases?'

'So I was,' said Mr Burnham with a smile. 'Yes—my present cargo is the largest I have ever shipped.'

Bahram's eyes widened. 'You are not concerned then about these recent attempts to impose a ban on the trade?'

'Not at all,' said Mr Burnham confidently. 'Indeed I have sent my ship, the *Ibis*, to Singapore to buy more. I am quite confident that the attempts to ban opium will wither in the face of growing demand. It is not within the mandarins' power to withstand the elemental forces of Free Trade.'

'You do not think the loss of Mr Jardine's steady hand will affect us adversely, here in Canton?'

'On the contrary,' said Mr Burnham. 'I think it is the best thing that could have happened. God willing, with our support Mr Dent will step into the breach. And Mr Jardine's presence in London will be a great asset for us. Being a man of extraordinary tact and address, he is sure to gain Lord Palmerston's ear. And he will be able to exert influence on the government in other ways as well. Jardine knows how to spend his money, you know, and has many friends in Parliament.'

Bahram nodded. 'Democracy is a wonderful thing, Mr Burnham,' he said wistfully. 'It is a marvellous tamasha that keeps the common people busy so that men like ourselves can take care of all matters of importance. I hope one day India will also be able to enjoy these advantages—and China too, of course.'

'Let us raise a glass to that!'

'Hear, hear!'

This was the most encouraging conversation Bahram had had in a long time and it greatly increased his enjoyment of the evening. The morbid humours that had beset him of late seemed to evaporate, leaving him free to lavish his attention on the meal—and the food was, without a doubt, the finest that had ever been served in the British Hong, with one excellent course following after another. By the end of it Bahram had done so much justice to the food and wine that it came as a relief when Mr Lindsay rang a bell and raised his glass.

The first toast was to the Queen and the next to the President of the United States.

'As a father glories in and rejoices over the strength, talents and enterprise of its children,' said Mr Lindsay, holding his glass aloft, 'so does Great Britain glory and rejoice in the healthy and growing vigour of her Western progeny!'

There followed a number of tributes to the departing Jardine; at intervals, in keeping with the festive mood, there were rollicking songs—'Money in Both Pockets', for example, and 'May We Ne'er Want a Friend or a Bottle to Give Him'. Then the band struck up 'Auld Lang Syne' and when the last notes had died away Jardine rose to speak.

'I rise,' said Jardine, 'to return my sincere thanks for the manner in which my health has been proposed. I shall carry away with me and remember while I have life your kindness this evening.'

Here, overcome by emotion, he paused to clear his throat.

'I have been a long time in this country and I have a few words to say in its favour; here we find our persons more efficiently protected by laws than in many other parts of the East or of the world; in China a foreigner can go to sleep with his windows open, without being in dread of either his life or property, which are well guarded by a most watchful and excellent police; business is conducted with unexampled facility and in general with singular good faith. Neither would I omit the general courtesy of the Chinese in all their intercourse and transactions with foreigners. These and some other considerations . . .'

At this point, it became clear that Jardine was deeply affected: his eyes strayed in the direction of his closest friends and his voice broke. Not a sound was heard in the hall, as Jardine struggled to regain his composure. After dabbing his face with a handkerchief he began again: 'These are the reasons that so many of us so oft revisit this country and stay in it for so long. I hold, gentlemen, the society of Canton high, yet I also know that this community has often heretofore and lately been accused of being a set of smugglers; this I distinctly deny. We are not smugglers, gentlemen! It is the Chinese government, it is the Chinese officers who smuggle and who connive at and encourage smuggling, not we; and then look at the East India Company: why, the father of all smuggling and smugglers is the East India Company!'

A storm of applause now swept through the hall, drowning out the rest of Jardine's speech. The noise continued even after he had sat down, and it took much bell-ringing and gong-banging to restore order. Then it was Dinyar Ferdoonjee's turn to speak, and as soon as he began Bahram knew that he had been right to entrust him with the speech: his announcement of the farewell gift was couched in rounded sentences, and perfectly delivered. The end was particularly impressive: 'Much has been said about the East India Company having showed us Parsis the way to China; this is undoubtedly true, but it was a mere circumstance of the time, of the age; for does anyone pretend to say that if the Company had never existed the spirit of Free Trade would not have found its way hither? No! We should most certainly have found our way to China long ago; and being now here, against much opposition, we want no extraneous aid to support us; for the spirit of Free Trade is self-dependent and all-sufficient for her own wide-extended, extending and flourishing existence!'

A great cheer went up, and one young man was so carried away by the passions of the moment that he jumped on a bench and proposed a toast to 'Free Trade, Universal Free Trade, the extinction of all monopolies, and especially the most odious one, the Hong monopoly!'

This was received with tumultuous acclaim, and nowhere more so than in the corner of the hall where Dent and his friends were seated. 'To Free Trade, gentlemen!' said Dent, raising his glass. 'It is the cleansing stream that will sweep away all tyrants, great and small!'

The ceremonies now being concluded, the stewards rushed in to clear a space for dancing. The band struck up a waltz and the crowd parted to allow Mr Jardine and Mr Wetmore to walk through the hall, arm-in-arm. On no one was it lost that these two old friends, who had grown grey in each other's company, might be dancing together for the last time. When they took their first turns on the floor there was scarcely a dry eye in the room.

Even Mr Slade was moved to shed a tear. 'Oh poor Jardine,' he cried. 'He does not yet understand how much he will miss our little Bulgaria.'

Seldom had Bahram been in such a mood for dancing, so he had already bespoken Dent's hand for the waltz. But what should have been the perfect conclusion to the evening, turned instead into a cause for confusion and embarrassment. Just as Bahram was about to seize Dent by the waist, an altercation broke out in a corner of the hall. Bahram turned around to discover that the Bombay contingent was embroiled in some kind of quarrel. Hurrying over, he saw that some of them were about to come to blows with a half-dozen young Englishmen. Fortunately Dinyar was not among the disputants. Between the two of them they were able to restore order. But seeing that feelings were still running high, Bahram decided it would be best to lead his contingent out of the hall.

Only when they were outside did Bahram stop to ask: What happened? What was going on in there?

Seth, those haramzadas were calling us all kinds of names. They said this was no place for monkeys and we should leave.

They were drunk, na? Why didn't you just ignore them?

How to ignore them, Seth? We gave all that money for the dinner and then they call us monkeys and niggers?

fourteen

February 20, 1839, Markwick's Hotel

My dear Maharanee of Pugglenagore—your servant Robin is proud to announce a Discovery! A most *astonishing* discovery—or perhaps it is only a conjecture, I cannot tell, and it does not matter, for along with it I also have some news—at last!—of your pictures. But I must start at the beginning . . .

The first part of this month flew by because of the Chinese New Year—for a fortnight nothing was done: the city was *convulsed* with celebrations and the lanes rang to the cry of 'Gong hei fa-tsai!' Scarcely had the festivities ceased when who should appear but Ah-med! You will remember him as the emissary who took me to Fa-Tee to meet Mr Chan (or Lynchong or Ah Fey or whatever you wish to call him). It had been so long since I last heard from Mr Chan that I had almost given up hope of seeing him again. That is why I was quite *inordinately* pleased to see Ah-med. I will not conceal from you, Puggly dear, that all my hopes in regard to the task Mr Penrose has entrusted to me are invested in Mr Chan—other than him I have not met a *soul* who has anything enlightening to offer on the subject of this mysterious golden camellia; no one has seen it, no one has heard of it; no one understands why anyone should think it worth a *smidgeon* of their attention. Indeed, so fruitless have my inquiries been that I had begun to wonder whether I ought not to consider returning the money Mr Penrose so generously advanced to me (but it really would not *suit*, dear, for it is already spent—a few weeks ago Mr Wong, the tailor, showed me an *exquisite* cloud-collar, trimmed with fur, and no sooner had I set eyes on it than I knew it would be a *perfect* New Year gift for Jacqua—and I was right. He loved it and thanked me so fulsomely, and in such interesting ways, that I could not imagine asking for its return . . .).

So there was Ah-med and there was I, and after we had gone through all the usual motions of chin-chinning, he told me that Mr Chan had returned to Canton for a few days and wanted to know if I had yet received any pictures from Mr Penrose. I said yes, they had been sent to me several weeks ago and I had been waiting impatiently all this while and would be glad to show them to Mr Chan at his earliest convenience. At this, Ah-med's smile grew broader still and he informed me that his employer was nearby and would be happy to meet with me at once.

'Can do, can do!' I replied. It took but a moment to fetch the pictures from my room and then off we went.

I had imagined that Ah-med would lead me to one of the many teashops and eateries that commonly serve as meeting-places in Canton—on Thirteen Hong Street perhaps, or somewhere in the vicinity of the city walls. But this was not to be: Ah-med turned instead in the direction of the river. I wondered perhaps whether we were once again to take a boat, but no—it turned out that we were to go to Shamian!

I think I have mentioned Shamian before—it is a tidal island, a mudbank that shows itself when the river runs low. It lies at one end of Fanqui-town, not far from the Danish Hong, and although it is only a sandbank it does enjoy a certain kind of renown in the city; this is by virtue of its being the favoured mooring-spot for some of Canton's brightest and most colourful 'flower-boats'. It was on one of these, evidently, that I was to meet with Mr Chan—and that too in the middle of the morning!

Flower-boats are among the largest—and certainly the gaudiest—vessels on the Pearl River. Were you to see them in some other place you would think them to be figments of your imagination, so fantastical is their appearance; they have pavilions and halls and terraces, covered and open; they are festooned with hundreds of lanterns and ornamented with decorations made of silk. At the entrance of each vessel is a tall gateway, brightly painted in red and gold and decorated with a bestiary of fabulous beings: writhing dragons, grinning demons and toothed gryphons. The purpose of these fearsome gargoyles is to announce to all who approach that beyond lies a world that is utterly unlike the dull reality of everyday experience—and at night, when the river is dark and the boats are illuminated by lights and lanterns, these boats do indeed seem to become floating realms of enchantment. But as I said, this was around mid-morning, and in the bright light of day they looked, I must admit, rather tired and melancholy, more tawdry than gaudy, humbled by the sun and ready to accept defeat in their unwinnable war against mundanity.

When the river is at its height, Shamian can only be reached by boat, but when the tide runs low a brick causeway emerges magically from the water: we crossed over on foot and Ah-med led me to one of the largest boats. The tall, gilded portals were firmly shut and the only person on deck was an elderly woman, busy with some washing. A shout from Ah-med brought her to her feet and a moment later the doors creaked open. I stepped inside, to find myself in a saloon that had the cluttered and disarranged air of a fairground after a long night. The floor was covered with rugs and laden with intricately carved wooden furniture; on the walls were scrolls with calligraphic characters and dream-like landscapes; the windows were shuttered and the room was fogged with the smell of smoke—of tobacco, incense and opium.

With hardly a pause, Ah-med led me through this saloon into the vessel's interior. Ahead lay a corridor with cabins on either side—but the doors were all closed and there was not a sound to be heard except the odd snore. Then we came to a dark stairway: here Ah-med came to a halt and gestured to me to go on up.

I was now in a state of no little trepidation, and I made my way up in a gingerly fashion, not knowing what to expect. I emerged on to a sunlit terrace to find Mr Chan reclining on a cushioned couch. He was dressed, as before, in Chinese costume, a grey gown and black cap, but it was not in the Celestial fashion that he greeted me but in a manner eminently English, with a handshake and a 'Holloa there!' There was a chair beside the couch: he signalled me to it and poured me a cup of tea. He was sorry, he said, about the great length of time that had elapsed between our last meeting and this one, but his circumstances had been such, of late, that he had been forced to travel a great deal &c. &c.

Mr Chan is not a man who gives the impression of being enamoured of small talk; at the first pause I handed over Ellen Penrose's illustrations of her father's collection. To my surprise, he did not even open the folder; laying it aside he said he would examine the pictures later; for the time being there was another matter he wished to discuss with me.

By all means, said I, at which he proceeded to explain that it had come to his ears that I was closely related to Mr George Chinnery, the famous English painter, and that I was myself an artist in the same style.

Yes, I said, this was all true. So then he asked whether I happened, by any chance, to be acquainted with a certain painting of Mr Chinnery's—a canvas that was generally known as 'The Portrait of an Eurasian'?

'Why yes,' I said, 'I certainly do!'—and this was no more than the truth for it is a fact that I know this picture very well indeed. Of the work Mr Chinnery has done in China, I like none better—and as you know, Puggly dear, it has long been a habit of mine to make copies of pictures that make an impression on me. Fortunately I had not neglected to do so in this instance: the copy is small, but, even if I say so myself, perfectly faithful to the original. I have it in front of me as I write: it depicts a young woman dressed in a cloak-like tunic of blue silk, and wide, white trousers. The garments are sumptuous, yet negligently worn; the face has the delicate contours of a heart-shaped leaf and the eyes are black and startlingly large, with a gaze that is at once gentle and direct. A pink chrysanthemum peeps out of her glistening black hair, which is parted in the middle and pulled back so that it falls over her temples in graceful, rounded curves. Behind her, serving as a frame within a frame, is a circular window; it outlines her head and provides a view of a pair of misted mountains in the distance. Every detail is chosen to evoke a Chinese interior—the shape of the sitter's chair, the tasselled lantern above her head, the high-legged teapoy and porcelain teapot. The face too, in the tint of the skin, and the angle of the cheekbones, is of a clearly Chinese cast—yet there is something about the woman's smile, her stance, her pose that suggests that she is also, in some way, foreign, an alien at least in part.

The painting is, to my mind, one of Mr Chinnery's finest, but I am not, as you know, Puggly dear, always the most impartial of judges. It may well be that my passion for this picture springs from a sense of sympathy with the subject—Adelina was her name—not only because she is of variegated parentage, but also because of what I know of the circumstances of her life and her death (and when you hear the story, as you presently shall, I think you too will agree that it is indeed impossible not to be *moved* . . .).

You will understand from this that my acquaintance with this painting is not of any ordinary measure (it took no little time and effort, I can tell you, to ferret the story out of Mr Chinnery's apprentices)—but fortunately I had the presence of mind not to betray to Mr Chan, the extent of my familiarity with it.

'I do know that painting,' said I. 'Why do you ask?'

'What do you think, Mr Chinnery, could you make a copy of it for me? I will pay handsomely.'

This put me in something of a quandary, for I know that my Uncle would be *incensed* if he found out—but on the other hand Mr Chan is such an elusive character that I cannot see how he *could* find out; and nor are my material circumstances such that I can afford to refuse commissions. I said yes, I would gladly do it.

'Very well then, Mr Chinnery,' said Mr Chan. 'I am leaving Canton tomorrow and will be away for four weeks. I would be most grateful if you could have the copy ready for me when I return. I will pay you a hundred silver dollars.'

This quite took my breath away—for the sum is not much less than my Uncle himself might expect for a painting—but you will be glad to know that I was not so nonplussed as to be unmindful of the matter that had brought me there. 'And what of Mr Penrose's pictures, sir?' said I. 'And the golden camellia?'

'Oh yes,' said he, in the most casual way. 'I will look at the pictures while I am away. We will talk about it again when I see you next, in four weeks.'

And that, my dear Puggly-devi, was the end of it.

I went straight back to my room and stretched a canvas upon a frame. But on making a start, I realized that the task would not be as easy as I had thought. Conjuring up that exquisite face was like raising a ghost from the dead: I began to feel haunted by her presence. For it was here that Adelina died, you know, in Canton, in the very river I can see from my window—almost within sight of the studio founded by her grandfather (it still stands, on Old China Street). This is the other thing I share with Adelina—she too was born of a line of artists. Her grandfather was indeed one of the greatest figures of the Canton School—his name was Chitqua and he was, in all things, a pioneer. While still in his thirties—in 1770 I think it was—he travelled to

London, where an exhibition of his work was mounted at the Royal Academy. It created a great sensation and he was feted everywhere he went: Zoffany painted him and he was invited to dine with the King and Queen. Not since Van Dyck had a foreign painter been accorded such a reception in London—and yet, despite his great success, Chitqua's life came to an inglorious end. On his return to Canton he fell in love with a young woman of humble origin—a boat-woman some say, while others allege her to have been a 'flower-girl'.

Chitqua was already the father of a substantial brood of children, begotten through many wives and concubines. Against the bitter opposition of his kin, far and near, he insisted on taking his newly found beloved under his protection. She bore him a son, and on this boy, as on his mother, he lavished his love as he never had on anyone before. This engendered, as you may imagine, many jealousies and also many apprehensions in regard to the disposal of the family property. Whether or not these fears had anything to do with Chitqua's death is not known but suffice it to say that when he suddenly ceased to breathe, after a banquet, there were many who whispered that the painter had been poisoned. The outcome in any event was that his young mistress and her son were left destitute, alone in the world except for a single servant.

The son had received some instruction in painting from his father and had the circumstances of his birth been different he would, no doubt, have been absorbed into one of Canton's many studios. But the artists of the city are a tight-knit lot, closely connected by blood, and they would not accept the boy into their midst. The lad kept himself alive by doing odd-jobs in Fanqui-town, working as an illustrator for botanists and collectors. The story goes that it was thus that his talent came to the notice of a wealthy American—a merchant who took him to Macau and helped him set up a studio of his own. It was there too that the lad adopted the name by which he would come to be known—Alantsae.

As is often the case with offspring who are born, so to speak, on the wrong side of the blanket, Alantsae proved to be more fully his father's heir than any of Chitqua's other sons. He quickly became the most celebrated portraitist in Macau and was much sought after by foreigners—merchants, sea-captains, and of course, the city's Portuguese funcíonarios, many of whom commissioned portraits from him: of themselves, their children and—need it be said?—their wives. Not the least of these luminaries was a fidalgo of ancient lineage and advanced years—one of those chirruping cockchafers who flourish in the dusty cracks of old empires, using their connections to cling for ever to their posts. This fine cavalheiro had previously served a term in Goa, Portugal's Asiatic metropolis, and while living there had lost one wife and acquired another: his first spouse having been carried away by malaria, he had married a girl of sixteen, some fifty years his junior. The bride belonged to a once-prominent mestiço family that had fallen on hard times: she was, by all accounts, a woman of exceptional loveliness, an otter-rose you might say, and her husband, overjoyed at having been able to pin such a prize upon his lapel, commissioned Alantsae to capture her likeness while she was still in the first freshness of her bloom.

I confess, Puggly dear, I am so fascinated by this tale, I sometimes feel I can see them with my own eyes: the lovely Indo-Portuguese Senhora and the handsome young Chinese painter; she in her mantillas and lace, he in his silken robe, dark-eyed and long-haired. Picture them if you will: the child-bride and the youthful painter, she the possession of a man too feeble to consummate his marriage and he, too virginal in his heart. Do you see how their eyes are drawn to each other, under the frowning gaze of the rosary-counting duennas who surround them? But to no avail alas! The Senhora is as pious as she is beautiful; no temptation can persuade her to stray, and the painter's passion, finding no release, is directed towards his easel. He caresses the canvas with his brush, strokes it, coaxes it, pours his pith upon it in hot, bright jets and lo! the seed is sown and life stirs within the likeness. It comes into the world like a love-child, a thing of such beauty that it deepens the attachment that was conceived during its making. And yet . . . and yet . . . there is nothing to be done—consummation is inconceivable. Society, ever censorious, has its eyes upon them. But heaven itself takes pity upon their love: the old cavalheiro is, as I have said, already in a state of advanced decrepitude and he does not long survive the completion of the painting (some say he is buried with it). After the old man's passing, the Senhora remains in Macau, purportedly to mourn by his grave, but the world soon discovers that a secret marriage has come about—the Senhora has wedded Alantsae!

You may imagine for yourself the scandal, the gossip, the vile innuendos—the couple are shunned by everyone they know: Chinese, European and Goan alike. The artist, once so much sought after, is now a pariah; his stream of commissions runs suddenly dry and he is forced to eke out a living by painting shop-signs and lurid murals. Yet the couple are not unhappy for they have each other after all, and their passion is rewarded, before long, with another precious gift: a daughter—Adelina. But little do they know, as they rejoice in their babe, that the end of their happiness is near: Alantsae has not much longer to live—grim death is creeping up on him, clothed in the garb of typhus.

After Alantsae's passing the Senhora struggles on, long enough to see her child into the threshold of adulthood—but then she too goes to an untimely grave, and the young Adelina is consigned to the Misericordia, where orphans and the children of the indigent are suffered to subsist, on public charity.

Well, Puggly dear, suffice it to say that Adelina—or Adelie as she was known—was not the kind of girl who could be expected to live for ever within the walls of a charitable institution. She escaped and became in time the most celebrated courtesan in Macau (this, they say, is how she came to Mr Chinnery's notice . . . and what else they say you can well imagine!).

As often happens with famous beauties, there were many men with whom it sat ill that they should have to share a woman like Adelina with others. A fierce struggle broke out amongst her lovers—many of them were rich and powerful, but victory went to a man who had an advantage that no one else could match. It appears that at some point in her past, Adelie had become a dedicated dragon-chaser, consuming copious amounts of opium—it was the man who kept her supplied who claimed her, a person whose position was such that he lived like a shadow, nameless and unseen, being known only as 'Elder Brother'. Once in his keeping, Adelie became, as you can imagine, a bird in a gilded cage, utterly alone and cut off from the world she had known before; so protective was her new master, so jealous of her fidelity, that he moved her away from Macau to an estate in Canton, where he would visit her when his affairs permitted. But such men, no matter how much they may desire it, are seldom free to lavish their time upon their mistresses: when he could not wait upon her himself, he would send her gifts of money and jewellery and opium with one of his most trusted lieutenants—this young man became her only other connection with the world beyond, her lifeline.

What this led to I need scarcely spell out: inevitably they were discovered; the young man disappeared without trace, and as for Adelina—well, they say that rather than live without her lover she threw herself in the river . . .

Having read this far, Puggly dear, you will perhaps be posing to yourself the same questions that occur to me: why does Mr Chan want this portrait? Who was Adelie to him? Who *is* he? In seeking answers you will no doubt arrive at the same conjectures (or discoveries?) that have suggested themselves to me—the conclusions are inevitable and disturbing, but you must not imagine that they will deter me, either from fulfilling my commission, or from discharging my duty to Mr Penrose: your poor Robin is not as timid a creature as you may think . . .

In four weeks, my dear, dear Countess of Pugglenburg, you shall have my next letter—until then!

~

As the month of February advanced, reports began to trickle in about the southward journey of the newly appointed High Commissioner and Imperial Plenipotentiary. These accounts reached the Committee mainly through the agency of the Chamber's translator Samuel Fearon.

Mr Fearon was a blond, willowy young man: his bulletins were much sought after by some members of the Committee and his entry into the Club would often cause ripples of excitement. Mr Slade was particularly avid in his courtship of the young translator and one day, seeing him go by, he hooked the crook of his cane in his elbow and all but dragged him to his table. 'Well my boy—do you have anything new for us today?'

'Why yes, Mr Slade.'

'Well then, come and sit beside me—I would like to hear it from your own lips. Mr Burnham will yield his chair. Will you not, Benjamin?'

'Yes, of course.'

So Mr Fearon came to sit at Mr Slade's table, where Mr Dent and Bahram were also seated. He then disclosed something that astonished everyone present—apparently the approaching Commissioner was paying his travel expenses out of his own pocket! What was more, he was going to considerable lengths to ensure that no unnecessary costs were charged to the state exchequer.

This was received with exclamations of disbelief: the idea that a mandarin might refuse to enrich himself at the public expense seemed preposterous to everyone at the table. Many heads—Bahram's included—nodded in agreement when

Mr Burnham expressed the opinion that the Commissioner was merely posturing in order to dupe the gullible. 'Mark my words: the squeeze, when it comes, will be all the tighter because it is more subtly applied.'

This strange piece of intelligence was still being digested when Mr Fearon brought in another startling report.

This time, much to Mr Slade's chagrin, he was unsuccessful in claiming the translator for his table: he was pre-empted by Mr Wetmore. 'Ah Fearon!' cried the soon-to-be installed President. 'Have you got anything interesting for us today?'

'Yes, sir. I do.'

Immediately the other tables emptied and everyone gathered around the translator. 'Well what is it, Fearon? What have you learnt?'

'I am told, sir, that the High Commissioner's arrival has been delayed.'

'Is that so?' said Mr Slade acidly. 'Well, perhaps he is suffering from the after-effects of an overly riotous celebration of the New Year?'

'Oh no, sir,' said Mr Fearon. 'I believe he has been holding meetings with scholars and academicians, especially those who have some knowledge of realms overseas.'

This too was received with cries of amazement: the notion that there actually existed a group of Chinese scholars who took an interest in the outside world was unbelievable to many members of the Committee. Most in any case were inclined to agree with Mr Slade, who gave a great guffaw and said: 'Pon my sivvy! You may depend on it, gentlemen—it will be the rhubarb business all over again.'

This served to remind everyone that the mandarins' previous attempts to inform themselves about the ways of the red-headed barbarians had almost always led to absurd conclusions—as, for example, in the matter of rhubarb. This vegetable was only a minor item of export from Canton, but somehow the local officials had come to be convinced that it was an essential element of the European diet, and that fanquis would perish of constipation if denied it. More than once, in moments of confrontation, had they embargoed the export of rhubarb. The fact that not a single fanqui had swelled up with unexpurgated matter or burst his bowels, had not, apparently, given them any reason to doubt their theory.

To seal the matter, Mr Slade proceeded to recite a passage from an Imperial memorandum—one that could always be trusted to raise a laugh in the Club: 'Inquiries have served to show that the foreigners, if deprived for several days of the tea and rhubarb of China, are afflicted with dimness of sight and constipation of the bowels, to such a degree that life is endangered . . .'

When the laughter had died down, Mr Burnham wiped his eyes and declared: 'There is no denying it. Lord Napier had the measure of it when he said the Chinese are a race remarkable for their imbecility.'

At this Mr King, who had been stirring uneasily in his seat for a while, was moved to protest: 'Why sir, I do not believe that Lord Napier could possibly have expressed so uncharitable a sentiment: he was after all a pious Christian.'

'Let me remind you, Charles,' said Mr Burnham, 'that Lord Napier was also a scientist, and when his faculties of reason led him to an irrefutable conclusion, he was not the man to dissimulate.'

'Exactly, sir,' said Mr King. 'Lord Napier was not only a good Christian, but also one of the most distinguished sons of the Scottish Enlightenment. I cannot believe he would express such a sentiment.'

'Very well then,' said Mr Burnham. 'Let us have a wager.'

The Club's betting-book was immediately sent for and a sum of ten guineas was entered into its columns. Then Lord Napier's book on his experiences in China was fetched from the library and the passage was quickly found: 'It has pleased Providence to assign to the Chinese—a people characterized by a marvellous degree of imbecility, avarice, conceit, and obstinacy—the possession of a vast portion of the most desirable parts of the earth and a population estimated as amounting to nearly a third of the whole human race.'

Since the wording was not exactly as stipulated, it fell to the President to settle the wager. He adjudicated in favour of Mr Burnham, who then proceeded to earn himself much credit by donating his winnings to Reverend Parker's hospital.

Even though the evening ended on a light-hearted note, the rumours surrounding the Commissioner's arrival had the cumulative effect of disrupting the normal functioning of the Chamber and creating an atmosphere of expectation and anxiety. It was against this background that Mr Wetmore hosted a small dinner to thank the outgoing President, Mr Hugh Lindsay, for his services.

The rubicund and high-spirited Mr Lindsay was observed to be uncharacteristically pensive through the meal, and when he rose to make his farewell address it became clear that he was in an unquiet frame of mind. At the end of the meal, after the vote of thanks had been proposed, he rose to offer a few thoughts: 'That the trade in opium has hitherto held out great and profitable inducement, sufficient to warrant almost any risk, must be admitted. But it must be borne in mind also that the trade has hitherto been allowed, or connived at, by the Chinese authorities. It may be doubted however whether this is likely to be the case for the future. What then is the alternative? Either the trade must be given up altogether, or some mode adopted for carrying it on independent of Chinese interference. Let us be honest: the first of these propositions—of giving up the opium trade—will not be adopted while any other possibility remains open. So there is only one plain and obvious alternative. It is *the formation of a settlement under British rule on the coast of China*.'

Like many others in the room, Bahram greeted this with polite applause—but in fact there was nothing new about Mr Lindsay's proposal: similar suggestions had been heard many times before. The advantages of an offshore trading base were obvious: it would allow foreign merchants to send opium and other goods to China without any fear of the Chinese authorities. They would also be spared the risks and opprobrium of transporting their goods to the mainland—that part of it would be taken care of by local smugglers. Western respectability would thus be preserved and the burden of blame would fall clearly on the Chinese.

The one thing against the idea was that everyone seemed to have a different view as to where the new colony should be. Bahram had heard many strange proposals to this effect—but none so startling as the one Mr Lindsay now came up with.

'I need scarcely tell you,' intoned Mr Lindsay, 'that many unappropriated spots exist that are admirably suited to the purpose—but none, to my mind, is the equal of an archipelago that has but recently been seized by the British government: the Bonin Islands, which stretch between Japan and Formosa.'

Bahram had never heard of the Bonin Islands and was astonished to learn that they had been seized by the British government. He could not imagine that they would serve any useful purpose and was glad when Mr Slade offered a counter-proposal: 'Surely some better place might be found nearer to China—Formosa, for instance?'

Even as the room was pondering this, it became clear that Mr Slade had posed the question only for rhetorical effect. 'But no, sir!' he thundered suddenly, signalling a change of tack. 'After two centuries of commerce, it is impossible that we should abandon our factories and retreat from Canton. It is here that we must make our stand; we must show the Chinese that if they attempt to curtail foreign trade they will find their boasted power shaken to pieces. Is it not time to ask what may be the consequences to this empire of the ignorance and obstinacy of its rulers? Ignorance of everything beyond China, obstinate adherence to their own dogmas of government? The answers are clear: we must remain here, if for no other reason than only to protect the Chinese from themselves. I do not doubt that it will soon become necessary for the British government to intervene here as it has elsewhere, merely in order to quell civil commotion.'

A storm of applause broke out and everyone congratulated Mr Slade on once again having brought a difficult matter to a satisfactory conclusion.

~

At the end of February the weather began to warm up and by the first week of March the days had become swelteringly hot. A new kind of vendor now made an appearance in the Maidan, disbursing ice-cold syrups and frozen sweetmeats from an earthenware vessel that was insulated with hay and strips of cloth.

Towards sunset Neel would often step out into the Maidan to cool off with some chilled syrup. He was on his way there one evening when he collided with Compton, who was even more short-sighted than usual, being in such a hurry that he had neglected to clean his sweat-fogged glasses. 'Ah Neel! *Dím aa*?'

'Hou leng. And where are you going to so fitee-fitee Compton?'

'Jackass Point-mé. To rent sampan.'

'Sampan? Why?'

'Don't you know a-ma? Yum-chae coming Guangzhou tomorrow.'

'Who?'

'High Commissioner Lin. All Guangzhou people are renting boats to watch. You want come too maah? Can come with us. Be Jackass Point tomorrow, first part of dragon-hour.'

'Seven?'

'Yes; come there. Dak mh dak aa?'

'I don't know: I may have to work.'

Compton laughed. 'Oh don't worry-wo. No one work tomorrow; not even tai-pan.'

Somewhat to Neel's surprise Compton's prognosis was proved correct: later that evening Vico announced that the entire staff was being given the morning off. The Seth would not be breakfasting in his daftar as usual; he had been invited to observe the Commissioner's entry into the city from the veranda of the Consulate.

The next day it became clear very early that the city was in a mood of high expectation: drums and fireworks were heard in the distance, and at the morning hazri, in the mess, Mesto reported that the markets were deserted and not a shop was open on Thirteen Hong Street. Everyone, even the vendors and vagabonds, had rushed off to catch a glimpse of the Yum-chae.

By the time Neel stepped out on the Maidan, the verandas of the British and the Dutch Hongs were already abuzz with spectators. On reaching Jackass Point, he found it choked with people—it took him a good half-hour to locate Compton, who was herding a band of children along the ghat and into a waiting sampan.

Three of the boys were his sons, said Compton, and the rest were their friends. They had all evidently been warned against any wi-wi-woy-woy for they were on their best behaviour with Ah Neel: not one of them was heard to mutter the words 'Achha' or 'Mo-ro-chaa' or 'Haak-gwai'. They kept their eyes shyly lowered as they said their chin-chins, scarcely glancing at Neel's turban or angarkha. When the sampan began to move they were even heard to admonish children in other boats nearby, reproving them for staring or making rude comments.

. . . jouh me aa . . . ?

. . . mh gwaan neih sih!

Progress along the river was very slow because it was choked with boats; they inched along, gunwale to gunwale.

Neel was astonished by the size of the crowd. 'Why, it's like a festival day! Does this always happen when a high official comes to the city?'

Compton laughed. 'No! Is usually not like this at all—people go to hide. But Lin Zexu different—not like others . . .'

Commissioner Lin's arrival had been preceded, Compton explained, by a steady flow of reports about his southward journey. These accounts had created an extraordinary ferment in the province. The stories being told were such as to make people wonder whether the Yum-chae might not be the last of a breed of men that had long been thought to be extinct: an incorruptible public servant who was also a scholar and an intellectual—a state official like those memorialized in legend and parable.

While other mandarins travelled with enormous entourages, at public expense, the Yum-chae was travelling with a very small retinue—a half-dozen armed guards, a cook, and a couple of servants—all paid out of his own purse. While the retainers of other officials freely extorted money from all who wanted access to their bosses, Commissioner Lin's men had been warned they would face arrest if they were found to be taking bribes. At inns and resthouses his orders were that he was only to be served common fare—expensive luxuries, like birds' nests and sharks' fins, were banned from his table. On the road, instead of fraternizing with other high officials the Yum-chae had sought out scholars and knowledgeable men, asking their advice on how to deal with the situation in the southern provinces.

'My teacher also called to meet Yum-chae,' said Compton proudly.

'And who is he?'

'His name Chang Nan-shan,' said Compton, 'but-gwo I call him "Chang Lou-si" because he is my teacher. Chang Lou-si know everything about Guangdong. He write many books. Yauh he will be adviser for Yum-chae.'

'Is he travelling with the Commissioner?'

'Hai-le!' said Compton. 'Maybe you will see him—on the boat.'

In the meanwhile, the crowd had begun to stir sensing the approach of the Yum-chae's boat. Soon a large official barge hove slowly into view: sheets of crimson fabric shimmered upon its hull and flecks of gold glinted brightly in the sunlight. The crewmen were dressed in neat white uniforms, with red trim, and conical rattan hats.

The barge was almost alongside before Neel spotted Commissioner Lin: he was seated in the vessel's prow, in the shade of an enormous umbrella. To his rear were a few red- and blue-button mandarins; they were flanked by rows of troops with horsehair plumes.

In relation to the soldiers in his retinue, the Yum-chae seemed tiny, and his costume looked drab in comparison with the drapes and pennants that were fluttering around him.

The boat was moving quite fast, with scores of oars dipping rhythmically in the water, but Neel was able to get a good look at the Commissioner's face. He had expected a frowning, stiffly dignified personage—but there was nothing stern or stone-faced about the Commissioner: he was looking from side to side with a lively and curious expression; his face was full, his forehead high and smooth; he had a black moustache and a wispy beard; in his eyes was a look of keen and active intelligence.

Then Compton tugged at his elbow. 'Ah Neel! Look there! There is Chang Lou-si.'

Neel saw that he was pointing to a stooped, elderly man with twinkling eyes and a thin, white beard. He was standing in the stern, watching the crowd. Somehow, in the midst of the multitudes, he caught sight of Compton and they exchanged bows.

'You know him well then?' said Neel.

'Yes,' said Compton. 'He come often to my shop, talk to me. He very interested in English books and all what is written in *Canton Register*. Ho-yih one day you can meet him.'

Neel glanced again at the Commissioner's barge: the stooped figure in the stern seemed to him the very image of a Chinese scholar. He said: 'I would like to meet him very, very much.'

~

For those who were observing the new Commissioner's entry into the city from the veranda of the Consulate, the most striking moment of the ceremony came just before he disappeared from view. At the gates of the citadel he stopped to confer with local officials. Then, as if in response to a question, some of these lesser mandarins raised their hands to point in the direction of the foreign enclave. At this point the Commissioner himself turned around—and to Bahram and those beside him, it seemed as if he were looking directly at them.

To have their gaze returned was disconcerting to many of the Committee. No one disagreed with Dent when he remarked:

'Let us make no mistake, gentlemen: that man has not come here with peaceful intentions.'

Afterwards, along with several members of the Committee, Bahram proceeded to the Club, for tiffin. The weather being clear and warm, the meal was served in the shaded veranda. The ale flowed freely and the fare was excellent but there was little conviviality at the table: instead the gathering quickly took on the character of a council of war. It was agreed that they would meet regularly to pool whatever intelligence they were able to collect; Mr Wetmore, as the incoming President, was assigned the task of creating a system of runners so that the Committee could be summoned to the Chamber at any hour of day or night. It was settled that in the event of a crisis the bell of the British Factory's chapel would be used as a tocsin, to sound the alarm.

After these rather ominous deliberations it came as something of a let-down when there was no immediate call, either for runners or for bell-ringing. The early snippets of news provided no cause for alarm: the Commissioner was reported to be occupied merely in conducting meetings and setting his household in order. The only unsettling item came from Mr Fearon: it seemed that the High Commissioner had elected not to reside in the part of the city where soldiers and high officials were quartered; instead he had installed his household in one of Canton's most venerable seats of education, the Yueh Lin Academy.

None of the Committee had heard of this institution, and even Mr Fearon had no idea where it was located: the geography of the walled city was indeed something of a mystery to fanquis, for maps of Canton were hard to come by. A few did exist, however, and the most detailed of them happened to be in the safekeeping of the President of the Chamber of Commerce: based upon a two-hundred-year-old Dutch prototype, the map was annotated and added to whenever new information became available. For reasons of security it was kept in the President's office, in a locked cupboard—at Mr Wetmore's invitation everyone trooped upstairs to take a look.

When rolled out, the map revealed Canton to be shaped like a bell or a dome. The top lay on a hill, to the north, with the apex being marked by the Sea-Calming Tower; the base ran along the river, in a more or less straight line. The citadel's walls were pierced by sixteen gateways and the area inside was so divided as to form a grid, with streets and avenues of varying width criss-crossing each other in a geometrical fashion.

The map showed the foreign enclave and the official quarter to be separated not only by the city walls but also by miles of densely packed habitations: Fanqui-town was but a tiny pendant, attached to the south-western corner of the citadel. The district where the mandarins and the Manchu bannermen lived was far away in the northern quadrant of the walled city. Canton's fanquis had always considered themselves fortunate in being well removed from local officialdom—and this was why the location of the High Commissioner's residence was perceived to be of some significance. When tracked upon the map it was seen to be uncomfortably close to the foreign factories.

'It is perfectly clear,' said Dent. 'He's steered his flagship to cross our bows. He's getting ready to deliver a broadside.'

At this Mr Slade puffed up his chest and delivered himself of one of his inspired bursts of eloquence. 'Well, sir,' said the Thunderer, 'our course too is clear now. The foreign community must remain perfectly quiet and passive; let the Chinese authorities act—let them commit themselves to the first step: this is the proceeding they always endeavour to force on their opponents; they know the great advantage it gives them: let us for once, endeavour to gain it.' Slade paused for effect before uttering his last sentence: 'We must be the willow, not the oak, in the lowering storm.'

There was an immediate chorus of assent: 'Quite right!' 'Well said, John!'

Bahram joined enthusiastically in the chorus: he had worried that the hotheads amongst the British might choose to take an overly aggressive stand; it came as a relief to hear one of the most aggressive among them expressing moderation.

'You have shot the bullseye John!' said Bahram. 'Definitely willow is better for now—why to go for oak already? Better to wait for storm.'

But still the predicted gale held off: the next few days brought instead confusing and apparently directionless crosswinds. There was a brief flurry of anxiety when it came to be known that the Commissioner had asked for several convicted opium-dealers to be produced before him—but the alarm subsided when it was learnt that he had actually commuted the offenders' sentences. This caused some speculation about whether the Commissioner's severity may have been somewhat overstated—but that too was confuted by the notice that followed. It was an announcement to the effect that the Yum-chae had left Canton in order to inspect the fortifications of the Pearl River.

The Committee breathed a collective sigh of relief and there followed several quiet days—but just as a sense of calm was beginning to return to Fanqui-town, the Commissioner returned. It was then that he made his opening move.

One morning, while Bahram was breakfasting, a runner came to the door of No. 1 Fungtai Hong. It was Vico who spoke with him and after listening to his message he went racing up to the daftar and entered without a knock.

Bahram was sitting at the breakfast table, sampling a plate of pakoras made from the newest spring vegetables. The munshi was reading from the latest issue of the *Register* but he stopped when Vico came in.

Patrão, a runner came just now: there is an emergency meeting at the Chamber.

Oh? A meeting of the Committee?

No, patrão; it's a meeting of the General Chamber. But only the Committee are being alerted.

Do you know what it's about?

The Co-Hong merchants have asked for it, patrão. They are already there; you must hurry.

Bahram drained his chai and rose from his chair: Get me my choga—a cotton one, but not too light.

The weather had been a little cool of late, and an unexpectedly chilly wind was blowing when Bahram stepped out into the Maidan. He was doing up the fastenings of his choga when he heard a shout—'Ah there you are, Barry!' He looked up to see Dent, Slade and Burnham heading towards the Chamber. He hurried over and fell in step.

The meeting was to be held in the Great Hall which was where the General Chamber usually assembled. They arrived there to find many rows of chairs facing a lectern. Seated in the front row, staring stonily ahead, were some half-dozen Co-Hong merchants, in formal regalia, with their buttons of rank fixed upon their hats; their linkisters and retainers were standing nearby, lined up against a wall.

The chairs around the Co-Hong delegation were mainly empty, the first couple of rows being customarily reserved for members of the Committee. As the new arrivals went to take their seats, they spotted the Chamber's President, Mr Wetmore. He was conferring urgently with Mr Fearon. They both looked tired and flustered, especially Mr Wetmore, who was unshaven and dishevelled, not at all his usual well-groomed self.

'Good heavens!' said Dent. 'They look as though they've been up all night!'

Mr Slade's lip curled sardonically: 'Perhaps,' he said, 'Wetmore has started offering lessons in Bulgarian.'

No sooner had they seated themselves than Mr Wetmore advanced to the lectern and picked up a gavel. The hall fell silent at the first knock.

'Gentlemen,' said Mr Wetmore, 'I am grateful to you for coming here at such short notice. I assure you I would not have requested your presence if this were not a matter of the gravest importance—a matter that has been brought to our attention by our friends of the Co-Hong guild, some of whom, as you will see, are present here today. They have asked me to inform you that the entire Co-Hong was summoned yesterday to the residence of the lately arrived Imperial Plenipotentiary, High Commissioner Lin Tse-hsü. They were detained there until late in the night. In the small hours they sent me an edict from the Commissioner, addressed to the foreign merchants of Canton—to us, in other words. I immediately summoned our translator, Mr Fearon, and he has spent the last several hours working on it. His translation is not yet complete, but he assures me that he will be able to communicate the gist of the most important parts of the document.'

Mr Wetmore glanced across the room: 'Are you ready, Mr Fearon?'

'Yes, sir.'

'Come then; let us hear it.'

Mr Fearon laid a sheaf of papers on the podium and began to read.

'"Proclamation to Foreigners from the Imperial Commissioner, His Excellency Lin Zexu.

'"It is common knowledge that the foreigners who come to Canton to trade have reaped immense profits. This is evidenced by the facts. Your ships which in former years amounted annually to no more than several tens now number vastly more. Let us ask if in the wide earth under heaven there is any other commercial port that yields rewards as rich as this? Our tea and rhubarb are articles without which you foreigners from afar cannot preserve your lives . . ."'

'Ah!' Mr Slade grinned in satisfaction. 'Did I not predict the rhubarb?'

'"Are you foreigners grateful for the favours shown you by the Emperor? You must then respect our laws and in seeking profit for yourselves you must not do harm to others. How does it happen then that you bring opium to our central land, chousing people out of their substance and involving their very lives in destruction? I find that with this thing you have seduced and deluded the people of China for tens of years past; and countless are the unjust hoards that you have thus accumulated. Such conduct rouses indignation in every human heart and it is utterly inexcusable in the eyes of heaven . . ."'

Mr Burnham, who was seated beside Bahram, was so incensed now that he began to mutter under his breath: 'And what of you, you damned hypocrite of a mandarin? Have you and your rascally colleagues played no part in these matters?'

'". . . at one time the prohibitions against opium were comparatively lax, but now the wrath of the great Emperor has been fully aroused and he will not stay his hand until the evil is completely and entirely done away with. You foreigners who have come to our land to reside, ought, in reason, to submit to our statutes as do the natives of China themselves."'

Here incredulous murmurs could be heard in the hall:

'. . . submit to Long-tail law . . . ?'

'. . . be collared with the cangue, as in the dark ages . . . ?'

'. . . be strangled, like Ho Lao-kin . . . ?'

That name again! Bahram flinched and his gaze strayed towards the Co-Hong merchants and their retinues. One of the linkisters seemed to drop his eyes, as if to avoid being caught staring. Bahram's heartbeat quickened in panic and his fingers tightened involuntarily on his cane. He sensed that the linkister was looking at him again and forced himself to be still. By the time he regained his composure Mr Fearon's recital was much advanced.

'". . . I, the Imperial envoy, am from Fujian, on the borders of the sea, and I thoroughly understand all the arts and ingenious devices of you foreigners. I find that you now have many scores of ships anchored at Lintin and other places, in which are several tens of thousands of chests of opium. Your intention is to dispose of them clandestinely. But where will you sell it? This time opium is indeed prohibited and cannot circulate; every man knows that it is a deadly poison; why then should you heap it up in your foreign cargo ships and keep them anchored, thereby wasting much money and exposing them to the chance of storms, of fire and other accidents?"'

Now Mr Fearon paused to take a deep breath.

'"Uniting all these circumstances, I now issue my edict; when it reaches the foreigners, let them immediately and with due respect take all the opium in their cargo ships and deliver it up to the officers of the government. Let the merchants of the Co-Hong examine clearly which man by name gives up how many chests, the total weight and so on, and make out a list to that effect so that the officers can openly take possession of the whole and have it burned and destroyed so as to cut off its power of doing mischief. A single atom must not be hidden or concealed . . ."'

A groundswell of protest had been gathering in the hall and it now grew loud enough to silence the translator.

'. . . surrender our entire cargoes . . . ?'

'. . . so they can be burned and destroyed . . . ?'

'. . . why sir, these are the ravings of a madman, a tyrant . . . !'

Mr Wetmore raised both his arms. 'Please, please, gentlemen; this is not all. There is more.'

'Yet more?'

'Yes, the Commissioner has another demand,' said Mr Wetmore. 'He has asked for a bond.' He turned to the translator. 'Please, Mr Fearon, let us hear that part of the edict.'

'Yes, Mr Wetmore.' Mr Fearon turned to his notes again.

'"I have heard it said that in the ordinary transactions of life you foreigners attach a great deal of importance to the words 'good faith'. So let a bond be duly prepared, written in the Chinese and Foreign character, stating clearly that the ships afterwards to arrive here shall never, to all eternity, dare to bring any opium. Should any ship after this bring it, then her whole cargo shall be confiscated and her people put to death . . ."'

'Shame!'

'. . . this is intolerable, sir . . .'

The hall was now filled with such an outcry that the Co-Hong merchants took alarm; leaving their seats they sought shelter behind their respective entourages.

Mr Wetmore could no longer make himself heard and his gavel too was ineffective against the uproar. Approaching the first row, he held a hurried consultation with the members of the Committee. 'There's no point going on with this,' he said. 'Nothing can be decided here anyway. The Committee must convene at once. The Co-Hong needs an immediate answer.'

'Will their delegation wait?' said Dent.

'Yes, they insist on it; they say they cannot return without an answer.'

'Well, let's get to it then.'

Under cover of the noise, the Committee and the Co-Hong delegation slipped out of the hall, through a back door, and made their way up to the third floor. While the Committee filed into the boardroom the Co-Hong merchants were left to wait in the commodious withdrawing-room that adjoined the President's office.

As they went to take their seats, many members of the Committee were surprised, and some not a little put out, to see that the young translator, Mr Fearon, had accompanied the President into the room. 'Why, sir,' said Mr Slade to Mr Wetmore, 'have you become so attached to your young friend that you've put him on the Committee?'

Mr Wetmore glared at him coldly. 'Mr Fearon is here to read us the rest of the edict.'

'Is there more?' Dent asked.

'So there is.' Mr Wetmore nodded to the translator, who began to read.

'"In reference to those vagabond foreigners who reside in the foreign hongs and are in the habit of selling opium, I already know their names full well. Those good foreigners who do not deal in opium, I am no less acquainted with them also."'

At the mention of 'good foreigners' several pairs of eyes turned to glare angrily at Charles King. He pretended not to notice and looked stonily ahead.

'"Those who can point out the vagabond foreigners and compel them to deliver up their opium, those who first step forward and give the bond, these are the good foreigners, and I, the Imperial envoy, will speedily bestow upon them some distinguishing mark of my approbation."'

Now, unable to contain himself, Mr Slade burst out: 'Why, the utter loathsomeness of it—he is promising to reward the traitors in our midst.'

Since he was looking directly at Charles King, there could be no doubt of who he was referring to. Mr King's face turned colour and he was about to respond when Mr Wetmore broke in, once again.

'Please, gentlemen,' said Mr Wetmore, 'Mr Fearon is not yet finished—and may I remind you that he is not a member of the Committee and ought not to be privy to *any part* of our deliberations?'

The rebuke silenced Mr Slade. Mr Fearon, thoroughly rattled, continued to read:

'"Woe and happiness, disgrace and honour are in your hands! It is you who must choose for yourselves. I have ordered the Hong merchants to go to your factories and explain the matter to you. I have set, as the limit, three days within which they must let me have a reply. And at the same time the bond, mentioned before, must also be produced. Do not indulge in delay and expectation!"'

By the time the last words were read, the room was stirring with indignation. Nothing was said, however, until the young translator had been thanked and shown to the door. Then Mr Wetmore took his chair again, and gave Mr Burnham the nod.

Mr Burnham sank back into his chair and stroked his silky beard. 'Let us be clear about what we have just heard,' he said calmly. 'An open threat has been issued against us: our lives, our property, our liberty are in jeopardy. Yet the only offence cited against us is that we have obeyed the laws of Free Trade—and it is no more possible for us to be heedless of these laws than to disregard the forces of nature, or disobey God's commandments.'

'Oh come now, Mr Burnham,' said Charles King. 'God has scarcely asked you to send vast shipments of opium into this country, against the declared wishes of its government and in contravention of its laws?'

'Oh please, Mr King,' snapped Mr Slade, 'need I remind you that the force of law obtains only between civilized nations? And the Commissioner's actions of today prove, if proof were needed, that this country cannot be included in that number?'

'Are you of the opinion then,' said King, 'that no civilized nation would seek to ban opium? That is contrary to fact, sir, as we know from the practices of our own governments.'

'I fear, Miss King,' said Slade in a voice that was dripping with innuendo, 'that your Celestial sympathies may have robbed you of your ability to comprehend plain English. You have misinterpreted my meaning. It is the nature of the Commissioner's threats that show him to be a creature beyond the pale of civilization. Does he not, in his letter, threaten to incite the population against us? Does he not imply that he holds our property and lives at his mercy? I assure you, sir, that such proud, ostentatious and unheard-of assumptions would not be made against us by the representatives of any civilized government.'

'Gentlemen, gentlemen,' Mr Wetmore broke in. 'This is neither the time nor the place to conduct a debate on the nature of civilized government. Let me remind you that we have been issued an ultimatum and our friends from the Co-Hong are awaiting our answer.'

'"Ultimatum"?' said Mr Slade. 'Why, that very word is repugnant to British ears. To respond to it in any form would be to countenance an insult to the Queen herself.'

At this point Dent tapped the table with his forefinger. 'I am not of a mind with you on this, Slade. To me, this ultimatum seems a most welcome development.'

'Indeed? Pray why?'

'The enemy has hoisted his colours and fired his first broadside. It falls to us now to respond.'

'And what do you propose we do?' said Mr Burnham.

Dent looked around the table with a smile. 'Nothing. I propose we do nothing.'

'Nothing?'

'Yes. Let us inform our friends in the Co-Hong that this is a matter of the gravest import and cannot be proceeded upon without due consideration and consultation. Let us tell them this process will take several days—that will give us time to see what this man Lin is made of. An ultimatum is easy to issue but difficult to act upon.'

Having had his say, Dent leant back in his chair and began to doodle upon a piece of paper. It was Mr Burnham who broke the silence. 'Why Dent, you're right! It is a stroke of genius. That is what we must do—nothing. Let us see if this Commissioner's bite is as bad as his bark.'

Mr Wetmore shook his head in disagreement. 'I don't think our friends from the Co-Hong will be satisfied with such an answer. And let me remind you that they are expected shortly to return to the Consoo House, with a response from us.'

'Well then, Wetmore,' said Dent with a smile. 'You must go to the Consoo House with them—you, and of course Mr King since he is so greatly beloved of the mandarins. I do not expect that you will have the slightest difficulty in explaining to them that we need a few days to consider the Commissioner's demands; it is in every way an eminently reasonable proposition.'

fifteen

Markwick's: March 20, 1839

My dearest Puggly, you will remember that I said I would write to you again in four weeks? Well, it has been slightly longer than that—but what I have to tell you today will make up for all of it, I promise you! And you must not imagine that you have been absent from my thoughts in the meantime: I have been perusing your letters with the *greatest* eagerness and was *fascinated* to learn of all that has been happening on *Redruth*—most particularly of your discovery of a promising patch of land on Hong Kong, and of Mr Penrose's decision to transfer a part of his collection to that spot. If this island of yours is as well-watered as you say, then it makes perfect sense that your poor plants should be given a holiday from their life aboard the *Redruth*. After all, plants were not *meant* to grow on ships, were they, Puggly dear? and it does seem cruel to deprive them of their natural element when it lies so close at hand. Indeed I can think of no reason why Mr Penrose should not contemplate setting up a little nursery on the island—I talked about this with Baburao and he says he might well be able to arrange for him to have the use of a suitable plot of land.

Just consider, my dear Principessa Puggliogne, how thrilling it would be to have a branch of the Penrose Nurseries sitting upon the edge of this vast continent: you could have all manner of plants shuttling back and forth between Cornwall and China, could you not? For all you know, it might become an exceedingly lucrative business—and if it does I hope you will remember to thank your poor Robin for planting the idea in your head!

But enough of all that: I'm sure you are impatient to learn of my doings in Canton—and I am *delighted* to inform you that these weeks have not gone by in vain: indeed, the principal reason for my silence is that I have had hardly a minute to spare. From the moment I accepted Mr Chan's commission I knew he would be back exactly when he said and I was determined to have the picture of Adelie done in time for his return—and there, precisely, lay the rub, for the undertaking proved to be more ambitious than I had envisioned. After labouring for a week I realized that I would need help if my commission was to be properly and punctually discharged. I then conceived the idea of asking Jacqua to assist me (in return, of course, for an extremely generous fee), and this proved a *capital* notion: every day, when his work at Lamqua's studio ended, Jacqua would come to my room for a while—and so *agreeably* did we contrive to spend our time together that it would be no exaggeration to say that those were some of the happiest and most instructive hours of my life! But whether the purpose of advancing the painting was always well served is perhaps better not asked: it is forever a temptation, you know, when Artists work in close proximity, to expatiate upon painterly matters—and in this regard we may have sinned a little more than most. The more time we spent together, the more curious we became about one another's artistic inclinations; no length of time seemed excessive if it extended our understanding of each other's methods and equipment. Why, even to place our hands upon each other's brushes—at once so familiar and so different—was to experience the thrill of discovery! Never had we imagined, Puggly dear, that we had so much yet to learn about these beloved tools of ours: every minute seemed well-used if it furthered our knowledge of the subtle variations of their hairs and bristles; not a minute felt wasted if it was spent in exploring the feel of their slender but sturdy shafts; not an hour was be grudged that was expended in learning how to coax out the wondrous luminosities that lie hidden within them.

I am, as you know, Puggly dear, always *greedy* to learn, and Jacqua has taught me things that are sublimely ingenious (how I envy him his education and experience!). I have learnt to create extraordinary effects through subtle variations of the rhythms of the hand; I have seen how, through the regulation of the breath, the vital energies of the body can be brought to bear upon each movement of the brush; I have been initiated into the meditative art of emptying and concentrating the mind so as to make the most of the moment of *attack*; I have learnt to time my strokes so that they build up to epiphanic conclusions, with the very essence of each creation being both captured and expressed in the final, climactic thrust of the brush.

But it would be idle to deny that we were often distracted: there was so much to learn that the beautiful Adelina was sometimes not accorded the attention that was her due. Not until a few days ago did it come to my notice that she still lacked her draperies and her shoes; that the circular window and the distant view of mountains had yet to appear in the background; that her teapoy possessed but a single leg! So then we set upon the canvas with a will, toiling night and day—and to such good effect did we work that I woke yesterday morning to find the picture almost finished! This was a great relief for I judged this to be the day when Ah-med would again present himself at the hotel. Knowing that there was no time to waste, I sprang from my bed and set myself to the task of applying the last dabs and finishing touches. But of course this is a task without end—for no sooner have you placed a little spot of colour *here* than it seems imperative for it to be balanced with another *there*—and in this fashion I might well have gone on for hours had I not been interrupted by a knock on my door.

It was the doleful Mr Markwick, holding in his hands a note that had just been delivered for me: it is not often that I get such missives and my pleasure was doubled when I recognized the seal to be that of Charlie King! It was an invitation of sorts—March 19th was the anniversary, said he, of the death of his Friend, James Perit, who had passed away in Canton seven years before. On this day it was his custom to go to French Island to lay flowers on his grave. He had intended to set off in the morning, but his plans had been disrupted by some urgent meetings; he now expected to leave in the late afternoon—and if I had the time and inclination to join him in this expedition he would gladly reserve a place in his boat—&c. &c.

For the life of me I could not have declined to participate in such a mission! I penned my acceptance at once and would have delivered it in person—but who should arrive right then but Ah-med? But it was still early in the day, and being sure that I would return in time for the expedition, I entrusted my note of acceptance to a peon. Then I hurried off to ready my canvas and when it was properly wrapped, in rolls of paper, we set off, with Ah-med in the lead.

And where to this time? you are no doubt asking yourself. This was certainly the question uppermost in my own mind, and on addressing it to Ah-med I learnt that we were to go once again to Fa-Tee. But the journey there was an altogether different business this time—it was an oddly furtive affair, and for that reason, not without a little *frisson* (or is it *soupçon*? I can never remember) of excitement. We went in a large boat, with a covered house, and most of the way we stayed inside, hidden from the view of the policemen who stopped our vessel from time to time, to interrogate the poor boatmen about their doings.

You may be puzzled to learn of this heightened vigilance, so I should explain that in the last couple of weeks, while Jacqua and I were happily absorbed in our own pursuits, the rest of Canton has been preoccupied with matters of an altogether different order. Although I had paid scant attention to these developments, I was not wholly oblivious to them for Zadig Bey has been kind enough to pass on a few little snippets.

The long-awaited Yum-chae—the Imperial Commissioner—arrived ten days ago with a great deal of fanfare (the whole city was given a holiday—for which Jacqua and I were *most* grateful since it allowed us to devote an entire day to our artistic pursuits!). It seems that the Commissioner has been sent here with an explicit mandate to put an end to the opium trade and he appears to be quite determined to do exactly that. It is because of his edicts that the local mandarins and policemen have become a great deal more officious of late.

But whether these considerations had anything to do with the precautions of our journey I forbore to ask, knowing full well that a truthful answer would be impossible to obtain. In any event, it was not till our boat turned into the tranquil creeks of Fa-Tee that Ah-med and I emerged once again into the daylight—and now I discovered that our destination was not the Pearl River Nursery, as I had thought, but rather the walled estate that sits hidden in its lee. You will remember perhaps that I had earlier described this compound as having the look of a fortress? In no way would I amend that description except to say that it now had the look of a citadel under siege, with armed men posted all around it.

We approached the compound not by land, but by water—for the compound has its own jetty, hidden away at the back. There we were met by a paltan of grim-faced men who led us quickly to the great red gates that pierce the walls. It was all rather disconcerting and peculiar but when the heavy gates swung open everything changed.

Nowhere on earth, I suspect, is the importance of portals as well understood as in China. In this country, gateways are not merely entrances and exits—they are tunnels between different dimensions of existence. Here, as at the threshold of Punhyqua's garden, I was visited by the feeling that I was stepping into a realm that existed on some plane other than the ordinary.

Ahead lay a garden, not unlike Punhyqua's, an artfully made landscape of streams and bridges, lakes and hills, rocks and forests, with winding pathways and wave-like walls. A part of the enchantment of these gardens is that they amplify the effects of the seasons. I had seen Punhyqua's garden in November, when it was cloaked in the wistful hues of autumn; now, spring was all around us, and nowhere more so than here—the trees and plants were bright with bloom and the air was perfumed with the scent of flowers.

If not for my escort, I would gladly have wandered for hours among the pathways—but Ah-med would not let me stray from his heels. He led me directly to a 'hill' that was topped by what seemed to be a pavilion, built of some unearthly material, translucent in appearance and mauve in colour. Only on approaching closer did I realize that the pavilion was actually an enormous wisteria bush, supported by a kind of pergola. The flowers hung down in thick clusters, emanating a sweet, heady odour; set out in the dappled shade beneath were some chairs, teapoys and a couple of long divans. On one of the couches lay Mr Chan, dressed in his customary gown.

I thought at first that he was asleep, but when I stepped beneath the wisteria he opened his eyes and sat up.

'Holloa there, Mr Chinnery: are you well?'

The voice no longer came as a surprise, although it was, as ever, strangely at odds with the setting. 'Yes, Mr Chan,' said I. 'And you?'

'Oh can't complain, can't complain,' he muttered, like some rheumatic old pensioner. 'And the painting?'

'I have it here.'

I had brought the canvas still stretched upon its wooden frame: I propped it on a chair and placed it in front of him.

The moment of unveiling commissions to clients is always fraught with worry: you find yourself anxiously scanning their faces in an effort to gauge their response; you hope to see some indication of their feelings, a softening of the eyes perhaps, or a smile. No such signs were visible on Mr Chan's countenance; for an instant I thought I saw a slight sharpening in his gaze, and then he nodded and motioned to me to seat myself on the other couch. When I had done so he clapped his hands and a couple of minutes later a servant appeared, to lay a covered tray on the table beside him. Removing the cover, Mr Chan picked up a cloth pouch and handed it over: 'Your fee, Mr Chinnery.'

Abrupt though this was, I was hugely relieved to find that my work had passed muster. 'Why thank you, sir,' I said, with unfeigned gratitude (for I will not conceal from you, Puggly dear, that in the last few weeks I have sometimes found myself just a *little* short).

'Good,' said he, 'and now that I have my painting and you have your fee, perhaps you would like to share a pipe with me?'

It was only now I realized that the tray which had been presented to Mr Chan contained also a pipe, a needle, a lamp, and a small ivory box. The function of these objects was not unfamiliar to me for I have seen their like often enough in my Uncle's house. I was well aware also that to share an occasional pipe of opium with a guest is considered a courtesy by many Chinese. I could think of no reason to decline—and yet I was not so bold as to throw all caution to the winds. When Mr Chan handed me the pipe I took only a small draught, expecting that it would sting the throat in the same way as tobacco. But it was quite different: the smoke was as unctuous and heavy as an expensive oil, and just as silkily smooth. No less of a surprise was the swiftness of its effect. Within an instant, or so it seemed, I was floating away, into the canopy of wisteria.

I have heard it said that opium is unpredictable in its effects: although it makes most people torpid and silent, there are also some who become uncharacteristically loquacious under its influence. The truth of this was immediately demonstrated to me—for even as my own tongue grew heavy, Mr Chan seemed to become more communicative. I do not exactly know how it happened but suddenly he was talking to me about his journey to England, three decades before.

I listened to Mr Chan with my eyes closed, but not a word escaped me—except that after a while it was as if I were not listening at all, but actually *seeing* his narrative unfold before my eyes. Such are the miraculous powers of the drug that it was as if I had become a fifteen-year-old gardener called Ah Fey: there I was, on the deck of an East India Company ship, a lone Chinese boy, travelling westwards through the oceans, towards England.

My plant cases are as precious to me as life itself: I water them by day and sleep beside them at night; and when the weather grows hot, I build little huts over them, with my own sparse clothing; when we are beset by tempests and storms I shield them with my own body. At every turn the other crewmen do their best to thwart me. Some are lascars and some are English seamen, and they are often at each other's throats: the one matter in which they are united is their hatred of me—to them I am little better than a monkey. When we cross the equator I submit tamely to their rituals—dunkings and daubings—but suddenly I find myself pinioned and spreadeagled on the deck. Then I hear a scraping sound: they are shearing off my queue with an unsharpened knife.

I struggle at first, but then I realize that I am only making the pain worse; I lie still and let them finish—but I take note of who they are, and afterwards I plan my revenge. The ringleader is a burly foretopman—late one night, during the dogwatch, when everyone is half-asleep, I make my way up to his foot-rope and scrape it thin. Two days later, in the midst of a gale, the rope snaps and he is lost at sea . . .

I arrive at Kew bringing with me more Chinese plants than anyone has succeeded in transporting before. These are plants that I myself have obtained for Mr Kerr in Canton: he has no more idea of where to find them than he has of buying opium—in all things I am his pander and procurer. But the successful delivery of the plants is attributed not to me but to Mr Kerr; I am but the monkey who travelled with them.

I say nothing: I have grown almost mute; months have passed since I was able to make myself properly understood. The foreman whose house I live in hands out daily beatings to his own children and I am not exempted from his floggings; the food is a vile pap and I am never free of hunger. In my eyes, Kew is not a garden but an untended wilderness. One night I break into a greenhouse and uproot some shrubs—I half hope to be caught, and I am. I am sent to live with a clergyman who I come to hate even more than the gardeners; one night, while he lies slumped over his brandywine, I help myself to the contents of his purse and make my escape. I walk towards Greenwich, guided by the lights of the fairground; for the first time in months I am able to disappear into a crowd. Under a tent people are dancing; I slip inside unseen and somehow I am drawn into the dance; the people who pull me in are of a kind familiar to me—barrow-pushers and pedlars, costermongers and gypsies. They show no surprise at having me in their midst; at dawn I cross the Thames with them and it is as if I were going from Honam to Guangzhou. In the rookeries of East London everything is familiar: the close-packed hovels, the bare feet, the barrows, the ordure on the streets, the smell of roasting chestnuts, the toffs in their sedan chairs, the nippers running wild: it is as if, after travelling all the way around the world, I had found my way home . . .

What a journey!

Is it not amazing, Puggly dear, that whenever we begin to congratulate ourselves on the breadth of our knowledge of the world, we discover that there are *multitudes* of people, in every corner of the earth, who have seen vastly more than we can ever hope to?

I do not know whether it was because of the narcotic effects of the opium or the enchantment of Mr Chan's narrative, but I was positively *crushed* when it came time for me to leave. Mr Chan walked me back to the sampan, and before I knew it I was back at Markwick's Hotel. It was as if weeks, or months, had gone by since I left—yet there was still plenty of daylight outside. My head was spinning and I was about to lie down when my eyes strayed to my desk, to alight upon Charlie's note. I woke to my senses in a panic, recalling the projected expedition to the cemetery on French Island.

Had Charlie left already? Was he lingering in wait for me? Pausing only to splash some water on my face, I ran to his lodgings in the American Hong. And there, to my astonishment, I learnt that he had yet to return from the meeting of that morning! I was told that he had gone, with Mr Wetmore, the President of the Chamber of Commerce, to deliver a letter to the merchants of the Co-Hong; they had been admitted into the Consoo House several hours before and had not been seen since.

You can scarcely imagine, my dear Pagla-hawa, the *alarm* that was sowed in me by these reports. For what purpose could my friend have been so long detained? Was he under arrest? And if so, for what offence?

I went at once to the Consoo House but arrived there only to find the gates firmly locked: no one could tell me anything except that the delegates were still inside.

Oh! What a day!

I came back to my room fully expecting to return to the Consoo House an hour later—but evidently the drug had yet to release its grip on me for I fell fast asleep.

On waking this morning I went at once to Charlie's

lodgings and was told that he had been released from the Consoo House late in the night and had gone straight to Mr Wetmore's house. He had returned to his rooms only at dawn, completely exhausted; he had yet to awake.

So envision if you will, Puggly dear, my state as I write this: my head is in such a whirl that I have omitted to give you a very important piece of news . . .

. . . but wait, I hear a knock . . .

~

The Club was as full that evening as Bahram had ever seen it. Since morning everyone had been waiting to hear, from Mr Wetmore's own mouth, the tale of the delegation's extended confinement at the Consoo House. Now, the better part of a day having gone by without a word, a large number of curious members had converged upon the Chamber, fully expecting that Mr Wetmore would emerge from his self-imposed seclusion in time for his accustomed glass of negus.

But that hour came and went and there was no sign of Mr Wetmore or any of the other delegates: all that was learnt of him was that he had been closeted with Mr Fearon through much of the night and most of the day.

This piece of news did nothing to sweeten Mr Slade's humour. With a quiver of his jowls he issued one of his cryptic pronouncements: 'Well, if our Achilles is to sulk in his tent, I suppose he cannot be without his Patroclus.'

'"Patroclus"?' Bahram frowned in puzzlement. 'What is "Patroclus"? Some new kind of medicine, is it?'

'I suppose some would call it that.'

'But what about Charlie King?' said Bahram. 'Why is he absent? Is he taking Patroclus also?'

'That possibility,' said Mr Slade gravely, 'cannot be dismissed, certainly. *Ab ore maiori discit arare minor.*'

'Baap-re! What does that mean, John?'

'"From the older ox the younger learns to plough."'

'My goodness!' said Bahram. 'It is unbelievable! Time is running away and they are busy ploughing and all? How much longer before the Commissioner's ultimatum expires?'

'Two more days,' said Mr Slade. 'But you cannot expect such considerations to weigh with them—Bulgarians are famously heedless of time, you know.'

Dinner was served and removed, and there was still no news of Mr Wetmore or any of the other delegates. After lingering a little over a glass of port, Bahram decided it was time to retire.

It was early yet, so the others were surprised when he made to rise.

'To bed so soon, Barry?'

'You're not keeping country hours nowadays, are you?'

Bahram was already on his feet and he answered with a bow. 'I am sorry, gentlemen, but today I must end up early. Tomorrow is my community's most important festival—we call it Navroze. It is our New Year, so I must be up at dawn.' He smiled as he looked around the table. 'Of course there will also be a burra-khana. You are most welcome to join us—lunch will be served at noon, in my house.'

Mr Burnham and Mr Slade exchanged glances. 'Thank you, Barry,' said Mr Burnham, shifting uneasily in his seat. 'But for myself I must confess I have no taste for heathenish festivities—and besides we wouldn't want to get in your way.'

Bahram laughed. 'Good night, gentlemen—and remember, if you change your minds, you are most welcome.'

'Good night.'

On returning to the Achha Hong, Bahram went immediately to bed. Rising at dawn the next day he lit some incense and made a fumigatory round of his house. Back in his bedroom he set energetically to work, wiping and tidying his altar: from his earliest childhood he had been taught that Navroze was a day for cleansing and cleanliness—the day when the dark shadow of Ahriman was driven from the farthest corners of the house. Even though he knew that his would be only a token effort, the feel of the duster in his hands brought back many warm memories of Navrozes past.

After an hour of cleaning, when he had worked himself into a sweat, he rang for hot water and took a long bath; then, summoning the valet-duty khidmatgar, he changed into the new clothes his family had sent from Bombay.

For breakfast Mesto had made some of his favourite Parsi dishes: a meltingly soft akoori of eggs; crisp *bhakra*; stuffed *dar-ni-pori* pastries, with a filling of sweetened lentils; hard-boiled eggs; a fillet of fried pomfret; *khaman-na-larva* dumplings, bursting with sweetened coconut; and sweet *ravo*—semolina cooked in milk and ghee.

On other days Bahram would have lingered over the meal, but today there was too much to be done. As the doyen of the community, he had invited every Parsi in Canton to assemble in his house. A large, empty storeroom on the ground floor had already been cleaned and prepared for the ceremony, but before the guests came he would have to put together a proper Navroze altar.

Vico! Where is that lace tablecloth?

Here, patrão—I've got it already.

Scarcely had the altar been put in place, complete with the *sés* tray, bearing rosewater, betel-nuts, rice, sugar, flowers, a sandalwood fire and a picture of the Prophet Zarathustra, than the first guests began to arrive. Bahram stood by the door, greeting each of them in turn, with an embrace and a hearty *Sal Mubarak!*

One of the guests was from a priestly family, and in deference to his lineage, Bahram had asked him to lead the prayers and preside over the Jashan. He discharged his duties unexpectedly well, pronouncing the ancient language so clearly that even Bahram, who was by no means well-versed in scriptural matters, was able to follow some of the verses: . . . *zad shekasteh baad ahreman*—'May Ahriman be smitten and defeated . . .'

As far back as Bahram could remember this passage had had an extraordinary effect on him, conjuring up more vividly than any other, the conflict between Good and Evil. Today the dread and awe inspired by those words was so powerful that he began to tremble: he closed his eyes and it was as if his head, his whole body, were afire with the flames of that struggle. His knees went weak and he had to hold on to the back of a chair to prevent himself from falling. Somehow he managed to hold himself upright for the rest of the ceremony, and when it ended he wasted no time in ushering the company into the formal dining room, which had been especially opened up and decorated for the occasion.

At this point, the company was joined by Zadig, who had celebrated Navroze in the Achha Hong many times before. Comforted by his friend's familiar presence Bahram seated him to his right and served him Mesto's offerings with his own hands: fish of several kinds, crisply fried and steamed in a wrapping of leaves; *jardalu ma gosht*, mutton cooked with apricots; kid in a creamy almond sauce; *goor per eeda*—eggs on mutton marrow; cutlets of many kinds, some frilly with tomato gravy and some made of lamb brains, crisp on the outside and meltingly soft within; kebabs of prawn and rice-flour rotis; *khaheragi pulao* with dried fruit, nuts and saffron—and much else. All through the meal wine, red and white, flowed freely, and at the end, Mesto served cakes, custards and sweet pancakes with coconut. He had even succeeded in obtaining some yogurt, from the Tibetans across the river—he served the dahi with sugar and spices, layered with a fine dusting of powdered nutmeg and cinnamon.

Afterwards, when everyone had left, Zadig stayed on, for a tumbler of chai in the daftar.

What a feast, Bahram-bhai! One of the best I've had under your roof—you could have fed an army!

The compliment, following as it did on the strangely mixed emotions of the day, threw Bahram into a mood of reflection. His eyes wandered to the small portrait of his mother that hung on his wall.

You know, Zadig Bey, he mused, when I was a little boy there were times when all there was in our house was a few rotlis made from bajra. We had so little money that when my mother cooked rice, she would even make us drink the 'pagé'—

the water in which it was cooked. Often we would eat the rice only with raw onions and chillies, and perhaps a little methioo, which is a kind of mango pickle. Once or twice a month we would share a few pieces of dried fish and that we would consider a feast. And now . . .

Bahram broke off to look around his daftar: I wish my mother could have seen all this, Zadig Bey. I wonder what she would have said.

Zadig looked at him with a teasing smile: And what would she have said, Bahram-bhai, if she'd known that it had all come from opium?

Although the question had been asked in a jocular way, Bahram was stung; a sharp retort rose to his lips, but he bit it back. He lowered his tumbler of chai and answered in a steady voice: I'll tell you what she would have said, Zadig Bey: she would have said that a lotus cannot bloom unless its roots are planted in the mud. She would have understood that opium is not important in itself: it is just mud—it is what grows out of it that is important.

And what will grow out of it, Bahram-bhai?

Bahram calmly returned his friend's gaze. The future, Zadig Bey, he said; that's what will grow out of it. If things go well and I am able to make a profit on my investments I'll be able to forge a new way ahead—for myself, and maybe for all of us.

What way? What are you talking about?

Don't you see, Zadig Bey? We are living in a world not of our own making. If we refuse to take advantage of the few opportunities that are open to us, we will not be able to keep up. In the end we will be driven out of business. I saw the start of this with my father-in-law and I won't let it happen to me.

What do you mean, Bahram-bhai? What happened to your father-in-law?

Bahram took a sip of his chai. I'll tell you a story, Zadig Bey, he said. It is about the *Anahita*. You've seen how beautifully the ship is built? Let me tell you why my late father-in-law took so much care over this vessel. For years he had been building ships for the English—for the East India Company and for the Royal Navy. Five frigates he built, and three ships of the line and any number of smaller vessels. He could build them better and cheaper in Bombay than they could in Portsmouth and Liverpool—and with all the latest technical improvements too. And when the shipbuilders of England realized this, what do you think happened? They talk of Free Trade when it suits them—but they made sure that the rules were changed so that the Company and the Royal Navy could no longer order ships from us. Then they created new laws which made it much more expensive to use India-built ships in the overseas trade. My father-in-law was among the first to understand what was happening. He knew that under these conditions the Bombay shipbuilding trade would not survive for long. That is why he wanted the *Anahita* to be the best and the most beautiful ship he had ever built. He used to say to me in those days: Bahram, you see what is happening to our shipyards? The same thing will happen also to all our other trades and crafts. We have to find alternatives or it is just a matter of time before we are driven out of business.

But what does that mean, Bahram-bhai?

It means we have to find a way Zadig Bey, our own way. We have to move our businesses to places where the laws can't be changed to shut us out.

What places?

I don't know. Maybe England itself. Or elsewhere in Europe. Perhaps even China. Or perhaps—here Bahram flashed Zadig a sly smile—perhaps we could have a place of our own. With enough money we might be able to buy a country, no? A small one?

Zadig burst out laughing. Bahram-bhai—it sounds as if you're preaching sedition!

Sedition? Bahram laughed too, but mostly in astonishment. Arré, what bakwaas! I am the most loyal of the Queen's subjects . . .

Before he could say any more, the door flew open.

Patrão!

Vico had climbed the stairs so fast he had to stop and catch his breath.

Patrão—a runner has just come! From Mr Wetmore. A meeting has been called. You must go at once!

~

March 21

Once again, Puggly dear, I find myself resuming an interrupted letter—and I cannot say I am at all sorry, for never was an interruption more welcome than this last! Suffice it to say that shortly after I responded to the knock on my door, I found myself in a boat with Charlie King, sailing towards French Island!

French Island lies behind Honam, in the direction of Whampoa: it is a considerable body of land, with hills, valleys and plains, all thickly cultivated. The foreigners' cemetery lies on a wooded slope, a short distance from the river. It is a tranquil spot and seems all the more so because the busy waters of the Pearl River are so close by, scarcely a mile away. A stream runs past the cemetery and its shores are lined with tall trees that throw their shadows upon the graves. The scene has something of the clouded melancholy that haunts the rural landscapes of Mr Constable: some of the headstones are tilted and overgrown, and some are cocooned in moss. To read the inscriptions is a *piteous* thing, for like James Perit, many of those who lie there were snatched away when scarcely past their boyhood—I could not help reflecting that were I to be laid there now, I would be older than many.

Mr Perit's grave is among the few that are well-tended (Charlie pays a nearby villager to look after it). He had brought flowers with him, and when he knelt to say a prayer I saw a tear escape his eye and go rolling down his cheek.

I must not dwell too long on this, Puggly dear, or else I too will not be able to restrain my tears: I shall content myself with saying merely that it was as tender a scene as I have ever witnessed (and you may be sure that I was not as composed then as I am now—indeed my handkerchief was quite *ruined*).

Afterwards, when we were making our way back, Charlie spoke at some length about his departed Friend, and I understood that this loss is in no small part responsible for his deep attachment to China. Mr Perit's grave has become for him an anchor, as it were, tying him to this land. For that reason, and many others, it is impossible for him to think of the Chinese as a race apart: he sees them as a people who have their virtues and their failings, as do people everywhere—but to exploit the more feeble-minded among them by pandering to their weaknesses seems to him just as unconscionable here as it would be anywhere else. And the worst of it, in his view, is that the foreign trade has created, in the eyes of the Chinese, an inseparable linkage between opium and Christianity. Since many of the men who peddle the drug are loud in proclaiming their piety it is inevitable that the Chinese should draw the inference that there is no conflict between trafficking in opium and the strict observance of Christianity. It is intolerable to Charlie that a simple moral principle should be clearer to pagans than to Christians.

In speaking of these things Charlie's mien became so troubled that I knew some event of recent provenance was weighing on him—and I was right.

Jacqua and I have been so sequestered of late, Puggly dear (and so happily so), that I had but little notion of all that has been happening in Fanqui-town—although it must be said that I doubt it would have been much different had I been out and about (for I am scarcely the kind of fellow who is likely to be included in the deliberations of Serious Men). But unlike me, Charlie is absolutely in the *thick* of it, largely by virtue of his membership in the Committee. What he told me about the most recent developments came as a complete revelation (and I cannot conceal from you, Puggly dear, that I find it rather *thrilling* to be taken into his confidence on such weighty matters).

It appears that the Chamber of Commerce has recently received an edict from the newly arrived Commissioner demanding that they surrender *all* the opium that is currently stored in their ships; they have also been asked to furnish bonds, pledging that they will never again smuggle opium into China. This has caused, as you may imagine, quite a flutter in the Committee: many of them have *enormous* cargoes of opium stored in their ships, and they are not the kind of men who will tamely surrender vast quantities of wealth in response to a mere edict, no matter how sternly couched. At their last meeting Charlie exerted himself to explain to the others that their losses would only be temporary and could be quickly offset by trading in other articles—his own firm, Olyphant & Co., has demonstrated for all the world to see that it is perfectly possible to make substantial profits even without dealing in opium.

But, of course, no man can see reason if he is blindfolded by his wallet. Charlie was brushed rudely aside and the Committee decided instead to follow Mr Dent's advice, which was to send a letter to the Consoo House saying that the Chamber was giving due and respectful consideration to the Commissioner's edict, but the matter would require several more days of deliberation, investigation, consultation &c. &c.

Charlie was not at all in accord with Mr Dent's letter—yet such were the circumstances that he found himself in the unfortunate position of having to accompany the delegation that delivered it to the Consoo House. It so happens, you see, that Charlie is from Brooklyn, the same city as the President of the Chamber, Mr Wetmore. Their families are acquainted with each other and Mr Wetmore has known Charlie since he was a boy. He has always had a fondness for Charlie and has often gone out of his way to be of help to him. This was why Charlie could not refuse

Mr Wetmore when he asked him to go with him to the Consoo House.

On arriving there they were met by Howqua, Mowqua and several other members of the Co-Hong guild, including Punhyqua (who has at last been set free). These men are all old friends of theirs, so it was with heavy hearts that they communicated to them the contents of the Chamber's letter—but their regrets were as nothing compared to the shock and grief of the Co-Hong merchants.

Howqua, Mowqua and their colleagues are all shrewd businessmen, of course, but they are perhaps overly trusting of their foreign friends: evidently they had persuaded themselves that the foreigners would not fail to take account of the great danger they were in. When they understood that the Chamber had decided, in effect, to deliberately disregard the Commissioner's deadline, they were utterly *stricken*: they are certain that the Commissioner will execute some of their number and it was unimaginable to them that the foreigners would put their lives in jeopardy for a sum of money that is, in the context of the fortunes they have all earned over their lifetimes, quite small. Their lamentations were terrible to behold, said Charlie; and the worst of it was to observe the grief of their sons and retainers, many of whom wept unashamedly.

As if this were not trying enough, the delegation was then taken to meet with a group of mandarins: Commissioner Lin was not present himself, but several of his most trusted deputies and lieutenants were there. When informed of the contents of the Chamber's letter they too were utterly shocked—they understood at once that the Chamber's intention was to delay and prevaricate, and they warned the foreigners that Commissioner Lin was not a man who would yield to such tactics. They then proceeded to question the delegates closely—yet at no point, said Charlie, were the foreigners subjected to the least discourtesy: indeed, when the meeting finally ended they were all given *presents*—silk and tea!

This is perhaps the most telling part of it, says Charlie; throughout this affair the behaviour of the Chinese has been absolutely exemplary: they have made the most reasonable of requests—that the foreign merchants surrender their contraband and pledge never to smuggle opium again, which is not much to ask. The foreigners, on the other hand, have conducted themselves in such a fashion as to utterly discredit their claims of belonging to a Higher Civilization: they know full well that if any Chinese were to attempt to smuggle drugs into their countries, they would be sent instantly to the gallows.

But all is not lost: Charlie was able to retrieve one small victory from the ashes of the day. On being released from the Consoo House Mr Wetmore, who was in a great state, fairly *begged* Charlie to accompany him to his house. This he agreed to do, and a very good thing it turned out to be. Now that Mr Jardine's baneful influence has been removed, Mr Wetmore has become much more malleable (at one point he broke into tears and absolutely *clung* to Charlie!). After several hours of persuasion and many appeals to his conscience Charlie was able to bring him around to his own point of view! Right there they drew up a letter formally acceding to Commissioner Lin's demands! It is to be presented to the Committee today so Mr Wetmore has spent the whole morning with Mr Fearon, the translator, so that a copy may be dispatched to the Commissioner as soon as it is signed by the rest of the Committee. But of course there is no knowing whether they will indeed agree to sign it. There will be quite a battle, Charlie thinks, but now that he has Mr Wetmore on his side he feels that victory may be within his grasp! The outcome will depend on one or two members and Charlie is hopeful of being able to sway at least one of them—Mr Bahram Moddie. He is, at heart, a good man, says Charlie—he went to see him a few weeks ago, and he seemed to be utterly *haunted* by the events of the last few months. At the very mention of the opium-dealer who was executed on December 12th he started as if he had seen a ghost! This is a sign, Charlie claims, that Mr Moddie's conscience has been touched: it is not impossible therefore that at the moment of decision he will choose to do what is right.

I confess, Puggly dear, that I cannot but marvel at the unflinching way in which Charlie has stepped into the battle. When I look at his face I see the delicately cast countenance of the young Géricault—but this is, I think, *utterly* deceptive: he is at heart the fiercest of warriors. When I ask him where he finds the strength to stand alone against all his tribe, he quotes a line of Scripture: *Thou shalt not follow a multitude to do evil!* If ever any man was an army of one, it is he.

. . . and I do believe the drums of war are about to sound! I can see from my window the members of the Committee, heading towards the Chamber of Commerce! There is Mr Wetmore, flanked by Charlie—and there is Mr Slade, on the war path as usual, and there, in the van, is Mr Moddie!

Who would ever have thought that a Chamber of Commerce could be the scene of such storms and convulsions? Unlike Charlie I am neither a sepoy nor a bawhawder but this is one instance in which I would dearly love to ride beside him, shoulder to shoulder (or should it be saddle to saddle?). Can you imagine the scene, Puggly dear: your poor Robin charging into a boardroom to do battle with a paltan of banyans?

And speaking of drama, my sweet Puggli-billi, you are certainly well enough acquainted with me to know that I would save the best for the last—and so I have, but I must get to it now for Baburao is leaving for the Islands this afternoon and he has promised to make sure that this letter gets to you tomorrow!

You will understand, I am sure, that my memory of what passed between me and Mr Chan is obscured just a little by the fumes of that shared pipe. But I do recall that he told me, as I was leaving, that he is eager to see your plants and has put together a collection that will also be of interest to you. Unfortunately there is very little time, for Mr Chan fears that he may soon have to travel again—and besides, the situation here is so uncertain that no one knows how long the river will remain open. In sum the exchange must be done *at once* if it is to happen at all.

Since neither you nor Mr Penrose are able to travel to Canton at this time, I fear you have no choice but to trust me to conduct this exchange on your behalf. I suggest you send a set of five or six plants to me with Baburao, and I will undertake to obtain for you the best bargain I can get. I should warn you, however, that I do not know whether I will be able to procure your golden camellias—I did ask Mr Chan whether he had succeeded in obtaining a specimen, but as I recall, he was very evasive about this matter.

In any event, Your Puggliness, you must make haste!

~

Bahram was among the last to enter the boardroom. Mr Wetmore was already in his seat, at the head of the table: his grooming, Bahram noticed, was as fastidious as ever, but his face was lined and weary, and at one end of his mouth an odd little tic had appeared, tugging his lips into spasmodic grimaces.

Bahram went to his usual place and was surprised to see that the chair beside his was still empty. He leant over to Mr Slade and whispered: 'Where is Dent?'

Mr Slade shrugged. 'Probably detained by some urgent business—it's not like him to be late.'

With everyone else present, Mr Wetmore waited for only a minute or two before asking for the doors to be closed. 'Gentlemen,' he began, 'I am sorry Mr Dent is not here yet, but I fear we cannot wait any longer: our time is short and I am sure you are all eager to know the outcome of our recent visit to the Consoo House. I beg your indulgence if I have tried your patience in this regard, but as you will see, certain documents needed to be translated before we could meet. These I will presently circulate, but let me begin by providing you with a brief account of what transpired. On entering the Consoo House we were met by several of our friends from the Co-Hong, among them Mowqua, Punhyqua, Mingqua, Puankhequa and others. They were, I might add, in a state of extraordinary perturbation—something akin to terror. I think Mr King will bear me out on this.'

Charles King was seated at the other end of the table; turning to look at him Bahram saw that his face too was drawn with fatigue. His voice, however, was firm and clear: 'I have had the misfortune before of looking into the eyes of men who have been seized by mortal fear. I cannot convey to you, gentlemen, how painful it was to see that very look in the eyes of these old friends of ours—friends at whose tables we have supped, friends who have made us rich and to whom we owe the comforts we enjoy.'

These words were still hanging in the air when the door opened to admit Dent.

'Gentlemen, my apologies—please excuse my tardiness.'

'You have come in good time, Mr Dent,' said Mr Wetmore. 'I am sure you will be interested in the document I am about to read out.' He picked up a sheet of paper and looked around the table. 'This is the edict the Imperial Commissioner has served upon the Co-Hong guild: it is this document that has struck terror into their hearts. I think it behoves us, gentlemen, to give our attention to the Commissioner's own words.'

Mr Wetmore looked around the table: 'With your permission, gentlemen?'

'Go ahead.'

'Let's hear what he has to say.'

'"While opium is pervading and filling with its poisonous influence the whole empire, the Hong merchants still continue to indiscriminately give sureties for foreign traders declaring that their ships have brought none of it. Are they not indeed dreaming, and snoring in their dreams? What is this but to 'shut the ear while the jingling bell is stolen'? The original Co-Hong merchants were men of property and family and would never have descended to this stage of degradation; yet all now are equally involved in the stench of it. Truly I burn with shame for you, the present incumbents of the Co-Hong: with you there seems to be no other consideration than that of growing rich.

'"The utter annihilation of the opium trade is now my first object and I have given commands to the foreigners to deliver up to the government all the opium which they have on board their warehousing vessels. I have called on them also to sign a bond, in Chinese and in foreign languages, declaring that henceforth they will never venture to bring opium into China again; and if any should again be brought, their property shall be confiscated by the government. These commands are now given to you Co-Hong merchants, that you may convey them to the foreign factories and plainly make them known. It is imperative that the forceful character of the commands be made clearly to appear. It is imperative for you Co-Hong merchants to act with energy and loftiness of purpose to unite in enjoining these commands upon the foreign merchants. Three days are prescribed within which you must obtain the required bonds and merchandise. If it is found that this matter cannot be resolved by you immediately, then it will be inferred that you are acting in concert with foreign criminals, and I, the High Commissioner, will forthwith solicit the royal death warrant and select for execution one or two of you. Do not claim you did not receive timely notice."'

A murmur of disbelief went around the table now. Bahram, who thought he had misheard, said: 'Did you say "execution", Mr Wetmore?'

'Yes I did, Mr Moddie.'

'Are you are telling us,' said Mr Lindsay, 'that the Commissioner may send two Hongists to the gallows if we do not surrender our goods and furnish this bond?'

'No, sir,' said Mr Wetmore. 'I mean they will be beheaded, not hung. And our friends Howqua and Mowqua are persuaded that they will be the first to die.'

A collective gasp was heard around the table. Then Mr Burnham said: 'There can be no doubt of it: this Commissioner Lin is a monster. None but a madman or monster could have such scant regard for human life as to consider executing two men for such a crime.'

'Indeed, Mr Burnham?' It was Mr King, speaking from the other end of the table. 'You are evidently greatly solicitous of human life, which is undoubtedly a most commendable thing. But may I ask why your concern does not extend to the lives you put in jeopardy with your consignments of opium? Are you not aware that with every shipment you are condemning hundreds, maybe thousands of people to death? Do you see nothing monstrous in your own actions?'

'No, sir,' answered Mr Burnham coolly. 'Because it is not my hand that passes sentence upon those who choose the indulgence of opium. It is the work of another, invisible, omnipotent: it is the hand of freedom, of the market, of the spirit of liberty itself, which is none other than the breath of God.'

At this Mr King's voice rose in scorn: 'Oh shame on you, who call yourself a Christian! Do you not see that it is the grossest idolatry to speak of the market as though it were the rival of God?'

'Please, please, gentlemen!' Mr Wetmore thumped the table in an effort to restore order. 'This is not the time for a theological debate. May I remind you that we are here to consider the High Commissioner's ultimatum, and that there are lives at stake?'

'But that is exactly the problem, Wetmore,' said Mr Burnham. 'If Commissioner Lin is what I believe him to be, a monster or madman, there is nothing to be gained from dealing with him, is there?'

Before Mr Wetmore could speak, Mr Slade broke in: 'Here I must beg to differ with you, Burnham. In my view, the High Commissioner is neither a monster nor a madman, but merely a mandarin of exceptional craftiness. His intention is to intimidate us with threats and braggadocio, so that he may boast of his exploits to the Emperor and earn himself a brighter button for his hat. For myself, I do not credit any of it—neither the menaces of the Commissioner nor the professions of terror on the part of our friends of the Co-Hong. It is obvious to me that the Co-Hong is thoroughly in league with the High Commissioner—they are clearly enacting this little pantomime together. The Hongists have assumed these masks of terror in the hope of getting us to part with our goods at no cost to themselves: that is all it is—a charade like those we are treated to every time we cross the Square. It is the usual Celestial humbug and we cannot be taken in.'

'But what do you propose we do, Mr Slade?' said Bahram. 'What are your suggestions?'

'What I propose,' said Slade, 'is that we stand fast and show that we are not to be budged. Once they understand this, Howqua and Mowqua will sort out the matter soon enough. They will dole out a few cumshaws and grease a few palms and that will be the end of it. Their heads will remain on their shoulders and we shall still be in possession of our goods. If we show signs of softness we will all lose: this above all is a moment when we must cleave to our principles.'

'Principles?' retorted Mr King in astonishment. 'I fail to see what principle can underlie the smuggling of opium.'

'Well then, you have chosen to blind yourself, sir!' Mr Burnham's fist landed loudly on the table. 'Is freedom not a principle as well as a right? Is there no principle at stake when free men claim the liberty to conduct their affairs without fear of tyrants and despots?'

'By that token, sir,' said Mr King, 'any murderer could claim that he is but exercising his natural rights. If the charter of your liberties entails death and despair for untold multitudes, then it is nothing but a licence for slaughter.'

Mr King and Mr Burnham were both on their feet now, staring at each other across the table.

Mr Wetmore thumped the table again. 'Please, gentlemen! May I remind you that this is a matter of the utmost urgency? We do not have the leisure to conduct debates on abstract principles. The time at our disposal is so short that to speed matters along, Mr King and I have taken the liberty of drafting a reply to the Commissioner's edict, on behalf of all of us.'

'Have you indeed?' said Dent with a quizzical smile. 'Well, you have certainly been busy, Wetmore! And what does your letter say?'

'In essence, Mr Dent, it seeks to assure the High Commissioner that we are willing to accede to his terms, but with certain reservations.'

'Does it now?' said Dent, smiling thinly. 'So are we to understand, Mr Wetmore, that you and your little friend Charlie have taken it upon yourselves to write a letter on our behalf but without consulting us? A letter that pledges to end a trade that has existed since before any of us were born? A trade that has conferred enormous wealth upon yourself and your friends, not least Mr Jardine?'

The reference to Jardine seemed to rattle Mr Wetmore, and his voice grew a little shaky. 'Well,' he said, 'our letter explains, of course, that there was, in the past, some ambiguity in regard to the Chinese government's position on the opium trade. At one time it was widely believed that the government might even legalize the trade. But whatever doubts may have existed in the past have certainly been removed by the Commissioner's deeds and words. There is no reason now to hesitate in providing the pledge that he demands.'

'Oh really?' said Dent with silky smoothness. 'And what of the ships that are already anchored around Hong Kong and the other outer harbours? Are we to meekly empty their holds and send the contents to the Commissioner?'

'Not at all,' said Wetmore. 'Our letter explains that while the ships might belong to us, their cargoes do not. They are in effect the property of our investors, in Bombay, Calcutta and London. To surrender the cargoes is impossible: what we will do instead is send the ships back to India.'

For Bahram, this was the prospect most to be feared. 'Send our cargoes back to India?' he cried in alarm. 'But you know, no, Mr Wetmore, the price of opium has fallen to the floor in

Bombay? And production has increased like anything. Where will our cargoes go? Who will buy? To send them to India will bring ruin.'

Bahram looked around the table and it seemed to him that many eyes had narrowed at the sound of the last word: if there was one thing he knew about the English language it was that nothing was more harmful to a merchant's credit than the word 'ruin'. He hastened to undo the damage. 'I don't mean any of us here, of course. We are all amply supplied with capital and will manage to get by. But what about small investors? We have to think of them, no? Many have put in whole life-savings. What of them?'

'Exactly!' cried Slade. 'It seems to me from the sentimental tenor of what I have heard here that the vision of the Hongists' blood spilt on the ground has blinded some of us from contemplating the consequences of surrendering our cargoes. Mr King and Mr Wetmore are so considerate of the sufferings of the Chinese that they are willing to drag down all those engaged in the opium traffic. But what of the ruination and destitution of those who have invested their savings in our shipments? What of their fall in station and society, leading perhaps to debtor's prison, to workhouse alms and probably death by starvation?'

'But surely, Mr Slade,' interjected Mr King, 'you are not suggesting that your investors are people of meagre means, who are in danger of being packed off to debtor's prison? Why would a man who is on the brink of poverty sink his last few pennies into a speculation in a commodity such as opium? In my experience, no one invests in such ventures unless they have capital to spare—they are no more likely to be forced into the workhouse than you or I. This is indeed the cruellest aspect of this trade—that a few rich men, in order to grow richer, are willing to sacrifice millions of lives.'

Slade threw up his hands. 'It is exactly as I suspected: Mr King's heart bleeds for his Celestial friends, but he is utterly indifferent to the sufferings of his fellow merchants and their investors. And for what this readiness to plunge his fellow merchants into certain and immense loss of property? Why forsooth! Because Howqua has said at a private meeting at the Consoo Hall that his head would be taken off if we did not do his bidding. But Howqua, as we well know, is a consummate businessman, and he will say whatever is necessary to protect his own profits.'

Mr Wetmore broke in wearily: 'I assure you, Mr Slade, Howqua believes with all his heart that his will be the first head to roll. It wrung my heart to see him at the Consoo House—I have never seen a more piteous picture.'

'Oh please, Wetmore!' snapped Mr Slade. 'Spare us these Bulgarian vapours! You must remember that you are the President of this Chamber, and not some old biddy presiding over a congress of dowagers.'

'Your language, Mr Slade, is unbecoming of a member of the Committee,' said Mr Wetmore stiffly. 'But I will let it pass because of the urgency of the matter at hand. But of this you should have no doubt—that Howqua, Mowqua and several other Hongists were indeed utterly struck down with fear when we saw them at the Consoo House.'

'Howqua?' Dent interrupted with a shrill, somewhat forced laugh. 'But I saw Howqua this very morning, on Old China Street: that was what delayed me in coming to this meeting. He said that he and his colleagues of the Co-Hong had received certain threats from the Yum-chae, but these were just threats and no more than that. Howqua is an uncommonly shrewd man and I suspect he greatly exaggerated his fears for the benefit of Mr King and Mr Wetmore, knowing them to be, shall we say, somewhat softer in nature than most men. He would not of course attempt anything like that with me, or indeed most of us. When I ran into him a short while ago he appeared to be in perfectly good spirits—this Committee has my word on that.'

A silence fell on the table as everyone tried to absorb the import of this. Then Mr King, whose face had turned red, declared: 'That is a bald-faced lie, Mr Dent!'

Now an audible hiss issued from Mr Slade's lips. 'If I were you, Miss King,' he said, 'I would watch what I say. There are certain words, you know, that entail a form of shorthand called pistolography.'

'Be that as it may, sir,' said Mr King, 'I shall not, for fear of it, silence myself. I too have but recently seen Howqua, and I assure you that his apprehensions were not factitious but real; I saw with my own eyes that he was crushed down to the ground by his terrors. I give you my word that the Hong merchants are in instant fear of their lives and properties. It is not my part to defend despotic measures; I wish only to remind you that once a chain of events is set in motion, it is not in our power to make reparation or atonement. I beg you to remember that the property lost under the present dispensation can easily and in a short time be put together again—but blood once shed is like water spilt upon the ground and can never again be gathered up. The present circumstances are directly destructive to the lives of our fellow creatures; we may occasionally have called the Hongists hard names but they are still our friends and neighbours. What reasonable man could conceive of putting the pocket of an investor in competition with the neck of a neighbour?'

Mr King had invested his words with great passion but their effect upon the Committee was to a considerable extent blunted by Dent, who through the duration of his speech had been looking around the table as if to count heads and assess his support. When Mr King had finished, he said, matter-of-factly: 'Well, it is clear that we have a profound disagreement. Mr King is of the opinion that Howqua and his ilk are in mortal fear of their lives; I, on the other hand, am equally convinced that this is just another instance of Celestial chicanery. It is my opinion that our friends of the Co-Hong are working upon the feelings of those of us who are not, by nature and inclination, imbued with the usual degree of masculine fortitude.'

'What does masculinity have to do with it?' said Mr King.

'Masculinity has everything to do with it,' said Mr Burnham. 'It is surely apparent to you, is it not, that effeminacy is the curse of the Asiatic? It is what makes him susceptible to opium; it is what makes him so fatefully dependent on government. If the gentry of this country had not been weakened by their love of painting and poetry China would not be in the piteous state that she is in today. Until the masculine energies of this country are replenished and renewed, its people will never understand the value of freedom; nor will they appreciate the cardinal importance of Free Trade.'

'Do you really believe,' retorted Mr King, 'that it is the doctrine of Free Trade that has given birth to masculinity? If that were so, then men would be as rare as birds of paradise.'

Now Mr Wetmore broke in again: 'Please, please, gentlemen—let us keep to the matter at hand.'

'I agree,' said Dent. 'There is no point in letting this matter drag on. Let us not waste any more time: Mr Wetmore has informed us about the contents of the letter he has drafted. I have an alternative to propose: it is my suggestion that we write to the Co-Hong in general terms. Let us assure them that we too are persuaded of the need to eventually bring a halt to the trade in opium; let us tell them that in order to determine how best that end might be achieved we will set up a committee. This will amply serve all our purposes; the High Commissioner will have a pretext for ceasing his oppressions and we will have yielded nothing.' Dent stopped to look around the table and then turned to Mr Wetmore. 'So there you have it, Mr President, your resolution against mine. Let us put it to the vote.'

Mr King too had glanced around the table, and seeing that Dent's words had met with many nods and murmured ayes, he gripped the edge of the table and pulled himself to his feet.

'Wait,' he said. 'I beg that you allow me a few more minutes for one last appeal. This is a matter that cannot be decided merely by a show of hands—not only because we are about to take a step that will have consequences far beyond this room and beyond this day, but also because there is present among us someone who sits here as the only representative of a very large population—he is indeed the only man here who can speak for the territories that produce the goods in question.'

Mr King turned now to Bahram. 'I refer of course to you, Mr Moddie. Amongst all of us it is you who bears the greatest responsibility, for you must answer not only to your own homeland but also to its neighbours. The rest of us are from faraway countries—our successors will not have to live with the outcome of today's decision in the same way that yours will. It is your children and grandchildren who will be called into account for what transpires here today. I beg you, Mr Moddie, to consider carefully the duty that confronts you at this juncture: your words and your vote will carry great weight in this Committee. You yourself have spoken to me of your faith and your beliefs. More than once have you said to me that no religion recognizes more clearly than yours, the eternal conflict between Good and Evil. Consider now the choice before you, Mr Moddie; I conjure you to look into the precipice before which you stand. Think not of this moment but of the eternity ahead.' He paused and lowered his voice: 'Who will you choose, Mr Moddie? Will you choose the light or the darkness, Ahura Mazda or Ahriman?'

The last words struck Bahram like a thunderbolt. His hands began to shake and he withdrew them quickly into the sleeves of his choga. Really, it was unfair, profoundly unfair, that Charlie King should pull such a trick on him; to speak not only of continents and countries, but of his faith. And what did continents and countries matter to him? He had to think first of those who were closest to him, did he not? And what conceivable good could result for them if he brought ruin upon himself? For his children, his daughters and Freddy, he would gladly sacrifice his well-being in the hereafter: indeed he could think of no duty more pressing than this, even if it meant that the bridge to heaven would forever be barred to him.

By force of habit, his right hand slipped inside his angarkha, to seek the reassurance of his kasti. He took a deep breath and cleared his throat. Then he raised his head and looked Mr King directly in the eye.

'My vote,' said Bahram, 'is with Mr Dent.'

sixteen

~

Spasms of rheumatism had kept Fitcher confined to bed for the last several days so it fell to Paulette to gather together the plants that were to be sent to Canton with Baburao.

Time being short they decided, after a quick discussion, to send a collection of six: a Douglas fir sapling; a redcurrant bush and two specimens from the north-western coast of America—a yard-high bush of the Oregon grape, now covered with yellow flowers, and a pot of *Gaultheria shallon*, with glossy leaves and clusters of delicate, bell-like sepals. Also included were two recently introduced plants from Mexico—the Mexican Orange, with pretty white blooms, and a beautiful fuchsia that was one of Fitcher's treasures: *Fuchsia fulgens*.

Paulette had grown attached to each of these plants, especially to the Oregon grape which had proved exceptionally vigorous. It pained her to see them being removed to the *Redruth*'s gig, to be transferred to Baburao's junk; like a parent at a time of parting, she doubted that her children would be properly looked after.

'Sir, I know I cannot go to Canton,' she said to Fitcher, 'but could I not travel with the plants a part of the way?'

Fitcher scratched his beard and mumbled, 'Ee could go as far as Lintin Island; ee'd be all right as long as ee don't get up to no flaygerries there.'

'Really, sir?'

'Yes. The junk can tow the gig behind it and the men'll bring ee back afterwards.'

‘Oh thank you, sir. Thank you.’

She ran on deck and signalled to the gig to wait.

The junk was close by, wallowing in the water: when the gig pulled up, Baburao lowered a wooden shelf for the plants. Paulette held her breath as the pots were being winched up, and was hugely relieved when the operation was concluded without mishap. Then a ladder was thrown down for her and she climbed up on deck.

This was the first time Paulette had stepped on Baburao’s junk, and her initial response was one of disappointment. The *Redruth* had been anchored off Hong Kong long enough that she had come to recognize some of the unusual vessels that plied those waters: caterpillar-like passenger boats, long and thin, with seats arranged in rows; ‘funeral-boats’, piled high with coffins; two-masted ‘ducktail’ junks, with tiered houses; and perhaps the most eye-catching of all—whale-like ‘pole-junks’, over a hundred feet in length, with mouths that looked as though they were sieving food from the water.

In a place where such vessels abounded Baburao’s junk was not a craft likely to attract much notice: she was a *sha-ch’uan*—a ‘sand-ship’—which his grandfather had acquired very cheap, somewhere up north. The ship’s name was too long for Paulette to remember, but it didn’t matter anyway, because in her hearing Baburao always referred to his junk as the *Kismat*—the word was the exact equivalent, he said, of the Chinese characters painted on the junk’s bows.

Like every other vessel on the Pearl River, the *Kismat* sported an enormous eye on each side of her bows—a gigantic oculus that seemed to be keeping watch for prey and predators. In size she was smaller than both the *Ibis* and the *Redruth*, being only about sixty feet in length, yet she had more masts than either of those vessels, being fitted with no less than five. Their arrangement was as odd as their appearance: they leant this way and that, like the tapers on a windblown candle-stand. Only two of the masts were planted squarely in the vessel and even these were slanted at strange, irregular angles, one leaning forward and the other tilting back. As for the three smaller poles, they looked more like sticks than masts, and were attached not to the deck but to the deck rails, being placed seemingly at random around the edges of the hull. The placement of the rudder was equally strange, to Paulette's eyes at least, for it was fitted not into the centre of the stern, but on one side of the hull, and was controlled not by a wheel, but by a huge tiller that stuck out over the roof of the deckhouse.

In short, with her raised stern, her miscellaneous masts and barrel-shaped hull, the *Kismat* projected an image of wallowing ungainliness. But this was deceptive: once the mats were up on the masts, the junk provided as smooth a ride as any vessel of her size.

The journey started with a ceremony that seemed, in the beginning, to be very like the pujas Paulette had seen in Calcutta, with incense being offered to T'ien-hou and Kuan-yin (who were benevolent goddesses, explained Baburao, like Lakshmi and Saraswati in India). But then the ritual suddenly exploded, quite literally, into a spectacular tamasha with popping fireworks, banging gongs and the lighting of innumerable strips of red-and-gold paper (to frighten away the bhoots, rakshasas and other demons, said Baburao helpfully). All this, combined with the noise of alarmed ducks, crying babies and snuffling pigs, created an atmosphere such that Paulette would not have been surprised to see the junk flying off like a rocket. But instead, as the noise built to a climax, the *Kismat*'s matted sails went soaring up and she began to move ahead, leaving behind a long trail of smoke.

The waters at the mouth of the Pearl River were torn by cross-cutting currents and there were so many boats swarming about that the junk needed careful handling. Watching the crew as they went about their work, Paulette realized that it was not just the *Kismat*'s appearance that made her different from the *Ibis* and the *Redruth*: there was a marked contrast also in the way she was manned and crewed. Paulette had thought that the laodah of a junk was something like the nakhoda of an Indian boat—someone who combined, in part or whole, the functions of captain, supercargo and shipowner.

But Baburao's way of commanding his vessel was nothing like that of the nakhodas and sea-captains she had observed on the Hooghly and in the Bay of Bengal; and nor could the *Kismat* be said to be 'manned'—for her crew included several women whose duties were no different from those of the men. And no matter whether male or female, none of the crew would put up with barked orders and peremptory hookums: Baburao usually spoke to them in a tone of mild cajolery, as if he were trying to persuade them of the wisdom of doing as he asked. Stranger still was the fact that much of the time he said nothing at all: everyone seemed to know what they had to do without being told, and when Baburao did choose to interfere, the others did not hesitate to question his orders. When arguments broke out, they were usually resolved not by a display of authority or a show of force, but through the intervention of one of the women.

For several hours the junk threaded a slow and careful path through fleets of fishing boats, sharp-toothed reefs and small, wave-pounded islands. Then her bows turned towards a looming crag, fringed by a line of angry surf.

This, said Baburao, is Lintin Island.

The junk worked its way slowly around to a bay on the eastern side of the island, where two vessels of unusual appearance lay at anchor. The hulls were like those of Western sailships, but their masts had been cut off and their rigging removed, so they looked like barrels that had been cut lengthwise in half.

These were the last of the 'hulks' of Lintin, Baburao explained: in the past, they had been used solely for the purpose of storing and distributing opium. One of them was British, the other American, and they had been stationed at Lintin for many years, so that foreign opium-carriers could rid themselves of their wares before heading towards the customs houses that guarded the mouth of the Pearl River. Even a few years before, he said, there would have been many foreign vessels anchored in this bay, busily emptying their holds of 'Malwa' and 'Bengal'; a flotilla of swift fast-crabs would have been sitting here too, waiting to whisk the cargo to the mainland.

Despite the ominous, eerie presence of the misshapen hulks, the bay was a wild and beautiful place, with clouds blowing past the island's steeply rising heights. Baburao anchored the junk in the middle of the bay, manoeuvring her patiently into place, and choosing his spot with great care.

Now followed another ceremony, with incense, offerings and burnt paper.

Is this another puja? asked Paulette, and unlike the last time, Baburao was slow to answer. She had begun to regret having asked the question when he said, all of a sudden: Yes, it is a puja; but not like the last one. This is different.

O? Why?

Yes, this one is for my dada-bhai, my older brother, who died here . . .

It had happened many years before, Baburao explained, but he still could not pass that way without making a stop. The brother he was speaking of was his oldest, and he too had grown up on the *Kismat*, doing what his father and grandfather had done before him. But one day someone said to him: You're a strong boy, why don't you trying rowing a fast-crab? You'll earn well, better than by fishing or sailing. How could anyone stop him? Every now and then he would go off to work the oars on one of those fast-crabs. It was hard work, but at the end of each run he would be given a little bit of opium as a cumshaw. He could have sold these, of course, and taken the money, but he was just a boy and often he ended up smoking his cumshaw instead. Soon he was working not for the pay but for the opium, and the harder he worked, the more he needed it. In a few years his body was wasted and his mind vacant; he could not row any longer and nor could he do anything else. He spent his time lying like a shadow on the *Kismat*'s foredeck. One day, when the junk was anchored in this spot he rolled over into the water and was never seen again.

I was the chhota-bhai, said Baburao, the little one, the youngest of four. When my brother died I was very small. My father decided that it would be best for me to go away so he found me a job as a chokra on a Manila-bound ship. He knew that if I stayed here I too would lose myself in the smoke, like my brothers.

Your older brother was not the only one then?

No, said Baburao. My two other brothers, they too went that way. Even though they saw what happened to my oldest brother, they could not stop themselves: they got greedy for money and went to work on the fast-crabs. One of them was found beheaded, his body floating in a creek near Whampoa. To this day we don't know who killed him or why, but what's for sure is that it had something to do with the 'black mud'. The other brother lived longer, he married and had children. But he was a smoker too, and he died when he was in his mid-twenties. After that my father wanted to sell this junk—he said the mud had turned this river into a stream of poison. I was in Calcutta when this came to my ears. I could not bear the thought of selling the *Kismat*; I had grown up on it. I loved these waters and I decided it was time to come back.

And are you glad you did? said Paulette.

I used to be, but to tell you the truth, I don't know now. The more I see, the more it worries me. I worry about my sons, my grandchildren. How can they live on this river without being choked by the smoke?

Here Baburao broke off and tapped her on the shoulder: Come, I'll show you something.

Leading her up to the most elevated part of the poop-deck, he handed her a telescope.

Look there, he said, pointing upriver. You'll see a big fort, down by the water, right at the river's mouth. The lascars call it 'Sher-ka-mooh', the Tiger's Mouth; the Angrez call it the Bogue. It was built just a few years ago, to defend the river, and to look at it you would think no one could ever get into such a stronghold. But at night you or I or anyone else could walk in, without anyone stopping us. The soldiers are all lost in smoke, and their officers too. This is a plague from which no one can escape.

~

Within a few hours, it was common knowledge in Fanquitown that the Dent faction had triumphed in the boardroom. The Achha Hong received the details through Vico, who predicted a celebration and sure enough, it was soon learnt that some of the Seth's friends would be coming by later in the day.

This set off something of a panic in the kitchen, but by the time the guests began to arrive Mesto had everything in hand: bottles of champagne had been chilled and several batches of croquettes, pakoras and samosas had been prepared and were ready to serve.

Mr Dent and Mr Burnham were the first to be shown up to the daftar; Mr Slade arrived soon afterwards, accompanied by several others. As the celebration got under way, the khidmatgars who were serving the guests kept the rest of the staff informed of what was happening up there: now Mr Burnham was offering a prayer of thanks for the divine guidance that had led their faction to victory; now Sethji was raising a toast to Mr Dent, congratulating him on his leadership.

Vico was the only one to express any reservations: The outcome's not decided yet, he muttered darkly; Mr Dent may have outmanoeuvred Mr King, but the Yum-chae may not be so easy to fool. Patrão knows this: he is raising toasts all right, but I know he's worried.

Towards the end of the evening the khidmatgars reported that the Seth was indeed looking a little strained. This was confirmed at dinner time, when Dent and his cronies left for the Club: despite being entreated to join them Bahram elected to stay at home and went straight to bed.

Down in the kitchen there was plenty of champagne left and a lot of food as well; with the Seth safely tucked away in his bedroom no one had to worry about keeping quiet. Glasses were quaffed and trays emptied and then Vico decided to teach everyone the basics of ballroom dancing: 'Come, munshiji, let me show you a few steps. We will start with waltz.'

Mesto began to beat time on a huge brass dekchi and the others started to clap. Neel's protests were drowned out and he was soon lumbering around the kitchen with Vico, trying to stay in step.

The sight of their cavorting quickly reduced the others to helpless laughter. A pitcher of grog appeared and was quickly emptied and then the others began to join in too—khidmatgars, chowkidars, kitchen-chokras, even the solemn shroffs; soon, except for Mesto, they were all whirling around the kitchen like children at a mela. Then, at a word from Vico, the tempo of the music changed. The new dance, announced the purser, was called a quadrille and under his instructions they formed themselves into two lines. With their arms interlinked, they rushed at each other, with such force that many were knocked down. They lay on the floor, laughing, and marvelling at the thought that something so ridiculous could pass for a dance.

Then, as the laughter faded away, a furious pounding made itself heard. Vico picked himself up off the ground and went to the front door to investigate. When he came back all trace of merriment was gone from his face.

The Chamber has sent a runner, he said. An extraordinary meeting has been called; the Seth is needed there immediately.

The chapel clock had begun to ring as Vico was speaking: it was eleven at night.

A meeting? said Neel. At this time?

Yes, said Vico. It's an emergency—the Co-Hong merchants have just returned from a meeting with Commissioner Lin. They've asked the foreigners to gather together because they have something very important to tell them.

Vico had already started for the staircase, but on reaching it he turned around: Who's on valet-duty tonight? Tell him to come quickly.

The man was more than a little tipsy and water had to be splashed on his face before he could be allowed to go upstairs. A half-hour later, the Seth came sweeping down, in a dark choga: his turban, everyone was glad to note, was properly tied, his clothing impeccable.

It was too late to arrange for a lantern-bearer; instead it was Vico who accompanied the Seth to the Chamber, torch in hand.

Now began a long vigil in the kitchen: it was almost two o'clock when the Seth and Vico returned to the Hong. They went straight up to the Seth's bedroom and another half-hour passed before Vico came down again.

By this time Neel, who had stayed up to work on the *Chrestomathy*, was the only man awake. Vico fetched a bottle of mao-tai liquor and poured out two stiff measures.

So what happened at the meeting?

Vico drained his glass and poured himself another: Munshiji, it seems patrão and his friends celebrated a little too early.

Why?

Munshiji, you would not have believed all the hungama . . .

They had arrived at the Chamber of Commerce to find the main hall all lit up, with people milling about as if it were a public theatre. This was fortunate because Vico was able to watch the proceedings from the back.

Twelve members of the Co-Hong were in attendance, seated in a row. Howqua, Mowqua and Punhyqua were there, of course, but so were several of the younger merchants, amongst them Yetuck, Fontai and Kinqua. They had all brought their servants and linkisters with them and there were dozens of lanterns bobbing over their heads, casting dancing shadows upon the walls. The foreigners were on the dimmer side of the room, some sitting and some standing, their faces looming out of a darkness that seemed barely to yield to the flickering sconces that lined the hall. In the no-man's-land between the two groups stood the translators—a phalanx of linkisters on one side and on the other, the tall, youthful Mr Fearon.

The meeting began with the announcement that the Hongists had come to tell the foreigners about the Yum-chae's response to the Chamber's letter: this being a matter of life and death they had decided to use translators instead of speaking pidgin. The result was that every word had to be filtered through many pairs of lips.

'We took your letter to the High Commissioner and he gave it to his deputy to examine. After it had been read out aloud His Excellency said: "The foreigners are merely trifling with the Co-Hong guild. They should not attempt to do the same with me." Then he declared: "If no opium is delivered up tomorrow, I shall be at the Consoo Hall at ten o'clock and then I will show what I will do."'

What does this mean?

It means, munshiji, that he saw right through Mr Dent's little game: he told the Hongists that if no opium was surrendered by tomorrow morning he would carry out his threat.

Of executions?

So the Hongists said—and to tell you the truth, munshiji, even I, watching from the back of the hall, could see they were not joking. Their hands were shaking; their servants were weeping; some actually fainted and had to be carried away. But still the Chamber was not convinced. Led by Dent and Burnham, they kept arguing, questioning every detail, asking how the Hongists could be sure that they would really be beheaded—as if any sane man could lie about such a thing. Every member of the Co-Hong said yes, yes, if no opium was surrendered by ten o'clock tomorrow two of them would lose their heads. But still the Chamber went on questioning. Back and forth they went until someone came up with a suggestion: instead of giving up all the opium, why not surrender a thousand chests? Maybe that would keep the Yum-chae happy?

Did they all agree to that?

In the end, yes, but they—the foreigners—bargained and bargained as if it were a matter of buying fish at a bazar. They even tried to get the Co-Hong to pay for the surrendered chests: 'Why should we pay?' they demanded to know. 'This is the price of your own heads—you should bear the costs.'

They said that?

More or less.

Vico shook his head in bemusement. See, munshiji, when you're in business, you need to think about your profits, everyone knows that. Sometimes you have to do a little hera-pheri, a little under-the-table business. That's all in the game. Some days you'll make money and on some days you'll also lose a little—that's normal too, for most of us. But these Burnhams and Dents and Lindsays, they don't look at it like that. They've made more money here than anyone can count, and all of it with the help of Howqua, Mowqua and others of the Co-Hong. But now, when it's a matter of life and death for the Hongists, they're still bargaining with a ferocity that would put fishwives to shame. It makes you think, if that's the value they put on their friends' lives, what would you or I be worth?

But wait, said Neel. What about Mr King? Surely he wasn't going along with the rest?

No, said Vico. He was talking about the Chamber's obligations to the Co-Hong, about old friendships and so on—but those weren't the arguments that weighed with the others. It was another man who got them to change their minds—an English translator. He told them that feelings were running very high in the city and there might be a riot if any of the Co-Hong merchants came to harm. That scared them a little and they decided to offer the Commissioner a thousand chests, as a kind of ransom.

Do you think he will accept?

Vico shrugged. We won't know till tomorrow morning. That's when the world will find out if the Hongists are going to keep their heads.

Vico poured himself a shot of mou-tai and held out the bottle. Another one, munshiji?

Neel waved the bottle away: it was very late and he wanted to be up in time to be at the gates of the Consoo House when the Commissioner came. After such a long day it was unlikely that Bahram would rise at his usual hour and even if he did he would not begrudge an absence occasioned by khabar-dari.

Next morning, on stepping out into the Maidan, Neel quickly became aware of a subtle change in atmosphere. Today there was nothing jocular about the shouts of the swarming urchins:

. . . *hak gu lahk dahk, laan lan hoi* . . .
. . . *mo-lo-chaa, diu neih louh mei* . . .
. . . *haak-gwai, faan uk-kei laai hai* . . .

For once even the usual cumshaws had little effect. A snot-nosed gang hung on Neel's heels as he hurried through the Maidan; in their shouts there was nothing playful or teasing, but instead a touch of real venom. At the entrance to Old China Street the boys dropped away. But here, too, Neel sensed something different in the regard of the watching bystanders; there was an anger in their eyes that reminded him of the rioters who had poured into Fanqui-town after the attempted execution.

Halfway down the lane, Neel heard a shout: 'Ah Neel! Ah Neel!'

It was Ahtore, Compton's oldest son: 'Jou-sahn Ah Neel! Bah-bah say come chop-chop.'

'Why?'

Ahtore shrugged. 'Come, Ah Neel. Come.'

'All right.'

On reaching the print-shop Neel was led straight through to the inner part of Compton's house. Even more than before, the courtyard seemed like an oasis of serenity: since Neel's last visit the cherry tree in the centre had burst into bloom and it was as if a fountain of white petals had erupted from a fissure in the paved floor.

Compton was sitting near the tree, under the shade of an overhanging roof; in the chair beside him was the white-bearded scholar he had pointed out on the day of the Commissioner's arrival.

Jou-sahn, Ah Neel, said Compton.

Jou-sahn, Compton.

'Come meet my teacher, Chang Lou-si.'

Both men rose and bowed and Neel reciprocated as best he could.

Compton and Chang Lou-si had been sitting around a low, stone table, drinking tea. Compton now ushered Neel to an empty chair and they spent a few minutes inquiring after each other's health. Then Compton said: 'So-yih, Ah Neel, perhaps you know what happen at the meeting last night?'

Neel nodded. 'Yes, they offered to give up a thousand chests of opium.'

'Jeng; that is right. Early this morning the Co-Hong go to Yum-chae to tell about offer.'

'What happened? Was His Excellency satisfied?'

'No. Yum-chae understand very well what it is—jik-haih foreigners are trying to bargain. They think he can be bought off, like other mandarin before. But Yum-chae cast their offer aside at once.'

'So what will happen then?' said Neel. 'Are Howqua and Mowqua to face execution?'

'No,' said Compton. 'His Excellency understand Co-Hong have gone as far as they can. He understand also that some foreigners do not object to surrender of opium. Only a few make trouble. Now time has come to move against those men—the worst criminals, ones who make most trouble.'

'Who do you mean?'

'Who you think, Ah Neel?'

'Dent? Burnham?'

Compton nodded. 'Jardine gone, so now Dent is the worst. We follow his doings over many years; he smuggle, he bribe; he is the black hand behind everything.'

'So what will be done to him?'

Compton glanced at Chang Lou-si, and then turned back to Neel. 'All this ji-haih for you, Ah Neel. You understand ne? Cannot speak to anyone.'

'Yes. Of course.'

'Dent must answer questions. He will be brought in.'

'What about Burnham?'

'No. Not him. Just one British enough for now la.' He paused. 'But one other man also will be arrested.'

Neel took a sip of his tea: it was a strong pu-er and made his mouth pucker. 'Who?'

Compton exchanged a word with Chang Lou-si before turning back to Neel. 'Listen, Ah Neel: again I say this just to you la? Many people here say that one from Hindusthan must be arrested also. Almost all opium come from there, ne? Without them opium cannot come. They too must be stopped. Best way is to hold up one Hindusthani so others can take warning. Houh-chih with Dent.'

'And who are you thinking of?'

'Can be only one man, ne? Leader of Canton Achhas.'

Neel was surprised to find that his throat had gone dry; he had to take another sip of his tea before he could speak. 'Seth Bahramji?'

Compton nodded. 'Deui-me-jyuh Neel, but he is responsible for do bad things; a lot of information has come out. And dou, he is allied with Dent.'

Neel looked into his cup and tried to think of Seth Bahram being led off to prison with a cangue around his neck, like Punhyqua. He remembered how, at one time, he had been amused by the devotion of the Seth's entourage. It was with a start of surprise that he realized that he too had now come to regard him with a loyalty that bordered on love. It was almost as if the tie of blood between Ah Fatt and his father had become his own, making it impossible for him to sit in judgement upon the Seth. He knew then that if he were to play a part in bringing harm upon Bahram, he would be haunted by it ever afterwards.

'Look,' said Neel, 'it is not surprising that you should think of taking this step. But you should know that even if Seth Bahramji and every other Achha trader were to stop trading opium it would make no difference. The drug may come from India, but the trade is almost entirely in British hands. In the Bengal Presidency, the cultivation of opium is their monopoly: few Achhas play any part in it, apart from the peasants who are made to grow it—and they suffer just as much as the Chinese who buy the drug. In Bombay, the British were not able to set up a monopoly because they were not in control of the entire region. That is why local merchants like Seth Bahramji were able to enter the trade. Their earnings are the only part of this immense commerce that trickles back to Hindusthan—all the rest goes to England and Europe and America. If Bahramji and all the other Bombay Seths stopped trading opium tomorrow, all that would happen is that the drug trade would become another British monopoly. It was not the Achhas who started sending opium to China: it was the

British. Even if every Achha washed his hands of opium, nothing would change in China; the British and Americans would make sure that opium continued to pour in.'

Neel waited for Compton to translate this and then he laid out the argument that he had saved for the last: 'And you know what will happen if you include Seth Bahramji's name with Dent's?'

'What?'

'The Chamber will save Dent by giving up Bahramji instead. Dent will slip out of your grasp.'

'Haih me! Would they do that?'

'I am sure of it. After all, they owe much more to the Co-Hong than to Bahramji. If they are willing to risk the lives of their Hongist friends, why would they not give up the Seth?'

He left the words hanging in the air and sat back to sip his tea. In a while, Compton said: 'Chang Lou-si asks if you and Mr Moddie are from same province? Dihng-hai same clan?'

'No,' said Neel. 'His province and mine are far away—like Manchuria and Kwangtung. We are not even born into the same religion.'

'Cheng-mahn, Neel, can I ask why you are so loyal to him? Gam, what is difference between him and Dent and Burnham?'

'Seth Bahram is not like Dent and Burnham,' said Neel. 'In other circumstances he would have been a pioneer, a genius even. It is his misfortune that he comes from a land where it is impossible even for the very best men to be true to themselves.'

'You mean Hindusthan, Ah Neel?'

'Yes. Hindusthan.'

A look of pity came into Chang Lou-si's eyes when Compton translated this for him. He said something which seemed to be addressed mostly to himself.

'Chang Lou-si says: it is so China does not become another Hindusthan that the Yum-chae must do what he has to do.'

'That is right,' said Neel with a nod. 'That is why I am sitting here with you.'

~

The meeting at the Chamber had ended so late, amidst so much ill-feeling, that Bahram would have had no sleep that night if not for a generous dose of laudanum. Having once drifted off, he slept deeply and awoke just as the chapel clock was striking eleven.

The windows of the bedroom were shuttered and except for the lamp on the altar it was completely dark. Still fuzzy from the laudanum, Bahram wondered whether he had slept right through the day and into the night. Then he saw glimmers of sunlight filtering in through the gaps in the window frames and suddenly the events of the night before came rushing back to him: the arguments and counter-arguments; the broken faces of Howqua and Mowqua, and Dent's warning that giving up a single chest would quickly lead to the surrender of them all; and then he remembered the intervention that had clinched the matter: Mr Thom's prediction that there would be riots if any harm came to Howqua, Mowqua or any other Co-Hong merchant. That was when Wetmore had suggested that the Chamber offer up a thousand chests of opium as ransom for the Hongists' lives.

Like the other tai-pans Bahram had agreed to contribute his fair share of crates—but there was no surety, of course, that Commissioner Lin would accept the offer: not till ten in the morning would it be known whether he was going to carry out his threats.

And now it was eleven, the hour well past: for all he knew Howqua and Mowqua were already dead.

Reaching for the bell-rope, Bahram tugged hard and within minutes a khidmatgar appeared at the door.

Where's Vico? said Bahram.

He went out, Sethji.

And the munshi?

He's in the daftar, Sethji. Waiting for you.

Bahram gestured to the man to step inside. Lay out my clothes, jaldi.

Dressing hurriedly, Bahram crossed the corridor and stepped into the daftar.

Munshiji, did you go to the Consoo House this morning?

Ji, Sethji.

What happened? Did Commissioner Lin announce his verdict?

No, Sethji. I was there till half past ten. Commissioner Lin didn't come to the Consoo House. There was no verdict. Nothing.

Are you sure?

Ji, Sethji, I am sure.

Giddy with relief, Bahram reached for the door jamb to steady himself. If Commissioner Lin hadn't come to the Consoo House, it could only mean that he had accepted the Chamber's offer. A thousand chests was no small thing, after all: even a year earlier that quantity of opium would have fetched three hundred and twenty-five thousand taels—equivalent to about eleven and a half tons of silver bullion, in other words. If Commissioner Lin were only to keep a fraction of it for himself, it would still be enough to provide for generations of his descendants. There was scarcely a man on earth who would not have been tempted.

A great weight seemed to rise off Bahram's shoulders. He looked around the daftar and was glad to see that everything was as it should be: breakfast was on the table and Mesto was waiting with a napkin over his arm. A sense of calm came over him as he seated himself at the table: for once, he felt no desire to know more about the news; all he wanted was to eat his breakfast in peace.

Sethji, shall I read from the *Register*?

No, munshiji, not today. It would be better if you went to find Vico.

Ji, Sethji.

The munshi's voice receded as Bahram ran his eyes over the table. It was clear at a glance that Mesto had made an extra effort that morning: he had evidently done a round of the Maidan's food vendors for Bahram could see char-siu-baau buns, light, fluffy and filled with roast pork, and a few chiu-chau dumplings as well, of the kind he liked best, stuffed with peanuts, garlic, chives, dried shrimp and mushrooms. Mesto had also prepared one of Bahram's Parsi favourites, *kolmi bharelo poro*, an omelette with a filling of stewed tomatoes and succulent prawns.

Bahram tasted it and gave Mesto a smile. Excellent! Almost as good as my mother's!

Mesto grinned with pleasure and pushed the dumplings towards him. Try these, Sethji; they're really fresh.

Bahram ate slowly, lingering over every dish. The better part of an hour passed but neither Vico nor the munshi had returned by the time he finished his meal.

What's taking them so long? Mesto, send a boy to look for them.

Mesto had been gone only a few minutes when Vico and Neel burst in, flushed and out of breath.

Patrão, a paltan of Manchu soldiers has gone to Mr Dent's place! The Weiyuen is with them.

The Weiyuen was the head of the local constabulary, a figure who rarely ventured into Fanqui-town.

Impossible! said Bahram. Why would he go there?

It was the munshi who answered: They've got a warrant for Mr Dent, Sethji. He's been charged with smuggling and many other things.

What other things?

They say he's been spying and trying to foment trouble in the country.

Are they arresting him?

They want to take him into the old city, for questioning.

Bahram frowned as he looked at the munshi. How do you know all this?

Mr Burnham's gomusta told me, Sethji; Mr Burnham's house is in the same hong, the Paoushun. The gomusta-baboo saw it all.

Bahram pushed his chair back and rose to his feet. Have they arrested Dent already? Or is he still there?

He's still there, patrão, said Vico. The other tai-pans are all heading to his place now.

I must go too, said Bahram. Where's my choga and cane?

The Paoushun Hong was only four doors from the Fungtai and it took Bahram just a few minutes to walk over. Stepping through the entrance, he found his way blocked by a detachment of guardsmen, tall soldiers with plumed helmets. Fortunately, one of the Co-Hong's linkisters, Young Tom, was with them; he recognized Bahram and persuaded the soldiers to let him pass.

Dent's lodgings were at the back of the factory compound, overlooking Thirteen Hong Street. To get there, Bahram had to pass through several courtyards: usually abuzz with people, these too were empty—all but the last which led to Dent's lodgings. This one, in marked contrast to the others, was filled with people, almost all of them Chinese; most were squatting dejectedly on the paved floor of the courtyard, under the watchful eyes of a detachment of Manchu soldiers.

As he was pushing his way through, Bahram felt a tug on his sleeve.

'Mr Moddie, Mr Moddie—please help . . . '

Bahram was astonished to recognize Howqua's youngest son, Attock: usually suave and reserved he was now in a state of complete dishevelment, his face streaked with dirt.

'What is happening, Attock?' said Bahram. 'Is your father here also? In Mr Dent's house?'

'Yes. Also Punhyqua. Yum-chae say he cuttee allo head if Mr Dent not go. Please Mr Moddie, please talkee Mr Dent.'

'Of course. I will do all what I can.'

Bahram was at the entrance to Dent's lodgings now; the door was wide open and no one stopped him from stepping inside.

Dent's lodgings, like Bahram's, consisted of a vertical set of rooms, distributed over three floors. As was the custom in Fanqui-town, the storage spaces were on the lowest level. The room that adjoined the entrance was in fact a godown, filled with objects that had accumulated there over a period of several decades. The contents consisted of the usual melange of things that passed through Fanqui-town—tall clocks from Europe, lacquerware, locally made renditions of European furniture and suchlike—except that in this instance they also included a number of other curiosities: stuffed animals, pottery and so on.

Now the dusty, dimly lit godown was crowded with people as well as objects. Seated in the centre, on a dainty Chippendale love-seat, was a glowering, stiff-backed mandarin, with a scroll in one hand and a fan in the other. On one side of him loomed the stuffed head of an enormous rhinoceros; on the other side were Howqua and Punhyqua. The two Hongists were crouched on the floor and both had chains around their necks. Their tunics were so begrimed that they looked as if they had been dragged through miles of dust. Their caps were conspicuously devoid of their buttons of rank.

Bahram could remember a time when mandarins would appear before Howqua and Punhyqua as supplicants: the sight of these two immensely wealthy men crouching beside the Weiyuen, like beggars, was so incomprehensible that he felt compelled to look more closely, to see if they were really who they seemed to be.

Only after several minutes had passed did Bahram realize that Dent, Burnham, Wetmore and several other foreign merchants were on the other side of the room, standing clustered around Mr Fearon. He made his way over and was just in time to hear Burnham say: 'Jurisdiction—that is the principle we must cling to, at all costs. You must explain to the Weiyuen that he does not have jurisdiction over Mr Dent. Or any other British merchant for that matter.'

'I have tried, sir, as you know,' said Mr Fearon patiently. 'And the Weiyuen's response was that he is acting on the authority of the High Commissioner, who has been invested with special powers by the Emperor himself.'

'Well, you must explain to him then,' said Burnham, 'that nobody, not even the Grand Manchu himself, can claim jurisdiction over a subject of the Queen of England.'

'I doubt that he will accept that, sir.'

'But nonetheless, you must make this clear to him, Mr Fearon.'

'Very well.'

As Mr Fearon stepped away, Dent ran a hand over his face. Bahram saw now that he looked pale and ill; his fingernails were bitten to shreds.

'My dear Dent!' said Bahram, extending a hand. 'This is terrible. What do they want of you?'

Dent was evidently too shaken to speak, for it was Burnham who answered. 'They say they want to escort him to the old city, to ask him a few questions. But it is likely that their real intentions are quite different.'

'The rumour,' added Wetmore, 'is that the Commissioner has asked that a cook, specializing in European food, be provided by the Co-Hong.'

'What does it mean?' said Bahram. 'Are they planning to keep Dent? Put him in jail?'

'Perhaps,' said Burnham with a grim smile. 'Or it could be something worse still—maybe they're planning to throw him a Last Supper.'

'Oh please, Benjamin,' said Dent, wringing his hands. 'Must you speak of that?'

'Sir!'

Mr Fearon was back now. 'The Weiyuen says it is clearly stated in the Emperor's decrees that all foreign residents in China must abide by Chinese law.'

'But that has not been the custom,' said Wetmore. 'In Canton, it has always been understood that foreigners would conduct their affairs according to their own laws. Please explain that to the Weiyuen, Mr Fearon.'

'Very well, sir.'

Mr Fearon was hardly gone before he was back. 'The Weiyuen asks that you approach him. He wishes to address you directly.'

'Approach him?' cried Slade indignantly. 'So he may rub in our faces the degradation he has inflicted on Howqua and Punhyqua? Why, it is the most abominable impudence!'

'He insists, sir.'

'We had better go,' said Dent, 'there's no need to provoke him.'

The others followed him across the room and positioned themselves so they could address the Weiyuen without being directly confronted with the two chained Hongists.

'The Weiyuen asks if in your country foreigners are exempted from observing the laws of the land.'

'No,' said Mr Wetmore. 'They are not.'

'Why then should you consider yourselves exempt from Chinese law?'

'Because it has been the custom for the foreign community in Canton to regulate itself.'

'The Weiyuen says: this custom holds only so long as you do not flout the laws of the land. We have given you warning after warning, issued edicts and proclamations, and yet you have continued to bring opium ships to our coast, in defiance of the law. Why then should you not be treated as criminals?'

'Please explain to the Weiyuen,' said Mr Wetmore, 'that as Englishmen and Americans, we enjoy certain freedoms under the laws of our own countries. These require us to be subject, in the first instance, to our own laws.'

This took a while to explain.

'The Weiyuen says he cannot believe that any country would be so barbaric as to allow its merchants the freedom to harm and despoil the people of a foreign realm. This is not freedom—it is akin to piracy. No government could possibly condone it.'

Mr Slade's patience had worn thin by now, and he had begun to tap his cane loudly on the floor. 'Oh for heaven's sake!' he cried. 'Can we not dispense with this mealy-mouthed cant? Please tell him, Mr Fearon, that he will know what freedom means when he sees it coming at him from the barrel of a sixteen-pounder.'

'Oh I cannot say that to him, sir,' said Mr Fearon.

'No, of course not,' said Dent. 'But I do believe Slade has a point. The time has come when we must seek Captain Elliott's intervention.'

Mr King had been listening to this exchange with a wry smile, and he broke in now: 'But Mr Dent! It is you and

Mr Slade who have always wanted to keep Captain Elliott at a distance from Canton. Am I wrong to think that it was you who said that the involvement of a government representative would be a perversion of the laws of Free Trade?'

'This is no longer a matter of trade, Mr King,' said Dent coldly. 'As you can see, it now concerns our persons, our safety.'

'Oh I see!' said Mr King with a laugh. 'The government is to you what God is to agnostics—only to be invoked when your own well-being is at stake!'

'Please, sir,' Mr Fearon broke in. 'The Weiyuen is waiting. What am I to say to him?'

The answer was provided by Mr Wetmore. 'Tell him that it is impossible for us to do anything without consulting with the English Representative, Captain Elliott, who is currently in Macau. Please inform him that we have sent word to him. He will be here soon.'

Absorbed in this exchange, Bahram had become totally oblivious to everything else that was going on around him; he was startled when he heard Zadig's voice in his ear.

Please Bahram-bhai, can I have a word with you?

Yes. Of course.

They retreated to a quiet corner, behind a huge armoire.

There's something I must tell you, Bahram-bhai.

Yes. What is it?

Zadig leant closer. I have it on good authority that your name was also on the arrest warrant.

What warrant? What are you talking about?

The same warrant that has been served on Dent. I have it on good authority that your name was on it this morning. You too were to be arrested. I believe your name was removed just before the Weiyuen set off to fetch Dent.

Bahram's eyes opened wide in disbelief: But why would they want to arrest me? What have I done?

They are evidently well informed about what has been going on at the Chamber. Clearly they know that Dent has been opposing the surrender of the opium. Perhaps they have learnt of your opposition too.

But how could they know? said Bahram. And if they do, then why did they remove my name?

Perhaps they felt the Chamber might give you up in exchange for Dent.

Bahram's voice fell to a whisper. But the Committee would not allow it surely? he said. Would they?

Listen, Bahram-bhai, you are not an American or an Englishman. You don't have any warships behind you. If the Chamber had to surrender you or Dent, who do you think they would pick?

Bahram stared at him: his throat had gone dry but he managed to say: What shall I do then, Zadig Bey? Tell me?

You had better go back to your hong, Bahram-bhai. And maybe you should stay out of sight for a while.

Although not entirely persuaded, Bahram decided to follow Zadig's advice. He slipped away and on the way back he had the distinct impression that the guardsmen were scrutinizing him with special care; while crossing the Maidan his instinct told him he was being watched. Everywhere he looked, eyes seemed to be following him: although he strode along as fast as he could, the two-minute walk seemed to last an hour.

Even the safety of his daftar brought little comfort to Bahram: it was as if the familiar surroundings had become a cage. When he looked out of the window, squads of guardsmen seemed to appear out of nowhere, to return his gaze; when he sat at his desk, he began to wonder what would have happened if his name had remained on the warrant. What if Howqua and Mowqua had come to the Achha Hong, with chains draped around their necks, to beg him to give himself up to the Yum-chae? He could almost hear Dinyar and the other Parsis clicking their tongues and whispering at a safe distance: Poor Shireenbai . . . husband in the chokey . . . just imagine the shame . . .

That night even laudanum failed to have its usual effect: the draught he took was strong enough that he was able to shut his eyes, but the sleep that came from it was neither continuous nor untroubled. At one point he imagined that his *fravashi*, his guardian spirit, was taking leave of him, abandoning him to make his way alone through the rest of his days on earth. He sat up to find the room plunged into a funereal darkness: even the lamp in his altar had gone out. He got groggily out of bed and kept striking matches until the divo lit up again. Barely had he closed his eyes—or so it seemed—when he was visited by another, even more disturbing vision: he saw himself stepping on to the bridge of heaven, *Chinvat-pul*; he saw that his way was barred by the angel of judgement, Meher Davar; he heard himself mouthing the words *Kâm nemon zâm, kuthrâ nemon ayem?*—'To which land shall I turn, where shall I go?'—he saw the angel's hand turning to point to the darkness under the bridge; he saw himself tumbling off the edge, falling into the fathomless chasm below.

He woke to find himself drenched in sweat—yet never had he been so glad to wake from a dream. Reaching for the bell-rope he pulled on it so hard that Vico came running up the stairs.

What's the matter, patrão? What happened?

Vico—I want you to go to the Paoushun Hong. See what you can learn about what's going on with Dent. And take the munshi with you too.

Vico looked at him in surprise. No work today, patrão?

No. I don't feel well; tell them to bring my breakfast to the bedroom.

Yes, patrão.

Through the rest of the morning, Vico and the munshi took it in turns to keep Bahram informed: now the Hongists were at Dent's house; now they were at the Chamber pleading with the members to persuade Dent to give himself up.

'But we do not possess the authority to coerce any of our members,' insisted the Committee.

'What is the purpose of a Chamber then,' responded the Hongists, 'if it has no influence over its members?'

In the early afternoon the munshi reported that he had just seen Zadig Bey—he was accompanying a delegation of translators and mediators; they were on their way to visit the mandarins.

A few hours later, Zadig dropped by himself, looking exhausted but also strangely exhilarated.

What happened? Where did you go? To the Consoo House?

No, said Zadig. We went into the walled city—for the first time ever in my life . . .

They had entered by the Choolan Gate and were taken to the temple of Kuan-yin. They had seated themselves in the first courtyard, in the shade of an immense tree. Soon they were led into the temple's interior, to the courtyard where the priests lived, and there they were served tea, fruit and other refreshments. After a while several senior mandarins arrived, including the treasurer of the province, the salt commissioner, the grain inspector and a judge.

Some of them had hoped, and some had feared, that the Yum-chae would be there too—but such was not the case; only these other officials were present.

They were asked their names, their countries and so on, and then the mandarins said: 'Why doesn't Mr Dent obey the Yum-chae?'

It was Mr Thom, the translator, who spoke for them: 'The foreigners are convinced that Mr Dent would be arrested and detained if he went into the old city.'

It was the judge who answered. He said: 'The High Commissioner's eyes are very sharp and his ears very long. He knows this Dent to be a very rich capitalist. The High Commissioner holds positive orders from the Emperor to put down the opium trade; he wishes to admonish this Dent and also to inquire into the nature of his business. If this Dent does not consent to come before him, he shall be dragged out of his house by force. If he resists he will be killed.'

To this the delegation made no response so the treasurer said: 'Why do you continue to shield this Dent? Is the trade with China not dear to you foreigners?'

'Yes,' answered Mr Thom. 'But Dent's life is still dearer.'

And then, said Zadig, a very strange thing happened, Bahram-bhai. They liked Mr Thom's answer so much they began to clap! Can you believe . . .

Before he could finish, Vico burst in. Patrão—look out of the window!

With Zadig beside him, Bahram went to the window and looked down: a crowd had gathered around the entrance to the British Factory. Visible over the heads of the milling spectators were the turbans of a paltan of sepoys; some of them had guns on their shoulders and the man in the lead was carrying the Union Jack.

'Captain Elliott,' said Zadig. 'It must be him!'

'Oh thank God, thank God,' said Bahram. Closing his eyes, he murmured a prayer of gratitude; for the first time in many days he felt safe; having the British Representative nearby was like being granted a reprieve.

seventeen

March 25, 1839
Markwick's Hotel, Canton

Dearest Puggly, bad news is always hard to convey, but never more so than when one is hard-pressed for time. You will understand then why this letter is doubly difficult: for not only have I to tell you about a *most* unfortunate development, it appears that I must do so with the greatest possible dispatch—for there are signs that something ominous is brewing in Fanqui-town today. I can hear disturbing sounds even as I write—on the roof of this hong, hammers are pounding, feet are running urgently to and fro—these are reminders that I have but little time and must be brief . . .

You will be glad to know that yesterday, under the most trying circumstances, Baburao succeeded in bringing your precious plants safely to Canton. The traffic on the river was all at sixes and sevens, he said, because Captain Elliott, the British Representative, was speeding down to Canton from Macau, trying to stay ahead of the Chinese authorities. Baburao actually saw Captain Elliott go past, at a bend in the river—he was in a swift cutter, rowed by a team of lascars, with a paltan of sepoys for an escort: when approached by mandarin boats, they forced their way past, more or less at gunpoint.

The Captain's haste was occasioned—and this will serve to give you an idea of the Tumult that has seized

Fanqui-town of late—by a rescue mission of sorts: Mr Dent has been asked to appear in person before the Commissioner and is terrified out of his wits! He believes he will be detained and has refused to leave his house; all his cronies have gathered around to support him, fearing that they may be next.

I was told about this yesterday by Charlie King, who was in Mr Dent's lodgings when it happened: it appears the Commissioner has recognized that the foreign merchants would liefer sacrifice the lives of the Co-Hong merchants than part with their opium. As a consequence he has decided to move directly against them: he has stopped issuing travel permits, which means that they cannot run away from Canton; he has also decided to confront the biggest and most unregenerate smuggler of all, Lancelot Dent. This has taken Mr Dent and his allies completely by surprise: evidently, they had assumed that being Europeans they would never be asked to personally answer for their crimes.

Charlie says that Mr Dent's face was quite a sight when the warrant was served on him. Within minutes he became a pathetic shell of a man; his vaunted doctrine of Free Trade was forgotten in a flash, and he lost no time in seeking refuge within the skirts of his government. He and his Free-Trader cronies are full of braggadocio and false conceit, but in fact they are the rankest of cowards—men who would count for nothing if they did not have the British Army and Navy to stand behind them as the guarantor of their profits.

In light of this you will understand, Puggly dear, what a great hubbub was occasioned by Captain Elliott's arrival in Fanqui-town. A huge crowd, of Chinese as well as foreigners, gathered to watch as he went from his cutter to the Consulate where he proceeded to hoist the flag. Then, surrounded by his sepoys, he went off to the Paoushun Hong, from wherein he shortly emerged with poor Mr Dent, who was, by this time, shivering like a leaf.

Under the Captain's protection, he crossed the Maidan and went into the British Factory: this has now become Mr Dent's lair and refuge. Charlie says it is a matter of shame and infamy for Britain that a known criminal should be given the shelter of her flag.

Not long afterwards a meeting of all foreign merchants was called in the British Hong—it was perhaps not my place to attend, but you know how *nosy* I am. I would not have missed it for the world! I went with Zadig Bey—and you cannot imagine, Puggly dear, what a tamasha and goll-maul there was, with foreigners of every stripe jostling for seats! We had to fight our way in.

I wish I could say the Captain's speech lived up to the excitement—but unfortunately it was the usual Burra Sahib stuff: he made no mention at all of the ways in which his government has connived in the smuggling of opium; nor did he speak of the charges levelled against Dent and the other smugglers. He announced instead that he would forthwith demand travel permits for all foreigners; if these were denied, he declared, he would consider it an act of war (does it not put you in mind, Puggly dear, of a dacoit leader marching into a courtroom and demanding the immediate and unconditional release of his gang?). Then—and this was the most alarming part—the Captain urged us all to move our belongings to the English ships that are currently anchored at Whampoa. This led everyone to believe that he would soon order an evacuation—and I am sure you can imagine, Puggly dear, how *upset* I was by that. The prospect of leaving Jacqua, of abandoning the one place on earth that has offered me some small measure of Happiness is, needless to add, utterly *abhorrent* to me . . .

Cast into the deepest melancholy, I was sitting in my room, wondering what to do next when who should arrive but Baburao.

I was very glad of course to learn that your consignment of plants had been safely transported to Canton—but I confess (and I trust you will not think any less of me for this, Puggly dear) that the news could not have come at a less opportune moment. Never had plants been further from my mind: what was I to do with them? How was I to get them to the Pearl River Nursery, without Ah-med's guidance? How could I even be sure that Mr Chan was still in the city? I have seen nothing of either him or Ah-med since my last visit.

And yet, it was clear that if the exchange of plants was to be effected at all it would have to be done at once—for the foreign merchants have now well and truly thrown down the gauntlet, not only refusing to surrender their opium, but declining even to be questioned. It was evident that there would be Consequences.

Baburao was perfectly in agreement with me on this score: the Commissioner was not a man to be lightly defied, he said: he was sure to shut down the river. It was imperative that the exchange be concluded before that happened.

Night had already fallen, so it was too late to set off for Fa-Tee immediately; we agreed instead that we would leave early the next day. So this morning I went down to the river and there, as arranged, was Baburao, in a covered sampan with your six pots carefully stowed in the shade (for it has been *dreadfully* hot here of late). We left at once, and I am glad to say I was not as hapless a guide as I had feared: on approaching Fa-Tee I was able to point out the creek which led, so far as I remembered, to the Pearl River Nursery.

It was only after we had entered the creek that we became aware of something *very* alarming. There were several officious-looking boats positioned ahead of us and the shores were swarming with troops.

You will not be surprised to learn, Puggly dear, that Baburao displayed greater presence of mind than your poor Robin: he pushed me under the sampan's covering and told me to conceal myself amongst the plants. This I proceeded to do with the greatest celerity: I curled up like a kitten and *cowered* between your pots (no easy matter, I might add, Puggly dear, for that nasty Douglas fir of yours did not take kindly to my presence—not for nothing, I discovered, is it said to be armoured with 'needles').

Baburao, in the meanwhile, had kept our sampan on a steady course with the intention of declaring, if asked, that he was merely passing through the creek on the way to some other destination. Sure enough, shortly before the nursery, we were intercepted. Baburao was then questioned at length by an officer. You cannot conceive, Puggly dear, how terrifed I was—and not only was I *palpitating* with fear, I had also to suffer the most extreme discomfort (for your vile little currant bush had somehow succeeded in inserting a leaf into my nose—it was all I could do not to erupt into a paroxysm of sneezes).

But fortunately Baburao's presence of mind did not fail him: I did not of course understand what he said to the officers, but it must have been persuasive for our sampan was allowed to proceed without being searched.

Baburao rowed on, at a steady pace, and as we were drawing abreast of the nursery I found a chink in the boat's bamboo covering and put my eye to it. I should have been prepared by this time for the sight that met my eyes but alas, I was not: what I saw made my blood freeze. Suffice it to say that the citadels had been breached! The gates of the nursery, and the garden beyond, had been battered down, and many of Mr Chan's men were lined up in a row, along the bund, with their hands tied behind their backs—to meet what fate I dare not think.

Of Mr Chan and Ah-med, I saw no sign, but nor did I look too closely, for the sight of that cordon of soldiers had filled my head, I must admit, with horrid imaginings: what if I had been there when it happened? What would have become of me?

Oh I dare not speak of it, Puggly dear—my belly quakes; I fear if I dwell too long on all the dreadful possibilities my trowsers will become a crêperie.

I had suspected for a while that Mr Chan—alias Lynchong, alias Ah Fey—is, let us say, a man of many parts. If this had not deterred me from seeking him out, it was only because of my incorrigible curiosity. I cannot deny that the intriguing story of Mr Chan's life had piqued my interest: it seemed to me exceedingly *peculiar* that a man should love flowers as well as opium—and yet I see now that there is no contradiction in this, for are they not perhaps both a means to a kind of intoxication? Could it not even be said that one might lead inevitably to the other? Certainly there could be no opium without flowers—and of what else do dragon-chasers dream but of gardens of unearthly delight?

Be that as it may, Baburao and I could not but count ourselves singularly fortunate in having so lightly escaped from this little misadventure. On the way back we decided that the plants must be returned to you *at once*, for Baburao doubts that he will be able to keep them alive for long—and we know how precious they are to you and how far they have travelled. So for the nonce, Puggly dear, it may be best to plant them in your island nursery so that they may grow and propagate while awaiting more propitious times. I know this will come as a grievous disappointment to you and Mr Penrose—but it is some consolation, is it not, that the plants have lived to be traded another day? All is not lost yet, Puggly dear: if it seems so then I conjure you to reflect, if you will, on a Chinese aphorism that Jacqua taught me when we were together exploring the Way of the Brush: To gain, you must yield; to grasp, let go; to win, lose . . .

I have carried on at too great a length (as you can see, the shocks of this morning have not cured me of my *chatterbox* habits). Ominous portents have continued to accumulate even during the hour I have spent at my desk. The pounding on the roof has grown louder—Mr Markwick believes the authorities are constructing bridges, to connect the factories to the buildings on the other side of Thirteen

Hong Street. This will allow them better access to the hongs and sentries will be posted on each roof, to keep the enclave under watch . . .

. . . and now, looking up from my desk I see dozens of men fleeing from the hongs. They are all local men—the cleaners and cooks and coolies who worked as servants for the fanquis. They are carrying bundles and bowlas on their heads and running as if from the plague . . .

. . . and now someone is pounding on my door . . . Baburao must have come to the hotel to snatch this letter away . . . not another word . . . here I must end.

~

It was unusually hot that afternoon so Neel and several others were sitting in the coolest room in the house—the empty godown that adjoined the kitchen—when one of the khidmatgars came running in.

Arré, come and see what's happening outside!

Knocking over tumblers of water and sherbet, they jumped to their feet and went racing to the front door. On opening it, they found a stream of Chinese workmen hurrying through the covered corridor, on the far side of the courtyard: they were heading towards the hong's gates, carrying their mats and clothes, pots and pans.

Amongst the foreigners who sojourned regularly in Canton, Bahram was one of the few who travelled with his own entourage of servants. Since it was far cheaper to employ local men, most of the other merchants relied on their compradors to provide them with cooks, cleaners and coolies—it was these men who were now on the move, all of them at the same time. It was as if they had received warning of an impending eruption and were racing to get away.

Jostling for a place in the throng, Neel found himself shoulder to shoulder with one of the coolies who regularly delivered provisions to the Achha Hong. 'Attay! What for all you-fellow walkee chop-chop?'

'Yum-chae have talkee—all China-yan must makee go. Can-na stay.'

They were at the Fungtai Hong's gates now: on stepping into the Maidan, Neel saw that similar streams of coolies and servants were pouring out of all thirteen hongs. Many foreigners had gathered in knots, to watch the spectacle. Neel spotted Baboo Nob Kissin's saffron-clad figure, standing under one of the flagpoles, and went to join him.

What is happening, Nob Kissin Baboo?

Obvious, isn't it? said the gomusta. They are moving out all the natives. The enclave is going to be cut off and isolated from the city.

The exodus of the servants took only half an hour. Shortly after it ended several detachments of the local constabulary entered the Maidan. Some of the policemen fanned out, shouting orders and making announcements. Almost at once the barbers began to fold up their portable sunshades. The food vendors doused their fires and the men who hosted tabletop cricket-fights coaxed their insects back into their cages. While the hawkers and hucksters were packing up their gear, the other denizens of Fanqui-town—the touts and twicers and trolls—were also being rounded up and herded out.

In the meanwhile, on the other side of the Maidan, the river too was astir with activity. Several small flotillas of boats were being brought around to face the factories; when the manoeuvre was completed, it was seen that the vessels had been arranged to form a three-tiered barricade: the first and second rows consisted of tea-barges, each with several dozen men on board; the third row was formed by a string of cargo-lighters: they were moored tightly together, forming a continuous line and leaving no room for even the smallest boat to pass between them. Then, as if to make it doubly clear that escape was not to be contemplated, a detachment of soldiers dragged all the foreign-owned boats out of the water and beached them on the embankment.

See, said Baboo Nob Kissin, see how carefully they have planned it? It is as if they want to make sure that not even a frog or mouse will get away.

Neel suggested a walk and Baboo Nob Kissin joined him in taking a turn around Fanqui-town. They quickly discovered that every thoroughfare that provided access to the enclave had been sealed off: Hog Lane, New China Street and Old China Street were all blocked at the mouth, by pickets; no one could pass through without producing the right chop.

Thirteen Hong Street had become a kind of no-man's-land: the rear entrances of the factories had been bricked up a while ago, and now infantrymen with matchlocks and cartouche-boxes had been stationed along the entire length of the street.

Around sunset, lantern-poles were set up all around the enclave: when the lanterns were lit the Maidan was bathed in an outpouring of light.

The atmosphere in the Achha Hong's kitchen was subdued that evening, and on the Seth's instructions Vico, Mesto and the kitchen-chokras spent a good deal of time compiling a complete inventory of the provisions in the pantry. It was found that there was enough daal, rice, sugar, flour and oil to last for a month, but the drinking water was down to a two-day supply.

What do you think they're planning? said Vico. Do you think they mean to starve us?

The discussion had scarcely begun when a line of coolies appeared at the front door: it turned out they had been sent by the authorities to disburse rations. No. 1 Fungtai Hong received, as its allotment, sixty live chickens, two sheep, four geese, fifteen tubs of drinking water, a tub of sugar, bags of biscuits, sacks of flour, jars of oil and much else.

I don't understand, said Vico, scratching his head. Are they trying to fatten us or starve us?

Outside there was no let-up in the activity: through the night the Maidan resounded to conch-shells, gongs, shouted orders and sudden, unnerving cries of *K'an-ch'o!* and *Tseaou-Ch'o!* as the officers exhorted their men to stay alert. Sleep was difficult that night.

In the morning, after choti-hazri had been served in the kitchen, Neel went again to look at the Maidan: the transformation was startling to behold—it was as if a carnival-site had been transformed overnight into a parade-ground. All the usual denizens were gone and there were armed men everywhere—five hundred of them or more—marching about or standing watchfully under the flags and pennants of their individual units.

The changes continued as the day progressed: around mid-morning a gang of workmen appeared and set up a tent in the middle of the Maidan. This was then occupied by a group of linkisters, led by Old Tom, who was the seniormost member of his profession.

What exactly were they doing there?

Neel was sent to investigate and came back to report that they had been posted there to deal with any inquiries and complaints the foreigners might have. Should any foreigner need to have any washing done, for instance, he had only to bring it to the tent—the linkisters would make sure that it was properly taken care of.

This made the Seth's mouth drop open. They are keeping us prisoners and they are worried about our laundry?

Ji, Sethji. They said they do not want any foreigner to suffer the least discomfort.

A short while later several large armchairs were carried out and placed in the shade of the British Hong's balcony. A number of Co-Hong merchants then trooped into the Maidan and occupied the chairs—there they remained, all day and night, keeping vigil in relays. It was as if they were being made to do penance for their failure to persuade their foreign partners to surrender their contraband.

Now, in ones and twos, a bedraggled little group of travellers came stumbling out into the Maidan: some were European sailors and some were lascars. They had come to Fanqui-town on shore leave the day before: having passed out in the dens of Hog Lane, they had only now awoken to the changed reality of the enclave. Being trapped in Fanqui-town, they were now offering themselves for employment.

Since many of the enclave's merchants had lost their servants, this news caused great excitement in the factories:

seasoned old traders came running half-dressed from the hongs and tripped over each other as they fell upon the mariners. None of the booze-befuddled sailors failed to find employment: in a matter of minutes they were dragged off to the hongs, to serve this master or that.

In the middle of the afternoon when the Maidan was baking in the glare of the sun, Baboo Nob Kissin burst into the Achha Hong with a cry for help: 'Bachao! Emergency! Rescue measures must be immediately implemented!'

'What has happened, Baboo Nob Kissin?'

'Cows! They are suffering from heat-strokes and sun-rashes!'

It turned out that the departure of the enclave's Chinese employees had deprived Fanqui-town's small herd of cows of their caretakers; they were now suffering dreadfully in the midday heat. Their plight had wrung the heart of the cow-loving milkmaid who lurked within Baboo Nob Kissin's bosom: he would not rest until Neel had recruited a team of khidmatgars to help him erect a makeshift shelter of bamboo matting over the cattle-pen.

Towards the end of the day a new militia made its appearance in the Maidan: it had been drafted almost entirely from the corps of men who had worked as servants in the foreign factories. Now they were armed with pikes, lances and staves and were smartly dressed in jackets with red cummerbunds. Every man was carrying a rattan shield; on every head was a sturdy conical hat, inscribed with large Chinese characters.

Neel recognized several of the men. He was taken aback by the change in their demeanour: while working as servants they had been scruffily clothed and subservient in manner; now, attired in their new uniforms, they formed as proud a troop as he had ever seen.

For dinner that night Mesto served up a chicken feast: batter-fried *marghi na farcha* and a savoury *alleti-paleti* made of gizzards; a creamy *marghi na mai vahala* with fine shreds of meat; and crisp frilly cutlets.

Why, it's a burra-khana! said Neel. Is there some reason for it?

Vico nodded: The Seth hasn't left the hong in days, not since he came back from Mr Dent's in such a hurry. Mesto has made some of his favourite Parsi dishes in the hope of rousing him from his gloom.

~

Next morning a notice, addressed to Bahram, was delivered to the Achha Hong by Captain Elliott's personal secretary. It was an urgent summons to a meeting at the Consulate. It could not be ignored so Bahram quickly changed his clothes and made his way to the doorway of the hong.

Although he had not been outside in the last few days, Bahram had observed the activity in the Maidan from his window and had some idea of what to expect—and yet, once at ground level, he realized that the atmosphere of the Maidan had changed even more than he had thought. He had never imagined that a day would come when he would find Fanqui-town empty of swadders and buttoners. Like many other foreigners he had always regarded the enclave's cheap-jacks as something of a nuisance and had often wished them gone—it had not occurred to him that their absence would leave the enclave so much diminished in spirit.

It was true, of course, that it had not been easy to cross the Maidan when it was a-swarm with mumpers and mucksnipes—but to do it now, under the frowning gaze of guardsmen, was more unpleasant by far. What made it worse still was that Bahram knew by sight many of the guards who were now patrolling the enclave with staves and pikes in hand. One, for instance, was a steward from the Club: it was strangely disconcerting to be stared at, as if you were some kind of escaped jailbird, by a man who had just the other day appeared at your elbow with a plate of roast duck. This was, in a way, the most unsettling part of it: it was as if the hidden mechanisms of Canton's economy had suddenly been laid bare for all to see; even the lowliest servants and tradesmen—people who had, in the past, fallen over themselves to please the fanquis—now had a look of judgement and appraisal in their eyes.

Nowhere was the cordon of security tighter than around the British Factory: ever since Dent had entered the Consulate, the whole compound had been kept under close watch, to prevent his escape. The Co-Hong merchants too had stationed themselves there, as if to shame their erstwhile partners into giving up their goods. To reach the entrance, Bahram had to step past their chairs; they nodded stiffly at each other, their faces unsmiling and impassive.

On entering the British Factory, Bahram was met by a detachment of sepoys: they were aware of who he was and one of them led him to the Consulate's library, where the meeting was to be held. This was a large, elegant room with tall shelves of leather-bound books ranged against the walls. At the far end, under a gilded mirror, was a fireplace and above it, a mantelpiece. The room was already full when Bahram arrived: glancing around it, Bahram saw that every member of the Committee was present and many others besides.

Captain Elliott was standing with his back to the mantelpiece, facing the gathering: he was dressed in full naval uniform and cut an imposing, soldierly figure, with a sword at his waist. He knew Bahram by sight and they exchanged nods as Bahram took a seat at the back.

The tip of the Captain's sword now rattled against the fireplace, as if to call the meeting to order. Holding himself stiffly erect, Captain Elliott said: 'Gentlemen, I have invited you here today so that you may be informed of the outcome of my attempts to negotiate with Commissioner Lin. I addressed a letter to the provincial authorities two days ago, asking that travel permits be issued to all of you. I stated also that if this was not done, I would reluctantly be driven to the conclusion that the men and ships of my country had been forcibly detained and would act accordingly. I noted further that the peace between our two countries has been placed in imminent jeopardy by the alarming proceedings of the authorities in Canton. At the same time I assured them also that it was my desire to keep the peace. My letter was duly transmitted to the High Commissioner. I am now in receipt of his reply.'

This roused a murmur of surprise, for all present were aware that the provincial authorities had long refused to communicate directly with the British Representative. Several people asked whether Commissioner Lin had addressed his letter to Captain Elliott himself, departing from past custom. The Captain shook his head and said that the reply had been communicated to him indirectly, by lesser officials, in a letter that quoted the Commissioner at great length.

'I thought,' said Captain Elliott, 'that you should hear at first hand what Commissioner Lin has to say. So I asked my translator, Mr Robert Morrison, to choose a few passages. He has done so and will read them out aloud.'

Yielding the mantel, the Captain went to sit down while the translator rose to face the gathering. He was a stout, sober-looking man in his late twenties: the son of a famous missionary, he had spent most of his life in China and was regarded as an authority on the language and culture of the country.

Now, producing a few sheets of paper, Mr Morrison smoothed them with the back of his hand. 'Gentlemen, these are Commissioner Lin's own words; I have tried to render them to the best of my ability.

'"I, High Commissioner Lin, find that the foreigners have, in their commercial intercourse with this country, long enjoyed gratifying advantages. Yet they have brought opium—that pervading poison—to this land, thus profiting themselves to the injury of others. As High Commissioner I issued an edict promising not to delve into the past but only requiring that the opium already here should be entirely delivered up and that further shipments should be effectually stopped from coming. Three days were prescribed within which to give a reply but none was received. As High Commissioner I had ascertained that the opium brought by Dent was comparatively in large quantity and summoned him to be examined. He too procrastinated for three days and the order was not obeyed. In consequence a temporary embargo was placed on the trade and the issuing of permits to go to Macau was stayed. In reading the letter of the English Superintendent I see no recognition of these circumstances, but only a demand for permits. I would ask: While my commands remain unanswered and my summonses unattended, how can permits be granted? Elliott has come into the territory of the Celestial Court as the English Superintendent. But his country, while itself interdicting the use of opium, has yet permitted the seduction and enticement of the Chinese people. The store-ships have long been anchored in the waters of Kwangtung yet Elliott has been unable to expel them. I would ask then what it is that Elliott superintends?'"

As the reading proceeded, Bahram had the odd impression that he was listening not to the translator, but to some other voice that had taken command of the young man's mouth and lips, a voice that was at once completely reasonable and utterly implacable. Bahram was astounded by this: how could the voice of this remote and distant figure, Lin Tse-hsü, have seized control of this youthful Englishman? Was it possible that some men possessed so great a force of character that they could stamp themselves upon their words such that no matter where they were read, or when, or in what language, their own distinctive tones would always be heard?

Who was this man, this Lin Tse-hsü? What gave him this peculiar power, this authority, this unalloyed certainty?

'"I have now merely to lay on Elliott the responsibility of speedily and securely arranging these matters: the delivery of the opium and the giving of bonds in obedience to my orders. If he can take the opium that is on board the store-ships and at once deliver it up, it will be my duty to give him encouragement. If he has aught to say, and it be not inconsistent with reason, let him make a clear statement of it. But if he speaks not according to reason and imagines, amid the darkness of night, to abscond with his men, it will show the conviction within him that he can have no face to encounter his fellow men. Will he be able to escape the meshes of the vast and wide net of heaven?"'

Here, Mr Morrison lowered his notes in some embarrassment: 'Shall I continue, Captain Elliott?'

Captain Elliott's face had reddened a little but he answered with a nod: 'Yes. Please go on.'

'"It needs to be enjoined upon Elliott that he should come to have a fear of crime and a purpose to repent and amend; that he should give clear commands to all the foreigners to obey the orders, requiring them to speedily deliver up all the opium that is on board their store-ships. Thenceforward all the foreigners will conduct a legitimate trade, rejoicing in the exhaustless gains thereof. But if, assuming a false garb of ignorance, Elliott voluntarily draws troubles upon himself the evil consequences will be of his own working out, and where shall he find a place of repentance afterwards?"'

~

Bahram had shut his eyes and on opening them now he was glad to see that the translator had finished reading and was returning to his seat.

Captain Elliott went again to stand by the mantelpiece. 'Well, gentlemen,' he said in his dry, unemphatic way, 'Commissioner Lin has had his say. There can be no further doubt that he intends to use every possible means to force the surrender of the opium that is currently stored on your ships. He knows very well that it would be impossible for him to seize your cargoes by main force—your ships would have no trouble in beating off an assault by his naval forces. So he intends instead to hold us hostage here until the opium is surrendered. And the truth is there is nothing we can do about it. Escape is clearly impossible: we are surrounded on all sides and under constant surveillance; our boats have been beached so we would not be able to get away even if we were to fight our way down to the river. A failed attempt would lead only to injury and humiliation. Nor at this moment can we contemplate the use of force: we have no warships at our disposal and no troops either. To assemble a suitable expeditionary force will take several months. And even if we did possess the necessary strength, an attack on Canton could not be contemplated at this time because it would place all our lives in jeopardy. Clearly no assault is possible until we are evacuated from this city, and to accomplish that in a manner that ensures the safety and security of all of Her Majesty's subjects is now my principal concern. I need hardly add that it is perfectly clear at this point that we will not be allowed to leave until the Commissioner's demands are met.'

Captain Elliott took a deep breath and ran a finger nervously over his moustache. 'So gentlemen, I am afraid the conclusion is inescapable: you will have to surrender all the opium that is currently stored on your ships.'

There was a stunned silence and then many voices began to speak, all at once.

'It is robbery, sir, plain robbery. It cannot be tolerated!'

'Are you aware, Captain Elliott, that you are speaking of goods worth many millions of dollars?'

'And what is more, they do not even belong to us. You are asking us to steal from our investors!'

Captain Elliott let the voices roll around him for a few minutes. When he broke in it was on a conciliatory note. 'Gentlemen, I do not for a moment dispute the truth of your arguments: that is not at issue here. The question is merely one of securing our release. The Commissioner has set his trap and we are caught in it; there is only one way in which we can escape his clutches and that is by surrendering the opium: there is no other option.'

This only added to the clamour.

'No option? For subjects of the world's most powerful nation?'

'Why, sir, you are a disgrace to your uniform!'

'Are we Frogs that we should throw up our arms in surrender at the first hint of trouble?'

With a grimace of resignation Captain Elliott glanced at Mr Slade who rose at once from his chair. The clamour continued as he went to the fireplace, cane in hand.

Then Mr Slade unloosed a roar: 'Gentlemen! Gentlemen, as you well know, no one is more in sympathy with you than I. But this is an instance when we would do well to recall the words *fallaces sunt rerum species*. We must pay heed to the immortal Seneca; we must look beyond appearances.'

Bahram understood now that Captain Elliott was far cleverer than he had thought: knowing that he commanded little authority in Fanqui-town, he had evidently taken the trouble to recruit some influential voices to speak in his support.

'A moment's reflection will reveal to you, gentlemen,' said Slade, 'that by seizing our property under threat the Commissioner is doing us a great service. For he is thereby offering Lord Palmerston exactly what he needs in order to declare war: a *casus belli*.'

At this, the protests began to fade away and quiet descended on the room.

'I have looked into the matter,' continued Mr Slade, 'and even a brief inquiry reveals several instances where the seizure of property belonging to British subjects has provided the grounds for a declaration of war. It happened after the massacre of Amboyna, in 1622, when the Dutch seized the property of the English residents of that island and subjected them to unspeakable tortures. Extensive reparations were later exacted. Similarly, the government of Spain has also been forced to indemnify British subjects for the seizure of their property on at least one occasion. But let me emphasize: I cite these examples only as precedents, because the history of commerce does not exhibit any instance of so extensive a robbery as is being contemplated now by Commissioner Lin—and that too on a specious plea of morality.'

'But Mr Slade!' The interjection was from Charles King who had risen to his feet. 'You have neglected to mention a crucial difference between these precedents and the case at hand—which is that the property in question here consists of *smuggled goods*. The prohibitions of Chinese law against opium are of nearly forty years' standing and their existence, and steadily increasing severity, is well known to all. Need I remind you, by way of comparison, that British law states that any person found harbouring prohibited goods shall forfeit treble their value? Need I add further that British law also states that any person who is found guilty of the offence of smuggling shall suffer death as a felon?'

'And need *I* remind *you*, Mr King,' said Mr Slade, 'that we are not in Britain but in China? Nothing remotely comparable to the processes of British law obtains here: no proceedings have been brought; no arrests made.'

'Ah! So that then is your objection?' retorted Mr King. 'Because instead of arresting the contrabandists and seizing the prohibited goods by force of arms, the Commissioner has, after repeated warnings, merely demanded their surrender? Because he has treated the owners not as individual felons but as a community in open insubordination against a regular government? But you would do well to note, sir, that the system of collective responsibility lies at the very heart of Chinese processes of law.'

Mr Slade's face had turned colour and his voice rose again to a roar. 'You disgrace yourself sir,' he thundered, 'by comparing English law with the whims of despots! If you, as an American, wish to submit to Manchu tyranny that is your business. But you cannot expect free men such as ourselves to join you in accepting the vagaries of Celestial misrule.'

'But . . .'

Before Mr King could say any more an outcry ripped through the room.

'. . . you've said enough already sir . . .'

'. . . don't even belong here . . .'

'. . . prating Yankee hypocrite . . . !'

Mr King cast a glance around the room and then, pushing back his chair, he quietly exited the room.

'. . . good riddance . . . !'

'. . . grow a long-tail sir, it'd suit you well . . .'

When silence had been restored Mr Dent rose to his feet and went to join Captain Elliott and Mr Slade at the fireplace. Turning to face the room he said: 'I am completely of a mind with Mr Slade: Commissioner Lin's demands amount to a straightforward act of robbery. But as Mr Slade has pointed out, there is a silver lining: if the Commissioner persists in this course he will present Her Majesty's government with an excellent opportunity to avenge the humiliations to which we have been subjected—and that while also placing our commercial relations with China on a sounder footing. What years of attempted negotiations have failed to achieve will be quickly settled by a few gunboats and a small expeditionary force.'

Mr Slade, not to be outdone, thumped his cane on the floor again: 'Let me remind you, gentlemen, of what King William the Fourth said when he sent his commissioners to the Canadas: "Remember, the Canadas must not be lost!" Needless to add that the British trade with China is of vastly greater commercial importance to Britain than the Canadas. It reaps an annual revenue of five million pounds and involves the most vital interests of the mercantile, manufacturing, shipping and maritime interests of the United Kingdom. It affects, in an eminent degree, the territorial revenue of our Indian empire. It must not be lost by any wavering imbecility in meeting the present difficulties.'

Now, seeing the tide turn in his favour, Captain Elliott permitted himself a smile: 'It will not be lost, gentlemen, I can assure you of that.'

Mr Dent nodded: 'If it comes to a passage of arms, as it surely will, no one who has any familiarity with the state of China's defences can doubt that our forces will prevail. Nor can there be any doubt that once the outcome is decided the British government will ensure that we are repaid for our losses, and at rates that are to our advantage.' Now, steepling his fingertips, Dent looked around the library. 'We are all businessmen here, so I need hardly explain to you the implications of this. In effect we will not be giving up our cargoes to Commissioner Lin.' Here he paused to flash a smile at his listeners: 'No, we will be extending him a loan—one that will be repaid at a rate of interest that will serve both as a punishment for his arrogance and a reward for our patience.'

Glancing around the room Bahram saw that many heads were nodding in agreement. He realized suddenly that he was alone in being utterly dismayed by this turn of events. His alarm grew deeper when not a single voice was raised in protest, even when Captain Elliott rose to his feet to say: 'I take it there are no further objections?'

To speak in public, in English, was not something Bahram had ever liked to do, but he could not stifle the cry that now burst from his throat. 'Yes, Captain Elliott! I object.'

Captain Elliott's face hardened as he turned to look in his direction. 'I beg your pardon?' he said with a raised eyebrow.

'You cannot give in, Captain Elliott!' cried Bahram. 'Please—you must stand fast. Surely you can see, no? If you give in now, this man will win—this Commissioner. He will win without harming a hair on our heads, without touching a weapon. He will win just by writing these things'—Bahram pointed at the papers in the translator's hands—'he will win by writing these, what do you call them? Hookums? Chitties? Letters?'

Captain Elliott's face creased into a smile. 'I assure you, Mr Moddie, the Commissioner's victory will be short-lived. As a naval officer I can tell you that battles are not won by letter-writers.'

'And still he has won, hasn't he?' said Bahram. 'At least this battle is his, is it not?' He had no other words in which to express his desolation, his sense of betrayal. He could not bear to look at Captain Elliott any more: how could he ever have imagined that this man would somehow conjure up an outcome that was favourable to himself?

Mr Burnham had swivelled around in his chair, and he broke in with a broad smile.

'But Mr Moddie, don't you see? The Commissioner's victory—if such it is—will be purely illusory. We will get back everything we give up, and more. Our investors stand to make handsome profits. It is just a matter of waiting.'

‘That is just it,’ said Bahram. ‘How long will we have to wait?’

Captain Elliott scratched his chin. ‘Perhaps two years. Maybe three.’

‘Two or three years!’

Bahram remembered the angry letters that had been accumulating in his office; he tried to think of how he would explain the circumstances to his investors; he thought of the reactions of his brothers-in-law when the news reached them; he could almost hear them exulting, in their discreet way; he could imagine what they would say to Shireenbai: We warned you; he's a speculator, you shouldn't have let him squander your inheritance . . .

‘Surely your investors would wait, Mr Moddie, would they not?’ Burnham insisted. ‘It is just a question of a little time after all.’

Time!

Every man in the room was looking in Bahram's direction now. He was too proud to tell them that time was the one thing he did not have; that a delay of two years would mean certain default; that for him the results of Captain Elliott's betrayal would be ruin, bankruptcy and debtor's prison.

None of this could be said, not here, not now. Somehow Bahram managed to summon a smile. ‘Yes,’ he said. ‘Of course. My investors will wait.’

The heads nodded and turned away. Once freed of their scrutiny Bahram tried to sit still, but it was impossible—his limbs would not obey him. Gathering the skirts of his angarkha together, he slipped noiselessly out of the library. With his head down he walked blindly through the Consulate's corridors and out of the compound. He passed the Co-Hong merchants without sparing them a glance and was halfway across the Maidan when he heard Zadig's voice behind him: Bahram-bhai! Bahram-bhai!

He stopped. Yes, Zadig Bey?

Bahram-bhai, said Zadig breathlessly. Is it true that Captain Elliott has asked everyone to surrender their opium?

Yes.

And they have agreed to do it?

Yes. They have.

So what will you do, Bahram-bhai?

What can I do, Zadig Bey? Tears had come to his eyes now, and he brushed them away. I will surrender my cargo, like everyone else.

Zadig took hold of his arm and they began to walk towards the river.

It is only money, Bahram-bhai. Soon you will recover your losses.

The money is the least of it, Zadig Bey.

What is it then?

Bahram could not speak; he had to stop and choke back a sob.

Zadig Bey, he said in a whisper, I gave my soul to Ahriman . . . and it was all for nothing. Nothing.

~

'Ah Neel! Ah Neel!'

Neel was crossing the Maidan when Young Tom called out to him from the linkisters' tent: 'Ah Neel, have got message for you, from Compton. He say tomorrow you come Old China Street, at noon. He meet there.'

'At the barricade?'

'Yes. At barricade.'

'All right.'

The next day, at the appointed time, Neel made his way to Old China Street. The barricade at the far end was a formidable-looking affair, and looked all the more so because the street was deserted and all the shops were shut: it was made of sharpened bamboo staves and the soldiers who were deployed around it were armed with matchlocks and cutlasses.

Neel's steps slowed involuntarily as he walked up to the picket: on the far side, on Thirteen Hong Street, a large crowd of curious onlookers had gathered. The spectators were packed closely together and Neel would not have caught sight of Compton if he hadn't held up a hand to wave: 'Hei! Neel! Ah Neel! Here!'

Compton was carrying a wooden chop, with a row of characters painted on it. When this was presented to the officer on duty, the barricade parted and Neel was allowed to go through.

After he had stepped across, Neel said: 'What's this, Compton? How is it that I was allowed to pass?'

'Something important. Gam you will see.'

They stepped into the print-shop and Compton opened a locked cabinet. Taking out a sheet of paper, he handed it to Neel. 'Here, Ah Neel; look at this.'

It was a list of eighteen names, each with a number beside it: the lettering was in Chinese, but there were annotations alongside each entry, in English. Neel saw at a glance that the names were those of Canton's leading foreign merchants.

'What do the numbers mean, Compton?'

'This how much opium they say have on their ships. You think is true ah?'

The first name was that of Lancelot Dent; his declared stock was by far the largest, numbering over six thousand crates. The second name was Bahram's and the figure beside it was 2,670 chests.

Seeing Neel hesitate, Compton said: 'Cheng-mahn, Ah Neel, you must be honest. Is this all opium he has got on his ship?'

'I can only guess,' said Neel, 'for I don't know the details. But my feeling is that the figure is right. I heard our purser say once that the Seth lost a little more than a tenth of his cargo in storm damage. Another time he mentioned that over three hundred crates had been lost. So if you work it out, the tally would be right.'

Compton nodded. 'It is a big loss for him—almost a million silver taels, cha-mh-do.'

'Really?' Neel gasped. 'As much as that?'

'Hai-bo! Big loss.' Compton tapped the sheet of paper. 'And what about others? Wa me ji—anyone else?'

Only one other name on the list was of interest to Neel: B. Burnham. The figure listed beside the name was relatively small: 1,000.

Neel smiled, exulting inwardly: here at last was an opportunity to exact a small measure of revenge for all he had suffered at the hands of Mr Burnham. 'This number is wrong,' he said.

'Dim-gaai? How you know that, Ah Neel?'

'Because Mr Burnham's accountant is my friend. He told me Mr Burnham's stock this year is bigger even than Seth Bahramji's.'

'Really?'

'Yes. I'm sure of it.'

'Dak! I will see that the Commissioner knows.'

~

As the days passed, sleep became harder and harder for Bahram. No matter how carefully the khidmatgars closed the shutters, the bright lights in the Maidan somehow filtered through, throwing shadows across his bedroom. When patrolling soldiers or guardsmen trooped past the Fungtai Hong, their ghostly reflections would flicker over his ceiling and his walls. Their voices too were impossible to shut out: even with the windows closed, the echoes of their cries and commands would waft through the room.

Every few hours Bahram would wake to the din of gongs and cymbals and lie still, watching ghostly shadows and listening to voices. Sometimes, the sounds seemed very close: he would hear footsteps in the corridors and whispers around his bed: there were moments when he found it hard not to reach for the bell-rope. But Vico was away now—he had gone to the *Anahita*, to arrange the transfer of her cargo to the Bogue, where the collection depot had been set up—and other than him there was no one that he could have talked to.

Even laudanum didn't help: if anything it made the sounds seem louder and the dreams more vivid. One night, after a copious dose, he dreamt that Chi-mei had come to the Achha

Hong to see him. This was something she had often threatened to do: it happened all the time, she said; flower-girls were often smuggled into factories. They dressed up in men's gowns and braided their hair and no one was any the wiser.

In Bahram's dream, it was a day like any other in Fanquitown: he was dressing to go the Club, in the evening, when Vico came into his bedroom.

Patrão, a Chinese gentleman has come to see you. One Li Sin-saang.

Who is he? Do I know him?

I don't know, patrão. I don't think he's been here before. But he said it was important.

All right then, show him into the daftar.

The daftar was empty, of course, at that time of day: the munshi was down in his cubicle and the khidmatgars had finished cleaning up. Bahram went to one of the big armchairs and sat down. Soon the door opened and a short, slight figure in a round cap and panelled gown came in.

The light in the daftar wasn't bright enough to illuminate the face, so Bahram did not recognize her immediately. With a formal bow, he said: 'Chin-chin Li Sin-saang.'

She said nothing until she was sure Vico was gone. Then she burst into peals of laughter. 'Mister Barry too muchi foolo.'

He was thunderstruck. 'Chi-mei? What-for come this-place? Chi-mei have done too muchi bad thing.'

Chi-mei paid no attention: picking up a lamp, she went around the daftar examining the objects that had accumulated in it. It was clear from her expression that not many of them met with her approval.

'Allo olo thing. What-for Mister Barry puttee here?'

The tone was comforting in its familiarity: she often spoke to him like this, in a register that was at once querulous and indulgent, as though she were trying to correct a child. He laughed.

The only object that seemed to please her was his desk, with its many locked drawers. She looked it over carefully, then tapped one of the drawers. 'What thing have got inside?'

Bahram pulled out a bunch of keys and opened the drawer. Inside was a large lacquered box.

'That box Chi-mei give Mister Barry, no?'

'Yes, Chi-mei have give that-thing.'

'What-for Mister Barry keepee here? No likee?'

'Likee. Likee.'

She lost interest in the desk and looked around the room again. 'What-place Mister Barry sleepee?' she said. 'Here bed no have got.'

'Sleepee bedroom,' he said, pointing involuntarily. 'But Chi-mei can-na go.'

Ignoring him she opened the door and crossed the corridor. He followed her into the bedroom, haplessly protesting. She paid him no mind: on seeing the bed, with its silken cover, she lay down and unbuttoned the fastenings of her gown. The sight of her breasts, emerging slowly from within the gown, mesmerized him. He went to lie beside her, but when he reached for her she changed her mind.

'Mister Barry bed no good. More better go boat. Come now, Mister Barry. We go boat. Come riverside. Ha-loy!'

'Why?' he said. 'Chi-mei here now. More better stay.'

'No,' she insisted. 'Time to go river now. Come, Mister Barry. Here no good.'

He was sorely tempted but something held him back. 'No. Not time now. Can-na go.' He reached for her hand. 'Stay here, Chi-mei; stay with Mister Barry.'

There was no answer and when he looked towards the window, she was gone: the shutters were open and the curtains were fluttering in the breeze.

He woke up in a sweat and found that the window had indeed blown open. He got out of bed and pushed it hurriedly shut.

He was shaking; to go back to bed was impossible in this state. He lit a candle, found his key-ring and carried it into the daftar. He went to his desk and unlocked the drawer: sure enough, the lacquer box that Chi-mei had given him was lying within, covered in dust. He took it out and wiped the dust away before removing the lid. Inside was a finely carved ivory pipe, a metal needle, and a small octagonal box, also made of ivory. The box was empty but Bahram remembered that at the start of the season Vico had brought him a container of prepared opium, as a sample: it was locked in another drawer. He found the key and opened the drawer: the container was still there.

He gathered everything up in his arms and went to his room. He placed the candle on his bedside table, opened the container and scooped up a droplet of the brown paste with the tip of the needle. Then he roasted the opium over the flame, and when it began to sizzle he placed it in the bowl of his pipe and took a deep draught.

When the last wisp of smoke was gone he blew out the candle and lay back against his pillows. He knew he would sleep well that night; he could not understand why he hadn't thought of doing this before.

The next day when he woke, it was well past the usual time. He could hear the khidmatgars conferring outside his door in hushed, worried voices. Rising quickly from the bed, he hid the pipe, the lacquered box and the container of opium inside one of his trunks. Then, opening the windows, he let the room air out for a couple of minutes before letting the khidmatgars in.

One of them said: Sethji, Mesto is in the daftar. He has served your hazri.

The thought of food made Bahram faintly nauseous. I'm not hungry, he said. Tell Mesto to take it away. All I want is chai.

Sethji, the munshi wanted to know if you have any work for him today. He said there were some letters to be answered.

No. Bahram shook his head. Tell the munshi there's no work for him today.

Ji, Sethji.

Bahram spent most of the morning in a chair by the window, looking in the direction of the river, gazing at the spot where Chi-mei's boat had once been moored.

Around midday some lascars came to the Maidan and put on a display of acrobatics, climbing up the flagpoles and doing tricks on top. The spectacle pleased Bahram and he thought of asking the shroffs to give the fellows some bakshish on his behalf. But to get up and pull the bell-rope was too much of an effort and he forgot about it. In the afternoon it was very hot and he decided to take a siesta—but when he went to lie down, it occurred to him that he would rest better after a pipe. So he fetched the paraphernalia and smoked a little before stretching himself out on his bed.

He had never felt so peaceful.

The days and nights began to melt into each other, and sometimes, when the chimes from the chapel came to his ears, it amazed him to think that this bell had once ruled his life.

One day a khidmatgar announced that Zadig had come to see him. Bahram did not much feel like making conversation, but there was nothing to be done for Zadig had already been shown up to the daftar. He changed his clothes and washed his face before crossing the corridor. But despite all that Zadig seemed to be shocked by his appearance.

Bahram-bhai! What has happened to you? You've become so thin.

Me? Bahram looked down at himself. Really? But I've been eating so much!

This was not a falsehood: nowadays a couple of mouthfuls were enough to make him feel that he was stuffed to bursting.

And you're so pale, Bahram-bhai. Your khidmatgars tell me you hardly ever leave your rooms. Why don't you go out more often, take a few turns around the Maidan?

Bahram was nonplussed by this. Go outside? But why? It's so hot out there. It's much better here, isn't it?

Bahram-bhai, there's always something interesting happening in the Maidan.

The daftar's window was open and turning towards it now Bahram heard a sound like that of something solid being hit by a plank of wood. He rose and went to the window. A game of cricket was under way in the Maidan: he saw to his surprise that there were several Parsis among the players. The batsman was Dinyar Ferdoonjee, dressed in white trousers and cap.

Zadig had come to stand beside him: Where did Dinyar learn to play cricket?

Here. I can't think where else he could have learnt.

See, Bahram-bhai. There's always something going on down there. You should step out and join in. It will be a change.

The thought of going out filled Bahram with a sense of deep fatigue.

What does it have to do with me, Zadig Bey? he said. I know nothing about cricket.

But still . . .

They watched for a while in silence, and then Bahram said: We're old men now, aren't we, Zadig Bey? It's these fellows who are the future—young men like Dinyar.

Down below there was a burst of applause: Dinyar had hit a ball all the way across the Maidan.

The boy looked splendidly self-confident, absolutely masterful as he leant on his bat and surveyed the field.

Bahram could not help feeling a twinge of envy.

When they make their future, do you think they will remember us, Zadig Bey? Do you think they will remember what we went through? Will they remember that it was the money we made here, the lessons we learnt and the things we saw that made it all possible? Will they remember that their future was bought at the price of millions of Chinese lives?

Down below Dinyar was running furiously between the wickets.

And what was it all for, Zadig Bey? Was it just for this: so that these fellows could speak English, and wear hats and trousers, and play cricket?

Bahram pulled the window shut, and the sounds faded away.

Perhaps that is what Ahriman's kingdom is, isn't it, Zadig Bey? An unending tamasha in a desert of forgetting and emptiness.

eighteen

~

June 5, House No. 1, American Hong, Canton

Queridísima Puggliosa, I feel as if an *epoch* had passed since I last sat down to write to you. During these last six weeks it was impossible for us even to *think* of corresponding with the outside world—we were warned that any courier who was caught carrying letters for us would be severely punished and under the circumstances it seemed *wrong* to write letters. Only a most *unfeeling* person would want anyone to risk the bastinado for the sake of their silly ramblings, wouldn't they, Puggly dear?

But that is all in the past now. Most of the opium has been rendered up and the Commissioner, in turn, has kept his word: from tomorrow onwards everyone who wishes to leave Canton will be allowed to do so—excepting only the sixteen foreigners who are considered the worst offenders. Zadig Bey will be leaving in a day or two and since I have elected to stay behind he has offered to carry my letters—so here I am, once again at my desk.

So much has happened in the interim, Puggly dear, that I do not quite know where to start. For me the greatest change was that I had to move out of Mr Markwick's hotel. On the day I last wrote to you, Fanqui-town lost all its workers, coolies and servants—every Chinese employed in the enclave was told to depart by the authorities. After that it became impossible for poor Mr Markwick to carry on and he decided to close down.

You can imagine the spot this put me in: I could not think where I would go. But I need not have worried: Charlie came to see me and offered me a room in his house (is he not the kindest man in existence?). I thought I should pay rent, but he would not hear of it and asked only that I make him some paintings, which I gladly undertook to do. Since then I have been installed in the American Hong, in a room twice as large and far more luxurious than the one I had before: and nor am I deprived of the view that I had at Markwick's, for here too I have a window that looks out on the Maidan! I have indeed been singularly fortunate: I miss Jacqua terribly, of course, but I do see him from time to time, across the barricades, and sometimes, when it is possible, he sends me things with one of the linkisters—jujubes and candied fruits. And to be living with Charlie is compensation of no small order: our time together has passed so agreeably that I am loath to see it end.

You have no doubt heard rumours about the privations we have had to endure during the last few weeks. You must not believe a *word* of it, Puggly dear. We have been lavishly supplied with food and drink—the lack of servants is the worst of the hardships we have had to suffer, and if you ask me, this has been in truth a most *salutary* thing. I can scarcely tell you how much pleasure it gives me to walk around the enclave and see these fanqui merchants, who have all grown rich and lazy on the fruits of their crimes, having to swab their own floors, make their own beds, boil eggs &c. &c. It is perhaps the only justice they will ever meet with.

You would not believe how *helpless*, indeed desperate, some of them are: why, just the other day, a fat old fellow came waddling after me in his sleeping gown and positively *begged* me to become his footman. Why no, sir, said I, drawing myself to my full height. I am the King's man and would not dream of serving anyone else.

I find endless amusement in watching the scenes that pass between the fanquis and the linkisters (who take it in turns to sit under a tent in the Maidan, right opposite my window). The linkisters have been instructed to address all our complaints and inquiries, and they are beset by fanquis at all times of day and night: Mr A. has dirtied his shirt and wants it to be sent to the dhobi; Mr B. is enraged because he has not received his daily ration of spring water; Mr C. has split his pantaloons while sweeping the floor and will not rest until the rent is sewn up by a tailor; Mr D. demands a basket of oranges and Mr E. swears that his rooms have been invaded by rats, and all his foodstuffs have been carried away, so he must *instantly* be given three hams and five loaves of bread. Now Mr F. arrives, in a great sweat, and declares he has seen a calf wandering through his corridor; he promises that if it happens again he will let fly with his blunderbuss, consequences be d——d; then comes Mr G. to complain of being insulted by a company of guardsmen; he swears that if the offenders are not suitably chastised he will annihilate them all with his whangee. To all this the linkisters listen with infinite patience, only breaking in to say from time to time: 'Hae yaw? How can do so? Mandarin too muchi angry, make big-big bobbery . . .' They are the most good-natured of fellows and do their utmost to hide their amusement.

One of the few merchants whose establishment has remained intact through this time is Mr Bahram Moddie, the Seth from Bombay (he travels in his own ship and is thus able to take his staff wherever he goes). Mr Moddie has been one of the greatest losers in the surrendering of opium (more than a tenth of all the chests are said to be his), and he is so downcast that he seldom emerges from his private quarters—even Zadig Bey, who is one of his oldest friends, hardly ever sees him any more.

But Mr Moddie's staff are a lively bunch, and through these last few weeks they have held a kind of open house, welcoming everyone who wants to eat at their table. I cannot tell you what a *boon* this has been to me, Puggly dear, for they have a peerless khansama and the food is unfailingly excellent—not till I ate at their table did I realize how much I miss my dholl and karibat!

The company too is most congenial: Mr Moddie's purser goes by the name of Vico and he is a jolly kind of fellow, always thinking of amusing ways to 'time-pass' (he has been away lately, supervising the transfer of Mr Moddie's opium to the authorities, and is much missed). Mr Moddie's munshi is an intriguing, rather mysterious man: he is a Bengali and claims to be from Tippera—but his Bangla accent speaks of a pure-bred Calcuttan, although he will not on any account admit this. (Speaking of Calcuttans I happened to mention to him that a Calcutta-born Miss, by the name of Paulette Lambert, was in the vicinity—and I swear, my dear Ranee of Pugglipur, that your name could not have been unknown to him. At the sound of it he turned quite *pale*, or at least as pale as his complexion would allow!)

Amongst those who frequent Mr Moddie's kitchen there are several Parsis and one of them is a most *fetching* young man by the name of Dinyar Ferdoonjee. We were thinking one night of things we might do to keep ourselves entertained and it occurred to me to suggest that we stage a play—and before we knew it, there we were, putting on 'Anarkali: The Doomed Nautch-Girl of Lahore' (as you may know, Puggly dear, this was my mother's favourite role, and I have always dreamt of playing it).

I wish I could tell you, my sweet chérie, how much *fun* we had! I made all my own costumes and the munshi took the role of the cruel old Emperor and played it exceedingly well (I must say, for a mofussil munshi he is rather well-informed about courtly etiquette). And Dinyar made a most splendid Jahangir, a perfect foil for my Anarkali: he is an excellent singer and dancer so I put in a couple of new songs, which we sang while chasing each other around a tree (it was just a pillar, of course). Such a grand old time did we have that Dinyar says that when he gets back to Bombay he will start a theatre company!

Dinyar is indeed a *whirlwind* of energy. One day he saw some Englishmen playing cricket in the Maidan and succeeded in persuading them to teach him this game (he says he has seen it being played by the British in Bombay, but it is impossible for a native to learn it there, since they are not allowed into the right clubs). Dinyar has become so proficient at the game that he has now taught it to several other Achhas and a week or two ago they actually challenged the British Hong to a match. But at the last minute they found themselves a man short—and you may not believe it, my dear Pug-wugs, but it was none other than your poor Robin who was dragooned into making up the deficit!

I need hardly tell you, Puggly dear, that I *loathe* most games and none more than cricket. But I could hardly refuse my Jahangir, especially when he put his arms around me and cajoled me in the most *beseeching* tones. He promised besides that he would keep me out of harm's way and for the most part it passed off quite peacefully: for the life of me I don't know how people can abide this game—nothing ever seems to *happen* (the Chinese guardsmen, I might add, were astonished by the goings-on and some of them even asked if we were being *paid* to run after the balls—they could not conceive of why else we would, which speaks rather well for them I think). But there came a moment when I heard everyone shouting 'Catch, Robin, catch!' I looked up at the sky and what should I see but a nasty little ball absolutely *hurtling* in my direction. My first thought was to run away of course, but I couldn't very well do that since I had my back to the cattle-pen. So I stood my ground and did what Jacqua had taught me to do—I emptied my mind of everything but the object of my desire . . . and lo! I managed somehow to snatch the vile little projectile out of the air! It was apparently a great thing to have done for it was the other side's leading batsman who had struck it—so to me went the credit of seizing not just his ball but also his wicket, thereby bringing victory to the

Achhas. Dinyar was hugely chuffed and has sworn that he will set up a cricket club for natives when he returns to Bombay—and I do hope he does. Can you imagine, my dear Puggly, how very *funny* it would be to watch bands of Achhas racing around in the hot sun in pursuit of each other's balls and wickets?

But you must not think, Puggly dear, that all my time has been spent on *frivolities*—it could scarcely be so when one is living under the roof of so high-minded a person as Charlie King! He would be mortified to hear me say so (for he is the most modest of men) but I am convinced that he is indeed a *great* man—for it does take greatness, I think, to stand resolutely against your own people, especially when you are alone, and especially when you know that even history will not be kind to you, since you will have forever given the lie to all the claims with which the High and the Mighty will try to exonerate themselves.

Oddly enough, I do believe that the only person who truly appreciates Charlie's courage and honesty is the High Commissioner. But perhaps it is not surprising that this should be so—for I suspect Commissioner Lin is in a position not dissimilar to Charlie's. His measures have not been universally popular, even among the Chinese, and I am told that he has made legions of enemies for himself. There are a great many people in this province who have grown rich on opium and I am sure they must *revile* the Commissioner just as so many of the fanquis revile Charlie. This perhaps is the bond between them: in a world where corruption and greed are the rule, they are both incorruptible—and it is not surprising that this should be hateful in the eyes of their peers.

Whatever the reason, there can be no doubt that there is indeed a bond between Commissioner Lin and Charlie. The Commissioner has even issued a public commendation to Charlie and it was for a while posted all around Fanqui-town (you can imagine the effect of this on Mr Dent and his ilk!).

When the destruction of the surrendered opium started, a few days ago, Charlie was one of the few foreigners who was present at the event. He described the scene to me in the most vivid detail and I was so taken with it that I have resolved to make a painting of it—I have already made a few sketches and Charlie tells me they are perfectly accurate!

The scene is set in a small village, not far from the Bogue. It is a flat, marshy place, intercut with creeks and surrounded by rice paddies. A field has been marked out, and trenches have been dug; the crates are stacked nearby as they arrive. The Commissioner is determined to prevent pilferage so the perimeter is guarded day and night and everyone who works there is searched, before they enter and when they leave.

Day by day the stocks of opium accumulate: the crates rise by the hundred until they reach a total of twenty thousand three hundred and eighty-one. Their combined value is almost beyond human imagining: Zadig Bey says that to buy it you would need hundreds of *tons* of silver! (Can you conceive of that, Puggly dear—a hillock of silver? And all this opium was intended for sale in a single season: does it not make the mind *boggle*?)

But there it is, this great haul of opium, and the day comes for Commissioner Lin to set in motion the process of its destruction. And on the eve of the ceremony, what does the Commissioner elect to do? Why, he sits down to write a *poem*—it is a prayer addressed to the God of the Sea asking that all the animals of the water be protected from the poison that will soon be pouring in.

When the time is right he goes to sit in the shade of a raised pavilion. From there he gives the signal for the work to start. The chests are opened, balls of opium are broken up and mixed with salt and lime and then thrown into the water-filled trenches; when the opium melts the sluices are opened and the opium is allowed to drain into the river. It is hard work: five hundred men, working long hours, can destroy only about three hundred chests a day.

Such was the scene that met Charlie's eyes when he went to the place. The Commissioner was seated in his pavilion and presently Charlie was taken there to meet him. This was the first time Charlie had been face-to-face with him and he was startled to find that the Commissioner was not at all the man his enemies had portrayed him to be: his manner was lively to the point of being vivacious, Charlie said, and he looked young for his age; he was short and rather stout, with a smooth full face, a thin black beard and sharp, black eyes. After exchanging a few pleasantries, the Commissioner asked Charlie who, amongst the Co-Hong merchants, he considered the most honest. When Charlie was unable to produce an immediate answer he burst into *peals* of laughter!

Is it not a most wonderful tableau, my dearest Puggly? I am of a mind to call it: 'Commissioner Lin and the River of Opium'.

Charlie was in transports of delight to see the drug being transformed, as he said, into heaps of ashes instead of kindling the fires of lust and frenzy in the brothels of a hundred cities. But his joy is tinged with a terrible sadness for he knows that the Commissioner's victory will not be long-lived: already several English and American battleships are on their way to China, and there can be little doubt of what the outcome will be if it comes to war. Charlie is so worried that he has written a long letter, addressed to Captain Elliott. It is, in my eyes, a most marvellous piece of writing, and being the inveterate copyist that I am, I could not refrain from noting down a few passages (I will slip them in with this letter when I send it off).

Charlie is often terribly downcast when he thinks of what lies ahead for he thinks that a great cataclysm is coming. Whether that is true or not I do not know—and nor, honestly, do I care. I am persuaded that this is a moment that should be savoured and celebrated. For it is a rare thing in this world, is it not, Puggly dear, when a couple of good men prevail against the forces arrayed against them?

As always, my dear Puggly, I have been overly prolix—it is a besetting sin. But I cannot end this letter without mentioning a very odd thing that happened last week.

One morning a bright red envelope, of the kind that is used in China for invitations, was found on the doorstep of this house. It was addressed to me, in English, and it was (or purported to be) from none other than Mr Chan (or Ah Fey or whatever you will). This is what it said:

'Dear Mr Chinnery, I have had to leave town on some pressing business and I do not know when I will be back. It is a pity because I had put together some good flowers for you. But you should know the golden camellia was not among them. That is because this plant does NOT exist. It was invented by Mr William Kerr. Like so many things that are said about China it is a HOAX. Mr Kerr made it up so that his sponsors would send him more money, that is all. The pictures were made by a painter called Alantsae. Mr Kerr taught him about botanical paintings. I know because I was their family servant and gardener—it was Alantsae's mother who sent me to work for Mr Kerr. I wanted to have the pleasure of telling Mr Penrose this myself, but I do not know if that will happen now.

'I bid you farewell. Lenny Chan (Lynchong).'

Frankly, Puggly dear, I don't know what to make of this and will not try. It is all so very *singular*—and yet perhaps it is not so for Canton.

Flowers and opium, opium and flowers!

It is odd to think that this city, which has absorbed so much of the world's evil, has given, in return, so much beauty. Reading your letters, I am amazed to think of all the flowers it has sent out into the world: chrysanthemums, peonies, tiger lilies, wisteria, rhododendrons, azaleas, asters, gardenias, begonias, camellias, hydrangeas, primroses, heavenly bamboo, a juniper, a cypress, climbing tea-roses and roses that flower many times over—these and many more. Were it in my power I would enjoin upon every gardener in the world that they remember, when they plant these blooms, that all of them came to their gardens by grace of this one city—this crowded, noisome, noisy, voluptuous place we call Canton.

One day all the rest will be forgotten—Fanqui-town and its Friendships, the opium and the flower-boats; even perhaps the paintings (for I doubt that anyone will ever love these pictures (and painters) as much as I do; this is, after all, a bastard art, neither sufficiently Chinese nor European, and thus likely to be displeasing to many).

But when all the rest is forgotten the flowers will remain, will they not, Puggly dear?

The flowers of Canton are immortal and will bloom for ever.

~

To Charles Elliott Esq., &c &c.

For nearly forty years, British merchants, led on by the East India Company, have been driving a trade in violation of the highest laws and the best interests of the Chinese empire. This course has been pushed so far as to derange its currency, to corrupt its officers, and ruin multitudes of its people. The traffic has become associated in the politics of the country, with embarrassments and evil omens; in its penal code, with the axe and the dungeon; in the breasts of men in private life, with the wreck of property, virtue, honour and happiness. All ranks, from the Emperor on the throne, to the people of the humblest hamlets, have felt its sting. To the fact of its descent to the lowest classes of society we are frequent witnesses; and the Court gazettes are evidence that it has marked out victims for disgrace and ruin even among the Imperial kindred.

Justice forbids that the steps taken by the Chinese, to arrest a system of wrongs practised on them, under the mask of friendship, be made pretence for still deeper injuries. Interest condemns the sacrifice of the lawful and useful trade with China, on the altar of illicit traffic. Still more loudly does it warn against the assumption of arms in an unjust quarrel, against—not the Chinese government only, but the Chinese people. Strong as Great Britain is she cannot war with success, or even safety, upon the consciences—the moral sense—of these three or four hundred million people.

The opium trade has dishonoured the name of God among the heathen more extensively than any other traffic of ancient or modern times. 'The flowing poison', the 'vile dirt', 'the dire calamity brought upon us by foreigners', these, and a hundred like them, are the names it bears, in the language of this empire. Its foreign origin has been bruited everywhere, and its introducers and their character branded in every city and hamlet throughout China.

What is it that has made the provinces of Malwa, Bihar, and Benares the chief localities of the opium cultivation? Why are vast tracts of land in those districts, formerly occupied with other articles, now covered with poppies? Although so wide-spread, why is the culture still rapidly on the increase?

The traffic is the creature of the East India Company, itself the organ of the British government. The revenues of India, the opium branch included, have repeatedly received the sanction of Parliament. The opium manufacture, and the trade inseparable from it, have received the highest sanction bestowable in one country, on an article proscribed in another. The British merchant went out from the high places of legislation to attend the sales of the East India Company. Authority, example, sympathy, were on his side; what cared he for the interdicts of the strange, despotic, repulsive government of China? Misled by Parliament he was confirmed in error by the decisions of society. No order of society was proof against this illusion. Will not the Stanhopes, the Noels, the Harrises take up this argument and tell the people of England that in the application of the principle of benevolence they are below the Chinese? Ought not this uprising of a Pagan empire against the demon of seduction, to react with power on Christians in the West? My oldest friend in China—a man familiar with the language—says: 'I have talked with many hundreds about the use of the drug, and never found *one*, to defend, or even palliate it.' Among all its victims it has no advocate. In England the licensed and gilded gin-palace courts every passer-by; the Chinese smoker threads his way to his secret haunt guilty and ashamed.

It is estimated that there are 80,000 chests of the drug in existence. Under this enormous accumulation, it is evident that the cultivation of the poppy, throughout India, should immediately cease. The lands which have been engrossed by this deleterious culture, should be returned to uses not incompatible with human life, virtue, and happiness.

Already, we are told, the use of the drug is insinuating itself into the habits of a morbid portion of Western society. (The consumption of Great Britain for 1831–32 was over 28,000 lbs per annum.) Such a taste once spread and fixed, by transmission through one or two generations, how shall it be eradicated?

It is undeniable that some of the most important ends of Providence in our day, are being brought about by the agency of national tastes. The manner in which England and China are, and have long been, bound together by the taste for tea is a good instance. And let it be remembered that the same Providence which uses these peculiar predilections as means of national friendship can turn them also to purposes of social chastisement. May it not happen that any such retributions—the recoil of a depraved taste, *the reaction of temptation on the tempter*—await the Western states in commerce with China.

The energies and truth of God go with us in every effort to hasten the reign of universal amity and freedom;

but that era must be coeval with the time when 'nation shall not lift up sword against nation, neither shall they learn war any more'.

I am, dear Sir
Ever truly yours
C.W. King

~

Suddenly one day it was over. The barricades came down and the shops on New and Old China Street began to open their doors and shutters.

But Fanqui-town was almost deserted now: only the sixteen merchants who had been refused permission to leave remained, with their employees.

The last period of detention, amidst the forlorn and empty factories, had been a trial for all who remained; there was great relief in the Achha Hong when it came to be known that the surrender of opium had finally been completed and everyone would soon be allowed to leave.

The day before their departure Neel did a last, solitary round of the enclave, bidding goodbye to Asha-didi and exchanging chin-chins with the linkisters, some of whom had become good friends. His last stop was at the print-shop; Compton led him into the inner courtyard and called for tea and snacks. They talked for a while of the still-unfinished *Chrestomathy* and then Compton handed him an envelope: 'Have got one last proof for you, Neel. It is a present.'

'What is it?'

'Letter.'

'But who is it from? And who is the writer?'

'Letter is from Lin Zexu to Queen of England.'

Neel started in surprise. 'Commissioner Lin has written a letter to Queen Victoria?'

'Haih! Translation also has been made and printed. Ho-yih can read later.'

'I will,' said Neel, rising to go. 'Thank you, Compton. Do-jeh!'

Mh sai!

At the door of the print-shop Neel came to a stop. 'Listen, Compton, there's something I've been meaning to ask you.'

'Yes, Ah Neel. Me-aa?'

'That day, when you introduced me to your teacher, Chang Lou-si, you said something that puzzled me.'

'What was it?'

'You said that you had found out something about Seth Bahramji—about the bad things he has been responsible for.'

Compton nodded. 'Yes. We found out because of Ho Lao-kin. You remember? Man who was executed?'

'Yes.'

'Before he die he very afraid, pale-face-white-lips, like gwai is after him. He talk a lot, lo-lo-so-so. Say many thing. He tell that it was Mister Moddie who first give him opium—that how he start in the business. That time Mister Moddie have woman here in Canton—aunt of Ho Lao-kin. Later he have son with her, ne? You savvy no-savvy all this, Ah Neel?'

'I've heard something about it. Go on.'

'This boy, when he grow up, he need work. Ho Lao-kin take him to Macau—help him join smuggler gang. He work for them some years but then he have trouble and want to leave. He ask his father to take to his country, but father say no, must stay here. Then things become very bad for him. Gang boss want to kill him, so he run away, come to Guangzhou, hide with his mother. Gang-men catch Ho Lao-kin and he tell them boy is with mother, on boat. They go there to catch him, but he is gone, ne? Only mother there.'

'And then?'

'Then they kill her and leave on boat.'

Compton pursed his lips in disapproval and shook his head: 'Mister Moddie not good; he have done too much harm. Low-low sek-sek, you should not work for him Ah Neel. Yauh-jyuh—watch out, all who are close to him will suffer for what he has done.'

Neel fell silent as he considered this. 'Maybe you're right,' he said. 'But you know, Compton, it is also true that amongst those who are close to Seth Bahramji there are very few who do not love him. And I am not one of them—for if there is one thing I know about the Seth it is that he has a large and generous heart. This is what makes him different from the Burnhams and Dents and Ferdoonjees and the rest of them. You mark my words, those men will lose nothing in the end. It is Seth Bahramji who will be the biggest loser—and the reason for that is just this: he has a heart.'

Compton smiled: 'You are loyal Neel. Sih-sih.'

'We Achhas are a loyal people—it is perhaps our greatest failing. It is a sin amongst us to break faith with those whose salt we have eaten.'

'Haih-bo?' Compton laughed. 'I will feed you salt when I see you next Neel.'

'No need,' said Neel smiling. 'I have eaten your salt already.'

Compton smiled and bowed. Joi-gin Ah Neel.

Joi-gin Compton. Joi-gin.

~

It was not till later that night, after all his things had been packed, that Neel opened the envelope Compton had given him. He read the Commissioner's letter to Queen Victoria several times, and then reached for a page of his unfinished *Chrestomathy*. Turning it over, on impulse, he translated a few passages into Bengali.

'The Way of Heaven is fairness to all; it does not suffer us to harm others in order to benefit ourselves. Men are alike in this all the world over: that they cherish life and hate what endangers life. Your country lies twenty thousand leagues away; but the Way of Heaven holds good for you as for us, and your instincts are not different from ours; for nowhere are there men so blind as not to distinguish between what brings life and what brings death, between what brings profit and what does harm.

'Our Heavenly Court treats all within the Four Seas as one great family; the goodness of our great Emperor is like Heaven, that covers all things. There is no region so wild or so remote that he does not cherish and tend it. Ever since the port of Canton was first opened, trade has flourished. For some hundred and twenty or thirty years the natives of the place have enjoyed peaceful and profitable relations with the ships that come from abroad.

'But there is a class of evil foreigner that makes opium and brings it for sale, tempting fools to destroy themselves, merely in order to reap profit. Formerly the number of opium-smokers was small; but now the vice has spread far and wide and the poison has penetrated deeper and deeper. For this reason we have decided to inflict very severe penalties on opium-dealers and opium-smokers, in order to put a stop forever to the propagation of this vice.

'It appears that this poisonous article is manufactured by certain devilish persons in places subject to your own rule. It is not of course either made or sold at your bidding, nor do all the countries you rule produce it, but only certain of them. We have heard that England forbids the smoking of opium within its dominions with the utmost rigour. This means you are aware of how harmful it is. Since the injury it causes has been averted from England, is it not wrong to send it to another nation? How can these opium-sellers bear to bring to our people an article which does them so much harm for an ever-grasping gain? Suppose those of another nation should go to England and induce its people to buy and smoke the drug—it would be right that You, Honoured Sovereign, should hate and abhor them. Hitherto we have heard that You, Honoured Sovereign, whose heart is full of benevolence, would not do to others that which you would not others should do to yourself. Better than to forbid the smoking of opium then would be to forbid the sale of it and, better still, to prohibit the production of it, which is the only way of cleansing the contamination at its source. So long as you do not take it upon yourselves to forbid the opium but continue to make it and tempt the people of China to buy it, you will be showing yourselves careful of your own lives, but careless of the lives of other people, indifferent in your greed for gain to the harm you do to others. Such conduct is repugnant to human feeling and at variance with the Way of Heaven.'

~

Whether by design or not, it happened that the chop-boats that carried the last foreigners to the Bogue followed a route that took them past the field where the surrendered opium was being destroyed. Had Bahram known beforehand, he would have closed the window of his cabin, but the sight was upon him before he could shut his eyes: hundreds of men were swarming over the compound, carrying crates and upending them into a tank.

He did not need to be told what they were doing: he had spent half a lifetime ferrying those familiar mango-wood crates across the seas; even at that distance they were easy to recognize. Looking at them now, he remembered the storm in the Bay of Bengal and how he had endangered his life for those precious crates; he remembered the months of effort it had taken to assemble that enormous consignment and the hopes he had invested in it. Even though he would have liked to be spared the sight of their destruction he could not tear his eyes away from the men who were standing waist-deep in the tank, stamping upon the opium: it was as if his own body were being trod upon until it melted into the water and flowed into the river—like the dark sludge that was spilling from the sluices.

His throat, head and chest began to ache with the craving for a pipe—but it was impossible to light one here, in sight of his own staff. He would have to wait till he reached the *Anahita*. He lay down and began to count the hours.

It was past midnight when he was finally alone in the Owners' Suite. He opened the window and locked the door before making himself a pipe. His fingers were trembling feverishly as he drank in the smoke. Within a few seconds his hands became steadier and his knotted muscles began to relax.

The night was hot and still: he had already taken off his angarkha, but his kasti and sadra were also drenched in sweat now. He took them off and lay bare-bodied on his bed, wearing nothing but a pair of pyjamas.

Through the window he could see the outlines of the desolate ridges and headlands of Hong Kong, looming above the ship, silhouetted against a brightly moonlit sky. The waters around the *Anahita* were crowded with ships and many small boats were paddling about. He could hear the splash of oars and the voices of boat-girls, raised in laughter and complaint. Their sound was very familiar, like echoes from the past; he was not in the least surprised when he heard his name being called: 'Mister Barry! Mister Barry!'

He went to the window and saw that a sampan had pulled up, under the overhang of the *Anahita*'s stern. There was a boy in the back, leaning against the yuloh; he was wearing a conical sun hat so his face was in darkness. But Bahram could hear him clearly, even though he was speaking in a whisper, so as not to alert the ship's crew: 'Come, Mister Barry. Come. She waiting you—waiting you inside.' He pointed to the sampan's covered hull.

The window of the Owners' Suite had been built, Bahram knew, to serve also as an escape hatch, in case of fire or other emergencies. Underneath was a glass-fronted box with a rope ladder. Bahram took the ladder out, attached the grapnels to the sill, and dropped it over the side. When the boy had taken hold of the bottom rung, Bahram swung his pyjama-clad leg over the sill and began to descend. He went down very carefully, rung by rung, watching every step.

'Come, Mister Barry. Ha-loy!'

The sampan was under his feet now, so he let go of the ladder and pushed it away.

The boy was pointing at the sampan's covered cabin: 'There, Mister Barry. She wait you there.'

Bahram crept under the bamboo matting and immediately a hand brushed against his bare chest. He recognized at once the feel of the rough, callused fingers.

'Chi-mei?' He heard her giggle, and stretched his arms into the darkness. 'Chi-mei! Come!'

Afterwards, as so often before, they crawled out on the prow. Lying flat on their bellies they looked at the moon's image, shimmering in the water. It was shining so brightly that her face too was illuminated by its reflected glow: she seemed to be looking up from under the water's surface, smiling at him, beckoning with a finger.

'Come, Mister Barry. Come. Ha-loy!'

He smiled. 'Yes, Chi-mei, I'm coming. It's time now.'

The water was so warm that it was as if they were still on the boat, lying in each other's arms.

~

The dangling rope ladder caught Paulette's attention early in the morning, soon after she had made her daily climb up the slopes of the island, to the plot of land Fitcher had rented for his plants.

The spot was high enough to provide her with a fine view of the strait and every morning, at the end of her climb, she would spend a few minutes in the shade of a tree, counting the ships in the bay and catching her breath.

Over the preceding weeks the channel between Hong Kong and Kowloon had become busier than ever before. Many British-owned ships had left Macau and moved there; most of Macau's British residents had left too and were now living on the anchored ships. As a result, a floating settlement had come into being in the shadows of Hong Kong's peaks and ridges; although its core was formed by the fleet of foreign ships, many boat-people had also gathered there, offering every kind of service, from laundry to provisioning; dozens of small boats were constantly on the prowl, hawking fruits, vegetables, meat, live chickens and much else.

In that motley assemblage of vessels the *Anahita* had stood out from the first by reason of her elegant lines and rakish masts. Paulette and Fitcher had passed the ship many times on their way to the eastern end of the island, where they often went to forage for plants. Often the *Anahita*'s lascar lookouts would wave to them as they went by.

Today it so happened that the *Anahita*'s stern was turned in Paulette's direction. This was why the ladder caught her eye: it made for an odd sight—a ladder hanging from a window in an anchored ship, with nothing below it but water. She wondered about it for a bit, then shrugged it off and busied herself with the plants.

The weather was hot and clammy and after an hour she had to take another break. Turning towards the *Anahita*, she saw that an uproar had broken out on the elegant three-master: the dangling ladder had been discovered and pulled in. The crew were swarming over the main deck, hoisting signals and shouting across the water, holding bungals to their mouths.

Around mid-morning, when it came time for Paulette to go down to meet the *Redruth*'s gig, she noticed that a yawl had been lowered from the *Anahita* and was now making its way towards Hong Kong. There were a dozen turbaned men inside, most of them lascars. They were pulling hard on the oars.

The trail that led down to the beach cut sharply back and forth across the hillside. Following it down, Paulette lost sight of the yawl for several minutes. When she glimpsed it again, it had already touched land: its passengers had leapt off and were running across the beach. They had evidently spotted something and were racing to get to it: what it was she could not tell for it was hidden by an overhang.

A minute or so later screams came echoing up the slope. The voices were distraught, shouting in frantic, high-pitched Hindusthani: *Yahan!* Here! Here! We've found him . . .

She quickened her pace and soon afterwards the men came into view. They were kneeling around a bare-bodied corpse that had washed up on the beach; some were weeping and some were striking their foreheads with the heels of their palms.

One of the men, bearded and turbaned, looked up and caught sight of her. His face did not look familiar but she could tell, from his widening eyes, that he had recognized her. He rose to his feet and came towards her.

'Miss Lambert?' he said softly.

She recognized the voice at once. *Apni?* she said in Bengali. Is it you? From the *Ibis*?

Yes, it's me.

She saw that his face was streaked with tears. What's happened here? she said. Who is that?

Do you remember Ah Fatt, from the *Ibis*?

She nodded. Yes. Of course.

It's his father. Seth Bahram Modi.

~

According to the legends of the Fami, it was entirely by chance that Neel came into possession of Robin Chinnery's letters.

The story goes that towards the end of his visit to the Colver farm Neel asked if he might spend a few nights in the place where Paulette had once stayed, down by the sea. This was a tin-roofed cabin, tucked inside a coconut grove: there was a charpoy inside, a rickety table and a chair or two; other than that the place was empty. Of Paulette's occupancy there was no trace at all, and yet, in the same way that a man can sometimes feel the gaze of another person resting upon his back, Neel felt that something of hers was staring him in the face. He got down on his knees and crawled over the tiled floor; he examined the walls; he went outside and rooted around in the sandy surroundings, hoping to find some shrub or flower that she might have planted. But other than coconuts and sea-grapes, not much would grow there and he found nothing.

Through all this, Neel grew ever more certain that something of Paulette's was hidden in plain view: what could it be and where was it? The thought nagged at his mind so persistently that he could not sleep properly. At some point in the night he pushed the pillow off the charpoy: that was when he noticed a bump in the mattress—something was hidden underneath. He lit a lamp and pulled back the mattress. Underneath lay a packet of some sort, wrapped in tarpaulin. He undid the knotted leather cord that was tied around it and gently removed the covering.

There was a sheaf of paper inside. The first sheet was yellow with age and covered with handwriting—large, flamboyantly sloped and a little faded.

Neel moved the lamp closer and began to read.

~

8 Rua Ignacio Baptista
Macau
July 6, 1839

Beloved Pugglee-shona, you cannot imagine how happy I was to receive your last, most recent letter. It provided me with the only bit of cheer I have had in a long while. It was nothing less than *thrilling* to learn that Zachary has been cleared of all charges and is on his way to China!

I am truly, truly glad for you, Puggly dear: I eagerly await even better and more joyful news—news that will allow me to call you 'Puggleebai'!—indeed I long for it, and I do hope I will receive it soon, for it is perhaps the only thing that could dispel the dark cloud that has settled on me these last few weeks.

Macau does not suit me at all, I find—or perhaps it is just that I do not like living in my Uncle's house. But no—it would be wrong of me to place the blame for my megrims on Macau or my 'uncle' or his house. The truth is that I miss Canton quite dreadfully: the Maidan, the factories, Hog Lane, Old China Street, Lamqua's shop—but most of all Jacqua. My only consolation is that he too is thinking of me. I know this because he sent me a present a couple of weeks ago: jujubes and candy, as usual, but they were wrapped in a most curious covering—a confection of silk that proved to be, on examination, the severed sleeve of one of his gowns! There was no accompanying letter, of course—since we share no written language I did not really expect one. But I confess I was *most* intrigued by that piece of silk: was it just a keepsake, I asked myself, or was it the vehicle of some coded message? The more I thought about it the more convinced I became that it was the latter, so I decided in the end to seek the assistance of some of my Uncle's Chinese assistants. Their response immediately confirmed my suspicions—they giggled and tittered and blushed and would not tell me what the message was. I had to resort to all kinds of bribery and cajolery to get the story out of them: apparently a long time ago there was an Emperor of China who was so greatly attached to his Friend that once, when he fell asleep on his arm, rather than disturb his rest he cut the sleeve off his priceless gown!

Is it not the most *touching* story? It ought to have cheered me but I confess it only made things worse: if I had missed Canton before, after this I found myself both *yearning* for it and *despairing* of ever seeing it again.

Seized by the blue-devils, I became prey also to nightmares: they started on the night of that fearsome storm that hit the coast a fortnight ago—you will remember it well, I am sure, for it must have given the *Redruth* quite a battering.

In any event, at some moment in that long, dreadful night, when the winds were easing off, I closed my eyes and thought myself to be back in Canton—but only to find it convulsed by another riot, like that of December 12th, except that it was even worse.

Something appalling had happened in the city and a great mob had poured into Fanqui-town; this time there were no troops at hand to control them and the crowd was bent on destruction. I saw men running into the Maidan with flaming torches; they broke into the factories and set fire to the godowns. I escaped from my room and ran along the city walls until I reached the Sea-Calming Tower. From the top I looked down and saw a line of flames leaping above the river; the factories were on fire and they burned through the night. In the morning when the sun rose, I saw that Fanqui-town had been reduced to ashes; it was gone; everything had disappeared—Markwick's Hotel and Lamqua's shop and the shamshoo-dens in Hog Lane and the flagpoles in the Maidan. They had all been wiped away and in their place there were only ashes . . .

I am haunted by these images, Puggly dear; they return to me almost every night. Even when I awake I cannot wipe this vision from my eyes. I can paint nothing else but this; I have done a dozen versions already—I will send you one with this letter.

I would have liked to bring it to you myself, Puggly dear, but I am too *stricken* at this time to consider making even this short journey. It has ever been so with us Chinnerys, you know—when we are happy we soar very high and when we are not we fall into the depths of an *abyss*. And so it is with me now, Puggly dear.

I do envy you your felicity, my sweet, sweet Empress of Puggledom, but not, I hope, in a *covetous* way. I am filled with gladness for you and only wish I could share your joy . . . but, yes, I will own also that I do not want you to be so joyful as to forget your poor Robin.

~

Neel read through the night, and in the morning, when Deeti came down to the hut, he showed her the packet. Since she had never learned to read, the letters were of no interest to her. But the paintings that Neel had found in the packet seized her attention immediately—especially the picture of Fanqui-town in flames.

What's this place? she demanded to know. Where is it?

It's a place you've heard a lot about, said Neel. Kalua and your brother Kesri Singh were there during the wars—they must have told you about it. And Jodu too—and Paulette as well.

Ah! Is it called Chin-kalan?

Yes. Canton in English.

Why is it burning?

It's a strange thing . . .

Turning the picture over Neel pointed to the bottom right-hand corner, where the words 'Pixt. E. Chinnery, July 1839' were written in tiny letters.

See, he said, the painter—Paulette's friend Robin Chinnery—has put down the date as July 1839. But the destruction of the Thirteen Factories did not happen until seventeen years later. But it seems that Robin saw it in a dream.

So the place doesn't exist any more?

Neel shook his head. No. It was burnt to the ground. One night during the wars, Canton was bombarded by British and French gunships. The townspeople saw that the foreign factories were the only part of the city that was unharmed and they were enraged. A mob set fire to the factories; they were razed and never rebuilt.

Have you been back there then?

Neel nodded. Yes. The last time was almost thirty years after my first visit. The place was changed beyond recognition. The site of the Maidan was a scene of utter desolation: the factories were gone—hardly a brick was left standing upon another. A new foreign enclave had been constructed nearby, on a mudbank that had been reclaimed and filled in. It was called Shamian Island and the houses the Europeans had built there were nothing like the Thirteen Hongs. Nor was the atmosphere of the new enclave anything like that of the Fanqui-town of old. It was a typical 'White Town' of the kind the British made everywhere they went—it was cut off from the rest of the city, and very few Chinese were allowed inside, only servants. The streets were clean and leafy, and the buildings were as staid and dull as the people inside them. But behind that façade of bland respectability the foreigners were importing more opium than ever from India—after winning the war the British had quickly put an end to Chinese efforts to prohibit the drug.

I hated the dull, European buildings of Shamian, with their prim façades and their pediments of murderous greed: the new enclave was like a monument built by the forces of evil to celebrate their triumphal march through history. I could not bear to linger there: it was so unlike the Canton of my memories that I began to wonder whether my recollections were only a dream. But then I went to Thirteen Hong Street, which was the only part of Fanqui-town that remained. There were still some shops there that sold paintings. In one of them I found a picture of the Maidan and the Thirteen Factories . . .

Neel looked down again at Robin's painting and a catch came into his throat.

The picture cost more than I could afford, he said, but I bought it anyway. I realized that if it were not for those paintings no one would believe that such a place had ever existed.

acknowledgements

This book follows Neel's khabar-dari in attending closely to the *Chinese Repository* and the *Canton Register* (which was edited, in this period, by John Slade). Apart from these journals it relies principally on books, memoirs, documents, travelogues and word-lists that were written and compiled by people who lived in or visited Canton at around the same time as Neel: David Abeel, Colin Campbell, C. Toogood Downing, Capt. Robert Elliot, Émile D. Forgues, Shen Fu, Thomas Gardiner, Henry Gribble, Charles Gutzlaff, William C. Hunter, J. Johnson, William Kershaw, Charles W. King, W. Lobscheid, Sir Anders Ljungstedt, Gideon Nye, Samuel Shaw, George Smith, Russell Sturgis, Harriet Low, William Henry Low and several other members of this well-travelled Brooklyn family.

Neel was a keen collector of documents relating to his experiences in China. His archive included parliamentary papers such as *The Sessional Papers Printed by Order of the House of Lords, Session 1840, Vol VIII, Correspondence Relating to China* (Presented to Both Houses of Parliament by Command of Her Majesty, printed by T.R. Harrison, London, 1840); and other related collections of documents like the *Statement of Claims of the British Subjects interested in Opium surrendered to Captain Elliot at Canton for the Public Service*, London, 1840. It also included compendia of Chinese official documents such as *Portfolio Chinensis: or A Collection of Authentic Chinese State Papers Illustrative of the History of the Present Position of Affairs in China*, Macao, 1840 (ed. J. Lewis Shuck).

Neel's archive was a testament to his catholic interests. It included, for example, some works of natural history, such as Cuthbert Collingwood's *Rambles of a Naturalist on the Shores and Waters of the China Sea* (John Murray, London, 1868); and several works on horticulture such as J.C. Loudon's magisterial *An Encyclopaedia of Gardening, Comprising the Theory and Practice of Horticulture, Floriculture, Arboriculture and Landscape-Gardening, including All the Latest Improvements, A General History of Gardening in All Countries and A Statistical View of Its Present State* (Longman et al., London, 1824) and Sir William Chambers' seminal work *A Dissertation on Oriental Gardening, To Which is Annexed An Explanatory Discourse By Tan Chet-qua of Quang-chew-fu, Gent* (London, 1773).

Neel was fortunate also in being able to acquire a copy of a book that illuminated his experiences on Great Nicobar Island: John Gottfried Haensel's *Letters on the Nicobar Islands* (London, 1812). He was not so fortunate in stumbling upon Elijah C. Bridgman's *A Chinese Chrestomathy in the Canton Dialect* (S.W. Williams, Macau, 1841). He subsequently gave up all hope of publishing his own *Celestial Chrestomathy* and took the work in a different direction (fragments of which are available on certain websites, including www.amitavghosh.com).

Much that is said by the characters in this book is taken from their own words. Some of John Slade's speeches are adapted from his editorials and articles, published in the *Canton Register*; some of Charles King's utterances are similarly adapted from the reports of the *Canton Register* and from his own writings, most notably *Opium Crisis: A Letter Addressed to Charles Elliot Esq.* (London, 1839). Some of the speeches given by Dinyar Ferdoonjee, William Jardine, Charles W. King and H.H. Lindsay are also adaptations based upon published accounts.

Quotations from edicts and proclamations issued by Chinese officials (including Commissioner Lin) are generally adapted from translations published contemporaneously in the *Chinese Repository*, the *Canton Register*, *Portfolio Chinensis* and *Correspondence Relating to China*. In rendering passages of Neel's Bengali version of Commissioner Lin's letter to Queen Victoria, I have relied partly on W.C. Hunter's translation; but mostly I have adapted it from Arthur Waley's beautiful translation in *The Opium War Through Chinese Eyes* (Stanford University Press, 1968).

As a supplement to Neel's library I have relied also on the work of many contemporary and near-contemporary scholars and historians. To list all the books, articles and essays that have enriched this narrative would be impossible here, but it would be remiss of me not to acknowledge my gratitude for, and indebtedness to, the work of the following: E.N. Anderson, Robert Antony, S.F. Balfour, Jack Beeching, David Bello, Henry and Sidney Berry-Hill, Kingsley Bolton, J.M. Braga, Lucile Brockway, Anne Bulley, Hsin-Pao Chang, Gideon Chen, Weng Eang Cheong, Craig Clunas, Alice Coats, Patrick Conner, A.H. Crook, Carl L. Crossman, Stephen Dobbs, Jacques M. Downs, Wolfram Eberhard, Mark Elvin, Fa-ti Fan, Amar Farooqui, Peter Ward Fay, R.W. Ferrier, S.N. Gajendragadkar, Valery M. Garrett, John Gascoigne, L. Gibbs, Martin Gregory, Basil Greenhill, Mary and John Gribbin, Amalendu Guha, Deyan Guo, G.A.C. Herklots, A.P. Hill, Bret Hinsch, Ke-en Ho, Nan Powell Hodges, A.W. Hummell, Robin Hutcheon, Christopher Hutton, Graham E. Johnson, Russell Jones, Maneck Furdoonji Kanga, Frank Kehl, Maggie Keswick, Jane Kilpatrick, Paul Kriwaczek, Roy Lancaster, Daniel Irving Larkin, Thomas N. Layton, Zhiwei Liu, Hosea Ballou Morse, H. Le Rougetel, Elma Loines, David R. MacGregor, Joyce Madancy, Pierre-Yves Manguin, John McCoy, Wilson Menard, Erik Mueggler, Yong Sang Ng, E.H. Parker, Glen D. Peterson, James Duncan Phillips, Behesti Minocher N. Pundol Saheb, Desmond Ray, Peter Raby, H.E. Richardson, Dingxu Shi, Asiya Siddiqi, Helen F. Siu, Anthony Xavier Soares, Tan Chung, Madhavi Thampi, Adrian P. Thomas, G.R. Tibbetts, G.H.R. Tillotson, Yun Hui Tsu, Peter Valder, Paul A. Van Dyke, Arthur Waley, Barbara E. Ward, Rubie S. Watson, Tyler Whittle, G.R. Worcester, Ching-chao Wu and Liu Yu.

For help with details of fact and language, for assistance in tracking down materials, and for their support, I am greatly beholden to Robert Antony, Pengyew Chin, Amar Farooqui, Atish Ghosh, Guoliang Guo, Ashutosh Kumar, Jiajing Liu, Ming Lu, Megha Majumdar, Cecil Pinto, Rahul Srivastava, Mo-lin Yee, Xu Xi and most particularly, Kingsley Bolton and Robert McCabe. To Shernaz Italia, Freny Khodaiji and their extended families, I owe an immense and very special debt of gratitude.

The long journey upriver would have been vastly more difficult without the unflagging support of Barney Karpfinger, my agent, and Roland Phillips, my publisher and editor in the UK; without Debbie, my wife and first reader, this vessel would almost certainly have run aground; without my children, Lila and Nayan it could not have kept to its course. My mother, Anjali Ghosh, taught me to read—without her the voyage would never have begun.

Praise for *Sea of Poppies*

'A grand narrative that gently reveals history . . . the strangers on the schooner [the *Ibis*] are not easily forgettable and could have you reaching for Book Two [of the trilogy], like an afeemkhor for abkari'—*Indian Express*

'If migration is the movement that animates history to the rhythm of the outcast's heartbeat, Amitav Ghosh is its most elegant choreographer'—*India Today*

'*Sea of Poppies* is riveting . . . [Ghosh] has gone from the highly readable to the unputdownable'—Khushwant Singh, *Hindustan Times*

'The cast is marvelous and the plot majestically serpentine, but the real hero is the English language, which rarely felt so alive and vibrant'—*Publishers Weekly* (starred review)

'[*Sea of Poppies*] is utterly involving and piles on the tension until the very last page . . . The next volume cannot come too soon'—*The Sunday Times* (London)

'Intoxicating stuff . . . Ordinary lives, extraordinary tales . . . [Ghosh] is a master at pitting stories of ordinary people against a historical swathe spanning generations and continents'
—*Financial Express*

Fiction
Rs 350